wanderings of the people
the great road
small roads
caravan routes
the generals' route
cliff
mountains
ocean currents

steppes
forests
swamp

# Sanctuary

# Sanctuary

THIEVES' WORLD

TALES FROM THE VULGAR UNICORN

SHADOWS OF SANCTUARY

**edited by Robert Lynn Asprin**

Nelson Doubleday, Inc.
*Garden City, New York*

# Contents

# Editor's Note

The perceptive reader may notice small inconsistencies in the characters appearing in these stories. Their speech patterns, their accounts of certain events, and their observations on the town's pecking order vary from time to time.

*These are not inconsistencies!*

The reader should consider the contradictions again, bearing three things in mind.

First; each story is told from a different viewpoint, and different people see and hear things differently. Even readily observable facts are influenced by individual perceptions and opinions. Thus, a minstrel narrating a conversation with a magician would give a different account than would a thief witnessing the same exchange.

Second; the citizens of Sanctuary are by necessity more than a little paranoid. They tend to either omit or slightly alter information in conversation. This is done more reflexively than out of premeditation, as it is essential for survival in this community.

Finally, Sanctuary is a fiercely competitive environment. One does not gain employment by admitting to being "the secondbest swordsman in town." In addition to exaggerating one's own status, it is commonplace to downgrade or ignore one's closest competitors. As a result, the pecking order of Sanctuary will vary depending on who you talk to . . . or more importantly, who you believe.

# Thieves' World

# *Contents*

# *Introduction*

## I
## The Emperor

"But surely Your Excellency can't dispute the facts of the matter!"

The robed figure of the Emperor never slackened its pacing as the new leader of the Rankan Empire shook his head in violent disagreement.

"I do not dispute the facts, Kilite," he argued, "but neither will I order the death of my brother."

"*Step*brother," his chief adviser corrected pointedly.

"The blood of our father flows in both our veins," the Emperor countered, "and I'll have no hand in spilling it."

"But Your Excellency," Kilite pleaded, "Prince Kadakithis is young and idealistic . . ."

". . . and I am not," the Emperor finished. "You belabor the obvious, Kilite. That idealism is my protection. He would no more lead a rebellion against the Emperor—against his brother—than I would order his assassination."

"It is not the Prince we fear, Your Excellency, it's those who would use him." The adviser was adamant. "If one of his many false-faced followers succeeded in convincing him that your rule was unjust or inhumane, that idealism would compel him to move against you even though he loves you dearly."

The Emperor's pacing slowed until finally he was standing motionless, his shoulders drooping slightly.

"You're right, Kilite. All my advisers are right." There was weary resignation in his voice. "Something must be done to remove my brother from the hotbed of intrigue here at the capital. If at all possible, however, I would hold any thoughts of assassination as a last resort."

"If Your Excellency has an alternate plan he wishes to suggest, I would be honored to give it my appraisal," Kilite offered, wisely hiding his feelings of triumph.

"I have no immediate plan," the Emperor admitted. "Nor will I be able to give it my full concentration until another matter is settled which weighs heavily on my mind. Surely the empire is safe from my brother for a few more days?"

"What is the other decision demanding your attention?" the adviser asked, ignoring his ruler's attempt at levity. "If it is something I might assist you in resolving . . ."

"It is nothing. A minor decision, but an unpleasant one nonetheless. I must appoint a new military governor for Sanctuary."

"Sanctuary?" Kilite frowned.

"A small town at the southern tip of the empire. I had a bit of trouble finding it myself—it's been excluded from the more recent maps. Whatever reason there was for the town's existence has apparently passed. It is withering and dying, a refuge for petty criminals and down-at-the-heels adventurers. Still, it's part of the empire."

"And they need a new military governor," Kilite murmured softly.

"The old one's retiring." The Emperor shrugged. "Which leaves me with a problem. As a garrisoned empire town, they are entitled to a governor of some stature—someone who knows the empire well enough to serve as their representative and go-between with the capital. He should be strong enough to uphold and enforce the law—a function I fear where the old governor was noticeably lax."

Without realizing it, he began to pace again.

"My problem is that such a man could be better utilized elsewhere in the empire. It seems a shame to waste someone on such an insignificant, out-of-the-way assignment."

"Don't say 'out-of-the-way,' Your Excellency," Kilite smiled. "Say 'far from the hotbed of intrigue.' "

The Emperor looked at his adviser for a long moment. Then both men began to laugh.

# II
# The Town

Hakiem the Storyteller licked the dust from his lips as he squinted at the morning sun. It was going to be hot again today—a wine day, if he could afford wine. The little luxuries, like wine, that he allowed himself were harder to come by as the caravans became fewer and more infrequent.

His fingers idly seeking a sandflea which had successfully found its way inside his rags, he settled himself wearily in his new roost at the edge of the bazaar. Previously, he had frequented the large wharf until the fishermen drove him off, accusing him of stealing. Him! With all the thieves that abound in this town, they chose him for their accusations.

"Hakiem!"

He looked about him and saw a band of six urchins descending on him, their eyes bright and eager.

"Good morning, children," he grimaced, exposing his yellow teeth. "What do you wish of old Hakiem?"

"Tell us a story," they chorused, surging around him.

"Be off with you, sandfleas!" he moaned, waving an arm. "The sun will be hot today. I'll not add to the dryness of my throat telling you stories for free."

"Please, Hakiem?" one whined.

"We'll fetch you water," promised another.

"I have money."

The last offer caught at Hakiem's attention like a magnet. His eyes fastened hungrily on the copper coin extended in a grubby hand. That coin and four of its brothers would buy him a bottle of wine.

Where the boy had gotten it mattered not—he had probably stolen it. What concerned Hakiem was how to transfer the wealth from the boy to himself. He considered taking it by force, but decided against it. The bazaar was rapidly filling with people, and open bullying of children would doubtless draw repercussions. Besides, the nimble urchins could outrun him with ease. He would just have to earn it honestly. Disgusting, the depths to which he had sunk.

"Very well, Ran-tu," he smiled extending his hand. "Give me the money, and you shall have any story you wish."

"After I hear the story," the boy announced haughtily. "You shall have the coin . . . if I feel the story is worth it. It is the custom."

"So it is." Hakiem forced a smile. "Come, sit here beside me so you can hear every detail."

The boy did as he was told, blissfully unaware that he was placing himself within Hakiem's long, quick reach.

"Now then, Ran-tu, what story do you wish to hear?"

"Tell us about the history of our city," the boy chirped, forgetting his pretended sophistication for the moment.

Hakiem grimaced, but the other boys jumped and clapped their hands with enthusiasm. Unlike Hakiem, they never tired of hearing this tale.

"Very well," Hakiem sighed. "Make room here!"

He shoved roughly at the forest of small legs before him, clearing a small space in the ground which he swept smooth with his hand. With quick, practiced strokes, he outlined the southern part of the continent and formed the north-south mountain range.

"The story begins here, in what once was the kingdom of Ilsig, east of the Queen's Mountains."

". . . which the Rankans call the World's End Mountains . . ." supplied an urchin.

". . . and the Mountain Men call Gunderpah . . ." contributed another.

Hakiem leaned back on his haunches and scratched absently.

"Perhaps," he said, "the young gentlemen would like to tell the story while Hakiem listens."

"No they wouldn't," insisted Ran-tu. "Shut up, everyone. It's my story! Let Hakiem tell it."

Hakiem waited until silence was restored, then nodded loftily to Ran-tu and continued.

"Afraid of invasion from the then young Rankan Empire across the mountains, they formed an alliance with the Mountain Tribes to guard the only known pass through the mountains."

He paused to draw a line on his map indicating the pass.

"Lo, it came to pass that their fears were realized. The Rankans turned their armies toward Ilsig, and they were forced to send their own troops into the pass to aid the Mountain Men in the kingdom's defense."

He looked up hopefully and extended a palm as a merchant paused to listen, but the man shook his head and moved on.

"While the armies were gone," he continued, scowling, "there was an uprising of slaves in Ilsig. Body-servants, galley slaves, gladiators, all united in an effort to throw off the shackles of bondage. Alas . . ."

He paused and threw up his hands dramatically.

". . . the armies of Ilsig returned early from their mountain campaign and put a swift end to the uprising. The survivors fled south . . . here . . . along the coast."

He indicated the route with his fingers.

"The kingdom waited for a while, expecting the errant slaves to return of their own volition. When they didn't, a troop of cavalry was sent to overtake them and bring them back. They overtook the slaves here, forcing them back into the mountains, and a mighty battle ensued. The slaves were triumphant, and the cavalry was destroyed."

He indicated a point in the southern portion of the mountain range.

"Aren't you going to tell about the battle?" Ran-tu interrupted.

"That is a story in itself . . . requiring separate payment," Hakiem smiled.

The boy bit his lip and said nothing more.

"In the course of their battle with the cavalry, the slaves discovered a pass through the mountains, allowing them to enter this green valley where game was plentiful and crops sprang from the ground. They called it Sanctuary."

"The valley isn't green," an urchin interrupted pointedly.

"That's because the slaves were dumb and overworked the land," countered another.

"My dad used to be a farmer, and he didn't overwork the land!" argued a third.

"Then how is it you had to move into town when the sands took your farm?" countered the second.

"I want to hear my story!" barked Ran-tu, suddenly towering above them.

The group subsided into silence.

"The young gentleman there has the facts of the matter right," smiled Hakiem, pointing a finger at the second urchin. "But it took time. Oh my, yes, lots of time. As the slaves exhausted the land to the north, they moved south, until they reached the point where the town stands today.

Here they met a group of native fishermen, and between fishing and farming managed to survive in peace and tranquility."

"That didn't last long," snorted Ran-tu, momentarily forgetting himself.

"No," agreed Hakiem. "The gods did not will it so. Rumors of a discovery of gold and silver reached the kingdom of Ilsig and brought intruders into our tranquility. First adventurers, and finally a fleet from the kingdom itself to capture the town and again bring it under the kingdom's control. The only fly in the kingdom's victory wine that day was that most of the fishing fleet was out when they arrived, and, realizing the fate of the town, took refuge on Scavengers' Island to form the nucleus of the Cape Pirates, who harass ships to this day."

A fisherman's wife passed by and, glancing down, recognized the map in the dust, smiled, and tossed two copper coins to Hakiem. He caught them neatly, elbowing an urchin who tried to intercept them, and secreted them in his sash.

"Blessings on your house, mistress," he called after his benefactor.

"What about the empire?" Ran-tu prompted, afraid of losing his story.

"What? Oh, yes. It seems that one of the adventurers pushed north seeking the mythical gold, found a pass through the Civa, and eventually joined the Rankan Empire. Later, his grandson, now a general in the empire, found his ancestor's journals. He led a force south over his grandfather's old route and recaptured the town. Using it as a base, he launched a naval attack round the cape and finally captured the kingdom of Ilsig, making it a part of the empire forever."

"Which is where we are today," one of the urchins spat bitterly.

"Not quite," corrected Hakiem, his impatience to be done with the story yielding to his integrity as a tale-spinner. "Though the kingdom surrendered, for some reason the Mountain Men continued to resist the empire's attempts to use the Great Pass. That was when the caravan routes were established."

A faraway look came into his eyes.

"Those were the days of Sanctuary's greatness. Three or four caravans a week laden with treasures and trade goods. Not the miserable supply caravans you see today—great caravans that took half a day just to enter town."

"What happened?" asked one of the awestruck urchins.

Hakiem's eyes grew dark. He spat in the dust.

"Twenty years ago, the empire succeeded in putting down the Moun-

tain Men. With the Great Pass open, there was no reason to risk major caravans in the bandit-ridden sands of the desert. Sanctuary has become a mockery of its past glory, a refuge for the scum who have nowhere else to go. Mark my words, one day the thieves will outnumber the honest citizenry, and then . . ."

"One side, old man!"

A sandaled foot came down on the map, obliterating its outlines and scattering the urchins.

Hakiem cowered before the shadow of one of the Hell-Hounds, the five new elite guards who had accompanied the new governor into town.

"Zalbar! Stop that!"

The unsmiling giant froze at the sound of the voice and turned to face the golden-haired youth who strode onto the scene.

"We're supposed to be governing these people, not bludgeoning them into submission."

It seemed strange, seeing a lad in his late teens chastising a scarred veteran of many campaigns, but the larger man merely dropped his eyes in discomfort.

"Apologies, Your Highness, but the Emperor said we were to bring law and order to this hellhole, and it's the only language these blackguards understand."

"The Emperor—my brother—put me in command of this town to govern it as I see fit, and my orders are that the people are to be treated kindly as long as they do not break the laws."

"Yes, Your Highness."

The youth turned to Hakiem.

"I hope we did not disturb your story. Here—perhaps this will make up for our intrusion."

He pressed a gold coin into Hakiem's hand.

"Gold!" Hakiem sneered. "Do you think one miserable coin can make up for scaring those precious children?"

"What?" roared the Hell-Hound. "Those gutter-rats? Take the Prince's money and be thankful I—"

"Zalbar!"

"But Your Highness, this man is only playing on your—"

"If he is, it's mine to give . . ."

He pressed a few more coins into Hakiem's outstretched hand.

"Now come along. I want to see the bazaar."

Hakiem bowed low, ignoring the Hell-Hound's black glare. When he straightened, the urchins were clustered about him again.

"Was that the Prince?"

"My dad says he's the best thing for this town."

"My dad says he's too young to do a good job."

"Izzat so!"

"The Emperor sent him here to get him out of the way."

"Sez who?"

"Sez my brother! He's been bribing guards here all his life and never had any trouble till the Prince came. Him and his whores and his Hell-Hounds."

"They're going to change everything. Ask Hakiem . . . Hakiem?"

The urchins turned to their chosen mentor, but Hakiem had long since departed with his new wealth for the cool depths of a tavern.

# III
# The Plan

"As you already know, you five men have been chosen to remain with me here in Sanctuary after the balance of the honor guard returns to the capital."

Prince Kadakithis paused to look each man in the face before he continued. Zalbar, Bourne, Quag, Razkuli, and Arman. Each of them a seasoned veteran, they doubtless knew their work better than the Prince knew his. Kadakithis' royal upbringing came to his rescue, helping him to hide his nervousness as he met their gazes steadily.

"As soon as the ceremonies are completed tomorrow, I will be swamped with problems in clearing up the backlog of cases in the civil court. Realizing that, I thought it best to give you your briefing and assignments now, so that you will be able to proceed without the delay of waiting for specific instructions."

He beckoned the men forward, and they gathered around the map of Sanctuary hung on the wall.

"Zalbar and I have done some preliminary scouting of the town. Though this briefing should familiarize you with the basic lay of the land, you should each do your own exploring and report any new observations to each other. Zalbar?"

The tallest of the soldiers stepped forward and swept his hand across the map.

"The thieves of Sanctuary drift with wind like the garbage they are," he began.

"Zalbar!" the Prince admonished. "Just give the report without asides or opinions."

"Yes, Your Highness," the man replied bowing his head slightly. "But there is a pattern here which follows the winds from the east."

"The property values change because of the smells," Kadakithis reported. "You can say that without referring to the people as garbage. They are still citizens of the empire."

Zalbar nodded and turned to the map once more.

"The areas of least crime are here, along the eastern edge of town," he announced, gesturing. "These are the richest mansions, inns, and temples, which have their own defenses and safeguards. West of them, the town consists predominantly of craftsmen and skilled workers. The crime in this area rarely exceeds petty theft."

The man paused to glance at the Prince before continuing.

"Once you cross the Processional, however, things get steadily worse. The merchants vie with each other as to who will carry the widest selection of stolen or illicit goods. Much of their merchandise is supplied by smugglers who openly use the wharves to unload their ships. What is not purchased by the merchants is sold directly at the bazaar."

Zalbar's expression hardened noticeably as he indicated the next area.

"Here is a tangle of streets known simply as the Maze. It is acknowledged by all to be the roughest section of town. Murder and armed robbery are commonplace occurrences day or night in the Maze, and most honest citizens are afraid to set foot there without an armed escort. It has been brought to our attention that none of the guardsmen in the local garrison will enter this area, though whether this is out of fear or if they have been bribed . . ."

The Prince cleared his throat noisily. Zalbar grimaced and moved on to another area.

"Outside the walls to the north of town is a cluster of brothels and gaming houses. There are few crimes reported in this area, though we believe this is due more to a reluctance on the part of the inhabitants to deal with authorities than from any lack of criminal activity. To the far west of town is a shantytown inhabited by beggars and derelicts known as the Downwinders. Of all the citizens we've encountered so far, they seem the most harmless."

His report complete, Zalbar returned to his place with the others as the Prince addressed them once again.

"Your priorities until new orders are issued will be as follows," he announced, eyeing the men carefully. "First, you are to make a concentrated effort to reduce or eliminate petty crime on the east side of town. Second, you will close the wharves to the smuggler traffic. When that is done, I will sign into law certain regulations enabling you to move against the brothels. By that time, my court duties should have eased to a point where we can formulate a specific plan of action for dealing with the Maze. Any questions?"

"Are you anticipating any problems with the local priesthood over the ordered construction of new temples to Savankala, Sabellia, and Vashanka?" Bourne asked.

"Yes, I am," the Prince acknowledged. "But the difficulties will probably be more diplomatic than criminal in nature. As such, I will attend to it personally, leaving you free to pursue your given assignments."

There were no further questions, and the Prince steeled himself for his final pronouncement.

"As to how you are to conduct yourselves while carrying out your orders . . ." Kadakithis paused dramatically while sweeping the assemblage with a hard glare. "I know you men are all soldiers and used to meeting opposition with bared steel. You are certainly permitted to fight to defend yourselves if attacked or to defend any citizen of this town. However, I will not tolerate brutality or needless bloodshed in the name of the empire. Whatever your personal feelings may be, you are not to draw a sword on any citizen unless they have proven—I repeat, *proven*—themselves to be criminal. The townsfolk have already taken to calling you Hell-Hounds. Be sure that title refers only to the vigor with which you pursue your duties and not to your viciousness. That is all."

There were mutters and dark glances as the men filed out of the room. While the Hell-Hounds' loyalty to the empire was above question, Kadakithis had pause to wonder if in their own minds they truly considered him a representative of that empire.

# Sentences of Death

## John Brunner

### 1

It was a measure of the decline in Sanctuary's fortunes that the scriptorium of Master Melilot occupied a prime location fronting on Governor's Walk. The nobleman whose grandfather had caused a fine family mansion to be erected on the site had wasted his substance in gambling, and at last was reduced to eking out his days in genteel drunkenness in an improvised fourth story of wattle and daub, laid out across the original roof, while downstairs Melilot installed his increasingly large staff and went into the book—as well as the epistle—business. On hot days the stench from the bindery, where size was boiled and leather embossed, bid fair to match the reek around Shambles Cross.

Not all fortunes, be it understood, were declining. Melilot's was an instance. Ten years earlier he had owned nothing but his clothing and a scribe's compendium; then he worked in the open air, or huddled under some tolerant merchant's awning, and his customers were confined to poor litigants from out of town who needed a written summary of their case before appearing in the Hall of Justice, or suspicious illiterate purchasers of goods from visiting traders who wanted written guarantees of quality.

On a never-to-be-forgotten day, a foolish man instructed him to write down matter relevant to a lawsuit then in progress, which would assuredly have convinced the judge had it been produced without the opposition being warned. Melilot realized that, and made an extra copy. He was richly rewarded.

Now, as well as carrying on the scribe's profession—by proxy, mostly —he specialized in forgery, blackmail, and mistranslation. He was ex-

actly the sort of employer Jarveena of Forgotten Holt had been hoping
for when she arrived, particularly since his condition, which might be
guessed at from his beardless face and roly-poly fatness, made him
indifferent to the age or appearance of his employees.

The services offered by the scriptorium, and the name of its proprietor, were clearly described in half a dozen languages and three distinct
modes of writing on the stone face of the building, a window and a door
of which had been knocked into one large entry (at some risk to the
stability of the upper floors) so that clients might wait under cover until
someone who understood the language they required was available.

Jarveena read and wrote her native tongue well: Yenized. That was
why Melilot had agreed to hire her. No competing service in Sanctuary
could offer so many languages now. But two months might go by—
indeed, they just had done so—without a single customer's asking for a
translation into or from Yenized, which made her pretty much of a status symbol. She was industriously struggling with Rankene, the courtly
version of the common dialect, because merchants liked to let it be
thought their goods were respectable enough for sale to the nobility
even if they had come ashore by night from Scavengers' Island, and she
was making good headway with the quotidian street-talk in which the
poorer clients wanted depositions of evidence or contracts of sale made
out. Nonetheless she was still obliged to take on menial tasks to fill her
time.

It was noon, and another such task was due.

Plainly, it was of little use relying on inscriptions to reach those who
were most in need of a scribe's assistance; accordingly Melilot maintained a squad of small boys with peculiarly sweet and piercing voices,
who paraded up and down the nearby streets advertising his service by
shouting, wheedling, and sometimes begging. It was a tiring occupation,
and the children frequently grew hoarse. Thrice a day, therefore, someone was commanded to deliver them a nourishing snack of bread and
cheese and a drink made of honey, water, a little wine or strong ale, and
assorted spices. Since her engagement, Jarveena had been least often involved in other duties when the time for this one arrived. Hence she was
on the street, distributing Melilot's bounty, when an officer whom she
knew by name and sight turned up, acting in a most peculiar manner.
He was Captain Aye-Gophlan, from the guardpost at the corner of Processional Way.

He scarcely noticed her as he went by, but that was less than surprising. She looked very much like a boy herself—more so, if anything, than the chubby-cheeked blond urchin she was issuing rations to. When Melilot took her on she had been in rags, and he had insisted on buying her new clothes of which, inevitably, the price would be docked from her miniscule commission on the work she did. She didn't care. She only insisted in turn that she be allowed to choose her garb: a short-sleeved leather jerkin cross-laced up the front; breeches to mid-calf; boots to tuck the breeches into; a baldric on which to hang her scribe's compendium with its reed-pens and ink-block and water-pot and sharpening knife and rolls of rough reed-paper; and a cloak to double as covering at night. She had a silver pin for it—her only treasure.

Melilot had laughed, thinking he understood. He owned a pretty girl a year shy of the fifteen Jarveena admitted to, who customarily boxed the ears of his boy apprentices when they waylaid her in a dark passageway to steal a kiss, and that was unusual enough to demand explanation.

But that had nothing to do with it. No more did the fact that with her tanned skin, thin build, close-cropped black hair, and many visible scars, she scarcely resembled a girl regardless of her costume. There were plenty of ruffians—some of noble blood—who were totally indifferent to the sex of the youngsters they raped.

Besides, to Jarveena such experiences were survivable; had they not been, she would not have reached Sanctuary. So she no longer feared them.

But they made her deeply—bitterly—angry. And someday one who deserved her anger more than any was going to pay for one at least of his countless crimes. She had sworn so . . . but she had been only nine then, and with the passage of time the chance of vengeance grew more and more remote. Now she scarcely believed in it. Sometimes she dreamed of doing to another what had been done to her, and woke moaning with shame, and she could not explain why to the other apprentice scribes sharing the dormitory that once had been the bedroom of the noble who now snored and vomited and groaned and snored under a shelter fit rather for hogs than humans the wrong side of his magnificently painted ceiling.

She regretted that. She liked most of her companions; some were from respectable families, for there were no schools here apart from temple schools whose priests had the bad habit of stuffing children's

heads with myth and legend as though they were to live in a world of
make-believe instead of fending for themselves. Without learning to
read and write at least their own language they would be at risk of
cheating by every smart operator in the city. But how could she befriend those who had led soft, secure lives, who at the advanced age of
fifteen or sixteen had never yet had to scrape a living from gutters and
garbage piles?

Captain Aye-Gophlan was in mufti. Or thought he was. He was by
no means so rich as to be able to afford clothing apart from his uniforms, of which it was compulsory for the guards to own several—this
one for the Emperor's birthday, that one for the feast of the regiment's
patron deity, another for day-watch duty, yet another for night-watch
duty, another for funeral drill . . . The common soldiers were luckier.
If they failed in their attire, the officers were blamed for stinginess. But
how long was it since there had been enough caravans through here for
the guard to keep up the finery required of them out of bribes? Times
indeed were hard when the best disguise an officer on private business
could contrive was a plum-blue overcloak with a hole in it exactly
where his crotch-armor could glint through.

Seeing him, Jarveena thought suddenly about justice. Or more
nearly, about getting even. Perhaps there was no longer any hope of
bringing to account the villain who had killed her parents and sacked
their estate, enslaved the able-bodied, turned loose his half-mad troops
on children to glut the lust of their loins amid the smoke and crashing
of beams as the village its inhabitants called Holt vanished from the
stage of history.

But there were other things to do with her life. Hastily she snatched
back the cup she had already allowed to linger too long in the grasp of
this, luckily the last of Melilot's publicity boys. She cut short an attempt
at complaint with a scowl which drew her forehead-skin down just far
enough to reveal a scar normally covered by her forelock. That was a
resource she customarily reserved until all else failed. It had its desired
effect; the boy gulped and surrendered the cup and went back to work,
pausing only to urinate against the wall.

2

Just as Jarveena expected, Aye-Gophlan marched stolidly around the block, occasionally glancing back as though feeling insecure without his regular escort of six tall men, and made for the rear entrance to the scriptorium—the one in the crooked alley where the silk-traders were concentrated. Not all of Melilot's customers cared to be seen walking in off a populous and sunny roadway.

Jarveena thrust the wine jar, dish, and cup she was carrying into the hands of an apprentice too young to argue, and ordered them returned to the kitchen—next to the bindery, with which it shared a fire. Then she stole up behind Aye-Gophlan and uttered a discreet cough.

"May I be of assistance, captain?"

"Ah—!" The officer was startled; his hand flew to something stick-shaped under his cloak, no doubt a tightly-rolled scroll. "Ah . . . Good day to you! I have a problem concerning which I desire to consult your master."

"He will be taking his noon meal," Jarveena said in a suitably humble tone. "Let me conduct you to him."

Melilot never cared to have either his meals or the naps which followed them interrupted. But there was something about Aye-Gophlan's behavior which made Jarveena certain that this was an exceptional occasion.

She opened the door of Melilot's sanctum, announced the caller rapidly enough to forestall her employer's rage at being distracted from the immense broiled lobster lying before him on a silver platter, and wished there were some means of eavesdropping on what transpired.

But he was infinitely too cautious to risk that.

At best Jarveena had hoped for a few coins by way of bonus if Aye-Gophlan's business proved profitable. She was much surprised, therefore, to be summoned to Melilot's room half an hour later.

Aye-Gophlan was still present. The lobster had grown cold, untouched, but much wine had been consumed.

On her entrance, the officer gave her a suspicious glare.

"This is the fledgling you imagine could unravel the mystery?" he demanded.

Jarveena's heart sank. What devious subterfuge was Melilot up to now? But she waited meekly for clear instructions. They came at once, in the fat man's high and slightly whining voice.

"The captain has a writing to decipher. Sensibly, he has brought it to us, who can translate more foreign tongues than any similar firm! It is possible that it may be in Yenized, with which you are familiar . . . though, alas, I am not."

Jarveena barely suppressed a giggle. If the document were in any known script or language, Melilot would certainly recognize it—whether or not he could furnish a translation. That implied—hmm! A cipher? How interesting! How did an officer of the guard come by a message in code he couldn't read? She looked expectant, though not eager, and with much reluctance Aye-Gophlan handed her the scroll.

Without appearing to look up, she registered a tiny nod from Melilot. She was to agree with him.

But—

What in the *world?* Only a tremendous self-control prevented her from letting fall the document. Merely glancing at it made her dizzy, as though her eyes were crossing against her will. For a second she had seemed to read it clearly, and a heartbeat later . . .

She took a firm grip on herself. "I believe this to be Yenized, as you suspected, sir," she declared.

"Believe?" Aye-Gophlan rasped. "But Melilot swore you could read it instantly!"

"Modern Yenized I can, captain," Jarveena amplified. "I recognize this as a high and courtly style, as difficult for a person like myself as Imperial Rankene would be for a herdsman accustomed to sleeping with the swine." It was always politic to imply one's own inferiority when talking to someone like this. "Luckily, thanks to my master's extensive library, I've gained a wider knowledge of the subject in recent weeks; and with the help of some of the books he keeps I would expect to get at least its gist."

"How long would it take?" Aye-Gophlan demanded.

"Oh, one might safely say two or three days," Melilot interpolated in a tone that brooked no contradiction. "Given that it's so unusual an assignment, there would naturally be no charge except on production of a satisfactory rendering."

Jarveena almost dropped the scroll a second time. Never in living memory had Melilot accepted a commission without taking at least half his fee in advance. There must be something quite exceptional about this sheet of paper—

And of course there was. It dawned on her that moment, and she had to struggle to prevent her teeth from chattering.

"Wait here," the fat man said, struggling to his feet. "I shall return when I've escorted the captain out."

The moment the door closed she threw the scroll down on the table next to the lobster—wishing, irrelevantly, that it were not still intact, so she might snatch a morsel without being detected. The writing writhed into new patterns even as she tried not to notice.

Then Melilot was back, resuming his chair, sipping from his half-full wine cup.

"You're astute, you little weasel!" he said in a tone of grudging admiration. "Are you quick-witted enough to know precisely why neither he nor I—nor you!—can read that writing?"

Jarveena swallowed hard. "There's a spell on it," she offered after a pause.

"Yes! Yes, there is! Better than any code or cipher. Except for the eyes of the intended recipient, it will never read the same way twice."

"How is it that the captain didn't realize?"

Melilot chuckled. "You don't have to read and write to become a captain of the guard," he said. "He can about manage to tell whether the clerk who witnesses his mark on the watch-report is holding the page right side up; but anything more complicated and his head starts to swim anyway."

He seized the lobster, tore off a claw, and cracked it between his teeth; oil ran down his chin and dripped on his green robe. Picking out the meat, he went on. "But what's interesting is how he came by it. Make a guess."

Jarveena shook her head.

"One of the imperial bodyguards from Ranke, one of the detachment who escorted the Prince along the Generals' Road, called to inspect the local guardhouse this morning at dawn. Apparently he made himself most unpopular, to the point that, when he let fall that scroll without noticing, Aye-Gophlan thought more of secreting it than giving it back. Why he's ready to believe that an imperial officer would carry a document in Old High Yenized, I can't guess. Perhaps that's part of the magic."

He thrust gobbets of succulent flesh into his mouth and chomped for a while. Jarveena tried not to drool.

To distract herself by the first means to mind, she said, "Why did he tell you all this . . . ? Ah, I'm an idiot. He didn't."

"Correct." Melilot looked smug. "For that you deserve a taste of lobster. Here!" He tossed over a lump that by his standards was generous, and a chunk of bread also; she caught both in mid-air with stammered thanks and wolfed them down.

"You need to have your strength built up," the portly scribe went on. "I have a very responsible errand for you to undertake tonight."

"Errand?"

"Yes. The imperial officer who lost the scroll is called Commander Nizharu. He and his men are billeted in pavilions in the courtyard of the governor's palace; seemingly he's afraid of contamination if they have to go into barracks with the local soldiery.

"After dark this evening you are to steal in and wait on him, and inquire whether he will pay more for the return of his scroll and the name of the man who filched it, or for a convincing but fraudulent translation which will provoke the unlawful possessor into some rash action. For all I can guess," he concluded sanctimoniously, "he may have let it fall deliberately. *Hm?*"


3


It was far from the first time since her arrival that Jarveena had been out after curfew. It was not even the first time she had had to scamper in shadow across the broad expanse of Governor's Walk in order to reach and scramble over the palace wall, nimble as a monkey despite the mass of scartissue where her right breast would never grow. Much practice enabled her to whip off her cloak, roll it into a cylinder not much thicker than a money-belt, fasten it around her, and rush up the convenient hand- and toeholds in the outer wall which were carefully not repaired, and for a fat consideration, when the chief mason undertook his annual repointing.

But it was definitely the first time she had had to contend with crack soldiers from Ranke on the other side. One of them, by ill chance, was relieving himself behind a flowering shrub as she descended, and needed to do no more than thrust the haft of his pike between her legs. She gasped and went sprawling.

But Melilot had foreseen all this, and she was prepared with her story and the evidence to back it up.

"Don't hurt me, please! I don't mean any harm!" she whimpered, making her voice as childish as possible. There was a torch guttering in a sconce nearby; the soldier heaved her to her feet by her right wrist, his grip as cruel as a trap's, and forced her toward it. A sergeant appeared from the direction of the pavilions which since her last visit had sprouted like mushrooms between the entry to the Hall of Justice and the clustered granaries on the northwest side of the grounds.

"What you got?" he rumbled in a threatening bass voice.

"Sir, I mean no harm! I have to do what my mistress tells me, or I'll be nailed to the temple door!"

That took both of them aback. The soldier somewhat relaxed his fingers and the sergeant bent close to look her over better in the wan torchlight.

"By that, I take it you serve a priestess of Argash?" he said eventually.

It was a logical deduction. On the twenty-foot-high fane of that divinity his most devoted followers volunteered, when life wearied them, to be hung up and fast unto death.

But Jarveena shook her head violently.

"N-no, sir! Dyareela!"—naming a goddess banned these thirty years owing to the bloodthirstiness of her votaries.

The sergeant frowned. "I saw no shrine to *her* when we escorted the prince along Temple Avenue!"

"N-no, sir! Her temple was destroyed, but her worshipers endure!"

"Do they now!" the sergeant grunted. "Hmm! That sounds like something the commander ought to know!"

"Is that Commander Nizharu?" Jarveena said eagerly.

"What? How do you know his name?"

"My mistress sent me to him! She saw him early today when he was abroad in the city, and she was so taken with his handsomeness that she resolved at once to send a message to him. But it was all to be in secret!" Jarveena let a quaver enter her voice. "Now I've let it out, and she'll turn me over to the priests of Argash, and . . . Oh, I'm done for! I might as well be dead right now!"

"Dying can wait," the sergeant said, reaching an abrupt decision.

"But the commander will definitely want to know about the Dyareelans. I thought only madmen in the desert paid attention to that old bitch nowadays . . . Hello, what's this at your side?" He lifted it into the light. "A writing-case, is it?"

"Yes, sir. That's what I mainly do for my mistress."

"If you can write, why deliver messages yourself? That's what I always say. Oh, well, I guess you're her confidante, are you?"

Jarveena nodded vigorously.

"A secret shared is a secret no longer, and here's one more proof of the proverb. Oh, come along!"

By the light of two lamps filled, to judge by their smell, with poor-grade fish oil, Nizharu was turning the contents of his pavilion upside-down, with not even an orderly to help him. He had cleared out two brassbound wooden chests and was beginning on a third, while the bedding from his fieldcouch of wood and canvas was strewn on the floor, and a dozen bags and pouches had been emptied and not repacked.

He was furious when the sergeant raised the tent flap and roared that he was not to be disturbed. But Jarveena took in the situation at a glance and said in a clear firm voice, "I wonder if you're looking for a scroll."

Nizharu froze, his face turned so that light fell on it. He was as fair a man as she had ever seen: his hair like washed wool, his eyes like chips of summer sky. Under a nose keen as a bird's beak, his thin lips framed well-kept teeth marred by a chip off the right upper front molar. He was lean and obviously very strong, for he was turning over a chest that must weigh a hundred pounds and his biceps were scarcely bulging.

"Scroll?" he said softly, setting down the chest. "What scroll?"

It was very hard for Jarveena to reply. She felt her heart was going to stop. The world wavered. It took all her force to maintain her balance. Distantly she heard the sergeant say, "She didn't mention any scroll to us!"

And, amazingly, she was able to speak for herself again.

"That's true, commander," she said. "I had to lie to those men to stop them killing me before I got to you. I'm sorry." Meantime she was silently thanking the network of informers who kept Melilot so well supplied with information that the lie had been credible even to these strangers. "But I think this morning you mislaid a scroll . . . ?"

Nizharu hesitated a single moment. Then he rapped, "Out! Leave the boy here!"

*Boy!* Oh, miracle! If Jarveena had believed in a deity, now was when she would have resolved to make sacrifice for gratitude. For that implied he hadn't recognized her.

She waited while the puzzled sergeant and soldier withdrew, mouth dry, palms moist, a faint singing in her ears. Nizharu slammed the lid of the chest he had been about to overturn, sat down on it, and said, "Now explain! And the explanation had better be a good one!"

It was. It was excellent. Melilot had devised it with great care and drilled her through it a dozen times during the afternoon. It was tinged with just enough of the truth to be convincing.

Aye-Gophlan, notoriously, had accepted bribes. (So had everyone in the guard who might possibly be useful to anybody wealthier than himself, but that was by the by.) It had consequently occurred to Melilot—a most loyal and law-abiding citizen, who as all his acquaintance would swear had loudly welcomed the appointment of the prince, the new governor, and looked forward to the city being reformed—it had occurred to him that perhaps this was part of a plan. One could scarcely conceive of a high-ranking imperial officer being so casual with what was obviously a top-secret document. *Could* one?

"Never," murmured Nizharu, but sweat beaded his lip.

Next came the tricky bit. Everything depended on whether the commander wanted to keep the mere existence of the scroll a secret. Now he knew Aye-Gophlan had it, it was open to him to summon his men and march down to the guardhouse and search it floor to rooftree, for—according to what Jarveena said, at any rate—Aye-Gophlan was far too cautious to leave it overnight in the custody of a mere scribe. He would return on his next duty-free day, the day after tomorrow or the day after that, depending on which of his fellow officers he could exchange with.

But Melilot had deduced that if the scroll were so important that Nizharu kept it by him even when undertaking a mundane tour of inspection, it must be very private indeed. He was, apparently, correct. Nizharu listened with close attention and many nods to the alternative plan of action.

For a consideration, Melilot was prepared to furnish a false translation designed to jar Aye-Gophlan into doing something for which Nizharu could safely arrest him, without it ever being known that he had enjoyed temporary possession of a scroll which by rights should have remained in the commander's hands. Let him only specify the terms, and it would be as good as done.

When she—whom Nizharu still believed a he, for which she was

profoundly glad—finished talking, the commander pondered awhile. At
length he started to smile, though it never reached his eyes, and in firm
clear terms expressed his conditions for entering into a compact along
the lines Melilot proposed. He capped all by handing over two gold
coins, of a type she did not recognize, with a promise that he would
have her (his) hide if they did not both reach Melilot, and a large silver
token of the kind used at Ilsig for *him*self.

Then he instructed a soldier she had not met to escort her to the gate
and across Governor's Walk. But she gave the man the slip as soon as
they were clear of the palace grounds and rushed toward the back entry,
via Silk Corner.

Melilot being rich, he could afford locks on his doors; he had given
her a heavy bronze key which she had concealed in her writing case.
She fumbled it into the lock, but before she could turn it the door
swung wide and she stepped forward as though impelled by another
person's will.

This was the street—or rather alley. This was the door with its
overhanging porch. Outside everything was right.

But inside everything was absolutely, utterly, unqualifiedly *wrong*.


4


Jarveena wanted to cry out, but found herself unable to draw enough
breath. A vast sluggishness took possession of her muscles, as though
she were descending into glue. Taking one more step, she knew, would
tire her to the point of exhaustion; accordingly she concentrated merely
on looking about her, and within seconds was wishing that she hadn't.

A wan, greyish light suffused the place. It showed her high stone
walls on either side, a stone-flagged floor underfoot, but nothing above
except drifting mist that sometimes took on an eerie pale color: pinkish,
bluish, or the sickly phosphorescent shade of dying fish. Before her was
nothing but a long table, immensely and ridiculously long, such that one
might seat a full company of soldiers at it.

A shiver tried to crawl down her spine, but failed thanks to the weird
paralysis that gripped her. For what she was seeing matched in every respect the descriptions, uttered in a whisper, which she had heard of the
home of Enas Yorl. In all the land there were but three Great Wiz-

ards, powerful enough not to care that their true names were noised abroad: one was at Ranke and served the needs of the court; one was at Ilsig and accounted the most skillful; the third, by reason of some scandal, made do with the slim pickings at Sanctuary, and that was Enas Yorl.

But how could he be here? His palace was on—or, more exactly, below—Prytanis Street, where the city petered out to the southeast of Temple Avenue.

Except . . .

The thought burgeoned from memory and she fought against it, and failed. Someone had once explained to her:

*Except when it is somewhere else.*

Abruptly it was as though the table shrank, and from an immense distance its farther end drew close and along with it a high-backed, thronelike chair in which sat a curious personage. He was arrayed in an enormously full, many-layered cloak of some dull brown stuff, and wore a high-crowned hat whose broad brim somehow contrived to shadow his face against even the directionless grey light that obtained here.

But within that shadow two red gleams like embers showed, approximately where a human's eyes would be.

This individual held in his right hand a scroll, partly unrolled, and with his left he was tapping on the table. The proportions of his fingers were abnormal, and one or two of them seemed either to lack, or to be overprovided with, joints. One of his nails sparkled luridly, but that ceased after a little.

Raising his head, after a fashion, he spoke.

"A girl. Interesting. But one who has . . . suffered. Was it punishment?"

It felt to Jarveena as though the gaze of those two dull red orbs could penetrate her flesh as well as her clothing. She could say nothing, but had nothing to say.

"No," pronounced the wizard—for surely it must be none other. He let the scroll drop on the table, and it formed itself into a tidy roll at once, while he rose and approached her. A gesture, as though to sketch her outline in the air, freed her from the lassitude that had hampered her limbs. But she had too much sense to break and run.

Whither?

"Do you know me?"

"I . . ." She licked dry lips. "I think you may be Enas Yorl."

"Fame at last," the wizard said wryly. "Do you know why you're here?"

"You . . . Well, I guess you set a trap for me. I don't know why, unless it has to do with that scroll."

"Hmm! A perceptive child!" Had he possessed eyebrows, one might have imagined the wizard raising them. And then at once: "Forgive me. I should not have said 'child.' You are old in the ways of the world, if not in years. But after the first century, such patronizing remarks come easy to the tongue . . ." He resumed his chair, inviting Jarveena with a gesture to come closer. She was reluctant.

For when he rose to inspect her, he had been squat. Under the cloak he was obviously thick-set, stocky, with a paunch. But by the time he regained his seat, it was equally definite that he was thin, light-boned, and had one shoulder higher than the other.

"You have noticed," he said. His voice too had altered; it had been baritone, while now it was at the most flattering a countertenor. "Victims of circumstance, you and I both. It was not I who set a trap for you. The scroll did."

"For me? But *why?*"

"I speak with imprecision. The trap was set not for you *qua* you. It was set for someone to whom it meant the death of another. I judge that you qualify, whether or not you know it. Do you? Make a guess. Trust your imagination. Have you, for example, recognized anybody who came to the city recently?"

Jarveena felt the blood drain from her cheeks. She folded her hands into fists.

"Sir, you are a great magician. I recognized someone tonight. Someone I never dreamed of meeting again. Someone whose death I would gladly accomplish, except that death is much too good for him."

"Explain!" Enas Yorl leaned an elbow on the table, and rested his chin on his fist . . . except that neither the elbow, nor the chin, let alone the fist, properly corresponded to such appellations.

She hesitated a second. Then she cast aside her cloak, tore loose the bow that held the cross-lacing of her jerkin at her throat, and unthreaded it so that the garment fell wide to reveal the cicatrices, brown on brown, which would never fade, and the great foul keloid like a turd where her right breast might have been.

"Why try to hide anything from a wizard?" she said bitterly. "He commanded the men who did this to me, and far far worse to many others. I thought they were bandits! I came to Sanctuary hoping that here if anywhere I might get wind of them—how could bandits gain access to Ranke or the conquered cities? But I never dreamed they would present themselves in the guise of imperial guards!"

"*They* . . . ?" Enas Yorl probed.

"Ah . . . No. I confess: it's only one that I can swear to."

"How old were you?"

"I was nine. And six grown men took pleasure of me, before they beat me with wire whips and left me for dead."

"I see." He retrieved the scroll and with its end tapped the table absently. "Can you now devine what is in this message? Bear in mind that it forced me hither."

"Forced? But I'd have thought—"

"I found myself here by choice? Oh, the contrary!" A bitter laugh rang out, acid-shrill. "I said we're both victims. Long ago when I was young I was extremely foolish. I tried to seduce away the bride of someone more powerful than me. When he found out, I was able to defend myself, but . . . Do you understand what a spell is?"

She shook her head.

"It's . . . activity. As much activity as a rock is passivity, which is conscious of being a rock but of nothing else. A worm is a little more aware; a dog or horse, much more; a human being, vastly more—but not infinitely more. In wildfire, storms, stars, can be found processes which with no consciousness of what they are act upon the outside world. A spell is such a process, created by an act of will, having neither aim nor purpose save what its creator lends. And to me my rival bequeathed . . . But no matter. I begin to sound as though I pity myself, and I know my fate is just. Shall we despise justice? This scroll can be an instrument of it. Written on it are two sentences.

"Of death."

While he spoke, there had been further changes under his concealing garb. His voice was now mellow and rich, and his hands, although very slender, possessed the ordinary number of joints. However, the redness still glowed.

"If one sentence is upon Commander Nizharu," Jarveena said firmly, "may it be executed soon."

"That could be arranged." A sardonic inflection colored the words. "At a price."

"The scroll doesn't refer to him? I imagined—"

"You imagined it spelt his doom, and that was why he was so anxious about its loss? In a way that's correct. In a way . . . And I can make certain that that shall be the outcome. At a price."

"What—price?" Her voice quavered against her will.

He rose slowly from his chair, shaking his cloak out to its fullest; it swept the floor with a faint rustling sound.

"Need you ask, of one who so plainly is obsessed by lust for women? That was the reason for my downfall. I explained."

Ice seemed to form around her heart. Her mouth was desert on the instant.

"Oh, why be so timid?" purred Enas Yorl, taking her hand in his. "You've endured many worse bedfellows. I promise."

It was true enough that the only means she had found to cross the weary leagues between Forgotten Holt and Sanctuary had been to yield her body: to merchants, mercenaries, grooms, guardsmen . . .

"Tell me first," she said with a final flare of spirit, "whose deaths are cited in the document."

"Fair," said the wizard. "Know, then, that one is an unnamed man, who is to be falsely convicted of the murder of another. And that other is the new governor, the prince."

Thereupon the light faded, and he embraced her unresisting.

5

She woke late, at least half an hour past dawn. She was in her own bed; the dormitory was otherwise empty. All her limbs were pervaded by a delicious languor. Enas Yorl had kept his promise. If he had been equally skilled when he was younger, small wonder his rival's bride had preferred him to her husband!

Reluctantly opening her eyes, she saw something on the rough pillow. Puzzled, she looked again, reached out, touched: green, iridescent, powdery—

*Scales!*

With a cry she leapt from the bed, just as Melilot marched in, red-faced with fury.

"So there you are, you little slut! Where were you all night? I watched until I could stay awake no longer! By now I was sure you'd been taken by the guard and thrown in jail! *What did Nizharu say?*"

Naked, bewildered, for a long moment Jarveena was at a loss. Then her eye fell on something infinitely reassuring. On the wooden peg over her bed hung her cloak, jerkin and breeches, and also her precious writing-case, just as though she herself had replaced them on retiring.

Seizing the case, she opened the compartment where she hid such things, and triumphantly produced the gold she had accepted from the commander—but not the silver he had allotted to herself.

"He paid this for a false rendering of the scroll," she said. "But you're not to make one."

"What?" Snatching the coins, Melilot made to bite them, but checked.

"How would you like to be scribe by appointment to the governor's household?"

"Are you crazed?" The fat man's eyes bulbed.

"Not in the least." Heedless of his presence, Jarveena reached under the bed for her chamber-pot and put it to its appropriate use. Meantime she explained the plot she had hatched.

"But this means you're claiming to have read the scroll," Melilot said slowly as he tried to digest her proposals. "It's enchanted! How could you?"

"Not I, but Enas Yorl."

Melilot's mouth worked and all his color drained away. "But his palace is guarded by basilisks!" he exclaimed at last. "You'd have been struck to stone!"

"It doesn't quite work like that," Jarveena said, pulling on her breeches, giving silent thanks that she could do so briskly. That dreadful paralysis would haunt her dreams for years. "To settle the argument, though, why don't you bring the scroll? I mean, why don't we go and take another look at it?"

They were in his sanctum a couple of minutes later.

"It's perfectly clear," Melilot said slowly when he had perused the document twice. "It's very stilted—formal Rankene—and I don't know anybody here or in the conquered cities who would use it for a letter. But it says exactly what you said it would."

A tremor of awe made his rolls of fat wobble.

"You're satisfied it's the same scroll? There's been no substitution?" Jarveena pressed.

"Yes! It's been all night in a locked chest! Only magic can account for what's happened to it!"

"Then," she said with satisfaction, "let's get on with the job."

\* \* \*

Each noon, in the grounds of the Governor's Palace before the Halls of Justice, the guard was inspected and rotated. This ceremony was open to the public—to everybody, in principle, but in practice only to those who could afford to bribe the gate guards. Hence most of the spectators were of the upper class, hangers-on of the nobility, or making an appearance at the law courts. Not a few bore a general resemblance, in figure or clothing and in their retinue, to Melilot, who was in any case a frequent visitor when transcripts of evidence were in demand.

Therefore his presence and Jarveena's were unremarkable. Moreover word had got about that today was the last day when the crack imperial guards would perform the ceremonial drill before fifteen of them were ordered back to Ranke. There was a much larger throng than usual awaiting the appearance of the governor, one of whose customary chores this was whenever he was in residence.

It was a warm, dry, dusty day. The sun cast strong dark shadows. Tents, pavilions, stone walls seemed all of a substance. So in a way did people, especially those in armor. Under closed visors, any soldier might have been mistaken for any other of like stature.

Strictly it was not the turn of a guard detachment from the watchhouse on Processional Way to take over from the Hell-Hounds. But a few bribes, and a sharp order from Aye-Gophlan, and the problem had been sorted out.

Jarveena composed her features and did her best to look as though she were just another casual passerby impressed by the standard of marching of troops from the capital, rather than a person whose dearest ambition for revenge bid fair to be fulfilled.

But her mouth kept wanting to snarl open like a wolf's.

The relieving guard marched in from the direction of Governor's Walk, exchanged salutes and passwords with the imperial troops, and formed up in the center of the courtyard. Attended by two armed orderlies, Commander Nizharu formally recognized his successor and took station at his side for the governor's inspection. As soon as it was over, the departing troops would retire by squads and march away with flying colors.

Less than ten minutes later, amid a ripple of applause at the precision drill of the Hell-Hounds, the prince was leaving the parade ground arm-in-arm with Nizharu. The latter was being posted back to the capital, but five of his comrades were to establish a bodyguard of local soldiers for the governor, trained to imperial standards.

So rumor said. Rumor had been known to lie.

With some care and ingenuity, Melilot had smiled and shoved his way to the front of the crowd, and as the two approached and all were bowing, he said very loudly and clearly, "Why, commander! What good luck! Now is my chance to return the scroll you dropped yesterday morning!"

Nizharu had raised his visor because of the heat. It could clearly be seen that his face grew pasty-pale. "I—I know nothing of any scroll!" he barked as soon as he could gather his wits.

"No? Oh, in that case, if it isn't yours, I'm sure the prince will accept it from me with a view to tracing its rightful owner!"

Fat though he was, Melilot could act briskly when he must. He whipped the scroll from under his robe and thrust it into Jarveena's eager hand. A heartbeat later, she was on her bended knee before the prince, gazing up into his handsome, youthful, and somewhat vacuous face.

"Read, Your Highness!" she insisted fiercely, and almost forced him to take hold of it.

The instant the prince caught its tenor, he froze. Nizharu did the opposite. Spinning on his heel, he shouted for his men and broke into a run.

The knife which Jarveena carried in her writing-case served other purposes than the sharpening of reed-pens. She withdrew it with a practiced flick, aimed, *threw*.

And, howling, Nizharu measured his length on the ground, pierced behind the right knee where there was only leather, not metal, to protect him.

The crowd shouted in alarm and seemed on the brink of panic, but the incoming guard had been warned. Throwing back his visor, Captain Aye-Gophlan ordered his men to surround and arrest Nizharu, and in a fine towering rage the prince bellowed at the onlookers to explain why.

"This message is from a traitor at the imperial court! It instructs Nizharu to assign one of his guards to murder me as soon as he has found someone on whom the charge can be falsely pinned! And it says that the writer is enchanting the message to prevent the wrong person's reading it—but there's no difficulty in reading this! It's the court writing I was first taught as a child!"

"We—ah—arranged for the magic to be eliminated," hinted Melilot. And added quickly, "Your Highness!"

"How came you by it?"

"It was dropped by Nizharu when he inspected our guardhouse."
That was Aye-Gophlan, marching smartly forward. "Thinking it important, I consulted Master Melilot, whom I've long known to be loyal and
discreet."

"And as for me . . ." Melilot gave a deprecating shrug. "I have certain *contacts*, let us say. It put me to no trouble to counteract the
spell."

True, thought Jarveena, and marveled at how cleverly he lied.

"You shall be well rewarded," declared the prince. "And, after due
trial, so shall he be! Attempting the life of one of the imperial blood—
why, it's as heinous a crime as anyone might name! It was a miracle
that he let fall the scroll. Surely the gods are on my side!" Raising his
voice again: "Tonight let all make sacrifice and give thanks! Under divine protection I have survived a dastardly assassin!"

If all gods, Jarveena thought, are no better than Melilot, I'm content
to be an unbeliever. But I do look forward to watching Nizharu fry.

6

"In view of how you must be feeling, Jarveena," said a soft voice at
her side, "I compliment you on the way you are concealing your emotions."

"It's not difficult," she answered with bitterness. The crowd was dispersing around them, heading away from the execution block where, according to the strict form, traitor Nizharu had paid for his many crimes
by beating, hanging, and lastly burning.

And then she started. The person who had addressed her was nobody
she recognized: tall, stooped, elderly, with wisps of grey hair, carrying a
market-basket . . .

Where eyes should be, a glint of red.

"Enas Yorl?" she whispered.

"That same." With a dry chuckle. "Inasmuch as I can ever make the
statement . . . Are you content?"

"I—I guess I'm not." Jarveena turned away and began to follow the
drift of the crowd. "I ought to be! I begged the privilege of writing the
authorization for his execution in my own hand, and I thought I might
include mention of my parents, my friends, the villagers he slaughtered

or enslaved, but my formal Rankene isn't good enough, so I had to make do copying a draft by Melilot!" She tossed her head. "And I hoped to stand up in open court, swear to what he did, watch the faces of the people change as they realized what a filthy villain came hither disguised as an imperial officer . . . They said there was no need for any other evidence after Aye-Gophlan's and Melilot's and the prince's."

"To speak after princes is a dangerous habit," opined the wizard. "But at all events, it appears to have dawned on you that revenge is never what you hope for. Take my own case. He who did to me what you know of was so determined to wreak his vengeance that he created one spell more than he could handle. To each he was obliged to cede a certain portion of his will; for as I told you, spells have no aim or purpose of their own. He thereby deprived himself of ordinary sense, and to his death sat blubbering and moaning like an infant."

"Why do you tell me this?" cried Jarveena. "I want to make the most of my moment of satisfaction, even if it can't be as rich and memorable as I dreamed."

"Because," said the wizard, taking her arm by fingers whose touch evoked extraordinary thrills all over her, "you paid a fair and honest price for the service I undertook. I shall not forget you. Scarred and branded you may be without; within you are beautiful."

"Me?" said Jarveena with genuine astonishment. "As well call a toad beautiful, or a mud wall!"

"As you like," Enas Yorl answered with a shrug. The movement revealed that he was no longer quite what he had been earlier. "At all events, there is a second reason."

"What?"

"You read the writing on the scroll, and previously I had described it to you. Nonetheless you're acting as though you have forgotten something."

For a brief moment she failed to take his point. Then her hand flew to her open mouth.

"Two deaths," she whispered.

"Yes, indeed. And I scarcely need tell you to whom a traitor in the imperial court would apply for a spell powerful enough to drag me into the matter willy-nilly. I could make the paper legible. I could not evade the consequences of undoing a colleague's work."

"Whose death? *Mine?*"

"It would be politic to minimize the danger, as for instance by taking employment with a seafarer. Many merchant-captains would be glad of

a skillful clerk, and after your apprenticeship with Melilot you're well
equipped for such a post. Moreover, your present master is inclined to
jealousy. You are half his age, yet already he regards you as a rival."

"He dissembles well," muttered Jarveena, "but now and then he's
acted in a fashion that makes me believe you."

"He might regard you more kindly were you to become a sort of foreign agent for him. I'm sure you could contrive—for a reasonable fee—to
supply him with commercially valuable information. He would scarcely
object to adding other strings to his bow: trading in spices, for instance."

For a while Jarveena had seemed enlivened by his discourse. Now
she fell back into gloom.

"Why should I want to make myself rich, let alone him? Ever since I
can remember I've had a purpose in life. It's gone—carried to the sky
with the stench of Nizharu!"

"It takes a very rich person to commission a spell."

"What would I want with magic?" she said contemptuously.

A second later, and it was as though fire coursed all over her body,
outlining every mark that defaced her, every whiplash, every burn,
every cut and scratch. She had forgotten until now, but sometime during
that extraordinary night when she had lain with him, he had taken the
trouble to trace her whole violent life-story from the map of her skin.

Now she also remembered thinking that it must be for some private
magical reason. Could she have been wrong? Could it have been simpler
than that—could it just have been that he sympathized with one whom
life had scarred in another way?

"You might wish," he was saying calmly, "to cleanse your body of
the past as I think you have now begun to cleanse your mind."

"Even. . . ?" She could not complete the question save by raising
her hand to the right side of her chest.

"In time. You are young. Nothing is impossible. But one thing is
much too possible. We've spoken of it. Now, act!"

They were almost at the gate, and the crowd was pressing and jostling; people were setting their hands to their money-belts and pouches,
for these were prime conditions for theft.

"I take it you'd not have spoken up unless you had a new employer
in mind for me?" Jarveena said at length.

"You're most perceptive."

"And if there were not some long-term advantage in it for yourself?"

Enas Yorl sighed. "There is a long-term purpose to everything. If there were not, spells would be impossible."

"So there was a purpose behind Nizharu's dropping of the scroll?"

"Dropping. . . ?"

"Oh! Why didn't I think of that?"

"In time, I'm sure you would have done. But you came to Sanctuary so recently, you could scarcely be expected to know that in his boyhood Aye-Gophlan was counted among the smartest dips and cutpurses in the city. How else do you think he managed to buy himself a commission in the guards? Does he talk as though he came from a wealthy background?"

They were at the gate, and being squeezed through. Clutching her writing-case tightly with one hand, keeping the other folded over the silver pin which fastened her cloak in a roll around her waist, Jarveena thought long and long.

And came to a decision.

Even though her main purpose in life up to now had vanished, there was no reason why she should not find another and maybe better ambition. If that were so, there were good reasons to try and prolong her life by quitting Sanctuary.

Although. . .

She glanced around in alarm for the magician, thinking them separated in the throng, and with relief was able to catch him by the arm.

"Will distance make any difference? I mean, if the doom is on me, can I flee from it?"

"Oh, it's not on you. It's merely that there were two deaths in the charm, and only one has happened. Any day of any year, scores of hundreds die in any city of this size. It's probable that the spell will work itself out locally; when there's a thunderstorm, the lightning strikes beneath it, not a hundred leagues away. Not inconceivably the other death may be that of someone who was as guilty as Nizharu in the sack of Forgotten Holt. He had soldiers with him, did he not?"

"Yes, they were all soldiers, whom I long mistook for bandits. . . ! Oh, what a pass this land has come to! You're quite right! I'm going away, as far as I can, whether or not it means I can outrun my death!"

She caught his hand, gave it a squeeze, and leaned close. "Name the ship that I must look for!"

The day the ship sailed it was unsafe for Enas Yorl to venture on the street; occasionally the changes working in him cycled into forms that

nobody, not with the kindest will in the world, could mistake for
human. He was therefore obliged to watch the tiring way, making use of
a scrying-glass, but he was determined to make certain that nothing had
gone wrong with his scheme.

All turned out well. He tracked the ship, with Jarveena at her stern,
until sea-mists obscured her, and then leaned back in what, for the time
being, could not exactly be a chair as most people thought of chairs.

"And with you no longer around to attract it," he murmured to the
air, "perhaps luck may lead that second death-sentence to be passed on
one who wearies beyond measure of mad existence, sport of a hundred
mindless spells, this miserable, this pitiable Enas Yorl."

Yet some hope glimmered, like the red pits he had to wear for eyes,
in the knowledge that at least one person in the world thought more
kindly of him than he did himself. At length, with a snorting laugh, he
covered the scrying-glass and settled down resignedly to wait out the
implacable transformation, a little comforted by knowing that so far he
had never been the same shape twice.

# The Face of Chaos

## Lynn Abbey

The cards lay face down in a wide crescent on the black-velvet-covered table Illyra used for her fortune-telling. Closing her eyes, she touched one at random with her index finger, then overturned it. The Face of Chaos, portrait of man and woman seen in a broken mirror. She had done a card-reading for herself; an attempt to penetrate the atmosphere of foreboding that had hung over the ramshackle cloth-and-wood structure she and Dubro, the bazaar smith, called home. Instead it had only brought more anxiety.

She went to another small table to apply a thick coating of kohl to her eyelids. No one would visit a young, pretty S'danzo to have their fortune told, and no stranger could enter her home for any other reason. The kohl and the formless S'danzo costume concealed her age in the dimly lit room, but if some love-deluded soldier or merchant moved too close, there was always Dubro under the canopy a few steps away. One sight of the brawny, sweating giant with his heavy mallet ended any crisis.

"Sweetmeats! Sweetmeats! Always the best in the bazaar. Always the best in Sanctuary!"

The voice of Haakon, the vendor, reached through the cloth-hung doorway. Illyra finished her toilette quickly. Dark masses of curly hair were secured with one pin under a purple silk scarf which contrasted garishly with each of the skirts, the shawl, and the blouse she wore. She reached deep within those skirts for her purse and removed a copper coin.

It was still early enough in the day that she might venture outside their home. Everyone in the bazaar knew she was scarce more than a girl, and there would be no city-folk wandering about for another hour, at least.

"Haakon! Over here!" She called from under the canopy where Dubro kept his tools. "Two . . . no, three, please."

He lifted three of the sticky treats on to a shell that she held out for them, accepting her copper coin with a smile. In an hour's time, Haakon would want five of the same coin for such a purchase, but the bazaar-folk sold the best to each other for less.

She ate one, but offered the other two to Dubro. She would have kissed him, but the smith shrank back from public affection, preferring privacy for all things which pass between a man and woman. He smiled and accepted them wordlessly. The big man seldom spoke; words came slowly to him. He mended the metalwares of the bazaar-folk, improving many as he did so. He had protected Illyra since she'd been an orphaned child wandering the stalls, turned out by her own people for the irredeemable crime of being a half-caste. Bright-eyed, quick-tongued Illyra spoke for him now whenever anything needed to be said, and in turn, he still took care of her.

The sweetmeats gone, Dubro returned to the fire, lifting up a barrel hoop he had left there to heat. Illyra watched with never-sated interest as he laid it on the anvil to pound it back into a true circle for Jofan, the wineseller. The mallet fell, but instead of the clear, ringing sound of metal on metal, there was a hollow clang. The horn of the anvil fell into the dirt.

Even Haakon was wide-eyed with silent surprise. Dubro's anvil had been in the bazaar since . . . since Dubro's grandfather for certain, and perhaps longer—no one could remember before that. The smith's face darkened to the color of the cooling iron. Illyra placed her hands over his.

"We'll get it fixed. We'll take it up to the Court of Arms this afternoon. I'll borrow Moonflower's ass-and-cart . . ."

"No!" Dubro exploded with one tortured word, shook loose her hands, and stared at the broken pieces of his livelihood.

"Can't fix an anvil that's broken like that one," Haakon explained softly to her. "It'll only be as strong as the seam."

"Then we'll get a new one," she responded, mindful of Dubro's bleak face and her own certain knowledge that no one else in the bazaar possessed an anvil to sell.

"There hasn't been a new anvil in Sanctuary since before Ranke closed down the sea-trade with Ilsig. You'd need four camels and a year to get a mountain-cast anvil like that one into the bazaar—if you had the gold."

A single tear smeared through the kohl. She and Dubro were well off by the standards of the bazaar. They had ample copper coins for Haakon's sweetmeats and fresh fish three times a week, but a pitifully small hoard of gold with which to convince the caravan merchants to bring an anvil from distant Ranke.

"We've got to have an anvil!" She exclaimed to the unlistening gods, since Dubro and Haakon were already aware of the problem.

Dubro kicked dirt over his fire and strode away from the small forge.

"Watch him for me, Haakon. He's never been like this."

"I'll watch him—but it will be your problem tonight when he comes home."

A few of the city-folk were already milling in the aisles of the bazaar; it was high time to hide in her room. Never before in her five years of working the S'danzo trade within the bazaar had she faced a day when Dubro did not lend his calm presence to the stream of patrons. He controlled their coming and going. Without him, she did not know who was waiting, or how to discourage a patron who had questions—but no money. She sat in the incense-heavy darkness waiting and brooding.

Moonflower. She would go to Moonflower, not for the old woman's broken-down cart, but for advice. The old woman had never shunned her the way the other S'danzo had. But Moonflower wouldn't know about fixing anvils, and what could she add to the message so clearly conveyed by the Face of Chaos? Besides, Moonflower's richest patrons arrived early in the day to catch her best "vibrations." The old woman would not appreciate a poor relation taking up her patrons' valuable time.

No patrons of her own yet, either. Perhaps the weather had turned bad. Perhaps, seeing the forge empty, they assumed that the inner chamber was empty also. Illyra dared not step outside to find out.

She shuffled and handled the deck of fortune-telling cards, acquiring a measure of self-control from their worn surfaces. Palming the bottom card, Illyra laid it face-up on the black velvet.

"Five of Ships," she whispered.

The card was a stylized scene of five small fishing boats, each with its net cast into the water. Tradition said that the answer to her question was in the card. Her gift would let her find it—if she could sort out the many questions floating in her thoughts.

"Illyra, the fortune-teller?"

Illyra's reverie was interrupted by her first patron before she had gained a satisfactory focus in the card. This first woman had problems with her many lovers, but her reading was spoiled by another patron stepping through the door at the wrong time. This second patron's reading was disrupted by the fish-smoker looking for Dubro. The day was everything the Face of Chaos had promised.

The few readings which were not disrupted reflected her own despair more than the patron's. Dubro had not returned, and she was startled by any sound from the outside canopy. Her patrons sensed the confusion and were unsatisfied with her performance. Some refused to pay. An older, more experienced S'danzo would know how to handle these things, but Illyra only shrank back in frustration. She tied a frayed rope across the entrance to her fortune-telling room to discourage anyone from seeking her advice.

"Madame Illyra?"

An unfamiliar woman's voice called from outside, undaunted by the rope.

"I'm not seeing anyone this afternoon. Come back tomorrow."

"I can't wait until tomorrow."

They all say that, Illyra thought. Everyone else always knows that they are the most important person I see and that their questions are the most complex. But they are all very much the same. Let the woman come back.

The stranger could be heard hesitating beyond the rope. Illyra heard the sound of rustling cloth—possibly silk—as the woman finally turned away. The sound jarred the S'danzo to alertness. Silken skirts meant wealth. A flash of vision illuminated Illyra's mind—this was a patron she could not let go elsewhere.

"If you can't wait, I'll see you now," she yelled.

"You will?"

Illyra untied the rope and lifted the hanging cloth to let the woman enter. She had surrounded herself with a shapeless, plain shawl; her face was veiled and shadowed by a corner of the shawl wound around her head. The stranger was certainly not someone who came to the S'danzo of the bazaar often. Illyra retied the rope after seating her patron on one side of the velvet-covered table.

A woman of means who wishes to be mysterious. That shawl might be plain, but it is too good for someone as poor as she pretends to be. She wears silk beneath it, and smells of roses, though she has tried to remove perfumes. No doubt she has gold, not silver or copper.

"Would you not be more comfortable removing your shawl? It is quite warm in here," Illyra said, after studying the woman.

"I'd prefer not to."

A difficult one, Illyra thought.

The woman's hand emerged from the shawl to drop three old Ilsig gold coins onto the velvet. The hand was white, smooth, and youthful. The Ilsig coins were rare now that the Rankan empire controlled Sanctuary. The woman and her questions were a welcome relief from Illyra's own thoughts.

"Well, then, what is your name?"

"I'd prefer not to say."

"I must have some information if I'm to help you," Illyra said as she scooped the coins into a worn piece of silk, taking care not to let her fingers touch the gold.

"My ser . . . There are those who tell me that you alone of the S'danzo can see the near future. I must know what will happen to me tomorrow night."

The question did not fulfill Illyra's curiosity or the promise of mystery, but she reached for her deck of cards.

"You are familiar with these?" she asked the woman.

"Somewhat."

"Then divide them into three piles and choose one card from each pile—that will show me your future."

"For tomorrow night?"

"Assuredly. The answer is contained within the moment of the question. Take the cards."

The veiled woman handled the cards fearfully. Her hands shook so badly that the three piles were simply unsquared heaps. The woman was visibly reluctant to touch the cards again and gingerly overturned the top card of each rather than handle them again.

Lance of Flames.

The Archway.

Five of Ships, reversed.

Illyra drew her hands back from the velvet in alarm. The Five of Ships—the card had been in her own hands not moments before. She did not remember replacing it in the deck. With a quivering foreknowledge

that she would see a part of her own fate in the cards, Illyra opened her
mind to receive the answer. And closed it almost at once.

Falling stones, curses, murder, a journey without return. None of the
cards was particularly auspicious, but together they created an image of
malice and death that was normally hidden from the living. The S'danzo
never foretold death when they saw it, and though she was but half-
S'danzo and shunned by them, Illyra abided by their codes and super-
stitions.

"It would be best to remain at home, especially tomorrow night.
Stand back from walls which might have loose stones in them. Safety
lies within yourself. Do not seek other advice—especially from the
priests of the temples."

Her visitor's reserve crumbled. She gasped, sobbed, and shook with
unmistakable terror. But before Illyra could speak the words to calm
her, the black-clad woman dashed away, pulling the frayed rope from
its anchorage.

"Come back!" Illyra called.

The woman turned while still under the canopy. Her shawl fell back
to reveal a fair-skinned blonde woman of a youthful and delicate beauty.
A victim of a spurned lover? Or a jealous wife?

"If you had already seen your fate—then you should have asked a
different question, such as whether it can be changed," she chided
softly, guiding the woman back into the incense-filled chamber.

"I thought if you saw differently . . . But Molin Torchholder will
have his way. Even you have seen it."

Molin Torchholder. Illyra recognized the name. He was the priestly
temple-builder within the Rankan prince's entourage. She had another
friend and patron living within his household. Was this the woman of
Cappen Varra's idylls? Had the minstrel finally overstepped himself?

"Why would the Rankan have his way with you?" she asked, prying
gently.

"They have sought to build a temple for their gods."

"But you are not a goddess, nor even Rankan. Such things should
not concern you."

Illyra spoke lightly, but she knew, from the cards, that the priests
sought her as part of some ritual—not in personal interest.

"My father is rich—proud and powerful among those of Sanctuary
who have never accepted the fall of the Ilsig kingdom and will never accept the empire. Molin has singled my father out. He has demanded our
lands for his temple. When we refused, he forced the weaker men not to

trade with us. But my father would not give in. He believes the gods of Ilsig are stronger, but Molin has vowed revenge rather than admit failure."

"Perhaps your family will have to leave Sanctuary to escape this foreign priest, and your home be torn down to build their temple. But though the city may be all you know, the world is large, and this place but a poor part of it."

Illyra spoke with far more authority than she actually commanded. Since the death of her mother, she had left the bazaar itself only a handful of times and had never left the city. The words were part of the S'danzo oratory Moonflower had taught her.

"My father and the others must leave, but not me. I'm to be part of Molin Torchholder's revenge. His men came once to my father's house. The Rankan offered us my full bride-price, though he is married. Father refused the 'honor.' Molin's men beat him senseless and carried me screaming from the house.

"I fought with him when he came to me that night. He will not want another woman for some time. But my father could not believe I had not been dishonored. And Molin said that if I would not yield to him, then no living man should have me."

"Such are ever the words of scorned men," Illyra added gently.

"No. It was a curse. *I* know this for certain. Their gods are strong enough to answer when they call.

"Last night two of their Hell-Hounds appeared at our estate to offer new terms to my father. A fair price for our land, safe conduct to Ilsig—but I am to remain behind. Tomorrow night they will consecrate the cornerstone of their new temple with a virgin's death. I am to be under that stone when they lay it."

Though Illyra was not specifically a truth-seer, the tale tied all the horrific visions into a whole. It would take the gods to save this woman from the fate Molin Torchholder had waiting for her. It was no secret that the empire sought to conquer the Ilsig gods as they had conquered their armies. If the Rankan priest could curse a woman with unbreachable virginity, Illyra didn't think there was much she could do.

The woman was still sobbing. There was no future in her patronage, but Illyra felt sorry for her. She opened a little cabinet and shook a good-sized pinch of white powder into a small liquid-filled vial.

"Tonight, before you retire, take this with a glass of wine."

The woman clutched it tightly, though the fear did fade from her eyes.

"Do I owe you more for this?" she asked.

"No, it is the least I could do for you."

There was enough of the cylantha powder to keep the woman asleep for three days. Perhaps Molin Torchholder would not want a sleeping virgin in his rite. If he did not mind, the woman would not awaken to find out.

"I can give you much gold. I could bring you to Ilsig."

Illyra shook her head.

"There is but one thing I wish—and you do not have it," she whispered, surprised by the sudden impulsiveness of her words. "Not all the gold in Sanctuary will find another anvil for Dubro."

"I do not know this Dubro, but there is an anvil in my father's stables. It will not return to Ilsig. It can be yours, if I'm alive to tell my father to give it to you."

The impulsiveness cleared from Illyra's mind. There were reasons now to soothe the young woman's fears.

"It is a generous offer," she replied. "I shall see you then, three days hence at your father's home—if you will tell me where it is."

And if you do, she added to herself, then it will not matter if you survive or not.

"It is the estate called 'Land's End,' behind the temple of Ils, Himself."

"Whom shall I ask for?"

"Marilla."

They stared at each other for a few moments, then the blonde woman made her way into the afternoon-crowded bazaar. Illyra knotted the rope across the entrance to her chambers with distracted intensity.

How many years—five at least—she had been answering the banal questions of city-folk who could not see anything for themselves. Never, in all that time, had she asked a question of a patron, or seen such a death, or one of her own cards in a reading. And in all the years of memory within the S'danzo community within the bazaar, never had any of them crossed fates with the gods.

No, I have nothing to do with gods. I do not notice them, and they do not see me. My gift is S'danzo. I am S'danzo. We live by fate. We do not touch the affairs of gods.

But Illyra could not convince herself. The thought circled in her mind that she had wandered beyond the realms of her people and gifts. She lit the incense of gentle-forgetting, inhaling it deeply, but the sound of Dubro's anvil breaking and the images of the three cards remained ungentle in her thoughts. As the afternoon waned, she convinced herself again to approach Moonflower for advice.

The obese S'danzo woman's three children squalled at each other in the dust while her dark-eyed husband sat in the shade holding his hands over his eyes and ears. It was not an auspicious moment to seek the older woman's counsel. The throngs of people were leaving the bazaar, making it safe for Illyra to wander among the stalls looking for Dubro.

"Illyra!"

She had expected Dubro's voice, but this one was familiar also. She looked closely into the crowd at the wineseller's.

"Cappen Varra?"

"The same," he answered, greeting her with a smile. "There was a rope across your gate today, and Dubro was not busy at his fire—otherwise I should have stopped to see you."

"You have a question?"

"No, my life could not be better. I have a song for you."

"Today is not a day for songs. Have you seen Dubro?"

"No. I'm here to get wine for a special dinner tomorrow night. Thanks to you, I know where the best wine in Sanctuary is still to be found."

"A new love?"

"The same. She grows more radiant with each day. Tomorrow the master of the house will be busy with his priestly functions. The household will be quiet."

"The household of Molin Torchholder must agree with you then. It is good to be in the grace of the conquerors of Ilsig."

"I'm discreet. So is Molin. It is a trait which seems to have been lost among the natives of Sanctuary—S'danzo excepted, of course. I'm most comfortable within his house."

The seller handed him two freshly washed bottles of wine, and with brief farewells, Illyra saw him on his way. The wineseller had seen Dubro earlier in the day. He offered that the smith was visiting every wineseller in the bazaar and not a few of the taverns outside it. Similar stories waited for her at the other winesellers. She returned to the forge-home in the gathering twilight and fog.

Ten candles and the oil stove could not cut through the dark emptiness in the chamber. Illyra pulled her shawls tightly around her and tried to nap until Dubro returned. She would not let herself think that he would not return.

"You have been waiting for me."

Illyra jumped at the sound. Only two of the candles remained lit; she had no idea how long she had slept, only that her home quivered with shadows and a man, as tall as Dubro but of cadaverous thinness, stood within the knotted rope.

"Who are you? What do you want?" She flattened against the back of the chair.

"Since you do not recognize me, then say, I have been looking for you."

The man gestured. The candles and stove rekindled and Illyra found herself staring at the blue-starred face of the magician Lythande.

"I have done nothing to cross you," she said, rising slowly from her chair.

"And I did not say that you had. I thought you were seeking me. Many of us have heard you calling today."

He held up the three cards Marilla had overturned and the Face of Chaos.

"I—I had not known my problems could disturb your studies."

"I was reflecting on the legend of the Five Ships—it was comparatively easy for you to touch me. I have taken it to myself to learn things for you.

"The girl Marilla appealed first to her own gods. They sent her to you since for them to act on her fate would rouse the ire of Sabellia and Savankala. They have tied your fates together. You will not solve your own troubles unless you can relieve hers."

"She is a dead woman, Lythande. If the gods of Ilsig wish to help her, they will need all their strength—and if that isn't enough, then there is nothing I can do for her."

"That is not a wise position to take, Illyra," the magician said with a smile.

"That is what I *saw*. S'danzo do not cross fates with the gods."

"And you, Illyra, are not S'danzo."

She gripped the back of the chair, angered by the reminder but unable to counter it.

"They have passed the obligation to you," he said.

"I do not know how to break through Marilla's fate," Illyra said simply. "I *see*, they must *change*."

Lythande laughed. "Perhaps there *is* no way, child. Maybe it will take two sacrifices to consecrate the temple Molin Torchholder builds. *You* had best hope there is a way through Marilla's fate."

A cold breeze accompanied his laughter. The candles flickered a moment, and the magician was gone. Illyra stared at the undisturbed rope.

Let Lythande and the others help her if it's so important. I want only the anvil, and that I can have regardless of her fate.

The cold air clung to the room. Already her imagination was embroidering upon the consequences of enraging any of the powerful deities of Sanctuary. She left to search for Dubro in the fog-shrouded bazaar.

Fog tendrils obscured the familiar stalls and shacks of the daytime bazaar. A few fires could be glimpsed through cracked doorways, but the area itself had gone to sleep early, leaving Illyra to roam through the moist night alone.

Nearing the main entrance she saw the bobbing torch of a running man. The torch and runner fell with an aborted shout. She heard lighter footsteps running off into the unlit fog. Cautiously, fearfully, Illyra crept toward the fallen man.

It was not Dubro, but a shorter man wearing a blue hawk-mask. A dagger protruded from the side of his neck. Illyra felt no sorrow at the death of one of Jubal's bully-boys, only relief that it had not been Dubro. Jubal was worse than the Rankans. Perhaps the crimes of the man behind the mask had finally caught up with him. More likely someone had risked venting a grudge against the seldom-seen former gladiator. Anyone who dealt with Jubal had more enemies than friends.

As if in silent response to her thoughts, another group of men appeared out of the fog. Illyra hid among the crates and boxes while five men without masks studied the dead man. Then, without warning, one of them threw aside his torch and fell on the warm corpse, striking it again and again with his knife. When he had had his fill of death, the others took their turns.

The bloody hawk-mask rolled to within a hand-span of Illyra's foot. She held her breath and did not move, her eyes riveted in horror on the unrecognizable body in front of her. She wandered away from the scene blind to everything but her own disbelieving shock. The atrocity seemed to be the final senseless gesture of the Face of Chaos in a day which had unraveled her existence.

She leaned against a canopy-post fighting waves of nausea, but Haakon's sweetmeats had been the only food she had eaten all day. The dry heaving of her stomach brought no relief.

" 'Lyra!"

A familiar voice roared behind her and an arm thrown protectively around her shoulder broke the spell. She clung to Dubro with clenched fingers, burying her convulsive sobs in his leather vest. He reeked of wine and the salty fog. She savored every breath of him.

" 'Lyra, what are you doing out here?" He paused, but she did not reply. "Did you begin to think I'd not come back to you?"

He held her tightly, swaying restlessly back and forth. The story of the hawk-masked man's death fell from her in wracked gasps. It took Dubro only a moment to decide that his beloved Illyra had suffered too much in his absence and to repent that he had gotten drunk or sought work outside the bazaar. He lifted her gently and carried her back to their home, muttering softly to himself as he walked.

Not even Dubro's comforting arms could protect Illyra from the nightmare visions that stalked her sleep once they had returned to their home. He shook off his drunkenness to watch over her as she tossed and fretted on the sleeping linens. Each time he thought she had settled into a calm sleep, the dreams would start again. Illyra would awaken sweating and incoherent from fear. She would not describe her dreams to him when he asked. He began to suspect that something worse than the murder had taken place in his absence, though their home showed no sign of attack or struggle.

Illyra did try to voice her fears to him at each waking interlude, but the mixture of visions and emotions found no expression in her voice. Within her mind, each redreaming of the nightmare brought her closer to a single image which both collected her problems and eliminated them. The first rays of a feeble dawn had broken through the fog when she had the final synthetic experience of the dream.

She saw herself at a place the dream-spirit said was the estate called Land's End. The estate had been long abandoned, with only an anvil chained to a pedestal in the center of a starlit courtyard to show that it had been inhabited. Illyra broke the chain easily and lifted the anvil as if it had been paper. Clouds rushed in as she walked away and a moaning wind began to blow dust-devils around her. She hurried towards the doorway where Dubro waited for his gift.

The steel cracked before she had traveled half the distance, and the anvil crumbled completely as she transferred it to him. Rain began to fall, washing away Dubro's face to reveal Lythande's cruel, mocking smile. The magician struck her with the card marked with the Face of Chaos. And she died, only to find herself captive within her body which was being carried by unseen hands to a vast pit. The dissonant music of priestly chants and cymbals surrounded her. Within the dream, Illyra opened her dead eyes to see a large block of stone descending into the pit over her.

"I'm already dead!" she screamed, struggling to free her arms and legs from invisible bindings. "I can't be sacrificed—I'm already dead!"

Her arms came free. She flailed wildly. The walls of the pit were glassy and without handholds. The lowered stone touched her head. She shrieked as the life left her body for a second time. Her body released her spirit, and she rose up through the stone, waking as she did.

"It was a dream," Illyra said before Dubro could ask.

The solution was safe in her mind now. The dream would not return. But it was like a reading with the cards. In order to understand what the dream-spirit had given her, she would have to meditate upon it.

"You said something of death and sacrifice," Dubro said, unmollified by her suddenly calmed face.

"It was a dream."

"What sort of dream? Are you afraid that I will leave you or the bazaar now that I have no work to do?"

"No," she said quickly, masking the fresh anxiety his words produced. "Besides, I have found an anvil for us."

"In your dream with the death and sacrifice?"

"Death and sacrifice are keys the dream-spirit gave me. Now I must take the time to understand them."

Dubro stepped back from her. He was not S'danzo, and though bazaar-folk, he was not comfortable around their traditions or their gifts. When Illyra spoke of "seeing" or "knowing," he would draw away from her. He sat, quiet and sullen, in a chair pulled into the corner most distant from her S'danzo paraphernalia.

She stared at the black-velvet covering of her table well past the dawn and the start of a gentle rain. Dubro placed a shell with a sweetmeat in it before her. She nodded, smiled, and ate it, but did not say anything. The smith had already turned away two patrons when Illyra finished her meditation.

"Are you finished now, 'Lyra?" he asked, his distrust of S'danzo ways not overshadowing his concern for her.

"I think so."

"No more death and sacrifice?"

She nodded and began to relate the tale of the previous day's events. Dubro listened quietly until she reached the part about Lythande.

"In my home? Within these walls?" he demanded.

"I saw him, but I don't know how he got in here. The rope was un-touched."

"No!" Dubro exclaimed, beginning to pace like a caged animal. "No, I want none of this. I will not have magicians and sorcerers in my home!"

"You weren't here, and I did not invite him in." Illyra's dark eyes flashed at him as she spoke. "And he'll come back again if I don't do these things, so hear me out."

"No, just tell me what we must do to keep him away."

Illyra dug her fingernails into the palm of one hand hidden in the folds of her skirts.

"We will have to—to stop the consecration of the cornerstone of the new temple for the Rankan gods."

" 'Gods,' 'Lyra, you would not meddle with the gods? Is this the meaning you found in 'death and sacrifice'?"

"It is also the reason Lythande was here last night."

"But, 'Lyra . . . ."

She shook her head, and he was quiet.

'He won't ask me what I plan to do,' she thought as he tied the rope across the door and followed her toward the city. 'As long as everything is in my head, I'm certain everything is possible and that I will succeed. But if I spoke of it to anyone—even him—I would hear how little hope I have of stopping Molin Torchholder or of changing Marilla's fate.'

In the dream, her already dead body had been offered to Sabellia and Savankala. Her morning's introspection had convinced her that she was to introduce a corpse into Molin Torchholder's ceremonies. They passed the scene of the murder, but Jubal's men had reclaimed their comrade. The only other source of dead men she knew of was the gov-ernor's palace where executions were becoming a daily occurrence under the tightening grip of the Hell-Hounds.

They passed by the huge charnel house just beyond the bazaar gates. The rain held the death smells close by the half-timbered building. Could Sabellia and Savankala be appeased with the mangled bones and fat of a butchered cow? Hesitantly she mounted the raised wooden walk over the red-brown effluvia of the building.

"What do the Rankan gods want from this place?" Dubro asked be-fore setting foot on the walkway.

"A substitute for the one already chosen."

A man emerged from a side door pushing a sloshing barrel which he dumped into the slow-moving stream. Shapeless red lumps flowed under the walkway between the two bazaar-folk. Illyra swayed on her feet.

"Even the gods of Ranke would not be fooled by these." Dubro lowered his hand toward the now-ebbing stream. "At least offer them the death of an honest man of Ilsig."

He held out a hand to steady her as she stepped back on the street, then led the way past the Serpentine to the governor's palace. Three men hung limply from the gallows in the rain, their crimes and names inscribed on placards tied around their necks. Neither Illyra nor Dubro had mastered the arcane mysteries of script.

"Which one is most like the one you need?" Dubro asked.

"She should be my size, but blonde," Illyra explained while looking at the two strapping men and one grandfatherly figure hanging in front of them.

Dubro shrugged and approached the stern-faced Hell-Hound standing guard at the foot of the gallows.

"Father," he grunted, pointing at the elderly corpse.

"It's the law—to be hung by the neck until sundown. You'll have to come back then."

"Long walk home. He's dead now—why wait?"

"There is *law* in Sanctuary now, peon, Rankan law. It will be respected without exception."

Dubro stared at the ground, fumbling with his hands in evident distress.

"In the rain I cannot see the sun—how shall I know when to return?"

Guard and smith stared at the steely-grey sky, both knowing it would not clear before nightfall. Then, with a loud sigh, the Hell-Hound walked to the ropes, selected and untied one, which dropped Dubro's "father" into the mud.

"Take him and begone!"

Dubro shouldered the dead man, walking to Illyra who waited at the edge of the execution grounds.

"He's—he's—" she gasped in growing hysteria.

"Dead since sunrise."

"He's covered with filth. He reeks. His face. . ."

"You wanted another for the sacrifice."

"But not like that!"

"It is the way of men who have been hung."

They walked back toward the charnel house where Sanctuary's un-

dertakers and embalmers held sway. There, for five copper coins, they
found a man to prepare the body. For another coin he would have
rented them a cart and his son as a digger to take the unfortunate ex-
thief to the common field outside the Gate of Triumph for proper
burial. Illyra and Dubro made a great show of grief, however, and
insisted that they would bury their father with their own hands.
Wrapped in a nearly clean shroud, the old man was bound to a plank.
Illyra held the foot-end, Dubro the other. They made their way back to
the bazaar.

"Do we take the body to the temple for the exchange?" he asked as
they pushed aside their chairs to make room for the plank.

Illyra stared at him, not realizing at first that his faith in her had
made the question sincere.

"During the night the Rankan priests will leave the governor's palace
for the estate called Land's End. They will bear Marilla with them. We
will have to stop them and replace Marilla with our corpse, without
their knowledge."

The smith's eyes widened with disillusion. " 'Lyra, it is not the same
as stealing fruit from Blind Jakob! The girl will be alive. He is dead.
Surely the priests will see."

She shook her head clinging desperately to the image she had found
in meditation. "It rains. There will be no moonlight, and their torches
will give more smoke than light. I gave the girl cylantha. They will have
to carry her as if she were dead."

"Will she take the drug?"

"Yes!"

But Illyra wasn't sure—couldn't be sure—until they actually saw the
procession. So many questions: if Marilla had taken the drug, if the
procession were small, unguarded and slowed by their burden, if the ritual were like the one in her dream. The cold panic she had felt as the
stone descended on her returned. The Face of Chaos loomed, laughing,
in her mind's eye.

"Yes! She took the drug last night," she said firmly, dispelling the
Face by force of will.

"How do you know this?" Dubro asked incredulously.

"I *know*."

There was no more discussion as Illyra threw herself into the prepa-
ration of a macabre feast that they ate on a table spread over their dead
guest. The vague point of sundown passed, leaving Sanctuary in a dark
rainy night, as Illyra had foreseen. The continuing rain bolstered her

confidence as they moved slowly through the bazaar and out the Common Gate.

They faced a long, but not difficult, walk beyond the walls of the city. As Dubro pointed out, the demoiselles of the Street of Red Lanterns had to follow their path each night on their way to the Promise of Heaven. The ladies giggled behind their shawls at the sight of the two bearing what was so obviously a corpse. But they did nothing to hinder them, and it was far too early for the more raucous traffic returning from the Promise.

Huge piles of stone in a sea of muddy craters marked the site of the new temple. A water-laden canopy covered sputtering braziers and torches; otherwise the area was quiet and deserted.

'It is the night of the Ten-Slaying. Cappen Varra told me the priests would be busy. Rain will not stop the dedication. Gods do not feel rain!' Illyra thought, but again did not *know* and sat with her back to Dubro quivering more from doubt and fear than from the cold water dripping down her back.

While she sat, the rain slowed to a misty drizzle and gave promise of stopping altogether. She left the inadequate shelter of the rockpile to venture nearer the canopy and braziers. A platform had been built above the mud at the edge of a pit with ropes dangling on one side that might be used to lower a body into the pit. A great stone was poised on logs opposite, ready to crush anything below. At least they were not too late—no sacrifice had taken place. Before Illyra had returned to Dubro's side, six torches appeared in the mist-obscured distance.

"They are coming," Dubro whispered as she neared him.

"I see them. We have only a few moments now."

From around her waist she unwound two coils of rope taken from the bazaar forge. She had devised her own plan for the actual exchange, as neither the dream-spirit nor her meditations had offered solid insight or inspiration.

"They will most likely follow the same path we did, since they are carrying a body also," she explained as she laid the ropes across the mud, burying them slightly. "We will trip them here."

"And I will switch our corpse for the girl?"

"Yes."

They said nothing more as each crouched in a mud-hole waiting, hoping that the procession would pass between them.

The luck promised in her dream held. Molin Torchholder led the small procession, bearing a large brass and wood torch from Sabellia's temple in Ranke itself. Behind him were three chanting acolytes bearing both incense and torches. The last two torches were affixed to a bier carried on the shoulders of the last pair of priests. Torchholder and the other three trod over the ropes without noticing them. When the first pallbearer was between the ropes Illyra snapped them taut.

The burdened priests heard the smack as the ropes lifted from the mud, but were tripped before they could react. Marilla and the torches fell toward Dubro, the priests toward Illyra. In the dark commotion, Illyra got safely to a nearby pile of building stones, but without being able to see if Dubro had accomplished the exchange.

"What's wrong?" Torchholder demanded, hurrying back with his torch to light the scene.

"The damned workmen left the hauling ropes strewn about," a mud-splattered priest exclaimed as he scrambled out of the knee-deep mud-hole.

"And the girl?" Molin continued.

"Thrown over there, from the look of it."

Lifting his robes in one hand, Molin Torchholder led the acolytes and priests to the indicated mud-pit. Illyra heard sounds she prayed were Dubro making his own way to the safe shadows.

"A hand here."

"Damned Ilsig mud. She weighs ten times as much now."

"Easy. A little more mud, a little sooner won't affect the temple, but it's an ill thought to rouse the Others." Torchholder's calm voice quieted the others.

The torches were relit. From her hideout, Illyra could see a mud-covered shroud on the bier. Dubro had succeeded somehow: she did not allow herself to think anything else.

The procession continued on toward the canopy. The rain had stopped completely. A sliver of moonlight showed through the dispersing clouds. Torchholder loudly hailed the break in the clouds as an omen of the forgiving, sanctifying presence of Vashanka and began the ritual. In due time the acolytes emptied braziers of oil on to the shroud, setting it and the corpse on fire. They lowered the flaming bier into the pit. The acolytes threw symbolic armloads of stone after it. Then they cut the ropes that held the cornerstone in its place at the edge. It slid from sight with a loud, sucking sound.

Almost at once, Torchholder and the other two priests left the platform to head back toward the palace, leaving only the acolytes to perform a night-long vigil over the new grave. When the priests were out of sight Illyra scrambled back to the mud-holes and whispered Dubro's name.

"Here," he hissed back.

She need only one glance at his moon-shadowed face to know something had gone wrong.

"What happened?" she asked quickly, unmindful of the sound of her voice. "Marilla? Did they bury Marilla?"

There were tears in Dubro's eyes as he shook his head. "Look at her!" he said, his voice barely under control.

A mud-covered shroud lay some paces away. Dubro would neither face it nor venture near it. Illyra approached warily.

Dubro had left the face covered. Holding her breath, Illyra reached down to peel back the damp, dirty linen.

For a heartbeat, she saw Marilla's sleeping face. Then it became her own. After a second of self-recognition, the face underwent a bewildering series of changes to portraits of people from her childhood and others whom she did not recognize. It froze for a moment in the shattered image of the Face of Chaos, then was still with pearly-white skin where there should have been eyes, nose, and mouth.

Illyra's fingers stiffened. She opened her mouth to scream, but her lungs and throat were paralyzed with fright. The linen fell from her unfeeling hands, but did not cover the hideous thing that lay before her.

*Get away! Get away from this place!*

The primitive imperative rose in her mind and would not be appeased by anything less than headlong flight. She pushed Dubro aside. The acolytes heard her as she blundered through the mud, but she ignored them. There were buildings ahead—solid stone buildings outlined in the moonlight.

It was a manor house of an estate long since abandoned. Illyra recognized it from her dream, but her panic and terror had been sated in the headlong run from the faceless corpse. An interior door hung open on rusty hinges that creaked when she pushed the door. She was unsurprised to see an anvil sitting on a plain wooden box in the center of a courtyard that her instincts told her was not entirely deserted.

'I'm only prolonging it now. The anvil, and the rest; they are there for me.'

She stepped into the courtyard. Nothing happened. The anvil was solid and far too heavy for her to lift.

"You've come to collect your reward?" a voice called.

"Lythande?" she whispered, waiting for the cadaverous magician to appear.

"Lythande is elsewhere."

A hooded man stepped into the moonlight.

"What has happened? Where is Marilla? Her family?"

The man gestured to his right. Illyra followed his movement and saw the tumbledown headstones of an old graveyard.

"But. . . ?"

"The priests of Ils seek to provoke the new gods. They created the homunculus, disguising it to appear as a young woman to an untrained observer. Had it been interred in the foundation of the new temple, it would have created a disruptive weakness. The anger of Savankala and Sabellia would reach across the desert. That is, of course, exactly what the priests of Ils wanted.

"We magicians—and even you gifted S'danzo—do not welcome the meddling feuds of gods and their priests. They tamper with the delicate balances of fate. Our work is more important than the appeasement of deities, so this time, as in the past, we have intervened."

"But the temple? They should have buried a virgin, then?"

"A forged person would arouse the Rankan gods, but not an imperfect virgin. When the temple of Ils was erected, the old priests sought a royal soul to inter beneath the altar. They wanted the youngest, and most loved, of the royal princes. The queen was a sorceress of some skill herself. She disguised an old slave, and his bones still rest beneath the altar."

"So the gods of Ilsig and Ranke are equal?"

The hooded man laughed. "We have seen to it that all gods within Sanctuary are equally handicapped, my child."

"And what of me? Lythande warned me not to fail."

"Did I not just say that our purpose—and therefore your purpose—was accomplished? You did not fail, and we repay, as Marilla promised, with a black-steel anvil. It is yours."

He laid a hand on the anvil and disappeared in a wisp of smoke.

"'Lyra, are you all right? I heard you speaking with someone. I buried that girl before I came looking for you."

"Here is the anvil."

"I do not want such an ill-gotten thing."

Dubro took her arm and tried to lead her out of the courtyard.

"I have paid too much already!" she shouted at him, wresting away from his grasp. "Take it back to the bazaar—then we will forget all this ever happened. Never speak of it to anyone. But don't leave the anvil here, or it's all worth nothing!"

"I can never forget your face on that dead girl . . . thing."

Illyra remained silently staring at the still-muddy ground. Dubro went to the anvil and brushed the water and dirt from its surface.

"Someone has carved a symbol in it. It reminds me of one of your cards. Tell me what it means before I take it back to the bazaar with us."

She stood by his side. A smiling Face of Chaos had been freshly etched into the worn surface of the metal.

"It is an old S'danzo sign of good luck."

Dubro did not seem to hear the note of bitterness and deceit in her voice. His faith in Illyra had been tried but not shattered. The anvil was heavy, an ungainly bundle in his arms.

"Well, it won't get home by itself, will it?" He stared at her as he started walking.

She touched the pedestal and thought briefly of the questions still whirling in her head. Dubro called again from outside the courtyard. The entire length of Sanctuary lay between them and the bazaar, and it was not yet midnight. Without glancing back, she followed him out of the courtyard.

# The Gate of
# the Flying Knives

## Poul Anderson

Again penniless, houseless, and ladyless, Cappen Varra made a brave sight just the same as he wove his way amidst the bazaar throng. After all, until today he had for some weeks been in, if not quite of, the household of Molin Torchholder, as much as he could contrive. Besides the dear presence of ancilla Danlis, he had received generous reward from the priest-engineer whenever he sang a song or composed a poem. That situation had changed with suddenness and terror, but he still wore a bright green tunic, scarlet cloak, canary hose, soft half-boots trimmed in silver, and plumed beret. Though naturally heartsick at what had happened, full of dread for his darling, he saw no reason to sell the garb yet. He could raise enough money in various ways to live on while he searched for her. If need be, as often before, he could pawn the harp that a goldsmith was presently redecorating.

If his quest had not succeeded by the time he was reduced to rags, then he would have to suppose Danlis and the Lady Rosanda were forever lost. But he had never been one to grieve over future sorrows.

Beneath a westering sun, the bazaar surged and clamored. Merchants, artisans, porters, servants, slaves, wives, nomads, courtesans, entertainers, beggars, thieves, gamblers, magicians, acolytes, soldiers, and who knew what else mingled, chattered, chaffered, quarreled, plotted, sang, played games, drank, ate, and who knew what else. Horsemen, cameldrivers, wagoners pushed through, raising waves of curses. Music tinkled and tweedled from wineships. Vendors proclaimed the wonders of their wares from booths, neighbors shouted at each other, and devotees chanted from flat rooftops. Smells thickened the air, of flesh, sweat, roast meat and nuts, aromatic drinks, leather, wool, dung, smoke, oils, cheap perfume.

Ordinarily, Cappen Varra enjoyed this shabby-colorful spectacle. Now he single-mindedly hunted through it. He kept full awareness, of course, as everybody must in Sanctuary. When light fingers brushed him, he knew. But whereas aforetime he would have chuckled and told the pickpurse, "I'm sorry, friend; I was hoping I might lift somewhat off *you*," at this hour he clapped his sword in such forbidding wise that the fellow recoiled against a fat woman and made her drop a brass tray full of flowers. She screamed and started beating him over the head with it. Cappen didn't stay to watch.

On the eastern edge of the marketplace he found what he wanted. Once more Illyra was in the bad graces of her colleagues and had moved her trade to a stall available elsewhere. Black curtains framed it, against a mud-brick wall. Reek from a nearby tannery well-nigh drowned the incense she burned in a curious holder, and would surely overwhelm any of her herbs. She herself also lacked awesomeness, such as most seeresses, mages, conjurers, scryers, and the like affected. She was too young; she would have looked almost wistful in her flowing, gaudy S'danzo garments, had she not been so beautiful.

Cappen gave her a bow in the manner of Caronne. "Good day, Illyra the lovely," he said.

She smiled from the cushion whereon she sat. "Good day to you, Cappen Varra." They had had a number of talks, usually in jest, and he had sung for her entertainment. He had hankered to do more than that, but she seemed to keep all men at a certain distance, and a hulk of a blacksmith who evidently adored her saw to it that they respected her wish.

"Nobody in these parts has met you for a fair while," she remarked. "What fortune was great enough to make you forget old friends?"

"My fortune was mingled, inasmuch as it left me without time to come down here and behold you, my sweet," he answered out of habit.

Lightness departed from Illyra. In the olive countenance, under the chestnut mane, large eyes focused hard on her visitor. "You find time when you need help in disaster," she said.

He had not patronized her before, or indeed any fortune-teller or thaumaturge in Sanctuary. In Caronne, where he grew up, most folk had no use for magic. In his later wanderings he had encountered sufficient strangeness to temper his native skepticism. As shaken as he already was, he felt a chill go along his spine. "Do you read my fate without even casting a spell?"

She smiled afresh, but bleakly. "Oh, no. It's simple reason. Word did filter back to the Maze that you were residing in the Jewelers' Quarter and a frequent guest at the mansion of Molin Torchholder. When you appear on the heels of a new word—that last night his wife was reaved from him—plain to see is that you've been affected yourself."

He nodded. "Yes, and sore afflicted. I have lost—" He hesitated, unsure whether it would be quite wise to say, "—my love" to this girl whose charms he had rather extravagantly praised.

"—your position and income," Illyra snapped. "The high priest cannot be in any mood for minstrelsy. I'd guess his wife favored you most, anyhow. I need not guess you spent your earnings as fast as they fell to you, or faster, were behind in your rent, and were accordingly kicked out of your choice apartment as soon as rumor reached the landlord. You've returned to the Maze because you've no place else to go, and to me in hopes you can wheedle me into giving you a clue—for if you're instrumental in recovering the lady, you'll likewise recover your fortune, and more."

"No, no, no," he protested. "You wrong me."

"The high priest will appeal only to his Rankan gods," Illyra said, her tone changing from exasperated to thoughtful. She stroked her chin. "He, kinsman of the Emperor, here to direct the building of a temple which will overtop that of Ils, can hardly beg aid from the old gods of Sanctuary, let alone from our wizards, witches, and seers. But you, who belong to no part of the empire, who drifted hither from a kingdom far in the West . . . you may seek anywhere. The idea is your own; else he would furtively have slipped you some gold, and you have engaged a diviner with more reputation than is mine."

Cappen spread his hands. "You reason eerily well, dear lass," he conceded. "Only about the motives are you mistaken. Oh, yes, I'd be glad to stand high in Molin's esteem, be richly rewarded, and so forth. Yet I feel for him; beneath that sternness of his, he's not a bad sort, and he bleeds. Still more do I feel for his lady, who was indeed kind to me and who's been snatched away to an unknown place. But before all else—" He grew quite earnest. "The Lady Rosanda was not seized by herself. Her ancilla has also vanished, Danlis. And—Danlis is she whom I love, Illyra, she whom I meant to wed."

The maiden's look probed him further. She saw a young man of medium height, slender but tough and agile. (That was due to the life he had had to lead; by nature he was indolent, except in bed.) His features were thin and regular on a long skull, clean-shaven, eyes bright blue, black hair banged and falling to the shoulders. His voice gave the language a melodious accent, as if to bespeak white cities, green fields and woods, quicksilver lakes, blue sea, of the homeland he left in search of his fortune.

"Well, you have charm, Cappen Varra," she murmured, "and how you do know it." Alert: "But coin you lack. How do you propose to pay me?"

"I fear you must work on speculation, as I do myself," he said. "If our joint efforts lead to a rescue, why, then we'll share whatever material reward may come. Your part might buy you a home on the Path of Money." She frowned. "True," he went on, "I'll get more than my share of the immediate bounty that Molin bestows. I will have my beloved back. I'll also regain the priest's favor, which is moderately lucrative. Yet consider. You need but practice your art. Thereafter any effort and risk will be mine."

"What makes you suppose a humble fortune-teller can learn more than the Prince Governant's investigator guardsmen?" she demanded.

"The matter does not seem to lie within their jurisdiction," he replied.

She leaned forward, tense beneath the layers of clothing. Cappen bent toward her. It was as if the babble of the marketplace receded, leaving these two alone with their wariness.

"I was not there," he said low, "but I arrived early this morning after the thing had happened. What's gone through the city has been rumor, leakage that cannot be calked, household servants blabbing to friends outside and they blabbing onward. Molin's locked away most of the facts till he can discover what they mean, if ever he can. I, however, I came on the scene while chaos still prevailed. Nobody kept me from talking to folk, before the lord himself saw me and told me to begone. Thus I know about as much as anyone, little though that be."

"And—?" she prompted.

"And it doesn't seem to have been a worldly sort of capture, for a worldly end like ransom. See you, the mansion's well guarded, and neither Molin nor his wife have ever gone from it without escort. His mission here is less than popular, you recall. Those troopers are from Ranke and not subornable. The house stands in a garden, inside a high wall whose top is patrolled. Three leopards run loose on the grounds after dark.

"Molin had business with his kinsman the Prince, and spent the night at the palace. His wife, the Lady Rosanda, stayed home, retired, later came out and complained she could not sleep. She therefore had Danlis wakened. Danlis is no chambermaid; there are plenty of those. She's amanuensis, adviser, confidante, collector of information, ofttimes guide or interpreter—oh, she earns her pay, does my Danlis. Despite she and I having a dawntide engagement, which is why I arrived then, she must now out of bed at Rosanda's whim, to hold milady's hand or take dictation of milady's letters or read to milady from a soothing book—but I'm a spendthrift of words. Suffice to say that they two sought an upper chamber which is furnished as both solarium and office. A single staircase leads thither, and it is the single room at the top. There is a balcony, yes; and, the night being warm, the door to it stood open, as well as the windows. But I inspected the façade beneath. That's sheer marble, undecorated save for varying colors, devoid of ivy or of anything that any climber might cling to, save he were a fly.

"Nevertheless . . . just before the east grew pale, shrieks were heard, the watch pelted to the stair and up it. They must break down the inner door, which was bolted. I suppose that was merely against chance interruptions, for nobody had felt threatened. The solarium was in disarray; vases and things were broken; shreds torn off a robe and slight traces of blood lay about. Aye, Danlis, at least, would have resisted. But she and her mistress were gone.

"A couple of sentries on the garden wall reported hearing a loud sound as of wings. The night was cloudy-dark and they saw nothing for certain. Perhaps they imagined the noise. Suggestive is that the leopards were found cowering in a corner and welcomed their keeper when he would take them back to their cages.

"And this is the whole of anyone's knowledge, Illyra," Cappen ended. "Help me, I pray you, help me get back my love!"

She was long quiet. Finally she said, in a near whisper, "It could be a worse matter than I'd care to peer into, let alone enter."

"Or it could not," Cappen urged.

She gave him a quasi-defiant stare. "My mother's people reckon it unlucky to do any service for a Shavakh—a person not of their tribe—without recompense. Pledges don't count."

Cappen scowled. "Well, I could go to a pawnshop and—But no, time may be worth more than rubies." From the depths of unhappiness, his grin broke forth. "Poems also are valuable, right? You S'danzo have your ballads and love ditties. Let me indite a poem, Illyra, that shall be yours alone."

Her expression quickened. "Truly?"

"Truly. Let me think. . . . Aye, we'll begin thus." And, venturing to take her hands in his, Cappen murmured:

> *My lady comes to me like break of day.*
> *I dream in darkness if it chance she tarries,*
> *Until the banner of her brightness harries*
> *The hosts of Shadowland from off the way—*

She jerked free and cried, "No! You scoundrel, that has to be something you did for Danlis—or for some earlier woman you wanted in your bed—"

"But it isn't finished," he argued. "I'll complete it for you, Illyra."

Anger left her. She shook her head, clicked her tongue, and sighed. "No matter. You're incurably yourself. And I . . . am only half S'danzo. I'll attempt your spell."

"By every love goddess I ever heard of," he promised unsteadily, "you shall indeed have your own poem after this is over."

"Be still," she ordered. "Fend off anybody who comes near."

He faced about and drew his sword. The slim, straight blade was hardly needed, for no other enterprise had site within several yards of hers, and as wide a stretch of paving lay between him and the fringes of the crowd. Still, to grasp the hilt gave him a sense of finally making progress. He had felt helpless for the first hours, hopeless, as if his dear had actually died instead of—of what? Behind him he heard cards riffled, dice cast, words softly wailed.

All at once Illyra strangled a shriek. He whirled about and saw how the blood had left her olive countenance, turning it grey. She hugged herself and shuddered.

"What's wrong?" he blurted in fresh terror.

She did not look at him. "Go away," she said in a thin voice. "Forget you ever knew that woman."

"But—but what—"

"Go away, I told you! Leave me alone!"

Then somehow she relented enough to let forth: "I don't know. I dare not know. I'm just a little half-breed girl who has a few cantrips and a tricksy second sight, and—and I saw that this business goes outside of space and time, and a power beyond any magic is there—Enas

Yorl could tell more, but he himself—" Her courage broke. "Go away!" she screamed. "Before I shout for Dubro and his hammer!"

"I beg your pardon," Cappen Varra said, and made haste to obey.

He retreated into the twisting streets of the Maze. They were narrow; most of the mean buildings around him were high; gloom already filled the quarter. It was as if he had stumbled into the same night where Danlis had gone . . . Danlis, creature of sun and horizons. . . . If she lived, did she remember their last time together as he remembered it, a dream dreamed centuries ago?

Having the day free, she had wanted to explore the countryside north of town. Cappen had objected on three counts. The first he did not mention; that it would require a good deal of effort, and he would get dusty and sweaty and saddle-sore. She despised men who were not at least as vigorous as she was, unless they compensated by being venerable and learned.

The second he hinted at. Sleazy though most of Sanctuary was, he knew places within it where a man and a woman could enjoy themselves, comfortably, privately—his apartment, for instance. She smiled her negation. Her family belonged to the old aristocracy of Ranke, not the newly rich, and she had been raised in its austere tradition. Albeit her father had fallen on evil times and she had been forced to take service, she kept her pride, and proudly would she yield her maidenhead to her bridegroom. Thus far she had answered Cappen's ardent declarations with the admission that she liked him and enjoyed his company and wished he would change the subject. (Buxom Lady Rosanda seemed as if she might be more approachable, but there he was careful to maintain a cheerful correctness.) He did believe she was getting beyond simple enjoyment, for her patrician reserve seemed less each time they saw each other. Yet she could not altogether have forgotten that he was merely the bastard of a minor nobleman in a remote country, himself disinherited and a footloose minstrel.

His third objection he dared say forth. While the hinterland was comparatively safe, Molin Torchholder would be furious did he learn that a woman of his household had gone escorted by a single armed man, and he no professional fighter. Molin would probably have been justified, too. Danlis smiled again and said, "I could ask a guardsman off duty to come along. But you have interesting friends, Cappen. Perhaps a warrior is among them?"

As a matter of fact, he knew any number, but doubted she would care to meet them—with a single exception. Luckily, Jamie the Red had no prior commitment, and agreed to join the party. Cappen told the kitchen staff to pack a picnic hamper for four.

Jamie's girls stayed behind; this was not their sort of outing, and the sun might harm their complexions. Cappen thought it a bit ungracious of the Northerner never to share them. That put him, Cappen, to considerable expense in the Street of Red Lanterns, since he could scarcely keep a paramour of his own while wooing Danlis. Otherwise he was fond of Jamie. They had met after Rosanda, chancing to hear the minstrel sing, had invited him to perform at the mansion, and then invited him back, and presently Cappen was living in the Jewelers' Quarter. Jamie had an apartment nearby.

Three horses and a pack mule clopped out of Sanctuary in the newborn morning, to a jingle of harness bells. That merriment found no echo in Cappen's head; he had been drinking past midnight, and in no case enjoyed rising before noon. Passive, he listened to Jamie:

"—Aye, milady, they're mountaineers where I hail from, poor folk but free folk. Some might call us barbarians, but that might be unwise in our hearing. For we've tales, songs, laws, ways, gods as old as any in the world, and as good. We lack much of your Southern lore, but how much of ours do you ken? Not that I boast, please understand. I've seen wonders in my wanderings. But I do say we've a few wonders of our own at home."

"I'd like to hear of them," Danlis responded. "We know almost nothing about your country in the Empire—hardly more than mentions in the chronicles of Venafer and Mattathan, or the *Natural History* of Kahayavesh. How do you happen to come here?"

"Oh-ah, I'm a younger son of our king, and I thought I'd see a bit of the world before settling down. Not that I packed any wealth along to speak of. But what with one thing and another, hiring out hither and yon for this or that, I get by." Jamie paused. "You, uh, you've far more to tell, milady. You're from the crown city of the Empire, and you've got book learning, and at the same time you come out to see for yourself what land and rocks and plants and animals are like."

Cappen decided he had better get into the conversation. Not that Jamie would undercut a friend, nor Danlis be unduly attracted by a wild highlander. Nevertheless—

Jamie wasn't bad-looking in his fashion. He was huge, topping Cappen by a head and disproportionately wide in the shoulders. His loose-jointed appearance was deceptive, as the bard had learned when they sported in a public gymnasium; those were heavy bones and oak-hard muscles. A spectacular red mane drew attention from boyish face, mild blue eyes, and slightly diffident manner. Today he was plainly clad, in tunic and cross-gaitered breeks; but the knife at his belt and the ax at his saddlebow stood out.

As for Danlis, well, what could a poet do but struggle for words which might embody a ghost of her glory? She was tall and slender, her features almost cold in their straight-lined perfection and alabaster hue —till you observed the big grey eyes, golden hair piled on high, curve of lips whence came that husky voice. (How often he had lain awake yearning for her lips! He would console himself by remembering the strong, delicately blue-veined hand that she did let him kiss.) Despite waxing warmth and dust puffed up from the horses' hoofs, her cowled riding habit remained immaculate and no least dew of sweat was on her skin.

By the time Cappen got his wits out of the blankets wherein they had still been snoring, talk had turned to gods. Danlis was curious about those of Jamie's country, as she was about most things. (She did shun a few subjects as being unwholesome.) Jamie in his turn was eager to have her explain what was going on in Sanctuary. "I've heard but the one side of the matter, and Cappen's indifferent to it," he said. "Folk grumble about your master—Molin, is that his name—?"

"He is not my master," Danlis made clear. "I am a free woman who assists his wife. He himself is a high priest in Ranke, also an engineer."

"Why is the Emperor angering Sanctuary? Most places I've been, colonial governments know better. They leave the local gods be."

Danlis grew pensive. "Where shall I start? Doubtless you know that Sanctuary was originally a city of the kingdom of Ilsig. Hence it has built temples to the gods of Ilsig—notably Ils, Lord of Lords, and his queen Shipri the All-Mother, but likewise others—Anen of the Harvests, Thufir the tutelary of pilgrims—"

"But none to Shalpa, patron of thieves," Cappen put in, "though these days he has the most devotees of any."

Danlis ignored his jape. "Ranke was quite a different country, under quite different gods," she continued. "Chief of these are Savankala the Thunderer, his consort Sabellia, Lady of Stars, their son Vashanka the Tenslayer, and his sister and consort Azyuna—gods of storm and war. According to Venafer, it was they who made Ranke supreme at last. Mattathan is more prosaic and opines that the martial spirit they inculcated was responsible for the Rankan Empire finally taking Ilsig into itself."

"Yes, milady, yes, I've heard this," Jamie said, while Cappen reflected that if his beloved had a fault, it was her tendency to lecture.

"Sanctuary has changed from of yore," she proceeded. "It has become polyglot, turbulent, corrupt, a canker on the body politic. Among its most vicious elements are the proliferating alien cults, not to speak of necromancers, witches, charlatans, and similar predators on the people. The time is overpast to restore law here. Nothing less than the Imperium can do that. A necessary preliminary is the establishment of the Imperial deities, the gods of Ranke, for everyone to see: symbol, rallying point, and actual presence."

"But they *have* their temples," Jamie argued.

"Small, dingy, to accommodate Rankans, few of whom stay in the city for long," Danlis retorted. "What reverence does that inspire, for the pantheon and the state? No, the Emperor has decided that Savankala and Sabellia must have the greatest fane, the most richly endowed, in this entire province. Molin Torchholder will build and consecrate it. Then can the degenerates and warlocks be scourged out of Sanctuary. Afterward the Prince's Government can handle common felons."

Cappen didn't expect matters would be that simple. He got no chance to say so, for Jamie asked at once, "Is this wise, milady? True, many a soul hereabouts worships foreign gods, or none. But many still adore the old gods of Ilsig. They look on your, uh, Savankala as an intruder. I intend no offense, but they do. They're outraged that he's to have a bigger and grander house than Ils of the Thousand Eyes. Some fear what Ils may do about it."

"I know," Danlis said. "I regret any distress caused, and I'm sure Lord Molin does too. Still, we must overcome the agents of darkness, before the disease that they are spreads throughout the Empire."

"Oh, no," Cappen managed to insert, "I've lived here awhile, mostly down in the Maze. I've had to do with a good many so-called magicians, of either sex or in between. They aren't that bad. Most I'd call pitiful. They just use their little deceptions to scrabble out what living they can, in this crumbly town where life has trapped them."

Danlis gave him a sharp glance. "You've told me people think ill of sorcery in Caronne," she said.

"They do," he admitted. "But that's because we incline to be rationalists, who consider nearly all magic a bag of tricks. Which is true. Why, I've learned a few sleights myself."

"You have?" Jamie rumbled in surprise.

"For amusement," Cappen said hastily, before Danlis could disapprove. "Some are quite elegant, virtual exercises in three-dimensional geometry." Seeing interest kindle in her, he added, "I studied mathematics in boyhood; my father, before he died, wanted me to have a gentleman's education. The main part has rusted away in me, but I remember useful or picturesque details."

"Well, give us a show, come luncheon time," Jamie proposed.

Cappen did, when they halted. That was on a hillside above the White Foal River. It wound gleaming through farmlands whose intense green denied that desert lurked on the rim of sight. The noonday sun baked strong odors out of the earth: humus, resin, juice of wild plants. A solitary plane tree graciously gave shade. Bees hummed.

After the meal, and after Danlis had scrambled off to get a closer look at a kind of lizard new to her, Cappen demonstrated his skill. She was especially taken—enchanted—by his geometric artifices. Like any Rankan lady, she carried a sewing kit in her gear; and being herself, she had writing materials along. Thus he could apply scissors and thread to paper. He showed how a single ring may be cut to produce two that are interlocked, and how a strip may be twisted to have but one surface and one edge, and whatever else he knew. Jamie watched with pleasure, if with less enthusiasm.

Observing how delight made her glow, Cappen was inspired to carry on the latest poem he was composing for her. It had been slower work than usual. He had the conceit, the motif, a comparison of her to the dawn, but hitherto only the first few lines had emerged, and no proper structure. In this moment—

> —the banner of her brightness harries
> The hosts of Shadowland from off the way
> That she now wills to tread—for what can stay
> The triumph of that radiance she carries?

Yes, it was clearly going to be a rondel. Therefore the next two lines were:

> My lady comes to me like break of day.
> I dream in darkness if it chance she tarries.

He had gotten that far when abruptly she said: "Cappen, this is such a fine excursion, such splendid scenery. I'd like to watch sunrise over the river tomorrow. Will you escort me?"

*Sunrise?* But she was telling Jamie, "We need not trouble you about that. I had in mind a walk out of town to the bridge. If we choose the proper route, it's well guarded everywhere, perfectly safe."

And scant traffic moved at that hour; besides, the monumental statues along the bridge stood in front of bays which they screened from passersby—"Oh, yes, indeed, Danlis, I'd love to," Cappen said. For such an opportunity, he could get up before cockcrow.

—When he reached the mansion, she had not been there.

Exhausted after his encounter with Illyra, Cappen hied him to the Vulgar Unicorn and related his woes to One-Thumb. The big man had come on shift at the inn early, for a fellow boniface had not yet recovered from the effects of a dispute with a patron. (Shortly thereafter, the patron was found floating face down under a pier. Nobody questioned One-Thumb about this; his regulars knew that he preferred the establishment safe, if not always orderly.) He offered taciturn sympathy and the loan of a bed upstairs. Cappen scarcely noticed the insects that shared it.

Waking about sunset, he found water and a washcloth, and felt much refreshed—hungry and thirsty, too. He made his way to the taproom below. Dusk was blue in windows and open door, black under the rafters. Candles smeared weak light along counter and main board and on lesser tables at the walls. The air had grown cool, which allayed the stenches of the Maze. Thus Cappen was acutely aware of the smells of beer—old in the rushes underfoot, fresh where a trio of men had settled down to guzzle—and of spitted meat, wafting from the kitchen.

One-Thumb approached, a shadowy hulk save for highlights on his bald pate. "Sit," he grunted. "Eat. Drink." He carried a great tankard and a plate bearing a slab of roast beef on bread. These he put on a corner table, and himself on a chair.

Cappen sat also and attacked the meal. "You're very kind," he said between bites and draughts.

"You'll pay when you get coin, or if you don't, then in songs and magic stunts. They're good for trade." One-Thumb fell silent and peered at his guest.

When Cappen was done, the innkeeper said, "While you slept, I sent out a couple of fellows to ask around. Maybe somebody saw something that might be helpful. Don't worry—I didn't mention you, and it's natural I'd be interested to know what really happened."

The minstrel stared. "You've gone to a deal of trouble on my account."

"I told you, I want to know for my own sake. If deviltry's afoot, where could it strike next?" One-Thumb rubbed a finger across the toothless part of his gums. "Of course, if you should luck out—I don't expect it, but in case you do—remember who gave you a boost." A figure appeared in the door and he went to render service.

After a bit of muttered talk, he led the newcomer to Cappen's place. When the minstrel recognized the lean youth, his pulse leaped. One-Thumb would not have brought him and Hanse together without cause; bard and thief found each other insufferable. They nodded coldly but did not speak until the tapster returned with a round of ale.

When the three were seated, One-Thumb said, "Well spit it out, boy. You claim you've got news."

"For him?" Hanse flared, gesturing at Cappen.

"Never mind who. Just talk."

Hanse scowled. "I don't talk for a single lousy mugful."

"You do if you want to keep on coming in here."

Hanse bit his lip. The Vulgar Unicorn was a rendezvous virtually indispensable to one in his trade.

Cappen thought best to sweeten the pill: "I'm known to Molin Torchholder. If I can serve him in this matter, he won't be stingy. Nor will I. Shall we say—hm—ten gold royals to you?"

The sum was not princely, but on that account plausible. "Awright, awright," Hanse replied. "I'd been casing a job I might do in the Jewelers' Quarter. A squad of the watch came by toward morning and I figured I'd better go home, not by the way I came, either. So I went along the Avenue of Temples, as I might be wanting to stop in and pay my respects to some god or other. It was a dark night, overcast, the reason I'd been out where I was. But you know how several of the temples keep lights going. There was enough to see by, even upward a ways. Nobody else was in sight. Suddenly I heard a kind of whistling, flapping noise aloft. I looked and—"

He broke off.

"And what?" Cappen blurted. One-Thumb sat impassive.

Hanse swallowed. "I don't swear to this," he said. "It was still dim, you realize. I've wondered since if I didn't see wrong."

"What was it?" Cappen gripped the table edge till his fingernails whitened.

Hanse wet his throat and said in a rush: "What it *seemed* like was a huge black thing, almost like a snake, but bat-winged. It came streaking from, oh, more or less the direction of Molin's, I'd guess now that I think back. And it was aimed more or less toward the temple of Ils. There was something that dangled below, as it might be a human body or two. I didn't stay to watch, I ducked into the nearest alley and waited. When I came out, it was gone."

He knocked back his ale and rose. "That's all," he snapped. "I don't want to remember the sight any longer, and if anybody ever asks, I was never here tonight."

"Your story's worth a couple more drinks," One-Thumb invited.

"Another evening," Hanse demurred. "Right now I need a whore. Don't forget those ten royals, singer." He left, stiff-legged.

"Well," said the innkeeper after a silence, "what do you make of this latest?"

Cappen suppressed a shiver. His palms were cold. "I don't know, save that what we confront is not of our kind."

"You told me once you've got a charm against magic."

Cappen fingered the little silver amulet, in the form of a coiled snake, he wore around his neck. "I'm not sure. A wizard I'd done a favor for gave me this, years ago. He claimed it'd protect me against spells and supernatural beings of less than godly rank. But to make it work, I have to utter three truths about the spellcaster or the creature. I've done that in two or three scrapes, and come out of them intact, but I can't prove the talisman was responsible."

More customers entered, and One-Thumb must go to serve them. Cappen nursed his ale. He yearned to get drunk and belike the landlord would stand him what was needful, but he didn't dare. He had already learned more than he thought the opposition would approve of— whoever or whatever the opposition was. They might have means of discovering this.

His candle flickered. He glanced up and saw a beardless fat man in an ornate formal robe, scarcely normal dress for a visit to the Vulgar Unicorn. "Greetings," the person said. His voice was like a child's.

Cappen squinted through the gloom. "I don't believe I know you," he replied.

"No, but you will come to believe it, oh, yes, you will." The fat man sat down. One-Thumb came over and took an order for red wine—"a decent wine, mine host, a Zhanuvend or Baladach." Coin gleamed forth.

Cappen's heart thumped. "Enas Yorl?" he breathed.

The other nodded. "In the flesh, the all too mutable flesh. I do hope my curse strikes again soon. Almost any shape would be better than this. I hate being overweight. I'm a eunuch, too. The times I've been a woman were better than this."

"I'm sorry, sir," Cappen took care to say. Though he could not rid himself of the spell laid on him, Enas Yorl was a powerful thaumaturge, no mere prestidigitator.

"At least I've not been arbitrarily displaced. You can't imagine how annoying it is, suddenly to find oneself elsewhere, perhaps miles away. I was able to come here in proper wise, in my litter. Faugh, how can anyone voluntarily set shoes to these open sewers they call streets in the Maze?" The wine arrived. "Best we speak fast and to the point, young man, that we may finish and I get home before the next contretemps."

Enas Yorl sipped and made a face. "I've been swindled," he whined. "This is barely drinkable, if that."

"Maybe your present palate is at fault, sir," Cappen suggested. He did not add that the tongue definitely had a bad case of logorrhea. It was an almost physical torture to sit stalled, but he had better humor the mage.

"Yes, quite probably. Nothing has tasted good since—Well. To business. On hearing that One-Thumb was inquiring about last night's incident, I sent forth certain investigators of my own. You will understand that I've been trying to find out as much as I can." Enas Yorl drew a sign in the air. "Purely precautionary. I have no desire whatsoever to cross the Powers concerned in this."

A wintry tingle went through Cappen. "You know who they are, what it's about?" His tone wavered.

Enas Yorl wagged a finger. "Not so hasty, boy, not so hasty. My latest information was of a seemingly unsuccessful interview you had with Illyra the seeress. I also learned you were now in this hostel and close to its landlord. Obviously you are involved. I must know why, how, how much—everything."

"Then you'll help—sir?"

A headshake made chin and jowls wobble. "Absolutely not. I told you I want no part of this. But in exchange for whatever data you possess, I am willing to explicate as far as I am able, and to advise you. Be

warned: my advice will doubtless be that you drop the matter and perhaps leave town."

And doubtless he would be right, Cappen thought. It simply happened to be counsel that was impossible for a lover to follow . . .
unless—O kindly gods of Caronne, no, no!—unless Danlis was dead.

The whole story spilled out of him, quickened and deepened by keen
questions. At the end, he sat breathless while Enas Yorl nodded.

"Yes, that appears to confirm what I suspected," the mage said most
softly. He stared past the minstrel, into shadows that loomed and flickered. Buzz of talk, clink of drinking ware, occasional gust of laughter
among customers seemed remoter than the moon.

"What was it?" broke from Cappen.

"A sikkintair, a Flying Knife. It can have been nothing else."

"A—what?"

Enas focused on his companion. "The monster that took the
women," he explained. "Sikkintairs are an attribute of Ils. A pair of
sculptures on the grand stairway of his temple represent them."

"Oh, yes, I've seen those, but never thought—"

"No, you're not a votary of any gods they have here. Myself, when I
got word of the abduction, I sent my familiars scuttling about and cast
spells of inquiry. I received indications. . . . I can't describe them to
you, who lack arcane lore. I established that the very fabric of space
had been troubled. Vibrations had not quite damped out as yet, and
were centered on the temple of Ils. You may, if you wish a crude analogy, visualize a water surface and the waves, fading to ripples and
finally to naught, when a diver has passed through."

Enas Yorl drank more in a gulp than was his wont. "Civilization was
old in Ilsig when Ranke was still a barbarian village," he said, as
though to himself; his gaze had drifted away again, toward darkness.
"Its myths depicted the home of the gods as being outside the world—
not above, not below, but outside. Philosophers of a later, more ra-
tionalistic era elaborated this into a theory of parallel universes. My
own researches—you will understand that my condition has made me especially interested in the theory of dimensions, the subtler aspects of
geometry—my own researches have demonstrated the possibility of
transference between these different spaces.

"As another analogy, consider a pack of cards. One is inhabited by a
king, one by a knight, one by a deuce, et cetera. Ordinarily none of the
figures can leave the plane on which it exists. If, however, a very thin
piece of absorbent material soaked in a unique kind of solvent were laid

between two cards, the dyes that form them could pass through: retain-
ing their configuration, I trust. Actually, of course, this is a less than
ideal comparison, for the transference is accomplished through a particular contortion of the continuum—"

Cappen could endure no more pedantry. He crashed his tankard
down on the table and shouted, "By all the hells of all the cults, will
you get to the point?"

Men stared from adjacent seats, decided no fight was about to erupt,
and went back to their interests. These included negotiations with
streetwalkers who, lanterns in hand, had come in looking for trade.

Enas Yorl smiled. "I forgive your outburst, under the circumstances," he said. "I too am occasionally young.

"Very well. Given the foregoing data, including yours, the infrastruc-
ture of events seems reasonably evident. You are aware of the conflict
over a proposed new temple, which is to outdo that of Ils and Shipri. I
do not maintain that the god has taken a direct hand. I certainly hope
he feels that would be beneath his dignity; a theomachy would not be
good for us, to understate the case a trifle. But he may have inspired a
few of his more fanatical priests to action. He may have revealed to
them, in dreams or visions, the means whereby they could cross to the
next world and there make the sikkintairs do their bidding. I hypothe-
size that the Lady Rosanda—and, to be sure, her coadjutrix, your in-
amorata—are incarcerated in that world. The temple is too full of
priests, deacons, acolytes, and lay people for hiding the wife of a mag-
nate. However, the gate need not be recognizable as such."

Cappen controlled himself with an inward shudder and made his
trained voice casual: "What might it look like, sir?"

"Oh, probably a scroll, taken from a coffer where it had long lain
forgotten, and now unrolled—yes, I should think in the sanctum, to
draw power from the sacred objects and to be seen by as few persons as
possible who are not in the conspiracy—" Enas Yorl came out of his
abstraction. "Beware! I deduce your thought. Choke it before it kills
you."

Cappen ran sandy tongue over leathery lips. "What . . . should we
. . . expect to happen, sir?"

"That is an interesting question," Enas Yorl said. "I can but conjecture. Yet I am well acquainted with the temple hierarchy and—I don't
think the Archpriest is privy to the matter. He's too aged and weak. On
the other hand, this is quite in the style of Hazroah, the High Flamen.
Moreover, of late he has in effect taken over the governance of the tem-

ple from his nominal superior. He's bold, ruthless—should have been a soldier—Well, putting myself in his skin, I'll predict that he'll let Molin stew awhile, then cautiously open negotiations—a hint at first, and always a claim that this is the will of Ils.

"None but the Emperor can cancel an undertaking for the Imperial deities. Persuading him will take much time and pressure. Molin is a Rankan aristocrat of the old school; he will be torn between his duty to his gods, his state, and his wife. But I suspect that eventually he can be worn down to the point where he agrees that it is, in truth, bad policy to exalt Savankala and Sabellia in a city whose tutelaries they have never been. He in his turn can influence the Emperor as desired."

"How long would this take, do you think?" Cappen whispered. "Till the women are released?"

Enas Yorl shrugged. "Years, possibly. Hazroah may try to hasten the process by demonstrating that the Lady Rosanda is subject to punishment. Yes, I should imagine that the remains of an ancilla who had been tortured to death, delivered on Molin's doorstep, would be a rather strong argument."

His look grew intense on the appalled countenance across from him. "I know," he said. "You're breeding fever-dreams of a heroic rescue. It cannot be done. Even supposing that somehow you won through the gate and brought her back, the gate would remain. I doubt Ils would personally seek revenge; besides being petty, that could provoke open strife with Savankala and his retinue, who're formidable characters themselves. But Ils would not stay the hand of the Flamen Hazroah, who is a most vengeful sort. If you escaped his assassins, a sikkintair would come after you, and nowhere in the world could you and she hide. Your talisman would be of no avail. The sikkintair is not supernatural, unless you give that designation to the force which enables so huge a mass to fly; and *it* is from no magician, but from the god.

"So forget the girl. The town is full of them." He fished in his purse and spilled a handful of coins on the table. "Go to a good whorehouse, enjoy yourself, and raise one for poor old Enas Yorl."

He got up and waddled off. Cappen sat staring at the coins. They made a generous sum, he realized vaguely: silver lunars, to the number of thirty.

One-Thumb came over. "What'd he say?" the taverner asked.

"I should abandon hope," Cappen muttered. His eyes stung; his vision blurred. Angrily, he wiped them.

"I've a notion I might not be smart to hear more." One-Thumb laid his mutilated hand on Cappen's shoulder. "Care to get drunk? On the house. I'll have to take your money or the rest will want free booze too, but I'll return it tomorrow."

"No, I—I thank you, but—but you're busy, and I need someone I can talk to. Just lend me a lantern, if you will."

"That might attract a robber, fellow, what with those fine clothes of yours."

Cappen gripped swordhilt. "He'd be very welcome, the short while he lasted," he said in bitterness.

He climbed to his feet. His fingers remembered to gather the coins.

Jamie let him in. The Northerner had hastily thrown a robe over his massive frame; he carried the stone lamp that was a night light. "Sh," he said. "The lassies are asleep." He nodded toward a closed door at the far end of this main room. Bringing the lamp higher, he got a clear view of Cappen's face. His own registered shock. "Hey-o, lad, what ails you? I've seen men poleaxed who looked happier."

Cappen stumbled across the threshold and collapsed in an armchair. Jamie barred the outer door, touched a stick of punk to the lamp flame and lit candles, filled wine goblets. Drawing a seat opposite, he sat down, laid red-furred right shank across left knee, and said gently, "Tell me."

When it had spilled from Cappen, he was a long span quiet. On the walls shimmered his weapons, among pretty pictures that his house-mates had selected. At last he asked low, "Have you quit?"

"I don't know, I don't know," Cappen groaned.

"I think you can go on a ways, whether or no things are as the witch-master supposes. We hold where I come from that no man can flee his weird, so he may as well meet it in a way that'll leave a good story. Be-sides, this may not be our death-day; and I doubt yon dragons are unkillable, but it could be fun finding out; and chiefly, I was much taken with your girl. Not many like her, my friend. They also say in my homeland, 'Waste not, want not.' "

Cappen lifted his glance, astounded. "You mean I should try to free her?" he exclaimed.

"No, I mean *we* should." Jamie chuckled. "Life's gotten a wee bit dull for me of late—aside from Butterfly and Light-of-Pearl, of course. Besides, I could use a share of reward money."

"I . . . I want to," Cappen stammered. "How I want to! But the odds against us—"

"She's your girl, and it's your decision. I'll not blame you if you hold back. Belike, then, in your country, they don't believe a man's first troth is to his woman and kids. Anyway, for you that was no more than a hope."

A surge went through the minstrel. He sprang up and paced, back and forth, back and forth. "But what could we *do*?"

"Well, we could scout the temple and see what's what," Jamie proposed. "I've been there once in a while, reckoning 'twould do no hurt to give those gods their honor. Maybe we'll find that indeed naught can be done in aid. Or maybe we won't, and go ahead and do it."

Danlis—

Fire blossomed in Cappen Varra. He was young. He drew his sword and swung it whistling on high. "Yes! We will!"

A small grammarian part of him noted the confusion of tenses and moods in the conversation.

The sole traffic on the Avenue of Temples was a night breeze, cold and sibilant. Stars, as icy to behold, looked down on its broad emptiness, on darkened buildings and weather-worn idols and rustling gardens. Here and there flames cast restless light, from porticoes or gables or ledges, out of glass lanterns or iron pots or pierced stone jars. At the foot of the grand staircase leading to the fane of Ils and Shipri, fire formed halos on the enormous figures, male and female in robes of antiquity, that flanked it.

Beyond, the god-house itself loomed, porticoed front, great bronze doors, granite walls rising sheer above to a gilt dome from which light also gleamed; the highest point in Sanctuary.

Cappen started up. "Halt," said Jamie, and plucked at his cloak. "We can't walk straight in. They keep guards in the vestibule, you know."

"I want a close view of those sikkintairs," the bard explained.

"Um, well, maybe not a bad idea, but let's be quick. If a squad of the watch comes by, we're in trouble." They could not claim they simply wished to perform their devotions, for a civilian was not allowed to bear more arms in this district than a knife. Cappen and Jamie each had that, but no illuminant like honest men. In addition, Cappen carried his rapier, Jamie a claymore, a visored conical helmet, and a knee-length byrnie. He had, moreover, furnished spears for both.

Cappen nodded and bounded aloft. Halfway, he stopped and gazed. The statue was a daunting sight. Of obsidian polished glassy smooth, it

might have measured thirty feet were the tail not coiled under the narrow body. The two legs which supported the front ended in talons the
length of Jamie's dirk. An upreared, serpentine neck bore a wickedly
lanceolate head, jaws parted to show fangs that the sculptor had rendered in diamond. From the back sprang wings, batlike save for their
sharp-pointed curvatures, which if unfolded might well have covered
another ten yards.

"Aye," Jamie murmured, "such a brute could bear off two women
like an eagle a brace of leverets. Must take a lot of food to power it. I
wonder what quarry they hunt at home."

"We may find out," Cappen said, and wished he hadn't.

"Come." Jamie led the way back, and around to the left side of the
temple. It occupied almost its entire ground, leaving but a narrow strip
of flagstones. Next to that, a wall enclosed the flower-fragrant sanctum
of Eshi, the love goddess. Thus the space between was gratifyingly
dark; the intruders could not now be spied from the avenue. Yet enough
light filtered in that they saw what they were doing. Cappen wondered if
this meant she smiled on their venture. After all, it was for love, mainly.
Besides, he had always been an enthusiastic worshiper of hers, or at any
rate of her counterparts in foreign pantheons; oftener than most men
had he rendered her favorite sacrifice.

Jamie had pointed out that the building must have lesser doors for
utilitarian purposes. He soon found one, bolted for the night and between windows that were hardly more than slits, impossible to crawl
through. He could have hewn the wood panels asunder, but the noise
might be heard. Cappen had a better idea. He got his partner down on
hands and knees. Standing on the broad back, he poked his spear
through a window and worked it along the inside of the door. After
some fumbling and whispered obscenities, he caught the latch with the
head and drew the bolt.

"Hoosh, you missed your trade, I'm thinking," said the Northerner as
he rose and opened the way.

"No, burglary's too risky for my taste," Cappen replied in feeble jest.
The fact was that he had never stolen or cheated unless somebody deserved such treatment.

"Even burgling the house of a god?" Jamie's grin was wider than
necessary.

Cappen shivered. "Don't remind me."

They entered a storeroom, shut the door, and groped through murk
to the exit. Beyond was a hall. Widely spaced lamps gave bare visibility.

Otherwise the intruders saw emptiness and heard silence. The vestibule and nave of the temple were never closed; the guards watched over a priest always prepared to accept offerings. But elsewhere hierarchy and staff were asleep. Or so the two hoped.

Jamie had known that the holy of holies was in the dome, Ils being a sky god. Now he let Cappen take the lead, as having more familiarity with interiors and ability to reason out a route. The minstrel used half his mind for that and scarcely noticed the splendors through which he passed. The second half was busy recollecting legends of heroes who incurred the anger of a god, especially a major god, but won to happiness in the end because they had the blessing of another. He decided that future attempts to propitiate Ils would only draw the attention of that august personage; however, Savankala would be pleased, and, yes, as for native deities, he would by all means fervently cultivate Eshi.

A few times, which felt ghastly long, he took a wrong turning and must retrace his steps after he had discovered that. Presently, though, he found a staircase which seemed to zigzag over the inside of an exterior wall. Landing after landing passed by—

The last was enclosed in a very small room, a booth, albeit richly ornamented—

He opened the door and stepped out—

Wind searched between the pillars that upheld the dome, through his clothes and in toward his bones. He saw stars. They were the brightest in heaven, for the entry booth was the pedestal of a gigantic lantern. Across a floor tiled in symbols unknown to him, he observed something large at each cardinal point—an altar, two statues, and the famous Thunderstone, he guessed; they were shrouded in cloth of gold. Before the eastern object was stretched a band, the far side of which seemed to be aglow.

He gathered his courage and approached. The thing was a parchment, about eight feet long and four wide, hung by cords from the upper corners to a supporting member of the dome. The cords appeared to be glued fast, as if to avoid making holes in the surface. The lower edge of the scroll, two feet above the floor, was likewise secured; but to a pair of anvils surely brought here for the purpose. Nevertheless the parchment flapped and rattled a bit in the wind. It was covered with cabalistic signs.

Cappen stepped around to the other side, and whistled low. That held a picture, within a narrow border. Past the edge of what might be a pergola, the scene went to a meadowland made stately by oak trees

standing at random intervals. About a mile away—the perspective was
marvelously executed—stood a building of manorial size in a style he
had never seen before, twistily colonaded, extravagantly sweeping of
roof and eaves, blood-red. A formal garden surrounded it, whose paths
and topiaries were of equally alien outline; fountains sprang in intricate
patterns. Beyond the house, terrain rolled higher, and snowpeaks thrust
above the horizon. The sky was deep blue.

"What the pox!" exploded from Jamie. "Sunshine's coming out of
that painting. I *feel* it."

Cappen rallied his wits and paid heed. Yes, warmth as well as light,
and . . . and odors? And were those fountains not actually at play?

An eerie thrilling took him. "I . . . believe . . . we've . . . found
the gate," he said.

He poked his spear cautiously at the scroll. The point met no resistance; it simply moved on. Jamie went behind. "You've not pierced it,"
he reported. "Nothing sticks out on this side—which, by the way, is
quite solid."

"No," Cappen answered faintly, "the spearhead's in the next world."
He drew the weapon back. He and Jamie stared at each other.

"Well?" said the Northerner.

"We'll never get a better chance," Cappen's throat responded for
him. "It'd be blind foolishness to retreat now, unless we decide to give
up the whole venture."

"We, uh, we could go tell Molin, no, the Prince what we've found."

"And be cast into a madhouse? If the Prince *did* send investigators
anyway, the plotters need merely take this thing down and hide it till
the squad has left. No." Cappen squared his shoulders. "Do what you
like, Jamie, but I am going through."

Underneath, he heartily wished he had less self-respect, or at least
that he weren't in love with Danlis.

Jamie scowled and sighed. "Aye, right you are, I suppose. I'd not
looked for matters to take so headlong a course. I awaited that we'd
simply scout around. Had I foreseen this, I'd have roused the lassies to
bid them, well, goodnight." He hefted his spear and drew his sword.
Abruptly he laughed. "Whatever comes, 'twill not be dull!"

Stepping high over the threshold, Cappen went forward.

It felt like walking through any door, save that he entered a mild
summer's day. After Jamie had followed, he saw that the vista in the
parchment was that on which he had just turned his back: a veiled
mass, a pillar, stars above a nighted city. He checked the opposite side

of the strip, and met the same designs as had been painted on its mate.

No, he thought, not its mate. If he had understood Enas Yorl aright, and rightly remembered what his tutor in mathematics had told him about esoteric geometry, there could be but a single scroll. One side of it gave on this universe, the other side on his, and a spell had twisted dimensions until matter could pass straight between.

Here too the parchment was suspended by cords, though in a pergola of yellow marble, whose circular stairs led down to the meadow. He imagined a sikkintair would find the passage tricky, especially if it was burdened with two women in its claws. The monster had probably hugged them close to it, come in at high speed, folded its wings, and glided between the pillars of the dome and the margins of the gate. On the outbound trip, it must have crawled through into Sanctuary.

All this Cappen did and thought in half a dozen heartbeats. A shout yanked his attention back. Three men who had been idling on the stairs had noticed the advent and were on their way up. Large and hard-featured, they bore the shaven visages, high-crested morions, gilt cuirasses, black tunics and boots, shortswords, and halberds of temple guards. "Who in the Unholy's name are you?" called the first. "What're you doing here?"

Jamie's qualms vanished under a tide of boyish glee. "I doubt they'll believe any words of ours," he said. "We'll have to convince them a different way. If you can handle him on our left, I'll take his feres."

Cappen felt less confident. But he lacked time to be afraid; shuddering would have to be done in a more convenient hour. Besides, he was quite a good fencer. He dashed across the floor and down the stair.

The trouble was, he had no experience with spears. He jabbed. The halberdier held his weapon, both hands close together, near the middle of the shaft. He snapped it against Cappen's, deflected the thrust, and nearly tore the minstrel's out of his grasp. The watchman's return would have skewered his enemy, had the minstrel not flopped straight to the marble.

The guard guffawed, braced his legs wide, swung the halberd back for an axhead blow. As it descended, his hands shifted toward the end of the helve.

Chips flew. Cappen had rolled downstairs. He twirled the whole way to the ground and sprang erect. He still clutched his spear, which had bruised him whenever he crossed above it. The sentry bellowed and hopped in pursuit. Cappen ran.

Behind them, a second guard sprawled and flopped, diminuendo, in what seemed an impossibly copious and bright amount of blood. Jamie had hurled his own spear as he charged and taken the man in the neck. The third was giving the Northerner a brisk fight, halberd against claymore. He had longer reach, but the redhead had more brawn. Thump and clatter rang across the daisies.

Cappen's adversary was bigger than he was. This had the drawback that the former could not change speed or direction as readily. When the guard was pounding along at his best clip, ten or twelve feet in the rear, Cappen stopped within a coin's breadth, whirled about, and threw his shaft. He did not do that as his comrade had done. He pitched it between the guard's legs. The man crashed to the grass. Cappen plunged in. He didn't risk trying for a stab. That would let the armored combatant grapple him. He wrenched the halberd loose and skipped off.

The sentinel rose. Cappen reached an oak and tossed the halberd. It lodged among boughs. He drew blade. His foe did the same.

Shortsword versus rapier—*much* better, though Cappen must have a care. The torso opposing him was protected. Still, the human anatomy has more vulnerable points than that. "Shall we dance?" Cappen asked.

As he and Jamie approached the house, a shadow slid across them. They glanced aloft and saw the gaunt black form of a sikkintair. For an instant, they nerved themselves for the worst. However, the Flying Knife simply caught an updraft, planed high, and hovered in sinister magnificence. "Belike they don't hunt men unless commanded to," the Northerner speculated. "Bear and buffalo are meatier."

Cappen frowned at the scarlet walls before him. "The next question," he said, "is why nobody has come out against us."

"Um, I'd deem those wights we left scattered around were the only fighting men here. What task was theirs? Why, to keep the ladies from escaping, if those are allowed to walk outdoors by day. As for yon manse, while it's plenty big, I suspect it's on loan from its owner. Naught but a few servants need be on hand—and the women, let's hope. I don't suppose anybody happened to see our little brawl."

The thought that they might effect the rescue—soon, safely, easily—went through Cappen in a wave of dizziness. Afterward—He and Jamie had discussed that. If the temple hierophants, from Hazroah on down, were put under immediate arrest, that ought to dispose of the vengeance problem.

Gravel scrunched underfoot. Rose, jasmine, honeysuckle sweetened the air. Fountains leaped and chimed. The partners reached the main door. It was oaken, with many glass eyes inset; the knocker had the shape of a sikkintair.

Jamie leaned his spear, unsheathed his sword, turned the knob left-handed, and swung the door open. A maroon sumptuousness of carpet, hangings, upholstery brooded beyond. He and Cappen entered. Inside were quietness and an odor like that just before a thunderstorm.

A man in a deacon's black robe came through an archway, his tonsure agleam in the dimness. "Did I hear—Oh!" he gasped, and scuttled backward.

Jamie made a long arm and collared him. "Not so fast, friend," the warrior said genially. "We've a request, and if you oblige, we won't get stains on this pretty rug. Where are your guests?"

"What, what, what," the deacon gobbled.

Jamie shook him, in leisured wise lest he quite dislocate the shoulder. "Lady Rosanda, wife to Molin Torchholder, and her assistant Danlis. Take us to them. Oh, and we'd liefer not meet folk along the way. It might get messy if we did."

The deacon fainted.

"Ah, well," Jamie said. "I hate the idea of cutting down unarmed men, but chances are they won't be foolhardy." He filled his lungs. *"Rosanda!"* he bawled. *"Danlis! Jamie and Cappen Varra are here! Come on home!"*

The volume almost bowled his companion over. "Are you mad?" the minstrel exclaimed. "You'll warn the whole staff—" A flash lit his mind: if they had seen no further guards, surely there were none, and nothing corporeal remained to fear. Yet every minute's delay heightened the danger of something else going wrong. Somebody might find signs of invasion back in the temple; the gods alone knew what lurked in this realm . . . . Yes, Jamie's judgment might prove mistaken, but it was the best he could have made.

Servitors appeared, and recoiled from naked steel. And then, and then—

Through a doorway strode Danlis. She led by the hand, or dragged, a half-hysterical Rosanda. Both were decently attired and neither looked abused, but pallor in cheeks and smudges under eyes bespoke what they must have suffered.

Cappen came nigh dropping his spear. "Beloved!" he cried. "Are you hale?"

"We've not been ill-treated in the flesh, aside from the snatching it-

self," she answered efficiently. "The threats, should Hazroah not get his
way, have been cruel. Can we leave now?"

"Aye, the soonest, the best," Jamie growled. "Lead them on ahead,
Cappen." His sword covered the rear. On his way out, he retrieved the
spear he had left.

They started back over the garden paths. Danlis and Cappen between
them must help Rosanda along. That woman's plump prettiness was
lost in tears, moans, whimpers, and occasional screams. He paid scant
attention. His gaze kept seeking the clear profile of his darling. When
her grey eyes turned toward him, his heart became a lyre.

She parted her lips. He waited for her to ask in dazzlement, "How
did you ever do this, you unbelievable, wonderful man?"

"What have we ahead of us?" she wanted to know.

Well, it was an intelligent query. Cappen swallowed disappointment
and sketched the immediate past. Now, he said, they'd return via the
gate to the dome and make their stealthy way from the temple, thence
to Molin's dwelling for a joyous reunion. But then they must act
promptly—yes, roust the Prince out of bed for authorization—and occupy the temple and arrest everybody in sight before new trouble got
fetched from this world.

Rosanda gained some self-control as he talked. "Oh, my, oh, my,"
she wheezed, "you unbelievable, wonderful men."

An ear-piercing trill slashed across her voice. The escapers looked
behind them. At the entrance to the house stood a thickset middle-aged
person in the scarlet robe of a ranking priest of Ils. He held a pipe to
his mouth and blew.

"Hazroah!" Rosanda shrilled. "The ringleader!"

"The High Flamen—" Danlis began.

A rush in the air interrupted. Cappen flung his vision skyward and
knew the nightmare was true. The sikkintair was descending. Hazroah
had summoned it.

"Why, you son of a bitch!" Jamie roared. Still well behind the rest,
he lifted his spear, brought it back, flung it with his whole strength and
weight. The point went home in Hazroah's breast. Ribs did not stop it.
He spouted blood, crumpled, and spouted no more. The shaft quivered
above his body.

But the sikkintair's vast wings eclipsed the sun. Jamie rejoined his
band and plucked the second spear from Cappen's fingers. "Hurry on,
lad," he ordered. "Get them to safety."

"Leave you? No!" protested his comrade.

Jamie spat an oath. "Do you want the whole faring to've gone for naught? Hurry, I said!"

Danlis tugged at Cappen's sleeve. "He's right. The state requires our testimony."

Cappen stumbled onward. From time to time he glanced back.

In the shadow of the wings, Jamie's hair blazed. He stood foursquare, spear grasped as a huntsman does. Agape, the Flying Knife rushed down upon him. Jamie thrust straight between those jaws, and twisted.

The monster let out a sawtoothed shriek. Its wings threshed, made thundercrack, it swooped by, a foot raked. Jamie had his claymore out. He parried the blow.

The sikkintair rose. The shaft waggled from its throat. It spread great ebon membranes, looped, and came back earthward. Its claws were before it. Air whirred behind.

Jamie stood his ground, sword in right hand, knife in left. As the talons smote, he fended them off with the dirk. Blood sprang from his thigh, but his byrnie took most of the edged sweep. And his sword hewed.

The sikkintair ululated again. It tried to ascend, and couldn't. Jamie had crippled its left wing. It landed—Cappen felt the impact through soles and bones—and hitched itself toward him. From around the spear came a geyser hiss.

Jamie held fast where he was. As fangs struck at him, he sidestepped, sprang back, and threw his shoulders against the shaft. Leverage swung jaws aside. He glided by the neck toward the forequarters. Both of his blades attacked the spine.

Cappen and the women hastened on.

They were almost at the pergola when footfalls drew his eyes rearward. Jamie loped at an overtaking pace. Behind him, the sikkintair lay in a heap.

The redhead pulled alongside. "Hai, what a fight!" he panted. "Thanks for this journey, friend! A drinking bout's worth of thanks!"

They mounted the death-defiled stairs. Cappen peered across miles. Wings beat in heaven, from the direction of the mountains. Horror stabbed his guts. "Look!" He could barely croak.

Jamie squinted. "More of them," he said. "A score, maybe. We can't cope with so many. An army couldn't."

"That whistle was heard farther away than mortals would hear," Danlis added starkly.

"What do we linger for?" Rosanda wailed. "Come, take us home!"

"And the sikkintairs follow?" Jamie retorted. "No. I've my lassies, and kinfolk, and—" He moved to stand before the parchment. Edged metal dripped in his hands; red lay splashed across helm, ringmail, clothing, face. His grin broke forth, wry. "A spaewife once told me I'd die on the far side of strangeness. I'll wager she didn't know her own strength."

"You assume that the mission of the beasts is to destroy us, and when that is done they will return to their lairs." The tone Danlis used might have served for a remark about the weather.

"Aye, what else? The harm they'd wreak would be in a hunt for us. But put to such trouble, they could grow furious and harry our whole world. That's the more likely when Hazroah lies skewered. Who else can control them?"

"None that I know of, and he talked quite frankly to us." She nodded. "Yes, it behooves us to die where we are." Rosanda sank down and blubbered. Danlis showed irritation. "Up!" she commanded her mistress. "Up and meet your fate like a Rankan matron!"

Cappen goggled hopelessly at her. She gave him a smile. "Have no regrets, dear," she said. "You did well. The conspiracy against the state has been checked."

*The far side of strangeness—check—chessboard—that version of chess were you pretend the right and left sides of the board are identical on a cylinder—*tumbled through Cappen. The Flying Knives drew closer fast. *Curious aspects of geometry—*

Lightning-smitten, he knew . . . or guessed he did . . . "No, Jamie, we go!" he yelled.

"To no avail save reaping of innocents?" The big man hunched his shoulders. "Never."

"Jamie, let us by! I can close the gate. I swear I can—I swear by—by Eshi—"

The Northerner locked eyes with Cappen for a span that grew. At last: "You are my brother in arms." He stood aside. "Go on."

The sikkintairs were so near that the noise of their speed reached Cappen. He urged Danlis toward the scroll. She lifted her skirt a trifle, revealing a dainty ankle, and stepped through. He hauled on Rosanda's wrist. The woman wavered to her feet but seemed unable to find her direction. Cappen took an arm and passed it into the next world for Danlis to pull. Himself, he gave a mighty shove on milady's buttocks. She crossed over.

He did. And Jamie.

Beneath the temple dome, Cappen's rapier reached high and slashed. Louder came the racket of cloven air. Cappen severed the upper cords. The parchment fell, wrinkling, crackling. He dropped his weapon, a-clang, squatted, and stretched his arms wide. The free corners he seized. He pulled them to the corners that were still secured, to make a closed band of the scroll.

From it sounded monstrous thumps and scrapes. The sikkintairs were crawling into the pergola. For them the portal must hang unchanged, open for their hunting.

Cappen gave that which he held a half-twist and brought the edges back together.

Thus he created a surface which had but a single side and a single edge. Thus he obliterated the gate.

He had not been sure what would follow. He had fleetingly supposed he would smuggle the scroll out, held in its paradoxical form, and eventually glue it—unless he could burn it. But upon the instant that he completed the twist and juncture, the parchment was gone. Enas Yorl told him afterward that he had made it impossible for the thing to exist.

Air rushed in where the gate had been, crack and hiss. Cappen heard that sound as it were an alien word of incantation: *"Möbius-s-s."*

Having stolen out of the temple and some distance thence, the party stopped for a few minutes of recovery before they proceeded to Molin's house.

This was in a blind alley off the avenue, a brick-paved recess where flowers grew in planters, shared by the fanes of two small and gentle gods. Wind had died away, stars glimmered bright, a half moon stood above easterly roofs and cast wan argence. Afar, a tomcat serenaded his intended.

Rosanda had gotten back a measure of equilibrium. She cast herself against Jamie's breast. "Oh, hero, hero," she crooned, "you shall have reward, yes, treasure, ennoblement, everything!" She snuggled. "But nothing greater than my unbounded thanks. . . ."

The Northerner cocked an eyebrow at Cappen. The bard shook his head a little. Jamie nodded in understanding, and disengaged. "Uh, have a care, milady," he said. "Pressing against ringmail, all bloody and sweaty too, can't be good for a complexion."

Even if one rescues them, it is not wise to trifle with the wives of magnates.

Cappen had been busy himself. For the first time, he kissed Danlis on her lovely mouth; then for the second time; then for the third. She responded decorously.

Thereafter she likewise withdrew. Moonlight made a mystery out of her classic beauty. "Cappen," she said, "before we go on, we had better have a talk."

He gaped. "What?"

She bridged her fingers. "Urgent matters first," she continued crisply. "Once we get to the mansion and wake the high priest, it will be chaos at first, conference later, and I—as a woman—excluded from serious discussion. Therefore best I give my counsel now, for you to relay. Not that Molin or the Prince are fools; the measures to take are for the most part obvious. However, swift action is desirable, and they will have been caught by surprise."

She ticked her points off. "First, as you have indicated, the Hell-Hounds"—her nostrils pinched in distaste at the nickname—"the Imperial elite guard should mount an immediate raid on the temple of Ils and arrest all personnel for interrogation, except the Archpriest. He's probably innocent, and in any event it would be inept politics. Hazroah's death may have removed the danger, but this should not be taken for granted. Even if it has, his co-conspirators ought to be identified and made examples of.

"Yet, second, wisdom should temper justice. No lasting harm was done, unless we count those persons who are trapped in the parallel universe; and they doubtless deserve to be."

They seemed entirely males, Cappen recalled. He grimaced in compassion. Of course, the sikkintairs might eat them.

Danlis was talking on: "—humane governance and the art of compromise. A grand temple dedicated to the Rankan gods is certainly required, but it need be no larger than that of Ils. Your counsel will have much weight, dear. Give it wisely. I will advise you."

"Uh?" Cappen said.

Danlis smiled and laid her hands over his. "Why, you can have unlimited preferment, after what you did," she told him. "I'll show you how to apply for it."

"But—but I'm no blooming statesman!" Cappen stuttered.

She stepped back and considered him. "True," she agreed. "You're valiant, yes, but you're also flighty and lazy and—Well, don't despair. I will mold you."

Cappen gulped and shuffled aside. "Jamie," he said, "uh, Jamie, I feel wrung dry, dead on my feet. I'd be worse than no use—I'd be a drogue on things just when they have to move fast. Better I find me a doss, and you take the ladies home. Come over here and I'll tell you how to convey the story in fewest words. Excuse us, ladies. Some of those words you oughtn't to hear."

A week thence, Cappen Varra sat drinking in the Vulgar Unicorn. It was mid-afternoon and none else were present but the associate tapster, his wound knitted.

A man filled the doorway and came in, to Cappen's table. "Been casting about everywhere for you," the Northerner grumbled. "Where've you been?"

"Lying low," Cappen replied. "I've taken a place here in the Maze which'll do till I've dropped back into obscurity, or decide to drift elsewhere altogether." He sipped his wine. Sunbeams slanted through windows; dustmotes danced golden in their warmth; a cat lay on a sill and purred. "Trouble is, my purse is flat."

"We're free of such woes for a goodly while." Jamie flung his length into a chair and signaled the attendant. "Beer!" he thundered.

"You collected a reward, then?" the minstrel asked eagerly.

Jamie nodded. "Aye. In the way you whispered I should, before you left us. I'm baffled why and it went sore against the grain. But I did give Molin the notion that the rescue was my idea and you naught but a hanger-on whom I'd slip a few royals. He filled a box with gold and silver money, and said he wished he could afford ten times that. He offered to get me Rankan citizenship and a title as well, and make a bureaucrat of me, but I said no, thanks. We share, you and I, half and half. But right this now, drinks are on me."

"What about the plotters?" Cappen inquired.

"Ah, those. The matter's been kept quiet, as you'd await. Still, while the temple of Ils can't be abolished, seemingly it's been tamed." Jamie's regard sought across the table and sharpened. "After you disappeared, Danlis agreed to let me claim the whole honor. She knew better—Rosanda never noticed—but Danlis wanted a man of the hour to carry her redes to the prince, and none remained save me. She supposed you were simply worn out. When last I saw her, though, she . . . um-m . . . she 'expressed disappointment.'" He cocked his ruddy head. "Yon's quite a girl. I thought you loved her."

Cappen Varra took a fresh draught of wine. Old summers glowed along his tongue. "I did," he confessed. "I do. My heart is broken, and in part I drink to numb the pain."

Jamie raised his brows. "What? Makes no sense."

"Oh, it makes very basic sense," Cappen answered. "Broken hearts tend to heal rather soon. Meanwhile, if I may recite from a rondel I completed before you found me—

> *"Each sword of sorrow that would maim or slay,*
> *My lady of the morning deftly parries.*
> *Yet gods forbid I be the one she marries!*
> *I rise from bed the latest hour I may.*
> *My lady comes to me like break of day;*
> *I dream in darkness if it chance she tarries."*

# A FEW REMARKS BY
## FURTWANCOINPINCH, MERCHANT

The first thing I noticed about him, just that first impression you understand, was that he couldn't be a poor man. Or boy, or youth, or whatever he was then. Not with all those weapons on him. From the shagreen belt he was wearing over a scarlet sash—a violently scarlet sash!—swung a curved dagger on his left hip and on the right one of those Ilbarsi "knives" long as your arm. Not a proper sword, no. Not a military man, then. That isn't all, though. Some few of us know that his left buskin is equipped with a sheath; the slim thing and knife-hilt appear to be only a decoration. Gift from a woman, I heard him tell Old Thumpfoot one afternoon in the bazaar. I doubt it.

(I've been told he has another sticker strapped less than comfortably to his inner thigh, probably the right. Maybe that's part of the reason he walks the way he does. Cat-supple and yet sort of stiff of leg all at once. A tumbler's gait—or a punk's swagger. Don't tell him I said!)

Anyhow, about the weapons and my first impression that he couldn't be poor. There's a throwing knife in that leather and copper armlet on his right upper arm, and another in the long bracer of black leather on that same arm. Both are short. The stickers I mean, not the bracers or the arms either.

All that armament would be enough to scare anybody on a dark night, or even a moonbright one. Imagine being in the Maze or someplace like that and out of the shadows comes this young bravo, swaggering, wearing all that sharp metal! Right at you out of the shadows that spawned him. Enough to chill even one of those Hell-Hounds. Even one of you-know-who's boys in the blue hawk-masks might step aside.

That was my impression. Shadowspawn. About as pleasant as gout or dropsy.

# Shadowspawn

## Andrew Offutt

His mop of hair was blacker than black and his eyes nearly so, under brows that just missed meeting above a nose not quite falcate. His walk reminded some of one of those red-and-black gamecocks brought over from Mrsevada. They called him Shadowspawn. No compliment was intended, and he objected until Cudget told him it was good to have a nickname—although he wished his own weren't Cudget Swearoath. Besides, *Shadowspawn* had a romantic and rather sinister sound, and that appealed to his ego, which was the largest thing about him. His height was almost average and he was rangy, wiry; swiftly wiry, with those bulgy rocks in his biceps and calves that other males wished they had.

Shadowspawn. It was descriptive enough. No one knew where he'd been spawned, which was shadowy, and he worked among shadows. Perhaps it was down in the shadows of the "streets" of Downwind and maybe it was over in Syr that he'd been birthed. It didn't matter. He belonged to Sanctuary and wished it belonged to him. He acted as if it did. If he knew or suspected that he'd come out of Downwind, he was sure he had risen above it. He just didn't have time for those street-gangs of which surely he'd have been chieftain.

He was no more sure of his age than anyone else. He might have lived a score of years. It might have been fewer. Had a creditable mustache before he was fifteen.

The raven-wing hair, tending to an indecisive curl, covered his ears without reaching his shoulders. He'd an earring under that hair, on the left. Few knew it. Had it done at fourteen, to impress her who took his virginity that year. (She was twoscore-and-two then, married to a man

like a building stone with a belly. She's a hag with a belly out to here,
now.)

"The lashes under those thick glossy brows of his are so black and
thick they look almost kohled, like a woman's or a priest over in Yenized," a man called Weasel told Cusharlain, in the Vulgar Unicorn.
"Some fool made that remark once, in his presence. The fellow wears
the scar still and knows he's lucky to be wearing tongue and life. Should
have known that a bravo who wears two throwing knives on his right
arm is dangerous, and left-handed. And with a name like Shadowspawn. . . !"

His name was not Shadowspawn, of course. True, many did not
know or no longer remembered his name. It was Hanse. Just Hanse.
Not Hanse Shadowspawn; people called him the one or the other or
nothing at all.

He seemed to wear a cloak about him at all times, a thoughtful
S'danzo told Cusharlain. Not a cloak of fabric; this one concealed his
features, his mind. Eyes hooded like a cobra's, some said. They weren't,
really. They just did not seem directed outward, those glittering black
onyxes he had for eyes. Perhaps their gaze was fixed on the plank-sized
chips on his shoulders. Mighty easily knocked off.

By night he did not swagger, save when he entered a public place.
Night of course was Hanse's time, as it had been Cudget's. By night . . .
"Hanse walks like a hungry cat," some said, and they might shiver a bit.
In truth he did not. He *glided*. His buskins' soft soles lifting only a
finger's breadth with each step. They came down on the balls of the
feet, not the heels. Some made fun of that—not to Hanse—because it
made for a sinuous glide strange in appearance. The better-born
watched him with an aesthetic fascination. And some horripilation.
Among females, highborn or otherwise, the fascination was often
layered with interest, however unwilling. Most then said the predictable: a distasteful, rather sexy animal; that Hanse, that Shadowspawn.

It had been suggested to him that a bit of committed practice could
make him a real swordslinger: he was a natural. Employment, a uniform . . . Hanse was not interested. Indeed he sneered at soldiers, at
uniforms. And now he hated them, with a sort of unreasoning reason.

These things Cusharlain learned, and he began to know him called
Shadowspawn. And to dislike him. Hanse sounded the sort of too-com-
petent young snot you would step aside for—and hate yourself for doing
it.

"Hanse is a bastard!" This from Shive the Changer, with a thump of his fist on the broad table on which he dealt with such as Hanse, changing loot into coin.

"Ah." Cusharlain looked innocently at him. "You mean by nature."

"Probably by birth too. A bastard both by birth and by nature! Better that all such cocky snotty stealthy arrogant bravos were stillborn!"

"He's bitten you then, Shive?"

"A bravo and a lowborn punk he is, and that's all."

"Punk?"

"Well . . . perhaps a cut above punk." Shive touched his mustachioes, which he kept curled like the horns of a mountain goat. "Cudget was a damned good thief. The sort of fellow who made the trade honorable. An art form. A pleasure doing business with. And Hanse was his apprentice, or nearly, sort of . . . and he has the potential of being an even better thief. Not man—thief." Shive wagged a finger made shiny by wax. "The potential, mind you. He'll never realize it." The finger paused on its way back to stroke one mustachio.

"You think not," Cusharlain said, drawing Shive out, pulling words from a man who knew how to keep his mouth shut and was alive and wealthy because he did.

"I think not. He'll absorb a foot or so of sharp metal long before. Or dance on the air."

"As, I remind you, Cudget did," Cusharlain said, noting that within the trade no one said "hanged."

Shive took umbrage. "After a long career! And Cudget was respected! He's respected still."

"Umm. Pity you admire the master but not the apprentice. He could use you, surely. And you him. If he's a successful thief, there'll be profit for the fence he chooses to—"

"Fence? Fence?"

"Sorry, Shive. The Changer he chooses to exchange his . . . goods with, for Rankan coin. There's always a profit to—"

"He cheated me!"

So. At last Shive admitted it. That's how he'd been bitten by this Hanse. Fat and fifty and the second most experienced Changer in Sanctuary, Shive had been cheated by a cocky youngster. "Oh," Cusharlain said. He rose, showing Shive a satirical little smile. "You know, Shive . . . you shouldn't admit that. You are after all a man with some twenty years' experience . . . and he has only that many years of life, if not less."

Shive stared after the customs inspector. An Aurveshan raised in

Sanctuary and now employed by their mutual conqueror, Ranke. As well as by an informal league of Changers and Sanctuary's foremost thieves; those so successful they employed other thieves. With a distinct curl of his lip—a cultivated artificial maneuver—and a brush of his double-curled left mustachio, Shive returned his attention to the prying of a nice ruby from its entirely too-recognizable setting.

Just now Cusharlain's prowling the Maze was in service of still another employer, for he was an ambitious and ever-hungry man. An amenable man, to opportunities for profit and new contracts. Today he was merely collecting information about the former apprentice of Cudget Swearoath, who had been swung shortly after the new Prince-Governor came out from Ranke to "whip this Thieves' World of a town into shape." Above bribery, beyond threat, the (very) young ass actually meant to govern Sanctuary! To clean it up! Young Kadakithis, whom they called Kittycat!

So far he had angered the priesthood and every thief and Changer in Sanctuary. And a good three-fifths of the taverners. And even a number of the garrison soldiers, with those baby-clean, revoltingly competent Hell-Hounds of his. Some of the old villa-dwellers thought he was just wonderful.

Probably wets his bed, Cusharlain thought with a jerk of his head—at the same time as he expertly twitched his robe's hem away from the touch of a legless beggar. Cusharlain knew very well that the fellow's legs were single-strapped up under his long, long, tattered coat. Well, and well. So one boy of nineteen or twenty, a thief, hated another, a half-brother of the Emperor sent out here because it was the anus of the Empire, good and far from the Rankan imperial seat! This the customs inspector had learned today, while gathering information for his secretive and clandestine employer. Hanse, Hanse. In all his life this Hanse had held regard for one person other than his cocky self: Cudget Swearoath. Respected senior thief. And Cudget had been arrested, which certainly would not have happened in the old days. The days B. D. P., Cusharlain thought; Before this Damned Prince! Far more incredibly, if there could be grades of incredibility, Cudget had been hanged!

Prince Stupid!

"Ah, the lad knows he can't hope to do injury on the Prince," someone had told the night proprietor of the Golden Lizard, who had told Cusharlain's old friend Gelicia, proprietor of the popular House of

Mermaids. "He schemes to steal from the very Prince-Governor, and make a quick *large* profit in the doing."

Cusharlain stared at her. "This young gamecock means to try to rob the very palace?" he said, feeling stupid instantly; so she'd said, yes.

"Don't scoff, Cusher," Gelicia said, waving a doughy hand well leavened with rings. This noon she was wearing apple-green and purple and lavender and mauve and orange, all in a way that exposed a large portion of her unrivaled bosom, which resembled two white cushions for a large divan and which Cusharlain was singularly uninterested in viewing.

"If it can be done, Shadowspawn'll do it," she said. "Oh, go ahead, tip yourself some more wine. Did you hear about the ring he tugged from under Corlas's pillow—while Corlas's head was on it, sleeping? You know, Corlas the camel dealer. Or've you heard tell of how our boy Hanse clumb up and stole the eagle off the roof of Barracks Three for a lark?"

"I wondered what had happened to that!"

She nodded wisely with a trebling of chin and a flashing swing of earrings whose diameter was the same as his wine-cup—which was of silver. Her wine-cup, that is; the one he was using. "Shadowspawn," she said, "as Eshi is my witness. Had a prodigal offer from some richie up in Twand, too—and do you know Hanse wouldn't take it? Said he liked having the thing. Pisses on it every morning on rising, he says."

Cusharlain smiled. "And . . . if it can't be done? Roaching the palace, I mean."

Gelicia's shrug imparted to her bosom a quake of seismic proportions. "Why then Sanctuary will be minus one more cockroach, and no one'll miss him. Oh, my Lycansha will moon for a while, but she'll soon be over it."

"Lycansha? Who's Lycansha?"

Nine rings flashed on Gelicia's hands as she sketched a form in the air exactly as a man would have done. "Ah, the sweetest little Cadite oral-submissive you ever laid eyes on, who fancies that leanness and those midnight eyes of his, Cusher. Like to . . . meet her? She's at liberty just now."

"I'm on business, Gelicia." His sigh was carefully elaborate.

"Asking about our little Shadowspawn?" Gelicia's meaty face took on a businesslike expression, which some would have called crafty-furtive.

"Aye."

"Well. Whoever you're reporting to, Cusher—you haven't talked to me!"

"Of course not, Gelicia! Don't be silly. I haven't talked with anyone with a name, or an address, or a face. I enjoy my . . . relationship with some of you more enterprising citizens"—he paused for her mirthful snort—"and have no wish to jeopardize it. Or to lose the physical attributes necessary to my availing myself of your dear girls from time to time."

Her snickering laugh rose and went on up to whoops about the time he reached the street, assuring him that eventually the successful Gelicia had got his parting joke. Red Lanterns was a quiet neighborhood this time of day, after the sweeping up of the dust and tracks of last night's customers. Now sheets were being washed. A few deliveries made. A couple of workmen were occupied with a broken door-hasp at a House down the street. Cusharlain squinted upward. The Enemy, a horrid white ball in a horrid sky going the color of turmeric powder laced with saffron, was high, nigh to passing noon. One-Thumb should be stirring himself about now. Cusharlain decided to go and have a talk with him, too, and maybe he could get his report made by sunset. His employer did not seem as long on patience as on funds. The customs inspector of a fading city whose chief business was theft and the disposal of its product had learned the former, and was ever at work on increasing his share of the latter.

"Did what?" the startlingly good-looking woman said. "Roaching? What's roaching mean?"

Her companion, who was only little older than her seventeen or eighteen years, stiffened his neck to keep from looking anxiously around. "Sh—not so loud. When do cockroaches come out?"

She blinked at the dark, so intense young man. "Why—at night."

"So do thieves."

"Oh!" She laughed, struck her hands together with a jangling of bangles—gold, definitely—and touched his arm. "Oh, Hanse, I know so little! You know just about everything, don't you." Her face changed. "My, these hairs are soft." And she left her hand on that arm with its dark, dark hairs.

"The streets are my home," he told her. "They birthed me and gave me suck. I know quite a bit, yes."

He could hardly believe his luck, sitting here in a decent tavern out of the Maze with this genuinely beautiful Lirain who was . . . by the

Thousand Eyes and by Eshi, too, could it be?—one of the concubines
the Prince-Governor had brought over from Ranke! And she's obviously fascinated with me, Hanse thought. He acted as if he sat here in
the Golden Oasis every afternoon with such as she. What a coincidence,
what great good fortune to have run into her in the bazaar that way!
Run into her indeed! She had been hurrying and he'd been turning,
glancing back at one of those child-affrighters of Jubal's, and they had
slammed together and had to cling to each other to avoid falling. She
had been so apologetic and in seeming need to make amends and—here
they were, Hanse and a palace conky unguarded or watched, and a
beauty at that—and *wearing* enough to support him for a year. He
strove to be oh so cool.

"You certainly do like my gourds, don't you."

"Wha—"

"Oh, don't dissemble. I'm not mad. Really, Hanse. If I didn't want
'em looked at I'd cover 'em in high-necked homespun."

"Uh . . . Lirain, I've seen one other pearl-sewn halter of silk in my
life, and it didn't have those swirls of gold thread, or so many pearls. I
wasn't this close, either." *Damn,* he thought. *Should have complimented
her, not let her know my interest is greed for the container!*

"Oh! Here I am, one of seven women for one man and bored, and I
thought you were wanting to get into my bandeau, when what you really want is *it.* What's a poor girl to do, used to the flatteries of courtiers
and servants, when she meets a real man who speaks his real thoughts?"

Hanse tried not to let his preening show. Nor did he know how to
apologize, or to fancytalk beyond the level of the Maze. Besides, he
thought this pout-lipped beauty with her heart-shaped face and nice
woman's belly was having some fun with him. She knew that pout was
irresistible!

"Wear high-necked homespun," he said, and while she laughed, "and
try not to look that way. This real man knows what you're used to, and
that you can't be interested in Hanse the roach!"

Her expression became very serious. "You must not have access to a
mirror, Hanse. Why don't you try me?"

Hanse fought his astonishment and made swift recovery. With prickly
armpits and outward confidence, he said, "Would you like to take a
walk, Lirain?"

"Is there a more private room at the end of it?"

Holding her gaze as she held his, he nodded.

"Yes," she said, that quickly. Concubine of Prince Kadakithis! "Could anything as good as this bandeau be bought in the bazaar?"

He was rising. "Who'd buy it? No," he said, puzzled at the question.

"Then you must buy me the best we can find after a *short* search." She chuckled at the sight of his stricken face. The cocky creature thought she was a whore, to charge him some trifle like any girl! "So that I can wear it back to the palace," she said, and watched understanding brighten that frightening yet sensuous pair of onyxes he wore for eyes, all hard and cold and wary. She slid her hand into his, and they departed the Golden Oasis.

"Of *course* I'm sure, Bourne!" Lirain twitched off the blue-arabesqued bandeau of green silk Hanse had bought her, and hurled it at the man on the divan. He grinned so that his big brown beard writhed. "He has such *needs!* He is never relaxed, and wants and needs so badly, and so wants to be and to do. He is *so* impressed with who or rather what I am, and yet he would deny under torture that I was anything but another nice tumble. You and I both well know about lowborns who hunger for far more than food! He is completely taken in and he'll be the perfect tool, Bourne. My agent assured me that he is a competent sneak-thief, and that he wants to rob and gain a leg on Prince Kittycat so badly he can taste it. I saw that, right enough. Look, it's perfect!"

"A thief. And competent, you say." Bourne scratched his thigh under the tunic of his Hell-Hound's uniform. He glanced around the apartment she occupied on nights when the Prince might come—hours from now. "And he has a valuable halter of yours now, to sell. Perhaps to brag about and get you into trouble. That kind of trouble ends in death, Lirain."

"You find it hard to admit that I—a *woman*—have accomplished this, love? Look here, that gourd-holster was stolen today in the marketplace. Sliced through in back and snatched off, in a single act. Some child of about thirteen, a dirty girl who ran off with it like a racing dromedary. I did not tell anyone because I *so* hated its loss and am *so* mortified."

"All right. Maybe. That's not bad—forget the part about its being sliced in back, lest it turn up whole. Hmm—I guess it won't. Likely perfectly good silk will be dumped while the pearls and gold thread are sold. And how *competent* was he at the couching, Lirain?"

Lirain looked to the heavens. "O Sabellia, and we call Thee the
Sharp-Tongued One! Men! Plague and drought, Bourne, can't you be
more than a man? He was . . . fair. That's all. I was on business. *We*
are on business, love. Our assignment for those 'certain interested nobles' back in Ranke—my hind leg, it's the Emperor himself, worried
about his half-brother's pretty golden-haired magnetism!—is to embar-
rass His pretty golden-haired Highness Kadakithis! He's been doing
that well enough all by himself! Trying to implement civilized law in
this roach-nest of a town! Continuing to insist that temples to Savankala
and Sabellia have to be mightier than the one to the Ils these people
worship, and that Vashanka's must be equal to Ils's. Priests hate him
and merchants hate him and thieves hate him—and thieves make this
town go!"

Bourne nodded—and demonstrated his strength by drawing a fifteen-
inch dagger to clean his nails.

Lirain tossed her girdle of silver links onto a pile of cushions and idly
fingered her naval. "Now we provide the finishing touch. There will
never be a threat to the Emperor from this pretty boy's supporters
again! We help Hanse the roach into the palace."

"After which he is absolutely on his own," he said, pointing with the
dagger. "We've got to be uncompromised."

"Oh," she said flaunting, "*I* shall be a-couching with His Highness!
The while, Hanse steals his Rod of Authority: the Savankh of Ranke,
given him personally by the Emperor as symbol of full authority here!
Hanse will wish to negotiate a private, quiet trade with Kittycat. Rod
for a fat ransom, and his safety. We will be busily seeing that word gets
around. A thief broke into the palace and stole the Savankh! And the
Prince-Governor is the laughing stock of the capital! He'll either rot
here—or, worse still, be recalled in disgrace."

The big man lounging so familiarly on her divan nodded slowly. "I
do have to point out that you may well rot here with him."

"Oh, no. You and I are promised reprieve from this middenheap
town. And . . . Bourne . . . *particularly* if we heroically regain the
Savankh for the honor of the Empire. After its theft is just terribly well
known, of course."

"Now, that's good!" Bourne's brows tipped up and his lips pursed, a
rather obscene spectacle between the bushiness of brown mustache
and beard. "And how do we do that? You going to trade this Hanse another halter for it?"

She looked long at him. Coolly, brows arched above blue-lidded eyes. "What's that in your hand, Guardian; Hell-Hound so loyal to His Highness?"

Bourne regarded the dagger in his big hairy hand, looked at Lirain, and began to smile.

Though hardly beloved nor indeed particularly lovable, Hanse was a member of the community. Though a paid ally, the customs inspector was not. Hanse heard from three sources that Cusharlain had been asking after him, on behalf of someone else. After giving that thought, Hanse traded with a grimy little thief. First Hanse reminded him that he could easily take the five truly fine melons the boy had been so deft as to steal, all in an afternoon. The boy agreed to accept a longish, stiffish piece of braided gold thread, and Hanse gained four melons. With his hilt and then thumb, Hanse made a nice depression in the top of each. Into each he tucked a nice pearl; four of his thirty-four.

These he set before the hugely fat and grossly misnamed Moonflower, a S'danzo who liked food, melons, pearls, Hanse, and proving that she was more than a mere charlatan. Many others were. Few had the Gift. Even the cynical Hanse was convinced that Moonflower had.

She sat on a cushioned stool of extra width and sturdy legs. Her pile of red and yellow and green skirts overflowed it, while disguising the fact that so did her vast backside. Her back was against the east wall of the tired building wherein she and her man and seven of their brood of nine dwelt, and wherein her man sold . . . things. Hanse sat cross-legged before her. Looking boyish without his arm-sheaths and in a dusty tunic the color of an old camel. He watched a pearl disappear under Moonflower's shawl into what she called her treasure chest. He watched the melon disappear between her lavender-painted lips. Swiftly.

"You are such a good boy, Hanse." When she talked, Moonflower was a kitten.

"Only when I want something, passionflower."

She laughed and beamed and tousled his hair for he knew that such talk pleased her. Then he told her the story. Handed her, disguised in carefully smudged russet, a strip of silken cloth: two straps and two cupped circles bearing many thread-holes.

"Ah! You've been visiting a lady in the Path of Money! Nice of you to let Moonflower have four of the pearls you've laboriously sliced off this little sheath!"

"She gave it me for services rendered." He waved a hand.

"Oh, of course. Hmm." She folded it, unfolded it, fondled it, drew it through her dimple-backed hands, sniffed and tasted it with a dainty tongue-tip. A gross kitten at her divining. She closed her eyes and was very still. As Hanse was, waiting.

"She is indeed a c—— what you said," she told him, able to be discreet even though in something approaching a trance. "Oh, Shadowspawn! You are involved in a plot beyond your dreaming. Odd—this must be the Emperor I see, watching from afar. And this big man with your . . . acquaintance. A big man with a big beard. In a uniform? I think so. Close to our ruler, both. Yet . . . ahh . . . they are his enemies. Yes. They plot. She is a serpent and he a lion of no little craft. They seek . . . ah, I see. The Prince-Governor has become faceless. Yes. They seek to cost him face." Her eyes opened to stare wide at him, two big garnets set amid a heavy layer of kohl. "And you, Hanse my sweet, are their *tool*."

They stared at each other for a moment. "Best you vanish for a time, Shadowspawn. You know what becomes of tools once they are no longer needed."

"Discarded," he snarled, not even bemoaning the loss of Lirain's denuded bandeau, which Moonflower made vanish within a shawl-buried, vaster one.

"Or," she said, keeping him fixed by her gaze, "hung up."

Lirain and her (uniformed?) confederate were tools then, Hanse reasoned, prowling the streets. Prince Kadakithis was nice to look at, and charismatic. So his imperial half-brother had sent him way out here, to Sanctuary. Now he wanted him sorely embarrassed here. Hanse could see the wisdom of that, and knew that despite what any might say, the Emperor was no fool. So, then. They two plotted. Lirain gained enough knowledge of Hanse to employ Cusharlain to investigate him. She had found a way to effect their meeting. Yes; though it hurt his ego, he admitted to himself that she had made the approach and the decisions. So now he was their tool. A tool of tools!

Robbing Kadakithis, however, had been his goal before he met that cupiditous concubine. So long as she helped, he was quite willing to let her think he was her dupe. He wanted to be their tool, then—insofar as it aided him to gain easy entry to the palace. Forewarned and all that. There was definitely potential here for a clever man, and Hanse deemed himself twice as clever as he was, which was considerably. Finally, being made the tool of plotting tools was far too demeaning for the Hansean ego to accept.

Yes. He would gain the wand. Trade it to the Prince-Governor for gold—no, better make it the less intimidating silver—and freedom. From Suma or Mrsevada or someplace, he'd send a message back, anonymously informing Kadakithis that Lirain was a traitor. Hanse smiled at that pleasant thought. Perhaps he'd just go up to Ranke and tell the Emperor what a pair of incompetent agents he had down in Sanctuary. Hanse saw himself richly rewarded, an intimate of the Emperor . . .

And so he and Lirain met again, and made their agreement and plan.

A gate was indeed left open. A guard did indeed quit his post before a door of the palace. It did indeed prove to be unlatched. Hanse locked it after him. Thus a rather thick-waisted Shadowspawn gained entry to the palatial home of the governor of Sanctuary. Dark corridors led him to the appointed chamber. As the Prince was not in it, it was not specifically guarded. The ivory rod, carved to resemble rough-barked wood, was indeed there. So, unexpectedly enjoying the royal couch in its owner's absence, was Lirain's sister concubine. She proved not to have been drugged. She woke and opened her mouth to yell. Hanse reduced that to a squeak by punching her in the belly, which was shockingly convex and soft, considering her youth. He held a pillow over her face, sustaining a couple of scratches and a bruised shin. She became still. He made sure that she was limp but quite alive, and bound her with a gaiter off her own sandal. The other he pulled around so as to hold in place the silken garment he stuffed into her mouth, and tied behind her head. He removed the pendant from one ear. All in darkness. He hurried to wrap the rod of authority in the drape off a low table. Hitching up his tunic, he began drawing from around his waist the thirty feet of knotted rope he had deemed wise. Lirain had assured him that a sedative would be administered to the Hell-Hounds' evening libation. Hanse had no way of knowing that to be the truth; that not only had one of those big burly five done the administering, he had drunk no less than the others. Bourne and company slept most soundly. The plan was that Hanse would leave the same way he had entered. Because he knew he was a tool and was suspicious unto caution, Hanse had decided to effect a different exit.

One end of the rope he secured to the table whose drape he'd stolen. The other he tossed out the window. Crosswise, the table would hold the rope without following him through the window.

It proved true. Hanse went out, and down. Slipping out westward to wend his way among the brothels, he was aware of a number of scorpions scuttling up and down his back, tails poised. Evidently the bound occupant of His Highness's bed was not found. Dawn was still only a promise when Hanse reached his second-floor room in the Maze.

He was a long time wakeful. Admiring the symbol of Rankan authority, named for the god they claimed had given it them. Marveling at its unimposing aspect. A twiglike wand not two feet long, of yellowing ivory. He had done it!

Shortly after noon next day, Hanse had a talk with babbly old Hakiem, who had lately done much babbling about what a fine fellow His handsome Highness was, and how he had even spoken with Hakiem, giving him two pieces of good silver as well! Today Hakiem listened to Hanse, and he swallowed often. What could he do save agree?

Carrying a pretty pendant off a woman's earring, Hakiem hied him to the palace. Gained the Presence by sending in one word to the Prince, with the pendant. Assured him he had nothing to do with the theft. Most privily Hakiem stated what he'd been told, and the thief's terms. Ransom.

The Prince-Governor had to pay, and knew it. If he could get the damned Savankh back, he'd never have to let out that it had been stolen in the first place. Taya, who had spent a night in his bed less comfortable than she had expected, had no notion what had been taken. Too, she seemed to believe his promise to stretch or excise various parts of her anatomy should she flap her mouth to anyone at all.

Meanwhile the concubine Lirain and Hell-Hound Bourne were jubilant. Plotting. Grinning. Planning the Revelation that would destroy their employer. Indeed, they lost no time in despatching a message to their other employers, back in Ranke. That was premature, unwise, and downright stupid.

Next came the coincidence, though it wasn't all that much one. Zalbar and Quag were sword-happy hotheads. Razkuli complained of fire in the gut and had the runs besides. That left only two Hell-Hounds; whom else would the Prince entrust with this mission? After a short testing conference, he chose Bourne to implement the transaction with the thief. Bourne's instructions were detailed and unequivocal: all was to be effected precisely as the thief, through Hakiem, had specified. Bourne would, of course, receive a nice bonus. He was made to understand that it was also to serve as a gag. Bourne agreed, promised, saluted, louted, departed.

Once the villa had commanded a fine view of the sea and naturally terraced landscape flowing a league along the coast to Sanctuary. Once a merchant had lived here with his family, a couple of concubines who counted themselves lucky, servants, and a small army or defense force. The merchant was wealthy. He was not liked and did not care that many did not care for the way he had achieved wealth and waxed richer. One day a pirate attack began. Two days later the gorge that marked the beginning of rough country disgorged barbarians. They also attacked. The merchant's small army proved too small. He and his armed force and servants and unlucky concubines and family were wiped out. The manse he had called Eaglenest was looted and burned. The pirates had not been pirates and the barbarians had not been barbarians—technically, at least: they were mercenaries. Thus, forty years ago, had some redistribution of wealth been achieved by that clandestine alliance of Sanctuarite nobles and merchants. Others had called Eaglenest "Eaglebeak" then and still did, though now the tumbled ruins were occupied only by spiders, snakes, lizards, scorpions, and snails. As Eaglebeak was said to be haunted, it was avoided.

It was a fine place for a night meeting and transfer of goods, and to Eaglebeak came Bourne, alone, on a good big prancing horse that swished its tail for the sheer joy and pride of it. The horse bore Bourne and a set of soft saddlebags, weighty and jingling.

Near the scrubby acacia specified, he drew rein and glanced about at a drear pile and scatter of building stones and their broken or crumbled pieces. His long cloak he doffed before he dismounted. Sliding off his horse, he stood clear while he unbuckled his big weapons belt. The belt, with sheathed sword and dagger, he hung on his saddle-horn. He removed the laden bags. Made them jingle. Laid them on the ground. Stepping clear of horse and ransom, he held his arms well out from his body while he turned, slowly.

He had shown the ransom and shown himself unarmed. Now a pebble flew from somewhere to whack a big chunk of granite and go skittering. At that signal, Bourne squatted and, on clear ground in the moonlight, emptied both saddlebags in a clinking, chiming, shimmering, glinting pile of silver coinage amid which gleamed a few gold disks. Laboriously and without happiness, Bourne clinked them all back into the pouches of soft leather, each the size of a nice cushion. He paced forward to lay them, clinking, atop a huge square stone against which leaned another. All as specified.

"Very good." The voice, male and young, came out of the shadows somewhere; no valley floor was so jumbled with stones as this once-courtyard of Eaglebeak. "Now get on your horse and ride back to Sanctuary."

"I will not. You have something for me."

"Walk over to the acacia tree, then, and look toward Sanctuary."

"I will walk over to the tree and watch the saddlebags, thanks, thief. If you show up without that rod . . ."

Bourne did that, and the shadows seemed to cough up a man, young and lean and darkly dressed. The crescent moon was behind him so that Bourne could not see his face. The fellow pounced lithely atop a stone, and held high the stolen Savankh.

"I see it."

"Good. Walk back to your horse, then. I will put this down when I pick up the bags."

Bourne hesitated, shrugged, and began ambling toward his horse. Hanse, thinking that he was very clever indeed and wanting all that money in his hands, dropped from his granite dais and hurried to the bags. Sliding his right arm through the connecting strap, he laid down the rod he carried in his left. That was when Bourne turned around and charged. While he demonstrated how fast a big burly man in mailcoat could move, he also showed what a dishonest rascal he was. Down his back, inside his mailshirt, on a thong attached to the camel-hair torque he wore, was a sheath. As he charged, he drew a dagger long as his forearm.

His quarry saw that the weight of the silver combined with Bourne's momentum made trying to run not only stupid, but suicidal. Still, he was young, and a thief: supple, clever, and fast. Bourne showed teeth, thinking this *boy* was frozen with shock and fear. Until Hanse moved, fast as the lizards scuttling among these great stones. The saddlebags slam-jingled into Bourne's right arm, and the knife flew away while he was knocked half around. Hanse managed to hang onto his own balance; he bashed the Hell-Hound in the back with his ransom. Bourne fell sprawling. Hanse ran—for Bourne's horse. He knew Bourne could outrun him so long as he was laden with the bags, and he was not about to part with them. In a few bounds, he gained a great rock and from there pounced onto the horse's back, just as he'd seen others do. It was Hanse's first attempt to mount a horse. Inexperience and the weight of his ransom carried him right off the other side.

In odd silence, he rose, on the far side of the horse. Not cursing as anyone might expect. Here came Bourne, and his fist sprouted fifteen inches of sharp iron. Hanse drew Bourne's other dagger from the sheath on the saddle and threw the small flat knife from his buckskin. Bourne went low and left, and the knife clattered among the tumbled stones of Eaglebeak. Bourne kept moving in, attacking under the horse. Hanse struck at him with his own dagger. To avoid losing his face, Bourne had to fall. Under the horse. Hanse failed to check his swipe, and his dagger nicked the inside of the horse's left hind leg.

The animal squealed, bucked, kicked, tried to gallop. Ruins barred him, and he turned back just as Bourne rose. Hanse was moving away fast, hugging one saddlebag to him and half-dragging the other. Bourne and his horse ran into each other. One of them fell backward and the other reared, neighed, pranced—and stood still, as if stricken with guilt. The other, downed painfully in mail for the second time in two minutes, cursed horse, Hanse, luck, gods, and himself. And began getting up.

However badly it had been handled, Bourne had horse, sword, and, a few paces away, the rod of Rankan authority. Hanse had more silver than would comprise Bourne's retirement. Under its weight he could not hope to escape. He could drop it and run or be overtaken. Dragging sword from sheath, Bourne hoped the roach kept running. What fun to carve him for the next hour or so!

Hanse was working at a decision, too, but none of it fell out that way. Perhaps he should have done something about trying to buy off a god or two; perhaps he should have taken better note of the well, this afternoon, and not run that way tonight. He discovered it too late. He fell in.

He was far less aware of the fall than of utter disorientation—and of being banged in every part of his body, again and again, by the sides of the well, which were brick, and by the saddlebags. When his elbow struck the bricks, the bags were gone. Hanse didn't notice their splash; he was busy crashing into something that wasn't water. And he was hurting.

The well's old wooden platform of a cover and sawhorse affair had fallen down inside, or been so hurled by vandals or ghosts. They weren't afloat, those pieces of very old, damp wood; they were braced across the well, at a slant. Hanse hit, hurt, scrabbled, clung. His feet were in water, and his shins. The wood creaked. The well's former cover deflected the head-sized stone Bourne hurled down. The fist-sized one he next threw struck the well's wall, bounced to roll down Hanse's back, caught a moment at his belt, and dropped into the water. The delay in his hearing the splash led Bourne to misconstrue the well's depth. Hanse clung and dangled. The water was cold.

In the circle of dim light above, Hanse saw Bourne's helmeted head. Bourne, peering down into a well, saw nothing.

"If you happen to be alive, thief, keep the saddlebags! No one will ever find you or them—or the Savankh you stole! You treacherously tricked us all, you see, and fled with both ransom and Savankh. Doubtless I will be chastised severely by His pretty Highness—and once I'm in Ranke again, I'll be rewarded! You have been a fool and a tool, boy, because I've friends back home in Ranke who will be delighted by the way *I* have brought embarrassment and shame on Prince Kittycat!"

Hanse, hurting and scared that the wood would yield, played dead. Strange how cold water could be, forty feet down in a brick-walled shaft!

Grinning, Bourne walked over and picked up the Savankh, which His stupid Highness would never see. He shoved it into his belt. Stuck his sword into the ground. And began wrestling a huge stone to drop, just in case, down the well. His horse whickered. Bourne, who had left his sword several feet away, froze. He straightened and turned to watch the approach of two helmeted men. They bore naked swords. One was a soldier. The other was—*the Prince-Governor?!*

"We thank you for letting us hear your confession, Bourne, traitor."

Bourne moved. He gained his sword. No slouch and no fool, he slashed the more dangerous enemy. For an instant the soldier's mail held Bourne's blade. Then the man crumpled. The blade came free and Bourne spun, just in time to catch the Prince's slash in the side. Never burly, Kadakithis had learned that he had to put everything he had behind his practice strokes just so that his opponents would notice. He did that now, so wildly and viciously that his blade tore several links of Bourne's mailcoat and relocated them in his flesh. Bourne made an awful noise. Horribly shocked and knowing he was *hurt,* he decided it were best to fly. He staggered as he ran, and the Prince let him go.

Kadakithis picked up the fallen rod of authority and slapped it once against his leather-clad leg. His heart beat unconscionably rapidly as he knelt to help the trusted man he'd brought with him. That was not necessary. In falling, the poor wight had smashed his head open on a chunk of marble from a statue. Slain by a god. Kadakithis glanced after Bourne, who had vanished in darkness and the ruins.

The Prince-Governor stood thinking. At last he went to the well. He knelt and called down into blackness.

"I am Prince Kadakithis. I have the wand. Perhaps I speak uselessly to one dead or dying. Perhaps not, in which case you may remain there and die slowly, or be drawn up to die under torture, or . . . you can agree to help me in a little plan I have just devised. Well—speak up!"

No contemplation was required to convince Hanse that he would go along with anything that meant vacating the well and seeing his next birthday. Who'd have thought pretty Prince Kittycat would come out here, and helmeted, too! He wondered at the noises he had heard. And made reply. The wood creaked.

"You need promise only this," Kadakithis called down. "Be silent until you are under torture. Suffer a little, then tell all."

"Suffer? . . . Torture?"

"Come, come, you deserve both. You'll suffer only a little of what you have coming. Don't, and betray these words, roach, and you will die out of hand. No, make that slowly. Nor will anyone believe you, anyhow."

Hanse knew that he was in over his head, both literally and figuratively. Hanging onto creaky old wood that was definitely rotting away by the second, he agreed.

"I'll need help," the Prince called. "Hang on."

Hanse rolled his eyes and made an ugly face. He hung on. He waited. Daring not to pull himself up onto the wood. His shoulders burned. The water seemed to grow colder, and the cold rose up in his legs. He hung on. Sanctuary was only about a league away. He hoped Kitty—the Prince—galloped. He hung on. Though the sun never came up and the moon's position changed only a little, Hanse was sure that a week or two passed. Cold, dark, and sore, those weeks. Riches! Wealth! Cudget had *told* him that revenge was a stupid luxury the poor couldn't afford!

Then His clever Highness was back, with several men of the night watch and a lot of rope. While they hauled up a bedraggled, bruised Shadowspawn, the Prince mentioned a call of nature and strolled away amid the clutter of big stones. He did not lift his tunic. He *did* pause on the other side of a pile of rubble. He gazed earthward, upon a dead traitor, and slowly he smiled in satisfaction. His first kill! Then Kadakithis began puking.

Pitchy torches flickered to create weird, dancing shadows on stone walls grim as death. The walls framed a large room strewn with tables, chains, needles, pincers, gyves, ropes, nails, shackles, hammers, wooden wedges and blocks and splinters, pliers, fascinating gags, mouth- and tongue-stretchers, heating irons, wheels, two braziers, pulleys. Much of this charming paraphernalia was stained dark here and there. On one of the tables lay Hanse. He was bruised, cut, contused—and being stretched, all in no more than his breechclout. Also present were Prince Kadakithis, his bright-eyed consort, two severe Hell-Hounds, his oddly attired old adviser, and three Sanctuarite nobles from the council. And the palace smith. Massively constructed and black-nailed, he was an imposing substitute for the torturer, who was ill.

He took up a sledgehammer and regarded it thoughtfully. Milady Consort's eyes brightened still more. So did those of Zalbar the Hell-Hound. Hanse discovered that in his present posture a gulp turned his Adam's apple into a blade that threatened to cut his throat from the inside.

The smith put down the hammer and took up a pair of long-handled pincers.

"Does he have to keep that there rag on his jewels, Yer Highness?"

"No need to torture him there," Kadakithis said equably. He glanced at his wife, who'd gone all trembly. "*Yet.* Try a few less horrific measures. *First.*"

"Surely he isn't tall enough," Zalbar said hopefully. He stood about six inches from the crank of the rack on which Hanse lay, taut.

"Well do *something* to him!" Milady snapped.

The smith surprised everyone. The movement was swift and the crack loud. He drew back his whip from a white stripe across Hanse's stomach. It went pink, then darker, and began to rise. The smith raised his brows as if impressed with himself. Struck again, across the captive's chest. The whip cracked like a slack sail caught in a gust. Chains rattled and Hanse's eyes and mouth went wide. A new welt began to rise. The smith added one across the tops of his thighs. An inch from the jewels, that. Milady Consort breathed through a mouth gone open.

"I don' like whippin' a man," the smith said. "Nor thisun either. Think I'll just ease this arm out of its socket and turn it around t'other way."

"You needn't walk all the way around to this side," Zalbar rumbled. "I'll turn the crank."

To the considerable disappointment of Zalbar and Sanctuary's first lady, Hanse began to talk. He told them about Bourne and Lirain. He could not tell them of Bourne's death, as he did not know of it.

"The Prince-Governor of Sanctuary," Kadakithis said, "and representative of the Emperor of Ranke, is merciful to one who tells him of a plot. Release him and hold him here—without torture. Give him wine and food."

"Damn!" Zalbar rumbled.

"Might I be getting back to my wife now, Highness? This job ain't no work for me, and I got all that anchor chain to work on tomorrow."

Hanse, not caring who released or guarded or fed him, watched the exit of the royal party.

With Zalbar and Quag, the Prince went to Lirain's apartment. "Do you stay here," he said, and took Quag's sword. Neither Hell-Hound cared for that and Zalbar said so.

"Zalbar: I don't know if you had a big brother you hated or what, you're a mean hothead who really ought to be employed as royal wasp-killer. Now stand here and shut up and wait for me."

Zalbar came to attention. He and Quag waited, board-stiff save for a rolling of dark eyes, while their charge entered the chamber of his treacherous concubine. And closed the door. Zalbar was sure that a week or two passed before the door opened and Kadakithis called them in. Quag's sword dripped in his hand.

The Hell-Hounds hurried within and stopped short. Staring. Lirain lay not dead, but asleep, sprawled naked and dégagée on a rumpled couch, obviously a recent participant in lovemaking. Naked beside her lay Bourne, not alive, and freshly bloodied.

"I've knocked her unconscious," the Prince said. "Take her down to the less comfortable bed so recently vacated by that Hanse fellow, who is to be sent to my apartment. Here, Quag—oh." The Prince carefully wiped Quag's sword on Lirain's belly and thighs and handed it to his Hell-Hound. Both guards, impressed and pleased, saluted. And bowed as well. They looked passing happy with their prince. Prince Kadakithis looked flagrantly happy with himself.

Attired in a soft tunic that proved a thief could be the size of a prince, Hanse sipped wine from a goblet he wished he could conceal and carry off with him. He rolled his eyes to glance around this royal chamber for audiences most private. For that reason the door was open. By it sat a deaf woman plucking a lute.

"Both of us are overdue for sleep, Hanse. The day presses on to mid-morning."

"I am . . . more accustomed to night work than y—than His Highness."

The Prince laughed. "So you are, Shadowspawn! Amazing how many clever men turn to crime. Broke into the very palace! My very chamber! Enjoyed a royal concubine too, eh?" He sat gazing reflectively at the thief, very aware that they were nearly of an age. Peasant and prince; thief and governor. "Well, soon Lirain will be babbling her head off, and all will know there was a plot—and from home at that! Also that she was dishonoring her royal master's bed with her co-conspirator."

"And that His Heroic Highness not only slew the son of a toad, but showed a true noble ruler's mercy by sparing a thief," Hanse said hopefully.

"Yes, Hanse. That is being put into writing at this moment. Ah, and there were witnesses to everything! All of it!"

Hanse was overboldened to say, "Except . . . Bourne's death, my lord prince."

"Hoho! Would you like to know about that, Hanse? You know so much already. We have holds each on the other, you and I. I killed Bourne up at Eaglenest. With one stroke," Kadakithis added. After all, it had been his first.

Hanse stared.

"You do seem to be learning caution, Shadowspawn! I do hope you will accept the employment I'll soon be offering you. You avoid mentioning that when you came out of that well you saw no corpse. No; he tried to flee and died a few feet away. The moment we returned here, I drugged Lirain. Drank it herself; thought she was drinking poison! She has laid with no one this night. *I* arranged her on the couch. One absolutely loyal man and I went back and fetched Bourne. My lady wife and I placed the corpse beside Lirain. Along with a bladder of the blood of a—appropriately!—pig. I thrust my sword into it before I called in Quag and Zalbar."

Hanse continued to stare. This saffron-haired boy was clever enough to be a thief! Hanse bet he was dissembling still, too; doubtless a favored rug merchant had aided in the bringing of Bourne's corpse into the palace!

The Prince saw his stare, read it. "Perhaps I'm not Prince Kittycat after all? I will shortly have high respect in Sanctuary, and wide knowledge of the plot is a weapon against my enemies at home. You are a hero—ah." The Prince nodded toward the doorway, beckoned. An oldish man entered to hand him a sheet of parchment. It soon bore the governor's signature and seal. The secretary left. Kadakithis handed the document to Hanse with a small flourish and a smile that Hanse saw was distinctly royal. Hanse glanced at it—very impressive—and looked again at the Prince.

"Oh," Kadakithis said, and no more; a prince did not apologize to a thief for forgetting his lack of education. "It says that by my hand and in the name of the Emperor in Ranke, you are forgiven of all you may have done up to this day, Hanse. You aren't a quintuple murderer, are you?"

"I've never killed anyone, Highness."

"I have! This very night—last night, rather!"

"Pardon, Highness, but killing's the business of them that rule, not thieves."

Kadakithis looked long and thoughtfully at Hanse after that, and would likely quote Shadowspawn long hence. Hanse had twice to mention the ransom at the bottom of the well.

"Ah! Forgot that, didn't I. It's been a bit busy tonight—last night. I've things to do, Hanse. A busy day ahead on no sleep and much excitement. I fear I can't be bothered thinking about some coins someone may have lost down an old well. If you can get it out, do. And do return here to discuss employment with me."

Hanse rose. He felt the kinship between them and was not comfortable with it. "That . . . will need some . . . some thinking, Prince-Governor, sir. I mean . . . *work*. And for you! Uh, yourself, that is— Your Highness. First I have to try to get used to the fact that I can't hate you anymore."

"Well, Hanse, maybe you can help a few others not to. I could use the help. Unless you take it ill of me to remind you that half of salvage *found* in this demesne is the property of the government."

Hanse began to wonder about the possibility of transferring the few gold coins into one saddlebag. If he was able to get the bags out of the well. That would take time, and help. And that would require paying someone. Or cutting someone in . . .

Hanse left the palace wearing a soft new tunic, eyes narrowed. Planning, calculating. Plotting.

# The Price of Doing Business

## Robert Lynn Asprin

Jubal was more powerful than he appeared. Not that his form conveyed any softness or weakness. If anything, his shiny ebony skin stretched tight over lithe, firm muscles gave an immediate impression of quick strength, while his scarred, severe facial features indicated a mind which would not hesitate to use that strength to his own advantage.

Rather, it was his wealth and the shrewd mind that had accumulated it which gave Jubal power above and beyond his iron muscles and razor-edged sword. His money, and the fierce entourage of sell-swords it had bought him made him a formidable force in the social order of Sanctuary.

Blood had been the price of his freedom; great quantities of blood shed by his opponents in the gladiator pits of Ranke. Blood, too, had given him his start at wealth: seizing a poorly guarded slave caravan for later sale at a sinful profit.

Where others might be content with modest gains, Jubal continued to amass his fortune with fanatic intensity. He had learned a dear lesson while glaring through hate-slitted eyes at the crowds who cheered his gory pit victories: swords and those who wielded them were bought and sold, and thus accounted as nothing in the minds of Society. Money and Power, not skill and courage, were what determined one's standing in the social order of men. It was fear which determined who spat and who wiped in his world.

So Jubal stalked the world of merchants as he had stalked the pits, ruthlessly pouncing on each opportunity and vulnerability as he had pitilessly cut down crippled opponents in the past. To enter into a deal with Jubal was to match wits with a mind trained to equate failure with death.

With this attitude, Jubal's concerns prospered and flourished in Sanctuary. With the first of his profits, he purchased one of the old mansions to the west of town. There he resided like a bloated spider in a web, waiting for signs of new opportunities. His fangs were his sell-swords, who swaggered through the streets of Sanctuary, their features disguised by blue hawk-masks. His web was a network of informants, paid to pass the word of any incident, any business deal, or any shift in local politics, which might be of interest to their generous master.

Currently the network was humming with word of the cataclysm in town. The Rankan prince and his new ideas were shaking the very roots of Sanctuary's economic and social structure.

Jubal sat at the center of his web and listened.

* * * *

After a while, the status reports all began to run together, forming one boring monotone.

Jubal slouched in his thronelike chair staring vacantly at one of the room's massive incense burners, bought in an unsuccessful attempt to counter the stench carried from Sanctuary by the easterly winds. Still the reports droned on. Things had been different when he was just beginning. Then he had been able to personally manage the various facets of his growing enterprises. Now, he had to listen while others . . . Something in the report caught his attention.

"Who did you kill?" he demanded.

"A blind." Saliman repeated, blinking at the interruption. "An informer who was not an informer. It was done to provide an example . . . as you ordered."

"Of course." Jubal waved. "Continue."

He relied heavily on informants from the town for the data necessary to conduct his affairs. It was known that if one sold false information to Jubal, one was apt to be found with a slit throat and a copper piece clenched between the teeth. This was known because it happened . . . frequently. What was not widely known was that if Jubal felt his informants needed an example to remind them of the penalty for selling fabrications, he would order his men to kill someone at random and leave the body with the marks of a false informer. His actual informers were not target for these examples—good informants were hard to find. Instead, someone would be chosen who had never dealt with Jubal. As his informants did not know each other's identities, the example would work.

". . . was found this morning." Saliman plodded on in his tireless recitation voice. "The coin was stolen by the person discovering the body, so there will be no investigation. The thief will talk, though, so word will spread."

"Yes, yes." Jubal grimaced impatiently. "Go on with another item."

"There is some consternation along the Avenue of Temples over the new shrines being erected to Savankala and Sabellia—"

"Does it affect our operations?" Jubal interrupted.

"No," Saliman admitted. "But I thought you should know."

"Now I know," Jubal countered. "Spare me the details. Next item."

"Two of our men were refused service at the Vulgar Unicorn last night."

"By who?" Jubal frowned.

"One-Thumb. He oversees the place evenings from—"

"I know who One-Thumb is!" Jubal snapped. "I also know he's never refused service to any of my men as long as they had gold and their manners were good. If he moved against two of mine, it was because of their own actions, not because he has ill feelings toward me. Next item."

Saliman hesitated to reorganize his thoughts, then continued.

"Increased pressure from the Prince's Hell-Hounds has closed the wharves to the smugglers. It is rumored they will be forced to land their goods at the Swamp of Night Secrets as they did in the old days."

"An inconvenience which will doubtless drive their prices up," Jubal mused. "How well guarded are their landings?"

"It is not known."

"Look into it. If there's a chance we can intercept a few shipments in the Swamp, there'll be no reason to pay their inflated prices at the bazaar."

"But if the smugglers lose shipments, they will raise their prices all the more to recover the loss."

"Of course." Jubal smiled. "Which means when we sell the stolen goods, we will be able to charge higher prices and still undercut the smugglers."

"We shall investigate the possibility. But—"

"But what?" Jubal inquired, studying his lieutenant's face. "Out with it, man. Something's bothering you about my plan, and I want to know what it is."

"I fear we might encounter difficulty with the Hell-Hounds," Saliman blurted. "If they have also heard rumors of the new landing sites, they might plan an ambush of their own. Taking a shipment away from smugglers is one thing, but trying to take confiscated evidence away from the Hell-Hounds . . . I'm not sure the men are up to it."

"My men? Afraid of guardsmen?" Jubal's expression darkened. "I thought I was paying good gold to have the finest swords in Sanctuary at my disposal."

"The Hell-Hounds are not ordinary guardsmen," Saliman protested. "Nor are they from Sanctuary. Before they arrived, I would have said ours were the finest swords. Now . . ."

"The Hell-Hounds!" Jubal snarled. "It seems all anyone can talk about is the Hell-Hounds."

"And you should listen." Saliman bristled. "Forgive me, Jubal, but you yourself admit the men you hire are no newcomers to battle. When they speak of a new force at large in Sanctuary, you should listen instead of decrying their judgment or abilities."

For a moment, a spark of anger flared in Jubal's eyes. Then it died, and he leaned forward attentively in his chair.

"Very well, Saliman. I'm listening. Tell me about the Hell-Hounds."

"They . . . they are unlike the guardsmen we see in Sanctuary, or even the average soldier of the Rankan army," Saliman explained, groping for words. "They were handpicked from the Royal Elite Guard especially for this assignment."

"Five men to guard a royal prince," Jubal murmured thoughtfully. "Yes, they would have to be good."

"That's right," Saliman confirmed hurriedly. "With the entire Rankan army to choose from, these five were selected for their skill at arms and unswerving loyalty to the empire. Since their arrival in Sanctuary, every effort to bribe or assassinate them has ended in death for whoever attempted it."

"You're right." Jubal nodded. "They could be a disruptive force. Still, they are only men, and all men have weaknesses."

He lapsed into thoughtful silence for several moments.

"Withdraw a thousand gold pieces from the treasury," he ordered at last. "Distribute it to the men to spread around town, particularly to those working in the governor's palace. In exchange, I want information about the Hell-Hounds, individually and collectively. Listen especially for word of dissent within their own ranks . . . anything that could be used to turn them against each other."

"It shall be done," Saliman responded, bowing slightly. "Do you also wish a magical investigation commissioned?"

Jubal hesitated. He had a warrior's dread of magicians and avoided them whenever possible. Still, if the Hell-Hounds constituted a large enough threat . . .

"Use the money for normal informants," he decided. "If it becomes necessary to hire a magician, then I will personally—"

A sudden commotion at the chamber's entryway drew the attention of both men. Two blue-masked figures appeared, dragging a third between them. Despite their masks, Jubal recognized them as Mor-Am and Moria, a brother-and-sister team of sell-swords in his employment. Their apparent captive was an urchin, garbed in the dirty rags common to Sanctuary's street children. He couldn't have been more than ten years of age, but the sizzling vindictives he screeched as he struggled against his captors marked him as one knowledgeable beyond his years.

"We caught this gutter rat on the grounds," Mor-Am announced, ignoring the boy's protests.

"Probably out to steal something," his sister added.

"I wasn't stealing!" the boy cried, wrenching himself free.

"A Sanctuary street-rat who doesn't steal?" Jubal raised an eyebrow.

"Of course I steal!" the urchin spat. "Everyone does. But that's not why I came here."

"Then why did you come?" Mor-Am demanded, cuffing the boy and sending him sprawling. "To beg? To sell your body?"

"I have a message!" the boy bawled. "For Jubal!"

"Enough, Mor-Am," Jubal ordered, suddenly interested. "Come here, boy."

The urchin scrambled to his feet, pausing only to knuckle tears of anger from his eyes. He shot a glare of pure venom at Mor-Am and Moria, then approached Jubal.

"What is your name, boy?" Jubal prompted.

"I—am called Mungo," the urchin stammered, suddenly shy. "Are you Jubal?"

"I am," Jubal nodded. "Well, Mungo, where is this message you have for me?"

"It . . . it's not written down," Mungo explained, casting a hasty glance at Mor-Am. "I was to tell you the message."

"Very well, tell me," Jubal urged, growing impatient. "And also tell me who is sending the message."

"The message is from Hakiem," the boy blurted. "He bids me tell you that he has important information for sale."

"Hakiem?" Jubal frowned.

The old storyteller! He had often been of service to Jubal when people forgot that he could listen as well as talk.

"Yes, Hakiem. He sells stories in the bazaar . . ."

"I know, I know," Jubal snapped. For some reason, today everyone thought he knew nothing of the people in town. "What information does he have for me, and why didn't he come himself?"

"I don't know what the information is. But it's important. So important that Hakiem is in hiding, afraid for his life. He paid me to fetch you to him, for he feels the information will be especially valuable to you."

"Fetch me to him?" Jubal rumbled, his temper rising.

"One moment, boy," Saliman interceded, speaking for the first time since his report was interrupted. "You say Hakiem paid you? How much?"

"A silver coin," the boy announced proudly.

"Show it to us!" Saliman ordered.

The boy's hand disappeared within his rags. Then he hesitated.

"You won't take it from me, will you?" he asked warily.

"Show the coin!" Jubal roared.

Cowed by the sudden outburst, Mungo extended his fist and opened it, revealing a silver coin nestled in his palm.

Jubal's eyes sought Saliman, who raised his eyebrows in silent surprise and speculation. The fact the boy actually had a silver coin indicated many things.

First: Mungo was probably telling the truth. Street-rats rarely had more than a few coppers, so a silver coin would have had to come from an outside benefactor. If the boy had stolen it, he would himself be in hiding, gloating over his ill-gotten wealth—not displaying it openly as he had just done.

Assuming the boy was telling the truth, then Hakiem's information must indeed be valuable and the danger to him real. Hakiem was not the sort to give away silver coins unless he were confident of recouping the loss and making a healthy profit besides. Even then, he would save the expense and bring the information himself, were he not truly afraid for his life.

All this flashed through Jubal's mind as he saw the coin, and Saliman's reactions confirmed his thoughts.

"Very well. We shall see what information Hakiem has. Saliman, take Mor-Am and Moria and go with Mungo to find the storyteller. Bring him here and—"

"No!" the boy cried, interrupting. "Hakiem will only give the information to Jubal personally, and he is to come alone."

"What?" Saliman exclaimed.

"This sounds like a trap!" Moria scowled.

Jubal waved them to silence as he stared down at the boy. It could be a trap. Then again, there could be another reason for Hakiem's request. The information might involve someone in Jubal's own force! An assassin . . . or worse, an informer! That could explain Hakiem's reluctance to come to the mansion in person.

"I will go," Jubal said, rising and sweeping the room with his eyes. "Alone, with Mungo. Saliman, I will require the use of your mask."

"I want my knife back!" Mungo declared suddenly.

Jubal raised a questioning eyebrow at Mor-Am, who flushed and produced a short dagger from his belt.

"We took it from him when we caught him," the sell-sword explained. "A safety precaution. We had no intent to steal it."

"Give it back," Jubal laughed. "I would not send my worst enemy into the streets of Sanctuary unarmed."

"Jubal," Saliman murmured as he surrendered his hawk-mask. "If this should be a trap . . ."

Jubal dropped a hand to his sword hilt.

"If it is a trap," he smiled, "they'll not find me easy prey. I survived five-to-one odds and worse in the pits before I won my freedom."

"But—"

"You are not to follow," Jubal ordered sternly. "Nor allow any other to follow. Anyone who disobeys will answer to me."

Saliman drew a breath to answer, then saw the look in Jubal's eyes and nodded in silent acceptance.

Jubal studied his guide covertly as they left the mansion and headed toward the town. Though he had not shown it openly, he had been impressed with the boy's spirit during their brief encounter. Alone and unarmed in the midst of hostile swords . . . men twice Mungo's age had been known to tremble and grovel when visiting Jubal at his mansion.

In many ways, the boy reminded Jubal of himself as a youth. Fighting and rebellious, with no parents but his pride and stubbornness to guide him, he had been bought from the slaves pens by a gladiator trainer with an eye for cold, spirited fighters. If he had instead been purchased by a gentle master . . . if someone interceded in the dubious path Fate had chosen for Mungo . . .

Jubal halted that line of thought with a grimace as he realized where it was leading. Adopt the boy into his household? Ridiculous! Saliman and the others would think he had gone soft in his old age. More important, his competitors would see it as a sign of weakness, an indication that Jubal could be reached by sentimentality . . . that he had a heart. He had risen above his own squalid beginnings; the boy would just have to do the same!

The sun was high and staggering in its heat as Jubal followed the boy's lead into town. Sweat trickled in annoying rivulets from beneath his blue hawk-mask, but he was loath to acknowledge his discomfort by wiping them away. The thought of removing the mask never entered his mind. The masks were necessary to disguise those in his employment who were wanted by the law; to complete the camouflage, all must wear them. To exempt himself from his own rule would be unthinkable.

In an effort to distract himself from his discomfort, Jubal began to peer cautiously at the people about him as they approached the bazaar. Since they had crossed the bridge and placed the hovels of the Downwinders behind them, there was a marked improvement in the quality of clothes and manners of the citizenry.

His eye fell on a magician, and he wondered about the star tattooed on the man's forehead. Then, too, he noted that the mage was engaged in a heated argument with a brightly garbed young bravo who displayed numerous knives, their hilts protruding from arm-sheath, sash, and boot top in ominous warning.

"That's Lythande," Mungo informed him, noting his interest. "He's a fraud. If you're looking for a magician, there are better to be had . . . cheaper."

"You're sure he's a fraud?" Jubal asked, amused at the boy's analysis.

"If he were a true magician, he wouldn't have to carry a sword," Mungo countered, pointing to the weapon slung at the magician's side.

"A point well taken," Jubal acknowledged. "And the man he's arguing with?"

"Shadowspawn," the boy announced loftily. "A thief. Used to work with Cudget Swearoath before the old fool got himself hung."

"A magician and a thief," Jubal murmured thoughtfully, glancing at the two again. "An interesting combination of talents."

"Unlikely!" Mungo scoffed. "Whatever Shadowspawn's last venture was, it was profitable. He's been spending freely and often, so it's unlikely he'll be looking for more work. My guess would be they're arguing over a woman. They each fancy themselves to be a gift from the gods to womankind."

"You seem to be well informed," Jubal commented, impressed anew with the boy's knowledge.

"One hears much in the streets." Mungo shrugged. "The lower one's standing is, the more important information is for survival . . . and few are lower than my friends and I."

Jubal pondered this as the boy led the way past Shambles Cross. Perhaps he had overlooked a valuable information source in the street children when he built his network of informers. They probably would not hear much, but there were so many of them. Together they might be enough to confirm or quash a rumor.

"Tell me, Mungo," he called to his guide. "You know I pay well for information, don't you?"

"Everyone knows that." The urchin turned into the Maze and skipped lightly over a prone figure, not bothering to see if the man were asleep or dead.

"Then why is it that none of your friends come to me with their knowledge?"

Jubal stepped carefully over the obstacle and cast a wary glance about. Even in broad daylight, the Maze could be a dangerous place for a lone traveler.

"We street-rats are close," Mungo explained over his shoulder. "Even closer than the bazaar people or the S'danzo. Shared secrets lose their value, so we keep them for ourselves."

Jubal recognized the wisdom in the urchin's policy, but it only heightened his resolve to recruit the children.

"Talk it over with your friends," he urged. "A full stomach can . . . where are we going?"

They had left the dank Serpentine for an alley so narrow that Jubal had to edge sideways to follow.

"To meet Hakiem," Mungo called, not slackening his pace.

"But where is he?" Jubal pressed. "I do not know this rat run."

"If you knew it, it would not make a good hiding place." The boy laughed. "It's just a little farther."

As he spoke, they emerged from the crawlspace into a small courtyard.

"We're here," Mungo announced, coming to a halt in the center of the yard.

"Where?" Jubal growled standing beside him. "There are no doors or windows in these walls. Unless he is hiding in one of those refuse heaps . . ."

He broke off his commentary as the details of their surroundings sank into his mind. No doors or windows! The only other way out of the courtyard was another crawlspace as small as that they had just traversed . . . except that it was blocked by a pile of wooden cartons. They were in a cul-de-sac!

A sudden crash sounded behind them, and Jubal spun to face it, his hand going reflexively to his sword. Several wooden boxes had fallen from the roof of one of the buildings, blocking the entrance.

"It's a trap!" he hissed, backing toward a corner, his eyes scanning the rooftops.

There was a sudden impact on his back. He staggered slightly, then lashed backward with his sword, swinging blind. His blade encountered naught but air, and he turned to face his attacker.

Mungo danced lightly just out of sword range, his eyes bright with triumph and glee.

"Mungo?" Jubal asked, knowing the answer.

He had been wounded often enough to recognize the growing numbness in his upper back. A rasp of pain as he shifted his stance told the rest of the story. The boy had planted his dagger in Jubal's back, and there it remained. In his mind's eye, Jubal could see it protruding from his shoulder at an unnatural angle.

"I told you we were close," Mungo taunted. "Maybe the big folk are afraid of you, but we aren't. You shouldn't have ordered Gambi's death."

"Gambi?" Jubal frowned, weaving slightly. "Who is Gambi?"

For a moment, the boy froze in astonishment. Then his face contorted with rage and he spat.

"He was found this morning with his throat cut and a copper coin in his mouth. Your trademark! Don't you even know who you kill?"

The blind! Jubal cursed himself for not listening closer to Saliman's reports.

"Gambi never sold you *any* information," Mungo shouted. "He hated you for what your men did to his mother. You had no right to kill him as a false informer."

"And Hakiem?" Jubal asked, stalling for time.

"We guessed right about that, didn't we—about Hakiem being one of your informers?" the boy crowed. "He's on the big wharf sleeping off a drunk. We pooled our money for the silver coin that drew you out from behind your guards."

For some reason, this last taunt stung Jubal more than had the dagger thrust. He drew himself erect, ignoring the warm liquid dripping down his back from the knife wound, and glared down at the boy.

"I need no guard against the likes of you!" he boomed. "You think you know killing? A street-rat who stabs overhand with a knife? The next time you try to kill a man—if there is another time—thrust underhand. Go between the ribs, not through them! And bring friends—one of you isn't enough to kill a real man."

"I brought friends!" Mungo laughed, pointing. "Do you think they'll be enough?"

Jubal risked a glance over his shoulder. The gutter rats of Sanctuary were descending on the courtyard. Scores of them! Scrabbling over the wooden cases or swarming down from the roofs like spiders. Children in rags—none of them even half Jubal's height, but with knives, rocks, and sharp sticks.

Another man might have broken before those hate-filled eyes. He might have tried to beg or bribe his way out of the trap, claiming ignorance of Gambi's murder. But this was Jubal, and his eyes were as cold as his sword as he faced his tormentors.

"You claim you're doing this to avenge one death," he sneered. "How many will die trying to pull me down?"

"You feel free to kill us one at a time, for no reason," Mungo retorted, circling wide to join the pack. "If some of us die killing you, then at least the rest will be safe."

"Only if you kill me," Jubal corrected. Without taking his eyes from the pack, he reached his left hand over his right shoulder, found the knife hilt, and wrenched it free. "And for that, you'll need your knife back!"

Mungo saw the knife coming as Jubal whipped his left hand down and across his body, but he froze for a split second. In that split second, the knife took him full in the throat. The world blurred and he went down, not feeling the fall.

The pack surged forward, and Jubal went to meet them, his sword flashing in the sun as he desperately tried to win his way to the exit.

A few fell before his first rush—he didn't know how many—but the rest scattered and closed about him from all sides. Sticks jabbed at his face faster than he could parry them, and he felt the touch of knives as small forms darted from behind him to slash and duck away.

Realization came to him that the harassment would bring him down before he could clear the wooden cases; abandoning his charge, he paused, whirling and cutting, trying to clear a space around him. The urchins were sharp-toothed, elusive phantoms, disappearing from in front of him to worry him from behind. It flashed through his mind that he was going to die! The survivor of countless gladiator duels was going to meet his end at the hands of angry children!

The thought drove him to desperate action. With one last powerful cut, he broke off his efforts at defense and tried to sprint for a wall to get something solid at his back. A small girl grabbed his ankle and clung with all her strength. He stumbled, nearly falling, and cut downward viciously without looking. His leg came free, but another urchin leapt onto his back, hammering at his head with a rock.

Jubal lurched sideways, scraping the child off along the wall, then turned to face the pack. A stick pierced his mask, opening a gash in his forehead which began to drip blood in his eyes. Temporarily blinded, he laid about him wildly with his sword, sometimes striking something solid, sometimes encountering air. A rock caromed off his head, but he was past feeling and continued his sightless, mindless slashing.

Slowly it crept into his fogged brain that there was a new note in the children's screams. At the same time, he realized that his sword had not struck a target for ten or fifteen swings now. Shaking his head to clear it, he focused anew on the scene before him.

The courtyard was littered with small bodies, their blood a bright contrast to their drab rags. The rest of the pack was in full flight, pursued over the rubble piles by . . .

Jubal sagged against the wall, fighting for breath and numb from wounds too numerous to count. He watched as his rescuer strode to his side, sheathing a sword wet with fresh blood.

"Your . . . your name?" he gasped.

"Zalbar," the uniformed figure panted in return. "Bodyguard to His Royal Highness, Prince Kadakithis. Your wounds . . . are they . . . ?"

"I've survived worse." Jubal shrugged, wincing at the pain the movement caused.

"Very well." The man nodded. "Then I shall be on my way."

"A moment," Jubal asked, holding up a restraining hand. "You have saved my life . . . a life I value quite highly. I owe you thanks and more, for you can't spend words. Name your reward."

"That is not necessary," Zalbar sniffed. "It is my duty."

"Duty or not," Jubal argued, "I know no other guardsman who would enter the Maze, much less risk his life to save . . . Did you say a royal bodyguard: Are you . . ."

"A Hell-Hound," Zalbar finished with a grim smile. "Yes, I am. And I promise you, the day is not far off when we will not be the only guardsmen in the Maze."

He turned to go, but Jubal stopped him again, removing the hawk-mask to mop the blood from his eyes.

"Wait!" he ordered. "I have a proposal for you. I have need of men such as you. Whatever pay you receive from the empire, I'll double it . . . as well as adding a bonus for your work today. What say you?"

There was no answer. Jubal squinted to get the Hell-Hound's face in focus, and found the man was staring at him in frozen recognition.

"You are Jubal!" Zalbar said in a tone that was more statement than question.

"I am," Jubal nodded. "If you know that, you must also know that there is none in Sanctuary who pay higher than I for services rendered."

"I know your reputation," the Hell-Hound acknowledged coldly. "Knowing what I do, I would not work for you at any price."

The rebuff was obvious, but Jubal chose to ignore it. Instead, he attempted to make light of the comment.

"But you already have," he pointed out. "You saved my life."

"I saved a citizen from a pack of street-rats," Zalbar countered. "As I said before, it's my duty to my prince."

"But—" Jubal began.

"Had I known your identity sooner," the Hell-Hound continued, "I might have been tempted to delay my rescue."

This time, the slight could not be ignored. More puzzled than angry, Jubal studied his opponent.

"I sense you are trying to provoke a fight. Did you save me, then, to wreak some vengeance of your own?"

"In my position, I cannot and will not engage in petty brawls," Zalbar growled. "I fight only to defend myself or the citizens of the empire."

"And I will not knowingly raise a sword against one who has saved my life . . . save in self-defense," Jubal retorted. "It would seem, then, that we will not fight each other. Still, it seems you hold some grudge against me. May I ask what it is?"

"It is the grudge I hold against any man who reaps the benefits of Rankan citizenship while accepting none of the responsibility," the Hell-Hound sneered. "Not only do you not serve the empire that shelters you, you undermine its strength by openly flaunting your disrespect for its laws in your business dealings."

"What do you know of my business dealings that allows you to make such sweeping judgments?" Jubal challenged.

"I know you make your money in ways decent men would shun," Zalbar retorted. "You deal in slaves and drugs and other high-profit, low-moral commodities . . . but most of all, you deal in death."

"A professional soldier condemns *me* for dealing in death?" Jubal smiled.

The Hell-Hound flushed red at the barb. "Yes. I also deal in death. But a soldier such as myself fights for the good of the empire, not for selfish gain. I lost a brother and several friends in the mountain campaigns fighting for the empire . . . for the freedoms you and your kind abuse."

"Imagine that," Jubal mused. "The whole Rankan army defending us against a few scattered mountain tribes. Why, if you and your friends hadn't been there, the Highlanders certainly would have swept down out of the mountains they haven't left for generations and murdered us all in our sleep. How silly of me to think it was the empire trying to extend its influence into one more place it wasn't wanted. I should have realized it was only trying to defend itself from a ferocious attacker."

Zalbar swayed forward, his hand going to his sword hilt. Then he regained his composure and hardened his features.

"I am done talking to you. You can't understand the minds of decent men, much less their words."

He turned to go, but somehow Jubal was in his path—on his feet now, though he swayed from the effort. Though the soldier was taller by a head, Jubal's anger increased his stature to where it was Zalbar who gave ground.

"If you're done talking, Hell-Hound, then it's time I had my say," he hissed. "It's true I make money from distasteful merchandise. I wouldn't be able to do that if your 'decent men' weren't willing to pay a hefty price for it. I don't sell my goods at sword point. They come to me—so many of them, I can't fill the demand through normal channels."

He turned to gesture at the corpse-littered courtyard.

"It's also true I deal in death," he snarled. "Your benevolent Rankan masters taught me the trade in the gladiator pits of the capital. I dealt in death then for the cheers of those same 'decent men' you admire so.

"Those 'decent men' allowed me no place in their 'decent' society after I won my freedom, so I came to Sanctuary. Now I still deal in death, for that is the price of doing business here—a price I almost paid today."

For a fleeting moment, something akin to sympathy flashed in the Hell-Hound's eyes as he shook his head.

"You're wrong, Jubal," he said quietly. "You've already paid the price for doing business in Sanctuary. It isn't your life, it's your soul . . . your humanity. You've exchanged it for gold, and in my opinion, it was a poor bargain."

Their eyes met, and it was Jubal who averted his gaze first, unsettled by the Hell-Hound's words. Looking away, his glance fell on the body of Mungo—the boy he had admired and thought of bringing into his household—the boy whose life he had wanted to change.

When he turned again, the Hell-Hound was gone.

# Blood Brothers

## Joe Haldeman

*Smiling, bowing as the guests leave. A good luncheon, much reassuring talk from the gentry assembled: the economy of Sanctuary is basically sound.* Thank you, my new cook . . . he's from Twand, isn't he a marvel? *The host appears to be rather in need of a new diet than a new cook, though the heavy brocades he affects may make him look stouter than he actually is.* Good leave . . . certainly, tomorrow. Tell your aunt I'm thinking of her.

You will stay, of course, Amar. *One departing guest raises an eyebrow slightly, our host a boylover?* We do have business.

Enoir, you may release the servants until dawn. Give yourself a free evening as well. We will be dining in the city.

And thank you for the excellent service. Here.

*He laughs.* Don't thank me. Just don't spend it all on one woman. *As the servantmaster leaves, our host's bluff expression fades to one of absolute neutrality. He listens to the servantmaster's progress down the stone steps, overhears him dismissing the servants. Turns and gestures to the pile of cushions by the huge fireplace. The smell of winter's ashes masked by incense fumes.*

I have a good wine, Amar. Be seated while I fetch it.

Were you comfortable with our guests?

Merchants, indeed. But one does learn from other classes, don't you agree?

*He returns with two goblets of wine so purple it is almost black. He sets both goblets in front of Amar: choose. Even closest friends follow this ritual in Sanctuary, where poisoning is art, sport, profession.* Yes, it was the color that intrigued me. Good fortune.

No, it's from a grove in the mountains, east of Syr. Kalos or something; I could never get my tongue around their barbaric . . . yes. A good dessert wine. Would you care for a pipe?

*Enoir returns, jingling his bell as he walks up the steps.*

That will be all for today, thank you . . .

No, I don't want the hounds fed. Better sport Ilsday if they're famished. We can live with their whimpering.

*The heavy front door creaks shut behind the servantmaster.* You don't? You would not be the only noble in attendance. Let your beard grow a day or two, borrow some rags from a servant . . .

Well, there are two schools of thinking. Hungry dogs are weaker but fight with desperation. And if your dogs aren't fed for a week, there's a week they can't be poisoned by the other teams.

Oh, it does happen—I think it happened to me once. Not a killing poison, just one that makes them listless, uncompetitive. Perhaps a spell. Poison's cheaper.

*He drinks deeply, then sets the goblet carefully on the floor. He crosses the room and mounts a step and peers through a slot window cut in the deep wall.*

I'm sure we're alone now. Drink up; I'll fetch the krrf. *He is gone for less than a minute, and returns with a heavy brick wrapped in soft leather.*

Caronne's finest, pure black, unadulterated. *He unfolds the package: ebony block embossed all over its surface with a foreign seal.* Try some?

*He nods.* "A wise vintner who avoids his wares." You have the gold?

*He weighs the bag in his hand.* This is not enough. Not by half.

*He listens and hands back the gold.* Be reasonable. If you feel you can't trust my assay, take a small amount back to Ranke; have anyone test it. Then bring me the price we established.

*The other man suddenly stands and claws at his falchion, but it barely clears its sheath, then clatters on the marble floor. He falls to his hands and knees, trembling, stutters a few words, and collapses.*

No, not a spell, though nearly as swift, don't you think? That's the virtue of coadjuvant poisons. The first ingredient you had along with everyone else, in the sauce for the sweetmeats. Everyone but me. The second part was in the wine, part of its sweetness.

*He runs his thumbnail along the block, collecting a pinch of krrf, which he rubs between thumb and forefinger and then sniffs.* You really should try it. It makes you feel young and brave. But then you are young and brave, aren't you.

*He carefully wraps the krrf up and retrieves the gold.* Excuse me. I have to go change. *At the door he hesitates.* The poison is not fatal; it only leaves you paralyzed for a while. Surgeons use it.

*The man stares at the floor for a long time. He is conscious of drooling, and other loss of control.*

*When the host returns, he is barely recognizable. Instead of the gaudy robe, he wears a patched and stained houppelande with a rope for a belt. The pomaded white mane is gone; his bald scalp is creased with a webbed old scar from a swordstroke. His left thumb is missing from the second joint. He smiles, and shows almost as much gap as tooth.*

I am going to treat you kindly. There are some who would pay well to use your helpless body, and they would kill you afterwards.

*He undresses the limp man, clucking, and again compliments himself for his charity, and the man for his well-kept youth. He lifts the grate in the fireplace and drops the garment down the shaft that serves for disposal of ashes.*

In another part of town, I'm known as One-Thumb; here, I cover the stump with a taxidermist's imitation. Convincing, isn't it? *He lifts the man easily and carries him through the main door.* No fault of yours, of course, but you're distantly related to the magistrate who had my thumb off. *The barking of the dogs grows louder as they descend the stairs.*

Here we are. *He pushes open the door to the kennels. The barking quiets to pleading whines. Ten fighting hounds, each in an individual run, up against its feeding trough, slavering politely, yawning gray sharp fangs.*

We have to feed them separately, of course. So they don't hurt each other.

*At the far end of the room is a wooden slab at waist-level, with channels cut in its surface leading to hanging buckets. On the wall above it, a rack with knives, cleavers, and a saw.*

*He deposits the mute staring man on the slab and selects a heavy cleaver.*

I'm sorry, Amar. I have to start with the feet. Otherwise it's a terrible mess.

\* \* \*

There are philosophers who argue that there is no such thing as evil *qua* evil; that, discounting spells (which of course relieve an individual of responsibility), when a man commits an evil deed he is the victim himself, the slave of his progeniture and nurturing. Such philosophers might profit by studying Sanctuary.

Sanctuary is a seaport, and its name goes back to a time when it provided the only armed haven along an important caravan route. But the long war ended, the caravans abandoned that route for a shorter one, and Sanctuary declined in status—but not in population, because for every honest person who left to pursue a normal life elsewhere, a rogue drifted in to pursue *his* normal life.

Now, Sanctuary is still appropriately named, but as a haven for the lawless. Most of them, and the worst of them, are concentrated in that section of town known as the Maze, a labyrinth of streets and nameless alleys and no churches. There is communion, though, of a rough kind, and much of it goes on in a tavern named the Vulgar Unicorn, which features a sign in the shape of that animal improbably engaging itself, and is owned by the man who usually tends bar on the late shift, an ugly sort of fellow by the name of One-Thumb.

One-Thumb finished feeding the dogs, hosed the place down, and left his estate by way of a long tunnel, that led from his private rooms to the basement of the Lily Garden, a respectable whorehouse a few blocks from the Maze.

He climbed the long steps up from the basement and was greeted by a huge eunuch with a heavy glaive balanced insolently over his shoulder.

"Early today, One-Thumb."

"Sometimes I like to check on the help at the Unicorn."

"Surprise inspection?"

"Something like that. Is your mistress in?"

"Sleeping. You want a wench?"

"No, just business."

The eunuch inclined his head. "That's business."

"Tell her I have what she asked for, and more, if she can afford it. When she's free. If I'm not at the Unicorn, I'll leave word as to where we can meet."

"I know what it is," the eunuch said in a singsong voice.

"Instant maidenhead." One-Thumb hefted the leather-wrapped brick. "One pinch, properly inserted, turns you into a girl again."

The eunuch rolled his eyes. "An improvement over the old method."
One-Thumb laughed along with him. "I could spare a pinch or so, if
you'd care for it."

"Oh . . . not on duty." He leaned the sword against the wall and
found a square of parchment in his money-belt. "I could save it for my
off time, though." One-Thumb gave him a pinch. He stared at it before
folding it up. "Black . . . Caronne?"

"The best."

"You have that much of it." He didn't reach toward his weapon.

One-Thumb's free hand rested on the pommel of his rapier. "For
sale, twenty *grimales*."

"A man with no scruples would kill you for it."

Gap-toothed smile. "I'm doubly safe with you, then."

The eunuch nodded and tucked away the krrf, then retrieved the
broadsword. "Safe with anyone not a stranger." Everyone in the Maze
knew of the curse that One-Thumb expensively maintained to protect
his life: if he were killed, his murderer would never die, but live forever
in helpless agony:

> *Burn as the stars burn;*
> *Burn on after they die.*
> *Never to the peace of ashes,*
> *Out of sight and succour*
> *From men or gods or ghost:*
> *To the ends of time, burn.*

One-Thumb himself suspected that the spell would only be effective for
as long as the sorcerer who cast it lived, but that was immaterial. The
reputation of the sorcerer, Mizraith, as well as the severity of the spell,
kept blades in sheaths and poison out of his food.

"I'll pass the message on. Many thanks."

"Better mix it with snuff, you know. Very strong." One-Thumb
parted a velvet curtain and passed through the foyer, exchanging greetings with some of the women who lounged there in soft veils (the cut
and color of the veils advertised price and, in some cases, curious
specialties), and stepped out into the waning light of the end of day.

The afternoon had been an interesting array of sensations for a man
whose nose was as refined as it was large. First the banquet, with all its
aromatic Twand delicacies, then the good rare wine with a delicate tang
of half-poison, then the astringent krrf sting, the rich charnel smell of

butchery, the musty sweat of the tunnel's rock walls, perfume and incense in the foyer, and now the familiar stink of the street. As he
walked through the gate into the city proper, he could tell the wind was
westering; the earthy smell from the animal pens had a slight advantage
over the tanners' vats of rotting urine. He even sorted out the delicate
cucumber fragrance of freshly-butchered fish, like a whisper in a jabber-
ing crowd; not many snouts had such powers of discrimination. As ever,
he enjoyed the first few minutes within the city walls, before the reek
stunned even his nose to dullness.

Most of the stalls in the Farmer's Market were shuttered now, but he
was able to trade two coppers for a fresh melon, which he peeled as he
walked into the bazaar, the krrf inconspicuous under his arm.

He haggled for a while with a coppersmith, new to the bazaar, for a
brace of lamps to replace the ones that had been stolen from the Unicorn last night. He would send one of his urchins around to pick them
up. He watched the acrobats for a while, then went to the various wine
merchants for bids on the next week's ordinaries. He ordered a hun-
dredweight of salt meat, sliced into snacks, to be delivered that night,
and checked the guild hall of the mercenaries to find a hall guard more
sober than the one who had allowed the lamps to be stolen. Then he
went down to the Wideway and had an early dinner of raw fish and crab
fritters. Fortified, he entered the Maze.

As the eunuch had said, One-Thumb had nothing to fear from the
regular denizens of the Maze. Desperadoes who would disembowel children for sport (a sport sadly declining since the introduction of a fool-
proof herbal abortifacient) tipped their hats respectfully, or stayed out
of his way. Still, he was careful. There were always strangers, often hot
to prove themselves, or desperate for the price of bread or wine; and although One-Thumb was a formidable opponent with or without his rapier, he knew he looked rather like an overweight merchant whose ugliness interfered with his trade.

He also knew evil well, from the inside, which is why he dressed
shabbily and displayed no outward sign of wealth. Not to prevent violence, since he knew the poor were more often victims than the rich, but
to restrict the class of his possible opponents to those who would kill for
coppers. They generally lacked skill.

On the way to the Unicorn, on Serpentine, a man with the conspic-
uously casual air of a beginner pickpocket fell in behind him. One-
Thumb knew that the alley was coming up and would be in deep
shadow, and it had a hiding-niche a few paces inside. He turned into the

alley and, drawing the dagger from his boot, slipped into the niche and set the krrf between his feet.

The man did follow, proof enough, and when his steps faltered at the darkness, One-Thumb spun out of the niche behind him, clamped a strong hand over his mouth and nose, and methodically slammed the stiletto into his back, time and again, aiming for kidneys. When the man's knees buckled, One-Thumb let him down slowly, slitting his throat for silence. He took the money-belt and a bag of coin from the still-twitching body, cleaned and replaced his dagger, picked up the krrf, and resumed his stroll down the Serpentine. There were a few bright spatters of blood on his houppelande, but no one on that street would be troubled by it. Sometimes guardsmen came through, but not to harass the good citizens nor criticize their quaint customs.

Two in one day, he thought; it had been a year or more since the last time that happened. He felt vaguely good about it, though neither man had been much of a challenge. The cutpurse was a clumsy amateur and the young noble from Ranke a trusting fool (whose assassination had been commissioned by one of his father's ministers).

He came up the street south of the Vulgar Unicorn's entrance and let himself in the back door. He glanced at the inventory in the storeroom and noted that it must have been a slow day, and went through to his office. He locked up the krrf in a strongbox and then poured himself a small glass of lemony aperitif, and sat down at the one-way mirror that allowed him to watch the bar unseen.

For an hour he watched money and drink change hands. The bartender, who had been the cook aboard a pirate vessel until he'd lost a leg, seemed good with the customers and reasonably honest, though he gave short measures to some of the more intoxicated patrons—probably not out of concern for their welfare. He started to pour a third glass of the liqueur and saw Amoli, the Lily Garden's mistress, come in to the place, along with the eunuch and another bodyguard. He went out to meet them.

"Wine over here," he said to a serving wench, and escorted the three to a curtained-off table.

Amoli was almost beautiful, though she was scarcely younger than One-Thumb, in a trade that normally aged one rapidly. She came to the point at once: "Kalem tells me you have twenty *grimales* of Caronne for sale."

"Prime and pure."

"That's a rare amount." One-Thumb nodded. "Where, may I ask, did it come from?"

"I'd rather not say."

"You'd better say. I had a twenty-*grimale* block in my bedroom safe. Yesterday it was stolen."

One-Thumb didn't move or change expression. "That's an interesting coincidence."

She snorted. They sat without speaking while a pitcher of wine and four glasses were slipped through the curtain.

"Of course I'm not accusing you of theft," she said. "But you can understand why I'm interested in the person you bought it from."

"In the first place, I didn't buy it. In the second, it didn't come from Sanctuary."

"I can't afford riddles, One-Thumb. Who was it?"

"That has to remain secret. It involves a murder."

"You might be involved in another," she said tightly.

One-Thumb slowly reached down and brought out his dagger. The bodyguards tensed. He smiled, and pushed it across the table to Amoli. "Go ahead, kill me. What happens to you will be rather worse than going without krrf."

"Oh—" She knocked the knife back to him. "My temper is short nowadays. I'm sorry. But the krrf's not just for me; most of my women use it, and take part of their pay in it, which is why I like to buy in large amounts." One-Thumb was pouring the wine; he nodded. "Do you have any idea how much of my capital was tied up in that block?"

He replaced the half-full glasses on the round serving tray and gave it a spin. "Half?"

"And half again of that. I *will* get it back, One-Thumb!" She selected a glass and drank.

"I hope you do. But it can't be the same block."

"Let me judge that—have you had it for more than two days?"

"No, but it must have left Ranke more than a week ago. It came on the Anenday caravan. Hidden inside a cheese."

"You can't know for sure that it was on the caravan all the time. It could have been waiting here until the caravan came."

"I can hear your logic straining, Amoli."

"But not without reason. How often have you seen a block as large as twenty *grimales?*"

"Only this time," he admitted.

"And is a pressed design stamped all over it uniformly, an eagle within a circle?"

"It is. But that only means a common supplier, his mark."

"Still, I think you owe me information."

One-Thumb sipped his wine. "All right. I know I can trust the eunuch. What about the other?"

"I had a vassal spell laid on him when I bought him. Besides . . . show him your tongue, Gage." The slave opened his mouth and showed pink scar tissue nested in bad teeth. "He can neither speak nor write."

"We make an interesting table," he said. "Missing thumb, tongue, and tamale. What are you missing, Amoli?"

"Heart. And a block of krrf."

"All right." He drank off the rest of his small glass and refilled it. "There is a man high in the court of Ranke, old and soon to die. His son, who would inherit his title, is slothful, incompetent, dishonest. The old man's counselors would rather the daughter succeed; she is not only more able, but easier for them to control."

"I think I know the family you speak of," Amoli said.

"When I was in Ranke on other business, one of the counselors got in touch with me, and commissioned me to dispose of this young pigeon, but to do it in Sanctuary. The twenty *grimales* was my pay, and also the goad, the bait. The boy is no addict, but he is greedy, and the price of krrf is three times higher in the court of Ranke than it is in the Maze. It was arranged for me to befriend him and, eventually, offer to be his wholesaler.

"The counselor procured the krrf from Caronne and sent word to me. I sent back a tempting offer to the boy. He contrived to make the journey to Sanctuary, supposedly to be introduced to the Emperor's brother. He'll miss the appointment."

"That's his blood on your sleeve?" the eunuch asked.

"Nothing so direct; that was another matter. When he's supposed to be at the palace tomorrow, he'll be floating in the harbor, disguised as the shit of dogs."

"So you got the krrf and the boy's money as well," Amoli said.

"Half the money. He tried to croy me." He refilled the woman's glass. "But you see. There can be no connection."

"I believe there may be. Anenday was when mine disappeared."

"Did you keep it wrapped in a cheese?"

She ignored that. "Who delivered yours?"

"Marype, the youngest son of my sorcerer Mizraith. He does all of my caravan deliveries."

The eunuch and Amoli exchanged glances. "That's it! It was from Marype I bought the block. Not two hours after the caravan came in." Her face was growing red with fury.

One-Thumb drummed his fingers on the table. "I didn't get mine till evening," he admitted.

"Sorcery?"

"Or some more worldly form of trickery," One-Thumb said slowly. "Marype is studying his father's trade, but I don't think he's adept enough to transport material objects . . . could your krrf have been an illusion?"

"It was no illusion. I tried a pinch."

"Do you recall from what part of the block you took it?"

"The bottom edge, near one corner."

"Well, we can settle one thing," he said, standing. "Let's check mine in that spot."

She bade the bodyguards stay, and followed One-Thumb. At the door to his office, while he was trying to make the key work, she took his arm and moved softly up against him. "You never tarry at my place anymore. Are you keeping your own woman, out at the estate? Did we do something—"

"You can't have all my secrets, woman." In fact, for more than a year he had not taken a woman normally, but needed the starch of rape. This was the only part of his evil life that shamed him, and certainly not because of the women he had hurt and twice killed. He dreaded weakness more than death, and wondered which part would fail him next.

Amoli idly looked through the one-way mirror while One-Thumb attended to the strongbox. She turned when she heard him gasp.

"Gods!" The leather wrapping lay limp and empty on the floor of the box.

They both stared for a moment. "Does Marype have his father's protection?" Amoli asked.

One-Thumb shook his head. "It was the father that did this."

Sorcerers are not omnipotent. They can be bargained with. They can even be killed, with stealth and surprise. And spells cannot normally be maintained without effort; a good sorcerer might hold six or a dozen at once. It was Mizraith's fame that he maintained past a hundred, although it was well known that he did this by casting secondary spells on lesser sorcerers, tapping their power unbeknownst. Still, gathering all these strings and holding them, as well as the direct spells that protected his life and fortune, used most of his concentration, giving him a distracted air. The unwary might interpret this as senility—a half-century without sleep had left its mark—and might try to take his purse or life, as their last act.

But Mizraith was rarely seen on the streets, and certainly never near the noise and smell of the Maze. He normally kept to his opulent apartments in the easternmost part of town, flanked by the inns of Wideway, overlooking the sea.

One-Thumb warned the pirate cook that he might have to take a double shift, and took a bottle of finest brandy to give to Mizraith, and a skin of the ordinary kind to keep up their courage as they went to face the man who guarded his life. The emptied skin joined the harbor's flotsam before they'd gone half of Wideway, and they continued in grim silence.

Mizraith's eldest son let them in, not seeming surprised at their visit. "The bodyguards stay here," he said, and made a pass with one hand. "You'll want to leave all your iron here, as well."

One-Thumb felt the dagger next to his ankle grow warm; he tossed it away and also dropped his rapier and the dagger sheathed to his forearm. There was a similar scattering of weapons from the other three. Amoli turned to the wall and reached inside her skirts, inside herself, to retrieve the ultimate birth-control device, a sort of diaphragm with a spring-loaded razor attached (no one would have her without paying in some coin). The hardware glowed dull red briefly, then cooled.

"Is Marype at home?" One-Thumb asked.

"He was, briefly," the older brother said. "You came to see Father, though." He turned to lead them up a winding flight of stairs.

Velvet and silk embroidered in arcane patterns. A golden samovar bubbling softly in the corner; flower-scented tea. A naked girl, barely of childbearing age, sitting crosslegged by the samovar, staring. A bodyguard much larger than the ones downstairs, but slightly transparent. In the middle of this sat Mizraith, on a pile of pillows, or maybe of gold, bright eyes in dark hollows, smiling openmouthed at something unseeable.

The brother left them there. Magician, guardian, and girl all ignored them. "Mizraith?" One-Thumb said.

The sorcerer slowly brought his eyes to bear on him and Amoli. "I've been waiting for you, Lastel, or what is your name in the Maze, One-Thumb . . . I could grow that back for you, you know."

"I get along well enough—"

"And you brought me presents! A bottle and a bauble—more my age than this sweetmeat." He made a grotesque face at the naked girl and winked.

"No, Mizraith, this woman and I, we both believe we've been wronged by you. Cheated and stolen from," he said boldly, but his voice shook. "The bottle is a gift."

The bodyguard moved toward them, its steps making no noise. "Hold, spirit." It stopped, glaring. "Bring that bottle here."

As One-Thumb and Amoli walked toward Mizraith, a low table materialized in front of him, then three glasses. "You may serve, Lastel." Nothing had moved but his head.

One-Thumb poured each glass full; one of them rose a handspan above the table and drained itself, then disappeared. "Very good. Thank you. Cheated, now? My, oh my. Stolen? Hee. What could you have that I need?"

"It's only we who need it, Mizraith, and I don't know why you would want to cheat us out of it—especially me. You can't have many commissions more lucrative than mine."

"You might be surprised, Lastel. You might be surprised. *Tea!*" The girl decanted a cup of tea and brought it over, as if in a trance. Mizraith took it and the girl sat at his side, playing with her hair. "Stolen, eh? What? You haven't told me. What?"

"Krrf," he said.

Mizraith gestured negligently with his free hand and a small snowstorm of grey powder drifted to the rug, and disappeared.

"No." One-Thumb rubbed his eyes. When he looked at the pillows, they were pillows; when he looked away, they turned to blocks of gold. "Not conjured krrf." It had the same gross effect but no depth, no nuance.

"Twenty *grimales* of black krrf from Caronne," Amoli said.

"Stolen from both of us," One-Thumb said. "It was sent to me by a man in Ranke, payment for services rendered. Your son Marype picked it up at the caravan depot, hidden inside a cheese. He extracted it somehow and sold it to this woman, Amoli—"

"Amoli? You're the mistress of a . . . of the Slippery Lily?"

"No, the Lily *Garden*. The other place is in the Maze, a good place for pox and slatterns."

One-Thumb continued. "After he sold it to her, it disappeared. He brought it to me last night. This evening, it disappeared from my own strongbox."

"Marype couldn't do that," Mizraith said.

"The conjuring part, I know he couldn't—which is why I say that you must have been behind it. Why? A joke?"

Mizraith sipped. "Would you like tea?"

"No. Why?"

He handed the half-empty cup to the girl. "More tea." He watched her go to the samovar. "I bought her for the walk. Isn't that fine? From behind, she could be a boy."

"Please, Mizraith. This is financial ruin for Amoli and a gross insult to me."

"A joke, eh? You think I make stupid jokes?"

"I know that you do things for reasons I cannot comprehend," he said tactfully. "But this is serious—"

"*I* know that!" He took the tea and fished a flower petal from it; rubbed it away. "More serious than you think, if my son is involved. Did it all disappear? Is there any tiny bit of it left?"

"The pinch you gave to my eunuch," Amoli said. "He may still have it."

"Fetch it," Mizraith said. He stared slack-jawed into his tea for a minute. "I didn't do it, Lastel. Some other did."

"With Marype's help."

"Perhaps unwilling. We shall see . . . Marype is adept enough to have sensed the worth of the cheese, and I think he is worldly enough to recognize a block of rare krrf, and know where to sell it. By himself, he would not be able to charm it away."

"You fear he's betrayed you?"

Mizraith caressed the girl's long hair. "We have had some argument lately. About his progress . . . he thinks I am teaching him too slowly, withholding . . . mysteries. The truth is, spells are complicated. Being able to generate one is not the same as being able to control it; that takes practice, and maturity. He sees what his brothers can do and is jealous. I think."

"You can't know his mind directly?"

"No. That's a powerful spell against strangers, but the closer you are to a person, the harder it is. Against your own blood . . . no. His mind is closed to me."

Amoli returned with the square of parchment. She held it out apologetically. "He shared it with the other bodyguard and your son. Is this enough?" There was a dark patch in the center of the square.

He took it between thumb and forefinger and grimaced. "Markmor!" The second most powerful magician in Sanctuary—an upstart not even a century old.

"He's in league with your strongest competitor?" One-Thumb said.

"In league or in thrall." Mizraith stood up and crossed his arms. The bodyguard disappeared; the cushions became a stack of gold bricks. He mumbled some gibberish and opened his arms wide.

Marype appeared in front of him. He was a handsome lad: flowing silver hair, striking features. He was also furious, naked, and rampant.

"*Father!* I am *busy!*" He made a flinging gesture and disappeared.

Mizraith made the same gesture and the boy came back. "We can do this all night. Or you can talk to me."

Noticeably less rampant. "This is unforgivable." He raised his arm to make the pass again; then checked it as Mizraith did the same. "Clothe me." A brick disappeared, and Marype was wearing a tunic of woven gold.

"Tell me you are not in the thrall of Markmor."

The boy's fists were clenched. "I am not."

"Are you quite certain?"

"We are friends, partners. He is teaching me things."

"You know I will teach you everything, eventually. But—"

Marype made a pass and the stack of gold turned to a heap of stinking dung. "Cheap," Mizraith said, wrinkling his nose. He held his elbow a certain way and the gold came back. "Don't you see he wants to take advantage of you?"

"I can see that he wants access to *you*. He was quite open about that."

"Stefab," Mizraith whispered. "Nesteph."

"You need the help of my brothers?"

The two older brothers appeared, flanking Mizraith. "What I need is some sense out of you." To the others: "Stay him!"

Heavy golden chains bound his wrists and ankles to sudden rings in the floor. He strained and one broke; a block of blue ice encased him. The ice began to melt.

Mizraith turned to One-Thumb and Amoli. "You weaken us with your presence." A bar of gold floated over to the woman. "That will compensate you. Lastel, you will have the krrf, once I take care of this. Be careful for the next few hours. Go."

As they backed out, other figures began to gather in the room. One-Thumb recognized the outline of Markmor flickering.

In the foyer, Amoli handed the gold to her eunuch. "Let's get back to the Maze," she said. "This place is dangerous."

One-Thumb sent the pirate cook home and spent the rest of the night in the familiar business of dispensing drink and krrf and haggling over rates of exchange. He took a judicious amount of krrf himself—the domestic kind—to keep alert. But nothing supernatural happened, and nothing more exciting than a routine eye-gouging over a dice dispute. He did have to step over a deceased ex-patron when he went to lock up at dawn. At least he'd had the decency to die outside, so no report had to be made.

One reason he liked to take the death-shift was the interesting ambience of Sanctuary in the early morning. The sunlight was hard, revealing rather than cleansing. Litter and excrement in the gutters. A few exhausted revelers, staggering in small groups or sitting half-awake, blade out, waiting for a bunk to clear at first bell. Dogs nosing the evening's remains. Decadent, stale, worn, mortal. He took dark pleasure in it. Double pleasure this morning, a slight krrf overdose singing deathsong in his brain.

He almost went east, to check on Mizraith. "Be careful the next few hours"—that must have meant his bond to Mizraith made him somehow vulnerable in the weird struggle with Markmor over Marype. But he had to go back to the estate and dispose of the bones in the dogs' troughs, and then be Lastel for a noon meeting.

There was one drab whore in the waiting room of the Lily Garden, who gave him a thick smile and then recognized him and slumped back to doze. He went through the velvet curtain to where the eunuch sat with his back against the wall, glaive across his lap.

He didn't stand. "Any trouble, One-Thumb?"

"No trouble. No krrf, either." He heaved aside the bolt on the massive door to the tunnel. "For all I know, it's still going on. If Mizraith had lost, I'd know by now, I think."

"Or if he'd won," the eunuch said.

"Possibly. I'll be in touch with your mistress if I have anything for her." One-Thumb lit the waiting lamp and swung the door closed behind him.

Before he'd reached the bottom of the stairs, he knew something was wrong. Too much light. He turned the wick all the way down; the air was slightly glowing. At the foot of the stairs, he set down the lamp, drew his rapier, and waited.

The glow coalesced into a fuzzy image of Mizraith. It whispered, "You are finally in dark, Lastel. One-Thumb. Listen: I may die soon. Your charm, I've transferred to Stefab, and it holds. Pay him as you've paid me . . ." He wavered, disappeared, came back. "Your krrf is in this tunnel. It cost more than you can know." Darkness again.

One-Thumb waited a few minutes more in the darkness and silence (fifty steps from the light above) before relighting the lamp. The block of krrf was at his feet. He tucked it under his left arm and proceeded down the tunnel, rapier in hand. Not that steel would be much use against sorcery, if that was to be the end of this. But an empty hand was less.

The tunnel kinked every fifty steps or so, to restrict line-of-sight. One-Thumb went through three corners and thought he saw light at the fourth. He stopped, doused the lamp again, and listened. No footfalls. He set down the krrf and lamp and filled his left hand with a dagger, then headed for the light. It didn't have to be magic; three times he had surprised interlopers in the tunnel. Their husks were secreted here and there, adding to the musty odor.

But no stranger this time. He peered around the corner and saw Lastel, himself, waiting with sword out.

"Don't hold back there," his alter ego said. "Only one of us leaves this tunnel."

One-Thumb raised his rapier slowly. "Wait . . . if you kill me, you die forever. If I kill you, the same. This is a sorcerer's trap."

"No, Mizraith's dead."

"His son is holding the spell."

Lastel advanced, crabwise dueler's gait. "Then how am I here?"

One-Thumb struggled with his limited knowledge of the logic of sorcery. Instinct moved him forward, point in line, left-hand weapon ready for side parry or high block. He kept his eye on Lastel's point, krrf-steady as his own. The krrf sang doom, and lifted his spirit.

It was like fencing with a mirror. Every attack drew instant parry, remise, parry, remise, parry, re-remise, break to counter. For several minutes, a swift yet careful ballet, large twins mincing, the tunnel echoing clash:

One-Thumb knew he had to do something random, unpredictable; he lunged with a cutover, impressing to the right.

Lastel knew he had to do something random, unpredictable; he lunged with a double-disengage, impressing to the right.

They missed each other's blades.

Slammed home.

One-Thumb saw his red blade emerge from the rich brocade over Lastel's back, tried to shout and coughed blood over his killer's shoulder. Lastel's rapier had cracked breastbone and heart and slit a lung as well.

They clung to each other. One-Thumb watched bright blood spurt from the other's back and heard his own blood falling, as the pain grew. The dagger still in his left hand, he stabbed, almost idly. Again he stabbed. It seemed to take a long time. The pain grew. The other man was doing the same. A third stab, he watched the blade rise and slowly fall, and inching slide back out of the flesh. With every second, the pain seemed to double; with every second, the flow of time slowed by half. Even the splash of blood was slowed, like a viscous oil falling through water as it sprayed away. And now it stopped completely, a thick scarlet web frozen there between his dagger and Lastel's back—his own back—and as the pain spread and grew, marrow itself on fire, he knew he would look at that forever. For a flickering moment he saw the image of two sorcerers, smiling.

# Myrtis

## Christine DeWees

"I feel as young as I look. I could satisfy every man in this house if I took the notion to, or if any one of them had half the magnificence of Lythande."

So speaking, Myrtis, proprietor of the Aphrodisia House leaned over the banister outside her private parlor and cast judgment on the activity of her establishment below.

"Certainly, madame."

Her companion on the narrow balcony was a well-dressed young man lately arrived with his parents from the imperial capital. He eased as far from her as possible when she turned to smile at him.

"Do you doubt me, young man?"

The words rolled off Myrtis' tongue with an ease and inflection of majesty. To many of the long-time residents of Sanctuary, Myrtis was the city's unofficial royalty. On the Street of Red Lanterns she reigned supreme.

"Certainly not, madame."

"You have seen the girls now. Did you have a particular lady in mind, or would you prefer to explore my establishment further?"

Myrtis guided him back into her parlor with a slight pressure against his arm. She wore a high-necked dark gown which only hinted at the legendary figure beneath. The madam of the Aphrodisia House was beautiful, more beautiful than any of the girls working for her; fathers told this to their sons who were, in turn, passing this indisputable fact along to their sons. But a ravishing beauty which endured unchanging for three generations was awesome rather than desirable. Myrtis did not compete with the girls who worked for her.

The young man cleared his throat. It was clearly his first visit to any brothel. He fingered the tassels on the side of an immense wine-colored velvet love seat before speaking.

"I think I'll go a round with the violet-silks."

Myrtis stared at him until he fidgeted one of the tassels loose and his face flushed a deep crimson.

"Call Cylene. Tell her the Lavender Room."

A girl too young to be working jumped up from a cushion where she had waited in silence for such a command. The youth turned to follow her.

"Four pieces of silver—Cylene is *very* talented. And a name—I think that you should be known as Terapis." Myrtis smiled to reveal her even white teeth.

The youth, who would henceforth be known as Terapis within the walls of the Aphrodisia House, searched his purse to find a single gold piece. He stood arrogant and obviously well-rehearsed while Myrtis counted out his change. The young girl took his hand to lead him to Cylene for two hours of unimaginable bliss.

"Children!" Myrtis mumbled to herself when she was alone in her parlor again.

Four of the nine knobs on the night-candle had melted away. She opened a great leatherbound ledger and entered the youth's true name as well as the one she had just given him, his choice for the evening, and that he had paid in gold. It had been fifteen years or more since she had given the nom-de-guerre of Terapis to one of the house's gentlemen. She had a good memory for all those who lingered in the sybaritic luxury of the Aphrodisia House.

A gentle knocking on the parlor door awoke Myrtis late the next morning.

"Your breakfast is ready, madame."

"Thank you, child. I'll be down for it."

She lay still for a few moments in the semidarkness. Lythande had used careful spells to preserve her beauty and give her the longevity of a magician, but there were no spells to numb the memory. The girls, their gentlemen, all passed through Myrtis's mind in a blurred unchanging parade which trapped her beneath the silken bedclothes.

"Flowers for you, madame."

The young girl who had sat quietly on the cushion the previous evening walked nonchalantly into the boudoir bearing a large bouquet of
white flowers which she began arranging in a crystal vase.

"A slave from the palace brought them. He said they were from
Terapis."

A surprise. There were always still surprises, and renewed by that
comforting knowledge Myrtis threw back the bedcovers. The girl set
down the flowers and held an embroidered day-robe of emerald satin
for Myrtis to wrap around herself.

Five girls in their linen shifts busied themselves with restoring the
studied disorder of the lower rooms as Myrtis passed through them on
her way to the kitchen. Five cleaning, one too pregnant to be of any
use, another off nursing a newborn; that meant twenty girls were still in
the upper rooms. Twenty girls whose time was fully accounted for; in
all, a very good night for the Aphrodisia House. Others might be
suffering with the new regime, but the foreigners expected a certain
style and discretion which in Sanctuary could be found only at the
Aphrodisia.

"Madame, Dindan ordered five bottles of our best Aurvesh wine last
night. We have only a dozen bottles left . . ." A balding man stepped
in front of her with a shopping list.

"Then buy more."

"But, madame, since the Prince arrived it is almost impossible to
buy Aurvesh wines!"

"Buy them! But first sell the old bottles to Dindan at the new prices."

"Yes, madame."

The kitchen was a large, brightly lit room hidden away at the back of
the house. Her cooks and an assortment of tradesmen haggled loudly at
the back door while the half-dozen or so young children of her working
girls raced around the massive center table. Everyone grew quiet as
Myrtis took her seat in a sunlit alcove that faced a tiny garden.

Despite the chaos the children caused, she always let the girls keep
them if they wanted to. With the girl-children there was no problem
with their earning their keep; no virgin was ever too ugly. But the boy-
children were apprenticed off at the earliest possible age. Their wages
were garnished to support the on-going concern that was the Aphrodisia
House.

"There is a soldier at the front door, madame." One of the girls who
had been cleaning the lower rooms interrupted as Myrtis spread a thick
blue-veined cheese over her bread. "He demands to see you, madame."

"Demands to see me?" Myrtis laid down the cheese knife. "A soldier has nothing that 'demands' to see me at the front door. At this hour, soldiers are less use than tradesmen. Send him around to the back."

The girl ran back up the stairs. Myrtis finished spreading her cheese on the bread. She had eaten half of it when a tall man cast a shadow over her private dining alcove.

"You are blocking my sunlight, young man," she said without looking up.

"You are Madame Myrtis, proprietress of this . . . brothel?" he demanded without moving.

"You are blocking my sunlight and my view of the garden."

He stepped to one side.

"The girls are not available during the day. Come back this evening."

"Madame Myrtis, I am Zalbar, captain of Prince Kadakithis' personal guard. I have not come to inquire after the services of your girls."

"Then what have you come for?" she asked, looking up for the first time.

"By order of Prince Kadakithis, a tax of ten gold pieces for every woman living on the Street of Red Lanterns is to be levied and collected at once if they are to be allowed to continue to practice their trade without incurring official displeasure."

Only the slight tensing of Myrtis' hands betrayed her indignation at Zalbar's statement. Her voice and face remained dispassionately calm.

"The royal concubines are no longer pleasing?" she replied with a sneering smile. "You cannot expect every woman on the Street of Red Lanterns to have ten gold pieces. How do you expect them to earn the money for your taxes?"

"We do not expect them to be able to pay the tax, madame. We expect to close your brothel and every other house like it on the Street. The women, including yourself, will be sent elsewhere to lead more productive lives."

Myrtis stared at the soldier with a practiced contempt that ended their conversation. The soldier fingered the hilt of his sword.

"The tax will be collected, madame. You will have a reasonable amount of time to get the money for yourself and the others. Let us say, three days? I'll return in the evening."

He turned about without waiting for a reply and left through the back door in complete silence. Myrtis went back to her interrupted breakfast while the staff and the girls were hysterical with questions and the seeds of rumor. She let them babble in this manner while she ate; then she strode to the head of the common table.

"Everything shall continue as usual. If it comes to paying their tax, arrangements will be made. You older girls already have ample gold set aside. I will make the necessary adjustments for the newer girls. Unless you doubt me—in which case, I'll arrange a severance for you."

"But madame, if we pay once, they will levy the tax again and again until we can't pay it. Those Hell-Hounds . . ." A girl favored more by intelligence than beauty spoke up.

"That is certainly their desire. The Street of Red Lanterns is as old as the walls of Sanctuary itself. I can assure you that we have survived much worse than the Hell-Hounds." Myrtis smiled slightly to herself, remembering the others who had tried and failed to shut down the Street. "Cylene, the others will be coming to see me. Send them up to the parlor. I'll wait for them there."

The emerald day-robe billowed out from behind her as Myrtis ascended the staircase to the lower rooms and up again to her parlor. In the privacy of her rooms, she allowed her anger to surface as she paced.

"Ambutta!" she shouted, and the young girl who attended her appeared.

"Yes, madame?"

"I have a message for you to carry." She sat at the writing table composing the message as she spoke to the still-out-of-breath girl. "It is to be delivered in the special way as before. No one must see you leave it. Do you understand that? If you cannot leave it without being seen, come back here. Don't let yourself become suspicious."

The girl nodded. She tucked the freshly folded and sealed message into the bodice of her ragged cast-off dress and ran from the room. In time, Myrtis expected her to be a beauty, but she was still very much a child. The message itself was to Lythande, who preferred not to be contacted directly. She would not rely on the magician to solve the Street's problems with the Hell-Hounds, but no one else would understand her anger or alleviate it.

The Aphrodisia House dominated the Street. The Hell-Hounds would come to her first, then visit the other establishments. As word of the tax spread, the other madams would begin a furtive pilgrimage to the back entrance of the Aphrodisia. They looked to Myrtis for guidance, and she looked out the window for inspiration. She had not found one by the time her guests began to appear.

"It's an outrage. They're trying to put us on the streets like common whores!" Dylan of the artificially flaming red hair exclaimed before sitting in the chair Myrtis indicated to her.

"Nonsense, dear," Myrtis explained calmly. "They wish to make us slaves and send us to Ranke. In a way, it is a compliment to Sanctuary."

"They can't do such a thing!"

"No, but it will be up to us to explain that to them."

"How?"

"First we'll wait until the others arrive. I hear Amoli in the hall; the others won't be long in coming."

It was a blatant stall for time on Myrtis's part. Other than her conviction that the Hell-Hounds and their prince would not succeed where others had failed in the past, Myrtis had no idea how to approach the utterly incorruptible elite soldiers. The other madams of the Street talked among themselves, exchanging the insight Myrtis had revealed to Dylan, and reacting poorly to it. Myrtis watched their reflections in the rough-cut glass.

They were all old. More than half of them had once worked for her. She had watched them age in the unkind manner that often overtakes youthful beauty and transforms it into grotesquerie. Myrtis might have been the youngest of them—young enough to be working in the houses instead of running one of them. But when she turned from the window to face them, there was the unmistakable glint of experience and wisdom in her eyes.

"Well, it wasn't really a surprise," she began. "It was rumored before Kittycat got here, and we've seen what has happened to the others the Hell-Hounds have been turned loose on. I admit I'd hoped that some of the others would have held their ground better and given us a bit more time."

"Time wouldn't help. I don't have a hundred gold pieces to give them!" A woman whose white-paste makeup cracked around her eyes as she spoke interrupted Myrtis.

"You don't need a hundred gold pieces!" A similarly made-up woman snarled back.

"The gold is unimportant." Myrtis's voice rose above the bickering. "If they can break one of us, they can drive us all out."

"We could close our doors; then they'd suffer. Half of my men are from Ranke."

"Half of *all* our men are, Gelicia. They won the war and they've got the money," Myrtis countered. "But they'll kowtow to the Hell-Hounds,

Kittycat, and their wives. The men of Ranke are very ambitious. They'll give up much to preserve their wealth and positions. If the Prince is officially frowning on the Street, their loyalties will be less strained if we have closed our doors without putting up a fight."

Grudgingly the women agreed.

"Then what will we do?"

"Conduct your affairs as always. They'll come to the Aphrodisia first to collect the taxes, just as they came here first to announce it. Keep the back doors open and I'll send word. If they can't collect from me, they won't bother you."

There was mumbled disagreement, but no one dared to look straight at Myrtis and argue the point of her power on the Street. Seated in her high-backed chair, Myrtis smiled contentedly. She had yet to determine the precise solution, but the house madams of the Street of Red Lanterns controlled much of the gold within Sanctuary, and she had just confirmed her control of them.

They left her parlor quickly after the decision was rendered. If the Street was to function as usual, they all had work to do. She had work to do. The Hell-Hounds would not return for three days. In that time, the Aphrodisia House would earn far more than those three hundred gold pieces the empire wanted, and would spend only slightly less than that amount to maintain itself. Myrtis opened the ledger, making new notations in a clear, educated hand. The household sensed that order had been restored at least temporarily, and one by one they filed into the parlor to report their earnings or debts.

It was well into afternoon and Ambutta had not returned from placing her message behind a loose stone in the wall behind the altar at the temple of Ils. For a moment, Myrtis worried about the girl. The streets of Sanctuary were never truly safe, and perhaps Ambutta no longer seemed as childlike to all eyes. There was always an element of risk. Twice before girls had been lost in the streets, and not even Lythande's magic could find them again.

Myrtis put such thoughts aside and ate dinner alone in her parlor. She had thought a bribe or offer of free privileges might still be the way out of her problem with the taxes. Prince Kadakithis was probably sincere, though, in his determination to make Sanctuary the ideal city of his adviser's philosophies while the capital city of the empire displayed many of the same excesses that Sanctuary did. The young Prince had a wife and concubines with whom he was supposedly well pleased. There had never been any suspicion that he might partake of the delights of the Street himself. And as for the Hell-Hounds, their first visit had been to announce the taxes.

The elite guard were men made of a finer fiber than most of the soldiers or fighters Sanctuary had known. On reflection, Myrtis doubted that they could be bought or bribed, and knew for certain that they would never relent in their persecution of the Street if the first offer did not succeed in converting them.

It was gathering dusk. The girls could be heard throughout the house, giggling as they prepared for the evening. Myrtis kept no one who showed no aptitude or enjoyment of the profession. Let the other houses bind their girls with poverty or drugs; the Aphrodisia House was the pinnacle of ambition for the working girls of the Street.

"I got your message," a soft voice called from the drapery hung doorway near her bed.

"I was beginning to get worried. My girl has not returned."

Lythande walked to her side, draping an arm about her shoulders and taking hold of her hand.

"I've heard the rumors in the streets. The new regime has chosen its next enemy, it would seem. What is the truth of their demands?"

"They intend to levy a tax of ten gold pieces on every woman living on the Street."

Lythande's habitual smile faded, and the blue star tattooed forehead wrinkled into a frown. "Will you be able to pay that?"

"The intent is not that we pay, but that the Street be closed and that we be sent up to the empire. If I pay it once, they'll keep on levying it until I can't pay."

"You could close the house . . ."

"Never!" Myrtis pulled her hands away. "The Aphrodisia House is mine. I was running this house when the Rankan Empire was a collection of half-naked barbaric tribes!"

"But they aren't any longer," Lythande reminded her gently. "And the Hell-Hounds—if not the Prince—are making substantial changes in all our lives."

"They won't interfere with magic, will they?"

Myrtis's concern for Lythande briefly overshadowed her fears for the Aphrodisia House. The magician's thin-lipped smile returned.

"For now it is doubtful. There are men in Ranke who have the ability to affect us directly, but they have not followed the Prince to Sanctuary, and I do not know if he could command their loyalty."

Myrtis stood up. She walked to the leaded-glass window, with its thick, obscuring panes which revealed movement on the Street but very little else.

"I'll need your help, if it's available," she said without facing Lythande.

"What can I do?"

"In the past you've prepared a drug for me from a qualis-berry extract. I recall you said it was quite difficult to mix—but I should like enough for two people when it's mixed with pure qualis liqueur."

"Delicate and precise, but not particularly difficult. It is very subtle. Are you sure you will only need enough to serve two?"

"Yes, Zalbar and myself. I agree; the drug must be subtle."

"You must be very certain of your methods, then."

"Of some things, at least. The Street of Red Lanterns does not lie outside the walls of Sanctuary by accident—you know that. The Hell-Hounds and their prince have much more to lose by hindering us than by letting the Street exist in peace. If our past purpose were not enough to convince them, then surely the fact that much of the city's gold passes through my hands every year will matter.

"I will use the qualis-berry love potion to open Zalbar's eyes to reality, not to close them."

"I can have it for you perhaps by tomorrow evening, but more likely the day after. Many of the traders and smugglers of the bazaar are no longer well supplied with the ingredients I will need, but I can investigate other sources. When the Hell-Hounds drove the smugglers into the Swamp of Night Secrets, many honest men suffered."

Myrtis' eyes narrowed, she released the drapery she had clutched.

"And if the Street of Red Lanterns wasn't here . . . The mongers and merchants, and even the smugglers, might not want to admit it, but without us to provide them with their gold while 'respectable' people offer promises, they would suffer even more than they do now."

There was a gentle knocking on the door. Lythande stepped back into the shadows of the room. Ambutta entered, a large bruise visible on the side of her face.

"The men have begun to arrive, Madame Myrtis. Will you collect their money, or shall I take the ledger downstairs?"

"I shall attend to them. Send them up to me and, Ambutta—" She stopped the girl as she headed out of the parlor. "Go to the kitchen and find out how many days we could go without buying anything from any of the tradesmen."

"Yes, madame."

The room was suddenly empty, except for Myrtis. Only a slight rippling of the wall tapestries showed where Lythande had opened a concealed panel and disappeared into the secret passages of the Aphrodisia House. Myrtis had not expected the magician to stay, but despite all their years together, the magician's sudden comings and goings still unsettled her. Standing in front of a full-length mirror, Myrtis rearranged the pearl-and-gold pins in her hair, rubbed scented oils into her skin, and greeted the first gentleman-caller as if the day had been no different from any other.

Word of the taxation campaign against the Street had spread through the city much as Lythande had observed. The result was that many of their infrequent guests and visitors came to the house to pay their last respects to an entertainment that they openly expected would be gone in a very short time. Myrtis smiled at each of them as they arrived, accepted their money, and asked their second choice of the girls before assuring them that the Aphrodisia House would never close its doors.

"Madame?"

Ambutta peered around the doorway when the flow of gentlemen had abated slightly.

"The kitchen says that we have enough food for ten days, but less of ordinary wine and the like."

Myrtis touched the feather of her pen against her temple.

"Ten days? Someone has grown lax. Our storerooms can hold enough for many months. But ten days is all we will have, and it will have to be enough. Tell the kitchen to place no orders with the tradesmen tomorrow or the next day, and send word to the other backdoors.

"And, Ambutta, Irda will carry my messages in the future. It is time that you were taught more important and useful things."

A steady stream of merchants and tradesmen made their way through the Aphrodisia House to Myrtis' parlor late the next morning as the effects of her orders began to be felt in the town.

"But Madame Myrtis, the tax isn't due yet, and surely the Aphrodisia House has the resources. . . ." The puffy-faced gentleman who sent meat to half the houses on the Street was alternately irate and wheedling.

"In such unsettled times as these, good Mikkun, I cannot look to luxuries like expensive meats. I sincerely wish that this were not true. The taste of salted meat has always reminded me of poverty. But the gover-

nor's palace does not care about the poverty of those who live outside
its walls, though it sends its forces to tax us," Myrtis said in feigned
helplessness.

In deference to the sad occasion she had not put on one of the
brightly embroidered day-robes as was her custom but wore a soberly
cut dress of a fashion outdated in Sanctuary at least twenty years before. She had taken off her jewelry, knowing that its absence would
cause more rumors than if she had indeed sold a part of it to the gem-
cutters. An atmosphere of austerity enveloped the house and every
other on the Street, as Mikkun could attest, for he'd visited most of
them.

"But madame, I have already slaughtered two cows! For three years
I have slaughtered the cows first to assure you the freshest meat early
in the day. Today, for no reason, you say you do not want my meat!
Madame, you already have a debt to me for those two cows!"

"Mikkun! You have never, in all the years I've known you, extended
credit to any house on the Street and now . . . now you're asking me to
consider my daily purchases a debt to you!" She smiled disarmingly to
calm him, knowing full well that the butcher and the others depended
on the hard gold from the Street to pay their own debts.

"There will be credit in the future!"

"But we will not be here to use it!"

Myrtis let her face take on a mournful pout. Let the butcher and his
friends start dunning the "respectable" side of Sanctuary, and word
would spread quickly to the palace that something was amiss. A "something" which she would explain to the Hell-Hound captain, Zalbar,
when he arrived to collect the tax. The tradesman left her parlor muttering prophecies of doom she hoped would eventually be heard by those
in a position to worry about them.

"Madame?"

Ambutta's child-serious face appeared in the doorway moments after
the butcher had left. Her ragged dress had already been replaced with
one of a more mature cut, brighter color, and new cloth.

"Amoli waits to speak with you. She is in the kitchen now. Shall I
send her up?"

"Yes, bring her up."

Myrtis sighed after Ambutta left. Amoli was her only rival on the
Street. She was a woman who had not learned her trade in the upper
rooms of the Aphrodisia, and also one who kept her girls working for
her through their addiction to krrf, which she supplied to them. If any-

one on the Street was nervous about the tax, though, it was Amoli; she
had very little gold to spare. The smugglers had recently been forced by
the same Hell-Hounds to raise the price of a well-refined brick of the
drug to maintain their own profits.

"Amoli, good woman, you look exhausted."

Myrtis assisted a woman less than a third her age to the love seat.

"May I get you something to drink?"

"Qualis, if you have any." Amoli paused while Myrtis passed the
request along to Ambutta. "I can't do it, Myrtis—this whole scheme of
yours is impossible. It will ruin me!"

The liqueur arrived. Ambutta carried a finely wrought silver tray with
one glass of the deep red liquid. Amoli's hands shook violently as she
grasped the glass and emptied it in one gulp. Ambutta looked sagely to
her mistress; the other madam was, perhaps, victim of the same addiction as her girls?

"I've been approached by Jubal. For a small fee, he will send his
men up here tomorrow night to ambush the Hell-Hounds. He has been
looking for an opportunity to eliminate them. With them gone, Kittycat
won't be able to make trouble for us."

"So Jubal is supplying the krrf now?" Myrtis replied without sympathy.

"They all have to pay to land their shipments in the Night Secrets, or
Jubal will reveal their activities to the Hell-Hounds. His plan is fair. I
can deal with him directly. So can anyone else—he trades in anything.
But you and Lythande will have to unseal the tunnels so his men face
no undue risk tomorrow night."

The remnants of Myrtis' cordiality disappeared. The Golden Lily had
been isolated from the rat's nest of passages on the Street when Myrtis
realized the extent of krrf addiction within it. Unkind experience
warned her against mixing drugs and courtesans. There were always
men like Jubal waiting for the first sign of weakness, and soon the
houses were nothing more than slaver's dens; the madams forgotten.
Jubal feared magic, so she had asked Lythande to seal the tunnels with
eerily visible wards. So long as she—Myrtis—lived, the Street would be
hers, and not Jubal's, nor the city's.

"There are other suppliers whose prices are not so high. Or perhaps
Jubal has promised you a place in his mansion? I have heard he learned
things besides fighting in the pits of Ranke. Of course, his home is
hardly the place for sensitive people to live."

Myrtis wrinkled her nose in the accepted way to indicate someone who lived Downwind. Amoli replied with an equally understandable gesture of insult and derision, but she left the parlor without looking back.

The problems with Jubal and the smugglers were only just beginning. Myrtis pondered them after Ambutta removed the tray and glass from the room. Jubal's ruthless ambition was potentially more dangerous than any threat radiating directly from the Hell-Hounds. But they were completely distinct from the matters at hand, so Myrtis put them out of her mind.

The second evening was not as lucrative as the first, nor the third day as frantic as the second. Lythande's aphrodisiac potion appeared in the hands of a dazed street urchin. The *geas* the magician had placed on the young beggar dissipated as soon as the vial left his hands. He had glanced around him in confusion and disappeared at a run before the day-steward could hand him a copper coin for his inconvenience.

Myrtis poured the vial into a small bottle of qualis which she then placed between two glasses on the silver tray. The decor of the parlor had been changed subtly during the day. The red liqueur replaced the black-bound ledger which had been banished to the night-steward's cubicle in the lower rooms. The draperies around her bed were tied back, and a padded silk coverlet was creased to show the plump pillows. Musky incense crept into the room from burners hidden in the corners. Beside her bed, a large box containing the three hundred gold pieces sat on a table.

Myrtis hadn't put on any of her jewelry. It would only have detracted from the ebony low-cut, side-slit gown she wore. The image was perfect. No one but Zalbar would see her until the dawn, and she was determined that her efforts and planning would not be in vain.

She waited alone, remembering her first days as a courtesan in Ilsig, when Lythande was a magician's raw apprentice and her own experiences a nightmare adventure. At that time she had lived to fall wildly in love with any young lordling who could offer her the dazzling splendor of privilege. But no man came forward to rescue her from the ethereal, but doomed, world of the courtesan. Before her beauty faded, she had made her pact with Lythande. The magician visited her infrequently, and for all her boasting, there was no passionate love between them. The spells had let Myrtis win for herself the permanent splendor she had wanted as a young girl; a splendor no high-handed barbarian from Ranke was going to strip away.

"Madame Myrtis?"

A peremptory knock on the door forced her from her thoughts. She had impressed the voice in her memory and recognized it though she had only heard it once before.

"Do come in."

She opened the door for him, pleased to see by the hesitation in his step that he was unaware that he would be entering her parlor and boudoir.

"I have come to collect the taxes!" he said quickly. His military precision did not completely conceal his awe and vague embarrassment at viewing the royal and erotic scene displayed before him.

He did not turn as Myrtis shut the door behind him and quietly slid a concealed bolt into place.

"You have very nearly undone me, captain," she said with downcast eyes and a light touch on his arm. "It is not so easy as you might think to raise such a large sum of money."

She lifted the ebony box inlaid with pearl from the table beside her bed and carried it slowly to him. He hesitated before taking it from her arms.

"I must count it, madame," he said almost apologetically.

"I understand. You will find that it is all there. My word is good."

"You . . . you are much different now from how you seemed two days ago."

"It is the difference between night and day."

He began assembling piles of gold on her ledger table in front of the silver tray with the qualis.

"We have been forced to cut back our orders to the town's merchants in order to pay you."

From the surprised yet thoughtful look he gave her, Myrtis guessed that the Hell-Hounds had begun to hear complaints and anxious whinings from the respectable parts of town as Mikkun and his friends called back their loans and credit.

"Still," she continued, "I realize that you are doing only what you have been told to do. It's not you personally who is to blame if any of the merchants and purveyors suffer because the Street no longer functions as it once did."

Zalbar continued shuffling his piles of coins around, only half-listening to Myrtis. He had half the gold in the box neatly arranged when Myrtis slipped the glass stopper out of the qualis decanter.

"Will you join me in a glass of qualis, since it is not your fault and we still have a few luxuries in our larder. They tell me a damp fog lies heavy on the streets."

He looked up from his counting and his eyes brightened at the sight of the deep red liqueur. The common variety of qualis, though still expensive, had a duller color and was inclined to visible sediment. A man of his position might live a full life and never glimpse a fine, pure qualis, much less be offered a glass of it. Clearly the Hell-Hound was tempted.

"A small glass, perhaps."

She poured two equally full glasses and set them both on the table in front of him while she replaced the stopper and took the bottle to the table by her bed. An undetectable glance in a side mirror confirmed that Zalbar lifted the glass farthest from him. Calmly she returned and raised the other.

"A toast then. To the future of your prince and to the Aphrodisia House!"

The glasses clinked.

The potion Lythande had made was brewed in part from the same berries as the qualis itself. The fine liqueur made a perfect concealing dilutant. Myrtis could taste the subtle difference the charm itself made in the normal flavor of the intoxicant, but Zalbar, who had never tasted even the common qualis, assumed that the extra warmth was only a part of the legendary mystique of the liqueur. When he had finished his drink, Myrtis swallowed the last of hers and waited patiently for the faint flush which would confirm that the potion was working.

It appeared in Zalbar first. He became bored with his counting, fondling one coin while his eyes drifted off toward nothingness. Myrtis took the coin from his fingers. The potion took longer to affect her, and its action when it did was lessened by the number of times she had taken it before and by the age-inhibiting spells Lythande wove about her. She had not needed the potion, however, to summon an attraction toward the handsome soldier nor to coax him to his feet and then to her bed.

Zalbar protested that he was not himself and did not understand what was happening to him. Myrtis did not trouble herself to argue with him. Lythande's potion was not one to rouse a wild, blind lust, but one which endowed a lifelong affection in the drinker. The pure qualis played a part in weakening his resistance. She held him behind the curtains of her bed until he had no doubt of his love for her. Then she helped him dress again.

"I'll show you the secrets of the Aphrodisia House," she whispered in his ear.

"I believe I have already found them."

"There are more."

Myrtis took him by the hand, leading him to one of the drapery covered walls. She pushed aside the fabric; released a well-oiled catch; took a sconce from the wall; then led him into a dark, but airy, passage way.

"Walk carefully in my footsteps, Zalbar—I would not want to lose you to the oubliettes. Perhaps you have wondered why the Street is outside the walls and its buildings are so old and well-built? Perhaps you think Sanctuary's founders wished to keep us outside their fair city? What you do not know is that these houses—especially the older ones like the Aphrodisia—are not really outside the walls at all. My house is built of stone four feet thick. The shutters on our windows are aged wood from the mountains. We have our own wells and storerooms which can supply us—and the city—for weeks, if necessary. Other passages lead away from here toward the Swamp of Night Secrets, or into Sanctuary and the governor's palace itself. Whoever has ruled in Sanctuary has always sought our cooperation in moving men and arms if a siege is laid."

She showed the speechless captain catacombs where a sizable garrison could wait in complete concealment. He drank water from a deep well whose water had none of the brackish taste so common in the seacoast town. Above he could hear the sounds of parties at the Aphrodisia and the other houses. Zalbar's military eye took all this in, but his mind saw Myrtis, candle-lit in the black gown, as a man's dream come true, and the underground fortress she was revealing to him as a soldier's dream come true. The potion worked its way with him. He wanted both Myrtis and the fortress for his own to protect and control.

"There is so much about Sanctuary that you Rankans know nothing about. You tax the Street and cause havoc with trade in the city. You wish to close the Street and send all of us, including myself, to the slave pens or worse. Your walls will be breachable then. There are men in Sanctuary who would stop at nothing to control these passages, and they know the Swamp and the palace better than you or your children could ever hope to."

She showed him a wall flickering with runes and magic signs. Zalbar went to touch it and found his fingers singed for his curiosity.

"These warding walls keep us safe now, but they will fade if we are not here to renew them properly. Smugglers and thieves will find the entrances we have kept invulnerable for generations. And you, Zalbar, who wish that Sanctuary will become a place of justice and order, will know in your heart that you are responsible, because you knew what was here and let the others destroy it."

"No, Myrtis. So long as I live, none of this shall be harmed."

"There is no other way. Do you not already have your orders to levy a second tax?"

He nodded.

"We have already begun to use the food stored in these basements. The girls are not happy; the merchants are not happy. The Street will die. The merchants will charge higher prices, and the girls will make their way to the streets. There is nowhere else for them to go. Perhaps Jubal will take—"

"I do not think that the Street will suffer such a fate. Once the Prince understands the true part you and the others play, he will agree to a nominal tax which would be applied to maintaining the defense of Sanctuary and therefore be returned to you."

Myrtis smiled to herself. The battle was won. She held his arm tightly and no longer fought the effect of the adulterated qualis in her own emotions. They found an abandoned officer's quarters and made love on its bare wooden-slats bed, and again when they returned to the parlor of the Aphrodisia House.

The night-candle had burned down to its last knob by the time Myrtis released the hidden bolt and let the Hell-Hound captain rejoin his men. Lythande was in the room behind her as soon as she shut the door.

"Are you safe now?" the magician asked with a laugh.

"I believe so."

"The potion?"

"A success, as always. I have not been in love like this for a long time. It is pleasant. I almost do not mind knowing how empty and hurt I will feel as I watch him grow old."

"Then why use something like the potion? Surely the catacombs themselves would have been enough to convince a Hell-Hound?"

"Convince him of what? That the defenses of Sanctuary should not be entrusted to whores and courtesans? Except for your potion, there is nothing else to bind him to the idea that we—that I should remain here as I always have. There was no other way!"

"You're right," Lythande said, nodding. "Will he return to visit you?"

"He will care, but I do not think he will return. That was not the purpose of the drug."

She opened the narrow glass-paned doors to the balcony overlooking the emptying lower rooms. The soldiers were gone. She looked back into the room. The three hundred gold pieces still lay half-counted on the table next to the empty decanter. He might return.

"I feel as young as I look," she whispered to the unnoticing rooms. "I could satisfy every man in this house if I took the notion to, or if anyone of them had half the magnificence of my Zalbar."

Myrtis turned back to an empty room and went to sleep alone.

# The Secret of the Blue Star

## Marion Zimmer Bradley

On a night in Sanctuary, when the streets bore a false glamour in the silver glow of full moon, so that every ruin seemed an enchanted tower and every dark street and square an island of mystery, the mercenary-magician Lythande sallied forth to seek adventure.

Lythande had but recently returned—if the mysterious comings and goings of a magician can be called by so prosaic a name—from guarding a caravan across the Grey Wastes to Twand. Somewhere in the Wastes, a gaggle of desert rats—two-legged rats with poisoned steel teeth—had set upon the caravan, not knowing it was guarded by magic, and had found themselves fighting skeletons that howled and fought with eyes of flame; and at their center a tall magician with a blue star between blazing eyes, a star that shot lightnings of a cold and paralyzing flame. So the desert rats ran, and never stopped running until they reached Aurvesh, and the tales they told did Lythande no harm except in the ears of the pious.

And so there was gold in the pockets of the long, dark magician's robe, or perhaps concealed in whatever dwelling sheltered Lythande.

For at the end, the caraven master had been almost more afraid of Lythande than he was of the bandits, a situation which added to the generosity with which he rewarded the magician. According to custom, Lythande neither smiled nor frowned, but remarked, days later, to Myrtis, the proprietor of the Aphrodisia House in the Street of Red Lanterns, that sorcery, while a useful skill and filled with many aesthetic delights for the contemplation of the philosopher, in itself put no beans on the table.

A curious remark, that, Myrtis pondered, putting away the ounce of gold Lythande had bestowed upon her in consideration of a secret which lay many years behind them both. Curious that Lythande should speak of beans on the table, when no one but herself had ever seen a bite of food or a drop of drink pass the magician's lips since the blue star had adorned that high and narrow brow. Nor had any woman in the Quarter even been able to boast that a great magician had paid for her favors, or been able to imagine how such a magician behaved in that situation when all men were alike reduced to flesh and blood.

Perhaps Myrtis could have told if she would; some of her girls thought so, when, as sometimes happened, Lythande came to the Aphrodisia House and was closeted long with its owner; even, on rare intervals, for an entire night. It was said, of Lythande, that the Aphrodisia House itself had been the magician's gift to Myrtis, after a famous adventure still whispered in the bazaar, involving an evil wizard, two horse-traders, a caravan master, and a few assorted toughs who had prided themselves upon never giving gold for any woman and thought it funny to cheat an honest working woman. None of them had ever showed their faces—what was left of them—in Sanctuary again, and Myrtis boasted that she need never again sweat to earn her living, and never again entertain a man, but would claim her madam's privilege of a solitary bed.

And then, too, the girls thought, a magician of Lythande's stature could have claimed the most beautiful women from Sanctuary to the mountains beyond Ilsig; not courtesans alone, but princesses and noble-women and priestesses would have been for Lythande's taking. Myrtis had doubtless been beautiful in her youth, and certainly she boasted enough of the princes and wizards and travelers who had paid great sums for her love. She was beautiful still (and of course there were those who said that Lythande did not pay *her,* but that, on the contrary, Myrtis paid the magician great sums to maintain her aging beauty with strong magic) but her hair had gone grey and she no longer troubled to dye it with henna or goldenwash from Tyrisis-beyond-the-sea.

But if Myrtis were not the woman who knew how Lythande behaved in that most elemental of situations, then there was no woman in Sanctuary who could say. Rumor said also that Lythande called up female demons from the Grey Wastes, to couple in lechery, and certainly Lythande was neither the first nor the last magician of whom that could be said.

But on this night Lythande sought neither food nor drink nor the

delights of amorous entertainment; although Lythande was a great fre-
quenter of taverns, no man had ever yet seen a drop of ale or mead or
fire-drink pass the barrier of the magician's lips. Lythande walked along
the far edge of the bazaar, skirting the old rim of the governor's palace,
keeping to the shadows in defiance of footpads and cutpurses, that love
for shadows which made the folk of the city say that Lythande could
appear and disappear into thin air.

Tall and thin, Lythande, above the height of a tall man, lean to ema-
ciation, with the blue star-shaped tattoo of the magician-adept above
thin, arching eyebrows; wearing a long, hooded robe which melted into
the shadows. Clean-shaven, the face of Lythande, or beardless—none
had come close enough, in living memory, to say whether this was the
whim of an effeminate or the hairlessness of a freak. The hair beneath
the hood was as long and luxuriant as a woman's, but greying, as no
woman in this city of harlots would have allowed it to do.

Striding quickly along a shadowed wall, Lythande stepped through an
open door, over which the sandal of Thufir, god of pilgrims, had been
nailed up for luck; but the footsteps were so soft, and the hooded robe
blended so well into the shadows, that eyewitnesses would later swear,
truthfully, that they had seen Lythande appear from the air, protected
by sorceries, or by a cloak of invisibility.

Around the hearthfire, a group of men were banging their mugs together noisily to the sound of a rowdy drinking-song, strummed on a
worn and tinny lute—Lythande knew it belonged to the tavernkeeper,
and could be borrowed—by a young man, dressed in fragments of
foppish finery, torn and slashed by the chances of the road. He was sitting lazily, with one knee crossed over the other; and when the rowdy
song died away, the young man drifted into another, a quiet love-song
from another time and another country. Lythande had known the song,
more years ago than bore remembering, and in those days Lythande the
magician had borne another name and had known little of sorcery.
When the song died, Lythande had stepped from the shadows, visible,
and the firelight glinted on the blue star, mocking at the center of the
high forehead.

There was a little muttering in the tavern, but they were not unaccustomed to Lythande's invisible comings and goings. The young man
raised eyes which were surprisingly blue beneath the black hair elaborately curled above his brow. He was slender and agile, and Lythande
marked the rapier at his side, which looked well handled, and the
amulet, in the form of a coiled snake, at his throat. The young man

said, "Who are you, who has the habit of coming and going into thin air like that?"

"One who compliments your skill at song." Lythande flung a coin to the tapster's boy. "Will you drink?"

"A minstrel never refuses such an invitation. Singing is dry work." But when the drink was brought, he said, "Not drinking with me, then?"

"No man has ever seen Lythande eat or drink," muttered one of the men in the circle round them.

"Why, then, I hold that unfriendly," cried the young minstrel. "A friendly drink between comrades shared is one thing; but I am no servant to sing for pay or to drink except as a friendly gesture!"

Lythande shrugged, and the blue star above the high brow began to shimmer and give forth blue light. The onlookers slowly edged backward, for when a wizard who wore the blue star was angered, bystanders did well to be out of the way. The minstrel set down the lute, so it would be well out of range if he must leap to his feet. Lythande knew, by the excruciating slowness of his movements and great care, that he had already shared a good many drinks with chance-met comrades. But the minstrel's hand did not go to his sword hilt but instead closed like a fist over the amulet in the form of a snake.

"You are like no man I have ever met before," he observed mildly, and Lythande, feeling inside the little ripple, nerve-long, that told a magician he was in the presence of spellcasting, hazarded quickly that the amulet was one of those which would not protect its master unless the wearer first stated a set number of truths—usually three or five—about the owner's attacker or foe. Wary, but amused, Lythande said, "A true word. Nor am I like any man you will ever meet, live you never so long, minstrel."

The minstrel saw, beyond the angry blue glare of the star, a curl of friendly mockery in Lythande's mouth. He said, letting the amulet go, "And I wish you no ill; and you wish me none, and those are true sayings too, wizard, hey? And there's an end of that. But although perhaps you are like to no other, you are not the only wizard I have seen in Sanctuary who bears a blue star about his forehead."

Now the blue star blazed rage, but not for the minstrel. They both knew it. The crowd around them had all mysteriously discovered that they had business elsewhere. The minstrel looked at the empty benches.

"I must go elsewhere to sing for my supper, it seems."

"I meant you no offense when I refused to share a drink," said Lythande. "A magician's vow is not as lightly overset as a lute. Yet I may guest-gift you with dinner and drink in plenty without loss of dignity, and in return ask a service of a friend, may I not?"

"Such is the custom of my country. Cappen Varra thanks you, magician."

"Tapster! Your best dinner for my guest, and all he can drink tonight!"

"For such liberal guesting I'll not haggle about the service," Cappen Varra said, and set to the smoking dishes brought before him. As he ate, Lythande drew from the folds of his robe a small pouch containing a quantity of sweet-smelling herbs, rolled them into a blue-grey leaf, and touched his ring to spark the roll alight. He drew on the smoke, which drifted up sweet and greyish.

"As for the service, it is nothing so great; tell me all you know of this other wizard who wears the blue star. I know of none other of my order south of Azehur, and I would be certain you did not see me, nor my wraith."

Cappen Varra sucked at a marrow-bone and wiped his fingers fastidiously on the tray-cloth beneath the meats. He bit into a ginger-fruit before replying.

"Not you, wizard, nor your fetch or doppelganger; this one had shoulders brawnier by half, and he wore no sword, but two daggers cross-girt astride his hips. His beard was black; and his left hand missing three fingers."

"Ils of the Thousand Eyes! Rabben the Half-handed, here in Sanctuary! Where did you see him, minstrel?"

"I saw him crossing the bazaar; but he bought nothing that I saw. And I saw him in the Street of Red Lanterns, talking to a woman. What service am I to do for you, magician?"

"You have done it." Lythande gave silver to the tavernkeeper—so much that the surly man bade Shalpa's cloak cover him as he went—and laid another coin, gold this time, beside the borrowed lute.

"Redeem your harp; that one will do your voice no boon." But when the minstrel raised his head in thanks, the magician had gone unseen into the shadows.

Pocketing the gold, the minstrel asked, "How did he know that? And how did he go out?"

"Shalpa the swift alone knows," the tapster said. "Flew out by the smoke-hole in the chimney, for all I ken! That one needs not the night-dark cloak of Shalpa to cover him, for he has one of his own. He paid for your drinks, good sir; what will you have?" And Cappen

Varra proceeded to get very drunk, that being the wisest thing to do when one becomes entangled unawares in the private affairs of a wizard.

Outside in the street, Lythande paused to consider. Rabben the Half-handed was no friend; yet there was no reason his presence in Sanctuary must deal with Lythande, or personal revenge. If it were business concerned with the Order of the Blue Star, if Lythande must lend Rabben aid, or the Half-handed had been sent to summon all the members of the Order, the star they both wore would have given warning.

Yet it would do no harm to make certain. Walking swiftly, the magician had reached a line of old stables behind the governor's palace. There was silence and secrecy for magic. Lythande stepped into one of the little side alleys, drawing up the magician's cloak until no light remained, slowly withdrawing farther and farther into the silence until nothing remained anywhere in the world—anywhere in the universe but the light of the blue star ever glowing in front. Lythande remembered how it had been set there, and at what cost—the price an adept paid for power.

The blue glow gathered, fulminated in many-colored patterns, pulsing and glowing, until Lythande stood *within* the light; and there, in the Place That Is Not, seated upon a throne carved apparently from sapphire, was the Master of the Star.

"Greetings to you, fellow star, star-born, *shyryu.*" The terms of endearment could mean fellow, companion, brother, sister, beloved, equal, pilgrim; its literal meaning was *sharer of starlight.* "What brings you into the Pilgrim Place this night from afar?"

"The need for knowledge, star-sharer. Have you sent one to seek me out in Sanctuary?"

"Not so, *shyryu.* All is well in the Temple of the Star-sharers; you have not yet been summoned; the hour is not yet come."

For every adept of the Blue Star knows; it is one of the prices of power. At the world's end, when all the doings of mankind and mortals are done, the last to fall under the assault of Chaos will be the Temple of the Star; and then, in the Place That Is Not, the Master of the Star will summon all of the Pilgrim Adepts from the farthest corners of the world, to fight with all their magic against Chaos; but until that day, they have such freedom as will best strengthen their powers. The Master of the Star repeated, reassuringly, "The hour has not come. You are free to walk as you will in the world."

The blue glow faded, and Lythande stood shivering. So Rabben had not been sent in that final summoning. Yet the end and Chaos might well be at hand for Lythande before the hour appointed, if Rabben the Half-handed had his way.

*It was a fair test of strength, ordained by our masters. Rabben should bear me no ill-will.* . . . Rabben's presence in Sanctuary need not have to do with Lythande. He might be here upon his lawful occasions—if anything of Rabben's could be said to be lawful; for it was only upon the last day of all that the Pilgrim Adepts were pledged to fight upon the side of Law against Chaos. And Rabben had not chosen to do so before then.

Caution would be needed, and yet Lythande knew that Rabben was near . . .

South and east of the governor's palace, there is a little triangular park, across from the Street of Temples. By day the graveled walks and turns of shrubbery are given over to predicants and priests who find not enough worship or offerings for their liking; by night the place is the haunt of women who worship no goddess except She of the filled purse and the empty womb. And for both reasons the place is called, in irony, the Promise of Heaven; in Sanctuary, as elsewhere, it is well known that those who promise do not always perform.

Lythande, who frequented neither women nor priests as a usual thing, did not often walk here. The park seemed deserted; the evil winds had begun to blow, whipping bushes and shrubbery into the shapes of strange beasts performing unnatural acts; and moaning weirdly around the walls and eaves of the Temples across the street, the wind that was said in Sanctuary to be the moaning of Azyuna in Vashanka's bed. Lythande moved swiftly, skirting the darkness of the paths. And then a woman's scream rent the air.

From the shadows Lythande could see the frail form of a young girl in a torn and ragged dress; she was barefoot and her ear was bleeding where one jeweled earring had been torn from the lobe. She was struggling in the iron grip of a huge burly black-bearded man, and the first thing Lythande saw was the hand gripped around the girl's thin, bony wrist, dragging her; two fingers missing and the other cut away to the first joint. Only then—when it was no longer needed—did Lythande see the blue star between the black bristling brows, the cat-yellow eyes of Rabben the Half-handed!

Lythande knew him of old, from the Temple of the Star. Even then Rabben had been a vicious man, his lecheries notorious. Why, Lythande wondered, had the Masters not demanded that he renounce them as the price of his power? Lythande's lips tightened in a mirthless grimace; so notorious had been Rabben's lecheries that if he renounced them, everyone would know the Secret of his Power.

For the powers of an adept of the Blue Star depended upon a secret. As in the old legend of the giant who kept his heart in a secret place outside his body, and with it his immortality, so the adept of the Blue Star poured all his psychic force into a single Secret; and the one who discovered the Secret would acquire all of that adept's power. So Rabben's Secret must be something else . . . Lythande did not speculate on it.

The girl cried out pitifully as Rabben jerked at her wrist; as the burly magician's star began to glow, she thrust her free hand over her eyes to shield them from it. Without fully intending to intervene, Lythande stepped from the shadows, and the rich voice that had made the prentice-magicians in the outer court of the Blue Star call Lythande "minstrel" rather than "magician," rang out:

"By Shipri the All-Mother, release that woman!"

Rabben whirled. "By the nine-hundred-and-ninety-ninth eye of Ils! Lythande!"

"Are there not enough women in the Street of Red Lanterns, that you must mishandle girl-children in the Street of Temples?" For Lythande could see how young she was, the thin arms and childish legs and ankles, the breasts not yet full-formed beneath the dirty, torn tunic.

Rabben turned on Lythande and sneered, "You were always squeamish, *shyryu*. No woman walks here unless she is for sale. Do you want her for yourself? Have you tired of your fat madame in the Aphrodisia House?"

"You will not take her name into your mouth, *shyryu!*"

"So tender for the honor of a harlot?"

Lythande ignored that. "Let that girl go, or stand to my challenge."

Rabben's star shot lightnings; he shoved the girl to one side. She fell nerveless to the pavement and lay without moving. "She'll stay there until we've done. Did you think she could run away while we fought? Come to think of it, I never did see you with a woman, Lythande—is that your Secret, Lythande, that you've no use for women?"

Lythande maintained an impassive face; but whatever came, Rabben must not be allowed to pursue *that* line. "You may couple like an animal in the streets of Sanctuary, Rabben, but I do not. Will you yield her up, or fight?"

"Perhaps I should yield her to you; this is unheard of, that Lythande should fight in the streets over a woman! You see, I know your habits well, Lythande!"

*Damnation of Vashanka! Now indeed I shall have to fight for the girl!*

Lythande's rapier snicked from its scabbard and thrust at Rabben as if of its own will.

"Ha! Do you think Rabben fights street-brawls with the sword like any mercenary?" Lythande's sword-tip exploded in the blue star-glow, and became a shimmering snake, twisting back on itself to climb past the hilt, fangs dripping venom as it sought to coil around Lythande's fist. Lythande's own star blazed. The sword was metal again but twisted and useless, in the shape of the snake it had been, coiling back toward the scabbard. Enraged, Lythande jerked free of the twisted metal, sent a spitting rain of fire in Rabben's direction. Quickly the huge adept covered himself in fog, and the fire-spray extinguished itself. Somewhere outside consciousness Lythande was aware of a crowd gathering; not twice in a lifetime did two adepts of the Blue Star battle by sorcery in the streets of Sanctuary. The blaze of the stars, blazing from each magician's brow, raged lightnings in the square.

On a howling wind came little torches ravening, that flickered and whipped at Lythande; they touched the tall form of the magician and vanished. Then a wild whirlwind sent trees lashing, leaves swirling bare from branches, and battered Rabben to his knees. Lythande was bored; this must be finished quickly. Not one of the goggling onlookers in the crowd knew afterward what had been done, but Rabben bent, slowly, slowly, forced inch by inch down and down, to his knees, to all fours, prone, pressing and grinding his face farther and farther into the dust, rocking back and forth, pressing harder and harder into the sand. . .

Lythande turned and lifted the girl. She stared in disbelief at the burly sorcerer grinding his black beard frantically into the dirt.

"What did you—"

"Never mind—let's get out of here. The spell will not hold him long, and when he wakes from it he will be angry." Neutral mockery edged Lythande's voice, and the girl could see it, too, Rabben with beard and eyes and blue star covered with the dirt and dust—

She scurried along in the wake of the magician's robe; when they were well away from the Promise of Heaven, Lythande halted, so abruptly that the girl stumbled.

"Who are you, girl?"

"My name is Bercy. And yours?"

"A magician's name is not lightly given. In Sanctuary they call me Lythande." Looking down at the girl, the magician noted, with a pang, that beneath the dirt and dishevelment she was very beautiful and very young. "You can go, Bercy. He will not touch you again; I have bested him fairly upon challenge."

She flung herself on to Lythande's shoulder, clinging. "Don't send me away!" she begged, clutching, eyes filled with adoration. Lythande scowled.

Predictable, of course. Bercy believed, and who in Sanctuary would have disbelieved, that the duel had been fought for the girl as prize, and she was ready to give herself to the winner. Lythande made a gesture of protest.

"No—"

The girl narrowed her eyes in pity. "Is it then with you as Rabben said—that your secret is that you have been deprived of manhood?" But beyond the pity was a delicious flicker of amusement—what a tidbit of gossip! A juicy bit for the Streets of Women.

"Silence!" Lythande's glance was imperative. "Come."

She followed, along the twisting streets that led into the Street of Red Lanterns. Lythande strode with confidence, now, past the House of Mermaids, where, it was said, delights as exotic as the name promised were to be found; past the House of Whips, shunned by all except those who refused to go elsewhere; and at last, beneath the face of the Green Lady as she was worshiped far away and beyond Ranke, the Aphrodisia House.

Bercy looked around, eyes wide, at the pillared lobby, the brilliance of a hundred lanterns, the exquisitely dressed women lounging on cushions till they were summoned. They were finely dressed and bejeweled— Myrtis knew her trade, and how to present her wares—and Lythande guessed that the ragged Bercy's glance was one of envy; she had probably sold herself in the bazaars for a few coppers or for a loaf of bread, since she was old enough. Yet somehow, like flowers covering a dungheap, she had kept an exquisite fresh beauty, all gold and white, flowerlike. Even ragged and half-starved, she touched Lythande's heart.

"Bercy, have you eaten today?"

"No, master."

Lythande summoned the huge eunuch Jiro, whose business it was to conduct the favored customers to the chambers of their chosen women, and throw out the drunks and abusive customers into the street. He came—huge-bellied, naked except for a skimpy loincloth and a dozen

rings in his ear—he had once had a lover who was an earring-seller and
had used him to display her wares.

"How we may serve the magician Lythande?"

The women on the couches and cushions were twittering at one another in surprise and dismay, and Lythande could almost hear their
thoughts:

*None of us has been able to attract or seduce the great magician, and
this ragged street wench has caught his eyes?* And, being women, Lythande knew they could see the unclouded beauty that shone through
the girl's rags.

"Is Madame Myrtis available, Jiro?"

"She's sleeping, O great wizard, but for you she's given orders she's
to be waked at any hour. Is this—" no one alive can be quite so supercilious as the chief eunuch of a fashionable brothel—"*yours,* Lythande,
or a gift for my madame?"

"Both, perhaps. Give her something to eat and find her a place to
spend the night."

"And a bath, magician? She has fleas enough to louse a floorful of
cushions!"

"A bath, certainly, and a bath-woman with scents and oils," Lythande said, "and something in the nature of a whole garment."

"Leave it to me," said Jiro expansively, and Bercy looked at Lythande in dread, but went when the magician gestured to her to go. As
Jiro took her away, Lythande saw Myrtis standing in the doorway; a
heavy woman, no longer young, but with the frozen beauty of a spell.
Through the perfect spelled features, her eyes were warm and welcoming as she smiled at Lythande.

"My dear, I had not expected to see you here. Is that yours?" She
moved her head toward the door through which Jiro had conducted the
frightened Bercy. "She'll probably run away, you know, once you take
your eyes off her."

"I wish I thought so, Myrtis. But no such luck, I fear."

"You had better tell me the whole story," Myrtis said, and listened to
Lythande's brief, succinct account of the affair.

"And if you laugh, Myrtis, I take back my spell and leave your grey
hairs and wrinkles open to the mockery of everyone in Sanctuary!"

But Myrtis had known Lythande too long to take that threat very
seriously. "So the maiden you rescued is all maddened with desire for
the love of Lythande!" She chuckled. "It is like an old ballad, indeed!"

"But what am I to do, Myrtis? By the paps of Shipri the All-Mother, this is a dilemma!"

"Take her into your confidence and tell her why your love cannot be hers," Myrtis said.

Lythande frowned. "You hold my Secret, since I had no choice; you knew me before I was made magician, or bore the blue star—"

"And before I was a harlot," Myrtis agreed.

"But if I make this girl feel like a fool for loving me, she will hate me as much as she loves; and I cannot confide in anyone I cannot trust with my life and my power. All I have is yours, Myrtis, because of that past we shared. And that includes my power, if you ever should need it. But I cannot entrust it to this girl."

"Still she owes you something, for delivering her out of the hands of Rabben."

Lythande said, "I will think about it; and now make haste to bring me food, for I am hungry and athrist." Taken to a private room, Lythande ate and drank, served by Myrtis's own hands. And Myrtis said, "I could never have sworn your vow—to eat and drink in the sight of no man!"

"If you sought the power of a magician, you would keep it well enough," said Lythande. "I am seldom tempted now to break it; I fear only lest I break it unawares; I cannot drink in a tavern lest among the women there might be some one of those strange men who find diversion in putting on the garments of a female; even here I will not eat or drink among your women, for that reason. All power depends on the vows and the secret."

"Then I cannot aid you," Myrtis said, "but you are not bound to speak truth to her; tell her you have vowed to live without women."

"I may do that," Lythande said, and finished the food, scowling.

Later Bercy was brought in, wide-eyed, enthralled by her fine gown and her freshly washed hair, softly curling about her pink-and-white face and the sweet scent of bath oils and perfumes that hung about her.

"The girls here wear such pretty clothes, and one of them told me they could eat twice a day if they wished! Am I pretty enough, do you think, that Madame Myrtis would have me here?"

"If that is what you wish. You are more than beautiful."

Bercy said boldly, "I would rather belong to *you,* magician," and flung herself again on Lythande, her hands clutching and clinging, dragging the lean face down to hers. Lythande, who rarely touched anything living, held her gently, trying not to reveal consternation.

"Bercy, child, this is only a fancy. It will pass."

"No," she wept. "I love you, I want only you!"

And then, unmistakably, along the magician's nerves, Lythande felt that little ripple, that warning thrill of tension which said: *spellcasting is in use.* Not against Lythande. That could have been countered. But somewhere within the room.

Here, in the Aphrodisia House? Myrtis, Lythande knew, could be trusted with life, reputation, fortune, the magical power of the Blue Star itself; she had been tested before this. Had she altered enough to turn betrayer, it would have been apparent in her aura when Lythande came near.

That left only the girl, who was clinging and whimpering, "I will die if you do not love me! I will die! Tell me it is not true, Lythande, that you are unable to love! Tell me it is an evil lie that magicians are emasculated, incapable of loving woman . . ."

"That is certainly an evil lie," Lythande agreed gravely. "I give you my solemn assurance that I have never been emasculated." But Lythande's nerves tingled as the words were spoken. A magician might lie, and most of them did. Lythande would lie as readily as any other, in a good cause. But the law of the Blue Star was this: when questioned directly on a matter bearing directly on the Secret, the adept might not tell a direct lie. And Bercy, unknowing, was only one question away from the fatal one hiding the Secret.

With a mighty effort, Lythande's magic wrenched at the very fabric of Time itself; the girl stood motionless, aware of no lapse, as Lythande stepped away far enough to read her aura. And yes, there within the traces of that vibrating field, was the shadow of the blue star. Rabben's; overpowering her will.

Rabben. Rabben the Half-handed, who had set his will on the girl, who had staged and contrived the whole thing, including the encounter where the girl had needed rescue; put the girl under a spell to attract and bespell Lythande.

The law of the Blue Star forbade one adept of the Star to kill another; for all would be needed to fight side by side, on the last day, against Chaos. Yet if one adept could prise forth the secret of another's power . . . then the powerless one was not needed against Chaos and could be killed.

What could be done now? Kill the girl? Rabben would take that, too, as an answer; Bercy had been so bespelled as to be irresistible to any man; if Lythande sent her away untouched, Rabben would know that

Lythande's secret lay in that area and would never rest in his attempts to uncover it. For if Lythande was untouched by this sex-spell to make Bercy irresistible, then Lythande was a eunuch, or a homosexual, or . . . sweating, Lythande dared not even think beyond that. The Secret was safe only if never questioned. It would not be read in the aura; but one simple question, and all was ended.

*I should kill her,* Lythande thought. *For now I am fighting, not for my magic alone, but for my secret and for my life. For surely, with my power gone, Rabben would lose no time in making an end of me, in revenge for the loss of half a hand.*

The girl was still motionless, entranced. How easily she could be killed! Then Lythande recalled an old fairy-tale, which might be used to save the Secret of the Star.

The light flickered as Time returned to the chamber. Bercy was still clinging and weeping, unaware of the lapse; Lythande had resolved what to do, and the girl felt Lythande's arms enfolding her, and the magician's kiss on her welcoming mouth.

"You must love me or I shall die!" Bercy wept.

Lythande said, "You shall be mine." The soft neutral voice was very gentle. "But even a magician is vulnerable in love, and I must protect myself. A place shall be made ready for us without light or sound save for what I provide with my magic; and you must swear that you will not seek to see or to touch me except by that magical light. Will you swear it by the All-Mother, Bercy? For if you swear this, I shall love you as no woman has ever been loved before."

Trembling, she whispered, "I swear." And Lythande's heart went out in pity, for Rabben had used her ruthlessly; so that she burned alive with her unslaked and bewitched love for the magician, that she was all caught up in her passion for Lythande. Painfully, Lythande thought; *if she had only loved me, without the spell; then I could have loved . . .*

*Would that I could trust her with my secret! But she is only Rabben's tool; her love for me is his doing, and none of her own will . . . and not real . . .* And so everything which would pass between them now must be only a drama staged for Rabben.

"I shall make all ready for you with my magic."

Lythande went and confided to Myrtis what was needed; the woman began to laugh, but a single glance at Lythande's bleak face stopped her cold. She had known Lythande since long before the blue star was set between those eyes; and she kept the Secret for love of Lythande. It wrung her heart to see one she loved in the grip of such suffering. So

she said, "All will be prepared. Shall I give her a drug in her wine to
weaken her will, that you may the more readily throw a glamour upon
her?"

Lythande's voice held a terrible bitterness. "Rabben has done that already for us, when he put a spell upon her to love me."

"You would have it otherwise?" Myrtis asked, hesitating.

"All the gods of Sanctuary—they laugh at me! All-Mother, help
me! But I would have it otherwise; I could love her, if she were not
Rabben's tool."

When all was prepared, Lythande entered the darkened room. There
was no light but the light of the Blue Star. The girl lay on a bed,
stretching up her arms to the magician with exalted abandon.

"Come to me, come to me, my love!"

"Soon," said Lythande, sitting beside her, stroking her hair with a
tenderness even Myrtis would never have guessed. "I will sing to you a
love-song of my people, far away."

She writhed in erotic ecstasy. "All you do is good to me, my love, my
magician!"

Lythande felt the blankness of utter despair. She was beautiful, and
she was in love. She lay in a bed spread for the two of them, and they
were separated by the breadth of the world. The magician could not endure it.

Lythande sang, in that rich and beautiful voice; a voice lovelier than
any spell;

> *Half the night is spent; and the crown of moonlight*
> *Fades, and now the crown of the stars is paling;*
> *Yields the sky reluctant to coming morning;*
> *Still I lie lonely.*
> *I will love you as no woman has ever been loved.*

Lythande could see tears on Bercy's cheeks.

Between the girl on the bed, and the motionless form of the magician, as the magician's robe fell heavily to the floor, a wraith-form grew,
the very wraith and fetch, at first, of Lythande, tall and lean, with blazing eyes and a star between its brows and a body white and unscarred;
the form of the magician, but this one triumphant in virility, advancing
on the motionless woman, waiting. Her mind fluttered away in arousal,
was caught, captured, bespelled. Lythande let her see the image for a
moment; she could not see the true Lythande behind; then, as her eyes

closed in ecstatic awareness of the touch, Lythande smoothed light fingers over her closed eyes.

"See—what I bid you to see!

"Hear—what I bid you hear!

"Feel—only what I bid you feel, Bercy!"

And now she was wholly under the spell of the wraith. Unmoving, stony-eyed, Lythande watched as her lips closed on emptiness and she kissed invisible lips; and moment by moment Lythande knew what touched her, what caressed her. Rapt and ravished by illusion, that brought her again and again to the heights of ecstasy, till she cried out in abandonment. Only to Lythande that cry was bitter; for she cried out not to Lythande but to the man-wraith who possessed her.

At last she lay all but unconscious, satiated; and Lythande watched in agony. When she opened her eyes again, Lythande was looking down at her, sorrowfully.

Bercy stretched up languid arms. "Truly, my beloved, you have loved me as no woman has ever been loved before."

For the first and last time, Lythande bent over her and pressed her lips in a long, infinitely tender kiss. "Sleep, my darling."

And as she sank into ecstatic, exhausted sleep, Lythande wept.

Long before she woke, Lythande stood, girt for travel, in the little room belonging to Myrtis.

"The spell will hold. She will make all haste to carry her tale to Rabben—the tale of Lythande, the incomparable lover! Of Lythande, of untiring virility, who can love a maiden into exhaustion!" The rich voice of Lythande was harsh with bitterness.

"And long before you return to Sanctuary, once freed of the spell, she will have forgotten you in many other lovers," Myrtis agreed. "It is better and safer that it should be so."

"True." But Lythande's voice broke. "Take care of her, Myrtis. Be kind to her."

"I swear it, Lythande."

"If only she could have loved *me*"—the magician broke and sobbed again for a moment; Myrtis looked away, wrung with pain, knowing not what comfort to offer.

"If only she could have loved me as I am, freed of Rabben's spell! Loved me without pretense! But I feared I could not master the spell Rabben had put on her . . . nor trust her not to betray me, knowing . . ."

Myrtis put her plump arms around Lythande, tenderly.

"Do you regret?"

The question was ambiguous. It might have meant: *Do you regret that you did not kill the girl?* Or even: *Do you regret your oath and the secret you must bear to the last day?* Lythande chose to answer the last.

"Regret? How can I regret? One day I shall fight against Chaos with all of my order; even at the side of Rabben, if he lives unmurdered as long as that. And that alone must justify my existence and my secret. But now I must leave Sanctuary, and who knows when the chances of the world will bring me this way again? Kiss me farewell, my sister."

Myrtis stood on tiptoe. Her lips met the lips of the magician.

"Until we meet again, Lythande. May She attend and guard you forever. Farewell, my beloved, my sister."

Then the magician Lythande girded on her sword, and went silently and by unseen ways out of the city of Sanctuary, just as the dawn was breaking. And on her forehead the glow of the Blue Star was dimmed by the rising sun. Never once did she look back.

# The Making of Thieves' World

## Robert Lynn Asprin

*It was a dark and stormy night . . .*

Actually, that Thursday night before Boskone '78 was a very pleasant night. Lynn Abbey, Gordy Dickson, and I were enjoying a quiet dinner in the Boston Sheraton's Mermaid Restaurant prior to the chaos which inevitably surrounds a major science fiction convention.

As so often happens when several authors gather socially, the conversation turned to the subject of writing in general and specifically to problems encountered and pet peeves. Not to be outdone by my dinner companions, I voiced one of my long-standing gripes: that whenever one set out to write heroic fantasy, it was first necessary to reinvent the universe from scratch regardless of what had gone before. Despite the carefully crafted Hyborean world of Howard or even the delightfully complex town of Lankhmar which Leiber created, every author was expected to beat his head against the writing table and devise a world of his own. Imagine, I proposed, if our favorite sword-and-sorcery characters shared the same settings and time-frames. Imagine the story potentials. Imagine the tie-ins. What if . . .

What if Fafhrd and Mouser had just finished a successful heist. With an angry crowd on their heels, they pull one of their notorious double-back escapes and elude the pursuing throng. Now suppose this angry, torch-waving pack runs headlong into Conan, hot and tired from the trail, his dead horse a day's walk behind him. All he wants is a jug of wine and a wench. Instead, he's confronted with a lynch mob. What if his saddlebags are full of loot from one of his own ventures, yet undiscovered?

Or what if Kane and Elric took jobs marshaling opposite armies in the same war?

Why, I proclaimed, the possibilities are endless. Pouring a little more wine, I admitted that one of my pet projects under consideration was to do a collection of fantasy stories featuring not one, but an array of central characters. They would all share the same terrain and be peripherally aware of each other's existence as their paths crossed. The only problem: my writing schedule was filling up so fast I wasn't sure when or if I'd ever get a chance to write it.

More wine flowed.

Gordy sympathized eloquently, pointing out that this was a problem all writers encountered as they grew more and more successful. Time! Time to fulfill your commitments and still be able to write the fun things you really want to write. As an example, he pointed out that there were countless story potentials in his Dorsai universe, but that he was barely able to find the time to complete the Childe Cycle novels, much less pursue all the spinoffs.

More wine flowed.

The ideal thing, Lynn suggested, was to be able to franchise one's ideas and worlds out to other authors. The danger there, Gordy pointed out, was the danger of losing control. None of us were particularly wild about letting any Tom, Dick, or Harry play around with our pet ideas.

More wine flowed.

Anthologies! If we went to an anthology format, we could invite authors to participate, as well as having final say as to the acceptability of the stories submitted.

Gordy ordered a bottle of champagne.

Of course, he observed, you'll be able to get some topflight authors for this because it'll be fun. They'll do it more for the love of the idea than for the money.

I remarked on the ease with which *"our"* idea had become *"my"* anthology. As the weight of the project had suddenly come to rest on my shoulders, I asked whether he intended to assist or at least contribute to the anthology. His reply set the classic pattern for nearly all the contributors to *Thieves' World:*

I'd love to, but I don't have the time. It's a lovely idea, though.

(Five minutes later) I just thought of a character who would fit into this perfectly.

(Fifteen minutes later . . . thoughtful stare into nothingness converting into a smug grin) I've got my story!

During this last exchange, Lynn was saying very little. Unbeknownst to me, she had mentally dealt herself out of the project when Gordy proposed "established writers only." At that point in time, she had in her suitcase the manuscript for *Daughter of the Bright Moon,* hoping to find an interested editor at Boskone. She was far from being "established." It is to her credit, however, that she successfully hid her disappointment at being excluded, and accompanied Gordy and me as we finished the last of the champagne and went "trolling for editors."

It may seem to you that it was rather early to try to find a publisher for such a nebulous work. That's how it struck me at the time. Gordy pointed out, however, that if we could find an editor and nudge him into an appraisal of the dollar value of the idea, I would have a better feel for what my budget would be when I went to line up my authors. (The fact that this made sense to me at the time will serve as an indication of the lateness of the hour and the amount of wine we had consumed.)

To this end, we devised a subtle tactic. We would try to find an author and an editor in the same room, preferably in the same conversation. We would then pitch the idea to the author as a potential contributor and see if the editor showed interest.

We found such a duo and launched into our song and dance. The editor yawned, but the author thought it was a great idea. Of course, he didn't have the time to write anything. . . . Then he thought of a character! That's how John Brunner came on board.

The next morning, the effects of our dinner wine dissipated and I began to realize what I had let myself in for. A brand-new author, barely published, and I was going to try to edit an anthology? Soliciting contributions from the best in the field, yet! That revelation sobered me up faster than a bucket of ice water and a five-day hotel bill.

Still, the ball was already rolling, and I had story commitments from Gordy and John. I might as well see how far things could go.

FRIDAY: I ambushed Joe Haldeman over a glass of lunch. He thought it was a terrific idea, but he didn't have any time. Besides, he pointed out, he had never written heroic fantasy. I countered by reminding him of his stay in Viet Nam, courtesy of the U.S. Army. Surely, I pressed, there must be one or two characters he had encountered who would fit into a sword-and-sorcery setting with minimal rewriting. His eyes cleared. He had his character.

SATURDAY: I finally found out what was bothering Lynn and assured her of a place on the *Thieves' World* roster. I was confident she would be "established" before the anthology came out, and even if she wasn't, I knew she could produce a solid story. No, I don't have a crystal ball. Lynn and I both live in Ann Arbor and share workspace when we're writing. As such, I had been reading the manuscript of *Daughter of the Bright Moon* as she was writing it, and knew her writing style even before the editors saw it. [My prophecy proved correct. Ace/Sunridge bought her manuscript, and a major promo campaign is currently underway. The book should be on the stands when you see this anthology.]

SUNDAY: Wonder of wonders. Over cognac at the Ace dead-dog party, Jim Baen expresses a solid interest in the anthology . . . *if* I succeed in filling the remaining slots with authors of an equal quality as those already committed. Leaving the party, I encounter Jim Odbert in the hall and do a little bragging. He brings me down to earth by asking about the street map. I hadn't even thought about it, but he was right! It would be absolutely necessary for internal continuity. Thinking fast, I commission him on the spot and retire, harboring a nagging hunch that this project might be a bit more involved than I had imagined.

Back in Ann Arbor, I face the task of filling the remaining openings for the anthology. My magic wand for this feat is a telephone. Having been a fan for many years, I have had passing contact with several prominent authors, many of whom don't know that I'm writing now. I figure it will be easier to jog their memories over the phone than trying to do the same thing by letter.

The problem now is . . . who? Solid authors . . . that's a must. Authors who know me well enough that they won't hang up when I call. Authors who *don't* know me so well that they'll hang up when I call.

Andy! Andy Offutt. Our paths had crossed several times at cons, and I know we share a mutual admiration of Genghis Khan.

Andy doesn't have any time, but is super enthusiastic over the idea and has his character. Yes, that's all one sentence. If anything, I've condensed it. If you've ever talked to Andy on the phone, you'll understand.

Next will be Poul Anderson. Poul and I know each other mostly by reputation through Gordy and through a medieval reenactment organization known as the Society for Creative Anachronism, Inc. Sir Bela of Eastmarch and Yang the Nauseating. Hooboy, do we know each other. In spite of that, Poul agrees to do a story for me . . . if he gets the time . . . in fact, he has a character in mind.

The list is growing. Confident now that the impressive array of authors submitting stories will offset my own relative obscurity, I go for a few who may not remember me.

Roger Zelazny was Pro Guest of Honor at a convention in Little Rock, Arkansas, where I was Fan Guest of Honor. He remembers and listens to my pitch.

I spoke briefly with Marion Zimmer Bradley about the swordwork in *Hunter of the Red Moon*—when we passed in the hall at a Wester-Con in Los Angeles—two years ago. She remembers me and listens to my pitch.

Philip José Farmer and I have seen each other twice: once in Milwaukee and once in Minneapolis. Both times we were at opposite ends of a table with half a dozen people crowded between us. He acknowledges the memory, then listens in silence for fifteen minutes while I do my spiel. When I finally grind to a halt, he says okay and hangs up. I find out later that this is his way of expressing enthusiasm. If he hadn't been enthusiastic, he would have said no and hung up.

By this time it's Minicon. Jim Odbert passes me a set of maps. Then he, Gordy, Joe, Lynn, and I sit around half the night discussing the history of the city and the surrounding continent. A set of house rules is devised and agreed upon: (1) Each contributor is to send me a brief description of the main character of his/her story. (2) These descriptions will be copied and distributed to the other contributors. (3) Any author can use these characters in his/her story, providing they're not killed off or noticeably reformed.

I run all this through a typewriter and mail it out to all the contributors. It occurs to me that this isn't nearly as difficult as I had feared. My only worry is that the mails might slow communication with John Brunner in England, causing him to be late with his submission. Except for that, everything was going fine.

Then the fun began . . .

Andy, Poul, and John all send me notes in varying degrees of gentleness correcting my grammar and/or word usage in the flier. They are willing to accept without confirmation that my spelling was intended as a joke. These are the people I'm supposed to be editing! Riiiiight!

Poul sends me a copy of his essay, "On Thud and Blunder," to ensure the realism of the setting, particularly the economic structure of the town. He also wants to know about the judicial system in Sanctuary.

Andy wants to know about the deities worshiped, preferably broken down by nationality and economic class of worshipers. Fortunately, he includes a proposed set of gods, which I gleefully copy and send to the other contributors. He heads his ten-page letters with "To Colossus: The Asprin Project." It occurs to me that with his own insight as an anthology editor, this could be more truth than humor.

To make my job a little easier, some of the authors start playing poker with their character sketches: "I won't show you mine till you show me yours." They delay submitting their sketches until they see what the other authors turn in. One of these is Gordy. Remember him? He's the one who got me into this in the first place. He's the one who "had his character" before there was an anthology! Terrific!

John Brunner submits his story—a full year before the stated deadline. So much for transatlantic delays. I haven't gotten all the character descriptions yet. More important, I haven't gotten the advance money yet! His agent begins to prod gently for payment.

Roger reappraises his time commitments and withdraws from the project. Oh, well. You can't win them all.

Poul wants to know about the architectural style of Sanctuary.

Andy and Poul want to know about the structure and nationality of names.

A call comes in from Ace. Jim Baen wants the manuscript a full three months ahead of the contracted deadline. I point out that this is impossible—the new deadline would give me only two weeks between receiving the stories from the authors and submitting the complete manuscript to New York. If I encountered difficulties with any of the stories or if any of the submissions came in late, it would disrupt the schedule completely. They point out that if I can meet the new schedule, they'll make it their lead book for the month it's released. The avaricious side of me is screaming, but I stick to my guns and repeat that it's impossible to guarantee. They offer a contract for a second *Thieves' World* anthology, suggesting that if a couple stories are late, I can include them in the next book. Under attack now both from my publisher and my own greedy nature, I roll my eyes heavenward, swallow hard, and agree.

A new note is rapidly dispatched to the contributors, politely reminding them of the approaching deadline. Also included is Gordy's character sketch for Jamie the Red which he had finally submitted under mild duress (his arm will heal eventually).

Andy calls and wants to know the Prince's name. I haven't given it any thought, but am willing to negotiate. An hour later, I hang up. It occurs to me that I haven't written my story yet.

Gordy notifies me that he can't get his story done in time for the first book. Terrific! With Gordy and Roger both out of the first volume, it's starting to look a little short.

Andy's story comes in, as does Joe's and Poul's.

Andy's story includes a discussion with Joe's One-Thumb character. Joe has killed One-Thumb off in his story. A minor sequencing problem.

Poul's story has Cappen Varra going off on an adventure with Gordy's Jamie the Red. Gordie's Jamie the Red story won't be in the first book! A major sequencing problem! Oh, well. I owe Gordy one for talking me into editing this monster.

I look at the stories already in the bin and decide that the first draft of my story needs some drastic rewriting.

A note arrives from Phil Farmer. He had sent me a letter months ago, which apparently never arrived, withdrawing from the project. (It hadn't!) Realizing that withdrawing at this late date would leave me in a bad spot, he is now rearranging his writing schedule in order to send me "something." Of course, it will be a little late. I am grateful, but panicky.

Lynn finishes her story and starts to gloat. I threaten to beat her head in with my Selectric.

Ace calls again. They want additional information for the cover copy. They also want a word count. I explain the situation as calmly as I can. Halfway through my explanation, the phone melts.

Ma Bell fixes my phone in record time (I am rapidly becoming their favorite customer), and I hurriedly call Marion to ask for a rough word count on her unsubmitted story. She tells me she sent me a letter which must not have arrived. (It didn't.) She tells me she'll have to withdraw from the project because of time pressures in her other writing commitments. She tells me to stop gibbering and say something. I calm myself and explain I'd *really* like to have a story from her. I explain I really *need* her story. I mention that her character is on the cover of the book. She observes that the water gushing from the phone is threatening to flood her living room and agrees to try to squeeze the story into her writing schedule . . . before she flies to London in two weeks.

With steady hand but trembling mind, I call Ace and ask for Jim Baen. I explain the situation: I have six stories in hand (yes, I finally finished mine) and two more on the way . . . a little late . . . maybe. He informs me that with just six stories the book will be too short. He wants at least one more story and an essay from me about how much fun it was to edit the anthology. To calm my hysterics, he suggests I commission a backup story in case the two en route don't arrive in time. I point out that there are only two weeks remaining before the deadline. He concedes that with such a limited time-frame, I probably won't be able to get a story from a "name" author. He'll let me work with an "unknown," but the story had better be good!

Christine DeWees is a kindly, white-haired grandmother who rides a Harley and wants to be a writer. Lynn and I have been criticizing her efforts for some time and have repeatedly encouraged her to submit something to an editor. So far, she has resisted our proddings, insisting that she would be embarrassed to show her work to a professional editor. I decide to kill two birds with one stone.

In my most disarming "nothing can go wrong" tones, I give my spiel to Christine and pass her a *Thieves' World* package. Three hours later, my phone rings. Christine loves the character of Myrtis, the madam of the Aphrodisia House and is ready to do a story centering around her. I stammer politely and point out that Myrtis is one of Marion's characters and that she might object to someone else writing her characters. Christine cackles and tells me she's already cleared it with Marion (don't ask me how she got the phone number!), and everything is effervescent. Two days later, she hands me the story, and I still haven't gotten around to looking up "effervescent" in the dictionary.

With seven stories now in hand, I declare *Thieves' World I* to be complete and begin writing my "fun fun" essay. The stories from Marion and Phil can wait until the second book.

Then Marion's story arrives.

Marion's story interfaces so nicely with Christine's that I decide to use them both in the first book. Rather than cut one of the other stories, the volume is assembled with intros, maps, eight stories, and essay, crated, and shipped off to New York.

Endo volume one! Print it!

The whole whirlwind process of editing this monster child was only vaguely as I had imagined it would be. Still, in hindsight, I loved it. With all the worries and panics, the skyhigh phone bills and the higher bar bills, I loved every minute. I find myself actually looking forward to the next volume . . . and that's what worries me!

# Tales from the Vulgar Unicorn

# Contents

# Introduction

Moving his head with minute care to avoid notice, Hakiem the Story-teller studied the room over the untouched rim of his wine cup. This was, of course, done through slitted eyes. It would not do to have any-one suspect he was not truly asleep. What he saw only confirmed his growing feelings of disgust.

The Vulgar Unicorn was definitely going downhill. A drunk was snoring on the floor against the wall, passed out in a puddle of his own vomit, while several beggars made their way from table to table, inter-rupting the undertoned negotiations and hagglings of the tavern's nor-mal clientele.

Though his features never moved, Hakiem grimaced inside. Such go-ings on were never tolerated when One-Thumb was around. The bar-tender/owner of the Vulgar Unicorn had always been quick to evict such riffraff as fast as they appeared. While the tavern had always been shunned by the more law-abiding citizens of Sanctuary, one of the main reasons it was favored by the rougher element was that here a man could partake of a drink or perhaps a little larcenous conversation unin-terrupted. This tradition was rapidly coming to an end.

The fact that he would not be allowed to linger for hours over a cup of the tavern's cheapest wine if One-Thumb were here never entered Hakiem's mind. He had a skill. He was a storyteller, a tale-spinner, a weaver of dreams and nightmares. As such, he considered himself on a measurably better plane than the derelicts who had taken to frequenting the place.

One-Thumb had been missing for a long time now, longer than any of his previous mysterious disappearances. Fear of his return kept the tavern open and the employees honest, but the place was degenerating in his absence. The only way it could sink any lower would be if a Hell-Hound took to drinking here.

Despite his guise of slumber, Hakiem found himself smiling at that thought. A Hell-Hound in the Vulgar Unicorn! Unlikely at best. Sanctuary still chafed at the occupying force from the Rankan Empire, and the five Hell-Hounds were hated second only to the military governor, Prince Kadakithis, who they guarded. Though it was a close choice between Prince Kittycat with his naive lawmaking and the elite soldiers who enforced his words, the citizens of Sanctuary generally felt the military governor's quest to clean up the worst hellhole in the empire was stupid, while the Hell-Hounds were simply devilishly efficient. In a town where one was forced to live by wit as often as skill, efficiency could be grudgingly admired, while stupidity, particularly stupidity with power, could only be despised.

No, the Hell-Hounds weren't stupid. Tough, excellent swordsmen and seasoned veterans, they seldom set foot in the Maze, and never entered the Vulgar Unicorn. On the west side of town, it was said that one only came here if he was seeking death . . . or selling it. While the statement was somewhat exaggerated, it was true that most of the people who frequented the Maze either had nothing to lose or were willing to risk everything for what they might gain there. As rational men, the Hell-Hounds were unlikely to put in an appearance at the Maze's most notorious tavern.

Still, the point remained that the Vulgar Unicorn sorely needed One-Thumb's presence and that his return was long overdue. In part, that was why Hakiem was spending so much time here of late: hope of acquiring the story of One-Thumb's return and possibly the story of his absence. That alone would be enough to keep the storyteller haunting the tavern, but the stories he gained during his wait were a prize in themselves. Hakiem was a compulsive collector of stories, from habit as well as by profession, and many stories had their beginnings, middles, or ends within these walls. He collected them all, though he knew that most of them could not be repeated, for he knew the value of a story is in its merit, not in its saleability.

# Spiders of the Purple Mage

## Philip José Farmer

## 1

This was the week of the great rat hunt in Sanctuary.

The next week, all the cats that could be caught were killed and degutted.

The third week, all dogs were run down and disembowelled.

Masha zil-Ineel was one of the very few people in the city who didn't take part in the rat hunt. She just couldn't believe that any rat, no matter how big, and there were some huge ones in Sanctuary, could swallow a jewel so large.

But when a rumor spread that someone had seen a cat eat a dead rat and that the cat had acted strangely afterward, she thought it wise to pretend to chase cats. If she hadn't, people might wonder why not. They might think that she knew something they didn't. And then she might be the one run down.

Unlike the animals, however, she'd be tortured until she told where the jewel was.

She didn't know where it was. She wasn't even sure that there *was* an emerald.

But everybody knew that she'd been told about the jewel by Benna nus-Katarz. Thanks to Masha's blabbermouth drunken husband, Eevroen.

Three weeks ago, on a dark night, Masha had returned late from midwifing in the rich merchants' eastern quarter. It was well past midnight, but she wasn't sure of the hour because of the cloud-covered sky. The second wife of Shoozh the spice-importer had borne her fourth infant. Masha had attended to the delivery personally while Doctor Nadeesh had sat in the next room, the door only half-closed, and listened to her reports. Nadeesh was forbidden to see any part of a female client except for those normally exposed and especially forbidden to see the breasts and genitals. If there was any trouble with the birthing, Masha would inform him, and he would give her instructions.

This angered Masha, since the doctors collected half of the fee, yet were seldom of any use. In fact, they were usually a hindrance.

Still, half a fee was better than none. What if the wives and concubines of the wealthy were as nonchalant and hardy as the poor women, who just squatted down wherever they happened to be when the pangs started and gave birth unassisted? Masha could not have supported herself, her two daughters, her invalid mother, or her lazy alcoholic husband. The money she made from doing the more affluent women's hair and from her tooth-pulling and manufacture of false teeth in the marketplace wasn't enough. But midwifery added the income that kept her and her family just outside hunger's door.

She would have liked to pick up more money by cutting men's hair in the marketplace, but both law and ancient custom forbade that.

Shortly after she had burned the umbilical cord of the newborn to ensure that demons didn't steal it and had ritualistically washed her hands, she left Shoozh's house. His guards, knowing her, let her through the gate without challenge, and the guards of the gate to the eastern quarters also allowed her to pass. Not however without offers from a few to share their beds with her that night.

"I can do much better than that sot of a husband of yours!" one said.

Masha was glad that her hood and the darkness prevented the guards from seeing her burning face by the torchlight. However, if they could have seen that she was blushing with shame, they might have been embarrassed. They would know then that they weren't dealing with a brazen slut of the Maze but with a woman who had known better days and a higher position in society than she now held. The blush alone would have told them that.

What they didn't know and what she couldn't forget was that she had once lived in this walled area and her father had been an affluent, if not wealthy, merchant.

She passed on silently. It would have made her feel good to have told them her past and then ripped them with the invective she'd learned in the Maze. But to do that would lower her estimate of herself.

Though she had her own torch and the means for lighting it in the cylindrical leather case on her back, she did not use them. It was better to walk unlit and hence unseen into the streets. Though many of the lurkers in the shadows would let her pass unmolested, since they had known her when she was a child, others would not be so kind. They would rob her for the tools of her trade and the clothes she wore and some would rape her. Or try to.

Through the darkness she went swiftly, her steps sure because of long experience. The adobe buildings of the city were a dim whitish bulk ahead. Then the path took a turn, and she saw some small flickers of light here and there. Torches. A little further, and a light became a square. The window of a tavern.

She entered a narrow winding street and strode down its center. Turning a corner, she saw a torch in a bracket on the wall of a house and two men standing near it. Immediately she crossed to the far side and, hugging the walls, passed the two. Their pipes glowed redly; she caught a whiff of the pungent and sickly smoke of *kleetel,* the drug used by the poor when they didn't have money for the more expensive *krrf.* Which was most of the time.

After two or three pipefuls, the smokers would be vomiting. But they would claim that the euphoria would make the upchucking worth it.

There were other odors: garbage piled by the walls, slop jars of excrement, and puke from *kleetel* smokers and drunks. The garbage would be shoveled into goat-drawn carts by Downwinders whose families had long held this right. The slop-jars would be emptied by a Downwinder family that had delivered the contents to farmers for a century and would and had fought fiercely to keep this right. The farmers would use the excrement to feed their soil; the urine would be emptied into the mouth of the White Foal River and carried out to sea.

She also heard the rustling and squealing of rats as they searched for edible portions and dogs growling or snarling as they chased the rats or fought each other. And she glimpsed the swift shadows of running cats.

Like a cat, she sped down the street in a half-run, stopping at corners to look around them before venturing farther. When she was about a half-mile from her place, she heard the pounding of feet ahead. She froze and tried to make herself look like part of the wall.

2

At that moment the moon broke through the clouds.

It was almost a full moon. The light revealed her to any but a blind person. She darted across the street to the dark side and played wall again.

The slap of feet on the hard-packed dirt of the street came closer. Somewhere above her, a baby began crying.

She pulled a long knife from a scabbard under her cloak and held the blade behind her. Doubtless, the one running was a thief or else someone trying to outrun a thief or mugger or muggers or perhaps a throat-slitter. If it was a thief who was getting away from the site of the crime, she would be safe. He'd be in no position to stop to see what he could get from her. If he was being pursued, the pursuers might shift their attention to her.

If they saw her.

Suddenly, the pound of feet became louder. Around the corner came a tall youth dressed in a ragged tunic and breeches and shod with buskins. He stopped and clutched the corner and looked behind him. His breath rasped like a rusty gate swung back and forth by gusts of wind.

Somebody was after him. Should she wait here? He hadn't seen her, and perhaps whoever was chasing him would be so intent he or they wouldn't detect her either.

The youth turned his face, and she gasped. His face was so swollen that she almost didn't recognize him. But he was Benna nus-Katarz, who had come here from Ilsig two years ago. No one knew why he'd immigrated, and no one, in keeping with the unwritten code of Sanctuary, had asked him why.

Even in the moonlight and across the street, she could see the swellings and dark spots, looking like bruises, on his face. And on his hands. The fingers were rotting bananas.

He turned back to peer around the corner. His breathing became less heavy. Now she could hear the faint slap of feet down the street. His chasers would be here soon.

Benna gave a soft ululation of despair. He staggered down the street toward a mound of garbage and stopped before it. A rat scuttled out but stopped a few feet from him and chittered at him. Bold beasts, the rats of Sanctuary.

Now Masha could hear the loudness of approaching runners and words that sounded like sheets being ripped apart.

Benna moaned. He reached under his tunic with clumsy fingers and drew something out. Masha couldn't see what it was, though she strained. She inched with her back to the wall toward a doorway. Its darkness would make her even more undetectable.

Benna looked at the thing in his hand. He said something which sounded to Masha like a curse. She couldn't be sure; he spoke in the Ilsig dialect.

The baby above had ceased crying; its mother must have given it the nipple or perhaps she'd made it drink water tinctured with a drug.

Now Benna was pulling something else from inside his tunic. Whatever it was, he molded it around the other thing, and now he had cast it in front of the rat.

The big gray beast ran away as the object arced toward him. A moment later, it approached the little ball, sniffing. Then it darted forward, still smelling it, touched it with its nose, perhaps tasted it, and was gone with it in its mouth.

Masha watched it squeeze into a crack in the old adobe building at the next corner. No one lived there. It had been crumbling, falling down for years, unrepaired and avoided even by the most desperate of transients and bums. It was said that the ghost of old Lahboo the Tight-Fisted haunted the place since his murder, and no one cared to test the truth of the stories told about the building.

Benna, still breathing somewhat heavily, trotted after the rat. Masha, hearing that the footsteps were louder, went alongside the wall, still in the shadows. She was curious about what Benna had gotten rid of, but she didn't want to be associated with him in any way when his hunters caught up with him.

At the corner, the youth stopped and looked around him. He didn't seem able to make up his mind which route to take. He stood, swaying, and then fell to his knees. He groaned, and pitched forward, softening his fall with outstretched arms.

Masha meant to leave him to his fate. It was the only sensible thing to do. But as she rounded the corner, she heard him moaning. And then she thought she heard him say something about a jewel.

She stopped. Was that what he had put in something, perhaps a bit of cheese, and thrown to the rat? It would be worth more money than she'd earn in a lifetime, and if she could, somehow, get her hands on it. . . . Her thoughts raced as swiftly as her heart, and now she was breathing heavily. A jewel! A jewel? It would mean release from this terrible place, a good home for her mother and her children. And for herself.

And it might mean release from Eevroen.

But there was also a terrible danger very close. She couldn't hear the sounds of the pursuers now, but that didn't mean they'd left the neighborhood. They were prowling around, looking into each doorway. Or perhaps one had looked around the corner and seen Benna. He had motioned to the others, and they were just behind the corner, getting ready to make a sudden rush.

She could visualize the knives in their hands.

If she took a chance and lost, she'd die, and her mother and daughters would be without support. They'd have to beg; Eevroen certainly would be of no help. And Handoo and Kheem, three and five years old, would grow up, if they didn't die first, to be child whores. It was almost inevitable.

While she stood undecided, knowing that she had only a few seconds to act and perhaps not that, the clouds slid below the moon again. That made the difference in what she'd do. She ran across the street toward Benna. He was still lying in the dirt of the street, his head only a few inches from some stinking dog turds. She scabbarded her dagger, got down on her knees, and rolled him over. He gasped with terror when he felt her hands upon him.

"It's all right!" she said softly. "Listen! Can you get up if I help you? I'll get you away!"

Sweat poured into her eyes as she looked toward the far corner. She could see nothing, but if the hunters wore black, they wouldn't be visible at this distance.

Benna moaned and then said, "I'm dying, Masha."

Masha gritted her teeth. She had hoped that he'd not recognize her voice, not at least until she'd gotten him to safety. Now, if the hunters found him alive and got her name from him, they'd come after her. They'd think she had the jewel or whatever it was they wanted.

"Here. Get up," she said, and struggled to help him. She was small, about five feet tall and weighing eighty-two pounds. But she had the muscles of a cat, and fear was pumping strength into her. She managed to get Benna to his feet. Staggering under his weight, she supported him toward the open doorway of the building on the corner.

Benna reeked of something strange, an odor of rotting meat but unlike any she'd ever smelled. It rode over the stale sweat and urine of his body and clothes.

"No use," Benna mumbled through greatly swollen lips. "I'm dying. The pain is terrible, Masha."

"Keep going!" she said fiercely. "We're almost there!"

Banna raised his head. His eyes were surrounded with puffed-out flesh. Masha had never seen such edema; the blackness and the swelling looked like those of a corpse five days dead in the heat of summer.

"No!" he mumbled. "Not old Lahboo's building!"

3

Under other circumstances, Masha would have laughed. Here was a dying man or a man who thought he was dying. And he'd be dead soon if his pursuers caught up with him. (Me, too, she thought.) Yet he was afraid to take the only refuge available because of a ghost.

"You look bad enough to scare even The Tight-Fisted One," she said. "Keep going or I'll drop you right now!"

She got him inside the doorway, though it wasn't easy what with the boards still attached to the lower half of the entrance. The top planks had fallen inside. It was a tribute to the fear people felt for this place that no one had stolen the wood, an expensive item in the desert town.

Just after they'd climbed over, Benna almost falling, she heard a man utter something in the raspy tearing language. He was nearby, but he must have just arrived. Otherwise, he would have heard the two.

Masha had thought she'd reached the limits of terror, but she found that she hadn't. The speaker was a Raggah!

Though she couldn't understand the speech—no one in Sanctuary could—she'd heard Raggah a number of times. Every thirty days or so five or six of the cloaked, robed, hooded, and veiled desert men came to the bazaar and the farmers' market. They could speak only their own language, but they used signs and a plentitude of coins to obtain what they wanted. Then they departed on their horses, their mules loaded down with food, wine, *vuksibah* (the very expensive malt whiskey imported from a far north land), goods of various kinds: clothing, bowls, braziers, ropes, camel and horse hides. Their camels bore huge panniers full of feed for chickens, ducks, camels, horses, and hogs. They also purchased steel tools: shovels, picks, drills, hammers, wedges.

They were tall, and though they were very dark, most had blue or green eyes. These looked cold and hard and piercing, and few looked directly into them. It was said that they had the gift, or the curse, of the evil eye.

They were enough, in this dark night, to have made Masha marble with terror. But what was worse, and this galvanized the marble, they were the servants of the purple mage!

Masha guessed at once what had happened. Benna had had the guts— and the complete stupidity—to sneak into the underground maze of the mage on the river isle of Shugthee and to steal a jewel. It was amazing that he'd had the courage, astounding that he could get undetected into the caves, an absolute wonder that he'd penetrated the treasurehold, and fantastic that he'd managed to get out. What weird tales he could tell if he survived! Masha could think of no similar event, no analog, to the adventures he must have had.

"*Mofandsf!*" she thought. In the thieves' argot of Sanctuary, "Mind-boggling!"

At that moment Benna's knees gave, and it was all she could do to hold him up. Somehow, she got him to the door to the next room and into a closet. If the Raggah came in, they would look here, of course, but she could get him no further.

Benna's odor was even more sickening in the hot confines of the closet, though its door was almost completely open. She eased him down. He mumbled, "Spiders . . . spiders."

She put her mouth close to his ear. "Don't talk loudly, Benna. The Raggah are close by. Benna, what did you say about the spiders?"

"Bites . . . bites," he murmured. "Hurt . . . the . . . the emerald . . . rich. . . !"

"How'd you get in?" she said. She put her hand close to his mouth to clamp down on it if he should start to talk loudly.

"Wha. . . ? Camel's eye . . . bu. . . ."

He stiffened, the heels of his feet striking the bottom of the closet door. Masha pressed her hand down on his mouth. She was afraid that he might cry out in his death agony. If this were it. And it was. He groaned, and then relaxed. Masha took her hand away. A long sigh came from his open mouth.

She looked around the edge of the closet. Though it was dark outside, it was brighter than the darkness in the house. She should be able to make out anyone standing in the doorway. The noise the heels made could have attracted the hunters. She saw no one, though it was possible that someone had already come in and was against a wall. Listening for more noise.

She felt Benna's pulse. He was dead or so close to it that it didn't matter any more. She rose and slowly pulled her dagger from the scabbard. Then she stepped out, crouching, sure that the thudding of her heart could be heard in this still room.

So unexpectedly and suddenly that a soft cry was forced from her, a whistle sounded outside. Feet pounded in the room—there *was* someone here!—and the dim rectangle of the doorway showed a bulk plunging through it. But it was going out, not in. The Raggah had heard the whistle of the garrison soldiers—half the city must have heard it—and he was leaving with his fellows.

She turned and bent down and searched under Benna's tunic and in his loincloth. She found nothing except slowly cooling lumpy flesh. Within ten seconds, she was out on the street. Down a block was the advancing light of torches, their holders not yet visible. In the din of shouts and whistles, she fled hoping that she wouldn't run into any laggard Raggah or another body of soldiers.

Later, she found out that she'd been saved because the soldiers were looking for a prisoner who'd escaped from the dungeon. His name was Badniss, but that's another tale.

4

Masha's two-room apartment was on the third floor of a large adobe building which, with two others, occupied an entire block. She entered it on the side of the Street of the Dry Well, but first she had to wake up old Shmurt, the caretaker, by beating on the thick oaken door. Grumbling at the late hour, he unshot the bolt and let her in. She gave him a *padpool,* a tiny copper coin, for his trouble and to shut him up. He handed her her oil lamp, she lit it, and she went up the three flights of stone steps.

She had to wake up her mother to get in. Wallu, blinking and yawning in the light of an oil lamp in the corner, shot the bolt. Masha entered and at once extinguished her lamp. Oil cost money, and there had been many nights when she had had to do without it.

Wallu, a tall skinny sagging-breasted woman of fifty, with gaunt deeply-lined features, kissed her daughter on the cheek. Her breath was sour with sleep and goat's cheese. But Masha appreciated the peck; her life had few expressions of love in it. And yet she was full of it; she was a bottle close to bursting with pressure.

The light on the rickety table in the corner showed a blank-walled room without rugs. In a far corner the two infants slept on a pile of tattered but clean blankets. Beside them was a small chamberpot of baked clay painted with the black and scarlet rings-within-rings of the Darmek guild.

In another corner was her false-teeth making equipment, wax, molds, tiny chisels, saws, and expensive wire, hardwood, iron, a block of ivory. She had only recently repaid the money she'd borrowed to purchase these. In the opposite corner was another pile of cloth, Wallu's bed, and beside it another thundermug with the same design. An ancient and wobbly spinning wheel was near it; Wallu made some money with it, though not much. Her hands were gnarled with arthritis, one eye had a cataract, and the other was beginning to lose its sight for some unknown reason.

Along the adobe wall was a brass charcoal brazier and above it a wooden vent. A bin held charcoal. A big cabinet beside it held grain and some dried meat and plates and knives. Near it was a baked clay vase for water. Next to it was a pile of cloths.

Wallu pointed at the curtain in the doorway to the other room.

"He came home early. I suppose he couldn't cadge drinks enough from his friends. But he's drunk enough to suit a dozen sailors."

Grimacing, Masha strode to the curtain and pulled it aside.

"*Shewaw!*" (A combination of "Whew!", "Ugh!", and "Yech!")

The stink was that which greeted her nostrils when she opened the door to The Vulgar Unicorn Tavern. A blend of wine and beer, stale and fresh, sweat, stale and fresh, vomit, urine, frying blood-sausages, *krrf,* and *kleetel.*

Eevroen lay on his back, his mouth open, his arms spread out as if he were being crucified. Once, he had been a tall muscular youth, very broad-shouldered, slim-waisted, and long-legged. Now he was fat, fat, fat, double-chinned, huge-paunched with rings of sagging fat around his waist. The once bright eyes were red and dark-bagged, and the once-

sweet breath was a hellpit of stenches. He'd fallen asleep without changing into nightclothes; his tunic was ripped, dirty, and stained with various things, including puke. He wore cast-off sandals, or perhaps he'd
stolen them.

Masha was long past weeping over him. She kicked him in the ribs,
causing him to grunt and to open one eye. But it closed and he was
quickly snoring like a pig again. That, at least, was a blessing. How
many nights had she spent in screaming at him while he bellowed at her
or in fighting him off when he staggered home and insisted she lie with
him? She didn't want to count them.

Masha would have gotten rid of him long ago if she had been able to.
But the law of the empire was that only the man could divorce unless
the woman could prove her spouse was too diseased to have children or
was impotent.

She whirled and walked toward the wash basin. As she passed her
mother, a hand stopped her.

Wallu, peering at her with one half-good eye, said, "Child! Something has happened to you! What was it?"

"Tell you in a moment," Masha said, and she washed her face and
hands and armpits. Later, she regretted very much that she hadn't told
Wallu a lie. But how was she to know that Eevroen had come out of his
stupor enough to hear what she said? If only she hadn't been so furious
that she'd kicked him . . . but regrets were a waste of time, though
there wasn't a human alive who didn't indulge in them.

She had no sooner finished telling her mother what had happened
with Benna when she heard a grunt behind her. She turned to see
Eevroen swaying in front of the curtains, a stupid grin on his fat face.
The face once so beloved.

Eevroen reeled toward her, his hands out as if he intended to grab
her. He spoke thickly but intelligibly enough.

"Why'n't you go affer the rat? If you caught it, we coulda been rich?"

"Go back to sleep," Masha said. "This has nothing to do with you."

"Nothin do wi' me?" Eevroen bellowed. "Wha' you mean? I'm your
husband! Wha'ss yoursh ish mine. I wan' tha' jewel!"

"You damned fool," Masha said, trying to keep from screaming so
that the children wouldn't wake and the neighbors wouldn't hear, "I
don't have the jewel. There was no way I could get it—if there ever was
any."

Eevroen put a finger alongside his nose and winked the left eye. "If there wa' ever any, heh? Masha, you tryna hol' ou' on me? You go' the jewel, and you lyin' to you' mo . . . mo . . . mama."

"No, I'm not lying!" she screamed, all reason for caution having deserted her quite unreasonably. "You fat stinking pig! I've had a terrible time, I almost got killed, and all you can think about is the jewel! Which probably doesn't exist! Benna was dying! He didn't know what he was talking about! I never saw the jewel! And . . ."

Eevroen snarled, "You tryna keep i' from me!" and he charged her.

She could easily have evaded him, but something swelled up in her and took over, and she seized a baked-clay water jug from a shelf and brought it down hard over his head. The jug didn't break, but Eevroen did. He fell face forward. Blood welled from his scalp; he snored.

By then the children were awake, sitting up, wide-eyed, but silent. Maze children learned at an early age not to cry easily.

Shaking, Masha got down on her knees and examined the wound. Then she rose and went to the rag rack and returned with some dirty ones, no use wasting clean ones on him, and stanched the wound. She felt his pulse; it was beating steadily enough for a drunkard who'd just been knocked out with a severe blow.

Wallu said, "Is he dead?"

She wasn't concerned about him. She was worrying about herself, the children, and Masha. If her daughter should be executed for killing her husband, however justified she was, then she and the girls would be without support.

"He'll have a hell of a headache in the morning," Masha said. With some difficulty, she rolled Eevroen over so that he would be face down, and she turned his head sideways and then put some rags under the side of his head. Now, if he should vomit during the night, he wouldn't choke to death. For a moment she was tempted to put him back as he had fallen. But the judge might think that she was responsible for his death.

"Let him lie there," she said. "I'm not going to break my back dragging him to our bed. Besides, I wouldn't be able to sleep, he snores so loudly and he stinks so badly."

She should have been frightened of what he'd do in the morning. But, strangely, she felt exuberant. She'd done what she'd wanted to do for several years now, and the deed had discharged much of her anger—for the time being, anyway.

She went to her room and tossed and turned for a while, thinking of how much better life would be if she could get rid of Eevroen.

Her last thoughts were of what life could be if she'd gotten the jewel that Benna had thrown to the rat.


5


She awoke an hour or so past dawn, a very late time for her, and smelled bread baking. After she'd sat on the chamberpot, she rose and pushed the curtain aside. She was curious about the lack of noise in the next room. Eevroen was gone. So were the children. Wallu, hearing the little bells on the curtain, turned.

"I sent the children out to play," she said. "Eevroen woke up about dawn. He pretended he didn't know what had happened, but I could tell that he did. He groaned now and then—his head I suppose. He ate some breakfast, and then he got out fast."

Wallu smiled. "I think he's afraid of you."

"Good!" Masha said. "I hope he keeps on being afraid."

She sat down while Wallu, hobbling around, served her a half loaf of bread, a hunk of goat cheese, and an orange. Masha wondered if her husband also remembered what she'd said to her mother about Benna and the jewel.

He had.

When she went to the bazaar, carrying the folding chair in which she put her dental patients, she was immediately surrounded by hundreds of men and women. All wanted to know about the jewel.

Masha thought, "The damn fool!"

Eevroen, it seemed, had procured free drinks with his tale. He'd staggered around everywhere, the taverns, the bazaar, the farmers' market, the waterfront, and he'd spread the news. Apparently, he didn't say anything about Masha's knocking him out. That tale would have earned him only derision, and he still had enough manhood left not to reveal that.

At first, Masha was going to deny the story. But it seemed to her that most people would think she was lying, and they would be sure that she had kept the jewel. Her life would be miserable from then on. Or ended. There were plenty who wouldn't hesitate to drag her off to some secluded place and torture her until she told where the jewel was.

So she described exactly what had happened, omitting how she had tried to brain Eevroen. There was no sense in pushing him too hard. If he was humiliated publicly, he might get desperate enough to try to beat her up.

She got only one patient that day. As fast as those who'd heard her tale ran off to look for rats, others took their place. And then, inevitably, the governor's soldiers came. She was surprised they hadn't appeared sooner. Surely one of their informants had sped to the palace as soon as he had heard her story, and that would have been shortly after she'd come to the bazaar.

The sergeant of the soldiers questioned her first, and then she was marched to the garrison, where a captain interrogated her. Afterward, a colonel came in, and she had to repeat her tale. And then, after sitting in a room for at least two hours, she was taken to the governor himself. The handsome youth, surprisingly, didn't detain her long. He seemed to have checked out her movements, starting with Doctor Nadeesh. He'd worked out a timetable between the moment she left Shoozh's house and the moment she came home. So, her mother had also been questioned.

A soldier had seen two of the Raggah running away; their presence was verified.

"Well, Masha," the governor said. "You've stirred up a rat's nest," and he smiled at his own joke while the soldiers and courtiers laughed.

"There is no evidence that there was any jewel," he said, "aside from the story this Benna told, and he was dying from venom and in great pain. My doctor has examined his body, and he assures me that the swellings were spider bites. Of course, he doesn't know everything. He's been wrong before.

"But people are going to believe that there was indeed a jewel of great value, and nothing anyone says, including myself, will convince them otherwise.

"However, all their frantic activity will result in one great benefit. We'll be rid of the rats for a while."

He paused, frowning, then said, "It would seem, however, that this fellow Benna might have been foolish enough to steal something from the purple mage. I would think that that is the only reason he'd be pursued by the Raggah. But then there might be another reason. In any event, if there is a jewel, then the finder is going to be in great peril. The mage isn't going to let whoever finds it keep it.

"Or at least I believe so. Actually, I know very little about the mage, and from what I've heard about him, I have no desire to meet him."

Masha thought of asking him why he didn't send his soldiers out to the isle and summon the mage. But she kept silent. The reason was obvious. No one, not even the governor, wanted to provoke the wrath of a mage. And as long as the mage did nothing to force the governor into action, he would be left strictly alone to conduct his business—whatever that was.

At the end of the questioning, the governor told his treasurer to give a gold *sheboozh* to Masha.

"That should more than take care of any business you've lost by being here," the governor said.

Thanking him profusely, Masha bowed as she stepped back, and then walked swiftly homeward.

The following week was the great cat hunt. It was also featured, for Masha anyway, by a breakin into her apartment. While she was off helping deliver a baby at the home of the merchant Ahloo shik-Mhanukhee, three masked men knocked old Shmurt the doorkeeper out and broke down the door to her rooms. While the girls and her mother cowered in a corner, the three ransacked the place, even emptying the chamberpots on the floor to determine that nothing was hidden there.

They didn't find what they were looking for, and one of the frustrated interlopers knocked out two of Wallu's teeth in a rage. Masha was thankful, however, that they did not beat or rape the little girls. That may have been not so much because of their mercifulness as that the doorkeeper regained consciousness sooner than they had expected. He began yelling for help, and the three thugs ran away before the neighbors could gather or the soldiers come.

Eevroen continued to come in drunk late at night. But he spoke very little, just using the place to eat and sleep. He seldom saw Masha when she was awake. In fact, he seemed to be doing his best to avoid her. That was fine with her.

6

Several times, both by day and night, Masha felt someone was following her. She did her best to detect the shadower, but whether she got the feeling by day or night, she failed to do it. She decided that her nervous state was responsible.

Then the great dog hunt began. Masha thought this was the apex of hysteria and silliness. But it worried her. After all the poor dogs were gone, what would next be run down and killed and gutted? To be more precise, who? She hoped that the who wouldn't be she.

In the middle of the week of the dog hunt, little Kheem became sick. Masha had to go to work, but when she came home after sundown, she found that Kheem was suffering from a high fever. According to her mother, Kheem had also had convulsions. Alarmed, Masha set out at once for Doctor Nadeesh's house in the eastern quarter. He admitted her and listened to her describe Kheem's symptoms. But he refused to accompany her to her house.

"It's too dangerous to go into the Maze at night," he said. "And I wouldn't go there in the day unless I had several bodyguards. Besides, I am having company tonight. You should have brought the child here."

"She's too sick to be moved," Masha said. "I beg you to come."

Nadeesh was adamant, but he did give her some powders which she could use to cool the child's fever.

She thanked him audibly and cursed him silently. On the way back, while only a block from her apartment, she heard a sudden thud of footsteps behind her. She jumped to one side and whirled, drawing her dagger at the same time. There was no moon, and the nearest light was from oil lamps shining through some iron-barred windows in the second story above her.

By its faintness she saw a dark bulk. It was robed and hooded, a man by its tallness. Then she heard a low hoarse curse and knew it was a man. He had thought to grab or strike her from behind, but Masha's unexpected leap had saved her. Momentarily, at least. Now the man rushed her, and she glimpsed something long and dark in his uplifted hand. A club.

Instead of standing there frozen with fear or trying to run away, she crouched low and charged him. That took him by surprise. Before he could recover, he was struck in the throat with her blade.

Still, his body knocked her down, and he fell hard upon her. For a moment, the breath was knocked out of her. She was helpless, and when another bulk loomed above her, she knew that she had no chance.

The second man, also robed and hooded, lifted a club to bring it down on her exposed head.

Writhing, pinned down by the corpse, Masha could do nothing but await the blow. She thought briefly of little Kheem, and then she saw the man drop the club. And he was down on his knees, still gripping whatever it was that had closed off his breath.

A moment later, he was face down in the dry dirt, dead or unconscious.

The man standing over the second attacker was short and broad and also robed and hooded. He put something in his pocket, probably the cord he'd used to strangle her attacker, and he approached her cautiously. His hands seemed to be empty, however.

"Masha?" he said softly.

By then she'd recovered her wind. She wriggled out from under the dead man, jerked the dagger from the windpipe, and started to get up.

The man said, in a foreign accent, "You can put your knife away, my dear. I didn't save you just to kill you."

"I thank you, stranger," she said, "but keep your distance anyway."

Despite the warning, he took two steps toward her. Then she knew who he was. No one else in Sanctuary stank so of rancid butter.

"Smhee," she said, equally softly.

He chuckled. "I know you can't see my face. So, though it's against my religious convictions, I will have to take a bath and quit smearing my body and hair with butter. I am as silent as a shadow, but what good is that talent when anyone can smell me a block away?"

Keeping her eyes on him, she stooped and cleaned her dagger on the dead man's robe.

"Are you the one who's been following me?" she said. She straightened up.

He hissed with surprise, then said, "You saw me?"

"No. But I knew someone was dogging me."

"Ah! You have a sixth sense. Or a guilty conscience. Come! Let's get away before someone comes along."

"I'd like to know who these men are . . . were."

"They're Raggah," Smhee said. "There are two others fifty yards from here, lookouts, I suppose. They'll be coming soon to find out why these two haven't shown up with you."

That shocked her even more than the attack.

"You mean the purple mage wants *me?* Why?"

"I do not know. Perhaps he thinks as so many others do. That is, that Benna told you more than you have said he did. But come! Quickly!"

"Where?"

"To your place. We can talk there, can't we?"

They walked swiftly toward her building. Smhee kept looking back, but the place where they had killed the two men was no longer visible. When they got to the door, however, she stopped.

"If I knock on the door for the keeper, the Raggah might hear it," she whispered. "But I have to get in. My daughter is very sick. She needs the medicine I got from Dr. Nadeesh."

"So that's why you were at his home," Smhee said. "Very well. You bang on the door. I'll be the rearguard."

He was suddenly gone, moving astonishingly swiftly and silently for such a fat man. But his aroma lingered.

She did as he suggested, and presently Shmurt came grumbling to the door and unbolted it. Just as she stepped in she smelled the butter more strongly, and Smhee was inside and pushing the door shut before the startled doorkeeper could protest.

"He's all right," Masha said.

Old Shmurt peered with runny eyes at Smhee by the light of his oil lamp. Even with good vision, however, Shmurt couldn't see Smhee's face. It was covered with a green mask.

Shmurt looked disgusted.

"I know your husband isn't much," he croaked. "But taking up with this foreigner, this tub of rotten butter . . . *shewaw!*"

"It's not what you think," she said indignantly.

Smhee said, "I *must* take a bath. Everyone knows me at once."

"Is Eevroen home?" Masha said.

Shmurt snorted and said, "At this early hour? No, you and your stinking lover will be safe."

"Dammit!" Masha said. "He's here on business!"

"Some business!"

"Mind your tongue, you old fart!" Masha said. "Or I'll cut it out!"

Shmurt slammed the door to his room behind him. He called, "Whore! Slut! Adulteress!"

Masha shrugged, lit her lamp, and went up the steps with Smhee close behind her. Wallu looked very surprised when the fat man came in with her daughter.

"Who is this?"

"Someone *can't* identify me?" Smhee said. "Does she have a dead nose?"

He removed his mask.

"She doesn't get out much," Masha said. She hurried to Kheem, who lay sleeping on her rag pile. Smhee took off his cloak, revealing thin arms and legs and a body like a ball of cheese. His shirt and vest, made of some velvety material speckled with glittering sequins, clung tightly to his trunk. A broad leather belt encircled his paunch, and attached to it were two scabbards containing knives, a third from which poked the end of a bamboo pipe, and a leather bag about the size of Masha's head. Over one shoulder and the side of his neck was coiled a thin rope.

"Tools of the trade," he said in answer to Masha's look.

Masha wondered what the trade was, but she didn't have time for him. She felt Kheem's forehead and pulse, then went to the water pitcher on the ledge in the corner.

After mixing the powder with the water as Nadeesh had instructed and pouring out some into a large spoon, she turned. Smhee was on his knees by the child and reaching into the bag on his belt.

"I have some talent for doctoring," he said as she came to his side. "Here. Put that quack's medicine away and use this."

He stood up and held out a small leather envelope. She just looked at him.

"Yes, I know you don't want to take a chance with a stranger. But please believe me. This green powder is a thousand times better than that placebo Nadeesh gave you. If it doesn't cure the child, I'll cut my throat. I promise you."

"Much good that'd do the baby," Wallu said.

"Is it a magical potion?" Masha said.

"No. Magic might relieve the symptoms, but the disease would still be there, and when the magic wore off, the sickness would return. Here. Take it! I don't want you two to say a word about it, ever, but I was once trained in the art of medicine. And where I come from, a doctor is twenty times superior to any you'll find in Sanctuary."

Masha studied his dark shiny face. He looked as if he might be about forty years old. The high broad forehead, the long straight nose, the well-shaped mouth would have made him handsome if his cheeks weren't so thick and his jowls so baggy. Despite his fatness, he looked intelligent; the black eyes below the thick bushy eyebrows were keen and lively.

"I can't afford to experiment with Kheem," she said.

He smiled, perhaps an acknowledgment that he detected the uncertainty in her voice.

"You can't afford not to," he said. "If you don't use this, your child will die. And the longer you hesitate, the closer she gets to death. Every second counts."

Masha took the envelope and returned to the water pitcher. She set

the spoon down without spilling its contents and began working as
Smhee called out to her his instructions. He stayed with Kheem, one
hand on her forehead, the other on her chest. Kheem breathed rapidly
and shallowly.

Wallu protested. Masha told her to shut up more harshly than she'd
intended. Wallu bit her lip and glared at Smhee.

Kheem was propped up by Smhee, and Masha got her to swallow the
greenish water. Ten minutes or so later, the fever began to go down. An
hour later, according to the sandglass, she was given another spoonful.
By dawn, she seemed to be rid of it, and she was sleeping peacefully.


7


Meantime, Masha and Smhee talked in low tones. Wallu had gone to
bed, but not to sleep, shortly before sunrise. Eevroen had not appeared.
Probably he was sleeping off his liquor in an empty crate on the wharf
or in some doorway. Masha was glad. She had been prepared to break
another basin over his head if he made a fuss and disturbed Kheem.

Though she had seen the fat little man a number of times, she did
not know much about him. Nobody else did either. It was certain that
he had first appeared in Sanctuary six weeks (sixty days) ago. A merchant ship of the Banmalts people had brought him, but this indicated
little about his origin since the ship ported at many lands and islands.

Smhee had quickly taken a room on the second floor of a building,
the first of which was occupied by the Khabeeber or "Diving Bird" Tavern. (The proprietor had jocularly named it thus because he claimed
that his customers dived as deeply into alcohol for surcease as the
khabeeber did into the ocean for fish.) He did no work nor was he
known to thieve or mug. He seemed to have enough money for his purposes, whatever they were, but then he lived frugally. Because he
smeared his body and hair with rancid butter, he was called "The Stinking Butterball" or "Old Rotten," though not to his face. He spent time
in all the taverns and also was often seen in the farmers' market and the
bazaar. As far as was known, he had shown no sexual interest in men or
women or children. Or, as one wag put it, "not even in goats."

His religion was unknown though it was rumored that he kept an idol
in a small wooden case in his room.

Now, sitting on the floor by Kheem, making the child drink water every half-hour, Masha questioned Smhee. And he in turn questioned her.

"You've been following me around," Masha said. "Why?"

"I've also investigated other women."

"You didn't say why."

"One answer at a time. I have something to do here, and I need a woman to help me. She has to be quick and strong and very brave and intelligent. And desperate."

He looked around the room as if anybody who lived in it had to be desperate indeed.

"I know your history," he said. "You came from a fairly well-to-do family, and as a child you lived in the eastern quarter. You were not born and bred in the Maze, and you want to get out of it. You've worked hard, but you just are not going to succeed in your ambition. Not unless something unusual comes your way and you have the courage to seize it, no matter what the consequences might be."

"This has to do with Benna and the jewel, doesn't it?" she said.

He studied her face by the flickering light of the lamp.

"Yes."

He paused.

"And the purple mage."

Masha sucked in a deep breath. Her heart thudded far more swiftly than her fatigue could account for. A coldness spread from her toes to the top of her head, a not unpleasant coldness.

"I've watched in the shadows near your building," he said. "Many a night. And two nights ago I saw the Raggah steal into other shadows and watch the same window. Fortunately, you did not go out during that time to midwife. But tonight. . . ."

"Why would the Raggah be interested in me?"

He smiled slowly.

"You're smart enough to guess why. The mage thinks you know more than you let on about the jewel. Or perhaps he thinks Benna told you more than you've repeated."

He paused again, then said, "Did he?"

"Why should I tell you if he did?"

"You owe me for your life. If that isn't enough to make you confide in me, consider this. I have a plan whereby you can not only be free of the Maze, you can be richer than any merchant, perhaps richer than the governor himself. You will even be able to leave Sanctuary, to go to the capital city itself. Or anywhere in the world."

She thought, if Benna could do it, we can.

But then Benna had not gotten away.

She said, "Why do you need a woman? Why not another man?"

Smhee was silent for a long time. Evidently, he was wondering just how much he should tell her. Suddenly, he smiled, and something invisible, an unseen weight, seemed to fall from him. Somehow, he even looked thinner.

"I've gone this far," he said. "So I must go all the way. No backing out now. The reason I must have a woman is that the mage's sorcery has a weakness. His magical defenses will be set up to repel men. He will not have prepared them against women. It would not occur to him that a woman would try to steal his treasure. Or . . . kill him."

"How do you know that?"

"I don't think it would be wise to tell you that now. You must take my word for it. I do know far more about the purple mage than anyone else in Sanctuary."

"You might, and that still wouldn't be much," she said.

"Let me put it another way. I do know much about him. More than enough to make me a great danger to him."

"Does he know much about you?"

Smhee smiled again. "He doesn't know I'm here. If he did, I'd be dead by now."

They talked until dawn, and by then Masha was deeply committed. If she failed, then her fate would be horrible. And the lives of her daughters and her mother would become even worse. Far worse. But if she continued as she had, she would be dooming them anyway. She might die of a fever or be killed, and then they would have no supporter and defender.

Anyway, as Smhee pointed out, though he didn't need to, the mage was after her. Her only defense was a quick offense. She had no other choice except to wait like a dumb sheep and be slaughtered. Except that, in this situation, the sheep would be tortured before being killed.

Smhee knew what he was saying when he had said that she was desperate.

8

When the wolf's tail, the false dawn, came, she rose stiffly and went through to her room and looked out the window. Not surprisingly, the corpses of the Raggah were gone.

Shortly thereafter, Kheem awoke, bright-eyed, and asked for food. Masha covered her with kisses, and, weeping joyfully, prepared breakfast. Smhee left. He would be back before noon. But he gave her five *shaboozh* and some lesser coin. Masha wakened her mother, gave her the money, and told her that she would be gone for a few days. Wallu wanted to question her, but Masha told her sternly that she would be better off if she knew no more than she did now.

"If Eevroen wants to know where I am, tell him that I have been called to help deliver a rich farmer's baby. If he asks for the man's name, tell him it is Shkeedur sha-Mizl. He lives far out and only comes into town twice a year except on special business. It doesn't matter that it's a lie. By the time I get back—it'll be soon—we'll be leaving at once. Have everything we'll need for a long journey packed into that bag. Just clothes and eating utensils and the medicine. If Kheem has a relapse, give her Smhee's powders."

Wallu wailed then, and Masha had to quiet her down.

"Hide the money. No! Leave one *shaboozh* where Eevroen will find it when he looks for money. Conceal the rest where he can't find it. He'll take the *shaboozh* and go out to drink, and you won't be bothered with him or his questions."

When the flaming brass bowl of the noon sun had reached its apex, Smhee came. His eyes looked very red, but he didn't act fatigued. He carried a carpet bag from which he produced two dark cloaks, two robes, and the masks which the priests of Shalpa wore in public.

He said, "How did you get rid of your mother and the children?"

"A neighbor is keeping the children until mother gets back from shopping," she said. "Eevroen still hasn't shown up."

"Nor will he for a long time," Smhee said. "I dropped a coin as I passed him staggering this way. He snatched it, of course, and ran off to a tavern.

"The *Sailfish* will be leaving port in three days. I've arranged for passage on her and also to be hidden aboard her if her departure is delayed. I've been very busy all morning."

"Including taking a bath," she said.

"You don't smell too good yourself," he said. "But you can bathe when we get to the river. Put these on."

She went into her room, removed her clothes, and donned the priest's garb. When she came out, Smhee was fully dressed. The bag attached to his belt bulged beneath his cloak.

"Give me your old clothes," he said. "We'll cache them outside the city, though I don't think we'll be needing them."

She did so, and he stuffed them into the belt-bag.

"Let's go," he said.

She didn't follow him to the door. He turned and said, "What's the matter? Your liver getting cold?"

"No," she said. "Only . . . mother's very short-sighted. I'm afraid she'll be cheated when she buys the food."

He laughed and said something in a foreign tongue.

"For the sake of Igil! When we return, we'll have enough to buy out the farmers' market a thousand times over!"

"If we get back. . . ." she murmured. She wanted to go to Looza's room and kiss the children goodbye. But that was not wise. Besides, she might lose her determination if she saw them now.

They walked out while old Shmurt stared. He was the weakest point in their alibi, but they hoped they wouldn't need any. At the moment, he was too dumfounded at seeing them to say anything. And he would be afraid to go to the soldiers about this. He probably was thinking that two priests had magically entered the house, and it would be indiscreet to interfere in their business.

Thirty minutes later, they mounted the two horses which Smhee had arranged to be tied to a tree outside city limits.

"Weren't you afraid they'd be stolen?" she said.

"There are two stout fellows hidden in the grass near the river," he said. He waved toward it, and she saw two men come from it. They waved back and started to walk back to the city.

There was a rough road along the White Foal River, sometimes coming near the stream, sometimes bending far away. They rode over it for three hours, and then Smhee said, "There's an old adobe building a quarter-mile inland. We'll sleep there for a while. I don't know about you, but I'm weary."

She was glad to rest. After hobbling the horses near a stand of the tall brown desert grass, they lay down in the midst of the ruins. Smhee went to sleep at once. She worried about her family for a while, and suddenly she was being shaken by Smhee. Dawn was coming up.

They ate some dried meat and bread and fruit and then mounted again. After watering the horses and themselves at the river, they rode at a canter for three more hours. And then Smhee pulled up on the reins. He pointed at the trees a quarter-mile inland. Beyond, rearing high, were the towering cliffs on the other side of the river. The trees on this side, however, prevented them from seeing the White Foal.

"The boat's hidden in there," he said. "Unless someone's stolen it. That's not likely, though. Very few people have the courage to go near the Isle of Shugthee."

"What about the hunters who bring down the furs from the north?"

"They hug the eastern shore, and they only go by in daylight. Fast."

They crossed the rocky ground, passing some low-growing purplish bushes and some irontrees with grotesquely twisted branches. A rabbit with long ears dashed by them, causing her horse to rear up. She controlled it, though she had not been on a horse since she was eleven. Smhee said that he was glad that it hadn't been his beast. All he knew about riding was the few lessons he'd taken from a farmer after coming to Sanctuary. He'd be happy if he never had to get on another one.

The trees were perhaps fifteen or twenty deep from the river's edge. They dismounted, removed the saddles, and hobbled the beasts again. Then they walked through the tall cane-like plants, brushing away the flies and other pestiferous insects, until they got to the stream itself. Here grew stands of high reeds, and on a hummock of spongy earth was Smhee's boat. It was a dugout which could hold only two.

"Stole it," Smhee said without offering any details.

She looked through the reeds down the river. About a quarter of a mile away, the river broadened to become a lake about two and a half miles across. In its center was the Isle of Shugthee, a purplish mass of rock. From this distance, she could not make out its details.

Seeing it, she felt coldness ripple over her.

"I'd like to take a whole day and a night to scout it," he said. "So you could become familiar with it, too. But we don't have time. However, I can tell you everything I know. I wish I knew more."

She doffed her clothes and bathed in the river while Smhee unhobbled the horses and took them some distance up to let them drink. When she came back, she found him just returning with them.

"Before dusk comes, we'll have to move them down to a point oppo-site the isle," he said. "And we'll saddle them, too."

They left the horses to go to a big boulder outside the trees but dis-tant from the road. At its base was a hollow large enough for them to lie down in. Here they slept, waking now and then to talk softly or to eat a bite or to go behind the rock and urinate. The insects weren't so numerous here as in the trees, but they were bad enough.

Not once, as far as they knew, did anyone pass on the road.

When they walked the horses down the road, Smhee said, "You've been very good about not asking questions, but I can see you're about to explode with curiosity. You have no idea who the purple mage really is. Not unless you know more than the other Sanctuarians."

"All I know," she said, "is that they say that the mage came here about ten years ago. He came with some hired servants, and many boxes, some small, some large. No one knew what his native land was, and he didn't stay long in town. One day he disappeared with the ser-vants and the boxes. It was some time before people found out that he'd moved into the caves of the Isle of Shugthee. Nobody had ever gone there because it was said that it was haunted by the ghosts of the Shugthee. They were a little hairy people who inhabited this land long before the first city of the ancients was built here."

"How do you know he's a mage?" Smhee said.

"I don't, but everybody says he is. Isn't he?"

"He is," Smhee said, looking grim.

"Anyway, he sent his servants in now and then to buy cattle, goats, pigs, chickens, horses, vegetables, and animal feed and fruit. These were men and women from some distant land. Not from his, though. And then one day they ceased coming in. Instead, the Raggah came. From that day on, no one has seen the servants who came with the mage."

"He probably got rid of them," Smhee said. "He may have found some reason to distrust them. Or no reason at all."

"The fur trappers and hunters who've gone by the isle say they've seen some strange things. Hairy beast-faced dwarfs. Giant spiders."

She shuddered.

"Benna died of spider bites," Smhee said.

The fat little man reached into his belt-bag and brought out a metal jar. He said, "Before we leave in the boat tonight we'll rub the ointment in this on us. It will repel some of the spiders but not, unfortunately, all."

"How do you know that?"

"I know."

They walked silently for a while. Then he sighed, and said, "We'll get bitten. That is certain. Only . . . all the spiders that will bite us—I hope so, anyway—won't be real spiders. They'll be products of the mage's magic. Apparitions. But apparitions that can kill you just as quickly or as slowly and usually as painfully as the real spiders."

He paused, then said, "Benna probably died from their bites."

Masha felt as if she were turning white under her dark skin. She put her hands on his arm.

"But . . . but . . . !"

"Yes, I know. If the spiders were not real, then why should they harm him? That is because he thought they were real. His mind did the rest to him."

She didn't like that she couldn't keep her voice from shaking, but she couldn't help it.

"How can you tell which is real and which magical?"

"In the daylight the unreal spiders look a little transparent. By that I mean that if they stand still, you can see dimly through them. But then they don't stand still much. And we'll be in the dark of night. So. . . .

"Look here, Masha. You have to be strong stuff to go there. You have to overcome your fear. A person who lets fear conquer him or her is going to die even if he knows that the spider is unreal. He'll make the sting of the bite himself and the effects of the venom. And he'll kill himself. I've seen it happen in my native land."

"But you say that we might get bitten by a real spider. How can I tell which is which in the dark?"

"It's a problem."

He added after a few seconds, "The ointment should repulse most of the real spiders. Maybe, if we're lucky. You see, we have an advantage that Benna didn't have. I know what faces us because I come from the mage's land. His true name is Kemren, and he brought with him the real spiders and some other equally dangerous creatures. They would have been in some of the boxes. I am prepared for them, and so will you be. Benna wasn't, and any of these Sanctuary thieves will get the same fate."

Masha asked why Kemren had come here. Smhee chewed on his lower lip for a while before answering.

"You may as well know it all. Kemren was a priest of the goddess Weda Krizhtawn of the island of Sharranpip. That is far east and south of here, though you may have heard of it. We are a people of the water, of lakes, rivers, and the sea. Weda Krizhtawn is the chief goddess of water, and she has a mighty temple with many treasures near the sea.

"Kemren was one of the higher priests, and he served her well for years. In return, he was admitted into the inner circle of mages and taught both black and white magic. Though, actually, there is little difference between the two branches, the main distinction being whether the magician uses his powers for good or evil.

"And it isn't always easy to tell what is good and what is evil. If a mage makes a mistake, and his use turns out to be for evil, even if he sincerely thought it was for good, then there is a . . . backlash. And the mage's character becomes changed for the worse in proportion to the amount of magical energy used."

He stopped walking.

"We're opposite the isle now."

It wasn't visible from the road. The plain sloped upward from the road, becoming a high ridge near the river. The tall spreading blackish *hukharran* bush grew on top of it. They walked the horses up the ridge, where they hobbled them near a pool of rainwater. The beasts began cropping the long brownish grass that grew among the bushes.

The isle was in the center of the lake and seemed to be composed mostly of a purplish rock. It sloped gently from the shore until near the middle, where a series of peculiar formations formed a spine. The highest prominence was a monolith perforated near its top as if a tunnel had been carved through it.

"The camel's eye Benna spoke of," Smhee said. "Over there is the formation known as the ape's head, and at the other end is that which the natives call the dragon's tail."

On the edge of the isle grew some trees, and in the waters by it were the ubiquitous tall reeds.

There was no sight or sound of life on it. Even the birds seemed to shun it.

"But I floated down past it at night several times," he said, "and I could hear the lowing of some cattle and the braying of a donkey. Also, I heard a weird call, but I don't know if it was from a bird or an animal. And I heard a peculiar grunting sound, but it wasn't from pigs."

"That camel's eye looks like a good place for a sentry," she said. "I got the impression from Benna that that is where he entered the caves. It must've been a very dangerous climb, especially during the dark."

"Benna was a good man," Smhee said. "But he wasn't prepared enough. There are eyes watching now. Probably through holes in the rocks. From what I heard, the mage had his servants buy a number of excavating tools. He would have used them to enlarge the caves and to make tunnels to connect the caves."

She took a final look in the sunlight at the sinister purple mass and turned away.

## 9

Night had come. The winds had died down. The sky was cloudy, but the covering was thin. The full moon glowed through some of these, and now and then broke through. The nightbirds made crazy startling sounds. The mosquitoes hummed around them in dense masses, and if it hadn't been for Smhee's ointment would have driven them out of the trees within a few minutes. Frogs croaked in vast chorus; things plopped into the water.

They shoved the boat out to the edge of the reeds and climbed in. They wore their cloaks now but would take them off when they got to the isle. Masha's weapons were a dagger and a short thin sword used for thrusting only.

They paddled silently as possible, the current helping their rate of speed, and presently the isle loomed darkly to their right. They landed halfway down the eastern shore and dragged the dugout slowly to the nearest tree.

They put their cloaks in the boat, and Masha placed a coil of rope over her shoulder and neck.

The isle was quiet. Not a sound. Then came a strange grunting cry followed by a half-moaning, half-squalling sound. Her neck iced.

"Whatever that is," Smhee said, "it's no spider."

He chuckled as if he were making a joke.

They'd decided—what else could they do?—that the camel's eye would be too heavily guarded after Benna's entrance through it. But there had to be more accessible places to get in. These would be guarded, too, especially since they must have been made more security-conscious by the young thief.

"What I'd like to find is a secret exit," Smhee said. "Kemren must have one, perhaps more. He knows that there might come a time when he'll be sorely in need of it. He's a crafty bastard."

Before they'd taken the boat, Smhee had revealed that Kemren had fled Sharranpip with many of the temple's treasures. He had also taken along spiders' eggs and some of the temple's animal guardians.

"If he was a high priest," Masha had said, "why would he do that? Didn't he have power and wealth enough?"

"You don't understand our religion," the fat thief had said. "The priests are surrounded by treasures that would pop your eyes out of their sockets if you saw them. But the priests themselves are bound by vows to extreme poverty, to chastity, to a harsh bare life. Their reward is the satisfaction of serving Weda Krizhtawn and her people. It wasn't enough for Kemren. He must have become evil while performing some magic that went wrong. He is the first priest ever to commit such a blasphemy.

"And I, a minor priest, was selected to track him down and to make him pay for his crime. I've been looking for him for thirteen years. During that time, to effect the vengeance of Weda Krizhtawn, I have had to break some of my own vows and to commit crimes which I must pay for when I return to my land."

"Won't she pardon you for these because you have done them in her name?" Masha had said.

"No. She accepts no excuses. She will thank me for completing my mission, but I must still pay. Look at me. When I left Sharranpip, I was as skinny as you. I led a very exemplary life. I ate little, I slept in the cold and rain, I begged for my food, I prayed much. But during the years of my crimes and the crimes of my years, I have eaten too well so that Kemren, hearing of the fat fellow, would not recognize me. I have been reeling drunk, I have gambled—a terrible sin—I have fought with fists and blade, I have taken human lives, I. . . ."

He looked as if he were going to weep.

Masha said, "But you didn't quit smearing yourself with butter?"

"I should have, I should have!" he cried. "But, apart from lying with women, that is the one thing I could not bring myself to do, though it was the first I should have done! And I'll pay for that when I get home, even though that is the hardest thing for a priest to do! Even Kemren, I have heard, though he no longer worships Weda Krizhtawn, still butters himself!

"And the only reason I quit doing that is that I'm sure that he's conditioned his real spiders, and his guardian animals, to attack anyone who's covered with butter. That way he can make sure, or thinks he can make sure, that no hunter of him will ever be able to get close. That is why, though it almost killed me with shame and guilt, I bathed this morning!"

Masha would have laughed if she hadn't felt so sorry for him. That was why his eyes had looked so red when he'd shown up at her apartment after bathing. It hadn't been fatigue but tears that had done it.

They drew their weapons, Masha a short sword and Smhee a long dagger. They set out for the base of the ridge of formations that ran down the center of the isle like serrations on a dragon's back. Before they'd gone far, Smhee put a restraining hand on her arm.

"There's a spider's web just ahead. Between those two bushes. Be careful of it. But look out for other dangers, since one will be obvious enough to distract your attention from others. And don't forget that the thorns of these bushes are probably poisonous."

In the dim moonlight she saw the web. It was huge, as wide as the stretch of her arms. She thought, if it's so big, what about its spinner?

It seemed empty, though. She turned to her left and walked slowly, her head turned to watch it.

Then something big scuttled out from under the bush at her. She stifled her scream and leaped toward the thing instead of following her desire to run away from it. Her sword leaped out as the thing sprang, and it spitted itself. Something soft touched the back of her hand. The end of a waving leg.

Smhee came up behind it as she stood there holding the sword out as far as she could to keep the arachnid away. Her arm got heavy with its weight, and slowly the blade sank toward the ground. The fat man slashed the thing's back open with his dagger. A foul odor vented from it. He brought his foot down on a leg and whispered, "Pull your sword out! I'll keep it pinned!"

She did so and then backed away. She was breathing very hard.

He jumped up and came down with both feet on the creature. Its legs waved for a while longer, but it was dying if not already dead.

"That was a real spider," he said, "although I suppose you know that. I suspect that the false spiders will be much smaller."

"Why?" she said. She wished her heart would quit trying to leap up through her throat.

"Because making them requires energy, and it's more effective to make a lot of little spiders and costs less energy than to make a few big ones. There are other reasons which I won't explain just now."

"Look out!" she cried, far louder than she should have. But it had been so sudden and had taken her off guard.

Smhee whirled and slashed out, though he hadn't seen the thing. It bounded over the web, its limbs spread out against the dimness, its great round ears profiled. It came down growling, and it fell upon Smhee's blade. This was no man's-headsized spider but a thing as big as a large dog and furry and stinking of something—monkey?—and much more vital than the arachnid. It bore Smhee backward with its weight; he fell on the earth.

Snarling, it tried to bury its fangs in Smhee's throat. Masha broke from her paralysis and thrust with a fury and strength that only fear could provide. The blade went through its body. She leaped back, drawing it out, and then lunged again. This time the point entered its neck.

Smhee, gasping, rolled it off him and stood up. He said, "By Wishvu's whiskers! I've got blood all over me. A fine mess! Now the others will smell me!"

"What is it?" Masha said shakily.

"A temple guardian ape. Actually, it's not an ape but a very large tailless monkey. Kemren must have brought some cubs with him."

Masha got close to the dead beast, which was lying on its back. The open mouth showed teeth like a leopard's.

"They eat meat," he said. "Unlike other monkeys, however, they're not gregarious. Our word for them, translated, would be the solitary ape."

Masha wondered if one of Smhee's duties had been teaching. Even under these circumstances, he had to be pedantic.

He looked around. "Solitary or not, there are probably a number on this isle."

After dragging the two carcasses into the river, they proceeded cautiously. Smhee looked mostly ahead; Masha, behind. Both looked to both sides of them. They came to the base of the ridges of rock. Smhee said, "The animal pens are north. That's where I heard them as I went by in the boat. I think we should stay away from them. If they scent us and start an uproar, we'll have the Raggah out and on our asses very quickly."

Smhee stopped suddenly, and said, "Hold it!"

Masha looked around quickly. What had he seen or heard?

The fat man got down on his knees and pushed against the earth just in front of him

He rose and said, "There's a pit under that firm-looking earth. I felt it give way as I put my foot on it. That's why it pays not to walk swiftly here."

They circled it, Smhee testing each step before taking another. Masha thought that if they had to go this slowly, they would take all night before they got to the ridge. But then he led her to a rocky place, and she breathed easier. However, he said, "They could carve a pit in the stone and put a pivoting lid over it."

She said, "Why are we going this way? You said the entrances are on the north end."

"I said that I only observed people entering on the north end. But I also observed something very interesting near here. I want to check it out. It may be nothing for us, but again. . . ."

Still moving slowly but faster than on the earth, they came to a little pool. It was about ten feet in diameter, a dark sheet of water on which bubbles appeared and popped. Smhee crouched down and stared at its sinister-looking surface.

She started to whisper a question, but he said, "Shh!"

Presently, something scuttled with a clatter across the solid rock from the shore. She jumped but uttered no exclamation. The thing looked like a spider in the dark, an enormous one, larger than the one they'd killed. It paid no attention to them or perhaps it wasn't at all aware of them. It leaped into the pool and disappeared. Smhee said, "Let's get behind that boulder."

When they were in back of it, she said, "What's going on?"

"When I was spying, I saw some things going into and coming out of this hole. It was too far away to see what they were, though I suspected they were giant spiders or perhaps crabs."

"So?"

His hand gripped her wrist.

"Wait!"

The minutes oozed by like snails. Mosquitoes hummed around them, birds across the river called, and once she heard, or thought she heard, that peculiar half-grunt, half-squall. And once she started when something splashed in the river. A fish. She hoped that was all it was.

Smhee said softly, "Ah!"

He pointed at the pool. She strained her eyes and then saw what looked like a swelling of the water in its center. The mound moved toward the edge of the pool, and then it left the water. It clacked as it shot toward the river. Soon another thing came and then another, and all of a sudden at least twenty popped up and clattered across the rocks.

Smhee finally relieved her bursting question.

"They look like the *bengil* crab of Sharranpip. They live in that hole but they must catch fish in the river."

"What is that to us?"

"I think the pool must be an entrance to a cave. Or caves. The crabs are not water-breathers."

"Are they dangerous?"

"Only when in water. On land they'll either run or, if cornered, try to defend themselves. They aren't poisonous, but their claws are very powerful."

He was silent for a moment, then said, "The mage is using them to defend the entrance to a cave, I'm sure. An entrance which is also an exit. For him as well as for the crabs. That pool has to be one of his secret escape routes."

Masha thought, "Oh, no!" and she rolled her eyes. Was this fat fool really thinking about trying to get inside through the pool?

"How could the mage get out this way if the crabs would attack him?"

"He would throw poisoned meat to them. He could do any number of things. What matters just now is that he wouldn't have bothered to bring their eggs along from Sharranpip unless he had a use for them. Nor would he have planted them here unless he needed them to guard this pool. Their flesh is poisonous to all living things except the *ghoondah* fish."

He chuckled. "But the mage has outsmarted himself. If I hadn't noticed the *bengil,* I would never have considered that pool as an entrance."

While he had been whispering, another group had emerged and run for the river. He counted them, thirty in all.

"Now is the time to go in," he said. "They'll all be feeding. That crab you first saw was their scout. It found a good place for catching fish, determined that there wasn't any enemy around, and returned with the good news. In some ways, they're more ant than crab. Fortunately, their nests aren't as heavily populated as an anthole."

He said, however, that they should wait a few minutes to make sure that all had left. "By all, I mean all but a few. There are always a few who stay behind to guard the eggs."

"Smhee, we'll drown!"

"If other people can get out through the pool, then we can get in."

"You don't know for sure that the pool is an escape route! What if the mage put the crabs there for some other reason?"

"What if? What if? I told you this would be very dangerous. But the rewards are worth the risk."

She stiffened. That strange cry had come again. And it was definitely nearer.

"It may be hunting us," Smhee said. "It could have smelled the blood of the ape."

"What is it?" she said, trying to keep her teeth from chattering.

"I don't know. We're downwind from it, but it sounds as if it'll soon be here. Good! That will put some stiffening in our backbone, heat our livers. Let's go now!"

So, he was scared, too. Somehow, that made her feel a little better.

They stuck their legs down into the chilly water. They found no bottom. Then Smhee ran around to the inland side and bent down. He probed with his hand around the edge.

"The rock goes about a foot down, then curves inward," he said. "I'll wager that this was once a pothole of some sort. When Kemren came here, he carved out tunnels to the cave it led to and then somehow filled it with river water."

He stood up. The low strange cry was definitely closer now. She thought she saw something huge in the darkness to the north, but it could be her imagination.

"Oh, Igil!" she said. "I have to urinate!"

"Do it in the water. If it smells your urine on the land, it'll know a human's been here. And it might call others of its kind. Or make such an uproar the Raggah will come."

He let himself down into the water and clung to the stony edge.

"Get in! It's cold but not as cold as death!"

She let herself down to his side. She had to bite her lip to keep from gasping with shock.

He gave her a few hurried instructions and said, "May Weda Krizhtawn smile upon us!"

And he was gone.


10


She took a deep breath while she was considering getting out of the pool and running like a lizard chased by a fox to the river and swimming across it. But instead she dived, and as Smhee had told her to do, swam close to the ceiling of rock. She was blind here even with her eyes open, and, though she thought mostly about drowning, she had room to think about the crabs.

Presently, when her lungs were about to burst and her head rang and the violent urge to get air was about to make her breathe, her flailing hand was grasped by something. The next instant, she was pulled into air.

There was darkness all about. Her gaspings mingled with Smhee's.

He said, between the wheezings, "There's plenty of airspace between the water and the ceiling. I dived down and came up as fast as I could out of the water, and I couldn't touch the rock above."

After they'd recovered their wind, he said, "You tread water while I go back. I want to see how far back this space goes."

She didn't have to wait long. She heard his swimming—she hoped it was his and not something else—and she called out softly when he was near. He stopped and said, "There's plenty of air until just before the tunnel or cave reaches the pool. Then you have to dive under a downthrust ledge of rock. I didn't go back out, of course, not with that creature out there. But I'm sure my estimate of distance is right."

She followed him in the darkness until he said, "Here's another downthrust."

She felt where he indicated. The stone did not go more than six inches before ceasing.

"Does the rope or your boots bother you any?" he said. "If they're too heavy, get rid of them."

"I'm all right."

"Good. I'll be back soon—if things are as I think they are."

She started to call to him to wait for her, but it was too late. She clung to the rough stone with her fingertips, moving her legs now and then. The silence was oppressive; it rang in her ears. And once she gasped when something touched her thigh.

The rope and boots did drag her down, and she was thinking of at least getting rid of the rope when something struck her belly. She grabbed it with one hand to keep it from biting her and with the other reached for her dagger. She went under water of course, and then she realized that she wasn't being attacked. Smhee, diving back, had run into her.

Their heads cleared the surface. Smhee laughed.

"Were you as frightened as I? I thought sure a *bengil* had me!"

Gasping, she said, "Never mind. What's over there?"

"More of the same. Another air space for perhaps a hundred feet. Then another downcropping."

He clung to the stone for a moment. Then he said, "Have you noticed how fresh the air is? There's a very slight movement of it, too."

She had noticed but hadn't thought about it. Her experiences with watery caves was nil until now.

"I'm sure that each of these caves is connected to a hole which brings in fresh air from above," he said. "Would the mage have gone to all this trouble unless he meant to use this for escape?"

He did something. She heard him breathing heavily, and then there was a splash.

"I pulled myself up the rock and felt around," he said. "There is a hole up there to let air from the next cave into this one. And I'll wager that there is a hole in the ceiling. But it must curve so that light doesn't come in. Or maybe it doesn't curve. If it were day above, we might see the hole."

He dived; Masha followed him. They swam ahead then, putting their right hands out from side to side to feel the wall. When they came to the next downcropping, they went through beneath it at once.

At the end of this cave they felt a rock ledge that sloped gently upward. They crawled out onto it. She heard him fumbling around and then he said, "Don't cry out. I'm lighting a torch."

The light nevertheless startled her. It came from the tip of a slender stick of wood in his hand. By its illumination she saw him apply it to the end of a small pine torch. This caught fire, giving them more area of vision. The fire on the stick went out. He put the stick back into the opened belt-bag.

"We don't want to leave any evidence we've been here," he said softly. "I didn't mention that this bag contains many things, including another waterproof bag. But we must hurry. The torch won't last long, and I've got just one more."

They stood up and moved ahead. A few feet beyond the original area first illuminated by the torch were some dark bulks. Boats. Twelve of them, with light wood frameworks and skin-coverings. Each could hold three people. By them were paddles.

Smhee took out a dagger and began ripping the skins. Masha helped him until only one boat was left undamaged.

He said, "There must be entrances cut into the stone sections dividing the caves we just came through. I'll wager they're on the left-hand

side as you come in. Anyone swimming in would naturally keep to the
right wall and so wouldn't see the archways. The ledges where the crabs
nest must also be on the left. Remember that when we come back. But
I'd better find out for sure. We want to know exactly how to get out
when the time comes."

He set his torch in a socket in the front of the boat and pushed the
boat down the slope and into the water. While Masha held the narrow
craft steady, he got into it. She stood on the shore, feeling lonely with
all that darkness behind her while she watched him by the light of the
brand. Within a few minutes he came back, grinning.

"I was right! There's an opening cut into the stone division. It's just
high enough for a boat to pass through if you duck down."

They dragged the boat back up onto the ledge. The cave ended about
a hundred feet from the water. To the right was a U-shaped entrance.
By its side were piles of torches and flint and steel and punk boxes.
Smhee lit two, gave one to Masha, and then returned to the edge of the
ledge to extinguish his little one.

"I think the mage has put all his magic spiders inside the caves," he
said. "They'd require too much energy to maintain on the outside. The
further away they are from him, the more energy he has to use to maintain them. The energy required increases according to the square of the
distance."

Masha didn't ask him what he meant by "square."

"Stick close to me. Not just for your sake. For mine also. As I said,
the mage will not have considered women trying to get into his place, so
his powers are directed against men only. At least, I hope they are.
That way he doesn't have to use as much energy on his magic."

"Do you want me to lead?" she said, hoping he wouldn't say yes.

"If you had as much experience as I, I wouldn't hesitate a moment.
But you're still an apprentice. If we get out of here alive, you will be on
your way to being a master."

They went up the steps cut out of the stone. At the top was another
archway. Smhee stopped before it and held his torch high to look within
it. But he kept his head outside it.

"Ha!"

11

He motioned her to come to his side. She saw that the interior of the deep doorway was grooved. Above the grooves was the bottom of a slab of stone.

"If the mechanism is triggered, that slab will crash down and block off anyone chasing the mage," he said. "And it'd crush anyone in the portal. Maybe. . . ."

He looked at the wall surrounding the archway but could find nothing.

"The release mechanism must be in the other room. A time-delay device."

He got as near to the entrance as he could without going into it, and he stuck his torch through the opening.

"I can't see it. It must be just around the corner. But I do see what looks like webs."

Masha breathed deeply.

"If they're real spiders, they'll be intimidated by the torches," he said. "Unless the mage has conditioned them not to be or uses magic to overcome their natural fear. The magic spiders won't pay any attention to the flame."

She thought that it was all very uncertain, but she did not comment.

He bent down and peered at the stone floor just beyond the doorway. He turned. "Here. Your young eyes are better than my old ones. Can you see a thread or anything like it raised above the floor just beyond the door?"

She said, "No, I can't."

"Nevertheless."

He threw his torch through the doorway. At his order, she got down with her cheek against the stone and looked against the flame.

She rose, saying, "I can see a very thin line about an inch above the floor. It could be a cord."

"Just as I thought. An old Sharranpip trick."

He stepped back after asking her to get out of the way. And he leaped through the doorway and came down past the cord. She followed. As they picked up their torches, he said pointing, "There are the mechanisms. One is the time-delay. The other releases the door so it'll fall behind the first who enters and trap him. Anyone following will be crushed by the slab."

After telling her to keep an eye on the rest of the room, he examined the array of wheels, gears, and counterweights and the rope that ran from one device through a hole in the ceiling.

"The rope is probably attached to an alarm system above," he said. "Very well. I know how to actuate both of these. If you should by any foul chance come back alone, all you have to do is to jump through and then throw a torch or something on that cord. The door will come down and block off your pursuers. But get outside as fast as you can because. . . ."

Masha said, "I know why."

"Good woman. Now, the spiders."

The things came before the webs were clearly visible in the light. She had expected to see the light reflected redly in their eyes, but it wasn't. Their many eyes were huge and purplish and cold. They scuttled forward, waving the foremost pair of legs, then backed away as Smhee waved his torch at them. Masha walked half-turned away from him so that she could use the brand to scare away any attack from the rear or side.

Suddenly, something leaped from the edge of the darkness and soared toward her. She thrust the brand at it. But the creature seemed to go through the torch.

It landed on her arm and seized the hand that held the torch. She had clenched her teeth to keep from screaming if something like this happened. But she didn't even think of voicing her terror and disgust. She closed her hand on the body of the thing to crush it, and the fingers felt nothing.

The next moment, the spider disappeared.

She told Smhee what had happened.

"Thanks be to Klooshna!" he said. "You are invulnerable to them. If you weren't, you'd be swelling up now!"

"But what if it'd been a real spider?" she said as she kept waving her torch at the monsters that circled them. "I didn't know until my hand closed on it that it was not real."

"Then you'd be dying. But the fact that it ignored the brand showed you what it really was. You realized that even if you didn't think consciously about it."

They came to another archway. While she threw her torch through it and got down to look for another thread, Smhee held off the spiders.

"There doesn't seem to be any," she said.

"Seem isn't good enough," he said. "Hah, back, you creatures of evil! Look closely! Can you see any thin lines in the floor itself? Minute cracks?"

After a few seconds, she said, "Yes. They form a square."

"A trapdoor to drop us into a pit," he said. "You jump past it. And let's hope there isn't another trap just beyond it."

She said that she'd need a little run to clear the line. He charged the spiders, waving his torch furiously, and they backed away. When she called to him that she was safe, he turned and ran and leaped. A hairy, many-legged thing dashed through the entrance after him. Masha stepped up to the line and thrust her brand at it. It stopped. Behind it were masses that moved, shadows of solidity.

Smhee leaped toward the foremost one and jammed the burning red of his brand into the head. The stink of charred flesh assailed their nostrils. It ran backward but was stopped by those behind it. Then they retreated, and the thing, its eyes burned out, began running around and around, finally disappearing into the darkness. The others were now just beyond the doorway in the other cave. Smhee threw his torch into it.

"That'll keep them from coming through!" he said, panting. "I should have brought some extra torches, but even the greatest mind sometimes slips. Notice how the weight of those spiders didn't make the trapdoor drop? It must have a minimum limit. You only weigh eighty-five pounds. Maybe . . . ?"

"Forget it," she said.

"Right you are," he said, grinning. "But Masha, if you are to be a master thief, you must think of everything."

She thought of reminding him about the extra torches he'd forgotten but decided not to. They went on ahead through an enormous cavern and came to a tunnel. From its dark mouth streamed a stink like a newly opened tomb. And they heard the cry that was half-grunt, half-squall.

Smhee halted. "I hate to go into that tunnel. But we must. You look upward for holes in the ceiling, and I'll look everywhere else."

The stone, however, looked solid. When they were halfway down the bore, they were blasted with a tremendous growling and roaring.

"Lions?" Masha said.

"No. Bears."

12

At the opposite end were two gigantic animals, their eyes gleaming redly in the light, their fangs a dull white.

The two intruders advanced after waiting for the bears to charge. But these stayed by the doorway, though they did not cease their thunderous roaring nor their slashes at the air with their paws.

"The bears were making the strange cry," she said. "I've seen dancing bears in the bazaars, but I never heard them make a noise like that. Nor were they near as large."

He said, "They've got chains around their necks. Come on."

When they were within a few feet of the beasts, they stopped. The stench was almost overpowering now, and they were deafened by the uproar in the narrowness of the tunnel.

Smhee told her to hold her torch steady. He opened his belt-bag and pulled out two lengths of bamboo pipe and joined them. Then, from a small wooden case, he cautiously extracted a feathered dart. He inserted it in one and raised the blowpipe almost to his lips.

"There's enough poison on the tip of the dart to kill a dozen men," he said. "However, I doubt that it would do much harm, if any, if the dart sticks in their thick fat. So. . . ."

He waited a long time, the pipe now at his lips. Then, his cheeks swelled, and the dart shot out. The bear to the right, roaring even louder, grabbed at the missile stuck in its left eye. Smhee fitted another dart into the pipe and took a step closer. The monster on the left lunged against the restraining collar and chain. Smhee shot the second dart into its tongue.

The first beast struck fell to one side, its paws waving, and its roars subsided. The other took longer to become quiet, but presently both were snoring away.

"Let's hope they die," Smhee said. "I doubt we'll have time to shoot them again when we come back."

Masha thought that a more immediate concern was that the roaring might have alarmed the mage's servants.

They went through a large cavern, the floor of which was littered with human, cattle, and goat skeletons and bear dung. They breathed through their mouths until they got to an exit. This was a doorway which led to a flight of steps. At the top of the steps was another entrance with a closed massive wooden door. Affixed to one side was a great wooden bar.

"Another hindrance to pursuers," Smhee said. "Which will, in our case, be the Raggah."

After a careful inspection of the door, he gripped its handle and slowly opened it. Freshly oiled, it swung noiselessly. They went out into a very large room illuminated by six great torches at one end. Here streams of water ran out from holes in the ceiling and down wooden troughs and onto many wooden wheels set between metal uprights.

Against the right-hand side of the far wall was another closed door as massive as the first. It, too, could be barred shut.

Unlike the bare walls of the other caves, these were painted with many strange symbols.

"There's magic here," Smhee said. "I smell it."

He strode to the pool in which were set the wheels. The wheels went around and around impelled by the downpouring water. Masha counted aloud. Twelve.

"A magical number," Smhee said.

They were set in rows of threes. At one end of the axle of each were attached some gears which in turn were fixed to a shaft that ran into a box under the wheel. Smhee reached out to the nearest wheel from the pool edge and stopped it. Then he released it and opened the lid of the box beneath the wheel. Masha looked past him into the interior of the box. She saw a bewildering array of tiny gears and shafts. The shafts were connected to more gears at the axle end of tiny wheels on uprights.

Smhee stopped the wheel again and spun it against the force of the waterfall. The mechanism inside started working backward.

Smhee smiled. He closed the box and went to the door and barred it. He walked swiftly to the other side of the pool. There was a large box on the floor by it. He opened it and removed some metal pliers and wrenches.

"Help me get those wheels off their stands," he said.

"Why?"

"I'll explain while we work." He looked around. "Kemren would have done better to have set human guards here. But I suppose he thought that no one would ever get this far. Or, if they did, they'd not have the slightest idea what the wheels are for."

He told her what she was to do with the wheels, and they waded into the pool. The water only came to their ankles; a wide drain in the center ensured against overflow.

Masha didn't like being drenched, but she was sure that it would be worthwhile.

"These boxes contain devices which convert the mechanical power of the water-driven wheels to magical power," he said. "There are said to be some in the temple of Weda Krizhtawn, but I was too lowly to be allowed near them. However, I heard the high priests talking about them. They sometimes got careless in the presence of us lowly ones. Anyway, we were bound by vows to keep silent.

"I don't know exactly what these particular wheels are for. But they must be providing energy for whatever magic he's using. Part of the energy, anyway."

She didn't really understand what he was talking about, though she had an inkling. She worked steadily, ignoring the wetting and removed a wheel. Then she turned it around and reattached it.

The wheel bore symbols on each of the paddles set along its rims. There were also symbols painted on its side.

Each wheel seemed to have the same symbols but in a different sequence.

When their work was done, Smhee said, "I don't know what their reversal will do. But I'll wager that it won't be for Kemren's good. We must hurry now. If he's sensitive to the inflow-outflow of his magic, he'll know something's wrong."

She thought that it would be better not to have aroused the mage. However, Smhee was the master; she, the apprentice.

Smhee started to turn away from the wheels but stopped.

"Look!"

His finger pointed at the wheels.

"Well?"

"Don't you see something strange?"

It was a moment before she saw what had made her uneasy without realizing why. No water was spilling from the paddles down to the pool. The water just seemed to disappear after striking them.

She looked wonderingly from them to him. "I see what you mean."

He spread out his hands. "I don't know what's happening. I'm not a mage or a sorcerer. But . . . that water has to be going some place."

They put their boots back on, and he unshot the bar of the door. It led to another flight of steps, ending in another door. They went down a corridor the walls of which were bare stone. But there were also lit torches set in brackets on them.

At the end of the corridor they came to a round room. Light came down from torches; the room was actually a tall shaft. Looking up from the bottom, they could see a black square outlined narrowly by bright light at its top.

## 13

Voices came from above.

"It has to be a lift," Smhee whispered. He said something in his native tongue that sounded like a curse.

"We're stuck here until the lift comes down."

He'd no sooner spoken than they heard a squeal as of metal, and the square began descending slowly.

"We're in luck!" Smhee said. "Unless they're sending down men to see what's happened to the wheels."

They retreated through the door at the other end. Here they waited with their blades ready. Smhee kept the door open a crack.

"There are only two. Both are carrying bags and one has a haunch of meat. They're going to feed the bears and the spiders!"

Masha wondered how the men intended to get past the bears to the arachnids. But maybe the bears attacked only strangers.

"One man has a torch," he said.

The door swung open, and a Raggah wearing a red-and-black striped robe stepped through. Smhee drove his dagger into the man's throat. Masha came out from behind the door and thrust her sword through the other man's neck.

After dragging the bodies into the room, they took off the robes and put them on.

"It's too big for me," she said. "I look ridiculous."

"Cut off the bottom," he said, but she had already started doing that.

"What about the blood on the robes?"

"We could wash it out, but then we'd look strange with dripping robes. We'll just have to take a chance."

They left the bodies lying on the floor and went back to the lift. This was an open-sided cage built of light (and expensive) imported bamboo. The top was closed, but it had a trapdoor. A rope descended through it.

They looked up but could see no one looking down.

Smhee pulled on the rope, and a bell clanged. No one was summoned by it, though.

"Whoever pulls this up is gone. No doubt he, or they, are not expecting the two to return so early. Well, we must climb up the pull-ropes. I hope you're up to it."

"Better than you, fat one," Masha said.

He smiled. "We'll see."

Masha, however, pulled herself up faster than he. She had to climb up onto the beam to which the wheel was attached and then crawl along it and swing herself down into the entrance. Smhee caught her as she landed on the edge, though she didn't need his help.

They were in a hallway the walls of which were hung with costly rugs and along which was expensive furniture. Oil lamps gave an adequate illumination.

"Now comes the hard part," he said between deep breaths. "There is a staircase at each end of this hall. Which leads to the mage?"

"I'd take that one," she said, pointing.

"Why?"

"I don't exactly know why. I just feel that it's the right one."

He smiled, saying, "That's as good a reason as any for me. Let's go."

Their hands against each other inside their voluminous sleeves, but holding daggers, the hoods pulled out to shadow their faces, they walked up the stairs. These curved to end in another hall, even more luxuriously furnished. There were closed doors along it, but Smhee wouldn't open them.

"You can wager that the mage will have a guard or guards outside his apartment."

They went up another flight of steps in time to see the back of a Raggah going down the hall. At the corner, Masha looked around it. No one in sight. She stepped out, and just then a Raggah came around the corner at the right-hand end of the hall. She slowed, imperceptibly, she hoped, then resumed her stride. She heard Smhee behind her saying, "When you get close, within ten feet of her, move quickly to one side."

She did so just as the Raggah, a woman, noticed the blood on the front of her robe. The woman opened her mouth, and Smhee's thrown knife plunged into her belly. She fell forward with a thump. The fat man withdrew his knife, wiped it on the robe, and they dragged her through a doorway. The room was unlit. They dropped her near the door and went out, closing it behind them.

They went down to the end of the hall from which the woman had come and looked around the corner. There was a very wide and high-ceilinged corridor there, and from a great doorway halfway down it came much light, many voices, and the odor of cooking. Masha hadn't realized until then how hungry she was; saliva ran in her mouth.

"The other way," Smhee said, and he trotted toward the staircase. At its top, Masha looked around the corner. Halfway down the length of this hall a man holding a spear stood before a door. By his side crouched a huge black wolfish dog on a leash.

She told Smhee what she'd seen.

As excited as she'd ever seen him, he said, "He must be guarding the mage's rooms!"

Then, in a calmer tone, "He isn't aware of what we've done. He must be with a woman or a man. Sexual intercourse, you know, drains more out of a person than just physical energy. Kemren won't be sensitive to the wheels just now."

Masha didn't see any reason to comment on that. She said, "The dog didn't notice me, but we can't get close before he alerts the guard."

Masha looked behind her. The hall was still empty. But what if the mage had ordered a meal to be delivered soon?

She told Smhee what she'd just thought. After a brief consultation, they went back down the stairs to the hall. There they got an exquisitely silver-chased tray and put some small painted dishes and gold pitchers on it. These they covered with a golden cloth, the worth of which was a thousand times more than Masha could make if she worked as dentist and midwife until she was a hundred years old.

With this assemblage, which they hoped would look like a late supper tray, they went to the hall. Masha had said that if the mage was with a sexual partner, it would look more authentic if they carried two trays. But even before Smhee voiced his objections, she had thought that he had to have his hands free. Besides, one tray clattering on the floor was bad enough, though its impact would be softened by the thick rug.

The guard seemed half-asleep, but the dog, rising to its feet and growling, fully awakened him. He turned toward them, though not without a glance at the other end of the hall first. Masha, in front of Smhee, walked as if she had a right to be there. The guard held the spear pointing at them in one hand and said something in his harsh back-of-the-throat speech.

Smhee uttered a string of nonsense syllables in a low but equally harsh voice. The guard said something. And then Masha stepped to one side, dropping the tray. She bent over, muttering something guttural, as if she were apologizing for her clumsiness.

She couldn't see Smhee, but she knew that he was snatching the blowpipe from his sleeve and applying it to his lips. She came up from her bent position, her sword leaping out of her scabbard, and she ran toward the dog. It bounded toward her, the guard having released the leash. She got the blade out from the leather just in time and rammed it into the dog's open mouth as it sprang soundlessly toward her throat. The blade drove deep into its throat, but she went backward from its weight and fell onto the floor.

The sword had been torn from her grip, but the dog was heavy and unmoving on her chest. She pushed him off though he must have weighed as much as she. She rolled over and got quickly, but trembling, to her feet. The guard was sitting down, his back against the wall. One hand clutched the dart stuck in his cheek. His eyes were open but glazing. In a few seconds the hand fell away. He slumped to one side, and his bowels moved noisily.

The dog lay with the upper length of the sword sticking from its mouth. His tongue extended from the jaws, bloody, seeming almost an independent entity, a stricken worm.

Smhee grabbed the bronze handle of the door.

"Pray for us, Masha! If he's barred the door on the inside . . . !"

The door swung open.

Smhee bounded in, the dead man's spear in his hands. Masha, following, saw a large room the air of which was green and reeking of incense. The walls were covered with tapestries, and the heavy dark furniture was ornately carved with demon's heads. They paused to listen and heard nothing except a faint burbling noise.

"Get the bodies in quickly!" Smhee said, and they dragged the corpses inside. They expected the dreaded mage to walk in at any time, but he still had not appeared when they shut the door.

Smhee whispered, "Anyone coming by will notice that there is no guard."

They entered the next room cautiously. This was even larger and was obviously the bedroom. The bed was huge and round and on a platform with three steps. It was covered with a rich scarlet material brocaded in gold.

"He must be working in his laboratory," Smhee whispered.

They slowly opened the door to the next room.

The burbling became louder then. Masha saw that it proceeded from a great glass vessel shaped like an upside-down cone. A black-green liquid simmered in it, and large bubbles rose from it and passed out the open end. Beneath it was a brazier filled with glowing coals. From the ceiling above a metal vent admitted the fumes.

The floor was mosaic marble in which were set pentagrams and monograms. From the center of one rose a wisp of evil-smelling smoke. A few seconds later, the smoke ceased.

There were many tables holding other mysterious equipment and racks holding long thick rolls of parchment and papyrus. In the middle of the room was a very large desk of some shiny reddish wood. Before it was a chair of the same wood, its arms and back carved with human-headed dragons.

The mage, clad in a purple silk robe which was embroidered with golden centaurs and gryphons, was in the chair. His face was on the desk, and his arms were spread out on it. He stank of rancid butter.

Smhee approached him slowly, then grabbed the thin curly hair of the mage's topknot and raised the head.

There was water on the desk, and water ran from the dead man's nose and mouth.

"What happened to him?" she whispered.

Smhee did not reply at once. He lifted the body from the chair and placed it on the floor. Then he knelt and thumped the mage's chest.

The fat man rose smiling.

"What happened is that the reversal of the wheels' motion caused the water which should have fallen off the paddles to go instead to the mage. The conversion of physical energy to magical energy was reversed."

He paused.

"The water went into the mage's body. He *drowned!*"

He raised his eyes and said, "Blessed is Weda Krizhtawn, the goddess of water! She has her revenge through her faithful servant, Rhandhee Ghee!"

He looked at Masha. "That is my true name, Rhandhee Ghee. And I have revenged the goddess and her worshippers. The defiler and thief is dead, and I can go home now. Perhaps she will forgive some of my sins because I have fulfilled her intent. I won't go to hell, surely. I will suffer in a purgatory for a while and then, cleansed with pain, will go to the lowest heaven. And then, perhaps. . . ."

"You forget that I am to be paid," she said.

"No, I didn't. Look. He wears golden rings set with jewels of immense value. Take them, and let's be off."

She shuddered and said, "No. They would bring misfortune."

"Very well. The next room should be his treasure chamber."

It was. There were chests and boxes filled with emeralds, diamonds, turquoises, rubies, and many other jewels. There were golden and silver idols and statuettes. There was enough wealth to purchase a dozen of the lesser cities of the empire and all their citizens.

But she could only take what she could carry and not be hampered in the leaving.

Exclaiming ecstatics, she reached toward a coffer sparkling with diamonds.

At her touch, the jewels faded and were gone.

14

She cried out in anguish.

"They're products of his magic!" Smhee said. "Set here to fool thieves. Benna must have taken one of these, though how he got here and then away I've no idea! The jewel did not disappear because the mage was alive and his powers were strong. But I'll wager that not long after the rat carried the jewel off, it disappeared. That's why the searchers found no jewel though they turned the city upside down and inside out!"

"There's plenty of other stuff to take!" she said.

"No, too heavy. But he must have put his real jewels somewhere. The next room!"

But there were no other rooms.

"Don't you believe it," Smhee said. He tore down the tapestries and began tapping on the walls, which were of a dense-grained purplish wood erected over the stone. Presently, he said, "Ah!" and he moved his hands swiftly over the area. "Here's a hole in the wood just big enough to admit my little finger. I put my finger in thus, and I pull thus, and thus . . . !"

A section of the wood swung out. Masha got a burning lamp and thrust it into the room beyond. The light fell on ten open chests and twenty open coffers. Jewels sparkled.

They entered.

"Take two handsful," Smhee said. "That's all. We aren't out of here yet."

Masha untied the little bag attached to her belt, hesitated, then scooped out enough to fill the bag. It almost tore her heart apart to leave the rest, but she knew that Smhee's advice was wisdom. Perhaps, some day, she could come back for more. No. That would be stupid. She had far more than enough.

On the way out, Smhee stopped. He opened the mage's robe and revealed a smooth-shaven chest on which was tattooed a representation of a fearful six-armed four-legged being with a glaring long-tusked face. He cut around this and peeled the skin off and put it rolled and folded into a small jar of ointment. Replacing the jar in his bag, he rose, saying, "The goddess knows that I would not lie about his death. But this will be the proof if any is demanded."

"Maybe we should look for the mage's secret exit," she said. "That way, we won't run into the Raggah."

"No. At any moment someone may see that the guard is missing. Besides, the mage will have put traps in his escape route, and we might not elude those."

They made their way back to the corridor of the lift shaft without being observed. But two men stood in front of the entrance to the lift. They were talking excitedly and looking down the shaft. Then one ran down the corridor, away from the corner behind which the two intruders watched.

"Going to get help before they venture down to find out why the two feeders haven't come back," Smhee muttered.

The man who'd stayed was looking down the shaft. Masha and Smhee took him from behind, one cutting the throat, the other stabbing him in the back. They let themselves down on the ropes and then cut them before going down through the open trapdoor. But as they left the cage, a spear shot through the trapdoor and thudded point first into the floor. Men shouted above.

"They'll bring ropes and come down on those," Smhee said. "And they'll send others outside to catch us when we come out of the pool. Run, but remember the traps!"

And the spiders, she thought. And the crabs. I hope the bears are dead.

They were. The spiders, all real now that the mage was dead, were alive. These were driven back by the torches the two had paused to light, and they got to the skin-boat. They pushed this out and began paddling with desperation. The craft went through the first arch and then through the second. To their right now were some ledges on which were masses of pale-white things with stalked eyes and clacking pincers. The crabs. The two directed their boat away from these, but the writhing masses suddenly became individual figures leaping outward and splashing into the dark water. Very quickly, the ledges were bare. There was no sign of the monsters, but the two knew that these were swimming toward them.

They paddled even faster, though it had not seemed possible until then. And then the prow of the boat bumped into the wall.

"Swim for it!" Smhee bellowed, his voice rebounding from the far walls and high ceilings of the cave.

Masha feared entering the water; she expected to be seized by those huge claws. But she went over, the boat tipping, and dived.

Something did touch her leg as she went under the stone downcropping. Then her head was above the surface of the pool and Smhee's was beside her.

They scrambled out onto the hard stone. Behind them came the clacking, but none of the crabs tried to leave the pool.

The sky was black; thunder bellowed in the north; lightning traced white veins. A wind blew, chilling them in their wet clothes.

They ran toward the dugout but not in a straight line since they had to avoid the bushes with the poisonous thorns. Before they reached it, rain fell. They dragged the craft into the river and got aboard. Above them lightning cracked across the sky. Another bolt struck shortly thereafter, revealing two bears and a number of men behind them.

"They can't catch us now!" Smhee yelled. "But they'll be going back to put their horses on rafts. They'll go all the way into Sanctuary itself to get us!"

Save your breath, Masha thought. I know all that.

The wind-struck river was rough now, but they got through the waves to the opposite shore. They climbed panting up the ridge and found their horses, whinnying from fear of the lightning. When they got to the bottom of the ridge, they sped away, their passage fitfully lit by the dreadful whiteness that seemed to smash all around them. They kept their horses at a gallop for a mile, then eased them up.

"There's no way they can catch us!" Smhee shouted through the thunder. "We've got too much of a head-start!"

Dawn came. The rain stopped. The clouds cleared away; the hot winter sun of the desert rose. They stopped at the hut where they had slept, and the horses rested, and they ate bread and cheese.

"Three more hours will bring us within sight of Sanctuary," the fat man said. "We'll get your family aboard the *Swordfish,* and the Raggah can search for us in vain."

He paused, then said, "What do you intend to do about Eevroen?"

"Nothing," she said. "If he gets in my way I'll brain him again."

He laughed so much he choked on his bread. When he'd cleared his throat, he said, "You are *some* woman! Brave as the goddess makes them! And supple in mind, too! If I were not vowed to chastity, I would woo you! I may be forty-five and fat, but. . . ."

He stopped to stare down at his hand. His face froze into an expression of horror.

Masha became equally paralyzed.

A small purple spider was on Smhee's hand.

"Move slowly," he said softly through rigid lips. "I dare not move. Slap it when you've got your hand within a few inches of it."

She got up and took a step toward him. Where had the creature come from? There were no webs in the hut. Had it come from outside and crawled upon him?

She took another step, leaned over, and brought her hand slowly down at an angle toward the thing. Its eyes were black and motionless, seemingly unaware of her presence.

Maybe it's not poisonous, she thought.

Suddenly, Smhee screamed, and he crushed the spider with his other hand. He leaped up then, brushing off the tiny body.

"It bit me! It bit me!"

The dark swelling had started.

"It's not one of the mage's creatures," she said. "Its vemon may not be deadly."

"It's the mage's," he said. His face was white under the heavy pigment.

"It must have crawled into my bag. It couldn't have done it when we were on the way to the mage's rooms. It must have gotten in when I opened the bag to skin off the tattoo."

He howled. "The mage has gotten *his* revenge!"

"You don't know that," she said, but she was certain that it was as Smhee had said. She removed her small belt-bag and carefully poured out the jewels. But that was all it contained.

"It's beginning to hurt," Smhee said. "I can make it back to the city. Benna did, and he was bitten many times. But I know these spiders. I will die as surely as he did, though I will take longer. There is no antidote."

He sat down, and for a while he rocked back and forth, eyes closed, moaning. Then he said, "Masha, there is no sense in my going on with you. But, since I have made it possible for you to be as wealthy as a queen, I beg you to do one favor for me. If it is not too much to ask."

"What is that?" she said.

"Take the jar containing the tattooed skin to Sharranpip. And there tell our story to the highest priest of Weda Krizhtawn. He will pray for me to her, and a great tombstone will be erected for me in the courtyard of the peacocks, and pilgrims will come from all over Sharranpip and the islands around and will pray for me. But if you don't want . . ."

Masha knelt and kissed him on the mouth. He felt cold.

She stood up and said, "I promise you that I will do that. That, as you said, is the least I can do."

He smiled, though it cost him to do it.

"Good. Then I can die in peace. Go. May Weda Krizhtawn bless you."

"But the Raggah . . . they will torture you!"

"No. This bag contains a small vial of poison. They will find only a corpse. If they find me at all."

Masha burst into tears, but she took the jar, and after kissing Smhee again, she rode off, his horse trotting behind hers.

At the top of the hill she stopped to look behind at the hut.

Far off, coming swiftly, was a dark mass. The Raggah.

She turned away and urged her horse into a gallop.

# *Goddess*

## David Drake

"By Savankala and the Son!" Regli swore, "why can't she bear and be done with it? And why does she demand to see her brother but won't see me?" The young lord's sweat-stained tunic looked as if it had been slept in. Indeed, Regli would have slept in it if he had slept any during the two days he had paced outside the bedroom, now couching room, of his wife. Regli's hands repeatedly flexed the shank of his riding crop. There were those—and not all of them women—who would have said that agitation heightened Regli's already notably good looks, but he had no mind for such nonsense now. Not with his heir at risk!

"Now, now," said Doctor Mernorad, patting the silver-worked lapels of his robe. The older man prided himself as much on his ability to see both sides of a question as he did on his skill at physic—though neither ability seemed much valued today in Regli's townhouse. "One can't hurry the gods, you know. The child will be born when Sabellia says it should be. Any attempt to hasten matters would be sacrilege as well as foolishness. Why, you know there are some . . . I don't know what word to use, *practitioners,* who use forceps in a delivery? Forceps of *metal!* It's disgusting. I tell you, Prince Kadakithis makes a great noise about smugglers and thieves; but if he wanted to clean up a *real* evil in Sanctuary, he'd start with the so-called doctors who don't have proper connections with established temples."

"Well, damn it," Regli snapped, "you've got a 'proper connection' to the Temple of Sabellia in Ranke itself, and you can't tell me why my wife's been two days in labor. And if any of those bitch-midwives who've stood shift in there know"—he gestured toward the closed door—

"they sure aren't telling anybody." Regli knuckled the fringe of blond whiskers sprouting on his jawbone. His wealth and breeding had made him a person of some importance even in Ranke. Here in Sanctuary, where he served as Master of the Scrolls for the royal governor, he was even less accustomed to being balked. The fact that Fate, in the form of his wife's abnormally-prolonged labor, was balking him infuriated Regli to the point that he needed to lash out at something. "I can't imagine why Samlane insists on seeing no one but midwives from the Temple of Heqt," he continued, snapping his riding crop at specks on the mosaic walls. "That place has no very good reputation, I'm told. Not at all."

"Well, you have to remember that your wife is from Cirdon," said Mernorad reasonably, keeping a wary eye on his patron's lash. "Though they've been forty years under the empire, worship of the Trinity hasn't really caught on there. I've investigated the matter, and these women do have proper midwives' licenses. There's altogether too much loose talk among laymen about 'this priesthood' or 'that particular healer' not being competent. I assure you that the medical profession keeps very close watch on itself. The worst to be said on the record —the only place it counts—about the Temple of Heqt here in Sanctuary is that thirty years ago the chief priest disappeared. Unfortunate, of course, but nothing to discredit the temple."

The doctor paused, absently puffing out one cheek, then the other, so that his curly white sideburns flared. "Though I do think," he added, "that since you have engaged me anyway, that their midwives might consult with one of my, well, stature."

The door between the morning room and the hall was ajar. A page in Regli's livery of red and gold tapped the jamb deferentially. The two Rankans looked up, past the servant to the heavier man beyond in the hall. "My lord," said the page bowing, "Samlor hil Samt."

Samlor reached past the servant to swing the door fully open before Regli nodded entry. He had unpinned his dull travelling cloak and draped it over his left arm, close to his body where it almost hid the sheathed fighting knife. Northern fashion, Samlor wore boots and breeches with a long-sleeved over-tunic gathered at the wrists. The garments were plain and would have been a nondescript brown had they not been covered with white road dust. His sole jewelry was a neck-thonged silver medallion stamped with the toad face of the goddess Heqt. Samlor's broad face was deep red, the complexion of a man who will never tan but who is rarely out of the sun. He cleared his throat, rubbed his mouth with the back of his big fist, and said, "My sister sent for me. She's in there, the servant says?" He gestured.

"Why yes," said Regli, looking a little puzzled to find the quirt in his hands. The doctor was getting up from his chair. "Why, you're much older, aren't you?" the lord continued inanely.

"Fourteen years," Samlor agreed sourly, stepping past the two Rankans to the bedroom door. He tossed his cloak over one of the ivory-inlaid tables along the wall. "You'd have thought the folks would have guessed something when the five between us were still-born, but no, Hell, no. . . . And much luck the bitch ever brought them."

"I say!" Regli gasped at the stocky man's back. "You're speaking of my wife!"

Samlor turned, his knuckles already poised to rap on the door panel. "You had a choice," he said. "I'm the one who was running caravans through the mountains, trying to keep the Noble House of Kodrix afloat long enough to marry its daughter well—and her slutting about so that the folks had to go to Ranke to get offers from anybody but a brothel keeper. No wonder they drink." He hammered on the door.

Mernorad tugged the white-faced Regli back. "Master Samlor," the physician said sharply.

"It's Samlor, dammit!" the Cirdonian was shouting in response to a question from within the bedroom. "I didn't ride 500 miles to stand at a damned doorway, either." He turned to Mernorad. "Yes?" he asked.

The physician pointed. "Your weapon," he said. "The lady Samlane has been distraught. Not an uncommon thing for women in her condition, of course. She, ah, attempted to have her conditon, ah, terminated some months ago. . . . Fortunately, we got word before. . . . And even though she has since been watched at all times, she, ah, with a spoon. . . . Well. I'd simply rather that—things like your knife—not be where the Lady could snatch them, lest something untoward occur. . . ."

Within the bedroom, a bronze bar creaked as it was lifted from the door slots. Samlor drew his long dagger and laid it on an intaglio table. Only the edge of the steel winked. The hilt was of a hard, pale wood, smooth but wrapped with a webbing of silver wire for a sure grip. The morning room had been decorated by a former occupant. In its mosaic battle scenes and the weapons crossed on its walls, the room suited Samlor's appearance far better than it did that of the young Rankan lord who now owned it.

The door was opened inward by a sour, grey-haired woman in temple garb. The air that puffed from the bedroom was warm and cloying like the smell of an overripe peach. Two branches of the sextuple oil lamp within had been lighted, adding to the sunlight seeping through the stained glass separating the room from the inner court.

If the midwife looked harsh, then Samlane herself on the bed looked like Death. All the flesh of her face and her long, white hands seemed to have been drawn into the belly that now mounded her linen wrapper. A silk coverlet lay rumpled at the foot of the bed. "Come in, brother dear." A spasm rippled the wrapper. Samlane's face froze, her mouth half open. The spasm passed. "I won't keep you long, Samlor," she added through a false smile. "Leah, wait outside."

Midwife, husband, and doctor all began to protest. "Heqt's face, get out, *get out!*" Samlane shrieked, her voice rising even higher as a new series of contractions racked her. Her piercing fury cut through all objection. Samlor closed the door behind the midwife. Those in the morning room heard the door latched but not barred. Regli's house had been built for room-by-room defense in the days when bandits or a mob would burst into a dwelling and strip it, in spite of anything the government might attempt.

The midwife stood, stiff and dour, with her back to the door. Regli ignored her and slashed at the wall again. "In the year I've known her, Samlane hasn't mentioned her brother a dozen times—and each of those was a curse!" he said.

"You must remember, this is a trying time for the lady, too," Mernorad said. "With her parents, ah, unable to travel, it's natural that she wants her brother—"

"Natural?" Regli shouted. "It's *my* child she's bearing! My *son*, perhaps. What am I doing out here?"

"What would you be doing in there?" the doctor observed, tart himself in response to his patron's anger.

Before either could say more, the door swung open, bumping the midwife. Samlor gestured with his thumb. "She wants you to fix her pillows," he said curtly. He picked up his knife and began walking across the morning room toward the hall. The midwife eeled back into the bedroom, hiding all but a glimpse of Samlane's face. The lampstand beside the bed gave her flesh a yellow cast. The bar thudded back in place almost as soon as the door closed.

Regli grabbed Samlor's arm. "But what did she want?" he demanded. Samlor shook his arm free. "Ask her, if you think it's any of your business," he said. "I'm in no humor to chatter." Then he was out of the room and already past the servant who should have escorted him down the staircase to the front door."

Mernorad blinked. "Certainly a surly brute," he said. "Not at all fit for polite company."

For once it was Regli who was reasonable. "Oh, that's to be expected," he said. "In Cirdon, the nobility always prided itself on being useless—which is why Cirdon is part of the Rankan Empire and not the reverse. It must have bothered him very much when he had to go into trade himself or starve with the rest of his family." Regli cleared his throat, then patted his left palm with the quirt. "That of course explains his hostility toward Samlane and the absurd—"

"Yes, quite absurd," Mernorad agreed hastily.

"—absurd charges he leveled at her," the young noble continued. "Just bitterness, even though he himself had preserved her from the, oh, as he saw it, lowering to which he had been subjected. Actually, I have considerable mining and trading interests myself, besides my—very real —duties here to the State."

The diversion had settled Regli's mind only briefly. He resumed his pacing, the shuffle of his slippers and his occasional snappish comments being almost the only sounds in the morning room for an hour. "Do you hear something?" Mernorad said suddenly.

Regli froze, then ran to the bedroom door. "Samlane!" he shouted. "*Samlane!*" He gripped the bronze latch and screamed as his palm seared.

Acting with dreadful realization and more strength than was to be expected of a man of his age, Mernorad ripped a battle-axe from the staples holding it to the wall. He swung it against the door panel. The oak had charred to wafer thinness. The heavy blade splintered through, emitting a jet of oxygen into the superheated bedroom.

The room exploded, blasting the door away in a gout of fire and splinters. The flames hurled Mernorad against the far wall as a blazing husk before they curled up to shatter the plastered ceiling.

The flame sucked back, giving Regli a momentary glimpse into the fully-involved room. The midwife had crawled from the bed almost back to the door before she died. The fire had arched her back so that the knife wound in her throat gaped huge and red.

Samlane may have cut her own jugular as well, but too little remained of her to tell. She had apparently soaked the bedding in lamp oil and then clutched the open flame to her. All Regli really had to see, however, to drive him screaming from his house, was the boot knife.

The wooden hilt was burned off, and the bare tang poked upright from Samlane's distended belly.

Samlor had asked a street-boy where the Temple of Heqt was. The child had blinked, then brightened and said, "Oh—the Black Spire!" Sitting on a bench outside a tavern across from the temple, Samlor thought he understood why. The temple had been built of grey limestone, its walls set in a square but roofed with the usual hemispherical dome. The obelisk crowning the dome had originally commemorated the victories of Alar hil Aspar, a mercenary general of Cirdonian birth. Alar had done very well by his adopted city—and well enough for himself in the process to be able to endow public buildings as one form of conspicuous consumption. None of Alar's boasts remained visible through the coating three decades of wood and dung smoke had deposited on the spire. Still, to look at it, the worst that could be said about the Temple of Heqt was that it was ugly, filthy, and in a bad district—all of which were true of most other buildings in Sanctuary, so far as Samlor could tell.

As the caravan-master swigged his mug of blue john, an acolyte emerged from the main doorway of the temple. She waved her censer three times and chanted an evening prayer to the disinterested street before retreating back inside.

The tavern's doorway brightened as the tapster stepped out carrying a lantern. "Move, buddy, these're for customers," he said to the classically handsome young man sitting on the other bench. The youth stood but did not leave. The tapster tugged the bench a foot into the doorway, stepped onto it, and hung the lantern from a hook beneath the tavern's sign. The angle of the lantern limned in shadow a rampant unicorn, its penis engorged and as large as the horn on its head.

Instead of returning to the bench on which he had been sitting, the young man sat down beside Samlor. "Not much to look at, is it?" he said to the Cirdonian, nodding toward the temple.

"Nor popular, it seems," Samlor agreed. He eyed the local man carefully, wondering how much information he could get from him. "Nobody's gone in there for an hour."

"Not surprising," the other man said with a nod. "They come mostly after dark, you know. And you wouldn't be able to see them from here anyway."

"No?" said Samlor, sipping a little more of his clabbered milk. "There's a back entrance?"

"Not just that," said the local man. "There's a network of tunnels beneath the whole area. They—the worshippers—enter from inns or shops or tenements from blocks away. In Sanctuary, those who come to Heqt come secretly."

Samlor's left hand toyed with his religious medallion. "I'd heard that before," he said, "and I don't figure it. Heqt brings the Spring rains . . . she's the genetrix, not only in Cirdon but everywhere she's worshipped at all—except Sanctuary. What happened here?"

"You're devout, I suppose?" asked the younger man, eying the disk with the face of Heqt.

"Devout, devout," said Samlor with a grimace. "I run caravans, I'm not a priest. Sure, maybe I spill a little drink to Heqt at meals . . . without her, there'd be no world but desert, and I see enough desert already."

The stranger's skin was so pale that it looked yellow now that most of the light was from the lamp above. "Well, they say there was a shrine to Dyareela here before Alar tore it down to build his temple. There wouldn't be anything left, of course, except perhaps the tunnels, and they may have been old when the city was built on top of them. Have you heard there's supposed to be a demon kept in the lower crypts?"

Samlor nodded curtly. "I heard that."

"A hairy, long-tailed, fang-snapping demon," said the younger man with a bright smile. "Pretty much of a joke nowadays, of course. People don't really believe in that sort of thing. Still, the first priest of Heqt here disappeared. . . . And last year Alciros Foin went into the temple with ten hired bravos to find his wife. Nobody saw the bullies again, but Foin was out on the street the next morning. He was alive, even though every inch of skin had been flayed off him."

Samlor finished his mug of blue john. "Men could have done that," he said.

"Would you prefer to meet men like that rather than . . . a demon?" asked the local, smiling.

The two men stared in silence at the temple. "Do you want a drink?" Samlor asked abruptly.

"Not I," said the other.

"You say that fellow was looking for his wife?" the Cirdonian pressed, his eyes on the shadow-hidden temple and not on his companion.

"That's right. Women often go through the tunnels, they say. Fertility rites. Some say the priests themselves have more to do with any increase in conceptions than the rites do—but what man can say what women are about?"

"And the demon?"

"Aiding the conceptions?" said the local. Samlor had kept his face turned from the other so that he would not have to see his smile, but the smile freighted the words themselves stickily. "Perhaps, but some people will say anything. That would be a night for the . . . suppliant, wouldn't it?"

Samlor turned and smiled back, baring his teeth like a cat eying a throat vein. "Quite a night indeed," he said. "Are there any places known to have entrances to—that?" He gestured across the dark street. "Or is it just rumor? Perhaps this inn itself?"

"There's a hostel west of here a furlong," said the youth. "Near the Beef Market—The Man In Motley. They say there's a network beneath like worm tunnels, not really connected to each other. A man could enter one and walk for days without ever seeing another soul."

Samlor shrugged. He stood and whistled for attention, then tossed his empty mug to the tapster behind the bar. "Just curiosity," he said to his companion. "I've never been in Sanctuary before." Samlor stepped into the street, over a drain which held something long dead. When he glanced back, he saw the local man still seated empty-handed on the bench. In profile against the light, his face had the perfection of an ancient cameo.

Samlor wore boots and he was long familiar with dark nights and bad footing, so he did not bother to hire a linkman. When he passed a detachment of the Watch, the Imperial officer in command stared at the dagger the Cirdonian now carried bare in his hand. Still, Samlor looked to be no more than he was, a sturdy man who would rather warn off robbers than kill them, but who was willing and able to do either. I'll have to buy another boot knife, Samlor thought; but for the time he'd make do, make do. . . .

The Man In Motley was a floor lower than the four-story tenements around it. The ground level was well lighted. Across the street behind a row of palings, a slave gang worked under lamps scraping dung from the cobbles of the Beef Market. Tomorrow their load would be dried in the sun for fuel. The public room of the inn was occupied by a score of men. Mostly drovers in leather and homespun. A barmaid in her fifties was serving a corner booth. As Samlor entered, the host thrust through the hangings behind the bar with a cask on his shoulder.

Samlor had sheathed his knife. He nodded to the brawny innkeeper and ducked beneath the bar himself. "Hey!" cried the host.

"It's all right," Samlor muttered. He slipped behind the hangings.

A stone staircase, lighted halfway by an oil lamp, led down into the cellars. Samlor followed it, taking the lamp with him. The floor beneath the public room was of dirt. A large trap, now closed and bolted, gave access to deliveries from the street fronting the inn. The walls were lined with racked bottles, small casks, and great forty-gallon fooders set on end. One of the fooders was of wood so time-blackened as to look charred. Samlor rapped it with his knife hilt, then compared the sound to the duller note of the tun beside it.

The stairs creaked as the host descended. He held a bung-starter in one heavy fist. "Didn't they tell you to go by the side?" he rasped. "D'ye think I want the name of running a devil's brothel?" He took another step. "By Ils and his sisters, you'll remember the next time!"

Samlor's fingers moved on his knife hilt. He still held the point away from the innkeeper. "We don't have a quarrel," he said. "Let's leave it at that."

The host spat as he reached the bottom of the stairs. "Sure, I know you hot-pants folderols. Well, when I'm done with you, you take my greetings to your pandering psalm-singers and tell them there'll be no more customers through here!"

"The priests share their privileges for a price?" Samlor said in sudden enlightenment. "But I don't come for sex, friend."

Whatever the tavern-keeper thought he understood, it frightened him as sight of the dagger had not. He paused with the bung-starter half raised. First he swallowed. Then, with a guttural sound of pure terror he flung the mallet into the shadows and fled back up the stairs. Samlor frowned, shrugged, and turned again to the fooder.

There was a catch disguised as a knot, obvious enough if one knew something of the sort had to be there. Pressed, the side of the cask swung out to reveal a dry, dark tunnel sloping gently downward. Samlor's tongue touched his lips. It was, after all, what he had been looking for. He picked up the lamp, now burned well down. He stepped into the tunnel, closing the door behind him.

The passage twisted but did not branch. It was carven through dense, yellow clay, shored at intervals with timbers too blackened for Samlor to identify the wood. There were tiny skitterings which seemed to come from just beyond the light. Samlor walked slowly enough not to lose the lampflame, steadily enough not to lose his nerve. Despite the disgrace of his vocation, Samlor was a noble of Cirdon; and there was no one else in his family to whom he could entrust this responsibility.

There was a sound behind him. Without turning, Samlor lashed out with a boot. His hobnails ground into something warm and squealing where his eyes saw nothing at all. He paused for a moment to finger his medallion of Heqt, then continued. The skittering preceded him at a greater distance.

When the tunnel entered a shelf of rock it broadened suddenly into a low-ceilinged, circular room. Samlor paused. He held his lamp out at arm's length and a little back of his line of sight so that the glare would not blind him. The room was huge and empty, pierced by a score of doorways. Each but the one at which Samlor stood and one other was closed by an iron grate.

Samlor touched but did not draw his double-edged dagger. "I'll play your silly game," he whispered. Taking short steps, he walked around the circumference of the room and out the other open door. Another empty passage stretched beyond it. Licking his lips again, Samlor followed the new tunnel.

The double clang of gratings behind him was not really unexpected. Samlor waited, poised behind his knife point, but no one came down the stone boring from either direction. No one and no thing. Samlor resumed walking, the tunnel curving and perhaps descending slightly with each step. The stone was beginning to vibrate, a tremor that was too faint to be music.

The passage broadened again. This time the room so formed was not empty. Samlor spun to face what first seemed a man standing beside the doorway. The figure's only movement was the flicker of the lampflame over its metallic luster. The Cirdonian moved closer and prodded the empty torso. It was a racked suit of mail, topped by a slot-fronted helmet.

Samlor scratched at a link of the armor, urged by a suspicion that he did not consciously credit even as he attempted to prove it. The tightly-woven rings appeared to be of verdigrised copper, but the edge of Samlor's knife could not even mar the apparent corrosion. "Blood and balls," the caravan-master swore under his breath.

He was touching one of the two famed suits of armor forged by the sorcerer Hast-ra-kodi in the fire of a burning diamond. Forged with the help of two demons, legend had it; and if that was open to doubt by a modern rationalist, there could be no doubt at all that the indestructible armor had clothed heroes for three of the five ages of the world.

Then, twelve hundred years ago, the twin brothers Harash and Hakkad had donned the mail and marched against the wizard-prince Sterl. A storm overtook the expedition in the mountains; and in the clear light of dawn, all had disappeared—armor, brothers, and the three thousand men of their armament. Some said the earth had gaped; others, that everything had been swallowed by the still-wider jaws of airy monsters whose teeth flashed in the lightning and whose backs arched high as the thunderheads. Whatever the cause, the armor had vanished in that night. The reappearance of one of the suits in this underground room gave Samlor his first tangible proof of the power that slunk through the skittering passages.

From the opening across the room came the sound of metal scraping stone, scraping and jingling. Samlor backed against the wall, sucking his cheeks hollow.

Into the chamber of living rock stepped the other suit of Hast-ra-kodi's armor. This one fitted snugly about a man whom it utterly covered, creating a figure which had nothing human in it but its shape. The unknown metal glowed green, and the sword the figure bore free in one gauntleted hand blazed like a green torch.

"Do you come to worship Dyareela?" the figure asked in a voice rusty with disuse.

Samlor set his lamp carefully on the flooring and sidled a pace away from it. "I worship Heqt," he said, fingering his medallion with his left hand. "And some others, perhaps. But not Dyareela."

The figure laughed as it took a step forward. "I worshipped Heqt, too. I was her priest—until I came down into the tunnels to purge them of the evil they held." The tittering laughter ricocheted about the stone walls like the sound caged weasels make. "Dyareela put a penance on me in return for my life, my life, my life. . . . I wear this armor. That will be your penance too, Cirdonian: put on the other suit."

"Let me pass, priest," Samlor said. His hands were trembling. He clutched them together on his bosom. His fighting knife was sheathed.

"No priest," the figure rasped, advancing.

"Man! Let me pass!"

"No man, not man," said the thing, its blade rising and a flame that dimmed the oil lamp. "They say you keep your knife sharp, *suppliant*—but did gods forge it? Can it shear the mesh of Hast-ra-kodi?"

Samlor palmed the bodkin-pointed push dagger from his wrist sheath and lunged, his left foot thrusting against the wall of the chamber.

Armor or no armor, the priest was not a man of war. Samlor's left hand blocked the sword arm while his right slammed the edgeless dagger into the figure's chest. The bodkin slipped through the rings like thread through a needle's eye. The figure's mailed fist caught the Cirdonian and tore the skin over his cheek. Samlor had already twisted his steel clear. He punched it home again through armor, ribs, and the spongy lungs within.

The figure staggered back. The sword clanged to the stone flooring. "What—?" it began. Something slopped and gurgled within the indestructible helmet. The dagger hilt was a dark tumor against the glowing mail. The figure groped vainly at the knob hilt with both hands. "What are you?" it asked in a whisper. "You're not a man, not. . . ." Muscles and sinews loosened as the brain controlling them starved for lack of oxygen. One knee buckled and the figure sprawled headlong on the stone. The green glow seeped out of it like blood from a rag, staining the flooring and dripping through it in turn.

"If you'd been a man in your time," Samlor said harshly, "I wouldn't have had to be here now."

He rolled the figure over to retrieve his bodkin from the bone in which it had lodged. Hemorrhages from mouth and nose had smeared the front of the helmet. To Samlor's surprise, the suit of mail now gaped open down the front. It was ready to be stripped off and worn by another. The body within was shrivelled, its skin as white as that of the grubs which burrow beneath tree bark.

Samlor wiped his edgeless blade with thumb and forefinger. A tiny streak of blood was the only sign that it had slipped between metal links to do murder. The Cirdonian left both suits of armor in the room. They had not preserved other wearers. Wizard mail and its tricks were for those who could control it, and Samlor was all too conscious of his own humanity.

The passageway bent, then formed a tee with a narrow corridor a hundred paces long. The corridor was closed at either end by living rock. Its far wall was, by contrast, artificial—basalt hexagons a little more than a foot in diameter across the flats. There was no sign of a doorway. Samlor remembered the iron grates clanging behind him what seemed a lifetime ago. He wiped his right palm absently on his thigh.

The caravan-master walked slowly down and back the length of the corridor, from end to end. The basalt plaques were indistinguishable one from another. They rose ten feet to a bare ceiling which still bore the tool-marks of its cutting. Samlor stared at the basalt from the head of the tee, aware that the oil in his lamp was low and that he had no way of replenishing it.

After a moment he looked down at the floor. Struck by a sudden notion, he opened his fly and urinated at the base of the wall. The stream splashed, then rolled steadily to the right down the invisible trench worn by decades of footsteps. Thirty feet down the corridor the liquid stopped and pooled, slimed with patches of dust that broke up the reflected lamplight.

Samlor examined with particular care the plaques just beyond the pool of urine. The seeming music was louder here. He set his knife-point against one of the hexagons and touched his forehead to the butt-cap. Clearly and triumphantly rolled the notes of a hydraulic organ, played somewhere in the complex of tunnels. Samlor sheathed the knife again and sighted along the stones themselves, holding the light above his head. The polished surface of one waist-high plaque had been dulled by sweat and wear. Samlor pressed it and the next hexagon over hinged out of the wall.

The plaque which had lifted was only a hand's breadth thick, but what the lamp showed beyond it was a tunnel rather than a room: the remainder of the wall was of natural basalt columns, twenty feet long and lying on their sides. To go further, Samlor would have to crawl along a hole barely wide enough to pass his shoulders; and the other end was capped as well.

Samlor had spent his working life under an open sky. He had thus far borne the realization of the tons of rock above his head only by resolutely not thinking about it. This rat-hole left him no choice . . . but he would go through it anyway. A man had to be able to control his mind, or he wasn't a man. . . .

The Cirdonian set the lamp on the floor. It would gutter out in a few minutes anyway. If he had tried to take it into the tunnel with him, it would almost immediately have sucked all the life from the narrow column of air among the hexagons. He drew his fighting knife and, holding both arms out in front of him, wormed through the opening. His body blocked all but the least glimmer of the light behind him, and the black basalt drank even that.

Progress was a matter of groping with boot toes and left palm, fighting the friction of his shoulders and pelvis scraping the rock. Samlor took shallow breaths, but even so before he had crawled his own length the air became stale. It hugged him like a flabby blanket as he inched forward in the darkness. The music of the water organ was all about him.

The knife-point clinked on the far capstone. Samlor squirmed a little nearer, prayed to Heqt, and thrust outward with his left hand. The stone swung aside. Breathable air flooded the Cirdonian with the rush of organ music.

Too relieved to be concerned at what besides air might wait beyond the opening, Samlor struggled out. He caught himself on his knuckles and left palm, then scrabbled to get his legs back under him. He had crawled through the straight side of a semicircular room. Panels in the arched ceiling fifty feet above his head lighted the room ochre. It was surely not dawn yet. Samlor realized he had no idea of what might be the ultimate source of the clear, rich light.

The hydraulic organ must still be at a distance from this vaulted chamber, but the music made the walls vibrate with its intensity. There was erotic love in the higher notes, and from the lower register came fear as deep and black as that which had settled in Samlor's belly hours before. Lust and mindless hatred lilted, rippling and bubbling through the sanctuary. Samlor's fist squeezed his dagger hilt in frustration. He was only the thickness of the edge short of running amok in this empty room. Then he caught himself, breathed deeply, and sheathed the weapon until he had a use for it.

An archway in the far wall suggested a door. Samlor began walking toward it, aware of the scrapes the basalt had given him and the groin muscle he had pulled while wrestling with the figure in armor. I'm not as young as I was, he thought. Then he smiled in a way that meshed all too well with the pattern of the music: after all, he was likely through with the problems of aging very soon.

The sanctuary was strewn with pillows and thick brocades. There was more substantial furniture also. Its patterns were unusual but their function was obvious in context. Samlor had crossed enough of the world to have seen most things, but his personal tastes remained simple. He thought of Samlane; fury lashed him again. This time instead of gripping the knife, he touched the medallion of Heqt. He kicked at a rack of switches. They clattered into a construct of ebony with silken tie-downs. Its three hollow levels could be adjusted toward one another by the pulleys and levers at one end of it.

Well, it wasn't for her, Samlor thought savagely. It was for the house, the honor of the Lords Kodrix of Cirdon. And perhaps—perhaps for Heqt. He'd never been a religious man, always figured it'd be best if the gods settled things among themselves . . . but there were some things that *any* man—

Well, that was a lie. Not any man, just Samlor hil Samt for sure and probably no other fool so damned on the whole continent. Well, so be it then; he was a fool and a fanatic, and before the night finished he'd have spilled the blood of a so-called demon or died trying.

Because the illumination was from above, Samlor had noticed the bas reliefs only as patterns of shadows along the walls. The detail struck him as he approached the archway. He stopped and looked carefully.

The carvings formed a series of panels running in bands across the polished stone. The faces in each tableau were modeled with a precise detail that made it likely they were portraits, though none of the personages were recognizable to Samlor. He peered up the curving walls and saw the bands continuing to the roof vaults. How and when they had been carved was beyond estimation; the caravan-master was not even sure he could identify the stone, creamy and mottled but seemingly much harder than marble.

Time was of indeterminable importance. Knowing that he might have only minutes to live, Samlor began following some of the series of reliefs. One group of carvings made clear the unguessed unity between the 'sorcerer' Hast-ra-kodi and the 'goddess' Dyareela. Samlor stared at the conclusion of the pattern, swallowing hard but not speaking. He was unutterably glad he had not donned either suit of mail when he might have done so.

The panels reeked of bloodshed and repression. Kings and priests had stamped out the worship of Dyareela a hundred times in a hundred places. The rites had festered in the darkness, then burst out again—cancers metastasizing from the black lump here in the vaults beneath Sanctuary. A shrine in the wasteland before it was a city; and even as a city, a brawling, stinking, leaderless hive where no one looked too hard for Evil's heart since Evil's limbs enveloped all.

Alar hil Aspar—a brash outsider, a reformer flushed with his triumph over brigandage—had at last razed the fane of Dyareela here. Instead of salt, he had sown the ruins with a temple to Heqt, the goddess of his upbringing. Fool that he was, Alar had thought that ended it.

Just above the archway, set off from the courses around it by a border of ivy leaves, was a cameo that caught Samlor's eye as he returned sick and exhausted by what he had been looking at. A file of women led by a piper cavorted through the halls of a palace. The women carried small animals and icons of obviously more than symbolic significance, but it was to the piper's features that Samlor's gaze was drawn. The Cirdonian swore mildly and reached up to touch the stone. It was smooth and cold to his fingertips.

So much fit. Enough, perhaps.

Samlor stepped through the double-hung doors closing the archway. The crossbowman waiting beyond with his eyes on the staircase screamed and spun around. The patterned screen that would have concealed the ambush from someone descending the stairs was open to the archway—but judging from the bowman's panic, the mere sight of something approaching from the sanctuary would probably have flushed him anyway.

Samlor had survived too many attacks ever to be wholly unprepared for another. He lunged forward, shouting to further disconcert the bowman. The screen was toppling as the bowman jerked back from the fingers of Samlor's left hand thrusting for his eyes. The bowstring slapped and the quarrel spalled chips from the archway before ricocheting sideways through a swinging door-panel. Samlor, sprawled across his attacker's lower legs, slashed at the other's face with the knife he had finally cleared. The bowman cried out again and parried with the stock of his own weapon. Samlor's edge thudded into the wood like an axe in a firelog. Three of the bowman's fingers flew out into the room.

Unaware of his maiming, the bowman tried to club Samlor with his weapon. It slipped away from him. He saw the blood-spouting stumps of his left hand, the index finger itself half severed. Fright had made the bowman scream; mutilation now choked his voice with a rush of vomit.

Samlor squirmed forward, pinning his attacker's torso with his own. He wrestled the crossbow out of the unresisting right hand. There was a pouch of iron quarrels at the bowman's belt, but Samlor ignored them: they were on the left side and no longer a threat. The gagging man wore the scarlet and gold livery of Regli's household.

The Cirdonian glanced quickly around the room, seeing nothing but a helical staircase reaching toward more lighted panels a hundred feet above. He waggled his knife a foot from his captive's eyes, then brought the point of it down on the other's nose. "You tried to kill me," he said softly. "Tell me why or you're missing more than some fingers only."

"Sabellia, Sabellia," the maimed retainer moaned. "You've ruined me now, you bastard."

Samlor flicked his blade sideways, knowing that the droplet of blood that sprang out would force the other's eyes to cross on it. They would fill with its red proximity. "Talk to me, little man," the caravan-master said. "Why are you here?"

The injured man swallowed bile. "My lord Regli," he said, closing his eyes to avoid the blood and the dagger point. "He said you'd killed his wife. He sent us all after you."

Samlor laid the dagger point on the other's left eyesocket. "How many?" he demanded.

"A dozen," gabbled the other. "All the guards and us coachmen besides."

"The Watch?"

"Oh, gods, get that away from my eye," the retainer moaned. "I almost shook—" Samlor raised the blade an inch. "Not the Watch," the other went on. "My lord wants to handle this himself for the, the scandal."

"And where are the others?" The point dipped, brushed an eyelash, and rose again harmlessly.

The wounded man was rigid. He breathed through his mouth, quick gasps as if a lungful of air would preserve him in the moment the knife-edge sawed through his windpipe. "They all thought you'd run for Cir-don," he whispered. "You'd left your cloak behind. I slipped it away, took it to a S'danzo I know. She's a liar like all of them, but sometimes not. . . . I told her I'd pay her for the truth of where I'd find you, and I'd pay her for nothing; but I'd take a lie out of her hide if six of my friends had to hold down her blacksmith buddy. She, she described where I'd meet you. I recognized it, I'd taken the Lady Samlane—"

"Here?" Samlor's voice and his knife both trembled. Death slid closer to the room than it had been since the first slash and scramble of the fight.

"Lord, lord," the captive pleaded. "Only this far. I swear by my mother's bones!"

"Go on, then." The knife did not move.

The other man swallowed. "That's all. I waited here—I didn't tell anybody, Lord Regli put a thousand royals on your head . . . and . . . and the S'danzo said I'd live through the meeting. Oh gods, the slut, the slut. . . ."

Samlor smiled. "She hasn't lied to you yet," he said. The smile was gone, replaced with a bleakness as cruel as the face of a glacier. "Listen," he went on, rising to one knee and pinning his prisoner by psychological dominance in the stead of his body weight. "My sister asked me for a knife. I told her I'd leave her one if she gave me a reason to."

A spasm wracked the Cirdonian's face. His prisoner winced at the trembling of the dagger point. "She said the child wasn't Regli's," Samlor went on. "Well, who ever thought it would be, the way she sniffed around? But she said a demon had got it on her . . . and that bothered even her at the last. Being used, she said. Being used. She'd tried to have it aborted after she thought about things for a while, but a priest of Heqt was waiting with Regli in the shop where she'd gone to buy the drugs. After that, she wasn't without somebody watching her, asleep or awake. The Temple of Heqt wanted the child born. Samlane said she'd use the knife to end the child when they pulled it from her . . . and I believed that, though I knew she'd be in no shape for knifings just after she'd whelped.

"Seems she knew that too, but she was more determined than even I'd have given her credit for being. She could give a lot of folks points for stubborn, my sister."

Samlor shook himself, then gripped a handful of the captive's tunic. He ripped the garment with his knife. "What are you doing?" the retainer asked in concern.

"Tying you up. Somebody'll find you here in time. I'm going to do what I came here for, and when it's done I'll leave Sanctuary. If I've got that option still."

Sweat was washing streaks in the blood-flecks on the captive's face. "Sweet goddess, don't do that," he begged. "Not tied, not—that. You haven't been here when . . . others were here. You—" the injured man wiped his lips with his tongue. He closed his eyes. "Kill me yourself, if you must," he said so softly it was almost a matter for lip-reading to understand him. "Don't leave me here."

Samlor stood. His left hand was clenched, his right holding the dagger pointed down at a slight angle. "Stand up," he ordered. Regli's man obeyed, wide-eyed. He braced his back against the wall, holding his left hand at shoulder height but refusing to look at its ruin. The severed arteries had pinched off. Movement had dislodged some of the scabs, but the blood only oozed instead of spurting as it had initially. "Tell Regli that I'm mending my family's honor in my way, as my sister seems to have done in hers," Samlor said. "But don't tell him where you found me—or how. If you want to leave here now, you'll swear that."

"I swear!" the other babbled. "By anything you please!"

The caravan-master's smile flickered again. "Did you ever kill anyone, boy?" he asked conversationally.

"I was a coachman," the other said with a nervous frown. "I—I mean
. . . no."

"Once I pulled a man apart with hot pincers," Samlor continued
quietly. "He was headman of a tribe that had taken our toll payment
but still tried to cut out a couple horses from the back of our train. I
slipped into the village that night, jerked the chief out of his bed, and
brought him back to the laager. In the morning I fixed him as a display
for the rest." The Cirdonian reached forward and wiped his dagger
clean on the sleeve of the other man's tunic. "Don't go back on your
word to me, friend," he said.

Regli's man edged to the helical staircase. As he mounted each of the
first dozen steps, he looked back over his shoulder at the Cirdonian.
When the pursuit or thrown knife did not come as he had feared or expected, the retainer ran up the next twenty steps without pausing. He
looked down from that elevation and said, "One thing, master."

"Say it," responded Samlor.

"They opened the Lady Samlane to give the child separate burial."

"Yes?"

"And it didn't look to be demon spawn, as you say," Regli's man
called. "It was a perfect little boy. Except that your knife was through
its skull."

Samlor began to climb the steps, ignoring the scrabbling slippers of
the man above him on the twisting staircase. The door at the top thudded, leaving nothing of the hapless ambusher but splotches of his
blood on the railing. Should have stuck to his horses, Samlor thought.
He laughed aloud, well aware that the epitaph probably applied to himself as well. Still, he had a better notion than that poor fool of a coachman of what he was getting into . . . though the gods all knew how
slight were his chances of getting out of it alive. If the fellow he was
looking for was a real magician, rather than someone like Samlor himself who had learned a few spells while knocking around the world, it
was over for sure.

The door at the top of the stairs pivoted outward. Samlor tested it
with a fingertip, then paused to steady his heart and breathing. As he
stood there, his left hand sought the toad-faced medallion. The dagger
in his right hand pointed down, threatening nothing at the moment but—
ready.

He pushed the door open.

On the other side, the secret opening was only a wall panel. Its fres-
coes were geometric and in no way different from those of the rest of

the temple hallway. To the left, the hall led to an outside door heavily banded with iron. From his livery and the mutilation of his outflung left hand, the coachman could be recognized where he lay. The rest of the retainer appeared to have been razored into gobbets of flesh and bone, no other one of them as large as what remained of the left hand. Under the circumstances, Samlor had no sympathy to waste on the corpse.

The Cirdonian sighed and turned to the right, stepping through the hangings of brass beads into the sanctuary of Heqt. The figure he expected was waiting for him.

Soft, grey dawnlight crept through hidden slits in the dome. Mirrors had been designed to light the grinning, gilded toad-face of Heqt at the top of the dome beneath the spire. Instead, the light was directed downward onto the figure on the floral mosaic in the center of the great room. The hair of the waiting man glowed like burning wire. "Did the night keep you well, friend?" Samlor called as he stepped forward.

"Well," agreed the other with a nod. There was no sign of the regular priests and acolytes of Heqt. The room brightened as if the light fed on the beauty of the waiting man. "As I see she kept you, Champion of Heqt."

"No champion," Samlor said, taking another step as casual as the long knife dangling from his right hand. "Just a man looking for the demon who caused his sister's death. I didn't have to look any farther than the bench across the street last night, did I?"

The other's voice was a rich tenor. It had a vibrancy that had been missing when he and Samlor had talked of Heqt and Dyareela the night before. "Heqt keeps sending her champions, and I . . . I deal with them. You met the first of them, the priest?"

"I came looking for a demon," the Cirdonian said, walking very slowly, "and all it was was a poor madman who had convinced himself that he was a god."

"I am Dyareela."

"You're a man who saw an old carving down below that looked like him," Samlor said. "That worked on your mind, and you worked on other people's minds. . . . My sister, now, she was convinced her child would look like a man but be a demon. She killed it in her womb. The only way that she'd have been able to kill it, because they'd never have let her near it, Regli's heir, and her having tried abortion. But such a waste, because it was just a child, only a madman's child."

The sun-crowned man gripped the throat of his white tunic and ripped downward with unexpected strength. "I am Dyareela," it said.

Its right breast was pendulous, noticeably larger than the left. The male genitals were of normal size, flaccid, hiding the vulva that must lie behind them. "The one there," it said, gesturing toward the wall beyond which the coachman lay, "came to my fane to shed blood *without my leave.*" The naked figure giggled. "Perhaps I'll have you wash in his blood, Champion," it said. "Perhaps that will be the start of your penance."

"A mad little hermaphrodite who knows a spell or two," Samlor said. "But there'll be no penance for any again from you, little one. You're fey, and I know a spell for your sort. She wasn't much, but I'll have your heart for what you led my sister to."

"Will you conjure me by Heqt, then, Champion?" asked the other with its arms spread in welcome and laughter in its liquid voice. "Her temple is my temple, her servants are my servants . . . the blood of her champions is mine for a sacrifice!"

Samlor was twenty feet away, a full turn and half a turn. He clutched his medallion left-handed, hoping it would give him enough time to complete his spell. "Do I look like a priest to talk about gods?" he said. "Watch my dagger, madman."

The other smiled, waiting as Samlor cocked the heavy blade. It caught a stray beam of sunlight. The double edge flashed black dawn.

"By the Earth that bore this," Samlor cried, "and the Mind that gave it shape;

"By the crown of this hilt and the silver wire that laps it;

"By the cold iron of this blade and by the white-hot flames it flowed from;

"By the blood it has drunk and the souls it has eaten—

*know thy hour!*"

Samlor hurled the dagger. It glinted as it rotated. The blade was point-first and a hand's breadth from the smiling face when it exploded in a flash and a thunderclap that shook the city. The concussion hurled Samlor backward, bleeding from the nose and ears. The air was dense with flecks of paint and plaster from the frescoed ceiling.

Dyareela stood with the same smile, arms lifting in triumph, lips opening further in throaty laughter. *"Mine for a sacrifice!"*

A webbing of tiny cracks was spreading from the center of the dome high above. Samlor staggered to his feet, choking on dust and knowing that if he was lucky he was about to die.

Heqt's gilded bronze head, backed by the limestone spire, plunged down from the ceiling. It struck Dyareela's upturned face like a two-hundred ton crossbow bolt. The floor beneath disintegrated. The limestone column scarcely slowed, hurtling out of sight as the earth itself shuddered to the impact.

Samlor lost his footing in the remains of Regli's coachman. An earthshock pitched him forward against the door panel. It was unlocked. The Cirdonian lunged out into the street as the shattered dome followed its pinnacle into a cavern that gaped with a sound like the lowest note of an organ played by gods.

Samlor sprawled in the muddy street. All around him men were shouting and pointing. The Cirdonian rolled onto his back and looked at the collapsing temple.

Above the ruins rose a pall of shining dust. More than imagination shaped the cloud into the head of a toad.

# The Fruit of Enlibar

## Lynn Abbey

The hillside groves of orange trees were all that remained of the legendary glory of Enlibar. Humbled descendants of the rulers of an empire dwarfing Ilsig or Ranke eked out their livings among the gnarled, ancient trees. They wrapped each unripe fruit in leaves for the long caravan journey and wrapped each harvest in a fresh retelling of their legends. By shrewd storytelling these once proud families survived, second only to the S'danzo in their ability to create mystery, but like the S'danzo crones they flavored their legends with truth and kept the skeptics at bay.

The oranges of Enlibar made their way to Sanctuary once a year. When the fist-sized fruits were nearly ripe Haakon, the sweetmeat vendor of the bazaar, would fill his cart and hawk oranges in the town as well as in the stalls of the bazaar. During those few days he would make enough money to buy expensive trinkets for his wife and children, another year's lodgings for his mistress, and have enough gold left to take to Gonfred, the only honest goldsmith in town.

The value of each orange was such that Haakon would ignore the unwritten code of the bazaar and reserve the best of his limited supply for his patrons at the Governor's Palace. It had happened, however, that two of the precious fruits had been bruised. Haakon decided not to sell that pair at all but to share them with his friends the bazaar-smith, Dubro, and his young wife, the half-S'danzo Illyra.

He scored the peel deftly with an inlaid silver tool meant especially for this one purpose. When his fingers moved away the pebbly rind fell back from the deep-colored pulp and Illyra gasped with delight. She took one of the pulp sections and drizzled the juice onto the back of her hand, then lapped it up with the tip of her tongue: the mannerly way to savor the delicate flavor of the blood-red juice.

"These are the best; better than last year's," she exclaimed with a smile.

"You say that every year, Illyra. Time dulls your memory; the taste brings it back." Haakon sucked the juice off his hand with less delicacy: his lips showed the Stain of Enlibar. "And, speaking of time dulling your memory—Dubro, do you recall, about fifteen years back, a death-pale boy with straw hair and wild eyes running about the town?"

Haakon watched as Dubro closed his eyes and sank back in thought. The smith would have been a raw youth then himself, but he had always been slow, deliberate, and utterly reliable in his judgments. Illyra would have been a skirt-clinging toddler that long ago so Haakon did not think to ask her, nor to glance her way while he awaited Dubro's reply. Had he done so he would have seen her tremble and a blood-red drop of juice disappear into the fine dust beneath her chair.

"Yes," Dubro said without opening his eyes, "I remember one as that: quiet, pale . . . nasty. Lived a few years with the garrison, then disappeared."

"Would you know him again after all this time?"

"Nay. He was that sort of lad who looks childish until he becomes a man, then one never sees the child in his face again."

"Would you reckon 'Walegrin' to be his name?"

Ignored, beside them, Illyra bit down on her tongue and stifled sudden panic before it became apparent.

"It might be . . . nay, I could not be sure. I doubt as I ever spoke to the lad by name."

Haakon shrugged as if the questions had been idle conversation. Illyra ate her remaining share of the oranges, then went into the ramshackle stall where she lit three cones of incense before returning to the men with a ewer of water.

"Illyra, I've just asked your husband if he'd come with me to the Palace. I've got two sacks of oranges to deliver for the Prince and another set of arms would make the work easier. But he says he won't leave you here alone."

Illyra hesitated. The memories Haakon had aroused were still fresh in her mind, but all that had been fifteen years ago, as he had said. She stared at the clouded-over sky.

"No, there'll be no problem. It may rain today and, anyway, you've taken everyone's money this week with your oranges," she said with forced brightness.

"Well then, you see, Dubro—there's no problem. Bank the fires and we'll be off. I'll have you back sweating again before the first raindrops fall."

Illyra watched them leave. Fear filled the forge, fear left over from a dimly remembered childhood. Visions she had shared with no one, not even Dubro. Visions not even the S'danzo gifts could resolve into truth or illusion. She caught up her curly black hair with a set of combs and went back inside.

When the bed was concealed under layers of gaudy, bright cloth and her youth under layers of kohl, Illyra was ready to greet the townsfolk. She had not exaggerated her complaints about the oranges. It was just as well that Haakon's supply was diminishing. For two days now she had had no querents until late in the day. Lonely and bored she watched the incense smoke curl into the darkness of the room, losing herself in its endless variations.

"Illyra?"

A man drew back the heavy cloth curtain. Illyra did not recognize his voice. His silhouette revealed only that he was as tall as Dubro, though not as broad.

"Illyra? I was told I'd find Illyra, the crone, here."

She froze. Any querent might have cause to resent a S'danzo prophecy, regardless of its truth, and plot revenge against the seeress. Only recently she had been threatened by a man in the red-and-gold livery of the Palace. Her hand slid under the folds of the tablecloth and eased a tiny dagger loose from a sheath nailed to the table leg.

"What do you want?" She held her voice steady; greeting a paying querent rather than a thug.

"To talk with you. May I come in?" He paused, waiting for a reply and when there was none continued, "You seem unduly suspicious, S'danzo. Do you have many enemies here, Little Sister?"

He stepped into the room and let the cloth fall behind him. Illyra's dagger slid silently from her hand into the folds of her skirts.

"Walegrin."

"You remember so quickly? Then you did inherit *her* gift?"

"Yes, I inherited it, but this morning I learned that you had returned to Sanctuary."

"Three weeks past. It has not changed at all except, perhaps, for the worse. I had hoped to complete my business without disturbing you but

I have encountered complications, and I doubt any of the other S'danzo would help me."

"The S'danzo will never forget."

Walegrin eased his bulk into one of Dubro's chairs. Light from the candelabra fell on his face. He endured the exposure, though as Dubro had guessed, there was no trace of youth left in his features. He was tall and pale, lean in the way of powerful men whose gentler tissues have boiled away. His hair was sun-bleached to brittle straw, confined by four thick braids and a bronze circlet. Even for Sanctuary he cut an exotic, barbarian figure.

"Are you satisfied?" he asked when her gaze returned to the velvet in front of her.

"You have become very much like him," she answered slowly.

"I think not, 'Lyra. My tastes, anyway, do not run as our father's did —so put aside your fears on that account. I've come for your help. True S'danzo help, as your mother could have given me. I could pay you in gold, but I have other items which might tempt you more."

He reached under his bronze-studded leather kilt to produce a suede pouch of some weight which he set, unopened, on the table. She began to open it when he leaned forward and grasped her wrist tightly.

"It wasn't me, 'Lyra. I wasn't there that night. I ran away, just like you did."

His voice carried Illyra back those fifteen years sweeping the doubts from her memories. "I was a child then, Walegrin. A little child, no more than four. Where could I have run to?"

He released her wrist and sat back in the chair. Illyra emptied the pouch onto her table. She recognized only a few of the beads and bracelets, but enough to realize that she gazed upon all of her mother's jewelry. She picked up a string of blue glass beads strung on a creamy braided silk.

"These have been restrung," she said simply.

Walegrin nodded. "Blood rots the silk and stinks to the gods. I had no choice. All the others are as they were."

Illyra let the beads fall back into the pile. He had known how to tempt her. The entire heap was not worth a single gold piece, but no storehouse of gold could have been more valuable to her.

"Well, then, what do you want from me?"

He pushed the trinkets aside and from another pouch produced a palm-sized pottery shard which he placed gently on the velvet.

"Tell me everything about that: where the rest of the tablet is; how it came to be broken; what the symbols mean—everything!"

There was nothing in the jagged fragment that justified the change that came over Walegrin as he spoke of it. Illyra saw a piece of common orange pottery with a crowded black design set under the glaze; the sort of ware that could be found in any household of the empire. Even with her S'danzo gifts focused on the shard it remained stubbornly common. Illyra looked at Walegrin's icy green eyes, his thought-protruded brows, the set of his chin atop the studded grieve on his forearm, and thought better of telling him what she actually saw.

"Its secrets are locked deeply within it. To a casual glance its disguises are perfect. Only prolonged examination will draw its secrets out." She placed the shard back on the table.

"How long?"

"It would be hard to say. The gift is strengthened by symbolic cycles. It may take until the cycle of the shard coincides. . . ."

"I know the S'danzo! I was there with you and your mother—don't play bazaar-games with me, Little Sister. I know too much."

Illyra sat back on her bench. The dagger in her skirts clunked to the floor. Walegrin bent over to pick it up. He turned it over in his hands and without warning thrust it through the velvet into the table. Then, with his palm against the smooth of the blade, he bent it back until the hilt touched the table. When he removed his hand the knife remained bent.

"Cheap steel. Modern stuff; death to the one who relies on it," he explained, drawing a sleek knife from within the grieve. He placed the dark-steel blade with the beads and bracelets. "Now, tell me about my pottery."

"No bazaar-games. If I didn't know from looking at you, I'd say it was a broken piece of 'cotta. You've had it a long time. It shows nothing but its associations with you. I believe it is more than that, or you wouldn't be here. You know about the S'danzo and what you call 'bazaar-games,' but it's true—right now I see nothing; later I might. There are ways to strengthen the vision—I'll try them."

He flipped a gold coin onto the table. "Get what you'll need."

"Only my cards," she answered, flustered by his gesture.

"Get them!" he ordered without picking up the coin.

She removed the worn deck from the depths of her blouse and set the shard atop them while she lit more candles and incense. She allowed

Walegrin to cut the pack into three piles, then turned over the topmost card of each pile.

Three of Flames: a tunnel running from light to darkness with three candle sconces along the way.

The Forest: primeval, gnarled trunks; green canopy; living twilight.

Seven of Ore: red clay; the potter with his wheel and kiln.

Illyra stared at the images, losing herself in them without finding harmony or direction. The Flame card was pivotal, but the array would not yield its perspective to her; the Forest, symbolic of the wisdom of the ages, seemed unlikely as either her brother's goal or origin; and the Seven must mean more than was obvious. But, was the Ore card appearing in its creativity aspect? Or was red clay the omen of bloodletting, as was so often true when the card appeared in a Sanctuary-cast array?

"I still do not see enough. Bazaar-games or not, this is not the time to scry this thing."

"I'll come again after sundown—that would be a better time, wouldn't it? I've no garrison duties until after sunrise tomorrow."

"For the cards, yes, of course, but Dubro will have banked the forge for the night by then, and I do not want to involve him in this."

Walegrin nodded without argument. "I understand. I'll come by at midnight. He should be long asleep by then, unless you keep him awake."

Illyra sensed it would be useless to argue. She watched silently as he swept the pile of baubles, the knife, and the shard into one pouch, wincing slightly as he dribbled the last beads from her sight.

"As is your custom, payment will not be made until the question is answered."

Illyra nodded. Walegrin had spent many years around her mother learning many of the S'danzo disciplines and rousing his father's explosive jealousy. The leather webbing of his kilt creaked as he stood up. The moment for farewell came and passed. He left the stall in silence.

A path cleared when Walegrin strode through a crowd. He noticed it here, in this bazaar where his memories were of scrambling through the aisles, taunted, cursed, fighting, and thieving. In any other place he accepted the deference except here, which had once been his home for a while.

One of the few men in the throng who could match his height, a dark man in a smith's apron, blocked his way a moment. Walegrin studied him obliquely and guessed he was Dubro. He had seen the smith's short aquiline companion several times in other roles about the town without learning the man's true name or calling; they each glanced to one side to avoid a chance meeting.

At the entrance to the bazaar, a tumble-down set of columns still showing traces of the Ilsig kings who had them built, a man crept out of the shadows and fell in step beside Walegrin. Though this second had the manner and dress of the city-born, his face was like Walegrin's: lean, hard, and parched.

"What have you learned, Thrusher?" Walegrin began, without looking down.

"That man Downwind who claimed to read such things. . . ."

"Yes?"

"Runo went down to meet with him, as you were told. When he did not return for duty this morning Malm and I went to look for him. We found them both . . . and these." He handed his captain two small copper coins.

Walegrin turned them over in his palm, then threw them far into the harbor. "I'll take care of this myself. Tell the others we will have a visitor at the garrison this evening—a woman."

"Yes, captain," Thrusher responded, a surprised grin making its way across his jaw. "Shall I send the men away?"

"No, set them as guards. Nothing is going well. Each time we have set a rendezvous something has gone wrong. At first it was petty nuisance, now Runo is dead. I will not take chances in this city above all others. And, Thrusher . . ." Walegrin caught his man by the elbow, "Thrusher, this woman is S'danzo, my half-sister. See that the men understand this."

"They will understand, we all have families somewhere."

Walegrin grimaced and Thrusher understood that his commander had not suddenly weakened to admit family concerns.

"We have need of the S'danzo? Surely there are more reliable seers in Sanctuary than scrounging the aisles of the bazaar. Our gold is good and nearly limitless." Thrusher, like many men in the Rankan Empire, considered the S'danzo best suited to resolving love triangles among house-servants.

"We have need of this one."

Thrusher nodded and oozed back into the shadows as deftly as he had emerged. Walegrin waited until he was alone on the filthy streets before changing direction and striding, shoulders set and fists balled, into the tangled streets of the Maze.

The whores of the Maze were a special breed unwelcomed in the great pleasure houses beyond the city walls. Their embrace included a poison dagger and their nightly fee was all the wealth that could be removed from a man's person. A knot of these women clung to the doorway of the Vulgar Unicorn, the Maze's approximation to Town Hall, but they stepped aside meekly when Walegrin approached. Survival in the Maze depended upon careful selection of the target.

An aura of dark foul air enveloped Walegrin as he stepped down into the sunken room. A moment's quiet passed over the other guests, as it always did when someone entered. A Hell-Hound, personal puritan of the Prince, could shut down conversation for the duration of his visit, but a garrison officer, even Walegrin, was assumed to have legitimate business and was ignored with the same slit-eyed wariness the regulars accorded each other.

The itinerant storyteller, Hakiem, occupied the bench Walegrin preferred. The heavy-lidded little man was wilier than most suspected. Clutching his leather mug of small ale tenderly, he had selected one of the few locations in the room that provided a good view of all the exits, public and private. Walegrin stepped forward, intending to intimidate the weasel from his perch, but thought better of the move. His affairs in the Maze demanded discretion, not reckless bullying.

From a lesser location he signalled the bartender. No honest wench would work the Unicorn so Buboe himself brought the foaming mug, then returned a moment later with one of the Enlibar oranges he had arranged behind the counter. Walegrin broke the peel with his thumbnail; the red juice ran through the ridges of the peel forming patterns not unlike those on his pottery shard.

A one-armed beggar with a scarred face and a pendulant, cloudy eye sidled into the Unicorn, careful to avoid the disapproving glance of Buboe. As the ragged creature moved from table to table collecting copper pittance from the disturbed patrons, Walegrin noted the tightly wound tunic under his rags and knew the left arm was as good as the one that was snapping up the coins. Likewise, the scar was a self-induced disfigurement and the yellow rheum running down his cheek the result of seeds placed under his eyelids. The beggar announced his arrival at Walegrin's table with a tortured wheeze. Without looking up Walegrin tossed him a silver coin. He had run with the beggars himself and seen their cunning deceit become crippling reality many times too often.

Buboe split the last accessible louse in his copious beard between his grimy fingernails, looked up, and noticed the beggar, whom he threw into the street. He shuffled a few more mugs of beer to his patrons, then returned to the never-ending task of chasing lice.

The door opened again, admitting another who, like Walegrin, was in the Maze on business. Walegrin drew a small circle in the air with a finger and the newcomer hastened to his table.

"My man was slain last night by following your suggestions." Walegrin stared directly into the newcomer's eyes as he spoke.

"So I've heard, and the Enlibrite potter as well. I've rushed over here to assure you that it was not *my* doing (though I knew you would suspect me). Why, Walegrin, even if I did want to double-cross you (and I doubly assure you that such thoughts never go through my mind) I'd hardly have killed the Enlibrite as well, would I?"

Walegrin grunted. Who was to say what a man of Sanctuary might do to achieve his goals? But the information broker was likely to be telling the truth. He had an air of distracted indignation about him that a liar would not think to affect. And if he were truthful then, like as not, Runo had been the victim of coincidental outrage. The coins showed that robbery was not the motive. Perhaps the potter had enemies. Walegrin reminded himself to enter the double slaying in the garrison roster where, in due course, it might be investigated when the dozens preceding it had been disposed of.

"Still, once again, I have received no information. I will still make no payment." Walegrin casually spun the beer mug from one hand to the other as he spoke, concealing the import of his conversation from prying eyes.

"There're others who can bait your bear: Markmor, Enas Yorl, even Lythande, if the price is right. Think of this only as a delay, my friend, not failure."

"No! The omens here grow bad. Three times you've tried and failed to get me what I require. I conclude my business with you."

The information broker survived by knowing when to cut his losses. Nodding politely, he left Walegrin without a word and left the Unicorn before Buboe had thought to get his order.

Walegrin leaned back on his stool, hands clenched behind his head, his eyes alert for movement but his thoughts wandering. The death of Runo had affected him deeply, not because the man was a good soldier and long-time companion, though he had been both, but because the death had demonstrated the enduring power of the S'danzo curse on his family. Fifteen years before, the S'danzo community had decreed that all things meaningful to his father should be taken away or destroyed while the man looked helplessly on. For good measure the crones had extended the curse for five generations. Walegrin was the first. He dreaded that day when his path crossed with some forgotten child of his own who would bear him no better will than he bore his own ignominious sire.

It had been sheer madness to return to Sanctuary, to the origin of the curse, despite the assurances of the Purple Mage's protection. Madness! The S'danzo felt him coming. The Purple Mage, the one person Walegrin trusted to unravel the spell, had disappeared long before he and his men arrived in town. And now the Enlibrite potter and Runo were dead by some unknown hand. How much longer could he afford to stay? True, there were many magicians here, and any could be bought, but they all had their petty loyalties. If they could reconstruct the shard's inscription, they certainly could not be trusted to keep quiet about it. If Illyra did not provide the answers at midnight, Walegrin resolved to take his men somewhere far from this accursed town.

He would have continued his litany of dislike had he not been brought to alertness by the distress call of a mountain hawk: a bird never seen or heard within the walls of Sanctuary. The call was the alarm signal amongst his men. He left a few coins on the table and departed the Unicorn without undue notice.

A second call led him down a passageway too narrow to be called an alley, much less a street. Moving with stealth and caution, Walegrin eased around forgotten doorways suspecting ambush with every step. Only a third call and the appearance of a familiar face in the shadows quickened his pace.

"Malm, what is it?" he asked, stepping over some soft, stinking mass without looking down.

"See for yourself."

A weak shaft of light made its way through the jutting roofs of a half dozen buildings to illuminate a pair of corpses. One was the information broker who had just left Walegrin's company, a makeshift knife still protruding from his neck. The other was the beggar to whom he'd given the silver coin. The latter bore the cleaner mark of the accomplished killer.

"I see," Walegrin replied dully.

"The ragged one, he followed the other away from the Unicorn. I'd been following the broker since we found out about Runo, so I began to follow them both. When the broker caught on that he was being followed, he lit up this cul-de-sac—by mistake, I'd guess—and the beggar followed him. I found the broker like this and killed the beggar myself."

Two more deaths for the curse. Walegrin stared at the bodies, then praised Malm's diligence and sent him back to the garrison barracks to prepare for Illyra's visit. He left the corpses in the cul-de-sac where they might never be found. This pair he would not enter into the garrison roster.

Walegrin paced the length of the town, providing the inhibiting impression of a garrison officer actually on duty, though if a murder had occurred at his feet he would not have noticed. Twice he passed the entrance of the bazaar, twice hesitated, and twice continued on his way. Sunset found him by the Promise of Heaven as the priests withdrew into their temples and the Red Lanterns women made their first promenade. By full darkness he was on the Wideway, hungry and close in spirit to the fifteen-year-old who had swum the harbor and stowed away in the hold of an outbound ship one horrible night many years ago.

In the moonless night that memory returned to him with palpable force. In the grip of his depravities and obsessed by the imagined infidelity of his mistress, his father had tortured and killed her. Walegrin could recall that much. After the murder he had run from the barracks to the harbor. He knew the end of the story from campfire tales after he'd joined the army himself. Unsatisfied with murder, his father had dismembered her body, throwing the head and organs into the palace sewer-stream and the rest into the garrison stewpot.

Sanctuary boasted no criers to shout out the hours of the night. When there was a moon its progress gave approximate time, but in its absence night was an eternity, and midnight that moment when your joints grew stiff from sitting on the damp stone pilings of the Wideway and dark memories threatened the periphery of your vision. Walegrin bought a torch from the cadaverous watchman at the charnel house and entered the quiet bazaar.

Illyra emerged from the blacksmith's stall the second time Walegrin used the mountain hawk cry. She had concealed herself in a dark cloak which she held tightly around herself. Her movements betrayed her fears. Walegrin led the way in hurried silence. He took her arm at the elbow when they came into sight of the barracks. She hesitated, then continued without his urging.

Walegrin's men were nowhere to be seen in the common room that separated the men's and officers' quarters. Illyra paced the room like a caged animal, remembering.

"You'll need a table, candles, and what else?" he asked, eager to be on with the night's activity and suddenly mindful that he had brought her back to this place.

"It's so much smaller than I remember it," she said, then added, "just the table and candles, I've brought the rest myself."

Walegrin pulled a table closer to the hearth. While he gathered up candles she unfastened her cloak and placed it over the table. She wore somber woolens appropriate for a modest woman from the better part of town instead of the gaudy layers of the S'danzo costume. Walegrin wondered from whom she had borrowed them and if she had told her husband after all. It mattered little so long as she could pierce the spell over his shard.

"Shall I leave you alone?" Walegrin asked after removing the pottery fragment from the pouch and placing it on the table.

"No, I don't want to be alone in here." Illyra shuffled her fortune cards, dropping several in her nervousness, then set the deck back on the table and asked, "Is it too much to ask for some wine and information about what I'm supposed to be looking for?" A trace of the bazaar scrappiness returned to her voice and she was less lost within the room.

"My man Thrusher wanted to lay in an orgy feast when I told him I'd require the common room tonight. Then I told him I only wanted the men out—but it's a poor barracks without a flask in it, poorer than Sanctuary." He found a half-filled wineskin behind a sideboard, squirted some into his mouth, and swallowed with a rare smile. "Not the best vintage, but passable. You'll have to drink from the skin. . . ." He handed it to her.

"I drank from a skin before I'd seen a cup. It's a trick you never forget." Illyra took the wineskin from him and caught a mouthful of wine without splattering a drop. "Now, Walegrin," she began, emboldened by the musty wine, "Walegrin, I can't get either your pottery nor Haakon's oranges out of my mind. What is the connection?"

"If this Haakon peddles Enlibar oranges, then it's simple. I got the shard in Enlibar, in the ruins of the armory there. We searched three days and found only this. But, if anyone's got a greater piece he knows not what he has, else there'd be an army massing somewhere that'd have the empire quaking."

Illyra's eyes widened. "All from a piece of cheap red clay?"

"Not the pottery, my dear sister. The armorer put the formula for Enlibar steel on a clay tablet and had a wizard spell the glaze to conceal it. I sensed the spell, but I cannot break it."

"But this might only be a small piece." Illyra ran her finger along the fragment's worn edges. "Maybe not even a vital part."

"Your S'danzo gifts are heedless of time, are they not?"

"Well, yes—the past and future are clear to us."

"Then you should be able to scry back to when the glaze was applied and glimpse the entire tablet."

Illyra shifted uneasily. "Yes, perhaps, I could glimpse it but, Walegrin, I don't 'read,'" she shrugged and grinned with the wine.

Walegrin frowned, considering the near-perfect irony of the curse's functioning. No doubt Illyra could, would, see the complete tablet and be unable to tell him what was on it.

"Your cards, they have writing on them." He pointed at the runic verses hoping that she could read runes but not ordinary script.

She shrugged again. "I use the pictures and my gifts. My cards are not S'danzo work." She seemed to apologize for the deck's origin, turning the pile face down to hide the offensive ink trails. "S'danzo are artists. We paint pictures in fate." She squirted herself another mouthful of wine.

"Pictures?" Walegrin asked. "Would you see a clear enough image of the tablet to draw its double here on the table?"

"I could try. I've never done anything like that before."

"Then try now," Walegrin suggested, taking the wineskin away from her.

Illyra placed the shard atop the deck, then brought both to her forehead. Exhaling until she felt the world grow dim, the wine-euphoria left her and she became S'danzo exercising that capricious gift the primordial gods had settled upon her kind. She exhaled again and forgot that she was in her mother's death chamber. Eyes closed, she lowered the deck and pottery to the table and drew three cards, face up.

Seven of Ore: again, red clay; the potter with his wheel and kiln.

Quicksilver: a molten waterfall; the alchemic ancestor of all ores: the ace-card of the suit of Ores.·

Two of Ore: steel; war-card; death-card with masked men fighting. She spread her fingers to touch each card and lost herself in search of the Enlibrite forge.

The armorer was old, his hand shook as he moved the brush over the unfired tablet. An equally ancient wizard fretted beside him, glancing fearfully over her shoulder beyond the limits of Illyra's S'danzo gifts. Their clothing was like nothing Illyra had seen in Sanctuary. The vision wavered when she thought of the present and she dutifully returned to the armory. Illyra mimicked the armorer's motions as he covered the tablet with rows of dense, incomprehensible symbols. The wizard took the tablet and sprinkled fine sand over it. He chanted a sing-song language as meaningless as the ink marks. Illyra sensed the beginnings of the spell and withdrew across time to the barracks in Sanctuary.

Walegrin had removed the cloth from the table and placed a charcoal stylus in her hand without her sensing it. For a fleeting moment she compared her copying to the images still in her mind. Then the image was gone and she was fully back in the room, quietly watching Walegrin as he stared at the table.

"Is it what you wanted?" she asked softly.

Walegrin did not answer, but threw back his head in cynical laughter. "Ah, my sister! Your mother's people are clever. Their curse reaches back to the dawn of time. Look at this!"

He pointed at the copied lines and obediently Illyra examined them closely.

"They are not what you wanted?"

Walegrin took the card of Quicksilver and pointed to the lines of script that delineated the waterfall. "These are the runes that have been used since Ilsig attained her height, but this—" he traced a squiggle on the table, "this is older than Ilsig. By Calisard, Vortheld, and a thousand gods of long dead soldiers, how foolish I've been! For years I've chased the secret of Enlibar steel and never realized that the formula would be as old as the ruins we found it in."

Illyra reached across the table and held his clenched fists between her palms. "Surely there are those who can read this? How different can one sort of writing be from another?" she asked with an illiterate's innocence.

"As different as the speech of the Raggah is from yours."

Illyra nodded. It was not the time to tell him that when the Raggah came to trade they bargained with hand signals so none could hear their speech. "You could go to a scriptorium along Governor's Walk. They sell letters like Blind Jakob sells fruit—it won't matter what the letter says as long as you pay the price," she suggested.

"You don't understand, 'Lyra. If the formula becomes known again, ambition will seek it out. Rulers will arm their men with Enlibar steel and set out to conquer their neighbors. Wars will ruin the land and the men who live on it." Walegrin had calmed himself and begun to trace the charcoal scratches onto a piece of translucent parchment.

"But, *you* wish to have it." Illyra's tone became accusing.

"For ten years I've campaigned for Ranke. I've taken my men far north, beyond the plains. In those lands there're nomads with no cause to fear us. Swift and outnumbering us by thousands they cut through our ranks like a knife through soft cheese. We fell back and the Emperor had our commanders hung as cowards. We went forward again, with new officers, and were thrown back again with the same results. I was commissioned myself and feared we'd be sent forward a third time, but Ranke has discovered easier gold to conquer in the east and the army left its dead in the field to chase some other Imperial ambition.

"I remembered the stories of Enlibar. I hid there when I first escaped this town. With Enlibar steel my men's swords would reap nomad blood and I would not be deemed a coward.

"I found men in the capitol who listened to my plans. They knew the army and knew the battlefield. They're no friends of a hidebound Emperor who sees no more of war than a parade ground, but they became my friends. They gave me leave to search the ruins with my men and arranged for the garrison posts here when all omens said the answer lay in Sanctuary. If I can return to them with the formula the army won't be the whipping-boy of lazy Emperors. Someday men who understand steel and blood would rule . . . but, I've failed them. The damned S'danzo curse has preceded me! The mage was gone when I got here and my dreams have receded further with each step I decided to take."

"Walegrin," Illyra began, "the S'danzo are not that powerful. Look at the cards. I cannot read your writing, but I can read them and there are no curses in your fate. You've found what you came for. Red clay yields steel through the Ore-ruler, Quicksilver. True, Quicksilver is a deceiver, but only because its depths are concealed. Quicksilver will let you change this scribbling into something more to your liking." She was S'danzo again, dispensing wisdom amid her candles, but without the bright colors and heavy kohl her words had a new urgent sincerity.

"*You* are touched by the same curse! *You* lie with your husband yet have no children."

Illyra shrank back ashamed. "I . . . I use the S'danzo gifts; I must believe in their powers. But you seek the power of steel and war. You need not believe in S'danzo; you need not fear them. You run away— you escaped! The only curse upon you is that of your own guilt."

She averted her eyes from his face and collected her cards carefully lest her trembling fingers send the deck flying across the rough-hewn floors. She shook out her cloak, getting relief from her anger in the whip-like snap of the heavy material.

"I've answered your questions. I'll take my payment, if you please." She extended her hand, still not looking at his face.

Walegrin unfastened the suede pouch from his belt and placed it on the table. "I'll get the torch and we can leave for the bazaar."

"No, I'll take the torch and go alone."

"The streets are no place for a woman after dark."

"I'll get by—I did before."

"I'll have one of my men accompany you."

"All right," Illyra agreed, inwardly relieved by the compromise.

From the speed with which the soldier appeared Illyra guessed he had been right outside all along and party to everything that had passed. Regardless, the man took the torch and walked slightly ahead of her, attentive to duty but without any attempt at conversation until they reached the bazaar gates where Illyra had to step forward to guide them both through the maze of stalls.

She took her leave of the man without farewell and slipped into the darkness of her home. Familiarity obviated need for light. She moved quickly and quietly, folding the clothes into a neat bundle and storing the precious pouch with her few other valuables before easing into the warm bed.

"You've returned safely. I was ready to pull on my trousers and come looking for you. Did he give you all that he promised?" Dubro whispered, settling his arms around her.

"Yes, and I answered all his questions. He has the formula now for Enlibar steel, whatever that is, and if his purposes are true he'll make much of it." Her body released its tension in a series of small spasms and Dubro held her tighter.

"Enlibar steel," he mused softly. "The swords of legend were of Enlibar steel. The man who possesses such steel now would be a man to be reckoned with . . . even if he were a blacksmith."

Illyra pulled the linen over her ears and pretended not to hear.


"Sweetmeats! Sweetmeats! Always the best in the bazaar! Always the best in Sanctuary!"

Mornings were normal again with Haakon wheeling his cart past the blacksmith's stall before the crowds disrupted the community. Illyra, one eye ringed with kohl and the other still pristine, raced out to purchase their breakfast treats.

"There's news in the town," the vendor said as he dropped three of the pastries onto Illyra's plate. "Twice news in fact. All of last night's watch from the garrison took its leave of the town during the night and the crippled scribe who lived in the Street of Armorer's was carried off amid much screaming and commotion. Of course, there was no watch to answer the call. The Hell-Hounds consider it beneath them to patrol the law-abiding parts of town." Haakon's ire was explained, in part, by his own residence in the upper floors of a house on the Street of Armorers.

Illyra looked at Dubro, who nodded slowly in return.

"Might they be connected?" she asked.

"Pah! What would fleeing garrison troops want with a man who reads fifteen dead languages but can't pass water without someone to guide his hands?"

What indeed?

Dubro went back to his forge and Illyra stared over the bazaar walls to the palace which marked the northern extent of the town. Haakon, who had expected a less mysterious reaction to his news, muttered farewell and wheeled his cart to another stall for a more sympathetic audience.

The first of the day's townsfolk could be heard arguing with other vendors. Illyra hurried back into the shelter of the stall to complete her daily transformation into a S'danzo crone. She pulled Walegrin's three Ore cards from her deck and placed them in the pouch with her mother's jewelry, lit the incense of gentle-forgetting, and greeted the first querent of the day.

# The Dream of the Sorceress

## A. E. van Vogt

The scream brought Stulwig awake in pitch darkness. He lay for a long moment stiff with fear. Like any resident of old, decadent Sanctuary his first fleeting thought was that the ancient city, with its night prowlers, had produced another victim's cry of terror. This one was almost as close to his second-floor, greenhouse residence as—

His mind paused. Realization came, then, in a flickering self-condemnation.

Did it again!

His special nightmare. It had come out of that shaded part of his brain where he kept his one dark memory. Never a clear recall. Perhaps not even real. But it was all he had from the night three years and four moons ago when his father's death cry had come to him in his sleep.

He was sitting up, now, balancing himself on the side of the couch. And thinking once more, guiltily: if only that first time I had gone to his room to find out.

Instead, it was morning before he had discovered the dead body with its slit throat and its horrifying grimace. Yet there was no sign of a struggle. Which was odd. Because his father at fifty was physically a good example of the healer's art he and Alten both practiced. Lying there in the light of day after his death, his sprawled body looked as powerful and strong as that of his son at thirty.

The vivid images of that past disaster faded. Stulwig sank back and down onto the sheep fur. Covered himself. Listened in the continuing dark to the sound of wind against a corner of his greenhouse. It was a strong wind; he could feel the bedroom tremble. Moments later, he was still awake when he heard a faraway muffled cry—someone being murdered out there in the Maze?

Oddly, that was the final steadying thought. It brought his inner world into balance with the outer reality. After all, this was Sanctuary where, every hour of each night, a life ended violently like a candle snuffed out.

At this time of early, early morning he could think of no purpose that he could have about anything. Not with those dark, dirty, dusty, windblown streets. Nor in relation to the sad dream that had brought him to shocked awareness. Nothing for him to do, actually, but turn over, and—

He woke with a start. It was daylight. And someone was knocking at his outer door two rooms away.

"One moment!" he called out.

Naturally, it required several moments. A few to tumble out of his night robe. And even more to slip into the tunic, healer's gown, and slippers. Then he was hurrying through the bright sunlight of the greenhouse. And on into the dimness of the hallway beyond, with its solid door. Solid, that was, except for the vent at mouth level.

Stulwig placed his lips at his end of the slanted vent, and asked, "Who is it?"

The answering voice was that of a woman. "It's me. Illyra. Alone."

The seeress! Stulwig's heart quickened. His instant hope: another chance for her favors. And alone—that was a strange admission this early in the morning.

Hastily, he unblocked the door. Swung it open, past his own gaunt form. And there she stood in the dimness, at the top of his stairway. She was arrayed as he remembered her, in her numerous skirts and S'danza scarfs. But the beautiful face above all those cloth frills was already shaded with creams and powders.

She said, "Alten, I dreamed of you."

There was something in her tone: an implication of darkness. Stulwig felt an instant chill. She was giving him a sorceress' signal.

Her presence, alone, began to make sense. What she had to offer him transcended a man's itching for a woman. And she expected him to realize it.

Standing there, just inside his door, Stulwig grew aware that he was trembling. A dream. The dream of a sorceress.

He swallowed. And found his voice. It was located deep in his throat, for when he spoke it was a husky sound: "What do you want?"

"I need three of your herbs." She named them: Stypia, gernay, dalin.

This was the bargaining moment. And in the world of Sanctuary there were few victims at such a time. From his already long experience, Stulwig made his offer: "The stypia and the gernay for the dream. For the dalin one hour in my bed tonight for an assignation."

Silence. The bright eyes seemed to shrink.

"What's this?" asked Stulwig. "Is it possible that with your seeress' sight you believe that this time there will be no evasion?"

Twice before, she had made reluctant assignation agreements. On each occasion, a series of happenings brought about a circumstance whereby he needed her assistance. And for that, release from the assignation was her price.

Stulwig's voice softened to a gentler tone: "Surely, it's time, my beautiful, that you discover how much greater pleasure it is for a woman to have lying on her the weight of a normal man rather than that monstrous mass of blacksmith's muscles, the possessor of which by some mysterious power captured you when you were still too young to know any better. Is it a bargain?"

She hesitated a moment longer. And then, as he had expected after hearing the name of the third drug, she nodded.

A business transaction. And that required the goods to be on hand. Stulwig didn't argue. "Wait!" he admonished.

Himself, he did not wait. Instead, he backed quickly out of the hallway and into the greenhouse. He presumed that, with her seeress' sight, she knew that he knew about the very special person who wanted the dalin. He felt tolerant. That prince—he thought. In spite of all the advice the women receive as to when they are, and are not, capable of accepting the male seed, the youthful governor evidently possesses his concubines so often that they are unable to divert his favors away from the one who—by sorceress' wisdom—is most likely in the time of pregnancy capability.

And so—a miscarriage was needed. An herb to bring it on.

Suppressing excitement, the dream almost forgotten in his state of overstimulation, the healer located all three herbs, in turn. The stypia came from a flowering plant that spread itself over one entire end of his big, bright room. Someone would be using it soon for a persistent headache. The gernay was a mixture of two roots, a flower, and a leaf, all ground together, to be made into a tea with boiling water, steeped, and drunk throughout the day. It was for constipation.

While he worked swiftly, deftly, putting each separately into a small pouch, Stulwig pictured Illyra leaving her little stall. At the opportune moment she had pushed aside the black curtains that blocked her away from the sight of curious passersby. His mental image was of a one-room dwelling place in a dreary part of the Maze. Coming out of that flimsy shelter at this hour of the morning was not the wisest act even for a seeress. But, of course, she would have some knowing to guide her. So that she could dart from one concealment to another at exactly the right moments, avoiding danger. And then, naturally, once she got to the narrow stairway leading up to his roof abode, there would be only the need to verify that no one was lurking on the staircase itself.

He brought the three bags back to the hallway, and placed two of them into her slender hands. And with that, there it was again, the reason for her visit. The special dream. For him.

He waited, not daring to say anything for, suddenly, there was that tenseness again.

She seemed not to need prompting. She said simply, "In my dream, Ils came to me in the form of an angry young man and spoke to me about you. His manner was ferocious throughout; and my impression is that he is displeased with you." She finished, "In his human form he had jet black hair that came down to his shoulders."

There was silence. Inside Stulwig, a blankness spread from some inner center of fear. A numbness seemed to be in all locations.

Finally: "Ils!" he croaked.

The impossible!

There were tales that reported the chief god of old Ilsig occasionally interfering directly in human affairs. But that he had done so in connection with Alten Stulwig brought a sense of imminent disaster.

Illyra seemed to know what he was feeling. "Something about your father," she said, softly, "is the problem."

Her hand and arm reached out. Gently, she took hold of the third pouch; tugged at it. Stulwig let go. He watched numbly, then as she turned and went rapidly down the stairway. Moments later there was a flare of light as the bottom door opened—and shut. Just before it closed he had a glimpse of the alley that was there, and of her turning to go left.

Ils!

All that morning, after the sick people started to arrive, Stulwig tried to put the thought of the god out of his mind. There were several persons who talked excessively about their ailments; and for a change he let them ramble on. The sound of each person's voice, in turn, distracted him for a precious time from his inner feeling of imminent disaster. He was accustomed to pay attention, to compare, and decide. And, somehow, through all the numbness he managed to hold onto that ability.

A persistent stomach ache—"What have you been eating?" The flower of the agris plant was exchanged for a silver coin.

A pain in the chest. "How long? Where, exactly?" The root of the dark melles was eaten and swallowed while he watched, in exchange for one small Rankan gold piece.

Persistently bleeding gums. The flower and seeds of a rose, and the light brown grindings from the husk of grain were handed over, with the instruction: "Take a spoonful of each morning and night."

There were a dozen like that. All were anxious and disturbed. And they took up his time until the morning was almost over. Suddenly, the visitors ceased to come. At once, there was the awful thought of Ils the Mighty, angry with him.

"What could he want of me?"

That was the persistent question. Not, what purpose could Alten Stulwig have in this awful predicament? But what intention did the super-being have in relation to him? Or what did he require of him?

It was almost the noon hour before the second possibility finally penetrated the madness of merely waiting for further signals. And the more personal thought took form.

"It's up to me. I should ask certain people for advice, or even—" sudden hope—"information."

Just like that he had something *he* could do.

At that moment there was one more patient. And then, as the rather stocky woman departed with her little leather bag clutched in one greasy hand, Stulwig hastily put on his street boots. Grabbed his stave. And, moments later, was heading down the stairs two at a time.

Arrived at the bottom; naturally, he paused. And peered forth cautiously. The narrow street, as he now saw it, pointed both left and right. The nearest crossing was an alleyway to the left. And Stulwig presumed, as his gaze flicked back and forth, Illyra, on her leave-taking that morning, had turned up that alley.

—Though it was still not clear why she had gone left when her stall was to the right. Going by the alley was, for her, a long, devious route home. . . .

His own destination, already decided, required Stulwig to pass her stall. And so, his stave at the ready, he walked rightward. A few dozen steps brought him to a crowded thoroughfare. Again, a pause. And, once more, his gaze flicking back and forth. Not that he felt in danger here, at this hour. What he saw was a typical throng. There were the short people who wore the sheeny satinish cloth of west Caronne. They mingled casually with the taller folk in dark tunics from the far south of the empire. Equally at ease were red-garbed sailors on shore leave from a Cleean vessel. Here and there a S'danzo woman in her rich attire reminded him of Illyra. There were other races, and other dress, of course. But these were more of a kind. The shabby poor. The thieves. The beggars. All too similar, one to the other, to be readily identified.

For a few moments, as he stood there, Stulwig's own problem faded from the forefront of his mind. In its place came a feeling he had had before: a sense of wonder.

Me! Here in this fantastic world.

All these people. This street, with its ancient buildings, its towers, and its minarets. And the meaning of it all going back and back into the dim reaches of a fabulous history.

Almost—standing there—Stulwig forgot where he was heading. And when the memory came again it seemed to have a different form.

A more practical form. As if what he had in mind was a first step of several that would presently lead him to—what?

Mental pause.

It was, he realized, the first dim notion of having a goal beyond mere information. First, of course, the facts; those he had to have.

Somehow, everything was suddenly clearer. As he started forward it was almost as if he had a purpose with a solution implicit in it.

Illyra's stall he passed a short time later. Vague disappointment, then, as he saw that the black curtains were drawn.

Stulwig stalked on, heading west out of town across the bridge which spanned the White Foal River. He ignored the hollow-eyed stares of the Downwinders as he passed their hovels, and only slowed his pace when he reached his destination, a large estate lorded over by a walled mansion. A sell-sword stood guard just inside the large, spreading yard. Theirs was a language Stulwig understood. He took out two coppers and held them forth.

"Tell Jubal that Alten Stulwig wishes to see him."

The coppers were skillfully palmed, and transferred to a slitted pocket in the tight-fitting toga. In a baritone voice the sell-sword called out the message—

Stulwig entered the throne room, and saw that gleaming-skinned black man sitting on the throne chair. He bowed courteously toward the throne. Whereupon Jubal waved one large arm, beckoning his visitor. And then he sat scowling as Stulwig told his story.

Despite the scowl, there was no resistance, or antagonism, in the bright, wicked eyes; only interest. Finally, as Stulwig fell silent, the merchant said, "You believe, as I understand you, that one or another of my numerous paid informants may have heard something at the time of your father's death that would provide a clue: information, in short, that is not even available from a sorceress."

"I so believe," acknowledged Stulwig.

"And how much will you pay if I can correctly recall something that was said to me in passing more than three long years ago?"

Stulwig hesitated; and hoped that his desperation did not show on that sunburned face of his; it was the one thing the chapped skin was good for: sometimes it enabled him to conceal his feelings. What he sensed now was a high cost; and the best outward show for that was to act as if this was a matter about which he was merely curious. "Perhaps," he said, in his best practical tone, "your next two visits for healing free—"

"For what I remember," said the big black, "the price is the medium Rankan gold piece *and* the two visits."

Long, unhappy pause. All this trouble and cost for an innocent man who, himself, had done nothing. It seemed unfair. "Perhaps," ventured Stulwig, "if you were to give me the information I could decide if the price is merited."

He was slightly surprised when Jubal nodded. "That seems reasonable. We're both men of our word." The big man twisted his lips, as if he were considering. Then: "The morning after your father died, a night prowler who watches the dark hours for me saw Vashanka come through your door—not out of it, through it. He was briefly a figure of dazzling light as he moved down the street. Then he vanished in a blinding puff of brightness akin to lightning. The flareup, since it lit up the entire street, was seen by several other persons, who did not know its origin."

Jubal continued, "I should tell you that there is an old story that a god can go through a wall or a door only if a second god is nearby on the other side. So we may reason that for Vashanka to be able to emerge in the fashion described there was another god outside. However, my informants did not see this second mighty being."

"Bu-u-t-t!" Stulwig heard a stuttering voice. And only when the mad sound collapsed into silence did he realize that it was his own mouth that had tried to speak.

What he wanted to say, what was trying to form in his mind and in his tongue was that, for Vashanka to have penetrated into the barricaded greenhouse in the first place, then there must already have been a god inside; who had somehow inveigled his way past his father's cautious resistance to nighttime visitors.

The words, the meaning, wouldn't come. The logic of it was too improbable for Stulwig to pursue the matter.

Gulping, he fumbled in his pocket. Identified the desired coin with his fingers. Brought it out. And laid it into the outstretched palm. The price was cheap—it was as if a voice inside him spoke his acceptance of that truth.

For a while after Stulwig left Jubal's grounds, his feeling was that he had now done what there was to do. He had the information he had craved. So what else was there? Go home and—and—

Back to normalcy.

It was an unfortunate way of describing the reality to himself. It brought a mental picture of a return to his daily routine as if no warning had been given. His deep, awful feeling was that something more was expected of him. What could it be?

It was noon. The glowing orb in the sky burned down upon Stulwig. His already miserably sunburned face itched abominably, and he kept scratching at the scabs; and hating himself because his sun-sensitive skin was his one disaster that no herb or ointment seemed to help. And here he was stumbling in the direct rays, making it worse.

He was walking unsteadily, half-blinded by his own inner turmoil and physical discomfort, essentially not heeding the crowds around him when . . . the part of him that was guiding him, holding him away from collisions, helping him find a pathway through an everchanging river of people—*that* part, still somehow observant, saw a familiar man's face.

Stulwig stopped short. But already the man was gone by; his feet scraping at the same dusty street as were the feet of a dozen other passers of the moment; scraping dust and breathing it in.

Normally, Stulwig would have let him go. But this was not a normal time. He spun around. He jammed his stave against the ground as a brace. And took four, long, swift steps. He reached.

Almost gently, then, his fingers touched the sleeve and, through it, the arm of the man. "Cappen Varra," Stulwig said.

The young man with the long black hair that rested on his shoulders, turned his head. The tone of Stulwig's voice was evidently not threatening; for Cappen merely paused without tensing. Nor did he make a quick reach of the hand toward the blade at his side.

But it took several moments before he seemed to realize who his interceptor was. Then: "Oh! the healer?" he spoke questioningly.

Stulwig was apologetic. "I would like to speak to you, sir. Though, as I recall it you only sought my services on one occasion. And I think somebody told me that you had recently departed from Sanctuary for a visit to your distant home."

The minstrel did not reply immediately. He was backing off, away from the main stream of that endlessly moving crowd; backing towards a small space between a fruit stand and a table on which stood a dozen small crates, each containing a half dozen or so small, live, edible, noisy birds.

Since Stulwig had shuffled after him, Cappen was able to say in a low voice, "It was a very decisive time for me. The herbs you gave me produced a series of regurgitations which probably saved my life. I still believe I was served poisoned food."

"I need advice," said Alten Stulwig.

"We can talk here," said Cappen.

It was not an easy story to tell. There was a rise and fall of street sounds. Several times he coughed from an intake of dust thrown at him by the heel of a passerby. But in the end he had completed his account. And it was then, suddenly, that the other man's eyes widened, as if a startling thought had come to him.

"Are you telling me that you are seriously pursuing the murderer of your father, despite that you have now discovered that the killer may well be the second most powerful Rankan god?"

It was the first time that meaning had been spoken so exactly. Stulwig found himself suddenly as startled as his questioner. Before he could say anything, the lean-faced, good-looking wandering singer spoke again: "What—what happens if he ever lets you catch up with him?"

The way the question was worded somehow steadied the healer. He said, "As we know, Vashanka can come to me any time he wishes. My problem is that I do not know why he came to my father, nor why he would come to me. If I could find that out, then perhaps I could go to the temple of Ils and ask the priests for help."

Cappen frowned, and said, "Since you seem to have these powerful purposes, perhaps I should remind you of the myth." He went on:

"You know the story. Vashanka is the god of warriors and weapons, the wielder of lightning, and other powerful forces. You know of this?"

"What I don't understand," Stulwig replied helplessly, "is why would such a being kill my father?"

"Perhaps—" a shrug—"they were rivals for the affection of the same woman." He went on, "It is well known that the gods frequently assume human form in order to have concourse with human females." The beautiful male face twisted. The bright eyes gazed into Stulwig's. "I have heard stories," Cappen said, "that you, as your father before you, often accept a woman's favors in exchange for your services as a healer; the woman having nothing else to give pays the price in the time-honored way of male-female. As a consequence you actually have many half-brothers out there in the streets, and you yourself—so it has been said—have sired a dozen sons and daughters, unacknowledged because of course no one can ever be sure who is the father of these numerous waifs, unless there is unmistakable facial resemblance."

Another shrug. "I'm not blaming you. These are the truths of our world. But—"

He stopped. His hand extended gingerly, and touched Stulwig's stave. "It's tough wood."

Stulwig was uneasy. "Awkward to handle in close quarters, and scarcely a weapon to ward off the god of lightning."

"Nevertheless," said Cappen, "it's your best defense. Use it firmly. Keep it between you and any attacker. Yield ground and flee only when there's a good moment."

"But," protested Stulwig, "suppose Vashanka seeks me out? Shall I pit my staff against the Rankan god of war?" When Cappen merely stood there, looking indifferent now, the healer continued in a desperate tone, "There are stories of how Ils helped individuals in battle in the old days. But I grew up after the Rankan conquest and—" he was gloomy—"somehow the powers of the defeated god of old Ilsig didn't seem worth inquiring about. So I'm ignorant of what he did, or how."

Abruptly, Cappen Varra was impatient. "You asked for my advice," he said curtly. "I have given it to you. Goodbye."

He walked off into the crowd.

. . . They brought Stulwig before the Prince, who recognized him. "Why, it's the healer," he said. Whereupon, he glanced questioningly at Molin Torchbearer.

The hall of justice was all too brightly lit by the mid-afternoon sun-light. The sun was at that location in the sky whereby its rays shone

directly through the slanting vents that were designed to catch, and si-
phon off, rain water . . . as the high priest said accusingly, "Your most
gracious excellency, we found this follower of Ils in the temple of
Vashanka."

With the brilliant light pouring down upon him, Stulwig started toward the dais—and the two Hell-Hounds, who had been holding him, let
him go.

He stopped only when he came to the long wooden barrier that separated the accused criminals from the high seat, where the Prince sat in
judgment. From that fence, Stulwig spoke his protest. "I did no harm,
your highness. And I meant no harm. Tell his excellency—" he
addressed Torchbearer—"that your assistants found me on my knees before the—" he hesitated; he had been about to say "the idol." Uneasily,
his mind moved over to the word, "statue." But he rejected that also,
shuddering. After a long moment he finished lamely—"before Vashanka
himself, praying for his assistance."

"Yes, but a follower of Ils praying to a son of Savankala—" Torchbearer was grim—"absolutely forbidden by the doctrines of our religion."

There seemed to be no answer that he could make. Feeling helpless,
Stulwig waited. It was a year since he had last seen the youthful governor, who would now decide his fate. Standing there, Stulwig couldn't
help but notice that there were changes in the young ruler's appearance
—for the better, it seemed to him.

The Prince, as all knew, was at this time 20 years old. He had been
representative in Sanctuary for his older half-brother, the emperor, for
only one of those years, but that year had brought a certain maturity
where once there had been softness. It was still a boyish face, but a year
of power had marked it with an appearance of confidence.

The young governor seemed undecided, as he said, "Well—it does not
look like a serious crime. I should think we would encourage converts
rather than punishing them." He hesitated, then followed the amenities.
"What penalty do you recommend?" He addressed the high priest of
Rankan deities courteously.

There was a surprisingly long pause. Almost, it was as if the older
man was having second thoughts. Torchbearer said finally, "Perhaps,
we should inquire what he was praying for. And then decide."

"An excellent idea," the Prince agreed heartily.

Once more, then, Stulwig told his story, ending in a humble tone,
"Therefore, sir, as soon as I discovered that, apparently, the great gods

themselves were involved in some disagreement, I decided to pray to Vashanka to ask what he wanted me to do; asked him what amends I could make for whatever my sin might be."

He was surprised as he completed his account to see that the Prince was frowning. And, in fact, moments later, the young governor bent down towards one of the men at a table below him to one side, and said something in a low voice. The aide's reply was equally inaudible.

The youngest ruler Sanctuary had ever had thereupon faced forward. His gaze fixed on Stulwig's face. "There are several people in these parts," he said in an alarmingly severe voice, "of whose whereabouts we maintain a continuing awareness. Cappen Varra, for several reasons, is one of these. And so, Mr. Healer, I have to inform you that Cappen left Sanctuary half a moon ago, and is not expected back for at least two more moons."

"B-b-bu-ut—" Stulwig began. And stopped. Then in a high pitched voice: "That man in the seeress' dream!" he stuttered. "Long black hair to the shoulders. Ils in human form!"

There was silence after he had spoken there in that great hall of justice, where a youthful Rankan prince sat in judgment, looking down from his high bench. Other offenders were waiting in the back of the room. They were guarded by slaves, with the two Hell-Hounds that had brought Stulwig acting as overseers.

So there would be witnesses to this judgment. The wisdom of it, whatever course it might take, would be debated when the news of it got out.

Standing there, Stulwig suppressed an impulse to remind his highness of a certain night thirteen moons ago. In the wee hours he had been called out of his bed, and escorted to the palace.

On that occasion he had been taken directly into the Prince's bedroom. There he found a frightened young man, who had awakened in the darkness with an extremely fast heartbeat—more than double normal, Stulwig discovered when he counted the pulse. The attending court healer had not been able, by his arts, to slow the madly beating organ. Stulwig had braced himself, and had taken the time to ask the usual questions, which produced the information that his highness had imbibed excessively all evening.

A minor heart condition was thus revealed. The cure: primarily time for the body to dispose of the alcohol through normal channels. But Stulwig asked, and was given, permission to return to his greenhouse. He raced there accompanied by a Hell-Hound. Arrived at his quarters, he procured the mixture of roots, nettles, and a large red flower which, when steeped in boiling water, and swallowed in mouthfuls every few minutes, within an hour had the heartbeat down, not to normal, but sufficiently to be reassuring.

He thereupon informed the young man that according to his father persons that he had attended when they were young, who had the same reaction, were still alive two decades later. The Prince was greatly relieved, and promised to limit himself to no more than one drink of an evening.

Remained, then, the task of saving face for the court healer. Which Stulwig did by thanking that disgraced individual for calling him for consultation; and, within the hearing of the Prince, adding that it took many individuals to accumulate experience of all the ills that men were heir to. "And one of these days I shall be asking your help."

. . . Would the youthful governor remember that night, and decide—hopeful thought—that Alten Stulwig was too valuable to penalize?

What the Prince did, first, was ask one more question. He said, "During the time you were with the person who seemed to be Cappen Varra, did he break into song, or recite a verse?"

The significance of the question was instantly apparent. The minstrel was known for his gaiety, and his free and easy renditions under all circumstances. Stulwig made haste to say, "No, highness, not a sound, or a poetic phrase. Contrariwise, he seemed very serious."

A few moments later, the Prince rendered his judgment. He said, "Since mighty Vashanka himself seems to be acting directly in this matter, it would be presumptuous of us to interfere."

The lean-faced young man glanced at Molin. The high priest hesitated, then nodded. Whereupon the Prince turned once more to Stulwig.

"Most worthy healer," he said, "you are released to whatever the future holds for you. May the gods dispense justice upon you, balancing your virtues against your sins."

"—So he does remember!" thought Stulwig, gratefully.

Surprisingly, after he had been escorted outside, Stulwig knew at once which was the proper place for him to go. Many times he had been confronted by grief or guilt, or the hopelessness of a slighted lover, or a betrayed wife. For none of these had his herbs ever accomplished more than a passing moment of sleep or unconsciousness.

So now, as he entered the Vulgar Unicorn, he muttered under his breath the bitter advice he had given on those special occasions for what his father had called ailments of the spirit. The words, heard only by himself, were: "What you need, Alten, is a good stiff drink."

It was the ancient prescription for calming the overwrought or the overemotional. In its fashion, however, liquor in fact was a concoction of brewed herbs, and so within his purview.

The smell of the inn was already in his nostrils. The dimly lit interior blanked his vision. But Stulwig could see sufficiently well so that he was aware of vague figures sitting at tables, and of the gleam of polished wood. He sniffed of the mingling odors of hot food cooking. And already felt better.

And he knew this interior sufficiently well. So he strode forward confidently toward the dividing barrier where the brew was normally dispensed. And he had his lips parted to give his order when his eyes, more accustomed to the light, saw who it was that was taking the orders.

*"One-Thumb!"* The name was almost torn out of his lips; so great was his surprise and delight.

Eagerly, he reached forward and grasped the other's thick hand. "My friend, you had us all worried. You have been absent—" He stopped, confused. Because the time involved even for a long journey was long. Much more than a year. He finished his greeting with a gulp, "You are right welcome, sir."

The owner of the Vulgar Unicorn had become more visible with each passing moment. So that when he gestured with one of his big hands at a helper, Stulwig perceived the entire action; even saw the youth turn and come over.

The rolypoly but rugged One-Thumb indicated a table in one corner. "Bring two cups of brew thither for my friend and myself," he said. To Alten he added, "I would have words with you, sir."

So there they sat presently. And, after several sips, One-Thumb said, "I shall say quickly what need be said. Alten, I must confess that I am not the real One-Thumb. I came because, with my sorcerer's seeing, when this past noon hour my body took on the form at which you are gazing, I had a visitor who informed me that the transformation to a known person was related to you."

It was a long explanation. Long enough for Stulwig to have a variety of reactions. First, amazement. Then, progressively, various puzzlements. And, finally, tentative comprehension, and acceptance.

And since he held a drink in his hand, he raised it, and said, "To the real One-Thumb, wherever he may be."

With that, still thinking hard as to what he could gain from this meeting, he sipped from his cup, took a goodly quaff from it, and set it down. All the while noticing that the other did not drink to the toast.

The false One-Thumb said unhappily, "My seeing tells me that the real One-Thumb is in some strange location. It is not quite clear that he is still dead; but he was killed."

Up came Stulwig's glass. "Very well, then, to Enas Yorl, the sorcerer, who in whatever shape seems to be willing to be my friend."

This time the other man's cup came up slowly. He sipped. "I suppose," he said, "no one can refuse to drink to himself; since my motives are worthy I shall do so."

Stulwig's mind was flickering again with the meanings of what had been said in that long explanation. So, now, he asked the basic question: "Enas," he mumbled, "in what way does your being in One-Thumb's body shape relate to me?"

The fleshy head nodded. "Pay careful heed," said the voice of One-Thumb. "The goddess Azyuna appeared to me as I was experiencing the anguish of changing form, and asked me to give you this message. You must go home before dark. But do not this night admit to your quarters any person who has the outward appearance of a man. Do this no matter how pitifully he begs for a healer's assistance, or how many pieces of gold he is prepared to pay. Tonight, direct all male visitors to other healers."

It took a while to drink to that, and to wonder about it aloud. And, of course, as Sanctuarites, they discussed once more the story of Azyuna. How Vashanka had discovered that she (his sister) and his ten brothers had plotted to murder the father-god of Ranke, Savankala. Whereupon, Vashanka in his rage slew all ten of the brothers; but his sister he reserved for a worse fate. She became his unwilling mistress. And at times when the winds moaned and sobbed, it was said that Azyuna was again being forced to pay the price of her intended betrayal of her parents.

And now she had come down from heaven to warn a mere human being against the brother who exacted that shame from her.

"How," asked Stulwig, after he had quaffed most of a second cup and had accordingly reached a philosophical state of mind, "would you, old wise Enas Yorl, explain why a goddess would take the trouble to warn a human being against some scheme of her god-brother-lover?"

"Because," was the reply, "she may be a goddess but she is also a woman. And as all men know, women get even in strange ways."

At that, Stulwig, remembering certain experiences of his own, shuddered a little, nodded agreement, and said, "I estimate that we have been imbibing for a goodly time, and so perhaps I had better take heed of your warning, and depart. Perhaps, there is something I can do for you. A fee, perhaps."

"Make it one free visit when one of my changing shapes becometh ill."

"But not this night." Stulwig stood up, somewhat lightheaded, and was even able to smile at his small jest.

"No, not this night," agreed One-Thumb, also standing up. The big man added quickly, "I shall appear to accompany you to the door as if to bid you goodbye. But in fact I shall go out with you. And so One-Thumb will vanish once more, perhaps this time forever."

"He has done nobly this day," said Stulwig. Whereupon he raised the almost empty third cup, and said, "To the spirit of One-Thumb, wherever it may be, my good wishes."

As it developed, Enas Yorl's plan of escape was made easy. Because as they emerged from the inn there, coming up, was a small company of Rankan military led by a Hell-Hound. The latter, a man named Quag, middle-aged, but with a prideful bearing, said to Stulwig, "Word came to his highness that you were imbibing heavily; and so he has sent me and this company to escort you to your residence."

Stulwig turned to bid farewell to the false One-Thumb. And at once observed that no such person was in sight. Quag seemed to feel that he was surprised. "He went around that corner." He indicated with his thumb. "Shall we pursue him?"

"No, no."

It was no problem at all for a man with three cups of brew in him to step forward, and walk beside a Hell-Hound like an equal.

And to say, "I'm somewhat surprised at his highness taking all this trouble for a person not of Ranke birth, or—" daringly—"religion."

Quag was calm, seemingly unoffended. "These are not matters about which I am qualified to have an opinion."

"Of course," Stulwig continued with a frown, "getting me back to my quarters could place me in a location where the mighty Vashanka could most easily find me."

They were walking along a side street in the Maze. But a goodly crowd pressed by at that moment. So if Quag were contemplating a reply it was interrupted by the passing of so great a number of individuals.

When they had wended through the mob, Stulwig continued, "After all, we have to remember that it is Ils that is the god of a thousand eyes. Which, presumably, means that he can see simultaneously where everybody in the world of Ilsig is at any one moment. No such claim—of many eyes—is made for either Savankala or his son, Vashanka. And so we may guess that Vashanka does not know that—"

He stopped, appalled. He had almost let slip that the goddess Azyuna had come to Enas Yorl with a warning. And, of course, her brother-lover, with his limited vision, would not know that she had done so.

"These are all fine points," Stulwig finished lamely, "and of concern only to an individual like myself who seems to have earned the displeasure of one of these mighty beings."

Quag was calm. "Having lived many years," he said, "it could be that I have some clarifying information for you, whereby you may judge the seriousness of your situation." He continued, after a moment of silence, "In Sanctuary, the reason for the gods interfering in human affairs can have only one underlying motive. Someone has got above himself. What would be above a healer? A woman of noble family taken advantage of. An insult to a priest or god. Was your father guilty of either sin?"

"Hmmm!" Stulwig did not resist the analysis. He nodded thoughtfully in the Sanctuary way of agreement, shaking his head from side to side. "No question," he said, "it was not a chance killing. The assassin by some means penetrated a barricaded residence, committed the murder, and departed without stealing any valuables. In a city where people are daily killed most casually for their possessions, when—as in this instance of my father's assassination—the possessions are untouched, we are entitled to guess a more personal motive."

He added unhappily, "I have to confess that the reason I did not run to his rescue when I heard his cry, was that he had established an agreement with me that neither of us would intrude upon the other during the night hours. So it could have been a lady of quality being avenged."

For a small time they walked silently. Then: "I advise you to abandon this search." Quag spoke earnestly. "Go back to your healing profession, and leave murderers to the authorities."

This time Stulwig did the up and down headshake, meaning no. He said unhappily, "When Ils himself manifests in a dream, which unmistakably commands me to track down the killer, I have no choice."

The Hell-Hound's craggy face was visibly unimpressed. "After all," he said dismissingly, "your Ils failed all his people in Sanctuary when he allowed the city to be overrun by armies that worshiped another god."

"The city is being punished for its sinfulness." Stulwig automatically spoke the standard explanation given by the priests of Ils. "When we have learned our lesson, and paid our penalty, the invader will be impelled to depart."

"When I left the palace," said Quag, "there was no sign of the Prince's slaves packing his goods." Shrugging. "Such a departure for such a reason is difficult for me to envision, and I suggest you build no hopes on it."

He broke off. "Ah, here we are. As soon as you are safely inside—and of course we'll search the place and make sure there is no one lurking in a dark corner—"

It was a few periods later. "Thank you," said a grateful Stulwig. He watched them, then, go down the stairs. When Quag paused at the bottom, and looked back questioningly, Stulwig dutifully closed and barricaded the door.

And there he was.

It was a quiet evening. Two men patients and one woman patient knocked on the door. Each, through the vent, requested healing service. Stulwig sent the men down the street to Kurd; and they departed in their considerably separated times, silently accepting.

Stulwig hesitated when he heard the woman's voice. She was a long-time patient, and would pay in gold. Nevertheless, he finally directed her to a healer named Nemis. When the woman objected, he gave as his excuse that he had eaten bad food, and was not well. She seemed to accept that; for she went off, also.

Shortly after midnight there was a fourth hesitant knock. It was Illyra. As he heard her whisper, something inside Stulwig leaped with excitement. She had come, she said, as they had agreed upon that morning.

An exultant Stulwig unlocked the door. Admitted her. Motioned her towards his bedroom. And, as she went with a heavy rustling of her numerous skirts, he barricaded the door again.

Moments later, he was snuffing out the candles, and flinging off his clothes. And then in pitch darkness he joined her in the bed. As he located her naked body, he had no sense of guilt; no feeling of being wrong.

In Sanctuary everybody knew the game. There were no prissies.

Every woman was someone's mistress whether she liked it or not. Every man was out for himself, and took advantage where he could. There were, true, codes of honor and religion. But they did not apply to love, liquor, or making a living. You drove the hardest bargain right now.

The opportunity seen. Instantly, the mind wildly scanned the possibilities. Then came the initial outrageous demand, thereupon negotiated downward by the equally determined defenses of the second party to the transaction.

And that was what had brought the beautiful Illyra into his embrace. Her own agreement that, unless something happened to interfere, she would be available for him in the man-woman relation.

Apparently, once she realized that the bargain was binding, she did not resist its meaning. In the darkness Stulwig found her naked body fully acceptant of him. Complete with many small motions and excitements. Most of the women who paid in kind for his services lay like frozen statues, occasionally vibrating a little in the final moments of the act. After which they hastily slipped out of bed. Dressed. And raced off down the stairs and out into the Maze.

With Illyra so different, even to the point of sliding her palms over his skin, Stulwig found himself thinking once more of the huge blacksmith who was her established lover. It was hard to visualize this female, even though she seemed somewhat larger than he would have guessed, with such a massive male on top of her. Although—

A sudden realization: there were surprisingly strong muscles that lay under him. . . . This woman is no weakling. In fact—

Presently, as he proceeded with the lovemaking, Stulwig found himself mentally shaking his head. . . . Those voluminous S'danzo skirts, he thought, conceal more than slender flesh—his sudden impression was that, in fact, Illyra was on the plump side. And that obviously she wore the skirts to hide a considerably heavier body than she wanted onlookers to know about. Not hard to do, with her face so thin and youthful.

No mind. She was a woman who had not been easy to capture. And here she was, actually responding. Interesting, also, that her skin felt unusually warm, almost as if she had a temperature.

He was coming to the climax. And so the size of her was temporarily blanked out. Thus, the awareness of a transformation of her plump body into that of an Amazon, was like coming out of a glorious dream into a nightmare.

His sudden impossible impression: he was lying on top of a woman over six feet tall, with hips that spread out beneath him at least a foot wider than he was.

His stunned thought, immediately spoken: "Illyra, what is this? Some sorceress' trick?"

In a single, sliding motion he disengaged from that massive female body. Slid off onto the floor. And scrambled to his feet.

As he did so there was a flash of incredible brightness. It lit up the entire room, revealing an oversized, strange, naked woman in his couch, sitting up now.

And revealing, also, a man's huge lighted figure coming through a door that, before his father's death, had been a private entrance to Alten's bedroom. It was an entrance that he had, long ago now, sealed up. . . . Through it came the shining figure into the bedroom.

One incredulous look was all Stulwig had time for. And many, many desperate awarenesses: the glowing one, the being who shone with a fiery body brightness—was Vashanka.

By the time he had that thought, he had numbly grasped his stave. And, moments later, was backing naked through the doorway that led out to the greenhouse.

Inside the bedroom a god was yelling in a deep, baritone voice at the nude Amazon, who was still sitting on the edge of the bed. And the Amazon was yelling back in a voice that was like that of a male tenor. They spoke in a language that was not Ilsig.

In his time Stulwig had learned several hundred basic medically useful words in half a dozen dialects of the Rankan Empire. So now, after a few familiar words had come through to him—suddenly, the truth.

The woman was Azyuna. And Vashanka was berating her for her infidelity. And she was yelling back, accusing him of similar infidelities with human women.

The revelation dazzled Stulwig. So the gods, as had so often been suggested in vague tales about them, were like humans in their physical needs. Fleshly contacts. Angry arguments. Perhaps even intake of food with the consequent digestion and elimination by stool and urination.

But much more important for this situation was the intimate act she had sought with a human male. . . . Trust a woman! thought Stulwig. Hating her incestuous relationship. Degraded. Sad. Hopeless. But nevertheless jealous when her god-husband-brother went off to earth, and, as gods have done since the beginning of time, lay with a human woman. Or two. Or a hundred.

So she had got even. Had taken the form of a human woman. And had cunningly enticed a male—this time, himself; three and a half years ago, his father—to lie with her. Not too difficult to do in lustful Sanctuary.

And thus, Ten-Slayer, in his jealous rage, had become Eleven-Slayer —if humans like the elder Stulwig counted in the arithmetic of the divine ones.

Standing, now, in the center of the greenhouse, with no way at all that he could use as a quick escape (it always required a fair time to unbarricade his door) Stulwig braced himself. Clutched his stave. And waited for he knew not what.

He grew aware, then, that the word battle in the bedroom had come to an ending. The woman was standing now, hastily wrapping the S'danzo skirts around her huge waist. That was a momentary revelation. So such skirts could fit all female sizes without alteration.

Moments later, the woman came out. She had three of the filmy scarfs wrapped around her upper body. Her eyes avoided looking at Stulwig as she thudded past him on bare feet. And then he heard her at the door, removing the barricade.

That brought a sudden, wild hope to the man. Perhaps, if he backed in that direction, he also might make it through the doorway, once it was unblocked.

But his belief was: he dared not move. Dared not turn his head.

As Stulwig had that tense realization, the brightness—which had been slightly out of his line of vision—moved. There was an awesome sound of heavy, heavy footsteps. And then—

Vashanka strode into view.

There was no question in Stulwig's numbed mind. What he was seeing, suddenly, was clearly a sight not given to many men to observe so close up. The Rankan god, Vashanka. Maker of lightning in the sky. Master of weaponry. Killer of ten god-brothers. Murderer of Jutu Stulwig (father of Alten).

The mighty being stood now, poised in the doorway leading from the bedroom. And he literally had to stoop down so that his head did not strike the top of the door jamb.

He was a massive figure whose every stretch and fold of skin was lit up like a fire. The light that enveloped him from head to foot actually seemed to flicker, as if tiny tongues of white heat were burning there.

Those innumerable fires suffused the greenhouse with a brightness greater than daylight.

Clearly, a human confronted by a god should not rely on force alone.

At no time was that realization a coherent thought in Stulwig's mind. But the awful truth of it was there in his muscles and bones. Every movement he made reflected the reality of a man confronting an over-whelming power.

Most desperately, he wanted to be somewhere, far away.

Which was impossible. And so—

Stulwig heard his voice stuttering out the first meaning of those defensive thought-feelings: "I'm innocent. I didn't know who she was."

It was purpose of a desperate sort. Avoid this incredible situation by explaining. Arguing. Proving.

The baleful eyes stared at him after he had spoken. If the being behind those eyes understood the words, there was no clear sign.

The man stammered on: "She came as a sorceress with whom I had arranged a rendezvous for this night. How could I know that it was a disguise?"

The Ilsig language, suddenly, did not seem to be a sufficient means of communication. Stulwig had heard that its verbal structure was despised by Rankans who had learned the speech of the conquered race. The verbs—it was said—were regarded by Rankans as lacking force. Whereas the conqueror's tongue was alive with verbs that expressed intense feeling, absolute purpose, uttermost determination.

Stulwig, fleetingly remembering those comparisons, had the thought: "To Vashanka it will seem as if I'm begging for mercy, whereas all I want is understanding."

Feeling hopeless, the man clung to his stave. It was all he had. So he held it up between himself and the great fire-god. But each passing instant he was recalling what Quag, the Hell-Hound, had said—about Ils having failed his people of Sanctuary.

Suddenly, it was hard to believe that the minor magic of a failed god, as projected into a wooden stick—however tough the wood—could withstand even one blow from the mighty Vashanka.

As he had that cringing thought, Stulwig grew aware that the god had extended one hand. Instantly, the flame of the arm-hand grew brighter. Abruptly, it leaped. And struck the stave.

Utter confusion of brightness.

And confusion in his dazzled eyes as to what was happening, or what had happened.

Only one thing was clear: the attack of the god against the man had begun.

. . . He was still alive; that was Stulwig's first awareness. Alive with, now, a vague memory of having seen the lightning strike the stave. And of hearing a base-voiced braying sound. But of what exactly had happened at the moment of the fire interacting with the stave there was no after-image in his eyes.

Uncertain, still somehow clinging miraculously to the stave, Stulwig took several steps backward before the awful brightness let go of his vision centers. And there, striding toward him, was the fire-god.

Up came the stave, defensively. But even as he was remembering the words of Cappen Varra, about holding the stave in front of him, Stulwig —the stave fighter—instinctively swung the stave in a hitting motion.

Swung it at the great being less than five feet away. And felt a momentary savage surge of hope, as mighty Vashanka actually ducked to avoid the blow.

Stave fighting! He had done a lot of it out there in the wilderness, where he either tended wild herbs, or gathered herbs for his greenhouse. Amazing how often a wandering nomad or two, seeing him alone, instantly unsheathed swords and came in for the kill.

In such a battle it would be deathly dangerous merely to prod with the stave. Used as a prod, the stave could be snatched. At which, it was merely a tussle of two men tugging for possession. And virtual certainty that some wild giant of a man would swiftly wrestle it away from the unwise person who had mistakenly tried to use it as if it also were a sword.

By Ils—thought a jubilant Stulwig—there is power in this stave. And he, the lightning-god, perceives it as dangerous.

With that realization, he began to swing with all the force he could muster: whack, whack, whack! Forgotten was Cappen Varra's admonishment to use the stave only as a barrier.

It was fascinating—and exciting—to Stulwig to notice that Vashanka jumped back from the stave whenever it swung toward him. Once, the god actually leaped way up to avoid being hit. The stave went by almost two foot-lengths beneath his lowest extremity.

—But why is he staying? Why isn't he trying to get away if the stave is dangerous to him? . . . That thought came suddenly, and at once brought a great diminishment to Stulwig's battle impulse.

The fear that hit the man abruptly was that there had to be a reason why Vashanka continued to fight by avoidance. Could it be that he expected the power in the stave to wear off?

The awful possibility brought back the memory of what Ils-Cappen Varra had said. The instant shock of what must already have happened to the stave's defense power sent Stulwig backing at top speed toward the hallway leading to the stairs. He gulped with joy, then, as he glanced back for just an instant, and saw that the normally barricaded door had been left wide open by Azyuna.

With that, he spun on his heels, and almost literally flung himself down the stairs, taking four, and once five, steps at a time. He came to the bottom. And, mercifully, that door also was open. It had been hard to see as he made his wild escape effort.

At that ultimate last moment, the entire stairwell suddenly lit up like day. And there was instantly no question but that the demon-god had belatedly arrived, and was in hot pursuit.

Out in that night, so dark near his entrance, Stulwig ran madly to the nearest corner. Darted around it. And then ran along the street until he came to a main thoroughfare. There he stopped, took up position with his back against a closed stall, and his stave in front of him.

Belated realization came that he was still stark naked.

There were people here even at this late hour. Some of them looked at Stulwig. But almost everybody stopped and stared in the direction from which Stulwig had come—where a great brightness shone into the sky, visible above a long, low building with a dozen projecting towers.

Everywhere, now, voices were expressing amazement. And then, even as Stulwig wondered if Vashanka would actually continue his pursuit— abruptly, the brilliant light winked out.

It took a while, then, to gather his courage. But the feeling was: even though I made the mistake of fighting, I won—

Returning took a while longer. Also, the streets were darker again; and so his nakedness was not so obvious. Passersby had to come close before, in a city where so many were skimpily dressed, they could see a naked man at night. Thus he was able to act cautiously, without shame.

Finally, then, holding his stave in front of him, Stulwig climbed the stairs up to his darkened quarters. Found the candle that was always lit (and replaced, of course, at proper intervals) at the bottom of a long tube in his office. And then, when he had made certain that the place was, indeed, free of intruders, he hastily replaced the barricade.

A little later.

Stulwig lay sprawled on his bed, unable to sleep. He considered taking one of the herbs he normally prescribed for light sleepers. But that might send him off into a drugged unconsciousness. And for this night that seemed a last resort. Not to be done casually.

Lying there, tossing, he grew aware that there were sounds coming to him out of the night. Voices. Many voices. A crowd of voices.

Huh!

Up and over into the greenhouse. First, removing a shutter. And then, looking out and down.

The streets that he could see from his second floor were alive with torchlights. And, everywhere, people. Several times, as passersby went beneath his window, Stulwig leaned out and called stentoriously: "What is it? What's happening?"

From the replies that were yelled back, totalling at least as many as he could count on the fingers of both hands, he was able to piece together the reason for the celebration—for that was what it was.

The people of Sanctuary celebrating a victory.

What had occurred: beginning shortly after the brilliance of Vashanka had dwindled to darkness in a puff of vanishment, messengers began to run along the streets of the Maze and through all the lesser sections of the city.

The messengers were Jubal's spies and informants. And as a result of the message they spread—

Myrtis' women whispered into the ears of males, as each in turn received that for which he had paid. An electrifying piece of information it was, for the men flung on their clothes, grabbed their weapons, and charged off into the night distances of the Maze.

The worshipers at the bar of the Vulgar Unicorn suddenly drained their cups. And they, also, took to their heels—that was the appearance. An astonished barkeep ventured to the door. Peered out. And, hearing the pad of feet and the rustle of clothing, and seeing the torches, hastily locked up and joined the throngs that were streaming in one direction: toward the temple of Ils.

From his open shutter Stulwig could see the temple with its gilded dome. All the portions that he could see were lit up, and the light was visible through numerous glass reflectors. A thousand candles must be burning inside for there to be so many shining surfaces.

And inside the temple the priests were in a state of excitement. For the message that Jubal's informants carried to all Sanctuary was that Ils had engaged in battle with the lightning god of the Rankans, and had won.

There would be exultant worshiping until the hour of dawn: that was the meaning that Stulwig had had shouted up to him.

As the meaning finally came to him, Stulwig hastily closed the shutter. And stood there, shivering. It was an inner cold, not an outer one. Was this wise?—he wondered. Suppose the people in the palace came out to learn what all the uproar was? Suppose Vashanka, in his rage at being made to appear a loser, sent his lightning bolts down upon the city. Come to think of it, the sky above had already started to look very cloudy and threatening.

His entire body throbbing with anxiety, Stulwig nonetheless found himself accepting the celebration as justified. It was true. Ils was the victor. And he had deliberately sought the opportunity. So it could be that the ancient god of Ilsig was at long last ready for—what?

What could happen? How could the forces of the Rankan Empire be persuaded to depart from Sanctuary?

Stulwig was back in bed, the wonder and the mystery of it still seething inside him.

And he was still awake, later, when there came a gentle knock on his outer door.

Instant shock. Fear. Doubt. And then, trembling, he was at the vent asking the question: "Who is it?"

The voice of Illyra answered softly, "I am here, Alten, as we agreed this morning, to pay my debt in kind."

Long pause. Because the doubt and shock, and the beginning of disappointment, were absolutely intense. So long a pause that the woman spoke again: "My blacksmith, as you call him, has gone to the temple of Ils and will not be back until morning."

On one level—the level of his desire—it had the ring of truth. But the denying thought was stronger. Suppose this was Azyuna, forced by her shamed brother-lover to make one more entrance into the home of the healer; so that the brother could use some mysterious connection with her to penetrate hard walls. Then, when death had been dealt, Ils would again be disgraced.

Thinking thus, a reluctant Stulwig said, "You are freed of your promise, Illyra. Fate has worked once more to deny me one of the great joys of life. And once more enabled you to remain faithful to that hulking monster."

The healer uttered a long sigh; finished: "Perhaps, I shall have better fortune next time."

As he returned to his sheepskin he did have the male thought that a night when a man made love to a goddess, could surely not be considered a total loss.

In fact—

Remembering, suddenly, that the affair had also included embracing, in its early stages, an Illyra look-alike, Stulwig began to relax.

It was then that sweet sleep came.

# Vashanka's Minion

## Janet Morris

### 1

The storm swept down on Sanctuary in unnatural fury, as if to punish the thieves for their misdeeds. Its hailstones were large as fists. They pummeled Wideway and broke windows on the Street of Red Lanterns and collapsed the temple of Ils, most powerful of the conquered Ilsigs' gods.

The lightning it brought snapped up from the hills and down from the devilish skies and wherever it spat the world shuddered and rolled. It licked round the dome of Prince Kadakithis's palace and when it was gone, the Storm God Vashanka's name was seared into the stone in huge hieratic letters visible from the harbor. It slithered in the window of Jubal's walled estate and circled round the slavetrader's chair while he sat in it, turning his black face blue with terror.

It danced on a high hill between the slaver's estate and the cowering town, where a mercenary named Tempus schooled his new Syrese horse in the art of death. He had bought the tarnished silver beast sight unseen, sending to a man whose father's life he had once saved.

"Easy," he advised the horse, who slipped in a sharp turn, throwing mud up into his rider's face. Tempus cursed the mud and the rain and the hours he would need to spend on his tack when the lesson was done. As for the screaming, stumbling hawk-masked man who fled ironshod hooves in ever-shortening circles, he had no gods to invoke—he just howled.

The horse wheeled and hopped; its rider clung tightly, reins flapping loose, using only his knees to guide his mount. If the slaver who kept a private army must flaunt the fact, then the mercenary-cum-Guardsman would reduce its ranks. He would teach Jubal the overweening flesh merchant that he who is too arrogant, is lost. He saw it as part of his duty to the Ranke Prince-Governor he was sworn to protect. Tempus had taken down a dozen hawk-masks. This one, stumbling and gibbering, would make thirteen.

"Kill," suggested the mercenary, tiring of his sport in the face of the storm.

The flattened ears of the misty horse flickered, came forward. It lunged, neck out. Teeth and hooves thunked into flesh. Screaming. Then screaming stopped.

Tempus let the horse pummel the corpse awhile, stroking the beast's neck and cooing soft praise. When bones showed in a lightning flash, he backed the horse off and set it at a walk toward the walled city.

It was then that the lightning came circling round man and mount.

"Stand, stand." The horse, though he shook like a newborn foal, stood. The searing red light violated Tempus's tight-shut lids and made his eyes tear. An awful voice rang inside his head, deep and thunderous: *"You are mine."*

"I have never doubted it," grated the mercenary.

*"You have doubted it repeatedly,"* growled the voice querulously, if thunder can be said to carp. *"You have been unruly, faithless though you pledged me your troth. You have been, since you renounced your inheritance, a mage, a philosopher, an auditing Adept of the Order of the Blue Star, a—"*

"Look here, God. I have also been a cuckold, a footsoldier in the ranks, a general at the end of that. I have bedded more iron in flesh than any ten other men who have lived as long as I. Now you ring me round with thunder and compass me with lightning though I am here to expand Your worship among these infidels. I am building Your accursed temple as fast as I can. I am no priest, to be terrified by loud words and bright manifestations. Get Thee hence, and leave this slum unenlightened. They do not deserve me, and they do not deserve You!"

A gust sighed fiercely, flapping Tempus's woolens against his mail beneath.

*"I have sent you hither to build me a temple among the heathens, O sleepless one! A temple you will build!"*

"A temple I will build. Yes, sir, Vashanka, lord of the Edge and the Point. If You leave me alone to do it." Damn pushy tutelary god. "You blind my horse, O God, and I will put him under Your threshold instead of the enemies slain in battle Your ritual demands. Then we will see who comes to worship there."

*"Do not trifle with me, Man."*

"Then let me be. I am doing the best I can. There is no room for foreign gods in the hearts of these Sanctuarites. The Ilsig gods they were born under have seen to that. Do something amazing: strike the fear of You into them."

*"I cannot even make you cower, O impudent human!"*

"Even Your visitations get old, after three hundred-fifty years. Go scare the locals. This horse will founder, standing hot in the rain."

The thunder changed its tune, becoming canny. *"Go you to the harbor, My son, and look upon what My Majesty hath wrought! And into the Maze, where I am making My power known!"*

With that, the corral of lightning vanished, the thunder ceased, and the clouds blew away on a west wind, so that the full moon shone upon the land.

"Too much krrf," the mercenary who had sold himself for a Hell-Hound sighed. "Hell-Hound" was what the citizenry called the Prince's Guard; as far as Tempus was concerned, Sanctuary was Hell. The only thing that made it bearable was krrf, his drug of choice. Rubbing a clammy palm across his mouth, he dug in his human-hide belt until searching fingers found a little silver box he always carried. Flipping it open, he took a pinch of black Caronne krrf and, clenching his fist, piled the dust into the hollow between his first thumb joint and the fleshy muscle leading to his knuckle. He sniffed deeply, sighed, and repeated the process, inundating his other nostril.

"Too much damn krrf," he chuckled, for the krrf had never been stepped on—he did not buy adulterated drugs—and all six and a half feet of him tingled from its kiss. One of these days he would have to stop using it—the same day he laid down his sword.

He felt for its hilt, patted it. He had taken to calling it his "Wriggly-be-good," since he had come to this Godforsaken warren of magicians and changelings and thieves. Then, the initial euphoria of the drug past, he kneed his horse homeward.

It was the krrf, not the instructions of the lightning or any fear of Vashanka, that made him go by way of the harbor. He was walking out his horse before taking it to the stable the Hell-Hounds shared with the barracks personnel. What had ever possessed him to come downcountry among the Ilsigs? It was not for his fee, which was exorbitant, that he had come, for the sake of those interests in the Rankan capital who underwrote him—those who hated the Emperor so much that they were willing to back such a loser as Kadakithis, if they could do it without becoming the brunt of too many jokes. It was not for the temple, though he was pleased to build it. It was some old, residual empathy in Tempus for a prince so inept as to be known far and wide as "Kitty" which had made him come. Tempus had walked away from *his* primogeniture in Azehur, a long time ago, leaving the throne to his brother, who was not compromised by palace politics. He had deposited a treatise on the nature of being in the temple of a favored goddess, and he had left. Had he ever, really, been that young? Young as Prince Kadakithis, whom even the Wrigglies disparaged?

Tempus had been around in the days when the Ilsigs had been the Enemy: the Wrigglies. He had been on every battlefield in the Rankan/Ilsig conflict. He had spitted more Ilsigs than most men, watched them writhe soundlessly until they died. Some said he had coined their derogatory nickname, but he had not, though he had doubtless helped spread it. . . .

He rode down Wideway, and he rode past the docks. A ship was being made fast, and a crowd had gathered round it. He squeezed the horse's barrel, urging it into the press. With only four of his fellow Hell-Hounds in Sanctuary, and a local garrison whose personnel never ventured out in groups of less than six, it was incumbent upon him to take a look.

He did not like what he saw of the man who was being helped from the storm-wracked ship that had come miraculously to port with no sail intact, who murmured through pale cruel lips to the surrounding Ilsigs, then climbed into a Rankan litter bound for the palace.

He spurred the horse. "Who?" he demanded of the eunuch-master whose path he suddenly barred.

"Aspect, the archmage," lisped the palace lackey, "if it's any business of yours."

Behind the lackey and the quartet of ebony slaves the shoulder-borne litter trembled. The viewcurtain with Kitty's device on it was drawn back, fell loose again.

"Out of my way, Hound," squeaked the enraged little pastry of a eunuch-master.

"Don't get flapped, Eunice," said Tempus, wishing he were in Caronne, wishing he had never met a god, wishing he were anywhere else. *Oh, Kitty, you have done it this time.* Alain Aspect, yet! Alchemist extraordinaire, assassin among magicians, dispeller of enchantments, in a town that ran on contract sorcery?

"Back, back, back," he counseled the horse, who twitched its ears and turned its head around reproachfully, but obeyed him.

He heard titters among the eunuchs, another behind in the crowd. He swung round in his saddle. "Hakiem, if I hear any stories about me I do not like, I will know whose tongue to hang on my belt."

The bent, news-nosed storyteller, standing amid the children who always clustered round him, stopped laughing. His rheumy eyes met Tempus's. "I have a story I would like to tell you, Hell-Hound. One you would like to hear, I humbly imagine."

"What is it, then, old man?"

"Come closer, Hell-Hound, and say what you will pay."

"How can I tell you how much it's worth until I hear?" The horse snorted, raised its head, sniffed a rank, evil breeze come suddenly from the stinking Downwind beach.

"We must haggle."

"Somebody else, then, old man. I have a long night ahead." He patted the horse, watching the crowd of Ilsigs surging round, their heads level with his hips.

"That is the first time I have seen *him* backed off!": a stage-whisper reached Tempus through the buzz of the crowd. He looked for the source of it, could not find one culprit more likely than the rest. There would be a lot more of that sort of talk, when word spread. But he did not interfere with sorcerers. Never again. He had done it once, thinking his tutelary god could protect him. His hand went to his hip, squeezed. Beneath his dun woolens and beneath his ring-mail he wore a woman's scarf. He never took it off. It was faded and it was ragged and it reminded him never to argue with a warlock. It was all he had left of her, who had been the subject of his dispute with a mage.

Long ago in Azehur. . . .

He sighed, a rattling sound, in a voice hoarse and gravelly from endless battlefield commands. "Have it your way tonight, then, Wriggly. And hope you live 'til morning." He named a price. The storyteller named another. The difference was split.

The old man came close and put his hand on the horse's neck. "The lightning came and the thunder rolled and when it was gone the temple of Ils was no more. The Prince has bought the aid of a mighty enchanter, whom even the bravest of the Hell-Hounds fears. A woman was washed up naked and half drowned on the Downwinders' beach and in her hair were pins of diamond."

"Pins?"

"Rods, then."

"Wonderful. What else?"

"The redhead from Amoli's Lily Garden died at moonrise."

He knew very well what whore the old man meant. He did not like the story, so far. He growled. "You had better astound me, quick, for the price you're asking."

"Between the Vulgar Unicorn and the tenement on the corner an entire building appeared on that vacant lot, where once the Black Spire stood—you know the one."

"I know it."

"Astounding?"

"Interesting. What else?"

"It is rather fancy, with a gilded dome. It has two doors, and above them two signs that read, 'Men,' and 'Women.'"

Vashanka had kept his word, then.

"Inside it, so the patrons of the Unicorn say, they sell weapons. Very special weapons. And the price is dear."

"What has this to do with me?"

"Some folk who have gone in there have not come out. And some have come out and turned one upon the other, dueling to the death. Some have merely slain whomsoever crossed their paths. Yet, word is spreading, and Ilsig and Rankan queue up like brothers before its doors. Since some of those who were standing in line were hawk-masks, I thought it good that you should know."

"I am touched, old man. I had no idea you cared." He threw the copper coins to the storyteller's feet and reined the horse sideways so abruptly it reared. When its feet touched the ground, he set it at a collected canter through the crowd, letting the rabble scatter before its iron-shod hooves as best they might.

2

In Sanctuary, enchantment ruled. No sorcerer believed in gods. But they believed in the Law of Correspondences, and they believed in evil.

Thus, since every negative must have its positive, they *implied* gods. Give a god an inch and he will take your soul. That was what the commoners and the second-rate prestidigitators lined up outside the Weaponshop of Vashanka did not realize, and that was why no respectable magician or Hazard Class Enchanter stood among them.

In they filed, men to Tempus's left, toward the Vulgar Unicorn, and women to his right, toward the tenement on the corner.

Personally, Tempus did not feel it wise or dignified for a god to engage in a commercial venture. From across the street, he took notes on who came and went.

Tempus was not sure whether he was going in there, or not.

A shadow joined the queue, disengaged, walked toward the Vulgar Unicorn in the tricky light of fading stars. It saw him, hesitated, took one step back.

Tempus leaned forward, his elbow on his pommel, and crooked a finger. "Hanse, I would like a word with you."

The youth cat-walked toward him, errant torchlight from the Unicorn's open door twinkling on his weapons. From ankle to shoulder, Shadowspawn bristled with armaments.

"What is it with you, Tempus? Always on my tail. There are bigger frogs than this one in Sanctuary's pond."

"Are you not going to buy anything tonight?"

"I'll make do with what I have, thanks. I do *not* swithe with sorcerers."

"Steal something for me?" Tempus whispered, leaning down. The boy had black hair, black eyes, and blacker prospects in this desperados' demesne.

"I'm listening."

"Two diamond rods from the lady who came out of the sea tonight."

"Why?"

"I won't ask you how, and you won't ask me why, or we'll forget it." He sat up straight in his saddle.

"Forget it, then," toughed Shadowspawn, deciding he wanted nothing to do with this Hell-Hound.

"Call it a prank, a jest at the expense of an old girlfriend."

The thief edged around where Tempus could not see him, into a dapple of deepest dark. He named a price.

The Hell-Hound did not argue. Rather, he paid half in advance.

"I've heard you don't really work for Kitty. I've heard your dues to the mercenaries' guild are right up to date, and that Kitty knows better than to give you any orders. If you are not arguing about my price, it must be too low."

*Silence.*

"Is it true that you roughed up that whore who died tonight? That Amoli is so afraid of you that you do whatever you want in her place and never pay?"

Tempus chuckled, a sound like the cracking of dry ice. "I will take you there, when you deliver, and you can see for yourself what I do."

There was no answer from the shadows, just a skittering of stones.

*Yes, I will take you there, young one. And yes, you are right. About everything. You should have asked for more.*

3

Tempus lingered there still, eating a boxed lunch from the Unicorn's kitchen, when a voice from above his head said, "The deal is off. That girl is a sorceress, if a pretty one. I'll not chance ensorcelment to lift baubles I don't covet, and for a pittance!"

*Girl?* The woman was nearly his own age, unless another set of diamond rods existed, and he doubted that. He yawned, not reaching up to take the purse that dangled over the lee of the roof, "I am disappointed. I thought Shadowspawn could steal."

The innuendo was not lost on the invisible thief. The purse was withdrawn. An impalpable something told him he was once again alone, but for the clients of Vashanka's Weaponshop. Things would be interesting in Sanctuary, for a good little while to come. He had counted twenty-three purchasers able to walk away with their mystical armaments. Four had died while he watched, intrigued.

It was possible that a career Hell-Hound such as Zalbar might have intervened. But Tempus wore Vashanka's amulet about his neck, and, if he did not agree with Him, he would at least bear with his god.

The woman he was waiting for showed there at dusk. He liked dusk; he liked it for killing and he liked it for loving. Sometimes if he was very lucky, the dusk made him tired and he could nap. A man who has been cursed by an archmage and pressed into service by a god does not sleep much. Sleep was something he chased like other men chased women. Women, in general, bored him, unless they were taken in battle, or unless they were whores.

This woman, her black hair brushing her doeskin-clad shoulders, was an exception.

He called her name, very softly. Then again: "Cime." She turned, and at last he was sure. He had thought Hakiem could mean no other: he had not been wrong.

Her eyes were gray as his horse. Silver shot her hair, but she was yet comely. Her hands rose, hesitated, covered a mouth pretending to hardness and tight with fear. He recognized the aborted motion of her hands: toward her head, forgetful that the rods she sought were no longer there.

He did not move in his saddle, or speak again. He let her decide, glance quickly about the street, then come to him.

When her hand touched the horse's bridle, he said: "It bites."

"Because you taught it to. It will not bite me." She held it by the muzzle, squeezing the pressure points that rode the skin there. The horse raised its head slightly, moaned, and stood shivering.

"What seek you in there?" He inclined his head toward Vashanka's; a lock of copper hair fell over one eye.

"The tools of my trade were stolen."

"Have you money?"

"Some. Not enough."

"Come with me."

"Never again."

"You have kept your vow, then?"

"I slay sorcerers. I cannot suffer any man to touch me except a client. I dare no love; I am chaste of heart."

"All these aching years?"

She smiled. It pulled her mouth in hard at its corners and he saw aging no potion or cosmetic spell could hide. "Every one. And you? You did not take the Blue Star, or I would see it on your brow. What discipline serves your will?"

"None. Revenge is fruitless. The past is only alive in us. I am not meant for sorcery. I love logic too well."

"So, you are yet damned?"

"If that is what you call it, I suppose—yes. I work for the Storm God, sometimes. I do a lot of wars."

"What brought you here, Cle—"

"Tempus, now. It keeps me in perspective. I am building a temple for Him." He pointed to Vashanka's Weaponshop, across the street. His finger shook. He hoped she had not seen. "You must not ply your trade here. I have employment as a Hell-Hound. Appearances must be preserved. Do not pit us against one another. It would be too sour a memory."

"For whomever survived? Can it be you love me still?" Her eyes were full of wonder.

"No," he said, but cleared his throat. "Stay out of there. I know His service well. I would not recommend it. I will get you back what you have lost. Meet me at the Lily Garden tonight at midnight, and you will have them. I promise. Just take down no sorcerers between now and then. If you do, I will not return them, and you cannot get others."

"Bitter, are you not? If I do what you are too weak to do, what harm is there in that?" Her right eyebrow raised. It hurt him to watch her.

"We are the harm. And we are the harmed, as well. I am afraid that you may have to break your fast, so be prepared. I will reason with myself, but I promise nothing."

She sighed. "I was wrong. You have not changed one bit."

"Let go of my horse."

She did.

He wanted to tell her to let go of his heart, but he was struck mute. He wheeled his mount and clattered down the street. He had no intention of leaving. He just waited in a nearby alley until she was gone.

Then he hailed a passing soldier, and sent a message to the palace.

When the sun danced above the Vulgar Unicorn's improbably engaged weather vane, support troops arrived, and Kadakithis's new warlock, Aspect, was with them.

"Since last night, and this is the first report you have seen fit to make?" The sorcerer's pale lips flushed. His eyes burned within his shadowed cowl.

"I hope you and Kadakithis had a talk."

"We did, we did. You are not still angry at the world after all these years?"

"I am yet living. I have your kind to blame or thank, whichever."

"Do you not think it strange that we have been thrown together as—equals?"

"I think that is not the right word for it, Aspect. What are you about, here?"

"Now, now, Hell-Hound—"

"Tempus."

"Yes, Tempus. You have not lost your fabled sense of irony. I hope it is a comfort."

"Quite, actually. Do not interfere with the gods, guildbrother of my nemesis."

"Our prince is justifiably worried. Those weapons—"

"—equal out the balance between the oppressors and the oppressed. Most of Sanctuary cannot afford your services, or the prices of even the lowliest members of the Enchanters' Guild. Let it be. We will get the weapons back, as their wielders meet their fates."

"I have to report to Kitt—to Kadakithis."

"Then report that I am handling it." Behind the magician, he could see the ranks whispering. Thirty men, the archmage had brought. Too many.

"You and I have more in common than in dispute, Tempus. Let us join forces."

"I would sooner bed an Ilsig matron."

"Well, I am going in there." The archmage shook his head and the cowl fell back. He was pretty, ageless, a blond. "With or without you."

"Be my guest," Tempus offered.

The archmage looked at him strangely. "We do the same services in the world, you and I. Killing, whether with natural or supernatural weapons, is still killing. You are no better than I."

"Assuredly not, except that I will outlive you. And I will make sure you do not get your requisite burial ritual."

"You would not!"

"Like you said, I yet bear my grudge—against every one of you."

With a curse that made the ranks clap their hands to their helmeted ears, the archmage swished into the street, across it, and through the door marked "Men" without another word. It was his motioned command which made the troops follow.

A waitress Tempus knew came out when the gibbous moon was high, to ask him if he was hungry. She brought him fish and he ate it, watching the doors.

When he had just about finished, a terrible rumble crawled up the street, tremors following in its wake. He slid from his horse and held its muzzle, and the reins up under its bit. The doors of Vashanka's Weaponshop grew shimmery, began taking color. Above, the moon went behind a cloud. The little dome on the shop rocked, grew cracks, crazed, steamed. The doors were ruby red, and melting. Awful wails and screams and the smell of sulphur and ozone filled the night.

Patrons began streaming out of the Vulgar Unicorn, drinks in hand. They stayed well back from the rocking building, which howled as it stressed larger, growing turgid, effluescing spectrums which sheeted and snapped and snarled. The doors went molten white, then they were gone. A figure was limned in the left-hand doorway, and it was trying to climb empty air. It flamed and screeched, dancing, crumbling, facing the street but unable to pass the invisible barrier against which it pounded. It stank: the smell of roasting flesh was overwhelming. Behind it, helmets crumpled, dripped onto the contorted faces of soldiers whose mustaches had begun to flare.

The mage who tried to break down the invisible door had no fists; he had pounded them away. The ranks were char and ash in infalling effigy of damnation. The doors which had been invisible began to cool to white, then to gold, then to red.

The street was utterly silent. Only the snorts of his horse and the squeals of the domed structure could be heard. The squeals fell off to growls and shudders. The doors cooled, turned dark.

People muttered, drifted back into the Unicorn with mumbled wardings, tracing signs and taking many backward looks.

Tempus, who could have saved thirty innocent soldiers and one guilty magician, got out his silver box and sniffed some krrf.

He had to be at the Lily Garden soon.

When he got there, the mixed elation of drug and death had faded.

What if Shadowspawn did not appear with the rods? What if the girl Cime did not come to get them back? What if he still could hurt, as he had not hurt for more than three hundred years?

He had had a message from the palace, from Prince Kadakithis himself. He was not going up there, just yet. He did not want to answer any questions about the archmage's demise. He did not want to appear involved. His only chance to help the Prince-Governor effectively lay in working his own way. Those were his terms, and under those terms Kitty's supporters in the Rankan capital had employed him to come down here and play Hell-Hound and see what he would do. There were no wars, anywhere. He had been bored, his days stretching out neverending, bleak. So he had concerned himself with Kitty, for something to do. The building of Vashanka's temple he oversaw for himself more than Kadakithis, who understood the necessity of elevating the state cult above the Ilsig gods, but believed only in wizardry, and his noble Ranke blood.

He was not happy about the spectacle at Vashanka's Weaponshop.

Sloppy business, this sideshow melting and unmelting. The archmage must have been talented, to make his struggles visible to those outside.

Wisdom is to know the thought which steers all things through all things, a friend of his who was a philosopher had once said to him. The thought that was steering all things through Sanctuary was muddled, unclear.

That was the hitch, the catch, the problem with employing the supernatural in a natural milieu. Things got confused. With so many spells at work, the fabric of causality was overly strained. Add the gods, and Evil and Good faced each other across a board game whose extent was the phenomenal world. He wished the gods would stay in their heavens and the sorcerers in their hells.

Oh, he had heard endless persiflage about simultaneity; iteration—the constant redefining of the now by checking it against the future—; alchemical laws of consonance. When he had been a student of philosophy and Cime had been a maiden, he had learned the axiom that Mind is unlimited and self-controlled, but all other things are connected; that nothing is completely separated off from any other thing, nor are things divided one from the other, except Mind.

The sorcerers put it another way: they called the consciousness of all things into service, according to the laws of magic.

Not philosophy, nor theology, nor thaumaturgy held the answer for Tempus; he had turned away from them, each and all. But he could not forget what he had learned.

And none of the adepts likes to admit that no servitor can be hired without wages. The wages of unnatural life are unnatural death.

He wished he could wake up in Azehur, with his family, and know that he had dreamed this impious dream.

But instead he came to Amoli's whorehouse, the Lily Garden. Almost, but not quite, he rode the horse up its stairs. Resisting the temptation, he reflected that in every age he had ever studied, doom-cryers abounded. No millennium is attractive to the man immured in it; enough prophecies have been made in antiquity that one who desires, in any age, to take the position that Apocalypse is at hand can easily defend it. He would not join that dour Order; he would not worry about anything but Tempus, and the matter awaiting his attention.

Inside Amoli's, Hanse the thief sat in full swagger, a pubescent girl on each knee.

"Ah," he waved. "I have something for you." Shadowspawn tumbled both girls off of him, and stood, stretching widely, so that every arm-dagger and belted sticker and thigh-sheath creaked softly. The girls at his feet stayed there, staring up at Tempus wide-eyed. One whimpered to Shadowspawn and clutched his thigh.

"Room key," Tempus snapped to no one in particular, and held out his hand. The concierge, not Amoli, brought it to him.

"Hanse?"

"Coming." He extended a hand to one girl.

"Alone."

"You are not my type," said the thief, suspicious.

"I need just a moment of your evening. You can do what you wish with the rest."

Tempus looked at the key, headed off toward a staircase leading to the room which bore a corresponding number.

He heard the soft tread of Shadowspawn close behind.

When the exchange had been made, the thief departed, satisfied with both his payment and his gratuity, but not quite sure that Tempus appreciated the trouble to which he had put himself, or that he had gotten the best of the bargain they had made.

He saw the woman he had robbed before she saw him, and ended up in a different girl's room than the one he had chosen, in order to avoid a scene. When he had heard her steps pass by, stop before the door behind which the big Hell-Hound waited, he made preclusive threats to the woman whose mouth he had stopped with the flat of his hand, and slipped downstairs to spend his money somewhere else, discreetly.

If he had stayed, he might have found out what the diamond rods were really worth; he might have found out what the sour-eyed mercenary with his high brow, suddenly so deeply creased, and his lightly carried mass, which seemed tonight too heavy, was worried about. Or perhaps he could have fathomed Tempus's enigmatic parting words:

"I would help you if I could, backstreeter," Tempus had rumbled. "If I had met you long ago, or if you liked horses, there would be a chance. You have done me a great service. More than that pouch holds. I am seldom in any man's debt, but you, I own, can call me anytime."

"You paid me, Hell-Hound. I am content," Hanse had demurred, confused by weakness where he had never imagined it might dwell. Then he saw the Hell-Hound fish out a snuffbox of krrf, and thought he understood.

But later, he went back to Amoli's and hung around the steps, cautiously petting the big man's horse, the krrf he had sniffed making him willing to dodge the beast's square, yellow teeth.

4

She had come to him, had Cime. She was what she was, what she had always been.

It was Tempus who was changed: Vashanka had entered into him, the Storm God who was Lord of Weapons who was Lord of Rape who was Lord of War who was Lord of Death's Gate.

He could not take her, gently. So spoke not his physical impotence, as he might have expected, but the cold wash of wisdom: he would not despoil her; Vashanka would accept no less.

She knocked and entered and said, "Let me see them," so sure he would have the stolen diamonds that her fingers were already busy on the lacings of her Ilsig leathers.

He held up a hide-wrapped bundle, slimmer than her wrist, shorter than her forearm. "Here. How were they thieved?"

"Your voice is hoarser than I have ever heard it," she replied, and: "I needed money; there was this man . . . actually, there were a few, but there was a tough, a streetbrawler. I should have known—he is half my apparent age. What would such as he want with a middle-aged whore? And he agreed to pay the price I asked, without quibbling. *Then* he robbed me." She looked around, her eyes, as he remembered them, clear windows to her thoughts. She was appalled.

"The low estate into which I have sunk?"

She knew what he meant. Her nostrils shivered, taking in the musty reek of the soiled bedding on which he sprawled fully clothed, smelling easily as foul. "The devolution of us both. That I would be here, under these circumstances, is surely as pathetic as you."

"Thanks. I needed that. Don't."

"I thought you wanted me." She ceased unlacing, looked at him, her tunic open to her waist.

"I did. I don't. Have some krrf." On his hips rode her scarf; if she saw it, then she would comprehend his degradation too fully. So he had not removed it, hoping its presence would remind him, if he weakened and his thoughts drowned in lust, that *this* woman he must not violate.

She sat on the quilt, one doe-gloved leg tucked under her.

"You jest," she breathed, then, eyes narrowed, took the krrf.

"It will be ill with you, afterward, should I touch you."

Her fingers ran along the flap of hide wrapped over her wands. "I am receiving payment." She tapped the package. "And I may not owe debts."

"The boy who pilfered these, did it at my behest."

"Must you pander for me?"

He winced. "Why do you not go home?" She smelled of salt and honey and he thought desperately that she was here only because he forced the issue: to pay her debt.

She leaned forward, touched his lips with a finger. "For the same reason that you do not. Home is changed, gone to time."

"Do you know that?" He jerked his head away, cracking it against the bed's wooden headboard.

"I believe it."

"I cannot believe anything, any more. I surely cannot believe that your hand is saying what it seems to be saying."

"I cannot," she said, between kisses at his throat he could not, somehow, fend off, "leave . . . with . . . debts . . . owing."

"Sorry," he said firmly, and got out from under her hands. "I am just not in the mood."

She shrugged, unwrapped the wands, and wound her hair up with them. "Surely, you will regret this, later."

"Maybe you are right," he sighed heavily. "But that is my problem. I release you from any debt. We are even. I remember past gifts, given when you still knew how to give freely." There was no way in the world he was going to hurt her. He would not strip before her. With those two constraints, he had no option. He chased her out of there. He was as cruel about it as he could manage to be, for both their sakes.

Then he yelled downstairs for service.

When he descended the steps in the cool night air, a movement startled him, on the gray's off side.

"It is me, Shadowspawn."

"It is I, Shadowspawn," he corrected, huskily. His face averted, he mounted from the wrong side. The horse whickered disapprovingly. "What is it, snipe?"

As clouds covered the moon, Tempus seemed to pull all night's shadows round him. Hanse might have the name, but this Tempus had the skill. Hanse shivered. There were no Shadow Lords any longer. . . . "I was admiring your horse. Bunch of hawk-masks rode by, saw the horse, looked interested. I looked proprietary. The horse looked mean. The hawk-masks rode away. I just thought I'd see if you showed soon, and let you know."

A movement at the edge of his field of vision warned him, even as the horse's ears twitched at the click of iron on stone. "You should have kept going, it seems," said Tempus quietly, as the first of the hawk-masks edged his horse out past the intersection, and others followed. Two. Three. Four. Two more.

"Mothers," whispered Cudget Swearoath's prodigy, embarrassed at not having realized that he was not the only one waiting for Tempus.

"This is not your fight, junior."

"I'm aware of that. Let's see if they are."

Blue night: blue hawk-masks: the sparking thunder of six sets of hooves rushing toward the two of them. Whickering. The gleam of frothing teeth and bared weapons: iron clanging in a jumble of shuddering, straining horses. The kill-trained gray's challenge to another stallion: hooves thudding on flesh and great mouths gaped, snapping; a blaring death-clarion from a horse whose jugular had been severed. Always watching the boy: keeping the gray between the hawk-masks and a thief who just happened to get involved; who just happened to kill two of them with thrown knives, one through an eye and the other blade, he recalled clearly, sticking out of a slug-white throat. Tempus would remember even the whores' ambivalent screams of thrill and horror, delight and disgust. He had plenty of time to sort it out:

Time to draw his own sword, to target the rider of his choice, feel his hilt go warm and pulsing in his hand. He really did not like to take unfair advantage. The iron sword glowed pink like a baby's skin or a just-born day. Then it began to react in his grip. The gray's reins, wrapped around the pommel, flapped loosely; he told it where he wanted it with gritted words, with a pressing knee, with his shifting weight. One hawk-mask had a greenish tinge to him: protected. Tempus's sword would not listen to such talk: it slit charms like butter, armor like silk. A blue wing whistled above his head, thrown by a compatriot of the man who fell so slowly with his guts pouring out over his saddle like cold molasses. While that hawk-mask's horse was in midair between two strides, Tempus's sword licked up and changed the color of the foe-seeking boomerang. Pink, now, not blue. He was content to let it return its death to the hand that threw it. That left just two.

One had the thief engaged, and the youth had drawn his wicked, twenty-inch Ibarsi knife, too short to be more than a temporizer against the hawk-mask's sword, too broad to be thrown. Backed against the

Lily Garden's wall, there was just time for Tempus to flicker the horse over there and split the hawk-mask's head down to his collarbones. Gray brains splattered him. The thrust of the hawk-mask, undiminished by death, shattered on the flat of the long, curved knife Shadowspawn held up in a two-fisted, desperate block.

"Behind you!"

Tempus had known the one last hawk-mask was there. But this was not the boy's battle. Tempus had made a choice. He ducked and threw his weight sideways, reining the horse down with all his might. The sword, a singing one, sonata'd over his head, shearing hairs. His horse, overbalanced, fell heavily, screaming, pitching, rolling onto his left leg. Pinned for an instant, he saw white anguish, then the last hawk-mask was leaping down to finish him, and the gray scrambled to its feet. "Kill," he shouted, his blade yet at ready, but lying in the dirt. His leg flared once again, then quieted. He tried it, gained his knees, dust in his eyes. The horse reared and lunged. The hawk-mask struck blindly, arms above his head, sword reaching for gray, soft underbelly. He tried to save it. He tried. He tackled the hawk-mask with the singing sword. Too late, too late: horse fluids showered him. Bellows of agony pealed in his ears. The horse and the hawk-mask and Tempus went down together, thrashing.

When Tempus sorted it out, he allowed that the horse had killed the hawk-mask at the same time the hawk-mask had disemboweled the horse.

But he had to finish it. It lay there thrashing pathetically, deep groans coming from it. He stood over it uncertainly, then knelt and stroked its muzzle. It snapped at him, eyes rolling, demanding to die. He acceded, and the dust in his eyes hurt so much they watered profusely.

Its legs were still kicking weakly when he heard a movement, turned on his good leg, and stared.

Shadowspawn was methodically stripping the hawk-masks of their arms and valuables.

Hanse did not notice Tempus, as he limped away. Or he pretended he did not. Whichever, there was nothing left to say.

5

When he reached the weapons shop, his leg hardly pained him. It was numb; it no longer throbbed. It would heal flawlessly, as any wound he took always healed. Tempus hated it.

Up to the weapons shop's door he strode, as the dawn spilled gore onto Sanctuary's alleys.

He kicked it; it opened wide. How he despised supernal battle, and himself when his preternatural abilities came into play.

"Hear me, Vashanka! I have had enough! Get this sidewalk stand out of here!"

There was no answer. Within, everything was dim as dusk, dim as the pit of unknowingness which spawned day and night and endless striving.

There were no weapons here for him to see, no counter, no proprietor, no rack of armaments pulsing and humming expectantly. But then, he already had his. One to a customer was the rule: one body; one mind; one swing through life.

He trod mists tarnished like the gray horse's coat. He trod a long corridor with light at its ending, pink like new beginnings, pink like his iron sword when Vashanka lifted it by Tempus's hand. He shied away from his duality; a man does not look closely at a curse of his own choosing. He was what he was, vessel of his god. But he had his own body, and that particular body was aching; and he had his own mind, and that particular mind was dank and dark like the dusk and the dusty death he dealt.

"Where are You, Vashanka, O Slaughter Lord?"

*Right here,* resounded the voice within his head. But Tempus was not going to listen to any internal voice. Tempus wanted confrontation.

"Materialize, you bastard!"

*I already have; one body; one mind; one life—in every sphere.*

"I am not you!" Tempus screamed through clenched teeth, willing firm footing beneath his sinking feet.

*No, you are not. But I am you, sometimes,* said the nimbus-wreathed figure striding toward him over gilt-edged clouds. Vashanka: so very tall with hair the color of yarrow honey and a high brow free from lines.

"Oh, no. . . ."

*You wanted to see Me. Look upon Me, servant!*

"Not so close, Pillager. Not so much resemblance. Do not torture me, my god! Let me blame it all on you—not *be* you!"

*So many years, and you yet seek self-delusion?*

"Definitely. As do You, if You think to gather worshipers in this fashion! O Berserker God, You cannot roast their mages before them: they are all dependent on sorcery. You cannot terrify them thusly, and expect them to come to You. Weapons will not woo them; they are not men of the armies. They are thieves, and pirates, and prostitutes! You have gone too far, and not far enough!"

*Speaking of prostitutes, did you see your sister? Look at me!*

Tempus had to obey. He faced the manifestation of Vashanka, and recalled that he could not take a woman in gentleness, that he could but war. He saw his battles, ranks parading in endless eyes of storm and blood bath. He saw the Storm God's consort, His own sister whom He raped eternally, moaning on Her couch in anguish that Her blood brother would ravish Her so.

Vashanka laughed.

Tempus snarled wordlessly through frozen lips.

*You should have let us have her.*

"Never!" Tempus howled. Then: "O God, leave off! You are not increasing your reputation among these mortals, nor mine! This was an ill-considered venture from the outset. Go back to Your heaven and wait. I will build Your temple better without Your maniacal aid. You have lost all sense of proportion. The Sanctuarites will not worship one who makes of their town a battlefield!"

*Tempus, do not be wroth with Me. I have My own troubles, you know. I have to get away every now and again. And you have not been warring,* whined the god, *for so very long. I am bored and I am lonely.*

"And you have caused the death of my horse!" Tempus spat, and broke free of Vashanka, wrenching his mind loose from the mirror mind of his god with an effort of will greater than any he had ever mounted before. He turned in his steps and began to retrace them. The god called to him over his shoulder, but he did not look back. He put his feet in the smudges they had left in the clouds as he had walked among them, and the farther he trudged, the more substantial those clouds became.

He trekked into lighter darkness, into a soft, new sunrise, into a pink and lavender morning which was almost Sanctuary's. He continued to walk until the smell of dead fish and Downwind pollution assailed his nostrils. He strode on, until a weed tripped him and he fell to his knees in the middle of a damp and vacant lot.

He heard a cruel laugh, and as he looked up he was thinking that he had not made it back at all—that Vashanka was not through punishing him.

But to his right was the Vulgar Unicorn, to his left the palimpsest tenement wall. And before him stood one of the palace eunuchs, come seeking him with a summons from Kittycat to discuss what might be done about the weapons shop said to be manifesting next to the Vulgar Unicorn.

"Tell Kadakithis," said Tempus, arduously gaining his feet, "that I will be there presently. As you can see . . ." He waved around him, where no structure stood or even could be proved ever to have stood. ". . . there is no longer any weapons shop. Therefore, there is no longer any problem, nor any urgency to attend to it. There is, however, one very irritable Hell-Hound in this vacant lot who wants to be left alone."

The blue-black eunuch exposed perfect, argent teeth. "Yes, yes, master," he soothed the honey-haired man. "I can see that this is so."

Tempus ignored the eunuch's rosy, outstretched palm, and his sneer at the Hell-Hound pretending to negotiate the humpy turf without pain. Accursed Wriggly.

As the round-rumped eunuch sauntered off, Tempus decided the Vulgar Unicorn would do as well as anyplace to sit and sniff krrf and wait for his leg to finish healing. It ought to take about an hour—unless Vashanka was more angry at him that he estimated, in which case it might take a couple of days.

Shying from that dismal prospect, he pursued diverse thoughts. But he fared little better. Where he was going to get another horse like the one he had lost, he could not conjecture, any more than he could recall the exact moment when the last dissolving wisps of Vashanka's Weaponshop blurred away into the mists of dawn.

# Shadow's Pawn

## Andrew Offutt

She was more than attractive and she walked with head high in pride and awareness of her womanhood. The bracelet on her bare arm flashed and seemed to glow with that brightness the gods reserve for polished new gold. She should have been walking amid bright lights illuminating the dancing waters of a fountain, turning its sparkling into a million diamonds and, with the aid of a bit of refraction, colorful other gemstones as well.

There was no fountain down here by the fish market, and the few lights were not bright. She did not belong here. She was stupid to be here, walking unescorted so late at night. She was stupid. Stupidity had its penalties; it did not pay.

Still, the watching thief appreciated the stupidity of others. It did pay; it paid him. He made his living by it, by his own cleverness and the stupidity of others. He was about to go to work. Even at the reduced price he would receive from a changer, that serpent-carved bracelet would feed him well. It would keep him, without the necessity of more such hard work as this damnable lurking, waiting, for—oh, probably a month.

Though she was the sort of woman men looked upon with lust, the thief would not have her. He did not see her that way. His lust was not carnal. The waiting thief was no rapist. He was a businessman. He did not even like to kill, and he seldom had to. She passed the doorway in whose shadows he lurked, on the north side of the street.

"G'night Praxy, and thanks again for all that beer," he called to no one, and stepped out onto the planking that bordered the street. He was ten paces behind the quarry. Twelve. "Good thing I'm walking—I'm in no condition to ride a horse t'night!" Fourteen paces.

Laughing giddily, he followed her. The quarry.

She reached the corner of the deserted street and turned north, onto the Street of Odors. Walking around two sides of the Serpentine! She *was* stupid. The dolt had no business whatever with that fine bracelet. Didn't have proper respect for it. Didn't know how to take care of it. The moment she rounded the corner, the thief stepped off the board-walk onto the unpaved street, squatted to snatch up his shoes the moment he stepped out of them, and *ran*.

Just at the intersection he stopped as if he had run into a wall, and dropped the shoes. Stepped into them. Nodded affably, drunkenly to the couple who came around off Stink Street—slat and slattern wearing three coppers' worth of clothing and four of "jewelry." He stepped onto the planking, noting that they noted little save each other. How nice. The Street of Odors was empty as far as he could see. Except for the quarry.

"Uhh," he groaned as if in misery. "Lady," he called, not loudly. "My lady?" He slurred a little, not overdoing. Five paces ahead, she paused and looked back. "H-hellp," he said, right hand clutching at his stomach.

She was too stupid to be down here alone at this time of night, all right. She came back! All solicitous she was, and his hand moved a little to the left and came out with a flat-bladed knife while his left hand clamped her right wrist, the unbraceleted one. The point of the knife touched the knot of her expensive cerulean sash.

"Do not scream. This is a throwing knife. I throw it well, but I *prefer* not to kill. Unless I have to, understand me? All I want is that nice little snake you're wearing."

"Oh!" Her eyes were huge and she tucked in her belly, away from the point of several inches of dull-silvery leaf-shape he held to her mid-dle. "It—it was a gift. . . ."

"I will accept it as a gift. Oh you are smart, very smart not to try yelling. I just hate to have to stick pretty women in the belly. It's messy, and it could give this end of town a bad name. I hate to throw a knife into their backs, for that matter. Do you believe me?"

Her voice was a squeak: "Yes." .

"Good." He released her wrist and kept his hand outstretched, palm up. "The bracelet then. I am not so rude as to tear such a pretty bauble off a pretty lady's pretty wrist."

Staring at him as if entranced, she backed a pace. He flipped the knife, caught it by the tip. His left palm remained extended, a waiting receptacle. The right hefted the knife in a throwing attitude and she swiftly twisted off the bracelet. Better than he had thought, he realized with a flash of green and gratification; the serpent's eyes appeared to be nice topazes! All right then, he'd let her keep the expensive sash.

She did not drop the bracelet into his palm; she placed it there. Nice hard cold gold, marvelously weighty. Only slightly warmed from a wrist the color of burnt sienna. Nice, nice. Her eyes leaped, flickered in fear when he flipped the knife to catch it by its leather-wrapped tang. It had no hilt, to keep that end light behind the weighted blade.

"You see?" he said, showing teeth. "I have no desire for your blood, understand me? Only this bauble."

The bracelet remained cold in his palm and when it moved he jerked his hand instinctively. Fast as he was he was only human, not a striking serpent; the bracelet, suddenly become a living snake, drove its fangs into the meaty part of his hand that was the inner part of his thumb. It clung, and it hurt. Oh it hurt.

The thief's smile vanished with his outcry of pain. Yet he saw her smile, and even as he felt the horror within him he raised the throwing knife to stab the filthy bitch who had trapped him.

That is, he tried to raise the knife, tried to shake his bitten hand to which the serpent clung. He failed. Almost instantly, the bite of that unnatural snake ossified every bone and bit of cartilage in his body and, stiffly, Gath the thief fell down dead.

His victim, still smiling, squatted to retrieve her property. She was shivering in excitement. She slipped the cold hard bracelet of gold onto her wrist. Its eyes, cold hard stones, scintillated. And a tremor ran all through the woman. Her eyes glittered and sparkled.

"Oooohh," she murmured with a shiver, all trembly and tingly with excitement and delight. "It was worth every piece of silver I paid, this lovely bauble from that lovely shop. I'm really glad it was destroyed. Those of us who bought these weapons of the god are so *unique*." She was trembling, excitement high in her and her heart racing with the thrill of danger faced and killing accomplished, and she stroked the bracelet as if it were a lover.

She went home with her head high in pride and continuing excitement, and she was not at all happy when her husband railed at her for being so late and seized her by the left wrist. He went all bright eyed and stiff and fell down dead. She was not at all happy. She had intended to kill only strangers for the thrill of it, those who deserved it.

Somewhere, surely, the god Vashanka smiled.

\* \* \*

"The god-damned city's in a mess and busy as a kicked anthill and I think you had more than a whit to do with it," the dark young man said. (Or was he a youth? Street-wise and tough and hooded of eyes and wearing knives as a courtesan wore gems. Hair blacker than black and eyes nearly so above a nose almost meant for a bird of prey.)

"'God-damned' city, indeed," said the paler, discomfitingly tall man, who was older but not old, and he came close to smiling. "You don't know how near you are to truth, Shadowspawn."

Around them in the charcoal dimness others neither heard nor were overheard. In this place, the trick was not to be overheard. The trick was to talk *under* everyone else. A bad tavern with a bad reputation in a bad area of a nothing town, the tavern called Vulgar Unicorn was an astonishingly quiet place.

"Just call me Hanse and stop being all cryptic and fatherly," the dark young man said. "I'm not looking for a father. I had one—I'm told. Then I had Cudget Swearoath. Cudget told me all I—all he knew."

The other man heard; "fatherly" used to mean "patronizing," and the flash of ego in the tough called Shadowspawn. Chips on his shoulders out to here. The other man did not smile. How to tell Hanse how many Hanses he had known, over so many years?

"Listen. One night a while ago I killed. Two men." Hanse did not lower his voice for that statement-not-admission; he kept it low. The shadow of a voice.

"Not men, Hanse. Hawk-masks. Jubal's bravoes. Hardly men."

"They were men, Tempus. They were all men. So is Hanse and even Kadaki—the prince-governor."

"Kittycat."

"I do not call him that," Hanse said, with austerity. Then he said, "It's you I'm not sure of, Tempus. Are you a man?"

"I'm a man," Tempus said, with a sigh that seemed to come from the weight of decades and decades. "Tonight I asked you to call me Thales. Go ahead, Hanse. You killed two men, while helping me. Were you, by the way? Or were you lurking around my horse that night thinking of laying hands on some krrf?"

"I use no drugs and little alcohol."

"That isn't what I asked," Tempus said, not bothering to refute.

Dark eyes met Tempus's, which impressed him. "Yes. That is why I was there, T—Thales. Why 'Thay-lees'?"

"Since all things are presently full of gods, why not 'Thales'? Thank you, Hanse. I appreciate your honesty. We can—"

"Honesty?" A man, once well built and now wearing his chest all over his broad belt and bulging under it as well, had been passing their small round table. "Did I hear something about Hanse's honesty? Hanse?" His laugh was a combination: pushed and genuine.

The lean youth called Shadowspawn moved nothing but his head. "How'd you like a hole in your middle to let out all that hot air, Abohorr?"

"How'd you like a third eye, Abohorr?" Hanse's tablemate said.

Abohorr betook himself elsewhere, muttering—and hurrying. Both Hanse's lean swift hands remained on the tabletop. "You know him, Thales?"

"No."

"You heard me say his name and so you said it right after me."

"Yes."

"You're sharp, Thales. Too . . . smart." Hanse slapped the table's surface. "I've been meeting too many sharp people lately. Sharp as . . ."

"Knives," Tempus said, finishing the complaint of a very very sharp young man. "You were mentioning that you were waiting for me to come out of that house-not-home, Hanse, because you knew I was carrying. And then Jubal's bravoes attacked—me—and you took down two."

"I was mentioning that, yes." Hanse developed a seemingly genuine interest in his brown-and-orange Saraprins mug. "How many men have you killed, Thales?"

"Oh *gods*. Do not ask."

"Many."

"Many, yes."

"And no scars on you."

Tempus looked pained. "No scars on me," he said, to his own big hands on the table. Bronzed, they were still more fair than Shadowspawn's. On a sudden thought, he looked up and his expression was of dawning revelation and disbelief. "Hanse? You saved my life that night. I saved yours—but they were after me to begin with. Hanse? How many men have you killed?"

Hanse looked away. Hair like a raven, nose of a young falcon. Profile carved out by a hand-ax sharper than a barber's razor, all planes and angles. A pair of onyxes for eyes, and just that hard. His look away was uncharacteristic and Tempus knew it. Tempus worked out of the palace and had access to confidential reports, one of which not even the prince-governor had seen. He wouldn't, either, because it no longer existed. Too, Tempus had dealt with this spawn of Downwind and the shadows. He was here in this murkily-lit tavern of humanity's dregs to deal with him again.

Hanse, looking away, said, "You are not to tell anyone."

Tempus knew just what to say. "Do not insult me again."

Hanse's nod was not as long as the thickness of one of his knives. (Were there five, or did he really wear a sixth on one of his thighs? Tempus doubted that; the strap wouldn't stay up.)

At last Hanse answered the question. "Two."

Two men. Tempus nodded, sighing, pushing back to come as close to slumping on his bench as his kind of soldier could. Damn. Who would have thought it? The *reputation* he had, this dark surly scary (to others, not the man currently calling himself Tempus) youth from the gutters he doubtless thought he had risen so far above. Tempus knew he had wounded a man or two, and he had assumed. Now Shadowspawn said he had never slain! That, from such a one, was an admission. *Because of me he has been blooded,* Tempus mused, and the weary thought followed: *Well, he's not the first. I had my first two, once. I wonder who they were, and where?* (But he knew, he knew. A man did not forget such. Tempus was older than anyone thought; he was not as world-weary old as he thought, or thought he thought.) Just now he wanted to put forth a hand and touch the much younger man. He certainly did not.

He said, "How do you feel about it?"

Hanse continued to gaze assiduously at something else. How could a child of the desert with such long long lashes and that sensuous, almost pretty mouth look so grim and thin-lipped? "I threw up."

"That proves you are human and is what you *did*. How *do* you feel about it?"

Hanse looked at him directly. After a time, he shrugged.

"Yes," Tempus sighed, nodding. He drained his cup. Raised a right arm on high and glanced in the general direction of the tap. The new nightman nodded. Though he had not looked at the fellow, Tempus lowered his arm and looked at Hanse. "I understand," he said.

"Do you. A while ago I told the Prince that it is a prince's business to kill, not a thief's. Now I have killed."

"What a wonderful thing to say to a bit of royalty! I wish you weren't so serious right now, so I could laugh aloud. Do not expect any gentle words from me about the kills, my friend. It happens. I didn't ask for your help—or for you to be waiting for me. You won't do that again."

"Not that way, no." Hanse leaned back while whatever-his-name-was (they called him "Two-Thumb") set two newly-filled mugs between them. He did not take the other two, or wait for payment. "I think things started when Bourne . . . died, and you came to Thieves' World."

"Thieves' World?"

Again that almost-embarrassed shrug. "It's what we call Sanctuary. Some of us. Now the whole city's in a mess and a turmoil and I think you have to do with that."

"I believe you said that."

"You led me astray, 'Thales.' That temple or store or whatever it was. It . . . collapsed?—erupted, like a volcano? Something. Next the Prince—"

"You really do respect him, don't you?"

"I don't work for him though," Hanse pointed out; Tempus did. "He impounded the . . . the god-weapons?—that place sold, or tried to. Hell-Hounds paying people for things they bought—or else! *Things!* New wealth in the city, because some of them had been stolen and now are bought from thieves. People are laughing at dealing with the new changer: the palace!"

Changer, Tempus knew, meant fence in this—*city?* O my God Vashanka—this? A city?!

"Two ships sitting out there in the harbor," Hanse went on, "guarded up to here. I know those Things, those dark weapons of sorcery, are being loaded aboard. Then what. Out to sea and straight to the bottom?"

"The very best place for them," Tempus said, turning and slowly turning his glazed earthenware mug. This one was striped garishly in yellow waves. "Believe it. There is too much power in those devices."

"Meanwhile some 'enforcers' from the mage-guild have been trying to get hands on them first."

That Tempus also knew. Three of the toughs had been eliminated in the past twenty hours, unless another or two had been slain tonight, by local Watchmen or those special guardsmen called Hell-Hounds. "Unions will try to protect their members, yes. No matter what. A union is a mindless animal."

"You paid me well—*fair,* to fetch you the diamond wand-things that woman wears in her hair. I did, and she has them back. You gave them back."

*Cime*. Cime's diamond-rods in her fine fine wealth of hair. "Yes. Did I?"

"You did. And strange things are happening in Sanctuary. Those were sorcerous weapons those hawk-masks used against you and me. A poor thief tried to snatch a woman's bracelet the other night, down in— never mind the street. She shouldn't have been there. The bracelet turned into a snake and killed him. I don't know what it did to him. He's dead and they say he weighs about twice as much as he did alive."

"It solidified his bones. It was obtained this morning. And when didn't strange things happen in Sanctuary, my friend?"

"That is twice you have called me that." Hanse's words had the sound of accusation about them.

"So I have. I must mean it, then."

Hanse became visibly uncomfortable. "I am Hanse. I was . . . apprentice to Cudget Swearoath. Prince *Kittycat* had him hanged. I am Shadowspawn. I have breached the palace and because of me a Hell-Hound is dead. I have no friends."

*And you slip and call him "Kittycat" when you think of your executed mentor, do you? Not seeking a father, eh? Do you know that all men do, and that I have mine, in Vashanka? Ah Hanse how you seek to be enigmatic and so cool—and are about as transparent as a pan of water caught from the sky!*

Tempus waved a hand. "Save all that. Just tell me not to be your friend. Not to call you friend."

A silence fell over them like a struck banner and something naked stared out of Hanse's eyes. By the time he knew he must speak into the silence, it was too late. That same silence was Tempus' answer.

"Yes," Tempus said, considerately-cleverly changing the subject. "What old whatsisname Torchholder yammers about is true. Vashanka Came, and He claimed Sanctuary. His name is branded into the palace, now. The very temple of Ils lies in rubble. Vashanka created the weapons shop, from nothing, and—"

"A pedlar-*god?*"

"I didn't think much of the tactic myself," Tempus said, hoping Vashanka heard him while noting how good the youth was at sneering. "And the weapons shop destroyed the mage the governor imported to combat him. Vashanka is not to be combatted."

Hanse snapped glances this way and that. "Say such things a time or two more in Sanctuary, *my friend,* and your body will be mourning the loss of its head."

The blond man stared at him. "Do you believe that?"

Hanse let that pass, while he rowed into the current of other conversations in the tavern. A current restless as a thief on a landing outside a window, and conversations just as stealthy and dark. He tuned it out again, stepping out of the flow yet flowing with it. Quietly.

"And how many of those fell Things do you think are still loose?"

"Too many. Two or four? You know our job is to collect them."

"Our?"

"The Hell-Hounds."

"Who's your bearded friend, Hanse?"

The speaker stood beside the table, only a bit older than Hanse and just as cocky. Older in years only; he had not benefited from those years and would never be so much as Hanse. Self-consciously he wore self-consciously tight black. Oh, a brilliant thief! About as unobtrusive as hives.

Hanse was staring at Tempus, who was pink and bronze of skin, gold and honey of hair, lengthy and lengthy of legs, and smoothshaven as a pair of doeskin leggings. Hanse did not take his dark-eyed gaze off the Hell-Hound, while his dark hand moved out to close on the (black-bracered) wrist of the other young man.

"What color would you say his beard is, Athavul?"

Athavul moved his arm and proved that his wrist would not come loose. His arrogance and mask of cocky confidence fled him faster than a street girl fled a man revealed poor. Tempus recognized Athavul's chuckle; nervousness and sham. Tempus had heard it a thousand or a million times. What was the difference? He reflected on temporality, even while this boy Athavul temporized.

"You going blind, Shadowspawn? You think myself is, and testing he and I?" With a harsh short laugh and a slap with his other hand on his own chest, Athavul said, "Black as this. Black as this!" He slapped his black leather pants—self-consciously.

Tempus, leaning a bit forward, elbows on the little table, big swordsman's shoulders hunched, continued to gaze directly at Hanse. Into Hanse's eyes. His face looked open because he made it that way. Beardless.

"Same's his hair?" Hanse said, and his voice sounded brittle as very old harness-leather. His eyes glittered.

Athavul swallowed. "Hair. . . ." He swallowed again, looking from

Hanse to Tempus to Hanse. "Ah . . . he's your, ah, friend, Hanse. Let go, will you? You twit him about his . . . head if you want to, but I won't. Sorry I stopped and tried to be civil."

Without looking away from Hanse, Tempus said, "It's all right, Athavul. My name is Thales and I am not sensitive. I've been this bald for years."

Hanse was staring at Tempus, blond Tempus. His hand opened. Athavul yanked his arm back so fast he hit himself in his (nearly inexistent) stomach. He made no pretense of grace; with a dark glance at Hanse, he betook himself elsewhere, sullenly silent.

"Nicely done," Tempus said, showing his teeth.

"Don't smile at me, stranger. What do you look like?"

"Exactly what you see, Hanse. Exactly."

"And . . . what did he see?" Hanse's wave of his arm was as tight as he had become inside. "What do they see here, talking with Hanse?"

"He told you."

"Black beard, no hair."

Blond, beardless Tempus nodded.

Neither had taken his gaze off the other's eyes. "What else?"

"Does it matter? I am in the employ of that person we both know. What you people call a Hell-Hound. I would not come here in that appearance! I doubt anyone else would be in this room, if they saw *me*. I was here when you came in, remember? Waiting for you. You were too cool to ask the obvious."

"They call me spawn of the shadows," Hanse said quietly, slowly, in a low tone. He was leaning back as if to get a few more centimeters between him and the tall man. "You're just a damned shadow!"

"It's fitting. I need your help, Shadowspawn."

Hanse said, enunciating distinctly, "Shit." And rising he added, "Sing for it. Dance in the streets for it." And he turned away, then back to add, "You're paying of course, Baldy," and then he betook himself elsewhere.

Outside, he glanced up and down the vermiform "street" called Serpentine, turned right to walk a few paces north. Automatically, he stepped over the broken plank in the boardwalk. He glanced into the tucked-in courtyard that was too broad and shallow to be dangerous for several hours yet. Denizens of the Maze called it variously The Outhouse, Tick's Vomitory, or, less seriously, Safehaven. From the pointed tail of the shortcloak on the man back within that three-sided box, Hanse recognized Poker the Cadite. From the wet sounds, he made an assumption as to Poker's activity. The man with the piebald beard glanced around.

"Come on in, Shadowspawn. Not much room left."

"Looking for Athavul. Said he was carrying and said I could join him." Lying was more than easy to Shadowspawn; it was almost instinctive.

"You're not mad at him?" Poker dropped his tunic's hem and turned from the stained rearmost wall.

"No no, nothing like that."

"He went south. Turned into Slick Walk."

"Thanks, Poker. There's a big-bearded man in the Unicorn with no hair on top. Get him to buy you a cup. Tell him I said."

"Ah. Enemy of yours, Hansey?"

"Right."

Hanse turned and walked a few paces north toward Straight, his back to Slick Walk (which led into the two-block L whose real name no one remembered. Nary a door opened onto it and it stayed dark as a sorcerer's heart. It smelled perpetually sour and was referred to as Vomit Boulevard). When Poker said the weather was sunny, turn up your cloak's hood against rain. When Poker said right, head left.

Hanse cut left through Odd Birt's Dodge, angling around the corner of the tenement owned by Furtwan the dealer in snails for dye—who lived way over on the east side, hardly in tenement conditions. Instantly Hanse vanished into the embrace of his true friend and home. The shadows.

Because he had kept his eyes slitted while he was in the light filtering down from Straight Street, he was able to see. The darkness deepened with each of his gliding westward steps.

He heard the odd tapping sound as he passed Wrong Way Park. What in all the—a blind man? Hanse smiled—keeping his mouth closed against the possible flash of teeth. This was a wonderful place for the blind! They could "see" more in three-quarters of the Maze than anyone with working eyes. He eased along toward the short streetlet called Tanner, hearing the noises from Sly's Place. Then he heard Athavul's voice, out in the open.

"Your pardon, dear lady, but if you don't hand myself your necklace and your wallet I'll put this crossbow bolt through your left gourd."

Hanse eased closer, getting himself nearer the triple "corner" where Tanner sort of intersected with Odd Birt's Dodge and touched the north-south wriggle of the Serpentine as well. Streets in the Maze, it has been said, had been laid out by two love-struck snakes, both soaring on krrf. Hanse heard the reply of Ath's intended prey:

"You don't *have* a crossbow, slime lizard, but see what *I* have!"

The scream, in a voice barely recognizable as Athavul's, raised the hairs on the back of Hanse's neck and sent a chill running all the way down his coccyx. He considered freezing in place. He considered the sensible course of turning and running. Curiosity urged him to edge two steps farther and peek around the building housing Sly's. Curiosity won.

By the time he looked, Athavul was whimpering and gibbering. Someone in a long cloak the color of red clay, hood up, stepped around him and Hanse thought he heard a giggle. Cowering, pleading, gibbering in horribly obvious fear—of what?—Athavul fell to his knees. The cloak swept on along Tanner toward the Street of Odors, and Hanse swallowed with a little effort. A knife had got itself into his hand; he didn't throw it. He edged down a few more steps to see which way the cloak turned. Right. Hanse caught a glimpse of the walking stick. It was white. The way the person in that cloak was moving, though, she was not blind. Nor was she any big woman.

Hanse put up his knife and started toward Athavul.

"No! Please plehehehease!" On his knees, Ath clasped his hands and pleaded. His eyes were wide and glassy with fear. Sweat and tears ran down his face in such profusion that he must soon have salt spots on his black jerkin. His shaking was wind-blown wash on the line and his face was the color of a priming coat of whitewash.

Hanse stood still. He stared. "What's the matter with you, Ath? I'm not menacing you, you fugitive from a dung-fueled stove! *Athavul!* What's the *matter*'th you?"

"Oh please pleohplease no no oh ohh ohohohono-o-o. . . ."

Athavul fell on his knees and his still-clasped hands, bony rump in the air. His shaking had increased to that of a whipped, starved dog.

Such an animal would have moved Hanse to pity. Athavul was just ridiculous. Hanse wanted to kick him. He was also aware that two or three people were peering out of the dump still called Sly's Place though Sly had taken dropsy and died two years back.

"Ath? Did she hurt you? Hey! You little piece of camel dropping— what did she *do* to you?"

At the angry, demanding sound of Hanse's voice, Athavul clutched himself. Weeping loudly, he rolled over against the wall. He left little spots of tears and slobber and a puddle from a spasming sphincter. Hanse swallowed hard. *Sorcery*. That damned Enas Y—no, he didn't

work this way. Ath was absolutely terrified. Hanse had always thought
him the consistency of sparrow's liver and chicken soup, with bird's
eggs between his legs. But *this*—not even this strutting ass could be *this*
hideously possessed by fear without preternatural aid. Just the sight of
it was scary. Hanse felt an urge to stomp or stick Ath just to shut him
up, and that was awful.

He glanced at the thirty-one strands of dangling Syrese rope (each
knotted thirty-one times) that hung in the doorway of Sly's. He saw
seven staring eyeballs, six fingers, and several mismatched feet. Even in
the Maze, noise attracted attention . . . but people had sense enough
not to go running out to see what was amiss.

"BLAAAH!" Hanse shouted, making a horrid face and pouncing at
the doorway. Then he rushed past the groveling, weeping Athavul. At
the corner he looked up Odors toward Straight, and he was sure he saw
the vermilion cloak. Maroon now, in the distance. Yes. Across Straight,
heading north now past the tanners' broad open-front sheds, almost to
the intersection with the Street Called Slippery.

Several people were walking along Odors, just walking, heading
south in Hanse's directon. The lone one carried a lanthorn.

All six walkers—three, one, and two—passed him going in the opposite direction. None saw him, though Hanse was hurrying. He heard the
couple talking about the hooded blind woman with the white staff. He
crossed well-lighted Straight Street when the red clay cloak was at the
place called Harlot's Cross. There Tanner's Row angled in to join the
Street of Odors at its mutual intersection with the broad Governor's
Walk. He passed the tiny "temple" of Theba and several shops to stop
outside the entrance of the diminutive Temple of Eshi Virginal—few
believed in *that*—and watched the cloak turn left. Northwest. A woman,
all right. Heading past the long sprawl of the farmers' market? Or one
of the little dwellings that faced it?

Heading for Red Lantern Road? *A woman who pretends to be blind
and who put a spell of terror on Athavul like nothing I ever saw.*

He had to follow her. He was incapable of not following her.

He was not driven only by curiosity. He wanted to know the identity
of a woman with such a device, yes. There was also the possibility of
obtaining such a useful wand. White, it resembled the walk-tap stick of
a sightless woman. Painted though, it could be the swagger stick of . . .
Shadowspawn. Or of someone with a swollen purse who could put it to
good use against Hanse's fellow thieves.

He looked out for himself; let them.

Hanse did not follow. He moved to intersect, and could anyone have done it as swiftly and surefootedly, it must have been a child who lived hereabouts and had no supervision.

He ran past Slippery—fading into a fig-pedlar's doorway while a pair of City Watchmen passed—then ran through two vacant lots, a common back yard full of dog droppings and the white patches of older ones, over an outhouse, around a fat tree and then two meathouses and through two hedges—one spiny, which took no note of being cursed by a shadow on silent feet—across a porch and around a rain barrel, over the top of a sleeping black cat that objected with more noise than the two dogs he had aroused—one was still importantly barking, puffed up and hating to leave off—across another porch ("Is that you, Dadisha? Where have you *been?*"), through someone's scraps and—long jump!— over a mulchpile, and around two lovers ("What was that, Wrenny?"), an overturned outhouse, a rain barrel, a cow tethered to a wagon he went under without even slowing down, and three more buildings.

One of the lovers and one of the dogs actually caught sight of the swift-fleeting shadow. No one else. The cow might have wondered.

On one knee beside a fat beanberry bush at the far end of Market Run, he looked out upon the long straight stretch of well-kept street that ran past the market on the other side. He was not winded.

The hooded cloak with the walking stick was just reaching this end of the long, long farmers' market. Hanse crimped his cheeks in a little smile. Oh he was so clever, so speedy! He was just in time to—

—to see the two cloakless but hooded footpads materialize from the deep jet shadows at the building's corner. They pounced. One ran angling, to grasp her from behind, while his fellow came at her face-on with no weapons visible. Ready to snatch what she had, and run. She behaved surprisingly; she lunged to one side and prodded the attacker in front. *Prodded,* that Hanse saw; she did not strike or stab with the white staff.

Instantly the man went to his knees. He was gibbering, pleading, quaking. A butterfly clinging to a twig in a windstorm. Or . . . Athavul.

Swiftly—not professionally fast, but swiftly for her, a civilian, Hanse saw (he was moving)—she turned to the one coming up behind her. He also adjusted rapidly. He went low. The staff whirred over his head while his partner babbled and pleaded in the most abject fear. The footpad had not stopped moving. (Neither had Hanse.) Up came the hooded man from his crouch and his right hand snapped out edge-on to strike her wrist while his other fist leaped to her stomach. That fist glittered in the moonlight, or something glittered in it. That silvery something went into her and she made a puking gagging throaty noise and while she fell the white stick slid from her reflexively opening fingers. He grabbed it.

That was surely ill-advised, but his hand closed on the staff's handle without apparent effect on him. He kicked her viciously, angrily—maybe she felt it, gutted, and maybe she did not—and he railed at his comrade. The latter, on his knees, behaved as Athavul had when Hanse shouted at him. He fell over and rolled away, assuming the foetal posture while he wept and pled.

The killer spat several expletives and whirled back to his victim. She was twitching, dying. Yanking open the vermilion cloak, he jerked off her necklace, ripped a twisted silver loop out of each ear, and yanked at the scantling purse on her girdle. It refused to come free. He sliced it with the swift single movement of a practiced expert. Straightening, he glanced in every direction, said something to his partner—who rolled foetally, sobbing.

"Theba take you, then," the thief said, and ran.

Back into the shadows of the market building's west corner he fled, and one of the shadows tripped him. As he fell, an elbow thumped the back of his neck.

"I want what you've got, you murdering bastard," a shadow-voice said from the shadows, while the footpad twisted to roll over. "Your kind gives thieves a bad name."

"Take it then!" The fallen man rammed the white staff into the shadow's thigh as it started to bend over him.

Instantly fear seized Hanse. Vised him; encompassed him; possessed him. Sickening, stomach-fluttering fear. His armpits flooded and his sphincter fluttered.

Unlike the stick's victims he had seen, he was in darkness, and he was Shadowspawn. He did not fall to his knees.

He fled, desperately afraid, sniveling, clutching his gut, babbling. Tears flowed to blind him, but he was in darkness anyhow. Staggering, weeping, horribly and obscenely afraid and even more horribly knowing all the while that he had no reason to be afraid, that this was sorcery; the most demeaning spell that could be laid on a man. He heard the killer laugh, and Hanse tried to run faster. Hoping the man did not pursue to confront him. Accost him. Snarl mean things at him. He could not stand that.

It did not happen that way. The thief who had slain without intending to kill laughed, but he too was scared, and disconcerted. He fled,
slinking, in another direction. Hanse stumbled-staggered-sniveled on,
on. Instinct was not gone but was heightened; he clung to the shadows
as a frightened child to its mother. But he made noise, noise.

Attracted at the same time as she was repulsed by that whining fearful gibbering, Mignureal came upon him. "What—it's Han—*what are
you doing?*"

He was seriously considering ending the terror by ending himself with
the knife in his fist. Anything to stop this enveloping, consuming agony
of fear. At her voice he dropped the knife and fell weeping to his knees.

"Hanse—*stop that!*"

He did not. He could not. He could assume the foetal. He did. Un-
comprehending, the garishly-dressed girl acted instinctively to save him.
Her mother liked him and to Mignureal he was attractive, a figure of ro-
mance. In his state, saving him was easy, even for a thirteen-year-old.
Though his hysterical sobbing pleas brought tears to her eyes, for him,
Mignureal tied his wrists behind him. The while, she breathed prayers
known only to the S'danzo.

"You come along now," she said firmly, leaking tears and gulping.
"Come along with me!"

Hanse obeyed.

She went straight along the well-lit Governor's Walk and turned
down Shadow Lane, conducting her bound, sniveling captive. At the
corner of Shadow and Slippery, a couple of uniformed men accosted
her.

"Why it's Moonflower's darter. What've you got there, Mineral?"

"Mignureal," she corrected. "Someone put a spell on him—over on
the Processional," she said, choosing an area far from where she had
found him. "My mother can help. Go with Eshi."

"Hmm. A spell of fear, huh? That damned Anus Yorl, I'll wager a
cup! Who is it, sniveling under your shawl that way?"

Mignureal considered swiftly. What had happened to Hanse was
awful. To have these City Watchmen know, and spread it about—that
would be insupportable. Again Mignureal lied. It was her brother An-
telope, she told them, and they made sympathetic noises and let her be
on her way, while they muttered about dam' sorcerers and the nutty
names S'danzo gave their get. Both men agreed; they would make a
routine check of Awful Alley and stop in at the Alekeep, just down the
street.

Mignureal led Hanse a half-block more and went into her parents'
shop-and-living-quarters. They were asleep. The tautly overweight
Moonflower did not heed summonses and did not make house calls.
Furthermore her husband was an irrepressibly randy man who bedded
early and insisted on her company. At her daughter's sobbing and shaking her, the seer awoke. That gently-named collection of talent and
adipose tissue and mammalia sufficient to nurse octuplets, simultaneously, sat erect. She reached comfortingly for her daughter. Soon she
had listened, was out of bed, and beside Hanse. Mignureal had ordered
him to remain on the divan in the shop.

"That just isn't Hanse, Mother!"

"Of course it isn't. Look on sorcery, and hate it."

"Name of Tiana Savior—it's awful, seeing him, hearing him this
way. . . ."

"Fetch my shawl," Moonflower said, one by one relieving Hanse of
his knives, "and do make some tea, sweetheart."

Moonflower held the quaking young man and crooned. She pillowed
his tear-wet face in the vastness of her bosom. She loosed his wrists,
drew his hands round, and held their wiry darkness in her large paler
dimple-backed ones. And she crooned, and talked low, on and on. Her
daughter draped her with the shawl and went to make tea.

The ray of moonlight that fell into the room moved the length of a
big man's foot while the seer sat there with him, and more, and Hanse
went to sleep, still shivering. She held his hands until he was still but for
his breathing. Mignureal hovered close, all bright of eye, and knew the
instant her mother went off. Sagging. Glassy-eyed. She began murmur-
ing, a woman small inside and huge without; a gross kitten at her divining.

"A yellow-furred hunting dog? Tall as a tree, old as a tree . . . he
hovers and with him is a god not of Ilsig. A god of Ranke—oh, it is a
Hell-Hound. Oh Hanse it is not wizard-sorcery but god-sorcery! And
who is thi—oh. Another god. But why is Theba involved, who has so
few adherents here? Oh!"

She shuddered and her daughter started to touch her; desisted.

"I see Ils Himself hiding His face . . . a shadow tall as a tree and
another, not nearly so big. A shadow and its pawn? Why it has no head,
this smaller shad—oh. It is afraid, that's it; it has no face left. It is Ha—I
will not say even though he sleeps. Oh Mignue, there is a corpse on the
street up in front of the farmers' market and—ahhh." Her relief was apparent in that great sigh. "Hanse did not kill her. Another did, and

Theba hovers over her. Hmm. I see—I s—I will not say what I s . . . it
fades, goes."

Again she sighed and sat still, sweating, overflowing her chair on
both sides. Gazing at the sleeping Shadowspawn. "He has spoken with
the governor who is the emperor's kinsman, Mignureal my dear, did
you know that? He will again. They are not enemies, our governor and
Shadowspawn."

"Oh." And Mignureal looked upon him, head to one side. Moonflower saw the look.

"You will go to bed and tomorrow you will tell me what you were
doing abroad so late, Mignue. You will *not* come near Hanse again, do
you understand?"

"Oh, mother." Mignureal met the level gaze only briefly. "Yes,
mother. I understand." And she went to bed.

Moonflower did not; she stayed beside Hanse. In the morning he was
all right and she told him what she had Seen. He would never be the
same again, she knew, he who had met quintessential fear, Lord Terror
himself, face to face. But he was Hanse again, and not afraid, and
Moonflower was sure that within a few hours he would have his gliding
swagger back. She did note that he was grim-facedly determined.

The message left at the little Watchpost at the corner of Shadow and
Lizard's Way suggested that the "tall as a tree Hell-Hound take a walk
between stinky market and the cat storage" at the time of the fifth night-
watch "when the shadows are spawning fear in all hearts." The message was delivered to Tempus, who ordered the sub-prefect to forget it,
and looked fierce. The wriggly agreed and got thence.

In private, his mind aided by a pinch of his powdered friend, Tempus
worked backward at the cipher. The last line had to be the signature:
Shadowspawn. Hanse wanted to meet him very privately, an hour past
midnight. Good. So . . . *where?* "Stinky market" could mean lots of
places. "Cat storage" meant nothing. Cat storage; cat—the granaries?—
where cats not only were kept but migrated, drawn by the mice drawn
by the grain? No; there was no way to walk *between* any of the granaries and anything deserving to be characterized as stinky market beyond any other stenchy place.

*What stinks most? Easy,* he answered himself. *The tanners—no!
Don't be stupid,* second thought told him. *Fish stink worse than anything.* Hmm. The fish market then, down on Red Clay Street—which
might as well be called Warehouse Street. So all the natives called it.

The stinking fish market, then, and . . . *cat storage?* He stared at the map.

Oh. Simple. The governor was called Kittycat and a warehouse was a place for storage. The Governor's Warehouse then, down beside the fish market. Not a block from the Watchpost at Shadow and Lizard, the rascal! Tempus shook his head, and hours and hours later he was there. He made sure no one tried to "help" him; twice he played thief, to watch his own trail. He was not followed. Wrinkling his nose at the stench and slipping on a discarded fishhead, he resolved to get a clean-up detail down here, and recommend a light as well.

"I am glad you look like you," the shadows said, from behind and above him.

"A god has marked me, Hanse," Tempus explained, without turning or looking up. "He helped me, in the Vulgar Unicorn. I didn't care to be seen there, compromising you. Did you leave the message because you have changed your mind?"

"There will be a bargain."

"I can appreciate that. Word is that you have bargained before, with my employer."

"That is as obviously impossible as breaking into the palace."

"Obviously. I am empowered to bargain, Hanse."

"A woman was found dead on Farmer's Run just at the west end of the market," the shadows said quietly. "She wore a cloak the color of red clay."

"Yes."

"She had a walking stick. It has a . . . *horrible* effect on a man. Her killer stole it, after she used it on his partner. He abandoned him."

"No thief's corpse was found."

"It does not kill. Its effect is . . . *obscene.*" A pause; while the shadow shuddered? "I saw it happen. They were hooded."

"Do you know who they are?"

"Not now. I can find out easily. Want the stick?"

"Yes."

"How many of those foul things remain in . . . circulation?"

"We think two. A clever fellow has done well for himself by counting the people who came out of the shop with a purchase, and recording the names of those he knew. What is the bargain, Hanse?"

"I had rather deal with him."

"I wish you would trust me. Setting up interviews with him takes time. "

"I trust you, Tempus, just as you trust me. Get me something in writing from him, then. Signed. Give it to the seer, Moonflower. This is costing me time, pulling me away from my work—"

"Work?"

"—and I shall have to have compensation. Now."

*O you damned arrogant boy,* Tempus thought, and without a word he made three coins clink as he dropped them. He was sure Hanse's ears could distinguish gold from copper or silver by the sound of the clink. He also dropped a short section of pig's intestine, stitched at one end and tied off at the other. He said, "Oops."

"I want assistance in recovering something of mine, Tempus. Just labor, that's all. What's to be recovered is mine, I guarantee it."

"I'll help you myself."

"We'll need tools, a horse, rope, strength. . . ."

"Done. I will get it in writing, but it is done. Deliver and I deliver. We have a bond between us."

"So have he and I. I do want that paper signed and slipped to the S'danzo seer. Very well then, Tempus. We have bargained."

"By mid-afternoon. Good night, spawn of shadows."

"Good night, shadow-man. You didn't say 'pawn,' did you?"

"No." And Tempus turned and walked back up between the buildings to light, and less stenchy air. Behind him, soundlessly, the three gold coins and little bag of krrf he had dropped vanished, into the shadows.

Next day not long after dawn Hanse gave Moonflower a great hug and pretended to find a gold piece in her ear.

"I Saw for you, not for coin," she told him.

"I understand. I know. Why look, here's another in your other ear, for Mignureal. I give you the gold because I found it, not because you helped me. And a message will be given you today, for me."

Moonflower made both coins disappear beneath her shawl into what she called her treasure chest. "Don't frown; Mignue shall have the one as her very own. Will you do something for me I would prefer to coin, Hanse?"

Very seriously, relaxing for once, he nodded. "Without question."

"My daughter is very young and thinks you are just *so* romantic a figure. Will you just pretend she is your sister?"

"Oh you would not want *that,* Passionflower," he said, in one of those rare indications of what sort of childhood he must have had. "She

is my friend's daughter and I shall call her cousin. Besides, she saw me
. . . that way. I may not be able to look her in the eyes again."

She took those lean restless hands of a thief proud never to have hurt
any he robbed. "You will, Hanse. You will. It was god-sorcery, and no
embarrassment. Will you now be careful?"

"I will."

She studied his eyes. "But you are going to find him."

"I am."


The adherents of the most ancient goddess Theba went hooded to
their little temple. This was their way. It also made it easier for the government to keep them under surveillance, and made it easy for Hanse to
slip among them. A little tilt to his shoulder, a slight favoring of one leg
under the dull brown robe, and he was not the lithely gliding Shadowspawn at all.

The services were dull and he had never liked the odor of incense. It
made him want to sneeze and go to sleep, both at once. Insofar as he
ever gave thought to religion, he leaned toward a sort of loyalty to the
demigod Rander Rehabilitatus. He endured, and he observed. This goddess' worship in Sanctuary included two blind adherents. Both carried
staffs. Though only one was white, it was not in the grip of a left-
handed man.

Finding his quarry really was as simple as that. On deserting his
partner, the murderous thief had sneered "Theba take you," and
Moonflower had Seen that goddess, or at least the likeness of her icons
and amulets. She had no more than forty worshipers here, and only this
one (part-time) temple. The thief had also struck away the terror-stick
with his right hand and used his left to drive the dagger into his victim—
and to use the staff on Hanse.

There came the time of Communing In Her. Hanse watched what the
others did. They mingled, and a buzz rose as they said nice silly loving
peace-things to each other in the name of Her. The usual meaningless
ritual; "peace" was a word and life and its exigencies were another matter. Hanse mingled.

"Peace and love to you, brother," a woman said from within her
wine-dark cowl, and her hand slipped into Hanse's robe and he caught
her wrist.

"Peace and defter fingers to you, sister," he said quietly, and went
around her toward his goal. To be certain, he came cowl to cowl with
the man with the white stick and, smiling, made a shamefully obscene

gesture. The cowl and the staff did not move; a hand moved gently out to touch him.

"Her peace remain on you, my brother," the blind man said in a high voice, and Hanse mouthed words, then turned.

"You rotten slime," a cowl striped in green and red hissed. "Poor blind Sorad has been among us for years and no one ever made such a nasty gesture to him. Who are you, anyhow?"

"One who thinks that other blind man is not blind and not one of us, and was testing—brother. Have you ever seen him before?"

His accoster—burly, in that striped Myrsevadan robe, looked around. "Well . . . no. The one in the gloves?"

"Yes. I think they are because his stick—yes, peace to you too, sister —has just been painted."

"You think it's a disguised weapon? That he's from the . . . palace?"

"No. I think the prince-governor couldn't care a rat's whisker about us." Substituting the pronoun was a last instant thought, and Hanse felt proud of that touch. Playing "I'm just like you but *he* is bad" had got him out of several scrapes. "I do think he is a spy, though. That priest from Ranke, who thinks every temple should be closed down except a glorious new one to Vash—Vashi—whatever they call him. I'll bet that's his spy."

That made the loyal Thebite quiver in rage! He went directly toward the man in the forest green cloak, with the brown stick. Hanse, edging along toward the entrance of what was by day a belt-maker's shop, watched Striped Robe speak to the man with the staff. An answer came, as Hanse moved.

Hanse didn't hear the reply; he heard "May all your days be bright in Her name and She take you when you are tired of life, brother." This from the fat man beside him, in a tent-sized cloak.

"Oh, *thank* you, brother. And on you, peace in Her n—" Hanse broke off when the terrified screaming began.

It was the big fellow in the robe of green and red stripes, and his cowl fell back to show his fear-twisted face. Naturally no one understood, and other cries arose amid the milling of robed, faceless people. Two did understand, and both moved toward the door. One was closer. He hurried forth, running—and outside, cut left out of view of the doorway and swung swiftly back. He already had the little jar of vinegar out of his dull brown robe, and the cork pulled. Inside the temple: clamor.

The man with the gloves and brown walking stick hurried through the door and turned left; had he not, Hanse would have called. The fellow had no time for anything before Hanse sent the vinegar sloshing within his hood.

"*Ah!*" Naturally the man ducked his head as the liquid drenched him and entered both eyes. Since he was not blind and not accustomed to carrying a staff as a part of him, he dropped it to rush both hands to his face. Hanse swallowed hard before snatching up the stick by its handle. He kicked the moaning fellow in the kneecap, and ran. The god-weapon seemed hummingly *alive* in his hand, so much that he wanted to throw it down and keeping running. He did not, and it exerted no other effect on him. Just around the corner he paused for an importuning beggar, who soon had the gift of a nice brown, cowled robe. Since it was thrown over him as he sat, he never saw the generous giver. He had been swallowed by the shadows once the beggar got his head free of the encumbering woolen.

"Here, you little lizard, where do you think you're running to, hah?"

That from the brutish swaggering desert tradesman who grabbed at Hanse as he ran by. Well, he was not of the city, and did not know who he laid big hand on. Nor was he likely to aught but hie himself out of Sanctuary, once he returned to normal—doubtless robbed. Besides, a test really should be made to be sure, and Hanse poked him.

This was the staff of ensorcelment, all right.

Hurrying on his way, Hanse began to smile.

He had the stick and the murdering thief who had used it on him would not be too nimble for a long, long time, and the robe he had snitched off a drying line was in the possession of a beggar who would be needing it in a few months, and Hanse had his little message from the prince-governor. It avowed—so Hanse was told, as he did not read—that "he you specify shall lend full aid in the endeavor you specify, provided it is legal in full, in return for your returning another wand to us."

Hanse had laughed when he read that last; even a prince had a sense of humor and could allude to Hanse's having stolen his Savankh, rod of authority, less than a month ago. And now Shadowspawn would have the aid of big strong super-legal Tempus in regaining two bags of silver coin from a well up in the supposedly haunted ruins of Eaglenest. Hanse hoped Prince Kadakithis would appreciate the humor in that, too: the bagged booty had come from him, as ransom for the official baton of his imperial authority in Sanctuary. Even Tempus' krrf had brought in a bit of silver.

And now . . . Hanse's grin broadened. Suppose he just went about a *second* illicit entry of the palace? Suppose a blind man showed up

among the swarm of alms-seekers to be admitted into the courtyard two
days hence, in accord with Kadakithis' people wooing custom? Shadowspawn would not only hand this awful staff to the prince-governor, he
would at the same time provide graphic demonstration of the palace's
pitiable security.

Unfortunately, Tempus had taken charge of security. The hooded
blind beggar was challenged at the gate two days thence, and the Hell-
Hound Quag suspiciously snatched the staff from him. When the disguised Hanse objected, he was struck with it. Well, at least that way it
was proven that he had brought the right stick in good faith, and that
way he did get to spend a night in the palace, however unpleasant in his
state of terror.

# To Guard the Guardians

## Robert Lynn Asprin

The Hell-Hounds were now a common sight in Sanctuary so the appearance of one in the bazaar created little stir, save for the concealment of a few smuggled wares and a price increase on everything else. However, when two appeared together, as they did today, it was enough to silence casual conversation and draw uneasy stares, though the more observant vendors noted that the pair were engrossed in their own argument and did not even glance at the stalls they were passing.

"But the man has offended me. . . ." the darker of the pair snarled.

"He offends everyone," his companion countered, "it's his way. I tell you, Razkuli, I've heard him say things to the Prince himself that would have other men flayed and blinded. You're a fool to take it personally."

"But, Zalbar. . . ."

"I know, I know—he offends you; and Quag bores you and Arman is an arrogant braggard. Well, this whole town offends me, but that doesn't give me the right to put it to the sword. Nothing Tempus has said to you warrants a blood-feud."

"It is done." Razkuli thrust one fist against his other palm as they walked.

"It is *not* done until you act on your promise, and if you do *I'll* move to stop you. I won't have the men in my command killing each other."

The two men walked silently for several moments, each lost in his own dark thoughts.

"Look, my friend," Zalbar sighed, "I've already had one of my men killed under scandalous circumstances. I don't want to answer for another incident—particularly if it involves you. Can't you see Tempus is trying to goad you into a fight?—a fight you can't win."

"No one lives that I've seen over an arrow," Razkuli said ominously, his eyes narrowing on an imaginary target.

"Murder, Razkuli? I never thought I'd see the day you'd sink to being an assassin."

There was a sharp intake of breath and Razkuli faced his comrade with eyes that showed a glint of madness. Then the spark faded and the small man's shoulders relaxed. "You're right, my friend," he said, shaking his head, "I would never do that. Anger speeds my tongue ahead of reason."

"As it did when you vowed blood-feud. You've survived countless foes who were mortal; don't try the favor of the gods by seeking an enemy who is not."

"Then the rumors about Tempus are true?" Razkuli asked, his eyes narrowing again.

"I don't know, there are things about him which are difficult to explain by any other logic. Did you see how rapidly his leg healed? We both know men whose soldiering career was ended after they were caught under a horse—yet he was standing duty again within the week."

"Such a man is an affront against Nature."

"Then let Nature take vengeance on him," Zalbar laughed, clapping a friendly hand on his comrade's shoulder, "and free us for more worthwhile pasttimes. Come, I'll buy you lunch. It will be a pleasant change from barracks food."

Haakon, the sweetmeats vendor, brightened as the two soldiers approached him and waited patiently while they made their selections from his spiced-meat turnovers.

"That will be three coppers," he smiled through yellowed teeth.

"Three coppers?" Razkuli exclaimed angrily, but Zalbar silenced him with a nudge in the ribs.

"Here, fellow . . ." the Hell-Hound commander dropped some coins into Haakon's outstretched hand, "take four. Those of us from the Capitol are used to paying full value for quality goods—though I suppose that this far from civilization you have to adjust the prices to accommodate the poorer folk."

The barb went home and Zalbar was rewarded by a glare of pure hatred before he turned away, drawing Razkuli with him.

"Four coppers! You were being overcharged at three!"

"I know." Zalbar winked. "But I refuse to give them the satisfaction of haggling. I find it's worth the extra copper to see their faces when I imply that they're selling below value—it's one of the few pleasures available in this hellhole."

"I never thought of it that way," Razkuli said with a laugh, "but you're right. My father would have been livid if someone deliberately overpaid him. Do me a favor and let me try it when we buy the wine."

Razkuli's refusal to bargain brought much the same reaction from the wineseller. The dark mood of their conversation as they had entered the bazaar had vanished and they were ready to eat with calm humor.

"You provided the food and drink, so I'll provide the setting," Razkuli declared, tucking the wine-flask into his belt. "I know a spot which is both pleasant and relaxing."

"It must be outside the city."

"It is, just outside the Common Gate. Come on, the city won't miss our presence for an hour or so."

Zalbar was easily persuaded though more from curiosity than belief. Except for occasional patrols along the Street of Red Lanterns he rarely got outside Sanctuary's North Wall and had never explored the area to the northwest where Razkuli was leading him.

It was a different world here, almost as if they had stepped through a magic portal into another land. The buildings were scattered, with large open spaces between them, in contrast to the cramped shops and narrow alleys of the city proper. The air was refreshingly free from the stench of unwashed bodies jostling each other in crowded streets. Zalbar relaxed in the peaceful surroundings. The pressures of patrolling the hateful town slipped away like a heavy cloak, allowing him to look forward to an uninterrupted meal in pleasant company.

"Perhaps you could speak to Tempus? We needn't like each other, but if he could find another target for his taunts, it would do much toward easing my hatred."

Zalbar shot a wary glance at his comrade, but detected none of the blind anger which he had earlier expressed. The question seemed to be an honest attempt on Razkuli's part to find a compromise solution to an intolerable situation.

"I would, if I thought it would help," he sighed reluctantly, "but I fear I have little influence on him. If anything, it would only make matters worse. He would redouble his attacks to prove he wasn't afraid of me either."

"But you're his superior officer," Razkuli argued.

"Officially, perhaps," his friend shrugged, "but we both know there are gaps between what is official and what is true. Tempus has the

Prince's ear. He's a free agent here and follows my orders only when it suits him."

"You've kept him out of the Aphrodisia House. . . ."

"Only because I had convinced the Prince of the necessity of maintaining the good will of that House before Tempus arrived," Zalbar countered, shaking his head. "I had to go to the Prince to curb Tempus' ill-conduct and earned his hatred for it. You notice he still does what he pleases at the Lily Garden—and the Prince looks the other way. No, I wouldn't count on my influence over Tempus. I don't think he would physically attack me because of my position in the Prince's bodyguard. I also don't think he would come to my aid if I were hard-pressed in a fight."

Just then Zalbar noticed a small flower garden nestled beside a house not far from their path. A man was at work in the garden, watering and pruning. The sight created a sudden wave of nostalgia in the Hell-Hound. How long had it been since he stood outside the Emperor's Palace in the Capitol, fighting boredom by watching the gardeners pampering the flowered grounds? It seemed like a lifetime. Despite the fact that he was a soldier by profession, or perhaps because he was a soldier, he had always admired the calm beauty of flowers.

"Let's eat there . . . under that tree," he suggested, indicating a spot with a view of the garden. "It's as good a place as any."

Razkuli hesitated, glancing at the gardened house and started to say something, then shrugged and veered toward the tree. Zalbar saw the mischievous smile flit briefly across his comrade's face, but ignored it, preferring to contemplate the peaceful garden instead.

The pair dined in the manner of hardened, but off-duty, campaigners. Rather than facing each other, or sitting side-by-side, the two assumed back-to-back positions in the shade of a spreading tree. The earthenware wine-flask was carefully placed to one side, but in easy reach of both. Not only did the arrangement give them a full circle of vision to insure that their meal would be uninterrupted, it also allowed a brief illusion of privacy for the individual—a rare commodity to those whose profession required that every moment be shared with at least a dozen colleagues. To further that illusion they ate in silence. Conversation would be neither attempted nor tolerated until both were finished with their meal. It was the stance of men who trusted each other completely.

Although his position allowed him a clear view of the flower garden, Zalbar found his thoughts wandering back to his earlier conversation with Razkuli. Part of his job was to maintain peace among the Hell-

Hounds, at least to a point where their personal differences did not interfere with the performance of their duties. To that end he had soothed
his friend's ruffled feathers and forestalled any open fighting within the
force . . . for the time being, at least. With peace thus preserved, Zalbar could admit to himself that he agreed wholeheartedly with Razkuli.

Loudmouthed bullies were nothing new in the army, but Tempus was
a breed apart. As a devout believer in discipline and law, Zalbar was
disgusted and appalled by Tempus' attitudes and conduct. What was
worse, Tempus did have the Prince's ear, so Zalbar was powerless to
move against him despite the growing rumors of immoral and illegal
conduct.

The Hell-Hound's brow furrowed as he reflected upon the things he
had heard and seen. Tempus openly used *krrf,* both on duty and off. He
was rapidly building a reputation for brutality and sadism among the
not easily shocked citizens of Sanctuary. There were even rumors that
he was methodically hunting and killing the blue-masked sell-swords
employed by the ex-gladiator, Jubal.

Zalbar had no love for that crime-lord who traded in slaves to mask
his more illicit activities, but neither could he tolerate a Hell-Hound
taking it upon himself to be judge and executioner. But he had been ordered by the Prince to allow Tempus free rein and was powerless to
even investigate the rumors: a fine state of affairs when the law-en-
forcers became the lawbreakers and the lawgiver only moved to shelter
them.

A scream rent the air, interrupting Zalbar's reverie and bringing him
to his feet, sword in hand. As he cast about, searching for the source of
the noise, he remembered he had heard screams like that before . . .
though not on any battlefield. It wasn't a scream of pain, hatred, or terror but the heartless, soulless sounds of one without hope and assaulted
by horror too great for the mind to comprehend.

The silence was completely shattered by a second scream and this
time Zalbar knew the source was the beautifully gardened house. He
watched in growing disbelief as the gardener calmly continued his work,
not even bothering to look up despite the now frequent screams. Either
the man was deaf or Zalbar himself was going mad, reacting to imaginary noises from a best-forgotten past.

Turning to Razkuli for confirmation, Zalbar was outraged to find his
friend not only still seated but grinning ear-to-ear.

"Now do you see why I was willing to pass this spot by?" the swarthy

Hell-Hound said with a laugh. "Perhaps the next time I offer to lead you won't be so quick to exert your rank."

"You were expecting this?" Zalbar demanded, unsoothed by Razkuli's humor.

"Of course, you should be thankful it didn't start until we were nearly finished with our meal."

Zalbar's retort was cut off by a drawn out piercing cry that rasped against ear and mind and defied human endurance with its length.

"Before you go charging to the rescue," Razkuli commented, ignoring the now fading outburst of pain, "you should know I've already looked into it. What you're hearing is a slave responding to its master's attentive care: a situation entirely within the law and therefore no concern of ours. It might interest you to know that the owner of that building is a. . . ."

"Kurd!" Zalbar breathed through taut lips, glaring at the house as if it were an archenemy.

"You know him?"

"We met once, back at the Capitol. That's why he's here . . . or at least why he's not still there."

"Then you know his business?" Razkuli scowled, a bit deflated that his revelations were no surprise. "I'll admit I find it distasteful, but there's nothing we can do about it."

"We'll see," Zalbar announced darkly, starting toward the house.

"Where're you going?"

"To pay Kurd a visit."

"Then I'll see you back at the barracks." Razkuli shuddered. "I've been inside that house once already, and I'll not enter again unless it's under orders."

Zalbar made no note of his friend's departure though he did sheathe his sword as he approached the house. The impending battle would not require conventional weapons.

"Ho there!" he hailed the gardener. "Tell your master I wish to speak with him."

"He's busy," the man snarled, "can't you hear?"

"Too busy to speak with one of the Prince's personal guard?" Zalbar challenged, raising an eyebrow.

"He's spoken to them before and each time they've gone away and I've lost pay for allowing the interruption."

"Tell him it's Zalbar . . ." the Hell-Hound ordered, ". . . your master will speak with me, or would you like to deal with me in his stead?"

Though he made no move toward his weapons Zalbar's voice and stance convinced the gardener to waste no time. The gnome-like man abandoned his chores to disappear into the house.

As he waited Zalbar surveyed the flowers again, but knowledge of Kurd's presence had ruined his appreciation of floral beauty. Instead of lifting his spirits, the bright blossoms seemed a horrifying incongruity, like viewing a gaily colored fungus growing on a rotting corpse.

As Zalbar turned away from the flowers, Kurd emerged into the daylight. Though it had been five years since they had seen each other, the older man was sufficiently unchanged that Zalbar recognized him instantly: the stained dishevelled dress of one who sleeps in his clothes, the unwashed, unkempt hair and beard, as well as the cadaverously thin body with its long skeletal fingers and pasty complexion. Clearly Kurd had not discontinued his habit of neglecting his own body in the pursuit of his work.

"Good day . . . citizen," the Hell-Hound's smile did not disguise the sarcasm poisoning his greeting.

"It *is* you," Kurd declared, squinting to study the other's features. "I thought we were done with each other when I left Ranke."

"I think you shall continue to see me until you see fit to change your occupation."

"My work is totally within the limits of the law." The thin man bristled, betraying, for a moment, the strength of will hidden in his outwardly feeble body.

"So you said in Ranke. I still find it offensive, without redeeming merit."

"Without redeeming. . . ." Kurd shrieked, then words failed him. His lips tightened, he seized Zalbar by the arm and began pulling him toward the house. "Come with me now," he instructed. "Let me show you my work and explain what I am doing. Perhaps then you will be able to grasp the importance of my studies."

In his career Zalbar had faced death in many guises and done it unflinchingly. Now, however, he drew back in horror.

"I . . . That won't be necessary," he insisted.

"Then you continue to blindly condemn my actions without allowing me a fair hearing?" Kurd pointed a bent, bony finger at the Hell-Hound, a note of triumph in his voice.

Trapped by his own convictions, Zalbar swallowed hard and steeled

himself. "Very well, lead on. But, I warn you—my opinions are not easily swayed."

Zalbar's resolve wavered once they entered the building and he was
assaulted by the smells of its interior. Then he caught sight of the gardener smirking at him from the doorway and set his face in an expres-
sionless mask as he was led up the stairs to the second floor.

All that the Hell-Hound had ever heard or imagined about Kurd's
work failed to prepare him for the scene which greeted him when the
pale man opened the door to his workshop. Half a dozen large, heavy
tables lined the walls, each set at a strange angle so their surfaces were
nearly upright. They were not unlike the wooden frames court artists
used to hold their work while painting. All the tables were fitted with
leather harnesses and straps. The wood and leather, both, showed dried
and crusted bloodstains. Four of the tables were occupied.

"Most so-called medical men only repeat what has gone before . . ."
Kurd was saying, ". . . the few who do attempt new techniques do so
in a slipshod, trial-and-error fashion borne of desperation and ignorance. If the patient dies, it is difficult to determine if the cause was the
original affliction, or the new treatment itself. Here, under controlled
conditions, I actually increase our knowledge of the human body and its
frailties. Watch your step, please. . . ."

Grooves had been cut in the floor, running along beneath the tables
and meeting in a shallow pit at the room's far end. As he stepped over
one, Zalbar realized that the system was designed to guide the flow of
spilled blood. He shuddered.

There was a naked man on the first table and when he saw them
coming he began to writhe against his bonds. One arm was gone from
the elbow down and he beat the stump against the tabletop. Gibberings
poured from his mouth. Zalbar noted with disgust that the man's tongue
had been cut out.

"Here," Kurd announced, pointing to a gaping wound in the man's
shoulder, "is an example of my studies."

The man had obviously lost control of his bodily functions. Excre-
tions stained his legs and the table. Kurd paid no attention to this, gesturing Zalbar closer to the table as he used his long fingers to spread the
edges of the shoulder wound. "I have identified a point in the body
which, if pressure like this. . . ."

The man shrieked, his body arching against the restraining straps.

"Stop!" Zalbar shouted, losing any pretense of disinterest.

It was unlikely he could be heard over the tortured sounds of the victim, but Kurd withdrew his bloody finger and the man sagged back on the table.

"Well, did you see it?" the pale man asked eagerly.

"See what?" Zalbar blinked, still shaken by what he had witnessed.

"His stump, man! It stopped moving! Pressure or damage to this point can rob a man of the use of his arm. Here, I'll show you again."

"No!" the Hell-Hound ordered quickly, "I've seen enough."

"Then you see the value of my discovery?"

"Ummm. . . . where do you get your . . . subjects?" Zalbar evaded.

"From slavers, of course." Kurd frowned. "You can see the brands quite clearly. If I worked with anything but slaves . . . well, that would be against Rankan law."

"And how do you get them onto the tables? Slaves or not, I should think they would fight to the death rather than submit to your knives."

"There is a herbalist in town," the pale man explained, "he supplies me with a mild potion that renders them senseless. When they awaken, it's too late for effective resistance."

Zalbar started to ask another question, but Kurd held up a restraining hand. "You still haven't answered *my* question: do you now see the value of my work?"

The Hell-Hound forced himself to look around the room again. "I see that you genuinely believe the knowledge you seek is worthwhile," he said carefully, "but I still feel subjecting men and women to this, even if they are slaves, is too high a price."

"But it's legal!" Kurd insisted. "What I do here breaks no Rankan laws."

"Ranke has many laws, you should remember that from our last meeting. Few live within all of them and while there is some discretion exercised between which laws are enforced and which are overlooked, I tell you now that I will be personally watching for anything which will allow me to move against you. It would be easier on both of us if you simply moved on now . . . for I won't rest while you are within my patrol-range."

"I am a law-abiding citizen." The pale man glared, drawing himself up. "I won't be driven from my home like a common criminal."

"So you said before." The Hell-Hound smiled as he turned to go. "But, you are no longer in Ranke—remember that."

"That's right," Kurd shouted after him, "we are no longer in Ranke. Remember that yourself, Hell-Hound."

*  *  *

Four days later Zalbar's confidence had ebbed considerably. Finishing his night patrol of the city he turned down the Processional toward the wharves. This was becoming a habit with him now, a final off-duty stretch-of-the-legs to organize his thoughts in solitude before retiring to the crowded barracks. Though there was still activity back in the Maze, this portion of town had been long asleep and it was easy for the Hell-Hound to lose himself in his ponderings as he paced slowly along the moon-shadowed street.

The Prince had rejected his appeal, pointing out that harassing a relatively honest citizen was a poor use of time, particularly with the wave of killings sweeping Sanctuary. Zalbar could not argue with the Prince's logic. Ever since that weapons shop had appeared, suddenly, in the Maze to dispense its deadly brand of magic, killings were not only more frequent but of an uglier nature than usual. Perhaps now that the shop had disappeared the madness would ease, but in the meantime he could ill afford the time to pursue Kurd with the vigor necessary to drive the vivisectionist from town.

For a moment Kurd's empassioned defense of his work flashed across Zalbar's mind, only to be quickly repressed. New medical knowledge was worth having, but slaves were still people. The systematic torture of another being in the name of knowledge was. . . .

"Cover!"

Zalbar was prone on the ground before the cry had fully registered in his mind. Reflexes honed by years in service to the empire had him rolling, crawling, scrabbling along the dirt in search of shelter without pausing to identify the source of the warning. Twice, before he reached the shadows of an alley, he heard the unmistakable *hisss-pock* of arrows striking nearby: ample proof that the danger was not imaginary.

Finally, in the alley's relative security, he snaked his sword from its scabbard and breathlessly scanned the rooftops for the bowman assassin. A flicker of movement atop a building across the street caught his eyes, but it failed to repeat itself. He strained to penetrate the darkness. There was a crying moan, ending in a cough; moments later, a poor imitation of a night bird's whistle.

Though he was sure someone had just died, Zalbar didn't twitch a muscle, holding his position like a hunting cat. Who had died? The assassin? Or the person whose call had warned him of danger? Even if it were the assassin there might still be an accomplice lurking nearby.

As if in answer to this last thought a figure detached itself from a darkened doorway and moved to the center of the street. It paused, placed hands on hips and hailed the alley wherein Zalbar had taken refuge.

"It's safe now, Hell-Hound. We've rescued you from your own carelessness."

Regaining his feet Zalbar sheathed his sword and stepped into the open. Even before being hailed he had recognized the dark figure. A blue hawk-mask and cloak could not hide the size or coloring of his rescuer, and if they had, the Hell-Hound would have known the smooth grace of those movements anywhere.

"What carelessness is that, Jubal?" he asked, hiding his own annoyance.

"You have used this route three nights in a row, now," the ex-gladiator announced. "That's all the pattern an assassin needs."

The Negro crime-lord did not seem surprised or annoyed that his disguise had been penetrated. If anything, Jubal gave an impression of being pleased with himself as he bantered with the Hell-Hound.

Zalbar realized that Jubal was right: on duty or off, a predictable pattern was an invitation for ambush. He was spared the embarrassment of making this admission, however, as the unseen savior on the rooftops chose this moment to dump the assassin's body to the street. The two men studied it with disdain.

"Though I appreciate your intervention," the Hell-Hound commented drily, "it would have been nice to take him alive. I'll admit a passing curiosity as to who sent him."

"I can tell you that." The hawk-masked figure smiled grimly. "It's Kurd's money that filled that assassin's purse, though it puzzles me why he would bear you such a grudge."

"You knew about this in advance?"

"One of my informants overheard the hiring in the Vulgar Unicorn. It's amazing how many normally careful people forget that a man can hear as well as talk."

"Why didn't you send word to warn me in advance?"

"I had no proof." The black man shrugged. "It's doubtful my witness would be willing to testify in court. Besides, I still owed you a debt from our last meeting . . . or have you forgotten you saved my life once?"

"I haven't forgotten. As I told you then, I was only doing my duty. You owed me nothing."

". . . And I was only doing my duty as a Rankan citizen in assisting you tonight." Jubal's teeth flashed in the moonlight.

"Well, whatever your motive, you have my thanks."

Jubal was silent a moment. "If you truly wish to express your gratitude," he said at last, "would you join me now for a drink? There's something I would like to discuss with you."

"I . . . I'm afraid I can't. It's a long walk to your . . . house and I have duties tomorrow."

"I was thinking of the Vulgar Unicorn."

"The Vulgar Unicorn?" Zalbar stammered, genuinely astonished. "Where my assassination was planned. I can't go in there."

"Why not?"

"Well . . . if for no other reason than that I am a Hell-Hound. It would do neither of us any good to be seen together publicly, much less in the Vulgar Unicorn."

"You could wear my mask and cloak. That would hide your uniform and face. Then, to any onlooker it would only appear that I was having a drink with one of my men."

For a moment Zalbar wavered in indecision, then the audacity of a Hell-Hound in a blue hawk-mask seized his fancy and he laughed aloud. "Why not?" he agreed, reaching for the offered disguise. "I've always wondered what the inside of that place looked like."

Zalbar had not realized how bright the moonlight was until he stepped through the door of the Vulgar Unicorn. A few small oil lamps were the only illumination and those were shielded toward the wall, leaving most of the interior in heavy shadow. Though he could see figures huddled at several tables as he followed Jubal into the main room, he could not make out any individual's features.

There was one, however, whose face he did not need to see, the unmistakably gaunt form of Hakiem the storyteller slouched at a central table. A small bowl of wine sat before him, apparently forgotten, as the tale-spinner nodded in near-slumber. Zalbar harbored a secret liking for the ancient character and would have passed the table quietly, but Jubal caught the Hell-Hound's eye and winked broadly. Withdrawing a coin from his sword-belt, the slaver tossed it in an easy arch toward the storyteller's table.

Hakiem's hand moved like a flicker of light and the coin disappeared in mid-flight. His drowsy manner remained unchanged.

"That's payment enough for a hundred stories, old man," Jubal rumbled softly, "but tell them somewhere else . . . and about someone else."

Moving with quiet dignity, the storyteller rose to his feet, bestowed a withering gaze on both of them, and stalked regally from the room. His bowl of wine had disappeared with his departure.

In the brief moment that their eyes met, Zalbar had felt an intense intelligence and was certain that the old man had penetrated both mask and cloak to coldly observe his true identity. Hastily revising his opinion of the gaunt tale-spinner, the Hell-Hound recalled Jubal's description of an informant whom people forgot could hear as well as see and knew whose spying had truly saved his life.

The slaver sank down at the recently vacated table and immediately received two unordered goblets of expensive qualis. Settling next to him, Zalbar noted that this table had a clear view of all entrances and exits of the tavern and his estimation of Hakiem went up yet another notch.

"If I had thought of it sooner, I would have suggested that your man on the rooftop join us," the Hell-Hound commented. "I feel I owe him a drink of thanks."

"That man is a woman, Moria; she works the darkness better than I do . . . and without the benefits of protective coloration."

"Well, I'd still like to thank her."

"I'd advise against it." The slaver grinned. "She hates Rankans, and the Hell-Hounds in particular. She only intervened at my orders."

"You remind me of several questions." Zalbar set his goblet down. "Why *did* you act on my behalf tonight? And how is it that you know the cry the army uses to warn of archers?"

"In good time. First you must answer a question of mine. I'm not used to giving out information for free, and since I told you the identity of your enemy, perhaps now you can tell me why Kurd would set an assassin on your trail?"

After taking a thoughtful sip of his drink, Zalbar began to explain the situation between himself and Kurd. As the story unfolded, the Hell-Hound found he was saying more than was necessary, and was puzzled as to why he would reveal to Jubal the anger and bitterness he had kept secret even from his own force. Perhaps, it was because, unlike his comrades whom he respected, Zalbar saw the slaver as a man so corrupt that his own darkest thoughts and doubts would seem commonplace by comparison.

Jubal listened in silence until the Hell-Hound was finished, then nodded slowly. "Yes, that makes sense now," he murmured.

"The irony is that at the moment of attack I was bemoaning my inability to do anything about Kurd. For a while, at least, an assassin is unnecessary. I am under orders to leave Kurd alone."

Instead of laughing, Jubal studied his opposite thoughtfully. "Strange you should say that." He spoke with measured care. "I also have a problem I am currently unable to deal with. Perhaps we can solve each other's problems."

"Is that what you wanted to talk to me about?" Zalbar asked, suddenly suspicious.

"In a way. Actually this is better. Now, in return for the favor I must ask, I can offer something you want. If you address yourself to my problem, I'll put an end to Kurd's practice for you."

"I assume that what you want is illegal. If you really think I'd. . . ."

"It is *not* illegal!" Jubal spat with venom. "I don't need your help to break the law, that's easy enough to do despite the efforts of your so-called elite force. No, Hell-Hound, I find it necessary to offer you a bribe to do your job—to enforce the law."

"Any citizen can appeal to any Hell-Hound for assistance." Zalbar felt his own anger grow. "If it is indeed within the law, you don't have to. . . ."

"Fine!" the slaver interrupted. "Then, as a Rankan citizen I ask you to investigate and stop a wave of murders—someone is killing my people; hunting blue-masks through the streets as if they were diseased animals."

"I . . . I see."

"And I see that this comes as no surprise," Jubal snarled. "Well, Hell-Hound, do your duty. I make no pretense about my people, but they are being executed without a trial or hearing. That's murder. Or do you hesitate because it's one of your own who's doing the killing?"

Zalbar's head came up with a snap and Jubal met his stare with a humorless smile.

"That's right, I know the murderer, not that it's been difficult to learn. Tempus has been open enough with his bragging."

"Actually," Zalbar mused drily, "I was wondering why you haven't dealt with him yourself if you know he's guilty. I've heard hawk-masks have killed transgressors when their offense was far less certain."

Now it was Jubal who averted his eyes in discomfort. "We've tried," he admitted, "Tempus seems exceptionally hard to down. Some of my men went against my orders and used magical weapons. The result was four more bloody masks to his credit."

The Hell-Hound could hear the desperate appeal in the slaver's confession.

"I cannot allow him to continue his sport, but the price of stopping him grows fearfully high. I'm reduced to asking for your intervention. You, more than the others, have prided yourself in performing your duties in strict adherence to the codes of justice. Tell me, doesn't the law apply equally to everyone?"

A dozen excuses and explanations leapt to Zalbar's lips, then a cold wave of anger swept them away. "You're right, though I never thought you'd be the one to point out my duty to me. A killer in uniform is still a killer and should be punished for his crimes . . . all of them. If Tempus is your murderer, I'll personally see to it that he's dealt with."

"Very well." Jubal nodded. "And in return, I'll fill my end of the bargain—Kurd will no longer work in Sanctuary."

Zalbar opened his mouth to protest. The temptation was almost too great—if Jubal could make good his promise—but, no, "I'd have to insist that your actions remain within the law," he murmured reluctantly. "I can't ask you to do anything illegal."

"Not only is it legal, it's done! Kurd is out of business as of now."

"What do you mean?"

"Kurd can't work without subjects," the slaver smiled, "and I'm his supplier—or I was. Not only have I ended his supply of slaves, I'll spread the word to the other slavers that if they deal with him I'll undercut their prices in the other markets and drive them out of town as well."

Zalbar smiled with new distaste beneath his mask. "You knew what he was doing with the slaves and you dealt with him anyway?"

"Killing slaves for knowledge is no worse than having slaves kill each other in the arena for entertainment. Either is an unpleasant reality in our world."

Zalbar winced at the sarcasm in the slaver's voice, but was unwilling to abandon his position.

"We have different views of fighting. You were forced into the arena as a gladiator while I freely enlisted in the army. Still, we share a common experience: however terrible the battle, however frightful the odds, we had a chance. We could fight back and survive—or at least take our foemen with us as we fell. Being trussed up like a sacrificial animal, helpless to do anything but watch your enemy—no, not your enemy—your tormentor's weapon descend on you again and again. . . . No being, slave or freedman, should be forced into that. I cannot think of an enemy I hate enough to condemn to such a fate."

"I can think of a few," Jubal murmured, "but then, I've never shared your ideals. Though we both believe in justice we seek it in different ways."

"Justice?" the Hell-Hound sneered, "that's the second time you've used that word tonight. I must admit it sounds strange coming from your lips."

"Does it?" the slaver asked. "I've always dealt fairly with my own or with those who do business with me. We both acknowledge the corruption in our world, Hell-Hound. The difference is that, unlike yourself, I don't try to protect the world—I'm hard-pressed to protect myself and my own."

Zalbar set down his unfinished drink. "I'll leave your mask and cloak outside," he said levelly, "I fear that the difference is too great for us to enjoy a drink together."

Anger flashed in the slaver's eyes. "But you will investigate the murders?"

"I will," the Hell-Hound promised, "and as the complaining citizen you'll be informed of the results of my investigation."

Tempus was working on his sword when Zalbar and Razkuli approached him. They had deliberately waited to confront him here in the barracks rather than at his favored haunt, the Lily Garden. Despite everything that had or might occur, they were all Army and what was to be said should not be heard by civilians outside their elite club.

Tempus favored them with a sullen glare, then brazenly returned his attention to his work. It was an unmistakable affront as he was only occupied with filing a series of saw-like teeth into one edge of his sword: a project that should run a poor second to speaking with the Hell-Hound captain.

"I would have a word with you, Tempus," Zalbar announced, swallowing his anger.

"It's your prerogative," the other replied without looking up.

Razkuli shifted his feet, but a look from his friend stilled him.

"I have had a complaint entered against you," Zalbar continued. "A complaint which has been confirmed by numerous witnesses. I felt it only fair to hear your side of the story before I went to Kadakithis with it."

At the mention of the Prince's name, Tempus raised his head and ceased his filing. "And the nature of the complaint?" he asked darkly.

"It is said you're committing wanton murder during your off-duty hours."

"Oh, that. It's not wanton. I only hunt hawk-masks."

Zalbar had been prepared for many possible responses to his accusations: angry denial, a mad dash for freedom, a demand for proof or witnesses. This easy admission, however, caught him totally off-balance. "You . . . you admit your guilt?" he managed at last, surprise robbing him of his composure.

"Certainly. I'm only surprised anyone has bothered to complain. No one should miss the killers I've taken . . . least of all you."

"Well, it's true I hold no love for Jubal or his sell-swords," Zalbar admitted, "but, there are still due processes of law to be followed. If you want to see them brought to justice you should have. . . ."

"Justice?" Tempus laughed. "Justice has nothing to do with it."

"Then why hunt them?"

"For practice," Tempus informed them, studying his serrated sword once more. "An unexercised sword grows slow. I like to keep a hand in whenever possible and supposedly the sell-swords Jubal hires are the best in town—though, to tell the truth, if the ones I've faced are any example, he's being cheated."

"That's all?" Razkuli burst out, unable to contain himself any longer. "That's all the reason you need to disgrace your uniform?"

Zalbar held up a warning hand, but Tempus only laughed at the two of them.

"That's right, Zalbar, better keep a leash on your dog there. If you can't stop his yapping, I'll do it for you."

For a moment Zalbar thought he might have to restrain his friend, but Razkuli had passed explosive rage. The swarthy Hell-Hound glared at Tempus with a deep, glowering hatred which Zalbar knew could not be dimmed now with reason or threats. Grappling with his own anger, Zalbar turned, at last, to Tempus.

"Will you be as arrogant when the Prince asks you to explain your actions?" he demanded.

"I won't have to." Tempus grinned again. "Kittycat will never call me to task for anything. You got your way on the Street of Red Lanterns, but that was before the Prince fully comprehended my position here. He'd even reverse that decision if he hadn't taken a public stance on it."

Zalbar was frozen by anger and frustration as he realized the truth of Tempus' words. "And just what *is* your position here?"

"If you have to ask," Tempus laughed, "I can't explain. But you must realize that you can't count on the Prince to support your charges. Save yourselves a lot of grief by accepting me as someone outside the law's jurisdiction." He rose, sheathed his sword and started to leave, but Zalbar blocked his path.

"You may be right. You may indeed be above the law, but if there is a god—any god—watching over us now, the time is not far off when your sword will miss and we'll be rid of you. Justice is a natural process. It can't be swayed for long by a prince's whims."

"Don't call upon the gods unless you're ready to accept their interference." Tempus grimaced. "You'd do well to heed that warning from one who knows."

Before Zalbar could react, Razkuli was lunging forward, his slim wrist-dagger darting for Tempus' throat. It was too late for the Hell-Hound captain to intervene either physically or verbally, but then, Tempus did not seem to require outside help.

Moving with lazy ease, Tempus slapped his left hand over the speeding point, his palm taking the full impact of Razkuli's vengeance. The blade emerged from the back of his hand and blood spurted freely for a moment, but Tempus seemed not to notice. A quick wrench with the already wounded hand and the knife was twisted from Razkuli's grip. Then Tempus' right hand closed like a vise on the throat of his dumbfounded attacker, lifting him, turning him, slamming him against a wall and pinning him there with his toes barely touching the floor.

"Tempus!" Zalbar barked, his friend's danger breaking through the momentary paralysis brought on by the sudden explosion of action.

"Don't worry, Captain," Tempus responded in a calm voice. "If you would be so kind?"

He extended his bloody hand toward Zalbar and the tall Hell-Hound gingerly withdrew the dagger from the awful wound. As the knife came clear the clotting ooze of blood erupted into a steady stream. Tempus studied the scarlet cascade with distaste, then thrust his hand against Razkuli's face.

"Lick it, dog," he ordered. "Lick it clean, and be thankful I don't make you lick the floor as well!"

Helpless and fighting for each breath, the pinned man hesitated only a moment before extending his tongue in a feeble effort to comply with the demand. Quickly impatient, Tempus wiped his hand in a bloody smear across Razkuli's face and mouth, then he examined his wound again.

As Zalbar watched, horrified, the seepage from the wound slowed from flow to trickle and finally to a slow ooze—all in the matter of seconds.

Apparently satisfied with the healing process, Tempus turned dark eyes to his captain. "Every dog gets one bite—but the next time your pet crosses me, I'll take him down and neither you nor the Prince will be able to stop me."

With that he wrenched Razkuli from the wall and dashed him to the floor at Zalbar's feet. With both Hell-Hounds held motionless by his brutality, he strode from the room without a backward glance.

The suddenness and intensity of the exchange had shocked even Zalbar's battlefield reflexes into immobility, but with Tempus' departure, control flooded back into his limbs as if he had been released from a spell. Kneeling beside his friend, he hoisted Razkuli into a sitting position to aid his labored breathing.

"Don't try to talk," he ordered, reaching to wipe the blood smear from Razkuli's face, but the gasping man jerked his head back and forth, refusing both the order and the help.

Gathering his legs under him, the short Hell-Hound surged to his feet and retained the upright position, though he had to cling to the wall for support. For several moments, his head sagged weakly as he drew breath in long ragged gasps, then he lifted his gaze to meet Zalbar's.

"I must kill him. I cannot . . . live in the same world and . . . breathe the same air with one who . . . shamed me so . . . and still call myself a man."

For a moment, Razkuli swayed as if speaking had drained him of all energy, then he carefully lowered himself onto a bench, propping his back against the wall.

"I must kill him," he repeated, his voice steadying. "Even if it means fighting you."

"You won't have to fight me, my friend," Zalbar sat beside him. "Instead accept me as a partner. Tempus must be stopped, and I fear it will take both of us to do it. Even then we may not be enough."

The swarthy Hell-Hound nodded in slow agreement. "Perhaps if we acquired one of those hellish weapons that have been causing so much trouble in the Maze?" he suggested.

"I'd rather bed a viper. From the reports I've heard they cause more havoc for the wielder than for the victim. No, the plan I have in mind is of an entirely different nature."

The bright flowers danced gaily in the breeze as Zalbar finished his lunch. Razkuli was not guarding his back today: that individual was back at the barracks enjoying a much earned rest after their night's labors. Though he shared his friend's fatigue, Zalbar indulged himself with this last pleasure before retiring.

"You sent for me, Hell-Hound?"

Zalbar didn't need to turn his head to identify his visitor. He had been watching him from the corner of his eyes throughout his dusty approach.

"Sit down, Jubal," he instructed. "I thought you'd like to hear about my investigations."

"It's about time," the slaver grumbled, sinking to the ground. "It's been a week—I was starting to doubt the seriousness of your pledge. Now, tell me why you couldn't find the killer."

The Hell-Hound ignored the sneer in Jubal's voice. "Tempus is the killer, just as you said," he answered casually.

"You've confirmed it? When is he being brought to trial?"

Before Zalbar could answer a terrible scream broke the calm afternoon. The Hell-Hound remained unmoved, but Jubal spun toward the sound. "What was that?" he demanded.

"That," Zalbar explained, "is the noise a man makes when Kurd goes looking for knowledge."

"But I thought . . . I swear to you, this is not my doing!"

"Don't worry about it, Jubal." The Hell-Hound smiled and waited for the slaver to sit down again. "You were asking about Tempus' trial?"

"That's right," the black man agreed, though visibly shaken.

"He'll never come to trial."

"Because of *that*?" Jubal pointed to the house. "I can stop. . . ."

"Will you be quiet and listen! The court will never see Tempus because the Prince protects him. That's why I hadn't investigated him before your complaint!"

"Royal protection!" The slaver spat. "So he's free to hunt my people still."

"Not exactly." Zalbar indulged in an extravagant yawn.

"But you said. . . ."

"I said I'd deal with him, and in your words 'it's done.' Tempus won't be reporting for duty today . . . or ever."

Jubal started to ask something, but another scream drowned out his words. Surging to his feet he glared at Kurd's house. "I'm going to find out where that slave came from, and when I do. . . ."

"It came from me, and if you value your people you won't insist on his release."

The slaver turned to gape at the seated Hell-Hound. "You mean. . . ."

"Tempus," Zalbar nodded. "Kurd told me of a drug he used to subdue his slaves, so I got some from Stulwig and put it in my comrade's *krrf*. He almost woke up when we branded him . . . but Kurd was willing to accept my little peace offering with no questions asked. We even cut out his tongue as an extra measure of friendship."

Another scream came—a low animal moan which lingered in the air as the two men listened.

"I couldn't ask for a more fitting revenge," Jubal said at last, extending his hand. "He'll be a long time dying."

"If he dies at all," Zalbar commented, accepting the handshake. "He heals very fast, you know."

With that the two men parted company, mindless of the shrieks that followed them.

# THE LIGHTER SIDE OF SANCTUARY

The reader response to the first volume of THIEVES' WORLD has been overwhelming and heartwarming. (For those of you who were not aware of it: you can write to me or any other author in care of their publisher.) The volume of correspondence helped to sell volumes two and three and prompted a THIEVES' WORLD war-game soon to be released from the Chaosium. It seems that none of our THIEVES' WORLD readers realize that anthologies in general don't sell and that fantasy anthologies specifically are sudden death.

While the letters received have been brimming with enthusiasm and praise, there has been one comment/criticism which has recurred in much of the correspondence. Specifically, people have noted that Sanctuary is incredibly grim. It seems that the citizens of the town never laugh, or when they do it is forcefully stifled . . . like the time Kittycat spilled wine down the front of his tunic while trying to toast the health of his brother, the Emperor.

This is a valid gripe. First of all because no town is totally dismal. Second, because those readers familiar with my other works are accustomed to finding *some* humor buried in the pages—even in a genocidal war between lizards and bugs. What's worse, in reviewing the stories in this second volume, I am painfully aware that the downward spiral of Sanctuary has continued rather than reversing itself.

As such I have taken it upon myself as editor to provide the reader with a brief glimpse of the bright side of the town—the benefits and advantages of living in the worst hellhole in the empire.

To this end let us turn to a seldom seen, never quoted document issued by the Sanctuary Chamber of Commerce shortly before it went out of business. The fact that Kittycat insisted the brochure contain some modicum of truth doubtless contributed to the document's lack of success. Nonetheless, for your enjoyment and edification, here are selected excerpts from

SANCTUARY
VACATION CAPITOL OF
THE RANKAN EMPIRE

*Every year tourists flock to Sanctuary by the tens, drawn by the rumors of adventure and excitement which flourish in every dark corner of the Empire. They are never disappointed that they chose Sanctuary. Our city is everything it is rumored to be—and more! Many visitors never leave and those that do can testify that the lives to which they return seem dull in comparison with the heartstopping action they found in this personable town.*

*If you, as a merchant, are looking to expand or relocate your business consider scenic Sanctuary. Where else can you find all these features in one locale?*

BUSINESS OPPORTUNITIES

*PROPERTY—Land in Sanctuary is cheap! Whether you want to build in the swamplands to the east of town, or west in the desert fringes, you'll find large parcels of land available at temptingly low prices. If you seek a more central location for your business, just ask. Most shop owners in Sanctuary are willing to surrender their building, stock and staff for the price of a one-way passage out of town.*

*LABOR—There is no shortage of willing workers in Sanctuary. You'll find most citizens are for hire and will do anything for a price. Moreover, the array of talents and skills available in our city is nothing short of startling. Abilities you never thought were marketable are bought and sold freely in Sanctuary—and the price is always right!*

*For those who prefer slave labor, the selection available in Sanctuary is diverse and plentiful. You'll be as surprised as the slaves themselves are by who shows up on the auction block. There, as everywhere in Sanctuary, bargains abound for one with a sharp eye . . . or sword.*

*MATERIALS—If the remoteness of the town's location makes you hesitate—never fear. Anything of value in the Empire is sold in Sanctuary. In fact, commodities you may have been told were not for sale often appear in the stalls and shops of this amazing town. Don't bother asking the seller how he got his stock. Just rest assured that in Sanctuary no one will ask how you came by yours, either.*

LIFESTYLES

*SOCIAL LIFE—As the ancients say, one does not live by bread alone. Similarly, a citizen of the Rankan Empire requires an active social life to balance his business activity. Here is where Sanctuary truly excels. It has often been said that day to day life in Sanctuary is an adventure without parallel.*

RELIGIONS—*For those with an eye for the afterlife, the religious offerings in a given area must withstand close scrutiny. Well, our town welcomes such scrutinizers with open arms. Every Rankan deity and cult is represented in Sanctuary, as well many not in open evidence elsewhere in the Empire. Old gods and forgotten rites exist and flourish alongside the more accepted traditions, adding to the town's quaint charm. Nor are our temples reserved for devout true-believers only. Most shrines welcome visitors of other beliefs and many allow—nay, require—audience participation in their curious native rituals.*

NIGHT LIFE—*Unlike many cities in the Empire which roll up their streets with the setting sun, Sanctuary comes to life at night. In fact, many of its citizens exist for the night life to a point where you seldom see them by the light of day. However conservative or jaded your taste in entertainment might be, you'll have the time of your life in the shadows of Sanctuary. Our Street of Red Lanterns alone offers a wide array of amusements, from the quiet elegance of the Aphrodisia House to the more bizarre pleasures available at the House of Whips. If slumming is your pleasure, you need look no further than your own doorstep.*

SOCIAL STATUS—*Let's face it: everybody likes to feel superior to somebody. Well, nowhere is superiority as easy to come by as it is in Sanctuary. A Rankan citizen of moderate means is a wealthy man by Sanctuary standards, and will be treated as such by its inhabitants. Envious eyes will follow your passing and people will note your movements and customs with flattering attentiveness. Even if your funds are less than adequate in your own opinion, it is still easy to feel that you are better off than the average citizen of Sanctuary—if only on a moral scale. We can guarantee, without reservation, that however low your opinion of yourself might be, there will be somebody in Sanctuary you will be superior to.*

A WORD ABOUT CRIME—*You have probably heard rumors of the high crime rate in Sanctuary. We admit to having had our problems in the past, but that's behind us now. One need only look at the huge crowds that gather to watch the daily hangings and impalements to realize that the citizens of Sanctuary's support for law and order is at an all-time high. As a result of the new Governor's anti-crime program, we are pleased to announce that last year the rate of reported crime, per day, in Sanctuary was not greater than that of cities twice our size.*

## IN SUMMARY

*Sanctuary is a place of opportunity for a far-thinking opportunist. Now is the time to move. Now, while property values are plummeting and the economy and the people are depressed. Where better to invest your money, your energies and your life than in this rapidly growing city of the future? Even our worst critics acknowledge the potential of Sanctuary when they describe it as a "town with nowhere to go but up!"*

# Shadows of Sanctuary

# Contents

# Introduction

## Robert Lynn Asprin

It was a slow night at the Vulgar Unicorn. Not slow in the sense that there had been no fights (there hadn't) or that there weren't many customers (there weren't) but rather a different kind of slow; the slow measured pace of a man on his way to the gallows, for the Unicorn was dying, as was the entire town of Sanctuary. More people were leaving every day and those left were becoming increasingly desperate and vicious as the economy dipped to new lows.

Desperate people were dangerous; they were quick to turn predator at the smallest imagined opportunity, which in turn made them vulnerable to the *real* predators drawn to the town like wolves to a sick animal. Anyone with an ounce of sense and a good leg to hobble on would have deserted Sanctuary long ago.

Such were the thoughts of Hakiem, the Storyteller, as he sat brooding over a cup of cheap wine. Tonight he did not even bother adopting his usual guise of dozing drunkenly while eavesdropping on conversations at the neighboring tables. He knew all the patrons present and not one of them was worth spying on—hence no need to fake disinterest.

He would leave Sanctuary tomorrow. He would go somewhere, anywhere, where people were freer with their money and a master storyteller would be appreciated. Hakiem smiled bitterly at himself even as he made the resolution—for he knew it to be a lie.

He loved this bedraggled town as he loved the tough breed of people it spawned. There was a raw, stubborn vitality that surged and ebbed just below the surface. Sanctuary was a storyteller's paradise. When he left, if he ever did, he would have stories enough for a lifetime . . . no, two lifetimes. Big stories and little ones, tailored to the buyer's purse. Stories of violent battle between warriors and between sorcerers. Tiny stories of people so common they would move the hearts of any who listened. From the princely military-governor with his Hell-Hound elite guard to the humblest thief, they were all grist for Hakiem's mill. If he had personally commanded their performances they could not have performed their roles better.

The storyteller's smile was more sincere as he raised his cup for another sip. Then his eye was caught by a figure lurching through the door and he froze in mid-movement.

One-Thumb!

The Vulgar Unicorn's owner had been absent for some time, causing no small question among the patrons about his fate. Now, here he was, large as life . . . well, not quite as large as life.

Hakiem watched with narrowed eyes as One-Thumb slumped against the bar, seizing a crock of wine while his normally practiced fingers fumbled with the stopper like a youth with his first woman. Unable to contain his curiosity longer, the old storyteller untangled himself from his chair and skuttled forward with a speed that belied his age.

"One-Thumb," he cackled with calculated joviality, "welcome back!"

The massive figure straightened and turned, focusing vacant eyes on the intruder. "Hakiem!" The fleshy face suddenly wrinkled with a wide smile. "By the gods—the world *is* normal."

To the storyteller's amazement, One-Thumb seemed on the verge of tears as he stepped forward, arms extended to embrace the old man like a long lost son. Recoiling, Hakiem hastily interposed his wine cup between them.

"You've been gone a long time," he said, abandoning all semblance of subtlety. "Where have you been?"

"Gone?" The eyes were vacant again. "Yes, I've been gone. How long has it been?"

"Over a year." The storyteller was puzzled, and insatiable.

"A year," One-Thumb murmured. "It seems like . . . the tunnels! I've been in the tunnels. It was . . ." He paused to take a long swallow of wine, then absently filled Hakiem's cup as he launched into his story.

Accustomed to piecing together tales from half-heard words and phrases, the storyteller rapidly grasped the essence of One-Thumb's ordeal.

He had been trapped by a magician's spell in the tangle of tunnels below Sanctuary's streets. Confronted by an image of himself, he had killed it and been slain in turn—over and over until this night when he miraculously found himself alone and unscathed.

As One-Thumb redoubled his lurid description, describing the feel of cold metal as it found its home in one's innards—again and again, Hakiem pondered the facts of the story. It fit.

Lately someone had been stalking wizards, slaying them in their own beds. Apparently the hunter's knife had struck down the spell-weaver who was holding One-Thumb in painful thrall, freeing him suddenly to his normal life. An interesting story, but totally useless to Hakiem.

First: One-Thumb was obviously willing to spill the tale to anyone who would stand still long enough to listen, ruining the market for second-hand renditions. Second, and more important: it was a bad story. Its motive was unclear; the ending hazy and inactive; there was no real interplay between the characters. The only real meat was the uniqueness of One-Thumb's ability to tell the tale in the first-person and even that weakened through repetition. In short, it was boring.

It didn't take a master storyteller to reach this conclusion. It was obvious. In fact, Hakiem was already growing weary listening to the whine and prattle.

"You must be tired," he interrupted. "It's wrong of me to keep you. Maybe we can talk again after you've rested." He turned to leave the Unicorn.

"What about the wine?" One-Thumb called angrily. "You haven't paid yet."

Hakiem's response was habitual: "Pay? I didn't order it. It was you who filled the cup. Pay for it yourself." He regretted the words immediately. One-Thumb's treatment of drinkers who refused to pay was legendary throughout the Maze. To his surprise, then, it was One-Thumb who gave ground.

"Well, all right," the big man grumbled. "Just don't make a habit of it."

The old storyteller felt a rare twinge of remorse as he left the Unicorn. While he had no love for One-Thumb, neither had he any reason to wish him ill.

The big man hadn't just lost a year of his life—he'd lost his fire—that core of ferocity which had earned him the respect of the town's underworld. Though One-Thumb was unmarked physically, he was only the empty shell of his former self. This town was no place for a man without the strength to back his bluster.

The end of One-Thumb's story was in sight—and it wouldn't be pleasant. Maybe with a few revisions the story—if not the man—had a future.

Lost in his thoughts, Hakiem faded once more into the shadows of Sanctuary.

# Looking for Satan

## Vonda N. McIntyre

The four travellers left the mountains at the end of the day, tired, cold, and hungry, and they entered Sanctuary.

The inhabitants of the city observed them and laughed, but they laughed behind their sleeves or after the small group passed. All its members walked armed. Yet there was no belligerence in them. They looked around amazed, nudged each other, and pointed at things, for all the world as if none had ever seen a city before. As, indeed, they had not.

Unaware of the amusement of the townspeople, they passed through the marketplace toward the city proper. The light was fading. The farmers culled their produce and took down their awnings. Limp cabbage leaves and rotten fruit littered the roughly cobbled street, and bits of unrecognizable stuff floated down the open central sewer.

Beside Wess, Chan shifted his heavy pack.

"Let's stop and buy something to eat," he said, "before everybody goes home."

Wess hitched her own pack higher on her shoulders and did not stop. "Not here," she said. "I'm tired of stale flatbread and raw vegetables. I want a hot meal tonight."

She tramped on. She knew how Chan felt. She glanced back at Aerie, who walked wrapped in her long dark cloak. Her pack weighed her down. She was taller than Wess, as tall as Chan, but very thin. Worry and their journey had deepened her eyes. Wess was not used to seeing her like this. She was used to seeing her freer.

"Our tireless Wess," Chan said.

"I'm tired, too!" Wess said. "Do you want to try camping in the street again?"

"No," he said. Behind him, Quartz chuckled.

In the first village they had ever seen—it seemed years ago now, but was only two months—they tried to set up camp in what they thought was a vacant field. It was the village common. Had the village possessed a prison, they would have been thrown into it. As it was they were escorted to the edge of town and invited never to return. Another traveller explained inns to them—and prisons—and now they all could laugh, with some embarrassment, at the episode.

But the smaller towns they had passed through did not even approach Sanctuary in size and noise and crowds. Wess had never imagined so many people or such high buildings or any odor so awful. She hoped it would be better beyond the marketplace. Passing a fish stall, she held her breath and hurried. It was the end of the day, true, but the end of a cool late fall's day. Wess tried not to wonder what it would smell like at the end of a long summer's day.

"We should stop at the first inn we find," Quartz said.

"All right," Wess said.

By the time they reached the street's end, darkness was complete and the market was deserted. Wess thought it odd that everyone should disappear so quickly, but no doubt they were tired too and wanted to get home to a hot fire and dinner. She felt a sudden stab of homesickness and hopelessness: their search had gone on so long, with so little chance of success.

The buildings closed in around them as the street narrowed suddenly. Wess stopped: three paths faced them, and another branched off only twenty paces farther on.

"Where now, my friends?"

"We must ask someone," Aerie said, her voice soft with fatigue.

"If we can find anyone," Chan said doubtfully.

Aerie stepped toward a shadow-filled corner.

"Citizen," she said, "would you direct us to the nearest inn?"

The others peered more closely at the dim niche. Indeed, a muffled figure crouched there. It stood up. Wess could see the manic glitter of its eyes, but nothing more.

"An inn?"

"The closest, if you please. We've travelled a long way."

The figure chuckled. "You'll find no inns in this part of town, foreigner. But the tavern around the corner—it has rooms upstairs. Perhaps it will suit you."

"Thank you." Aerie turned back, a faint breeze ruffling her short black hair. She pulled her cloak closer.

They went the way the figure gestured, and did not see it convulse with silent laughter behind them.

In front of the tavern, Wess puzzled out the unfamiliar script: The Vulgar Unicorn. An odd combination, even in the south where odd combinations were the style of naming taverns. She pushed open the door. It was nearly as dark inside as out, and smoky. The noise died as Wess and Chan entered—then rose again in a surprised buzz when Aerie and Quartz followed.

Wess and Chan were not startlingly different from the general run of southern mountain folk: he fairer, she darker. Wess could pass unnoticed as an ordinary citizen anywhere; Chan's beauty often attracted attention. But Aerie's tall white-skinned black-haired elegance everywhere aroused comment. Wess smiled, imagining what would happen if Aerie flung away her cloak and showed herself as she really was.

And Quartz: she had to stoop to come inside. She straightened up. She was taller than anyone else in the room. The smoke near the ceiling swirled a wreath around her hair. She had cut it short for the journey, and it curled around her face, red, gold, and sand-pale. Her gray eyes reflected the firelight like mirrors. Ignoring the stares, she pushed her blue wool cloak from her broad shoulders and shrugged her pack to the floor.

The strong heavy scent of beer and sizzling meat made Wess' mouth water. She sought out the man behind the bar.

"Citizen," she said, carefully pronouncing the Sanctuary language, the trade-tongue of all the continent, "are you the proprietor? My friends and I, we need a room for the night, and dinner."

Her request seemed ordinary enough to her, but the innkeeper looked sidelong at one of his patrons. Both laughed.

"A room, young gentleman?" He came out from behind the bar. Instead of replying to Wess, he spoke to Chan. Wess smiled to herself. Like all Chan's friends, she was used to seeing people fall in love with him on sight. She would have done so herself, she thought, had she first met him when they were grown. But they had known each other all their lives and their friendship was far closer and deeper than instant lust.

"A room?" the innkeeper said again. "A meal for you and your ladies? Is that all we can do for you here in our humble establishment? Do you require dancing? A juggler? Harpists and hautbois? Ask and it shall be given!" Far from being seductive, or even friendly, the innkeeper's tone was derisive.

Chan glanced at Wess, frowning slightly, as everyone within earshot burst into laughter. Wess was glad her complexion was dark enough to hide her blush of anger. Chan was bright pink from the collar of his homespun shirt to the roots of his blond hair. Wess knew they had been insulted but she did not understand how or why, so she replied with courtesy.

"No, citizen, thank you for your hospitality. We need a room, if you have one, and food."

"We would not refuse a bath," Quartz said.

The innkeeper glanced at them, an irritated expression on his face, and spoke once more to Chan.

"The young gentleman lets his ladies speak for him? Is this some foreign custom, that you are too high-bred to speak to a mere tavernkeeper?"

"I don't understand you," Chan said. "Wess spoke for us all. Must we speak in chorus?"

Taken aback, the man hid his reaction by showing them, with an exaggerated bow, to a table.

Wess dumped her pack on the floor next to the wall behind her and sat down with a sigh of relief. The others followed. Aerie looked as if she could not have kept on her feet a moment longer.

"This is a simple place," the tavern-keeper said. "Beer or ale, wine. Meat and bread. Can you pay?"

He was speaking to Chan again. He took no direct note of Wess or Aerie or Quartz.

"What is the price?"

"Four dinners, bed—you break your fast somewhere else, I don't open early. A piece of silver. In advance."

"The bath included?" Quartz said.

"Yes, yes, all right."

"We can pay," said Quartz, whose turn it was to keep track of what they spent. She offered him a piece of silver.

He continued to look at Chan, but after an awkward pause he shrugged, snatched the coin from Quartz, and turned away. Quartz drew back her hand, then, under the table, surreptitiously wiped it on the leg of her heavy cotton trousers.

Chan glanced over at Wess. "Do you understand anything that has happened since we entered the city's gates?"

"It is curious," she said. "They have strange customs."

"We can puzzle them out tomorrow," Aerie said.

A young woman carrying a tray stopped at their table. She wore odd clothes, summer clothes by the look of them, for they uncovered her arms and shoulders and almost completely bared her breasts. It *is* hot in here, Wess thought. That's quite intelligent of her. Then she need only put on a cloak to go home, and she will not get chilled or overheated.

"Ale for you, sir?" the young woman said to Chan. "Or wine? And wine for your wives?"

"Beer, please," Chan said. "What are 'wives'? I have studied your language, but this is not a word I know."

"The ladies are not your wives?"

Wess took a tankard of ale off the tray, too tired and thirsty to try to figure out what the woman was talking about. She took a deep swallow of the cool bitter brew. Quartz reached for a flask of wine and two cups, and poured for herself and Aerie.

"My companions are Westerly, Aerie, and Quartz," Chan said, nodding to each in turn. "I am Chandler. And you are—?"

"I'm just the serving girl," she said, sounding frightened. "You could not wish to be troubled with my name." She grabbed a mug of beer and put it on the table, spilling some, and fled.

They all looked at each other, but then the tavern-keeper came with platters of meat. They were too hungry to wonder what they had done to frighten the barmaid.

Wess tore off a mouthful of bread. It was fairly fresh, and a welcome change from trail rations—dry meat, flatbread mixed hurriedly and baked on stones in the coals of a campfire, fruit when they could find or buy it. Still, Wess was used to better.

"I miss your bread," she said to Quartz in their own language. Quartz smiled.

The meat was hot and untainted by decay. Even Aerie ate with some appetite, though she preferred meat raw.

Halfway through her meal, Wess slowed down and took a moment to observe the tavern more carefully.

At the bar, a group suddenly burst into raucous laughter.

"You say the same damned thing every damned time you turn up in Sanctuary, Bauchle," one of them said, his loud voice full of mockery.

"You have a secret or a scheme or a marvel that will make your fortune. Why don't you get an honest job—like the rest of us?"

That brought on more laughter, even from the large, heavyset young man who was being made fun of.

"You'll see, this time," he said. "This time I've got something that will take me all the way to the court of the Emperor. When you hear the criers tomorrow, you'll know." He called for more wine. His friends drank and made more jokes, both at his expense.

The Unicorn was much more crowded now, smokier, louder. Occasionally someone glanced toward Wess and her friends, but otherwise they were let alone.

A cold breeze thinned the odor of beer and sizzling meat and unwashed bodies. Silence fell suddenly, and Wess looked quickly around to see if she had breached some other unknown custom. But all the attention focused on the tavern's entrance. The cloaked figure stood there casually, but nothing was casual about the aura of power and self-possession.

In the whole of the tavern, not another table held an empty place.

"Sit with us, sister!" Wess called on impulse.

Two long steps and a shove: Wess' chair scraped roughly along the floor and Wess was rammed back against the wall, a dagger at her throat.

"Who calls me 'sister'?" The dark hood fell back from long, gray-streaked hair. A blue star blazed on the woman's forehead. Her elegant features grew terrible and dangerous in its light.

Wess stared up into the tall, lithe woman's furious eyes. Her jugular vein pulsed against the point of the blade. If she made a move toward her knife, or if any of her friends moved at all, she was dead.

"I meant no disrespect—" She almost said "sister" again. But it was not the familiarity that had caused offense: it was the word itself. The woman was travelling incognito, and Wess had breached her disguise. No mere apology would repair the damage she had done.

A drop of sweat trickled down the side of her face. Chan and Aerie and Quartz were all poised on the edge of defense. If Wess erred again, more than one person would die before the fighting stopped.

"My unfamiliarity with your language has offended you, young gentleman," Wess said, hoping the tavern-keeper had used a civil form of address, if not a civil tone. It was often safe to insult someone by the tone, but seldom by the words themselves. "Young gentleman," she said again when the woman did not kill her, "someone has made sport of me by translating *'frejôjan,'* 'sister.'"

"Perhaps," the disguised woman said. "What does *frejôjan* mean?"

"It is a term of peace, an offer of friendship, a word to welcome a guest, another child of one's own parents."

"Ah. 'Brother' is the word you want, the word to speak to men. To call a man 'sister,' the word for women, is an insult."

"An insult!" Wess said, honestly surprised.

But the knife drew back from her throat.

"You are a barbarian," the disguised woman said, in a friendly tone. "I cannot be insulted by a barbarian."

"There is the problem, you see," Chan said. "Translation. In our language, the word for outsider, for foreigner, also translates as 'barbarian.'" He smiled, his beautiful smile.

Wess pulled her chair forward again. She reached for Chan's hand under the table. He squeezed her fingers gently.

"I meant only to offer you a place to sit, where there is no other."

The stranger sheathed her dagger and stared down into Wess' eyes. Wess shivered slightly and imagined spending the night with Chan on one side, the stranger on the other.

*Or you could have the center, if you liked,* she thought, holding the gaze.

The stranger laughed. Wess could not tell if the mocking tone were directed outward or inward.

"Then I will sit here, as there is no other place." She did so. "My name is Lythande."

They introduced themselves, and offered her—Wess made herself think of Lythande as "him" so she would not damage the disguise again —offered him wine.

"I cannot accept your wine," Lythande said. "But to show I mean no offense, I will smoke with you." He rolled shredded herbs in a dry leaf, lit the construction, inhaled from it, and held it out. "Westerly, *frejôjan.*"

Out of politeness Wess tried it. By the time she stopped coughing her throat was sore, and the sweet scent made her feel lightheaded.

"It takes practice," Lythande said smiling.

Chan and Quartz did no better, but Aerie inhaled deeply, her eyes closed, then held her breath. Thereafter she and Lythande shared it while the others ordered more ale and another flask of wine.

"Why did you ask me, of all this crowd, to sit here?" Lythande asked.

"Because . . ." Wess paused to try to think of a way to make her intuition sound sensible. "You look like someone who knows what's going on. You look like someone who might help us."

"If information is all you need, you can get it less expensively than by hiring a sorcerer."

"Are you a sorcerer?" Wess asked.

Lythande looked at her with pity and contempt. "You child! What do your people mean, sending innocents and children out of the north!" He touched the star on his forehead. "What did you think this means?"

"I'll have to guess, but I guess it means you are a mage."

"Excellent. A few years of lessons like that and you might survive, a while, in Sanctuary—in the Maze—in the Unicorn!"

"We haven't got years," Aerie whispered. "We have, perhaps, overspent the time we *do* have."

Quartz put her arm around Aerie's shoulders, for comfort, and hugged her gently.

"You interest me," Lythande said. "Tell me what information you seek. Perhaps I will know whether you can obtain it less expensively— not cheaply, but less expensively—from Jubal the Slavemonger, or from a seer—" At their expressions, he stopped.

"Slavemonger!"

"He collects information as well. You needn't worry that he'll abduct you from his sitting-room."

They all started speaking at once, then fell silent, realizing the futility.

"Start at the beginning."

"We're looking for someone," Wess said.

"This is a poor place to search. No one will tell you anything about any patron of this establishment."

"But he's a friend."

"There's only your word for that."

"Satan wouldn't be here anyway," Wess said. "If he were free to come here he'd be free to go home. We'd have heard something of him, or he would have found us, or—"

"You fear he was taken prisoner. Enslaved, perhaps."

"He must have been. He was hunting, alone. He liked to do that, his people often do."

"We need solitude sometimes," Aerie said.

Wess nodded. "We didn't worry about him till he didn't come home for Equinox. Then we searched. We found his camp, and a cold trail . . ."

"We tried to hope for kidnapping," Chan said. "But there was no ransom demand. The trail was so old—they took him away."

"We followed, and we heard some rumors of him," Aerie said. "But the road branched, and we had to choose which way to go." She shrugged, but could not maintain the careless pose; she turned away in despair. "I could find no trace . . ."

Aerie, with her longer range, had met them after searching all day at each evening's new camp, ever more exhausted and more driven.

"Apparently we chose wrong," Quartz said.

"Children," Lythande said, "children, frejôjans—"

"*Frejôjani,*" Chan said authomatically, then shook his head and spread his hands in apology.

"Your friend is one slave out of many. You could not trace him by his papers, unless you discovered what name they were forged under. For someone to recognize him by a description would be the greatest luck, even if you had an homuncule to show. Sisters, brother, you might not recognize him yourselves, by now."

"I would recognize him," Aerie said.

"We'd all recognize him, even in a crowd of his own people. But that makes no difference. Anyone would know him who had seen him. But no one *has* seen him, or if they have they will not say so to us." Wess glanced at Aerie.

"You see," Aerie said, "he is winged."

"Winged!" Lythande said.

"Winged folk are rare, I believe, in the south."

"Winged folk are myths, in the south. Winged? Surely you mean . . ."

Aerie started to shrug back her cape, but Quartz put her arm around her shoulders again. Wess broke into the conversation quickly.

"The bones are longer," she said, touching the three outer fingers of her left hand with the forefinger of her right. "And stronger. The webs between fold out."

"And these people fly?"

"Of course. Why else have wings?"

Wess glanced at Chan, who nodded and reached for his pack.

"We have no homuncule," Wess said. "But we have a picture. It isn't Satan, but it's very like him."

Chan pulled out the wooden tube he had carried all the way from Kaimas. From inside it, he drew the rolled kidskin, which he opened out onto the table. The hide was carefully tanned and very thin; it had writing on one side and a painting, with one word underneath it, on the other.

"It's from the library at Kaimas," Chan said. "No one knows where it came from. I believe it is quite old, and I think it is from a book, but this is all that's left." He showed Lythande the written side. "I can decipher the script but not the language. Can you read it?"

Lythande shook his head. "It is unknown to me."

Disappointed, Chan turned the illustrated side of the manuscript page toward Lythande. Wess leaned toward it too, picking out the details in the dim candlelight. It was beautiful, almost as beautiful as Satan himself. It was surprising how like Satan it was, for it had been in the library since long before he was born. The slender and powerful winged man had red-gold hair and flame-colored wings. His expression seemed composed half of wisdom and half of deep despair.

Most flying people were black or deep iridescent green or pure dark blue. But Satan, like the painting, was the color of fire. Wess explained that to Lythande.

"We suppose this word to be this person's name," Chan said. "We cannot be sure we have the pronunciation right, but Satan's mother liked the sound as we say it, so she gave it to him as his name, too."

Lythande stared at the gold and scarlet painting in silence for a long time, then shook his head and leaned back in his chair. He blew smoke toward the ceiling. The ring spun, and sparked, and finally dissipated into the haze.

"Frejôjani," Lythande said, "Jubal—and the other slavemongers—parade their merchandise through the town before every auction. If your friend were in the coffle, everyone in Sanctuary would know. Everyone in the empire would know."

Beneath the edges of her cape, Aerie clenched her hands into fists.

Chan slowly, carefully, blankly, rolled up the painting and stored it away.

This was, Wess feared, the end of their journey.

"But it might be . . ."

Aerie looked up sharply, narrowing her deepset eyes.

"Such an unusual being would not be sold at public auction. He would be offered in private sale, or exhibited, or perhaps even offered to the emperor for his menagerie."

Aerie flinched, and Quartz traced the texture of her short-sword's bone haft.

"It's better, children, don't you see? He'll be treated decently. He's valuable. Ordinary slaves are whipped and cut and broken to obedience."

Chan's transparent complexion paled to white. Wess shuddered. Even contemplating slavery they had none of them understood what it meant.

"But how will we find him? Where will we look?"

"Jubal will know," Lythande said, "if anyone does. I like you, children. Sleep tonight. Perhaps tomorrow Jubal will speak with you." He got up, passed smoothly through the crowd, and vanished into the darkness outside.

In silence with her friends, Wess sat thinking about what Lythande had told them.

A well-set-up young fellow crossed the room and leaned over their table toward Chan. Wess recognized him as the man who had earlier been made sport of by his friends.

"Good evening, traveller," he said to Chan. "I have been told these ladies are not your wives."

"It seems everyone in this room has asked if my companions are my wives, and I still do not understand what you are asking," Chan said pleasantly.

"What's so hard to understand?"

"What does 'wives' mean?"

The man arched one eyebrow, but replied. "Women bonded to you by law. To give their favors to no one but you. To bear and raise your sons."

" 'Favors'?"

"Sex, you clapperdudgeon! Fucking! Do you understand me?"

"Not entirely. It sounds like a very odd system to me."

Wess thought it odd, too. It seemed absurd to decide to bear children of only one gender; and bonded by law sounded suspiciously like slavery. But—three women pledged solely to one man? She glanced across at Aerie and Quartz and saw they were thinking the same thing. They burst out laughing.

"Chan, Chan-love, think how exhausted you'd be!" Wess said.

Chan grinned. They often slept and made love all together, but he was not expected to satisfy all his friends. Wess enjoyed making love with Chan, but she was equally excited by Aerie's delicate ferocity, and by Quartz' inexhaustible gentleness and power.

"They're not your wives, then," the man said. "So how much for that one?" He pointed at Quartz.

They all waited curiously for him to explain.

"Come on, man! Don't be coy! You're obvious to everyone—why else bring women to the Unicorn? With that one, you'll get away with it till the madams find out. So make your fortune while you can. What's her price? I can pay, I assure you."

Chan started to speak, but Quartz gestured sharply and he fell silent.

"Tell me if I interpret you correctly," she said. "You think coupling with me would be enjoyable. You would like to share my bed tonight."

"That's right, lovey." He reached for her breast but abruptly thought better of it.

"Yet you speak, not to me, but to my friend. This seems very awkward, and very rude."

"You'd better get used to it, woman. It's the way we do things here."

"You offer Chan money, to persuade me to couple with you."

The man looked at Chan. "You'd best train your whores to manners yourself, boy, or your customers will help you and damage your merchandise."

Chan blushed scarlet, embarrassed, flustered, and confused. Wess began to think she knew what was going on, but she did not want to believe it.

"You are speaking to me, *man*," Quartz said, using the word with as much contempt as he had put into "woman." "I have but one more question for you. You are not ill-favored, yet you cannot get someone to bed you for the joy of it. Does this mean you are diseased?"

With an incoherent sound of rage, he reached for his knife. Before he touched it, Quartz' short-sword rasped out of its scabbard. She held its tip just above his belt-buckle. The death she offered him was slow and painful.

Everyone in the tavern watched intently as the man slowly spread his hands.

"Go away," Quartz said. "Do not speak to me again. You are not unattractive, but if you are not diseased you *are* a fool, and I do not sleep with fools."

She moved her sword a handsbreadth. He backed up three fast steps and spun around, glancing spasmodically from one face to another, to another. He found only amusement. He bolted, through a roar of laughter, fighting his way to the door.

The tavern-keeper sauntered over. "Foreigners," he said, "I don't know whether you've made your place or dug your graves tonight, but that was the best laugh I've had since the new moon. Bauchle Meyne will never live it down."

"I did not think it funny in the least," Quartz said. She sheathed her short-sword. She had not even touched her broadsword. Wess had never seen her draw it. "And I am tired. Where is our room?"

He led them up the stairs. The room was small and low-ceilinged. After the tavern-keeper left, Wess poked the straw mattress of one of the beds, and wrinkled her nose.

"I've got this far from home without getting lice, I'm not going to sleep in a nest of bedbugs." She threw her bedroll to the floor. Chan shrugged and dropped his gear.

Quartz flung her pack into the corner. "I'll have something to say to Satan when we find him," she said angrily. "Stupid fool, to let himself be captured by these creatures."

Aerie stood hunched in her cloak. "This is a wretched place," she said. "You can flee, but he cannot."

"Aerie, love, I know, I'm sorry." Quartz hugged her, stroking her hair. "I didn't mean it, about Satan. I was angry."

Aerie nodded.

Wess rubbed Aerie's shoulders, unfastened the clasp of her long hooded cloak, and drew it from Aerie's body. Candlelight rippled across the black fur that covered her, as sleek and glossy as sealskin. She wore nothing but a short thin blue silk tunic and her walking boots. She kicked off the boots, dug her clawed toes into the splintery floor, and stretched.

Her outer fingers lay close against the backs of her arms. She opened them, and her wings unfolded.

Only half-spread, her wings spanned the room. She let them droop, and pulled aside the leather curtain over the tall narrow window. The next building was very close.

"I'm going out. I need to fly."

"Aerie, we've come so far today—"

"Wess, I *am* tired. I won't go far. But I can't fly in the daytime, not here, and the moon is waxing. If I don't go now I may not be able to fly for days."

"It's true," Wess said. "Be careful."

"I won't be gone long." She slid sideways out the window and climbed up the rough side of the building. Her claws scraped into the adobe. Three soft footsteps overhead, the shushh of her wings: she was gone.

The others pushed the beds against the wall and spread their blankets, overlapping, on the floor. Quartz looped the leather flap over a hook in the wall and put the candle on the windowledge.

Chan hugged Wess. "I never saw anyone move as fast as Lythande. Wess, love, I feared he'd killed you before I even noticed him."

"It was stupid, to speak so familiarly to a stranger."

"But he offered us the nearest thing to news of Satan we've heard in weeks."

"True. Maybe the fright was worth it." Wess looked out the window, but saw nothing of Aerie.

"What made you think Lythande was a woman?"

Wess glanced at Chan sharply. He gazed back at her with a mildly curious expression.

He doesn't know, Wess thought, astonished. He didn't realize—

"I . . . I don't know," she said. "A silly mistake. I made a lot of them today."

It was the first time in her life she had deliberately lied to a friend. She felt slightly ill, and when she heard the scrape of claws on the roof above, she was glad for more reasons than simply that Aerie had returned. Just then the tavern-keeper banged on their door announcing their bath. In the confusion of getting Aerie inside and hidden under her cloak before they could open the door, Chan forgot the subject of Lythande's gender.

Beneath them, the noise of revelry in the Unicorn gradually faded to silence. Wess forced herself to lie still. She was so tired that she felt as if she were trapped in a river, with the current swirling her around and around so she could never get her bearings. Yet she could not sleep. Even the bath, the first warm bath any of them had had since leaving Kaimas, had not relaxed her. Quartz lay solid and warm beside her, and Aerie lay between Quartz and Chan. Wess did not begrudge Aerie or Quartz their places, but she did like to sleep in the middle. She wished one of her friends were awake, to make love with, but she could tell from their breathing that they were all deeply asleep. She cuddled up against Quartz, who reached out, in a dream, and embraced her.

The darkness continued, without end, without any sign of dawn, and finally Wess slid out from beneath Quartz' arm and the blankets, silently put on her pants and shirt, and, barefoot, crept down the stairs, past the silent tavern, and outside. On the doorstep, she sat and pulled on her boots.

The moon gave a faint light, enough for Wess. The street was deserted. Her heels thudded on the cobblestones, echoing hollowly against the close adobe walls. Such a short stay in the town should not make her uneasy, but it did. She envied Aerie her power to escape, however briefly, however dangerous the escape might be. Wess walked down the street, keeping careful track of her path. It would be very easy to get lost in this warren of streets and alleys, niches and blank canyons.

The scrape of a boot, instantly stilled, brought her out of her mental wanderings. They wished to try to follow her? Good luck to them.

Wess was a hunter. She tracked her prey so silently that she killed with a knife; in the dense rain forest where she lived, arrows were too uncertain. She had crept up on a panther and stroked its smooth pelt— then vanished so swiftly that she left the creature yowling in fury and frustration, while she laughed with delight. She grinned, and quickened her step, and her footfalls turned silent on the stone.

Her unfamiliarity with the streets hampered her slightly. A dead-end could trap her. But she found, to her pleasure, that her instinct for seeking out good trails translated into the city. Once she thought she would have to turn back, but the high wall barring her way had a deep diagonal fissure from the ground to its top. She found just enough purchase to clamber over it. She jumped into the garden the wall enclosed, scampered across it and up a grape arbor, and swung down into the next alley.

She ran smoothly, gladly, as her exhaustion lifted. She felt good, despite the looming buildings and twisted dirty streets and vile odors.

She faded into a shadowed recess where two houses abutted but did not line up. Listening, she waited.

The soft and nearly silent footsteps halted. Her pursuer hesitated. Grit scraped between stone and leather as the person turned one way, then the other, and, finally, chose the wrong turning and hurried off. Wess grinned, but she felt respect for any hunter who could follow her this far.

Moving silently through shadows, she started back toward the tavern. When she came to a tumbledown building she remembered, she found finger- and toe-holds and climbed to the roof of the next house. Flying was not the only talent Aerie had that Wess envied. Being able to climb straight up an undamaged adobe wall would be useful sometimes, too.

The rooftop was deserted. Too cold to sleep outside, no doubt; the inhabitants of the city went to ground at night, in warmer, unseen warrens.

The air smelled cleaner here, so she travelled by rooftop as far as she could. But the main passage through the Maze was too wide to leap across. From the building that faced the Unicorn, Wess observed the tavern. She doubted that her pursuer could have reached it first, but the possibility existed, in this strange place. She saw no one. It was near dawn. She no longer felt exhausted, just deliciously sleepy. She climbed down the face of the building and started across the street.

Someone flung open the door behind her, leaped out as she turned, and punched her in the side of the head.

Wess crashed to the cobblestones. The shadow stepped closer and kicked her in the ribs. A line of pain wrapped around her chest and tightened when she tried to breathe.

"Don't kill her. Not yet."

"No. I have plans for her."

Wess recognized the voice of Bauchle Meyne, who had insulted Quartz in the tavern. He toed her in the side.

"When I'm done with you, bitch, you can take me to your friends." He started to unbuckle his belt.

Wess tried to get up. Bauchle Meyne's companion stepped toward her, to kick her again.

His foot swung toward her. She grabbed it and twisted. As he went down, Wess struggled up. Bauchle Meyne, surprised, lurched toward her and grabbed her in a bear hug, pinioning her arms so she could not reach her knife. He pressed his face down close to hers. She felt his whisker stubble and smelled his yeasty breath. He could not hold her and force his mouth to hers at the same time, but he slobbered on her cheek. His pants slipped down and his penis thrust against her thigh.

Wess kneed him in the balls as hard as she could.

He screamed and let her go and staggered away, holding himself, doubled up and moaning, stumbling over his fallen breeches. Wess drew her knife and backed against a wall, ready for another attack.

Bauchle Meyne's accomplice rushed her. Her knife sliced quickly toward him, slashing his arm. He flung himself backwards and swore violently. Blood spurted between his fingers.

Wess heard the approaching footsteps a moment before he did. She pressed her free hand hard against the wall behind her. She was afraid to shout for help. In this place whoever answered might as easily join in attacking her.

But the man swore again, grabbed Bauchle Meyne by the arm, and dragged him away as fast as the latter, in his present distressed state, could go.

Wess sagged, sliding down the wall to the ground. She knew she was still in danger, but her legs would not hold her up anymore.

The footsteps ceased. Wess looked up, clenching her fingers around the handle of her knife.

"Frejôjan," Lythande said softly, from ten paces away, "sister, you led me quite a chase." She glanced after the two men. "And not only me, it seems."

"I never fought a person before," Wess said shakily. "Not a real fight. Only practice. No one ever got hurt." She touched the side of her head. The shallow scrape bled freely. She thought about its stopping, and the flow gradually ceased.

Lythande sat on his heels beside her. "Let me see." He probed the cut gently. "I thought it was bleeding, but it's stopped. What happened?"

"I don't know. Did you follow me? Did they? I thought I was eluding one person."

"I was the only one following you," Lythande said. "They must have come back to bother Quartz again."

"You know about that?"

"The whole city knows, child. Or anyway, the whole Maze. Bauchle will not soon live it down. The worst of it is he will never understand what it is that happened, or why."

"No more will I," Wess said. She looked up at Lythande. "How can you live here?" she cried.

Lythande drew back, frowning. "I do not live here. But that is not really what you are asking. We cannot speak so freely on the public street." He glanced away, hesitated, and turned back. "Will you come with me? I haven't much time, but I can fix your cut, and we can talk safely."

"All right," Wess said. She sheathed her knife and pushed herself to her feet, wincing at the sharp pain in her side. Lythande grasped her elbow, steadying her.

"Perhaps you've cracked a rib," he said. They started slowly down the street.

"No," Wess said. "It's bruised. It will hurt for a while, but it isn't broken."

"How do you know?"

Wess glanced at him quizzically. "I may not be from a city, but my people aren't completely wild. I paid attention to my lessons when I was little."

"Lessons? Lessons in what?"

"In knowing whether I am hurt, and what I must do if I am, in controlling the processes of my body—surely your people teach their children these things?"

"My people don't know these things," Lythande said. "I think we have more to talk about than I believed, frejôjan."

The Maze confused even Wess, by the time they reached the small building where Lythande stopped. Wess was feeling dizzy from the blow to her head, but she was confident that she was not dangerously hurt. Lythande opened a low door and ducked inside. Wess followed.

Lythande picked up a candle. The wick sparked. In the center of the dark room, a shiny spot reflected the glow. The wick burst into flame and the spot of reflection grew. Wess blinked. The reflection spread into a sphere, taller than Lythande, the color and texture of deep water, blue-gray, shimmering. It balanced on its lower curve, bulging slightly so it was not quite perfectly round.

"Follow me, Westerly."

Lythande walked toward the sphere. Its surface rippled at her approach. She stepped into it. It closed around her, and all Wess could see was a wavering figure, beyond the surface, and the spot of light from the candle flame.

She touched the sphere gingerly with her fingertip. It was wet. Taking a deep breath, she put her hand through the surface.

It froze her fast; she could not proceed, she could not escape, she could not move. Even her voice was captured.

After a moment Lythande surfaced. Her hair sparkled with drops of water, but her clothes were dry. She stood frowning at Wess, lines of thought bracketing the star on her forehead. Then her brow cleared and she grasped Wess' wrist.

"Don't fight it, little sister," she said. "Don't fight me."

The blue star glittered in the darkness, its points sparking with new light. Against great resistance, Lythande drew Wess' hand from the sphere. The cuff of Wess' shirt was cold and sodden. In only a few seconds the water had wrinkled her fingers. The sphere freed her suddenly and she nearly fell, but Lythande caught and supported her.

"What happened?"

Still holding her up, Lythande reached into the water and drew it aside like a curtain. She urged Wess toward the division. Unwillingly, Wess took a shaky step forward, and Lythande helped her inside. The surface closed behind them. Lythande eased Wess down on the platform that flowed out smoothly from the inside curve. Wess expected it to be wet, but it was resilient and smooth and slightly warm.

"What happened?" she asked again.

"The sphere is a protection against other sorcerers."

"I'm not a sorcerer."

"I believe you believe that. If I thought you were deceiving me, I would kill you. But if you are not a sorcerer, it is only because you are not trained."

Wess started to protest, but Lythande waved her to silence.

"Now I understand how you eluded me in the streets."

"I'm a hunter," Wess said irritably. "What good would a hunter be, who couldn't move silently and fast?"

"No, it was more than that. I put a mark on you, and you threw it off. No one has ever done that before."

"I didn't do it, either."

"Let us not argue, frejôjan. There isn't time."

She inspected the cut, then dipped her hand into the side of the sphere, brought out a handful of water, and washed away the sticky drying blood. Her touch was warm and soothing, as expert as Quartz'.

"Why did you bring me here?"

"So we could talk unobserved."

"What about?"

"I want to ask you something first. Why did you think I was a woman?"

Wess frowned and gazed into the depths of the floor. Her boot dimpled the surface, like the foot of a water-strider.

"Because you *are* a woman," she said. "Why you pretend you are not, I don't know."

"That is not the question," Lythande said. "The question is why you called me 'sister' the moment you saw me. No one, sorcerer, or otherwise, has ever glanced at me once and known me for what I am. You could place me, and yourself, in great danger. How did you know?"

"I just knew," Wess said. "It was obvious. I didn't look at you and wonder if you were a man or a woman. I saw you, and I thought, how beautiful, how elegant she is. She looks wise. She looks like she could help us. So I called to you."

"And what did your friends think?"

"They . . . I don't know what Quartz and Aerie thought. Chan asked whatever was I thinking of."

"What did you say to him?"

"I . . ." She hesitated, feeling ashamed. "I lied to him," she said miserably. "I said I was tired and it was dark and smoky, and I made a foolish mistake."

"Why didn't you try to persuade him you were right?"

"Because it isn't my business to deny what you wish known about yourself. Even to my oldest friend, my first lover."

Lythande stared up at the curved surface of the inside of the sphere. The tension eased in the set of her shoulders, the expression on her face.

"Thank you, little sister," she said, her voice full of relief. "I did not know if my identity were safe with you. But I think it is."

Wess looked up suddenly, chilled by insight. "You brought me here— you would have killed me!"

"If I had to," Lythande said easily. "I am glad it was not necessary. But I could not trust a promise made under threat. You do not fear me; you made your decision of your own free will."

"That may be true," Wess said. "But it isn't true that I don't fear you."

Lythande gazed at her. "Perhaps I deserve your fear, Westerly. You could destroy me with a thoughtless word. But the knowledge you have could destroy you. Some people would go to great lengths to discover what you know."

"I'm not going to tell them."

"If they suspected—they might force you."

"I can take care of myself," Wess said.

Lythande rubbed the bridge of her nose with thumb and forefinger. "Ah, sister, I hope so. I can give you very little protection." She—*he*, Wess reminded herself—stood up. "It's time to go. It's nearly dawn."

"You asked questions of me—may I ask one of you?"

"I'll answer if I can."

"Bauchle Meyne—if he hadn't behaved so stupidly, he could have killed me. But he taunted me till I recovered myself. He made himself vulnerable to me. His friend knew I had a knife, but he attacked me unarmed. I've been trying to understand what happened, but it makes no sense."

Lythande drew a deep breath. "Westerly," she said, "I wish you had never come to Sanctuary. You escaped for the same reason that I first chose to appear as I now must remain."

"I still don't understand."

"They never expected you to fight. To struggle a little, perhaps, just enough to excite them. They expected you to acquiesce to their wishes whether it was to beat you, to rape you, or to kill you. Women in Sanctuary are not trained to fight. They are taught that their only power lies in their ability to please, in bed and in flattery. Some few excel. Most survive."

"And the rest?"

"The rest are killed for their insolence. Or—" She smiled bitterly and gestured to herself. "Some few . . . find their talents are stronger in other areas."

"But why do you put up with it?"

"That is the way it is, Westerly. Some would say that is the way it must be—that it is ordained."

"It isn't that way in Kaimas." Just speaking the name of her home made her want to return. "Who ordains it?"

"Why, my dear," Lythande said sardonically, "the gods."

"Then you should rid yourselves of gods."

Lythande arched one eyebrow. "You should, perhaps, keep such ideas to yourself in Sanctuary. The gods' priests are powerful." She drew her hand up the side of the sphere so it parted as if she had slit it with a knife, and held the skin apart so Wess could leave.

Wess thought the shaky uncertain feeling that gripped her would disappear when she had solid ground beneath her feet again.

But it did not.

Wess and Lythande returned to the Unicorn in silence. As the Maze woke, the street began to fill with laden carts drawn by scrawny ponies, with beggars and hawkers and pickpockets. Wess bought fruit and meat rolls to take to her friends.

The Unicorn was closed and dark. As the tavern-keeper had said, he did not open early. Wess went around to the back, but at the steps of the lodging door, Lythande stopped.

"I must leave you, frejôjan."

Wess turned back in surprise. "But I thought you were coming up-stairs with me—for breakfast, to talk . . ."

Lythande shook his head. His smile was odd, not, as Wess had come to expect, sardonic, but sad. "I wish I could, little sister. For once, I wish I could. I have business to the north that cannot wait."

"To the north! Why did you come this way with me?" She had got her bearings on the way back, and while the twisted streets would not permit a straight path, they had proceeded generally southward.

"I wanted to walk with you," Lythande said.

Wess scowled at him. "You thought I hadn't enough sense to get back by myself."

"This is a strange place for you. It isn't safe even for people who have always lived here."

"You—" Wess stopped. Because she had promised to safeguard his true identity, she could not say what she wished: that Lythande was treating her as Lythande himself did not wish to be treated. Wess shook her head, flinging aside her anger. Stronger than her anger in Lythande's lack of confidence in her, stronger than her disappointment that Lythande was going away, was her surprise that Lythande had pretended to hint at finding Satan. She did not wish to think too deeply on the sorcerer's motives.

"You have my promise," she said bitterly. "You may be sure that my word is important to me. May your business be profitable." She turned away and fumbled for the latch, her vision blurry.

"Westerly," Lythande said gently, "do you think I came back last night only to coerce an oath from you?"

"It doesn't matter."

"Well, perhaps not, since I have so little to give in return."

Wess turned around. "And do you think I made that promise only because I hoped you could help us?"

"No," Lythande said. "Frejôjan, I wish I had more time—but what I came to tell you is this. I spoke with Jubal last night."

"Why didn't you tell me? What did he say? Does he know where Satan is?" But she knew she would have no pleasure from the answer. Lythande would not have put off good news. "Will he see us?"

"He has not seen your friend, little sister. He said he had no time to see you."

"Oh."

"I did press him. He owes me, but he has been acting peculiar lately.

He's more afraid of something else than he is of me, and that is very strange." Lythande looked away.

"Didn't he say *anything?*"

"He said . . . this evening, you should go to the grounds of the governor's palace."

"Why?"

"Westerly . . . this may have nothing to do with Satan. But the auction block is there."

Wess shook her head, confused.

"Where slaves are offered for sale."

Fury and humiliation and hope: Wess' reaction was so strong that she could not answer. Lythande came up the steps in one stride and put his arms around her. Wess held him, trembling, and Lythande stroked her hair.

"If he's there—is there no law, Lythande? Can a free person be stolen from their home, and . . . and . . ."

Lythande looked at the sky. The sun's light showed over the roof of the easternmost building.

"Frejôjan, I *must* go. If your friend is to be sold, you can try to buy him. The merchants here are not so rich as the merchants in the capital, but they are rich enough. You'd need a great deal of money. I think you should, instead, apply to the governor. He is a young man, and a fool— but he is not evil." Lythande hugged Wess one last time and stepped away. "Good-bye, little sister. Please believe I'd stay if I could."

"I know," she whispered.

Lythande strode away without looking back, leaving Wess alone among the early-morning shadows.

Wess returned to the room at the top of the stairs. When she entered, Chan propped himself up on one elbow.

"I was getting worried," he said.

"I can take care of myself!" Wess snapped.

"Wess, love, what's the matter?"

She tried to tell him, but she could not. Wess stood, silent, staring at the floor, with her back turned on her best friend.

She glanced over her shoulder when Chan stood up. The ripped curtain let in shards of light that cascaded over his body. He had changed, like all of them, on the long journey. He was still beautiful, but he was thinner and harder.

He touched her shoulder gently. She shrank away.

He saw the bloodstains on her collar. "You're hurt!" he said, startled. "Quartz!"

Quartz muttered sleepily from the bed. Chan tried to lead Wess over to the window, where there was more light.

"Just don't touch me!"

"Wess—"

"What's wrong?" Quartz said.

"Wess is injured."

Quartz padded barefoot toward them and Wess burst into tears and flung herself into her arms.

Quartz held Wess, as Wess had held her a few nights before, when Quartz had cried silently in bed, homesick, missing her children. "Tell me what happened," she said softly.

What Wess managed to say was less about the attack than about Lythande's explanations of it, and of Sanctuary.

"I understand," Quartz said after Wess had told her only a little. She stroked Wess' hair and brushed the tears from her cheeks.

"I don't," Wess said. "I must be going crazy, to act like this!" She started to cry again. Quartz led her to the blankets, where Aerie sat up, blinking and confused. Chan followed, equally bewildered. Quartz made Wess sit down, sat beside her and hugged her. Aerie rubbed her back and neck and let her wings unfold around them.

"You aren't going crazy," Quartz said. "It's that you aren't used to the way things are here."

"I don't want to get used to things here, I hate this place, I want to find Satan, I want to go home."

"I know," Quartz whispered. "I know."

"But I don't," Chan said.

Wess huddled against Quartz, unable to say anything that would ease the hurt she had given Chan.

"Just leave her alone for a little while, Chan," Quartz said to him. "Let her rest. Everything will be all right."

Quartz eased Wess down and lay beside her. Cuddled between Quartz and Aerie, with Aerie's wing spread over them all, Wess fell asleep.

At midmorning, Wess awoke. Her head ached fiercely and the black bruise across her side hurt every time she took a breath. She looked around the room. Sitting beside her, mending a strap on her pack, Quartz smiled down at her. Aerie was brushing her short smooth fur, and Chan stared out the window, his arm on the sill and his chin resting on his arm, his other shirt abandoned unpatched on his knee.

Wess got up and crossed the room. She sat on her heels near Chan. He glanced at her, and out the window, and at her again.

"Quartz explained, a little . . ."

"I was angry," Wess said.

"Just because barbarians act like . . . like barbarians, isn't a good reason to be angry with *me*."

He was right. Wess knew it. But the fury and bewilderment mixed up in her were still too strong to shrug off with easy words.

"You know—" he said, "you *do* know I couldn't act like that . . ."

Just for an instant Wess actually tried to imagine Chan acting like the innkeeper, or Bauchle Meyne, arrogantly, blindly, with his self-interest and his pleasure considered above everything and everyone else. The idea was so ludicrous that she burst out in sudden laughter.

"I know you wouldn't," she said. She had been angry at the person he *might* have been, had all the circumstances of his life been different. She had been angry at the person *she* might have been, even more. She hugged Chan quickly. "Chan, I've got to get free of this place." She took his hand and stood up. "Come, I saw Lythande last night, I have to tell you what he said."

They did not wait till evening to go to the governor's palace, but set out earlier, hoping to gain an audience with the Prince and persuade him not to let Satan be sold.

But no one else was waiting till evening to go to the palace, either. They joined a crowd of people streaming toward the gate. Wess' attempt to slip through the throng earned her an elbow in her sore ribs.

"Don't push, girl," said the ragged creature she had jostled. He shook his staff at her. "Would you knock over an old cripple? I'd never get up again, after I'd been trompled."

"Your pardon, citizen," she said. Ahead she could see that the people had to crowd into a narrower space. They were, more or less, in a line. "Are you going to the slave auction?"

"Slave auction? Slave auction! No slave auction today, foreigner. The carnival come to town!"

"What's the carnival?"

"A carnival! You've never heard of a carnival? Well, ne'mind, nor has half the people in Sanctuary, nor seen one neither. Two twelve-years since one came. Now the Prince is governor, we'll see more, I don't doubt. They'll come wanting an admission to his brother the emperor—out of the hinterlands and into the capital, if you know."

"But I still don't know what a carnival is."

The old man pointed.

Over the high wall of the palace grounds, the great drape of cloth that hung limply around a tall pole slowly began to spread, and open—like a huge mushroom, Wess thought. The guy ropes tightened, forming the canvas into an enormous tent.

"Under there—magic, foreign child. Strange animals. Prancing horses with pretty girls in feathers dancing on their backs. Jugglers, clowns, acrobats on high wires—and the freaks!" He chuckled. "I like the freaks best, the last time I saw a carnival they had a sheep with two heads and a man with two—but that's not a story to tell a young girl unless you're fucking her." He reached out to pinch her. Wess jerked back, drawing her knife. Startled, the old man said, "There, girl, no offense." She let the blade slide back into its sheath. The old man laughed again. "And a special exhibition, this carnival—special, for the Prince. They won't say what 'tis. But it'll be a sight, you can be sure."

"Thank you, citizen," Wess said coldly, and stepped back among her friends. The ragged man was swept forward with the crowd.

Wess caught Aerie's gaze. "Did you hear?"

Aerie nodded. "They have him. What else could their great secret be?"

"In *this* skyforsaken place, they might have overpowered some poor troll, or a salamander." She spoke sarcastically, for trolls were the gentlest of creatures, and Wess herself had often stretched up to scratch the chin of a salamander who lived on a hill where she hunted. It was entirely tame, for Wess never hunted salamanders. Their hide was too thin to be useful and no one in the family liked lizard meat. Besides, one could not pack out even a single haunch of fullgrown salamander, and she would not waste her kill. "In this place, they might have a winged snake in a box, and call it a great secret."

"Wess, their secret is Satan and we all know it," Quartz said. "Now we have to figure out how to free him."

"You're right, of course," Wess said.

At the gate, two huge guards glowered at the rabble they had been ordered to admit to the parade-ground. Wess stopped before one of them.

"I want to see the Prince," she said.

"Audience next week," he replied, hardly glancing at her.

"I need to see him before the carnival begins."

This time he did look at her, amused. "You do, do you? Then you've no luck. He's gone, won't be back till the parade."

"Where is he?" Chan asked.

She heard grumbling from the crowd piling up behind them.

"State secret," the guard said. "Now go in, or clear the way."

They went in.

The crowd thinned abruptly, for the parade-ground was enormous. Even the tent seemed small; the palace loomed above it like a cliff. If the whole population of Sanctuary had not come here, then a large proportion of every section had, for several merchants were setting up stalls: beads here, fruit there, pastries farther on; a beggar crawled slowly past; and a few paces away a large group of noblefolk in satins and fur and gold walked languidly beneath parasols held by naked slaves. The thin autumn sunlight was hardly enough to mar the complexion of the most delicate noble, or to warm the back of the most vigorous slave.

Quartz looked around, then pointed over the heads of the crowd. "They're making a pathway, with ropes and braces. The parade will come through that gate, and into the tent from this side." She swept her hand from right to left, east to west, in a long curve from the Processional gate. The carnival tent was set up between the auction block and the guards' barracks.

They tried to circle the tent, but the area beyond it all the way to the wall was blocked by rope barriers. In the front, a line of spectators already snaked back far beyond any possible capacity.

"We'll never get in," Aerie said.

"Maybe it's for the best," Chan said. "We don't need to be inside with Satan—we need to get him out."

The shadows lengthened across the palace grounds. Wess sat motionless and silent, waiting. Chan bit his fingernails and fidgeted. Aerie hunched under her cloak, her hood pulled low to shadow her face. Quartz watched her anxiously, and fingered the grip of her sword.

After again being refused an audience with the Prince, this time at the palace doors, they had secured a place next to the roped-off path. Across the way, a work crew put the finishing touches on a platform. When it was completed, servants hurried from the palace with rugs, a silk-fringed awning, several chairs, and a brazier of coals. Wess would not have minded a brazier of coals herself; as the sun fell, the air was growing chill.

The crowd continued to gather, becoming denser, louder, more and more drunk. Fights broke out in the line at the tent, as people began to realize they would never get inside. Soon the mood grew so ugly that criers spread among the people, ringing bells and announcing that the carnival would present one more performance, several more performances, until all the citizens of Sanctuary had the opportunity to glimpse the carnival's wonders. And the secret. Of course, the secret. Still, no one even hinted at the secret's nature.

Wess pulled her cloak closer. She knew the nature of the secret; she only hoped the secret would see his friends and be ready for whatever they could do.

The sun touched the high wall around the palace grounds. Soon it would be dark.

Trumpets and cymbals: Wess looked toward the Processional gate, but a moment later realized that all the citizens around her were straining for a view of the palace entrance. The enormous doors swung open and a phalanx of guards marched out, followed by a group of nobles wearing jewels and cloth of gold. They strode across the hard-packed ground. The young man at the head of the group, who wore a gold coronet, acknowledged his people's shouts and cries as if they all were accolades—which, Wess thought, they were not. But above the mutters and complaints, the loudest cry was, "The Prince! Long live the Prince!"

The phalanx marched straight from the palace to the new-built platform. Anyone shortsighted enough to sit in that path had to snatch up their things and hurry out of the way. The route cleared as swiftly as water parting around a stone.

Wess stood impulsively, about to sprint across the parade route to try once more to speak to the Prince.

"Sit down!"

"Out of the way!"

Someone threw an apple core at her. She knocked it away and crouched down again, though not because of the threats or the flying garbage. Aerie, too, with the same thought, started to her feet. Wess touched her elbow.

"Look," she said.

Everyone within reach or hearing of the procession seemed to have the same idea. The crowd surged in, every member clamoring for attention. The Prince flung out a handful of coins, which drew the beggars scuffling away from him. Others, more intent on their claims, continued to press him. The guards fell back, surrounding him, nearly cutting off the sight of him, and pushed at the citizens with spears held broadside.

The tight cordon parted and the Prince mounted the platform. Standing alone, he turned all the way around, raising his hands to the crowd.

"My friends," he cried, "I know you have claims upon me. The least wrong to one of my people is important to me."

Wess snorted.

"But tonight we are all privileged to witness a wonder never seen in the empire. Forget your troubles tonight, my friends, and enjoy the spectacle with me." He held out his hand, and brought a member of his party up beside him on the stage.

Bauchle Meyne.

"In a few days, Bauchle Meyne and his troupe will journey to Ranke, there to entertain the Emperor my brother."

Wess and Quartz glanced at each other, startled. Chan muttered a curse. Aerie tensed, and Wess held her arm. They all drew up their hoods.

"Bauchle goes with my friendship, and my seal." The Prince held up a rolled parchment secured with scarlet ribbons and ebony wax.

The Prince sat down, with Bauchle Meyne in the place of honor by his side. The rest of the royal party arrayed themselves around, and the parade began.

Wess and her friends moved closer together, in silence.

They would have no help from the Prince.

The Processional gates swung open to the sound of flutes and drums. The music continued for some while before anything else happened. Bauchle Meyne began to look uncomfortable. Then abruptly a figure staggered out onto the path, as if he had been shoved. The skeletally thin, red-haired man regained his balance, straightened up, and gazed from side to side. The jeers confounded him. He pushed his long cape off his shoulders to reveal his star-patterned black robe, and took a few hesitant steps.

At the rope barrier's first wooden supporting post, he stopped again. He gestured toward it tentatively and spoke a gutteral word.

The post sputtered into flame.

The people nearby drew back shouting, and the wizard lurched along the path, first to one side, then the other, waving his hands at each wooden post in turn.

The foggy white circles melded together to light the way. Wess saw that the posts were not, after all, burning. When the one in front of her began to shine, she brought her hand toward it, palm forward and fingers outspread. When she felt no heat she touched the post gingerly, then gripped it. It held no warmth, and it retained its ordinary texture, splintery rough-hewn wood.

She remembered what Lythande said, about her having a strong talent. She wondered if she could do the same thing. It would be a useful trick, though not very important. She had no piece of wood to try it on, nor any idea how to start to try in the first place. She shrugged and let go of the post. Her handprint—she blinked. No, it was her imagination, not a brighter spot that she had touched.

At the Prince's platform, the wizard stood staring vacantly around. Bauchle Meyne leaned forward intently, glaring, his worry clear and his anger barely held in check. The wizard gazed at him. Wess could see Bauchle Meyne's fingers tense around a circle of ruby chain. He twisted it. Wess gasped. The wizard shrieked and flung up his hands. Bauchle Meyne slowly relaxed his hold on the talisman. The wizard spread his arms. He was trembling. Wess, too, was shaking. She felt as if the chain had whipped around her body like a lash.

The wizard's trembling hands moved: the Prince's platform, the wooden parts of the chairs, the poles supporting the fringed awning, all burst suddenly into a fierce white fire. The guards leaped forward in fury and confusion, but stopped at a word from their prince. He sat calm and smiling, his hands resting easily on the bright arms of his throne. Shadowy flames played across his fingers, and the light spun up between his feet. Bauchle Meyne leaned back in satisfaction, and nodded to the wizard. The other nobles on the platform stood disconcerted, awash in the light from the boards between the patterned rugs. Nervously, but following the example of their ruler, they sat down again.

The wizard stumbled onward, lighting up the rest of the posts. He disappeared into the darkness of the tent. Its supports began to shine with the eerie luminescence. Gradually, the barrier-ropes and the carpets on the platform and the awning over the Prince and the canvas of the tent became covered with a soft gentle glow.

The Prince applauded, nodding and smiling toward Bauchle Meyne, and his people followed his lead.

With a sharp cry, a jester tumbled through the Processional gates and somersaulted along the path. After him came the flutists and drummers, and then three ponies with bedraggled feathers attached to their bridles. Three children in spangled shorts and halters rode them. The one in front jumped up and stood balanced on her pony's rump, while the two following did shoulder-stands, braced against the ponies' withers. Wess, who had never been on a horse in her life and found the idea quite terrifying, applauded. Others in the audience applauded, too, here and there, and the Prince himself idly clapped his hands. But nearby a large grizzled man laughed sarcastically and yelled, "Show us more!" That was the way most of the audience reacted, with hoots of derision and laughter. The child standing up stared straight ahead. Wess clenched her teeth, angry for the child but impressed by her dignity. Quartz' oldest child was about the same age. Wess took her hand, and Quartz squeezed her fingers gratefully.

A cage, pulled by a yoke of oxen, passed through the dark gate. Wess caught her breath. The oxen pulled the cage into the light. It carried an elderly troll, hunched in the corner on dirty straw. A boy poked the troll with a stick as the oxen drew abreast of the Prince. The troll leaped up and cursed in a high-pitched angry voice.

"You uncivilized barbarians! You, Prince—prince of worms, I say, of maggots! May your penis grow till no one will have you! May your best friend's vagina knot itself with you inside! May you contract water on the brain and sand in the bladder!"

Wess felt herself blushing: she had never heard a troll speak so. Ordinarily they were the most cultured of forest people, and the only danger in them was that one might find oneself listening for a whole afternoon to a discourse on the shapes of clouds or the effects of certain shelf-fungi. Wess looked around, frightened that someone would take offense at what the troll was saying to their ruler. Then she remembered that he was speaking the Language, the real tongue of intelligent creatures, and in this place no one but she and her friends understood.

"Frejôjan!" she cried on impulse. "Tonight—be ready—if I can—!"

He hesitated in the midst of a caper, stumbled, but caught himself and gamboled around, making nonsense noises till he faced her. She pulled her hood back so he could recognize her later. She let it fall again as the cart passed, so Bauchle Meyne would not see her from the other side of the path.

The gray-gold furry little being gripped the bars of his cage and looked out, making horrible faces at the crowd, horrible noises in reaction to their jeers. But between the shrieks and the gibberish, he said, "I wait—"

After he passed them, he began to wail.

"Wess—" Chan said.

"How could I let him go by without speaking to him?"

"He isn't a friend, after all," Aerie said.

"He's enslaved, just like Satan!" Wess looked from Aerie's face to Chan's, and saw that neither understood. "Quartz—?"

Quartz nodded. "Yes. You're right. A civilized person has no business being in this place."

"How are you going to find him? How are you going to free him? We don't even know how we're going to free Satan! Suppose he needs help?" Aerie's voice rose in anger.

"Suppose we need help?"

Aerie turned her back on Wess and stared blankly out into the parade. She even shrugged off Quartz' comforting hug.

Then there was no more time for arguing. Six archers tramped through the gate. A cart followed. It was a flatbed, curtained all around, and pulled by two large skewbald horses, one with a wild blue eye. Six more archers followed. A mutter of confusion rippled over the crowd, and then cries of "The secret! Show us the secret!"

The postillion jerked the draft horses to a standstill before the Prince. Bauchle Meyne climbed stiffly off the platform and onto the cart.

"My lord!" he cried. "I present you—a myth of our world!" He yanked on a string and the curtains fell away.

On the platform, Satan stood rigid and withdrawn, staring forward, his head high. Aerie moaned and Wess tensed, wanting to leap over the glowing ropes and lay about with her knife, in full view of the crowd, whatever the consequences. She cursed herself for being so weak and stupid this morning. If she had had the will to attack, she could have ripped out Bauchle Meyne's guts.

They had not broken Satan. They would kill him before they could strip him of his pride. But they had stripped him naked, and shackled him. And they had hurt him. Streaks of silver-gray cut across the red-gold fur on his shoulders. They had beaten him. Wess clenched her fingers around the handle of her knife.

Bauchle Meyne picked up a long pole. He was not fool enough to get within reach of Satan's talons.

"Show yourself!" he cried.

Satan did not speak the trade-language, but Bauchle Meyne made himself well enough understood with the end of the pole. Satan stared at him without moving until the young man stopped poking at him, and, with some vague awareness of his captive's dignity, backed up a step. Satan looked around him, his large eyes reflecting the light like a cat's. He faced the Prince. The heavy chains clanked and rattled as he moved.

He raised his arms. He opened his hands, and his fingers unfolded.

He spread his great red wings. Wizard-light glowed through the translucent webs. It was as if he had burst into flame.

The Prince gazed upon him with silent satisfaction as the crowd roared with surprise and astonishment.

"Inside," Bauchle Meyne said, "when I release him, he will fly."

One of the horses, brushed by Satan's wingtip, snorted and reared. The cart lurched forward. The postillion yanked the horse's mouth to a bloody froth and Bauchle Meyne lost his balance and stumbled to the ground. His face showed pain and Wess was glad. Satan barely shifted. The muscles tensed and slid in his back as he balanced himself with his wings.

Aerie made a high, keening sound, almost beyond the limits of human hearing. But Satan heard. He did not flinch; unlike the troll he did not turn. But he heard. In the bright white wizard-light, the short fur on the back of his shoulders rose. He made an answering cry, a sighing: a call to a lover. He folded his wing-fingers back along his arms. The webbing trembled and gleamed.

The postillion kicked his horse and the cart lumbered forward. For the crowd outside, the show was over.

The Prince stepped down from the platform, and, walking side by side with Bauchle Meyne and followed by his retinue, proceeded into the carnival tent.

The four friends stood close together as the crowd moved past them. Wess was thinking, They're going to let him fly, inside. He'll be free . . . She looked at Aerie. "Can you land on top of the tent? And take off again?"

Aerie looked at the steep canvas slope. "Easily," she said.

The area behind the tent was lit by torches, not wizard-light. Wess stood leaning against the grounds' wall, watching the bustle and chaos of the troupe, listening to the applause and laughter of the crowd. The show had been going on a long time now; most of the people who had not got inside had left. A couple of carnival workers kept a bored watch on the perimeter of the barrier, but Wess knew she could slip past any time she pleased.

It was Aerie she worried about. Once the plan started, she would be very vulnerable. The night was clear and the waxing moon bright and high. When she landed on top of the tent she would be well within range of arrows. Satan would be in even more danger. It was up to Wess and Quartz and Chan to create enough chaos so the archers would be too distracted to shoot either of the flyers.

Wess was rather looking forward to it.

She slipped under the rope when no one was looking and strolled through the shadows as if she belonged with the troupe. Satan's cart stood at the performers' entrance, but Wess did not go near her friend now. Taking no notice of her, the children on their ponies trotted by. In the torchlight the children looked thin and tired and very young, the ponies thin and tired and old. Wess slid behind the rank of animal cages. The carnival did, after all, have a salamander, but a piteous poor and hungry-looking one, barely the size of a large dog. Wess broke the lock on its cage. She had only her knife to pry with; she did the blade no good. She broke the locks on the cages of the other animals, the half-grown wolf, the pygmy elephant, but did not yet free them. Finally she reached the troll.

"Frejôjan," she whispered. "I'm behind you."

"I hear you, frejôjan." The troll came to the back of his cage. He bowed to her. "I regret my unkempt condition, frejôjan; when they captured me I had nothing, not even a brush." His golden gray-flecked hair was badly matted. He put his hand through the bars and Wess shook it.

"I'm Wess," she said.

"Aristarchus," he said. "You speak with the same accent as Satan—you've come for him?"

She nodded. "I'm going to break the lock on your cage," she said. "I have to be closer to the tent when they take him in to make him fly. It would be better if at first they didn't notice anything was going wrong . . ."

Aristarchus nodded. "I won't escape till you've begun. Can I be of help?"

Wess glanced along the row of cages. "Could you—would it put you in danger to free the animals?" He was old; she did not know if he could move quickly enough.

He chuckled. "All of us animals have become rather good friends," he said. "Though the salamander is rather snappish."

Wess wedged her knife into the padlock and wrenched it open. Aristarchus snatched it off the door and flung it into the straw. He smiled, abashed, at Wess.

"I find my own temper rather short in these poor days."

Wess reached through the bars and gripped his hand again. Near the tent, the skewbald horses wheeled Satan's cart around. Bauchle Meyne yelled nervous orders. Aristarchus glanced toward Satan.

"It's good you've come," he said. "I persuaded him to cooperate, at least for a while, but he does not find it easy. Once he made them angry enough to forget his value."

Wess nodded, remembering the whip scars.

The cart rolled forward; the archers followed.

"I have to hurry," Wess said.

"Good fortune go with you."

She moved as close to the tent as she could. But she could not see inside; she had to imagine what was happening, by the tone of the crowd. The postillion drove the horses around the ring. They stopped. Someone crawled under the cart and unfastened the shackles from below, out of reach of Satan's claws. And then—

She heard the sigh, the involuntary gasp of wonder as Satan spread his wings, and flew.

Above her, Aerie's shadow cut the air. Wess pulled off her cloak and waved it, signalling. Aerie dived for the tent, swooped, and landed.

Wess drew her knife and started sawing at a guy-rope. She had been careful enough of the edge so it sliced through fairly quickly. As she hurried to the next line, she heard the tone of the crowd gradually changing, as people began to notice something amiss. Quartz and Chan were doing their work, too. Wess chopped at the second rope. As the tent began to collapse, she heard tearing canvas above where Aerie ripped through the roof with her talons. Wess sliced through a third rope, a fourth. The breeze flapped the sagging fabric against itself. The canvas cracked and howled like a sail. Wess heard Bauchle Meyne screaming, "The ropes! Get the ropes, the ropes are breaking!"

The tent fell from three directions. Inside, people began to shout, then to scream, and they tried to flee. A few spilled out into the parade-ground, then a mob fought through the narrow opening. The shriek of frightened horses pierced the crowd-noise, and the scramble turned to panic. The skewbald horses burst through the crush, scattering people right and left, Satan's empty cart lurching and bumping along behind. More terrified people streamed out after them. All the guards from the palace fought against them, struggling to get inside to their prince.

Wess turned to rejoin Quartz and Chan, and froze in horror. In the shadows behind the tent, Bauchle Meyne snatched up an abandoned bow, ignored the chaos, and aimed a steel-tipped arrow into the sky. Wess sprinted toward him, crashed into him, and shouldered him off-balance. The bowstring twanged and the arrow fishtailed up, falling back spent to bury itself in the limp canvas.

Bauchle Meyne sprang up, his high complexion scarlet with fury.

"You, you little bitch!" He lunged for her, grabbed her, and back-handed her across the face. "You've ruined me for spite!"

The blow knocked her to the ground. This time Bauchle Meyne did not laugh at her. Half-blinded, Wess scrambled away from him. She heard his boots pound closer and he kicked her in the same place in the ribs. She heard the bone crack. She dragged at her knife but its edge, roughened by the abuse she had given it, hung up on the rim of the scabbard. She could barely see and barely breathe. She struggled with the knife and Bauchle Meyne kicked her again.

"You can't get away this time, bitch!" He let Wess get to her hands and knees. "Just try to run!" He stepped toward her.

Wess flung herself at his legs, moved beyond pain by fury. He cried out as he fell. The one thing he could never expect from her was attack. Wess lurched to her feet. She ripped her knife from its scabbard as Bauchle Meyne lunged at her. She plunged it into him, into his belly, up, into his heart.

She knew how to kill, but she had never killed a human being. She had been drenched by her prey's blood, but never the blood of her own species. She had watched creatures die by her hand, but never a creature who knew what death meant.

His heart still pumping blood around the blade, his hands fumbling at her hands, trying to push them away from his chest, he fell to his knees, shuddered, toppled over, convulsed, and died.

Wess jerked her knife from his body. Once more she heard the shrieks of frightened horses and the curses of furious men, and the howl of a half-starved wolf cub.

The tent shimmered with wizard-light.

I wish it were torches, Wess screamed in her mind. Torches would burn you, and burning is what you deserve.

But there was no fire, and nothing burned. Even the wizard-light was fading.

Wess looked into the sky. She raked her sleeve across her eyes to wipe away her tears.

The two flyers soared toward the moon, free.

And now—

Quartz and Chan were nowhere in sight. She could find only terrified strangers: performers in spangles, Sanctuary people fighting each other, and more guards coming to the rescue of their lord. The salamander lumbered by, hissing in fear.

Horses clattered toward her and she spun, afraid of being run down. Aristarchus brought them to a halt and flung her the second horse's reins. It was the skewbald stallion from Satan's cart, the one with the wild blue eye. It smelled the blood on her and snorted and reared. Somehow she kept hold of the reins. The horse reared again and jerked her off her feet. Bones ground together in her side and she gasped.

"Mount!" Aristarchus cried. "You can't control him from the ground!"

"I don't know how—" She stopped. It hurt too much to talk.

"Grab his mane! Jump! Hold on with your knees."

She did as he said, found herself on the horse's back, and nearly fell off his other side. She clamped her legs around him and he sprang forward. Both the reins were on one side of his neck—Wess knew that was not right. She pulled on them and he twisted in a circle and almost threw her again. Aristarchus urged his horse forward and grabbed the stallion's bridle. The animal stood spraddle-legged, ears flat back, nostrils flaring, trembling between Wess' legs. She hung onto his mane, terrified. Her broken ribs hurt so badly she felt faint.

Aristarchus leaned forward, blew gently into the stallion's nostrils, and spoke to him so quietly Wess could not hear the words. Slowly, easily, the troll straightened out the reins. The animal gradually relaxed, and his ears pricked forward again.

"Be easy on his mouth, frejôjan," the troll said to Wess. "He's a good creature, just frightened."

"I have to find my friends," Wess said.

"Where are you to meet them?"

Aristarchus' calm voice helped her regain her composure.

"Over there." She pointed to a shadowed recess beyond the tent. Aristarchus started for it, still holding her horse's bridle. The animals stepped delicately over broken equipment and abandoned clothing.

Quartz and Chan ran from the shadowed side of the tent. Quartz was laughing. Through the chaos she saw Wess, tagged Chan on the shoulder to get his attention, and changed direction to hurry toward Wess.

"Did you see them fly?" Quartz cried. "They outflew eagles!"

"As long as they outflew arrows," Aristarchus said dryly. "Hurry, you, the big one, up behind me, and you," he said to Chan, "behind Wess."

They did as he ordered. Quartz kicked the horse and he sprang forward, but Aristarchus reined him in.

"Slowly, children," the troll said. "Slowly through the dark, and no one will notice."

To Wess' surprise, he was quite correct.

In the city they kept the horses at the walk, and Quartz concealed Aristarchus beneath her cloak. The uproar fell behind them, and no one chased them. Wess clutched the stallion's mane, still feeling very insecure so high above the ground.

A direct escape from Sanctuary did not lead them past the Unicorn, or indeed into the Maze at all, but they decided to chance going back; the risk of travelling unequipped through the mountains this late in the fall was too great. They approached the Unicorn through back alleys, and saw almost no one. Apparently the denizens of the Maze were as fond of entertainments as anyone else in Sanctuary. No doubt the opportunity to watch their prince extricate himself from a collapsed tent was almost the best entertainment of the evening. Wess would not have minded watching that herself.

Leaving the horses hidden in shadow with Aristarchus, they crept quietly up the stairs to their room, stuffed belongings in their packs, and started out again.

"Young gentleman and his ladies, good evening."

Wess spun around, Quartz right beside her gripping her sword. The tavern-keeper flinched back from them, but quickly recovered himself.

"Well," he said to Chan, sneering. "I thought they were one thing, but I see they are your bodyguards."

Quartz grabbed him by the shirt front and lifted him off the floor. Her broadsword scraped from its scabbard. Wess had never seen Quartz draw it, in defense or anger; she had never seen the blade. But Quartz had not neglected it. The edge gleamed with transparent sharpness.

"I foreswore the frenzy when I abandoned war," Quartz said very quietly. "But you are very nearly enough to make me break my oath."

She opened her hand and he fell to his knees before the point of the sword.

"I meant no harm, my lady—"

"Do not call me 'lady'! I am not of noble birth! I was a soldier and I am a woman. If that cannot deserve your courtesy, then you cannot command my mercy!"

"I meant no harm, I meant no offense. I beg your pardon . . ." He looked up into her unreadable silver eyes. "I beg your pardon, northern woman."

There was no contempt in his voice now, only terror, and to Wess that was just as bad. She and Quartz could expect nothing here, except to be despised or feared. They had no other choices.

Quartz sheathed her sword. "Your silver is on the table," she said coldly. "We had no mind to cheat you."

He scrabbled up and away from them, into the room. Quartz grabbed the key from the inside, slammed the door, and locked it.

"Let's get out of here."

They clattered down the stairs. In the street, they tied the packs together and to the horses' harnesses as best they could. Above, they heard the innkeeper banging at the door, and when he failed to break it down, he came to the window.

"Help!" he cried. "Help, kidnappers! Brigands!" Quartz vaulted up behind Aristarchus and Chan clambered up behind Wess. "Help!" the innkeeper cried. "Help, fire! Floods!"

Aristarchus gave his horse its head and it sprang forward. Wess' stallion tossed his mane, blew his breath out hard and loud, and leaped from a standstill into a gallop. All Wess could do was hold on, clutching the mane and the harness, hunching over the horse's withers, as he careered down the street.

They galloped through the outskirts of Sanctuary, splashed across the river at the ford, and headed north along the river trail. The horses sweated into a lather and Aristarchus insisted on slowing down and breathing them. Wess saw the sense of that, and, too, she could detect no pursuit from the city. She scanned the sky, but darkness hid any sign of the flyers.

Abandoning the headlong pace, they walked the horses or let them jog. Each step jarred Wess' ribs. She tried to concentrate on pushing out the pain, but to do it well she needed to stop, dismount, and relax. That was impossible right now. The road and the night led on forever.

At dawn, they reached the faint abandoned trail Wess had brought them in on. It led away from the road, directly up into the mountains.

The trees, black beneath the slate-blue sky, closed in overhead. Wess felt as if she had fought her way out of a nightmare world into a world she knew and loved. She did not yet feel free, but she could consider the possibility of feeling free again.

"Chan?"

"I'm here, love."

She took his hand, where he held her gingerly around the waist, and kissed his palm. She leaned back against him, and he held her.

A stream gushed between the gnarled roots of trees, beside the nearly invisible trail.

"We should stop and let the horses rest," Aristarchus said. "And rest, ourselves."

"There's a clearing a little way ahead," Wess said. "It has grass. They eat grass, don't they?"

Aristarchus chuckled. "They do, indeed."

When they reached the clearing, Quartz jumped down, stumbled, groaned, and laughed. "It's a long time since I rode horseback," she said. She helped Aristarchus off. Chan dismounted and stood testing his legs after the long ride. Wess sat where she was. She felt as if she were looking at the world through Lythande's secret sphere.

The sound of great wings filled the cold dawn. Satan and Aerie landed in the center of the clearing and hurried toward them.

Wess twined her fingers in the skewbald's striped mane and slid off his back. She leaned against his shoulder, exhausted, taking short shallow breaths. She could hear Chan and Quartz greeting the flyers. But Wess could not move.

"Wess?"

She turned slowly, still holding the horse's mane. Satan smiled down at her. She was used to flyers' being lean, but they were sleek: Satan was gaunt, his ribs and hips sharp beneath his skin. His short fur was dull and dry, and besides the scars on his back he had marks on his ankles, and around his throat, where he had been bound.

"Oh, Satan—" She embraced him, and he enfolded her in his wings.

"It's done," he said. "It's over." He kissed her gently. Everyone gathered around him. He brushed the back of his hand softly down the side of Quartz' face, and bent down to kiss Chan.

"Frejôjani . . ." He looked at them all; then, as a tear spilled down his cheek, he wrapped himself in his wings and cried.

They held him and caressed him until the racking sobs ceased.

Ashamed, he scrubbed away the tears with the palm of his hand. Aristarchus stood nearby, blinking his large green eyes.

"You must think me an awful fool, Aristarchus, a fool, and weak."

The troll shook his head. "I think, when I can finally believe I'm free . . ." He looked at Wess. "Thank you."

They sat beside the stream to rest and talk.

"It's possible that we aren't even being followed," Quartz said.

"We watched the city, till you entered the forest," Aerie said. "We saw no one else on the river road."

"Then they might not have realized anyone but another flyer helped Satan escape. If no one saw us fell the tent—"

Wess reached into the stream and splashed her face, cupped her hand in the water, and lifted it to her lips. The first rays of direct sunlight pierced the branches and entered the clearing.

Her hand was still bloody. The blood was mixing with the water. She choked and spat, lurched to her feet, and bolted. A few paces away she fell to her knees and retched violently.

There was nothing in her stomach but bile. She crawled to the stream and scrubbed her hands, then her face, with sand and water. She stood up again. Her friends were staring at her, shocked.

"There was someone," she said. "Bauchle Meyne. But I killed him."

"Ah," Quartz said.

"You've given me another gift," Satan said. "Now I don't have to go back and kill him myself."

"Shut up, Satan, she's never killed anyone before."

"Nor have I. But I would have ripped out his throat if just once he'd left the chains slack enough for me to reach him!"

Wess wrapped her arms around herself, trying to ease the ache in her ribs. Suddenly Quartz was beside her.

"You're hurt—why didn't you tell me?"

Wess shook her head, unable to answer. And then she fainted.

She woke up at midafternoon, lying in the shade of a tall tree in a circle of her friends. The horses grazed nearby, and Aristarchus sat on a stone beside the stream, combing the tangles from his fur. Wess got up and went to sit beside him.

"Did you call my name?"

"No," he said.

"I thought I heard—" She shrugged. "Never mind."

"How are you feeling?"

"Better." Her ribs were bandaged tight. "Quartz is a good healer."

"No one is following. Aerie looked, a little while ago."

"That's good. May I comb your back for you?"

"That would be a great kindness."

In silence, she combed him, but she was paying very little attention. The third time the comb caught on a knot, Aristarchus protested quietly.

"Sister, please, that fur you're plucking is attached to my skin."

"Oh, Aristarchus, I'm sorry . . ."

"What's wrong?"

"I don't know," she said. "I feel—I want—I . . ." She handed him the comb and stood. "I'm going to walk up the trail a little way. I won't be gone long."

In the silence of the forest she felt easier, but there was something pulling her, something calling to her that she could not hear.

And then she did hear something, a rustling of leaves. She faded back off the trail, hiding herself, and waited.

Lythande walked slowly, tiredly, along the trail. Wess was so surprised that she did not speak as the wizard passed her, but a few paces on, Lythande stopped and looked around, frowning.

"Westerly?"

Wess stepped into sight. "How did you know I was there?"

"I felt you near . . . How did you find me?"

"I thought I heard someone call me. Was that a spell?"

"No. Just a hope."

"You look so tired, Lythande."

Lythande nodded. "I received a challenge. I answered it."

"And you won—"

"Yes." Lythande smiled bitterly. "I still walk the earth and wait for the days of Chaos. If that is winning, then I won."

"Come back to camp and rest and eat with us."

"Thank you, little sister. I will rest with you. But your friend—you found him?"

"Yes. He's free."

"You all escaped unhurt?"

Wess shrugged, and was immediately sorry for it. "I did crack my ribs this time." She did not want to talk about the deeper hurts.

"And now—are you going home?"

"Yes."

Lythande smiled. "I might have known you would find the Forgotten Pass."

They walked together back toward camp. A little scared by her own presumption, Wess reached out and took the wizard's hand in hers. Lythande did not draw away, but squeezed her fingers gently.

"Westerly—" Lythande looked at her straight on, and Wess stopped. "Westerly, would you go back to Sanctuary?"

Stunned and horrified, Wess said, "Why?"

"It isn't as bad as it seems at first. You could learn many things . . ."

"About being a wizard?"

Lythande hesitated. "It would be difficult, but—it might be possible. It is true that your talents should not be wasted."

"You don't understand," Wess said. "I don't want to be a wizard. I wouldn't go back to Sanctuary if that were the reason."

Lythande said, finally, "That isn't the only reason."

Wess took Lythande's hand between her own, drew it to her lips, and kissed the palm. Lythande reached up and caressed Wess' cheek. Wess shivered at the touch.

"Lythande, I can't go back to Sanctuary. You would be the only reason I was there—and it would change me. It *did* change me. I don't know if I can go back to being the person I was before I came here, but I'm going to try. Most of what I did learn there I would rather never have known. You must understand me!"

"Yes," Lythande said. "It was not fair of me to ask."

"It isn't that I wouldn't love you," Wess said, and Lythande looked at her sharply. Wess took as deep a breath as she could, and continued. "But what I feel for you would change, too, as I changed. It wouldn't be love anymore. It would be . . . need, and demand, and envy."

Lythande sat on a tree root, shoulders slumped, and stared at the ground. Wess knelt beside her and smoothed her hair back from her forehead.

"Lythande . . ."

"Yes, little sister," the magician whispered, as if she were too tired to speak aloud.

"You must have important work here." How could she bear it otherwise? Wess thought. She is going to laugh at you for what you ask her, and explain how foolish it is, and how impossible. "And Kaimas, my home . . . you would find it dull—" She stopped, surprised at herself for her hesitation and her fear. "You come with me, Lythande," she said abruptly. "You come home with me."

Lythande stared at her, her expression unreadable. "Did you mean what you said—"

"It's so beautiful, Lythande. And peaceful. You've met half my family already. You'd like the rest of them, too! You said you had things to learn from us."

"—about loving me?"

Wess caught her breath. She leaned forward and kissed Lythande quickly, then, a second time, slowly, as she had wanted to since the moment she saw her.

She drew back a little.

"Yes," she said. "Sanctuary made me lie, but I'm not in Sanctuary now. With any luck I'll never see it again, and never have to lie anymore."

"If I had to go—"

Wess grinned. "I might try to persuade you to stay." She touched Lythande's hair. "But I wouldn't try to hold you. As long as you wanted to stay, and whenever you wanted to come back, you'd have a place in Kaimas."

"It isn't your resolve I doubt, little sister, it's my own. And my own strength. I think I would not want to leave your home, once I'd been there for a while."

"I can't see the future," Wess said. Then she laughed at herself, for what she was saying to a wizard. "Perhaps you can."

Lythande made no reply.

"All I know," Wess said, "is that anything anyone does might cause pain. To oneself, to a friend. But you cannot do nothing." She stood up. "Come. Come sleep, with me and my friends. And then we'll go home."

Lythande stood up too. "There's so much you don't know about me, little sister. So much of it could hurt you."

Wess closed her eyes, wishing, like a child at twilight seeking out a star. She opened her eyes again.

Lythande smiled. "I will come with you. If only for a while."

They walked together, hand in hand, to join the others.

# Ischade

## C.J. Cherryh

### 1

Shadows slipped along the cobbles in this deepest sink of the Maze, in that small light of the moon which wended its way among the overhangs and glistened wetly off noisome moistures. A well-dressed woman had no place here, even shadow-clad in black, robed and hooded—but she went deliberately, weaving only from the course of the foulest and widest streams, stepping over most.

And a ruffler, a bravo, a sometime thief—Sjekso by name—he took to the alleys as a matter of course.

Sjekso belonged here, had been whelped here, wove in his steps too, but not from fastidiousness, as he came from the opposite direction down the web of dark ways. A handsome fellow, was Sjekso Kinzan, a blond youth with curling locks, a short and carefully kept beard, his shirt and jerkin open from the recent heat of the common room of the *Vulgar Unicorn*—from the heat, and, truth be told, from a certain vanity. He radiated sex, wine vapors, and a certain peevishness: was out of pocket from the dice, had lost even Minsy's purchasable favors to a bad throw . . . his absolute nadir of discomfort. Minsy was off with that whoreson Hanse, while he—

He staggered his hazed way back toward his lodgings and his own doorway off the Serpentine. He snuffed and faltered and lamented his misfortune with himself. He hated Hanse, at least for the evening, and plotted elaborate and public revenge . . . .

And blinking in the vapors up from the harbor and in the uncertain focus of his eyes, he found his way intersected with a woman's in the alleyway. No ordinary doxy, this: a courtesan of quality strayed from some rendezvous, an opportunity some fickle god had tossed into his path or him into hers.

"Well," he said, and flung wide his arms, leaned from one side of the way to the other to block her attempt to walk around him . . . a little fun, he reckoned. And again, owlishly: *"Well,"*—but she made a quick move to go past him and he seized her in that swift pass, grabbed and grasped and felt female roundnesses in delightful proportions. His prey writhed and pushed and kneed at him, and he gripped her hair through the hood, drew her head back and kissed her with fair aim and rising passion.

She struggled, which motion only felt the better in his hands, and she gave out muffled cries, which were far from loud, his mouth covering hers the while. He held her tight and sought with his eyes for some more convenient alcove among the broken amphorae and barrels, a place where they might not be disturbed.

All at once another sound penetrated the fog of sense and sound, the scuff of another foot near him. Sjekso started to spin himself and his victim about, went the least bit over to that foot and had a hand clamped onto his own chin, his head jerked back, and a deadly keen blade at his throat in the same instant.

"Let the lady go," a male whisper suggested, and he carefully, trading in all his remaining advantage, relaxed his hands and let them fall, wondering wildly all the while whether his only chance might be in some wild try at escape. The woman in the edge of his vision stepped back, brushed at her robes, adjusted her hood. The knife rode razor-edged at his throat and the hand which held his chin gave him nothing.

Mradhon Vis kept his grip and held the ruffian just off his balance, looked in a moment's distraction at the lady in question . . . at a severe and dusky face in the faint light of the alleyway. She was beautiful. His romantical soul was touched—that seldom-afforded self which launched itself mostly in the wake of more profitable motives. "Be off," he told Sjekso, and flung the villain a good several body lengths down the alley; and Sjekso scrambled up and set to his heels without stopping to see anything.

*"Wait!"* the woman called after Sjekso. The would-be rapist spun about with his back to a wall, ducking an imagined blow from behind. Mradhon Vis, dagger still in hand, stood facing him, utterly confounded.

"The boy and I are old friends," she said—and to Sjekso: "Isn't it so?"

Sjekso straightened with his back against the wall and managed a bow, if a wobbling one . . . managed a sneer, his braggadocio recovered in the face of a man he, after all, knew from the dice table that night—and Mradhon Vis took a tighter and furious grip on his dagger, knowing this vermin at least from the tables at the *Unicorn*.

But feminine fingers touched very lightly on his bare arm. "A misunderstanding," the woman said, very soft and low. "But thank you for stepping in, all the same. You have some skill, don't you? Out of the army, maybe—I ask you, sir . . . I have need to find someone . . . with that skill. To guard me. I have to come and go hereabouts. I could pay, if you could find me someone like yourself, a friend maybe—who might serve. . . ."

"At your service," Sjekso said, with a second grander flourish. "I know my way around."

But the woman never turned to see. Her eyes were all for Mradhon, dark and glittering in the night. "He's one, in fact, I might sometimes want protection *from*.—Do you know someone who might be interested?"

Mradhon straightened his back and took a superior stance. "I've served as bodyguard now and again. And as it happens, I'm at liberty."

"Ah," she said, a hand to her robed breast, which outlined female curves in the shadow. And she turned at once to the confused villain, who had taken advantage of the moment to slip toward the shadows and the corner. "No, no, wait. I did promise you this evening. I had no right to put you off; and I want to talk with you. Be patient."—A glance then back, her hand bringing a purse from beneath her robes. She loosed the strings and took out a gold coin that caught Mradhon's whole attention, the more so when she dropped the heavy purse into his hand. Only the one coin she held, it winking colorless bright in the moonlight, and she held that up like an icon for Sjekso's eyes—another look at Mradhon: "I lodge seventh down from this corner, the first steps you'll come to that have a newel on the rail: on your right as you go. Go there. Learn the place so you can find it tomorrow morning, and be waiting there for me at midmorning. I'll be there. And the purse is yours."

He considered the weight in his palm, heavy as with gold. "I'll find it," he said, and, less than confident of the situation at hand: "Are you sure you don't want me to stay about?"

Black brows drew together, a frown uncommonly grim. "I have no doubts to my safety.—Ah, your name, sir. When I pay, I like to know that."

"Vis. Mradhon Vis."

"From—"

"Northward. A lot of places."

"We'll talk. Tomorrow morning. Go on, now. Believe me, that the quarrel wasn't what it seemed."

"Lady," he murmured—he had known polite company once. He clenched the purse in his fist and turned off in the direction she had named—not without a backward look. Sjekso still waited where he had fixed himself against the wall; but the lady seemed to know he would look back, and turned a shadowy look on him.

Mradhon moved on quickly and further along the winding way, stopped and anxiously shook out the purse into his hand, a spill of five heavy pieces in gold and half a dozen of silver. Hot and cold went through him, like the shock of a blow, a tremor through things that were . . . A second glance back, but buildings had come between him and the woman and her bought-boy Sjekso. Well, he had hired to stranger folk and no few worse to look on. He gave a twitch of his shoulders at that proceedings back there and shrugged it off. There was gold in his possession, a flood of gold. His gallantry had come from his own poverty, from one look at the woman's fine clothing and a sure knowledge that Sjekso Kinzan was all hollow when pushed. And for that gold in his hand he would have waited in the alley all night, or beaten Sjekso to fine rags, no questions asked.

It occurred to him while he went that it might involve more than that, but he went, all the same.

The woman looked back at Sjekso and smiled, a fervid smile which made wider and wider chaos of Sjekso's grasp of the situation. He stood away from his wall and—sobered as he had been in the encounter, deprived of the vaporous warmth of the wine in his blood—still he recovered something of anticipation, reestimated his own considerable animal charm in the light of the lady's sultry dark eyes, in the moonlike gleam of the gold coin she held up before him. He grinned, his confidence restored, stood easier still as she came to him—it might have been the wine after all, this new blush of heat; it might have been her slim fingers which touched at his collar and drew a line with the edge of the coin down amongst the fine hairs of his chest, disturbing there the chain of the luckpiece he wore.

His luck had improved, he reckoned, laying it all to his way with women. She had liked it after all . . . they all did; and she might be parted from more than a golden coin, and if she thought of using him and that bastard northerner one against the other, good: there was a chance of paying off Mradhon Vis. He had skills the northerner did not; and he knew how to get the most out of them. He took most of his living from women, in one way or the other.

"What's your name?" she asked him.

"Sjekso Kinzan."

"Sjekso. I have a place . . . not the lodgings where I sent that fellow; that's business. But my real house . . . near the river. A little wine, a soft bed . . . I'll bet you're good."

He laughed. "I make it a rule never to go out of my own territory till I know the terms. Here's good enough. Right over here. And I'll bet you don't care."

"Mine's Ischade," she murmured distractedly, as he put his hands up under the robes. She swayed against him, her own hands on him, and he found the coin and took it from her unresisting fingers. She brushed his lips with her own and urged him on. "My name's Ischade."

2

A corpse was no uncommon sight in the Maze. But one sprawled in the middle of the Serpentine, in the first light of the sun—the potboy of the *Unicorn* found the blond male corpse when he came out to heave the slops, a corpse on the inn's very doorstep, a body quite stiff and cold, and he knew Sjekso Kinzan. He spun on his heel and started to run back in—thought again and darted back to search for valuables . . . after all, some less acquainted and deserving person might come along. He found the brass luckpiece, found the purse . . . empty, except for an old nail and a bit of lint—dropped the luckpiece down his own collar, jumped up and ran inside in breathless haste, to spill his news to the morning's first stirrers-forth in the tavern; and the fact of one of the *Unicorn's* regular patrons lying stiff at the door brought a stamping up and down the stair and a general outpouring of curious and half-awake overnighters.

That was how it came to Hanse, a disturbance under Minsy Zithyk's rented window next door.

The gathering around the body in the street was solemn . . . partly a kind of respect and partly morning headaches, more and more on-lookers arriving as the commotion became its own reason for being. Hanse was one of the first, stood with his arms clenched into a tight fold—he had his daggers: had them about his person natural as breath-ing. His scowl and awakened-owl stare at the corpse of Sjekso Kinzan, his arms about his ribs holding his spine stiff—warned Minsy Zithyk off. She stood snuffling and holding her own ribs, doubtless with the other half of a throbbing headache. Hanse wanted no hanging-on, now, of Sjekso's longtime woman. The dice game and the wager stuck in his mind and he felt eyes on him, himself part of the morning's gossip, with a man he had diced with lying cold in the soiled stream of a drain.

"Who got him?" Hanse asked finally, and there was a general shrug-ging of shoulders. "Who?" Hanse snapped, looking round at the onlookers. A corpse was indeed no novelty in the Maze, but an other-wise young and healthy one, with no mark of violence on it . . . but a man on the doorstep of the tavern he frequented, a turn or two of the alleys to his own lodgings . . . .

There were amenities like territory. A man was never assured . . . but there were places and places, and when he was in his own place, he was least likely to end up among the morning's debris. There were stirrings among the crowd, discomfort—with Hanse, for one, whose smallish size meant a temper backed with knives, a bad reputation for every kind of mischief.

And his sullen, headachy stare passed right round to a stranger in the territory—to one Mradhon Vis; to a new and frequent patron at the *Uni-corn.* "You," Hanse said. "You left about the same time last night. You see anything?"

A shrug. A useless question. No one in the Maze saw anything. But Vis looked too thin-lipped about the shrug and Hanse looked back with a blacker stare still—had sudden awareness of the silence of the crowd when he spoke, of eyes on him; and he unfolded his arms and thought of how they had jostled in a doorway last night, Sjekso and Mradhon Vis, and Sjekso had laughed and acted his usual flippant self at Vis' ex-pense. Hanse drew quiet conclusions—quiet because he cut a mean figure at the moment, having gotten off with a dead man's last cash and last pleasure . . . he swept a glance about at faces dour with their own private conclusions. No love lost on him or dead Sjekso; but Sjekso being local and dead was the focus of pity, while regarding himself— there was quite another thing in the air.

Vis started to leave, edging away through the crowd. "That's the one to look at," Hanse said. "Hey, you! You don't like the questions, do you? The garrison threw you out, hey? You come back here, whoreson coward, you don't turn your back on me."

"He's crazy," Vis said, stopped behind an unwilling screen of onlookers who were trying to melt in all directions, but Mradhon kept with the migrating cover. "Figure who got his money and his woman, you figure that and wonder who did for him, that's who . . . ."

Hanse went for the knives. "Wasn't no mark on him," a youngish voice was shrilling. The crowd was swinging wildly out of the interval Vis was busy preserving. Minsy yelled, and several strong and larger arms wound themselves into Hanse's elbows and about his middle. He heaved and kicked to no use while Mradhon Vis, in the clear, straightened his person and his clothing.

"Crazy," Vis said again, and Hanse poured invective on him and most especially on those holding him from his knives—cold, sweating afraid, because Vis might do anything, or the crowd might, and the knives were all he had. But Vis walked off then, at an increasing pace, and Hanse launched another kick and a torrent of abuse on those hold-ing him.

"Easy." The grip on his left was Cappen Varra's, an arm tucked elbow to elbow into his arm and a hand locked on his wrist; he had no grudge with the minstrel. It was a calm voice, a cultivated, better-than-thou voice: Hanse hated Varra at the moment, but the grip persuaded and the object of his rage was off down the street. He took his weight on his own feet and slowly, brushing off his clothes while he stood fairly shaking with his anger, Varra eased up and let him go. Igan on the other side, big, not very bright Igan, let go his other arm, and claps on his shoulders and sympathy offered . . . started to settle his stomach and persuade him he had some credit here. "Let's have a drink," Varra said. "The corpsetakers will get the rumor—do you want to be standing here conspicuous? Come on inside."

He went as far as the door of the *Unicorn,* looked back, and there was Minsy standing over Sjekso sniffling; and Sjekso lying there a great deal sadder, open-eyed, while the crowd started away under the same logic.

Hanse wanted the drink.

Mradhon Vis turned the corner, none following, stopped against an alley wall and let the tremors pass from his limbs. Ugly, that back there. Corpses, he had seen—had created his share, in and out of mercenary service. He had no wish to take on useless trouble . . . not now, not with gold in his boot and a real prospect of more. A bodyguard sometimes, but he was not big enough for hired muscle; and with a surly and foreign look—even guard jobs were hard come by. He meant to be on time for this one. A patron who could come up with a fistful of gold on a whim was one to cultivate—if only her throat was still uncut. And that thought worried him: that was what had drawn him, against his natural and wary instincts, to that noisy scene outside the *Vulgar Unicorn*—a body he had last seen alive and escorting the patron who was his latest and most fervent hope. He was more than concerned.

Other alarums sounded in his mind, warnings of greater complexity, but he refused them, because they led to suspicions of traps and connivances; he had a knife in his belt, his wits about him, and no little experience of employers of all sorts, no few of whom had had notions of refusing him his pay at the end . . . one way and the other.

3

The *Vulgar Unicorn* still thumped with comings and goings, an untidy lot of early-morning patrons and irregulars. For his own part Hanse drank down his ale and nursed his head back to size, across the table from Cappen. He had no inclination to talk or to be the center of anything at the moment.

"They've got him off," the potboy said from the door. So the corpse was gone. That cleared out some of the traffic. Inquiry and snoopery might be close behind the corpsetakers. "Excuse me," Cappen Varra said, likewise discreet, and left his place at the table, bound for the door. Hanse recovered his equilibrium and stood up from the bench amid the general flow of bodies outward.

Someone touched his arm, a feathery light hand. He looked back, expecting Minsy, in no mood for her—and looked up instead into eyes like a statue's eyes, as unfocused and as vague, in a male face old/young and beardless. The man was blind.

"Hanse called Shadowspawn?" The voice was like the man, smooth and sere.

"What's my business with you?"

"You lost a friend."

"Ha. No friend. Acquaintance. What's it to you and me?"

The groping hand caught his arm and directed it to the other hand, which caught his fingers—he began to resist this eerie familiarity, and then felt the unmistakable metal heaviness of a coin.

"I'm listening."

"My employer has more for you."

"Where?"

"Not here. Do you want a name? Come outside."

The blind man would have taken him out the front, among the others, following the crowd. Hanse pulled him instead to another door, out into the back alley where few had gone and those already vanished. "Now," Hanse said, taking the blind man by the arm and backing him against the wall. "Who?"

"Enas Yorl."

He dropped his hand from the blind man's arm. "*Him*. For what?"

"He wants to talk to you. You come—recommended. And you'll be paid."

Hanse took in his breath and fingered his coin, looked down at it a space, found it new minted and heavy silver, and reckoned uneasily in what quarters he was recommended. Coin of that denomination was not so easily come by . . . but Enas Yorl—the wizard took few visitors . . . and there were things lately amiss in Sanctuary. Things larger than Hanse Shadowspawn. Rumors filtered down into the Maze.

Sjekso dead, unmarked, and Enas Yorl—offering money to talk to a thief: the world was mad. He walked it for the narrow lane it was.

"All right," he said, because Yorl had a long reach and because ignorance scared him. "You show me."

The blind man took his hand, and they went, down the alley and out again. It was so unfaltering a progress, so lacking a blind man's moves, that Hanse inevitably suspected some sham, such as beggars used—an actor and a good one, he thought, appreciating art.

*   *   *

Mradhon Vis fretted, paced below the balcony at the wooden stairs he had found last night. It was a place as sordid as any in the Maze, unpainted boards and age-slimed stone, a place atilt toward the alley and propped on boards and braces. It breathed decrepitude.

And more and more as he waited in this unlikely place, he gnawed on the thought of his hoped-for patron . . . dead, it might be, victim along with Sjekso, lying unfound as yet in some other alleyway. He had been mad to have gone off and left a woman in the backways of the Maze; a cat among hounds, that piece . . . and gone, snatched up, swallowed up—with friends, gods, more than likely money like that had friends *and* enemies. His mind built more and grimmer fancies . . . of princes and politics and clandestine meetings, this Sjekso perhaps more than he had seemed, this woman casting about money to be rid of a witness too much for the man she was with, an expedience—

He built such fancies, paced, stalked finally halfway up the creaking length of the stairs and came back down in indecision—then up again, gathering his courage and his resolve. He reached the swaying balcony, tried the door.

It swung inward, never locked or barred. That startled him. He slipped the knife from his belt and pushed the door all the way open—smelled incense and spices, perfumes. He walked in, pushed the door very gently shut again. A dim light came from a milky parchmented casement, cast color slantwise on a couch spread with russet silk, on dusty draperies and stacks of cloth and oddments.

Wings snapped and rustled. He spun about into a crouch, found only a large black bird chained to a perch against the wall in which the door was set. His heart settled again. He straightened. He should have smelled the creature: no large bird lived in a place without some fetor . . . but the perfume and the incense were that strong, that he had not. He ignored the creature, poked about amid the debris on a table, feminine clutter of small boxes and brocade

And the steps creaked, outside. He cast about him in a sudden fright, knife at the ready, slid in amongst the abundant shadows of the room. The steps reached the top, and the bird stirred and beat his wings in gusts as the door opened.

Black robes cast a silhouette against the daylight; the lady turned unerringly in his direction, took no fright at him or the knife, merely closed the door and reached up and dropped her hood from a tumble of midnight hair about a somber face. "Mradhon Vis," she said quietly. She *belonged* in the dark of this place, amid the clutter of worn and beautiful things. It was incredible that she could ever have walked through sunlight.

"Here," he said, "lady."

"Ischade," she named herself. "Do you make free of my lodgings?"

"The man you were with last night. He's dead."

"I've heard, yes." The voice was unreadable and cool. "We parted company. Sad. A handsome boy." She walked to the slight illumination of the parchment panes, drew an incense wand from others in a dragon vase and added it to the one which was dying, a curl of pale smoke in the light. She looked back then. "So. I have employment for you. I trust you're not fastidious."

"Not often."

"You'll find rewards. Gold. And it might be—further employment."

"I don't shy off at much."

"I'll trust not." She walked near him, and he recalled the knife and flipped it into its sheath. Her eyes followed the move and looked up at him . . . grave, so very grave. Women of quality he had seen tended to flutter the eyes; this one stared eye to eye, and he found himself inclined to break the contact, to look down or elsewhere. She extended her hand, close to touching him, a move he thought might be an invitation to take liberties of his own.

And then she drew the hand back and the moment passed. She walked over and offered the bird a morsel from the cup at the side of the stand. The creature took it with a great flapping of wings.

"What do you have in mind?" he asked, vexed at this mincing about, with so much at stake. "It's not legal, I'll guess."

"It might involve powerful enemies. I can guarantee—equally powerful protections. And the reward. Of course that."

"Who's to die? Someone else . . . like that boy last night?"

She looked about, lifted a brow, then turned her attentions back to the bird, stroked black feathers with a forefinger. "Priests, perhaps. Does that bother you?"

"Not unduly. A man wonders—"

"The risk is mine. So are the consequences. Only I need someone to take care of physical difficulties. I assure you I know what I'm about."

There was more than the scent of incense about the place. Of a sudden there was quite another thing . . . the smell of wizardry. He gathered that, as he had been picking up the pieces all along. It was not a thing a man expected to find—everywhere. But it was here. And there were crimes done in the Maze, by that means and others. Spells, he had dealt with, at least at distance . . . had a hint then of more rewards than gold. "You have protections, do you?"

A second time that cool look. "I assure you it's well thought out."

"Protections for me as well."

"They'd be far less interested in you." She walked back to the table, to the light, a shadow against it. "This evening," she said, "you'll earn the gold I gave you. But perhaps, just perhaps, you ought to go out again. And come back again when I tell you. To prove you know that my door isn't yours."

Heat surged to his face, words into his mouth. He thought of the money and it stifled the rest.

"Now," she said. "About the other thing you have in mind . . . well, that might come later, mightn't it? But you choose, Mradhon Vis. There's gold . . . or other rewards. And you can tell me which you'd like. Ah. Both, perhaps. Ambition. But know me better, Mradhon Vis, before you propose anything aloud. You might not like my terms. Take the gold. The likes of Sjekso Kinzan is commoner than you. And far less to regret."

So she had killed the boy. Markless, and cold and stiff within sight of the doorway which might have saved him. He thought about it . . . and the ambition persisted. It was power. And that was more than the money, much more.

"You'll go now," she said very, very softly. "I wouldn't tempt you. Consider we have a bargain. Now get out."

No one talked to him after that fashion . . . at least not twice. But he found himself silenced and his steps tending to the door. He stopped there and looked back to prove he could.

"I've needed a man of your sort," she said, "in certain ways."

He walked out, into the sun.


4


It was one of those neighborhoods less frequented by the inhabitants of the Maze, and Hanse had a dislocated, uncomfortable feeling in this guide and this place, creeping as they did through the cleaner, wider back ways of Sanctuary at large. It was not his territory or close to any of his known boltholes.

And in the shadows of an alley far along the track, his guide paused and shed an inner and ragged cloak from beneath the outer one, proffering it. "Put it on. You'll not want to be noticed hereabouts for yourself."

Hanse took it, not without distaste: it was gray and a mass of patches. He swung it about his shoulders and it was long enough to hide him down to midcalf.

His guide held out a dingy bandage as well. "For your eyes. For your own safety. The house has . . . protections. If I told you only to shut your eyes, you'd forget at the worst moment. And my master wants you whole."

Hanse stared at the offered rag, liking all of this less and less; and very softly he drew the dagger from his arm sheath and extended the blade toward the guide's face.

Not a flinch or blink. That sent a prickling up his spine. He brought the point of the blade very close to the blind eyes and, truth, the man did not react. He flipped the blade into its sheath.

"If you have doubts," the blind man said, "accept my master's assurances. But don't under any account look from beneath the bandage once inside. My blindness . . . has reasons."

"Huh." Hanse took the dirty bandage, feeling far from assured; but he had dealt with nervous uptowners before, and under conditions and precautions more bizarre and hazardous. He wound it about his eyes and tied it firmly: it was true—about Enas Yorl's doorway there were rumors, and bad ones.

And when the blind man grasped his sleeve and began to guide him a quiet panic set in: he had no liking of this helplessness—they entered a street, he guessed, because he heard a change in the sound of their footsteps; he sensed watchers about, stumbled suddenly on an unevenness in the paving and heard the blind man hiss a warning, wrenching at his sleeve: "Three steps up."

Three steps to the top and a moment waiting while his guide opened a door. Then a tug at his sleeve drew him inside, where a cold draft blew on his face until the door boomed solidly shut behind him. Instinctively he put a hand on his wrist sheath, keeping the knife hilt comfortingly under his fingers. Again a tug at his sleeve drew him on . . . the guide; it must still be the guide and no stranger by him. He wanted a voice. "How much further with this?" he asked.

Claws scrabbled on stone on his left, a heavy body slithered closer in haste. He made a frantic move to get the knife out, but the guide jerked him to a standstill. "Don't offend it," the guide said. "Don't try to look. Come on."

A reptile hissed; and by that sound it was a big one. Something flicked over the surface of his boot and coiled about his ankle, instantly withdrawing. The guide drew him on, away from the touch and down a hall which echoed more closely on either hand, where the distance was all in front of them . . . and into a place which smelled of coals and hot metal and a strange, musky incense.

The guide stopped, on his right. "Shadowspawn," a new voice said, a throaty sigh, low, and to his left. He reached for the blindfold, hesitated. "Go ahead," the new voice invited him, and he pulled it down.

A robed and hooded form sat in this narrow marble hall—fine robes, in midnight blue and bright silver, in deep shadow, beside a heating brazier. Hanse blinked in the recent pressure on his eyes—the robes seemed to swell and sink in the vicinity of the chest, and the right arm, the hand resting visible . . . it went dark, that hand, and then, a deception of his abused eyes, went pale and young. "Shadowspawn." The voice too was clearer, younger. "You lost a friend last night. Do you want to know how?"

That unnerved him, a threat on a level he understood. His hand fidgeted toward his sheath-bearing wrist, his mind conjuring more and unblinded servants in the shadows.

"Ischade is her name," the voice of Enas Yorl continued, rougher now . . . and was the figure itself smaller and wider? "She's also a thief. And she killed Sjekso Kinzan. Do you want more?"

Hanse assumed a more careless stance, flipped the hand outward, palm up. "Money got me here. If you want more of my time to listen to this, it costs."

"She's in your own neighborhood. That information might be worth even more than money to you."

"What, this name of yours?"

"Ischade. A thief. She's better than you, Shadowspawn. Your knives might not stop her." The voice roughened further. "But you're good and you're smart. I've heard so. From—no matter. I have my sources. I'm told you're extraordinarily discreet." He moved the fingers, a gesture sideways. "Darous, give him the amulet."

The blind man drew something from the heart of his robes; Hanse's eyes darted nervously from the wizard he was trying to watch to that distraction, a gold teardrop that spun and dazzled on a chain.

"Take it," Enas Yorl said. A degree rougher yet. A sigh like the sea, or like hot iron plunging into water. "This Ischade—steals from wizards. Steals spells and suchlike. Her own abilities are small in that regard . . . but she made a mistake once, and the spell on Ischade is nothing small or harmless. A man who—shares her bed, shall we say? discovers that. He dies . . . of no apparent cause. Like your friend Kinzan. Like a number of others I know of. The curse affects her humor. Imagine—to pursue lover after lover and kill them all. If I hire you, Shadowspawn, you might be glad of such protections as I offer you. Take it."

"Who says I'm to hire?" Hanse looked unhappily from servant to master. The hand which now peeped from the shifting robe was woman-delicate. "Who says that a dozen Sjeksos are any of my concern? I'm my concern. *Me*. Hanse. I don't have any interest in Sjekso. So I just stay out of the whole business. That's what interests me."

"Then you'll run, will you, and find some safer place to steal." The voice ground like rocks tumbling. "And you'll ignore my gold and protection. Both of which you may need.—It's no great thing I ask, simply a matter of spying out where she is. Did I ask you to go against her yourself? No. A small favor, well paid. And you've done favors like that before. Would you have that known—that you've worked in high places? Your past patron wouldn't appreciate that publicity. He wouldn't retaliate against me, no. But you—how long do you think you'd live, thief, if your connections went public?"

Hanse had sucked in his breath. He forced a grin then, struck a lighter pose, hand on hip. "So, well, paid in gold, you said?"

"After."

"Now."

"Darous, give the man sufficient as earnest. And give him the amulet."

Hanse turned from the wizard, whose voice had acquired a hissing quality; and the hand—had vanished into one of those blinks of the eye that deceived the mind and memory that anything had—a moment earlier—been there. Hanse took the chain and put it over his head. The amulet itself hit his bare throat and it was bitter and burning cold. The servant held out a purse. Hanse took that, felt the weight in his hand, opened the neck of it and looked at the gold and silver abundance inside. His heart beat wildly, while against his neck the metal failed to be warmed as metal ought, stayed there like lump of ice. It sent a vague malaise through him, which changed character from moment to moment like—

"So what am I supposed to do?" he asked. "And where do I look?"

"A house," a woman's voice said to his right, and he looked, blinked, found only the hooded form in the chair. "Seventh in the alley called Snake. On the right as you go from the Serpentine at Acban's Passage. She lodges there. Mark what she does and where she goes. Don't attempt to prevent her. I only want to know the business that brought her to Sanctuary."

Hanse let go a sigh, relief, for all that the robes shifted again—felt a wild confidence in himself (it might have been the money) that he could get out of this easily, and with still more money, and an employer satisfied, who was powerful and rich. Hanse Shadowspawn, Hanse the thief, small Hanse the knife . . . had friends in high places, a condition unexpected. He expanded in this knowledge and stood loose, dropped the purse into his shirt, ignoring the chill at his neck. "So, then, and I come here from time to time and report to you."

"Darous will find you from time to time," the same voice said. The changing seemed to have settled for the moment. "Depend on that contact. Good day to you. Darous will show you out."

Hanse made a flourish of a bow, turned to the servant and indicated they should go.

"The blindfold," the blind servant said. "Use it, master thief. My master would regret an accident, especially now."

Hanse put his hand on the metal droplet that hung like ice at his throat, turned to glower at the wizard. "I thought this was supposed to take care of things like that."

"Did I say so? No, I didn't say. I wouldn't be rash in relying on it. Against some things it has no protection at all. My guardians in the hall, for instance, would never notice it."

"Then what good is it?"

"Much . . . in its right place. Afraid, thief?"

"Huh," Hanse said critically. Laughed and swung on his heel, caught the blind servant by the arm and started out with him. But remembering the movements in the outer hall, the thing which had brushed at his leg—"All right, all right," he said suddenly, and let go the man's arm to put the blindfold back in place. "All right, rot you, wait."

The thief went, and Enas Yorl rose from his chair. His shape had settled again into a form far more pleasant than most. He walked to a hall more interior to his house, examined hands delicate and fine, that were purest pleasure to touch—and all the worse when they would begin . . . next moment or next day . . . to change.

It was a revenge, a none too subtle revenge, but then the wizard who
had cursed him had never been much on subtleties, which was why his
young wife had had Enas Yorl in her bed in the first place—a younger
Enas Yorl in those days, but age meant nothing now. The forms his
affliction cast on him might be old or young, male or female, human or
—not. And the years frightened him. All the time he had had, to become
master of his arts, and his arts had no power to undo another's spell.
No one could. And some of his forms, still, were young, which
suggested that he did not age, that there was no end to this torment—
forever.

Yet wizards died, lately, in Sanctuary. Tell the thief that was the
name of the game, and even threats might not persuade him. But in
these deaths, Enas Yorl was desperately, passionately interested. Ischade . . . Ischade: the name tasted of vile rumor; a wizardous thief, a
preyer upon wizards, a conniver in shadows and dark secrets, this
Ischade, with reason to hate the prey she chose.

And all her lovers died, softly, gently for the most part; but Enas
Yorl was not particularly in that regard.

He paused a moment, hearing the great outer doors boom shut. The
thief was on his way, thief to take a thief. And Enas Yorl felt a sudden
cold. Wizards died, in Sanctuary, and this possibility fascinated him,
taunted him with hope and fear: with fear—because shapes like this he
wore turned him coward, reminding him there were pleasures to be had.
He feared death at such times . . . while the thief he had sent out went
to find it for him.

Darous came back, softly stopped on the marble paving. "Well
done," Enas Yorl said.

"Follow him, master?"

"No," Enas Yorl said. "No need. None at all." He looked distractedly about again, with the queasiness of impending change upon him.
He fled suddenly, his steps quicker and quicker on the pavings. Darous
could see nothing—Darous sensed, but that was another matter. There
was, however, pride.

And within the hour, in a dark recess of the house with the basilisks
prowling the halls unchecked, something gibbered within a pile of midnight robes, and with keen sense of beauty imprisoned in that moaning
heap, longed toward oblivion.

Darous, who saw nothing, sensed the essence of this change and kept
himself to other halls.

The basilisks, whose cold eyes saw very well, writhed scaly-lithe away in haste, outstared and overwhelmed.

5

Not many women came to the *Unicorn,* not many at least of the elevated sort, and this one took a table to herself and held it. One of the *Unicorn's* muddled regulars brushed by, and leaned close, and offered to sit down . . . but a long hand from beneath those black robes waved an idle and disinterested dismissal. A ring glinted there, a silver serpent, and the bully's bleared eyes stared at that, at immaculate long nails, into dark almond eyes beneath the shadowy hood. And a fog of alcohol seemed to grow thicker then, so that he forgot all the wittiness he had meant to say, forgot for a moment to close his mouth. A second wave of the thin, olive-skinned hand and he forgot everything and stumbled away in confusion.

"Acolyte," Cappen Varra thought in his own counsel, slouched on a bench in the nook nearest the back door. There was somewhat of chaos in the *Unicorn* of late, a certain lack of the authority which had held the peace, and *that* sort moved in, cheap muscle. But the woman—that was something extraordinary, like the *Unicorn* before; a woman, a stranger in the neighborhood . . . He was intrigued by the dark robes and the fineness of them, and his fingers moved restlessly on the moisture-ringed tabletop, thinking of a song, fingering imaginary strings of the harp he had pawned (again) and thinking—oddly—on Hanse Shadowspawn, in another and quite irrelevant train of thought, as Hanse had ridden his mind all day. Sjekso gone, Hanse vanished utterly, and night falling out-side . . . Hanse was up to no good, it was certain. There had been nei-ther sight nor sound of him all day long and certain whispers passed in the *Unicorn,* with more and more credibility: of revenge, of Hanse, about the likelihood of survival of one Mradhon Vis—or Hanse, should the two meet. And about a certain blind man who had found his way without aid into the *Unicorn* and out again, with Hanse in tow . . . a blind man and no beggar, for all his looks—but a man of darker rumor.

It was curious business, and more than mildly unpleasant. Cappen was not sanguine. Hanse stalking Vis—it was quite unlikely. Hanse was all temper and bluster. If anyone was doing the stalking it was likeliest

to be Vis, and Hanse was ill-advised to have prodded that surly-coun-
tenanced bastard . . . far more trouble than Hanse really wanted, that
was sure. Likely it was Hanse in hiding, if Vis had not yet got him.
Cappen picked up his cup again, and of a sudden his eyes hooded and
while his hand carrying his cup to his lips never faltered, the sip he took
was slow and studied: he watched a second man make attempt on the
lady's table.

And that was Mradhon Vis himself . . . who went up quietly, and
met no rebuff at all. The lady lifted her face and her eyes to him—a face
certainly worth a song, although a dark and somber one. And when her
eyes lit on Mradhon Vis, very quietly the lady got to her feet and in
Vis' still silent company . . . walked toward the back door of the
tavern. Only a few heads turned, of those at the other tables, and those
only casually. There was at the same time the faintest of pricklings at
Cappen's nape, a feeling he knew: he touched the amulet at his throat,
a silver coiled serpent . . . a gift, a protection against spells, more effi-
cacious than most priest-blessed gimcrack tokens . . . under its own
terms. He saw, with a touch of unease the greater because no one else
in the room seemed to see . . . how Mradhon Vis and his dark companion moved, with common purpose and peculiar menace.

Strangeness enough progressed in Sanctuary . . . deaths which made
a man naturally think on protections of the sorcerous kind, and to be
glad of them if he had them, because where the powerful died, wizardry
was about, selective of its victims thus far, but not—perhaps—exclusive
of them. There was Sjekso Kinzan, who had been no one. Cappen wondered did such protection as he possessed . . . protect or mark him;
and as the lady and Mradhon Vis came past his table by the door—

A moment Cappen was looking up and the lady looked down at him,
more familiar in that stare than he would have liked. The prickling
about the amulet became strong indeed while he stared, lost in those
dark eyes with a sense of deadly peril, of his whole life resting loose and
endangered, as if some small nudge on anyone's part might tumble it.
"You're beautiful," he murmured, because three truths was the rule of
the amulet if it was to work at all—"You're dangerous—and foreign
here."

She lingered, and reaching down picked up his cup where it sat; lifted
it, sipped and set it down again, all with an eerie hint of humor or menace flaunted at him, at him who alone in the room but Mradhon Vis—or
he exempt?—Alone of all the others, Cappen stared back at her with

his mind clear and with knowledge, with something gut-wrenching telling him that everything about this woman was askew.

She smiled at him, a parting of the lips on white teeth, a flash of dark
eyes, an impression that she admired what she saw . . . and all the
fineness he kept so studiously, his elegance, different from others about
him, his talents, his—if streetworn—finery. . . was suddenly perilous to
him, marking him out among all the rest. And most of all . . . she
knew he resisted her.

She left then, swept out the door which Mradhon Vis held open, a
gust of wind and a sudden thud of the door closing. Cappen wanted
wine . . . but his hand stopped short of the cup she had just set down
again, the metal she had had her lips to and the wine her mouth had
tasted. He pushed back from the table and the bench scraped loudly
over the noise of the other patrons. He hesitated looking at the door
which led out to the backways, not wanting to go out there, in the gathering dark.

But Mradhon Vis, linked with that, and Sjekso cold dead with no
mark on him; and Hanse outright disappeared, hunting Mradhon Vis,
as all the Maze surmised . . . .

Hanse had involved himself in something which was likely to be the
death of him, and what concern that was to Cappen Varra was unclear
to Cappen himself, only that he had drunk with Hanse of late, with a
short and lately successful thief and ruffian who had wanted—almost
pathetically—to acquire style, who spent most that came into his hands
on the finer things, a cloak—o gods! that cloak!—Cappen's aristocratic
soul shuddered. But of the unassuming ruffians in the lot, of what quality there was to be had in the Maze, in Hanse there existed at least the
hankering after something else.

The business had marked Hanse down—and now stopped and stared
at himself. It was always safer, he reckoned, to walk at a thing than to
have it walking up at his back—later and unforeseen. Cappen opened
the door carefully, went out into the backways, his hand on his rapier
hilt, recalling that Sjekso had used the same door last night. But there
was only the dark outside, amid the litter of old barrels and used bottles. The woman in black had vanished, and Vis with her, vanished, and
in what direction Cappen was in no wise certain.

Patience was rewarded. Vis, by the gods, and this Ischade . . . in
company; and Hanse crouched lower in the shadows of the alley, a chill
up his back, his fingers rubbing at the well polished hilt of his left boot

knife. That promised a revenge within his own grasp: so Yorl wanted the woman, and if Yorl settled with her, then Vis went in the same bargain. Hanse evened his breathing, calmed himself with wild hopes, first of getting out of this Yorl business and then of having Yorl to settle Vis —the means by which the street might be safe again for Hanse Shadowspawn. Report, Yorl had said, and by the gods, he was anxious to have it done, if only they went to earth for the night. . . .

They turned, not the way he had anticipated, toward the lodgings he had been watching, but the other way, toward the Serpentine. Hanse swore and slipped out from his concealment, shadowed them most carefully in their course through the debris of the alley and out onto the street. The moon was not yet up; the only light came from the city itself, a vague glimmering on a bank of fog toward the harbor which diffused across the sky and promised one of those nights in which light spread through milky mist, from whatever sources—a thieves' night, and a worse to come.

The pair tended on up the Serpentine, bold as dockside whores . . . but odd sights were common enough in the Maze by night, masks, cloaks, bright colors flaunted by night when the kindly dark masked the signs of wear and their threadbare condition. Man and woman, they were only conspicuous by their plainness, the woman shrouded by the robe and hood so that she might be instead some night-prowling priest with an unlikely and rough guard.

Hanse followed, in and out amongst the occasional walkers on the street, a kind of stalking at which he had some skill.

. . . So, well, it answered, at least, what Hanse had been up to, and upset all Cappen Varra's calculations about Hanse as bluster and no threat. Cappen stopped at the corner with the trio in view, glanced over his own shoulder with a touch of mad humor and the desperate thought that the whole was getting to be a procession in the dark streets . . . the woman and Vis, and Hanse, and now himself—but at least there was no fifth person that he could see, following him.

Hanse moved off, slipping casually down the street amid the ordinary traffic with a skill Cappen found amazing . . . he had never seen Hanse work, not after this fashion; had never particularly wanted to think at depth on the essence of the smallish thief, that there was in fact something more than the temper and the knives and the vanity which made this man dangerous. Having seen it, he reckoned to himself that the only sensible course for him now was to go back into the *Unicorn,* work

his way into whatever game might start—his current hope of prosperity—
and forget Hanse entirely, never minding a moment when Hanse turned
up as stiff and cold as Sjekso had, which was assuredly where he was
headed at the moment. But perhaps it was the poetry of the matter, the
suspicion that there might be something worth the witnessing . . . perhaps it was the assurance that Hanse was into far more than he knew,
and that somewhere up there, without untidy recourse to the rapier that
swung at his side . . . he might overtake the revenge-bound lunatic and
talk him out of it. Hanse—was the only likely ally in a situation of his
own; the woman had *looked* at him back there, and there was nagging
at him an unwelcome vision, Hanse lying at the doorstep in the morning
and himself there the day after—macabre fancy it might be, but the wind
still blew up his back. There was only the matter of catching Hanse to
stop him, and that was like putting one's hands on a shadow. Cappen
was not accustomed to feel awkward in his moves, looked down on the
louts and ne'er-do-wells who walked the Maze; possessed a grace
surpassing most—in any situation.

But not in walking the Maze by dark and unseen. Hanse was in his
element, and Cappen followed him artlessly, down the length of the Serpentine, and into territory of the city at large—where the law came, and
where a wanted thief was less than safe. The houses and shops here
were more sturdy, and finally magnificent, and those latter existed behind walls, and most with bars on the windows. Walkers grew scarce for
a time, and Cappen hung further back, afraid that he himself might attract the notice of the pair Hanse followed . . . which he earnestly did
not want.

One street and another, and sometimes a passage through narrower
ways where Cappen found Hanse going more carefully, where they four
were virtually alone and where a false move could alert the pair ahead.
Cappen stayed far back then, and once he thought he had lost them all
. . . but a quick move around a corner put them all in view again.
Hanse looked back in that instant, while Cappen tried to stay incon-
spicuously part of a stack of barrels, recalling Hanse's knives, and the
murk of the night. The fog was coming on and the light played tricks; a
light mist slicked the stones . . . and still the pair kept moving, out of
the merchant quarter and into the quarter of the gods, past the square
of the Promise of Heaven, where prostitutes, bedraggled in the mist, sat
their accustomed benches like rain-soaked birds—They swung past this
place and into the Avenue of Temples itself; and Cappen shrugged his
cloak about him with a genuinely wretched chill and marvelled at the

trio ahead, who moved, pursued and pursuer, with such a tireless purpose.

And then another alley, a sudden move aside, which almost caught
Hanse himself by surprise, near the magnificence of the dome of the
temple of Ils and Shipri.

There Hanse tucked himself away into shadow and Cappen quite lost
sight of him, among the buttresses and the statuary of the outthrust
wing of the temple . . . vanished.

Then the woman in black went out into the street, ascended the plain
center of the steps of Ils and Shipri, toward the temple guards who
warded the constantly open doors in these uneasy times . . . four men
and well armed, setting hands on hilts at once as they were approached.
The woman cast back her hood: swords stayed undrawn, hands unmoving, numb as the patrons of the *Unicorn*.

Then another shadow began to move, from the unwatched side of the
steps, a man from out of the shadows, knife in hand, a swift stalking
. . . which afforded Cappen even less of comfort and made him think
that a wayward minstrel perhaps should have spent a safer, drier night
in the *Unicorn*.

Follow, the wizard had said, and Hanse pressed himself close against
the wall, in the scant shadow afforded by a bit of brickwork, pressed
himself there and watched in chill discomfort—blinked in horror while it
happened, and four men died with swords still in sheath—only the last
attempted a defense, and Mradhon Vis cut his throat in one quick and
unmistakable move. Hanse blinked again and discovered to his consternation that the dark one, the woman, was gone, Mradhon Vis crouching
now in sole possession of that bloody threshold. Hanse fingered his belt
knife like a warding talisman; and wanted only to stay put, but all the
while the icy cold at the pit of his neck, more biting than the cold of the
mist, reminded him what he was there to do—what other power there
was to offend. And he waited, reckoning every small move Mradhon
Vis made, crouched over the bodies of the guards—every small shifting
of a man busy at corpse-looting, every glance about as some hardy passerby noised along the main avenue—but none saw, none came near.

The woman delayed about her business inside: it might have been a
moment, or far longer—time did tricks in his mind. Hanse shifted uneasily, finally gathered his nerve, slipped out of that safe concealment and,
in the turning of Vis' head toward a distraction on the street . . . he

eased past a gap in cover and into the alley Vis and the woman had left, along the temple itself.

He reached the first of three barred windows, and with utmost silence took the chance and seized the bars, hoisted himself up to see. The breath passed silently over his teeth and his gut knotted up—a robber of wizards, Enas Yorl had said: and now a thief who preyed on gods.

That struck hard . . . not that he darkened the doorway of his city gods with his presence or practiced alms; but there were territories, there were limits to a thief's audacity . . . or it went hard for all. It was his *craft,* by the gods, his *art* the woman involved; and they were old, those gods, and belonged in Sanctuary, as the Rankan emperor's new lot never would. And the woman, the foreigner, the witch-thief, climbed up to the lap of bearded Ils himself and lifted the fabled necklace of Harmony from about the marble neck.

"Shalpa," Hanse swore silently, and with chilling appropriateness—let himself ever so carefully down from his vantage with one chill throbbing about his neck and another one travelling his backbone. So Enas Yorl wanted a report. And the gods of old Ilsig were plundered by a foreign witch while the Rankans moved in with their new lot of deities down the block, with scaffolds and plans and the evident intent of overshadowing the gods of Ilsig. Prince Kadakithis and the Rankan gods; and: "recommended," Enas Yorl had said, sending a thief out to keep watch on this god-thievery.

Hanse flattened himself back into his concealment with a sense of a world amiss, of matters under way no mere thief wanted part of. He had mixed in Kittycat's connivances once to his discomfort . . . but now, now it was possible Enas Yorl had a side of his own.

And hired help.

A footstep toward the temple front warned him: he crouched low and held his breath—Ischade, rejoining Mradhon Vis. "Done," he heard her say; and "here's an end. Let's be gone, and quickly."

Of course an outsider like Mradhon Vis—of course a man not Ilsig, who would have no scruples in killing Ilsig priests or robbing Ilsig gods.

In the emperor's hire? Hanse wondered, which was far too much and too clear wondering for a thief; the sweat was coursing down his ribs despite the misty chill of the air. He was not sure at all now what side Yorl was . . . and it occurred to him to tear the amulet from his neck, drop it in the alley and run.

But how far? And how long? He thought a second and chilling time of the wizard and his connections; recalled Sjekso; and Kadakithis himself . . . a prince of some small gratitude for services a thief had rendered; but more than dangerous if certain rumors started, that Yorl could spread . . . effortlessly.

The pair headed back the way they had come, and he set out after them, seeing no other course.

More and more bizarre, this midnight wandering. Cappen went rigid in his hiding place first as the quarry passed, and then as he caught sight of Hanse again, padding after them as before.

So there was no encounter. They went out and they did murder and came back, while Hanse followed after having seen what Hanse had seen . . . very unlike Hanse. Cappen suspected motives ill-defined, gave shape to nothing, only sure it was something more than Hanse's private impulses that moved him now. He recalled the way in which the woman had passed a roomful of patrons at the *Unicorn,* in which she and her companion went where they liked on the street, in which guards died like slaughtered cattle. . . .

The relief Cappen felt at seeing Hanse mobile and not lying stiff in the alley further on, gave way to a horror at the silence of all that was done, the neatness of it; and a subtle dread of this pacing about the streets. The procession which had started to be humorous and might have become yet more so on the return . . . now assumed a thoroughly macabre character, such that he forbore to contact Hanse when he had, for one instant, the chance. Hanse's face too, in the small glimpse he had had of it as he passed, had the wan, set look of terror.

They went back very much the way they had come, and long before they came close to the alley behind the *Unicorn,* Cappen had a sure idea that such was their destination.

6

The pair of them went well enough where Hanse had figured they would go, in the alley behind the *Unicorn.* He held back as he had been doing and kept them in sight . . . wished anew that he had had the chance during the day to creep up to Ischade's lodgings and have a closer look, but she had been there most of the day, and daylight and the fact that it was the second story gave him no easy options. When

she had left, toward evening, he had been obliged to follow, having no
real idea of her motives and habitual movements . . . and well that he
had followed, since this evening had turned out as it had.

But there was still, as there had been, a presence on his trail—and
that was Cappen. Hanse knew that much, had caught sight of the minstrel out of his own territory and seen him more than once on streets
where Cappen had no business being.

And who had hired Cappen?

It was not Cappen's custom to take employment; he diced and he
sang songs; but never this kind of work. He was not suited for it. Enas
Yorl could have hired better. Far better.

But this Ischade—

Hanse refused the idea. And yet constantly nagging at him in that
small nook of his mind where he tucked coincidences, was Cappen's
presence that morning. But Cappen had been in the game too, like
Mradhon Vis and Sjekso; and Cappen had gotten off with some profit,
as Cappen usually did.

Cappen bought him a drink; and that was uncommon, that Cappen
had that much to spare. But it was in Cappen's nature to play the lord
and throw about what he had.

Cappen had ducked out of the *Unicorn* a scant moment before the
blind man came, having assured Hanse's presence there with that drink
. . . but that then circled the matter back to Yorl, where it made least
sense.

Hanse forbore another glance over his shoulder, reckoning that even
Cappen's unskilled stalking might pick that up. He kept his attention toward the pair in front of him, kept moving where necessary—watched
them reach the steps and both of them start up the stairs toward the
lady's lodgings, without any exchanged movement which might mean
the passing of the loot.

Now . . . now while the noise of the creaking stairs gave him sound
to rely on in tracking them—he had his chance, and took it, a path he
had marked out that afternoon. He carefully set his hands on a barrel,
levered himself up into a tuck and sought the next level of debris,
noiselessly, one after the other, holding his breath as one foothold
rocked and the next proved stable.

He made the roof as the pair made the door and opened it; he edged
along it with the greatest care—a wooden roof at least, and not the tiles
some fancied uptown. Even now he would have preferred to be rid of
the boots and to go barefoot, as he had worked in the days before pros-

perity, but he figured there was no time for such. He edged his way around the ell of the roof on wet shingles and out onto that section over the room itself.

There was noise inside, a sharp, animal sound which lifted his nape hairs and made him less certain he wanted near this place at all. He edged closer to the very edge of the eaves, put his head over, viewing upside down where only parchment covered the window and formed a scant barrier to sounds and voices from inside. He heard footsteps clearly, heard a flapping sound . . . and suddenly a jolt and crack as an aged shingle snapped in two under his hand on the edge. It flung him overbalance, but he caught himself on his belly, spread-eagled on the roof. "Hssst!" he heard from inside, and he swore silently by appropriate gods and began to work his way hastily back from the vulnerable edge.

His hands, his legs went numb; his breath grew short and the talisman at his throat became a lump of ice and fire. Magic, he thought, some warding spell flung his way . . . he dealt with wizards; and it was a trap. He strove to make his limbs do what they well knew how to do: carefully he put a knee on a wet and worn row of shingles on the slant.

One broke; he slipped, a rattling loud career down the layered face of the shingles, his feet swinging into empty air, his wild final thought that if he fought the fall now he might go head downward or onto his back. He let go, slid, expecting a dizzying long drop—the barrels, maybe, the debris of the alley might break his fall and save his back and legs—

He hit the edge of the porch unprepared, a shock that sent him tumbling a further few feet down the stairs backward—a ridiculous lot of noise, his battered mind was thinking through the pain, an embarrassing lot of noise . . .

And then the door was open above him, and he was lying sprawled on his back head downward on the narrow steps, looking up through his feet at Mradhon Vis, who came with the metal flash of a dagger in his fist.

Hanse went for the belt knife, curled up and threw it with all he had: Mradhon Vis staggered back with an oath, spun half about by the cast as Hanse twisted to get up, his feet higher than his head with a railing on his left and a wall at his right, which hindered more than helped. He got as far as his knee when the bravo's foot caught him under the jaw and hurled him back into the wall; and a knife followed—further humiliation—up against his throat while Mradhon Vis grabbed his hair and twisted. Hanse fought to get loose; he thought that he struggled, but the messages were slow getting to his limbs and the burning of the amulet at his throat distracted him with the feeling that he was choking—or was it the knife?

"Bring him up," a female voice said from the light of the doorway; and Hanse looked blurrily up into it, while a hand twisted into his hair jerked him up and the dagger shifted a keen point to his back under the ribs. He went up the stairs, and followed the blackrobed figure which retreated inside. There seemed little else at the moment that he could do, that he wanted to do, bruised as he was and with his wits leaden weighted. He blinked in the interior light, stared dully at the russet silks, at the clutter of objects separately beautiful, but which lay disarrayed—like bones in a nest, he thought distantly, thinking of something predatory; and he jerked at the sudden racket and flutter of wings, a fluttering of the lamplight in the commotion of a great black bird which sat on its perch over against the wall.

"You can go," the woman said, and Hanse's heart lifted for the instant. "You've been paid. Come back tomorrow." And then he knew she spoke to Mradhon Vis.

"Tomorrow."

"Then."

"Is that all there is? And leave this here?" A jab at Hanse's back. "I took a knife, woman; I've got a hole in my arm and you keep this and turn me out in the wet, do you?"

"Out," she said, in a lower tone.

And to Hanse's bewilderment the knife retreated. Hanse moved then, turned in the instant, thinking of a quick stab from behind, his own hand to his wrist sheath . . . and he had the blade out, facing Mradhon Vis—but somehow the rest of the move failed him, and he watched dully as Mradhon Vis turned away and sulked his way to the open door.

"Close it behind you," the woman said, and Mradhon Vis did so, not slamming it. Hanse blinked, and the amulet at his neck hurt more than any bruise he had taken. It burned, and he had no sense left to get rid of it.

Ischade smiled abstractedly at her guest, left him so a moment, having greater business at hand. "Peruz," she said softly, shook back her hood, and taking from her robes the necklace, she drew near the huge raptor . . . or the guise it wore. With the greatest of care she slipped the necklace into a small case which hung from the side of the stand and fastened the case in its turn to the scaly leg of the bird. Peruz stood still too, uncommonly so, his great wings folded. A last time she teased the breast feathers, the softness about the neck—she had grown fond of the creature in recent weeks, as anything that shared her life. She smiled at the regard of a cold topaz eye.

"Open the window," she instructed her intruder/guest, and he moved, slowly, with the look of a man caught in a bad dream. "Open it," and he did so. She launched Peruz and he flew, with a clap of wings, a hurtling out toward the dark, a lingering coolness of wind.

So he was sped. Her employer had all he had paid to have—and well paid. And she was alone. She let go her mental grip on the ruffian . . . and at once his face showed panic and he whipped up the knife he had in hand. She stopped that. He looked confused, as if he had quite forgotten what the dagger was doing in his hand. And that effort would cost her, come the morning: on the morrow would be a fearful headache and a mortal lassitude, so that she would want to do nothing for days but drowse. But now the blood was still quick in her veins, the excitement lingered, and in the threat of ennui and solitude which followed any completed task . . . she felt another kind of excitement, and looked on her uninvited visitor knowing, quite knowing that at such times she was mad, and what it cost to cure such madness for the time. . . .

Attractive. Her tastes were broad, but in that curiously compartmented mind of hers, it pleased her . . . the mission done . . . that there was room for Mradhon to go. Here stood instead an unmissable someone—he had all the marks of that condition. It was justice owed her for her pains . . . twice as sweet when it all came together just as it did now, her satisfaction and the last untidy threads of a business, tied together and nipped short.

She held out her hand and came closer, feeling that sweet/sad warmth that sex set into her blood . . . and had felt it, at every weakening moment, from the time she had robbed the wrong wizard and left him living. In the morning she would even feel some torment for it, a tangled regret: the handsome ones always left her with that, a sense of beauty wasted. But for the moment reason was quite gone.

And there had been so many before.

Hanse still held the knife and could not feel it; then heard the distant shock it made hitting the floor. There was no pain of the bruises, no sensation but of warmth and of the woman's nearness, her dark eyes regarding him, her perfume enveloping him. And the amulet at his throat,

which gave off a bitter cold: that was the one last focus of his discomfort. She put her arms about his neck and her fingers found the chain.
"You don't want this," she said, lifting it ever so gently over his head.
He heard it fall, far, far away. Truth, he did not want it. He wanted her.
It came to him that this was the way that Sjekso had gone, before he
had ended up dead and cold outside the *Unicorn,* and it failed to matter. Her lips pressed his and oh, gods, he wanted her.

The floor wavered, and a wind swept in, laden with sweetish incense . . .

"Pardon me," Enas Yorl said, and the couple on the verge of further
intimacies broke apart, the woman staring at him wide-eyed and Shadowspawn with a hazy desperation. The russet silks in the room still
billowed with the draft he had set up.

"Who are *you?*" the woman Ischade asked, and at once Enas Yorl
felt a small trial of his defenses, which he shrugged off. Ischade's expression at once took on a certain wariness.

"Let him go," Enas Yorl said with a backhanded wave toward Shadowspawn. "He's admirably discreet. And I'd take it kindly.—Go on,
Shadowspawn. Now. Quickly."

Shadowspawn edged toward the door, hesitated there with a look of
violated sanity.

"Out," Enas Yorl said.

The thief spun about and opened the door, a fresh gust of wind.

And fled.

Hanse hit the stairs running, hardly pausing for the steps, never saw
the figure loom up at the bottom until he was headed straight down at
the knife that aimed up at his gut.

He knocked the attacking blade aside and grabbed for arms or
clothes, whatever he could hold, fell, in the shock of the collision, tumbled with the attacker and the blade, and lost his purchase in the impact
with the ground. He hit on his back, desperately got a grip on the descending knife hand with Mradhon Vis' face coming down on him with
a weight of body a third again his own. It was his left hand he used on
the descending arm, left hand, knife hand, involved with that, and his
battered muscles shook under the strain while he plied his unaccustomed right hand trying to reach the knife strapped to his leg. His left
arm was buckling.

Suddenly Vis' weight shifted rightwards and came down on him, pinning his other arm—a limp weight, and in the space Vis' grimace had occupied, most improbably, Cappen Varra stood with a barrel stave in both his hands.

"Did you want rescue?" Cappen asked civilly. "Or is it all some new diversion?"

Hanse swore, kicked and writhed his way from under Vis' inert weight and went for his dagger in fright. Cappen checked his arm and the heat of anger went out of him, leaving only a sickly shiver. "Hang you," he said feebly, "couldn't you have hit him easier and given me a go?"

And then he realized the source of the light which was streaming down on them by way of the stairs, and that above them was the open door in which two wizards met. "Gods," he muttered, and scrambling up, grabbed Cappen by the arm.

And ran, for very life.

"Not my doing."

"No?" Enas Yorl felt his shoulders expand ever so slightly, his features shift, and in his pride he refused to look down at his hands to know. Perhaps it was not too terrible, this form: Ischade's eyes flickered, but seemed unappalled.

"None of the killings that interest you," she said, "are mine. They're not my style. I trust I'm somewhat known in the craft. As you are, Enas Yorl."

He gave a small bow. "I have some unwilling distinction."

"The story's known."

"Ah." Again he felt the shift, a wave of terror. He bent down and picked up the amulet which lay on the floor, saw his hand covered with a faint opalescence of scales. Then the scales faded and left only a young and shapely male hand. He tucked the amulet into his robes and straightened, looked at Ischade somewhat more calmly. "So you're not the one. I don't ask you then who hired you. I can guess, knowing what you did—ah, I do know. And by morning the priests will have discovered the loss and made some substitution—the wars of gods, after all, follow politics, don't they? And what matter a riot or two in Sanctuary? It interests neither of us."

"Then what is your interest?"

"How did they die, Ischade—your lovers? Do you know? Or don't you wonder?"

"Your curiosity—has it some specific grievance?"

"Ah, no grievance at all. I only ask."

"I do nothing. The fault's their own . . . their luck, a heart too fragile, a fall . . . who am I to know? They're well when they leave me, that's the truth."

"But they're dead by morning, every one."

She shrugged. "You should understand. I have nothing to do with it."

"Ah, indeed we have misfortunes in common. I know. And when I knew you'd come to Sanctuary—"

"It took me some few days to acclimate myself; I trust I didn't inconvenience you . . . and that we'll avoid each other in future."

"Ischade: how am I— presently?"

She tilted back her head and looked, blinked uncertainly. "Younger," she said. "And quite handsome, really. Far unlike what I've heard."

"So? Then you can look at me? I see that you can. And not many do."

"I have business," she declared, liking all of this less and less. She was not accustomed to feel fear . . . hunted the sensation in the alleys of cities in the hope of discovering a measure of life. But this was far from comfortable. "I have to be about it."

"What, some new employer?"

"Not killing wizards, if that's your worry. My business is private, and it need not intrude on yours."

"And if I engaged you?"

"In what regard?"

"To spend one night with me."

"You're mad."

"I might become so—I don't age, you see. And that's the difficulty."

"You're not afraid? You're looking to die? Is that the cause of all this?"

"Ah, I'm afraid at times. At times like this, when the shape is good. But it doesn't last. There are other times . . . and they come. And I never grow old, Ischade. I can't detect it if I do. And that frightens me."

She regarded him askance . . . he was handsome, very. She wondered if this had been his first shape, when he was young, that brought his trouble on him. It was a shape fine enough to have done that. The eyes were beautiful, full of pain. So many of her young men of the streets were full of that pain. It touched her as nothing else could.

"How long has it been," he asked, setting his hands on her shoulders, touching ever so gently, "since you had a lover worth the name? And

how long since I've had hope of anything? We might be each other's answer, Ischade. If I should die, then that's one way out for me; or if I
don't—then you're not doomed to lose them all, after all, are you,
Ischade? Some of my forms might not be to your taste, but others—I
have infinite variety, Ischade. And no dread of you at all."

"For this you hunted me down? That was it, wasn't it—the amulet, a
way to draw yourself to me—"

"It costs you nothing. No harm. So small a thing for you,
Ischade . . . ."

It tempted. He was beautiful, this moment, this one moment, and the
nights and the years were long.

And then the other chance occurred to her and she shivered, who had
not shivered in years. "No. No. Maybe you're set to die, but I'm not.
No. Oppose two curses the like of ours—half the city could go in that
shock, not to mention you and me. The chance of that, the merest
chance—No. I'm not done living . . . ."

He frowned, drew himself up with the least tremor about his lips, a
look of panic. "Ischade. . . ." The voice began to change, and of a sudden the features starting with the mouth wavered, as if the strain had
been too much, too long and dearly held. The scales were back; and
"No," he cried, and plunged his face into hands which were not
quite still hands. The draperies billowed, the very air rippled, and
"No . . . ." the air sighed after him, a vanishing moan, a sob.

A second time she shivered, and looked about her, distracted, but he
was quite gone.

So, well, she thought. He had had his answer, once for all. Her business took her here and there about the empire, but she discovered a liking for Sanctuary as for no other place she had known . . . and it was
well that Yorl took his answer, and that it was settled. New tasks might
come. But at the moment she thought of the river house. This lodging
was too well known for the time; and she might walk to the river . . .
might meet someone—along the way.

The wine splashed into the cup and such was Hanse's state of mind
that he never looked to see who served, only hoisted the cup and drank
a mouthful.

"That's good," he said; and Cappen Varra across the table in the
*Unicorn* watched him shake off the ghosts and lifted his own cup, thinking ruefully of a song abandoned, a tale best not sung at all, even in the
safe confines of the *Unicorn*. The city would be full of questions tomor-

row, and it was well to know nothing at all . . . as he was sure Hanse
planned to know least of all.

"A game," Cappen proposed.

"No. No dicing tonight." Hanse dug into his purse and came up with
a silver round, laid it carefully on the table. "That's for another pitcher
when this is done. And for a roof tonight."

Cappen poured again, topping off the cup—a wonder, that Hanse
bought drinks. Hanse flinging money about as if he wished to be rid of
it.

"Tomorrow on the game," Cappen said, in hope.

"Tomorrow," Hanse said, and lifted the cup.

Blind Darous poured, the cup held just so for his finger to feel the
coolth of the liquid . . . measured it carefully and extended the filled
goblet toward his seated master. The breathing was hoarse tonight. A
hand took the stem of the cup most delicately, not touching his fingers
at all, for which Darous was deeply grateful.

And toward the river, a house apart from others . . . which seemed
oddly discontinuous from its surrounds: in squalor, it had a garden, and
a wall; and yet had a quaint decrepitude. Mradhon Vis stood outside
the gate—sore and much out of sorts. *She* was there: she had found herself a young man much the image of Sjekso, who presently held the
warmth and the light inside.

He had walked that far.

And finally, knowing what he knew, he did the harder thing, and
walked away.

# A Gift in Parting

## Robert Lynn Asprin

The sun was a full two handspans above the horizon when Hort appeared on the Sanctuary docks; early in the day but late by fishermen's standard. The youth's eyes squinted painfully at the unaccustomed brightness of the morning sun. He fervently wished he were home in bed . . . or in someone else's bed . . . or anywhere but here. Still, he had promised his mother he would help the Old Man this morning. While his upbringing made it unthinkable to break that promise, his stubbornness required that he demonstrate his protest by being late.

Though he had roamed these docks since early childhood and knew them to be as scrupulously clean as possible, Hort still chose his path carefully to avoid brushing his clothes against anything. Of late he had been much more attentive to his personal appearance; this morning he had discovered he no longer had any old clothes suitable for the boat. While he realized the futility of trying to preserve his current garb through an entire day's work in the boat, newly acquired habits demanded he try to minimize the damage.

The Old Man was waiting for him, sitting on the overturned boat like some stately sea-bird sleeping off a full belly. The knife in his hand caressed the stray piece of wood he held with a slow, rhythmic cadence. With each pass of the blade a long curl of wood fell to join the pile at his feet. The size of the pile was mute testament to how long the Old Man had been waiting.

Strange, but Hort had always thought of him as the Old Man, never as Father. Even the men who had fished these waters with him since their shared boyhoods called him Old Man rather than Panit. He wasn't

really old, though his face was deceptive. Wrinkled and crisscrossed by
weather lines, the Old Man's face looked like one of those red clay
riverbeds one saw in the desert beyond Sanctuary: parched, cracked,
waiting for rain that would never fall.

No, that was wrong. The Old Man didn't look like the desert. The
Old Man would have nothing in common with such a large accumu-
lation of dirt. He was a fisherman, a creature of the sea and as much a
part of the sea as one of those weathered rocks that punctuated the
harbor.

The Old Man looked up at his son's approach then let his attention
settle back on the whittling.

"I'm here," Hort announced unnecessarily, adding, "sorry I'm late."

He cursed himself silently when that remark slipped out. He had
been determined not to apologize, no matter what the Old Man said,
but when the Old Man said nothing . . .

His father rose to his feet unhurriedly, replacing his knife in its
sheath with a gesture made smooth and unconscious by years of repetition.

"Give me a hand with this," he said, bending to grasp one end of the
boat.

Just that. No acceptance of the apology. No angry reproach. It was
as if he had expected his reluctant assistant would be late.

Hort fumed about this as he grunted and heaved, helping to right the
small boat and set it safely in the water. His annoyance with the whole
situation was such that he was seated in the boat, accepting the oars as
they were passed down from the dock, before he remembered that his
father had been launching this craft for years without assistance. His
son's inexpert hands could not have been a help, only a hindrance.

Spurred by this new irritation, Hort let the stern of the boat drift
away from the dock as his father prepared to board. The petty gesture
was in vain. The Old Man stepped into the boat, stretching his leg
across the water with no more thought than a merchant gives his keys in
their locks.

"Row that way," came the order to his son.

Gritting his teeth in frustration, Hort bent to the task.

The old rhythms returned to him in mercifully few strokes. Once he
had been glad to row his father's boat. He had been proud when he had
grown enough to handle the oars himself. No longer a young child to be
guarded by his mother, he had basked in the status of the Old Man's
boy. His playmates had envied his association with the only fisherman

on the dock who could consistently trap the elusive Nya—the small schooling fish whose sweet flesh brought top price each afternoon after the catch was brought in.

Of course, that had been a long time ago. He'd wanted to learn about the Nya then—he knew less now; his memories had faded.

As Hort had grown, so had his world. He learned that away from the docks no one knew of the Old Man, nor did they care. To the normal citizens of Sanctuary he was just another fisherman and fishermen did not stand high in the social structure of the town. Fishermen weren't rich, nor did they have the ear of the local aristocrats. Their clothes weren't colorful like the S'danzos'. They weren't feared like the soldiers or mercenaries.

And they smelled.

Hort had often disputed this latter point with the street urchins away from the docks until bloody noses, black eyes and bruises taught him that fishermen weren't good fighters, either. Besides, they did smell.

Retreating to the safety of the dock community Hort found that he viewed the culture which had raised him with a blend of scorn and bitterness. The only people who respected fishermen were other fishermen. Many of his old friends were drifting away—finding new lives in the crowds and excitement of the city-proper. Those that remained were dull youths who found reassurance in the unchanging traditions of the fish-craft and who were already beginning to look like their fathers.

As his loneliness grew, it was natural that Hort used his money to buy new clothes which he bundled and hid away from the fish-tainted cottage they called home. He scrubbed himself vigorously with sand, dressed and tried to blend with the townsfolk.

He found the citizens remarkably pleasant once he had removed the mark of the fishing community. They were most helpful in teaching him what to do with his money. He acquired a circle of friends and spent more and more time away from home until . . .

"Your mother tells me you're leaving."

The Old Man's sudden statement startled Hort, jerking him rudely from his mental wanderings. In a flash he realized he had been caught in the trap his friends had warned him about. Alone in the boat with his father he would be a captive audience until the tide changed. Now he'd hear the anger, the accusations and finally the pleading.

Above all Hort dreaded the pleading. While they had had their differences in the past, he still held a lingering respect for his father, a respect he knew would die if the Old Man was reduced to whining and begging.

"You've said it yourself a hundred times, Old Man," Hort pointed out with a shrug, "not everyone was meant to be a fisherman."

It came out harsher than he had intended, but Hort let it go without more explanations. Perhaps his father's anger would be stirred to a point where the conversation would be terminated prior to the litanies of his obligations to his family and tradition.

"Do you think you can earn a living in Sanctuary?" the Old Man asked, ignoring his son's baiting.

"We . . . I won't be in Sanctuary," Hort announced carefully. Even his mother hadn't possessed this last bit of knowledge. "There's a caravan forming in town. In four days it leaves for the capital. My friends and I have been invited to travel with it."

"The capital?" Panit nodded slowly. "And what will you do in Ranke?"

"I don't know yet," his son admitted, "but there are ten jobs in Ranke for every one in Sanctuary."

The Old Man digested this in silence. "What will you use for money on this trip?" he asked finally.

"I had hoped . . . There's supposed to be a tradition in our family, isn't there? When a son leaves home his father gives him a parting gift. I know you don't have much, but . . ." Hort stopped; the Old Man was shaking his head in slow negation.

"We have less than you think," he said sadly. "I said nothing before, but your fine clothes, there, have tapped our savings; the fishing's been bad."

"If you won't give me anything, just say so!" Hort exploded angrily. "You don't have to rationalize it with a long tale of woe."

"I'll give you a gift," the Old Man assured him. "I only wanted to warn you that it probably would not be money. More to the left."

"I don't need your money," the youth growled, adjusting his stroke. "My friends have offered to loan me the necessary funds. I just thought it would be better not to start my new life in debt."

"That's wise," Panit agreed. "Slow now."

Hort glanced over his shoulder for a bearing then straightened with surprise. His oars trailed loose in the water.

"There's only one float!" he announced in dumb surprise.

"That's right," the Old Man nodded. "It's nice to know you haven't forgotten your numbers."

"But one float means . . ."

"One trap," Panit agreed. "Right again. I told you fishing was bad. Still, having come all this way, I would like to see what is in my one trap."

The Old Man's dry sarcasm was lost on his son. Hort's mind was racing as he reflexively maneuvered the boat into position by the float.

One trap! The Old Man normally worked fifteen to twenty traps; the exact number always varied from day to day according to his instincts, but never had Hort known him to set less than ten traps. Of course the Nya were an unpredictable fish whose movements confounded everyone save Panit. That is—they came readily to the trap if the trap happened to be near them in their random wanderings.

One trap! Perhaps the schools were feeding elsewhere; that sometimes happened with any fish. But then the fishermen would simply switch to a different catch until their mainstay returned. If the Old Man were less proud of his ability and reputation he could do the same . . .

"Old Man!" The exclamation burst from Hort's lips involuntarily as he scanned the horizon.

"What is it?" Panit asked, pausing as he hauled his trap from the depths.

"Where are the other boats?"

The Old Man returned his attention to the trap. "On the dock," he said brusquely. "You walked past them this morning."

Open-mouthed, Hort let his memory roam back over the docks. He had been preoccupied with his own problems, but . . . yes! there had been a lot of boats lying on the dock.

"All of them?" he asked, bewildered. "You mean we're the only boat out today?"

"That's right."

"But why?"

"Just a minute . . . here!" Panit secured a handhold on the trap and heaved it onto the boat. "Here's why."

The trap was ruined. Most of the wooden slats which formed its sides were caved in and those that weren't dangled loose. If Hort hadn't been expecting to see a Nya trap he wouldn't have recognized this as something other than a tangle of scrap-wood.

"It's been like this for over a week!" the Old Man snarled with sudden ferocity. "Traps smashed, nets torn. That's why those who call themselves fishermen cower on the land instead of manning their boats!" He spat noisily over the side of the boat.

Was it also why his mother had insisted Hort give the Old Man a hand?

"Row for the docks, boy. Fishermen! They should fish in buckets where it's safe! Bah!"

Awed by the Old Man's anger, Hort turned the boat toward the shore. "What's doing it?" he asked.

There was silence as Panit stared off to the sea. For a moment Hort thought his question had gone unheard and was about to repeat it. Then he saw how deep the wrinkles on his father's face had become.

"I don't know," the Old Man murmured finally. "Two weeks ago I would have said I knew every creature that swam or crawled in these waters. Today . . . I just don't know."

"Have you reported this to the soldiers?"

"Soldiers? Is that what you've learned from your fancy friends? Run to the soldiers?" Panit fairly trembled with rage. "What do soldiers know of the sea? Eh? What do you want them to do? Stand on the shore and wave their swords at the water? Order the monster to go away? Collect a tax from it? Yes! That's it! If the soldiers declare a monster tax maybe it'll swim away to keep from being bled dry like the rest of us! Soldiers!"

The Old Man spat again and lapsed into a silence that Hort was loath to break. Instead he spent the balance of the return journey mentally speculating about the trap-crushing monster. In a way he knew it was futile; sharper minds than his, the Old Man's for example, had tried and failed to come up with an explanation. There wasn't much chance he'd stumble upon it. Still, it occupied his mind until they reached the dock. Only when the boat had been turned over in the late morning sun did Hort venture to reopen the conversation.

"Are we through for the day?" he asked. "Can I go now?"

"You can," the Old Man replied, turning a blank expression to his son. "Of course, if you do it might cause problems. The way it is now, if your mother asks me: 'Did you take the boat out today?' I can say yes. If you stay with me and she asks: 'Did you spend the day with the Old Man?' you can say yes. If, on the other hand, you wander off on your own, you'll have to say 'no' when she asks and we'll both have to explain ourselves to her."

This startled Hort almost more than the discovery of an unknown monster loose in the fishing grounds. He had never suspected the Old Man was capable of hiding his activities from his wife with such a calculated web of half-truths. Close on the heels of his shock came a wave of intense curiosity regarding his father's plans for a large block of time about which he did not want to tell his wife.

"I'll stay," Hort said with forced casualness. "What do we do now?"

"First," the Old Man announced as he headed off down the dock, "we visit the Wine Barrel."

The Wine Barrel was a rickety wharf-side tavern favored by the fishermen and therefore shunned by everyone else. Knowing his father to be a nondrinker, Hort doubted the Old Man had ever before been inside the place, yet he led the way into the shadowed interior with a firm and confident step.

They were all there: Terci, Omat, Varies; all the fishermen Hort had known since childhood plus many he did not recognize. Even Haron, the only woman ever accepted by the fishermen, was there, though her round, fleshy and weathered face was scarcely different from the men's.

"Hey, Old Man? You finally given up?"

"There's an extra seat here."

"Some wine for the Old Man!"

"One more trap-wrecked fisherman!"

Panit ignored the cries which erupted from various spots in the shadowed room at his entrance. He held his stride until he reached the large table custom reserved for the eldest fisherfolk.

"I told you, you'd be here eventually," Omat greeted him, pushing the extra bench out with his long, thin leg. "Now, who's a coward?"

The Old Man acknowledged neither the jibe nor the bench, leaning on the table with both hands to address the veterans. "I only came to ask one question," he hissed. "Are all of you, or any of you, planning to do anything about whatever it is that's driven you from the sea?"

To a man, the fishermen moved their gazes elsewhere.

"What can we do?" Terci scowled. "We don't even know what's out there. Maybe it will move on . . ."

". . . And maybe it won't," the Old Man concluded angrily. "I should have known. Scared men don't think; they hide. Well, I've never been one to sit around waiting for my problems to go away on their own. Not planning to change now."

He kicked the empty bench away and turned toward the door only to find Hort blocking his way.

"What are you going to do?" Terci called after him.

"I'm going to find an answer!" the Old Man announced, drilling the room with his scorn. "And I'll find it where I've always found answers —in the sea; not at the bottom of a winecup."

With that he strode out the door. Hort started to follow when some-one called his name and he turned back.

"I thought that was you under those city-clothes," Omat said without rancor. "Watch over him, boy. He's a little crazy and crazy people sometimes get killed before they get sane."

There was a low murmur of assent from those around the table. Hort nodded and hurried after his father. The Old Man was waiting for him outside the door.

"Fools!" he raged. "No money for a week and they sit drinking what little they have left. Pah!"

"What do *we* do now, Old Man?"

Panit looked around then snatched up a Nya trap from a stack on the dock. "We'll need this," he said, almost to himself.

"Isn't that one of Terci's traps?" Hort asked cautiously.

"He isn't using it, is he?" the Old Man shot back. "And besides we're only borrowing it. Now, you're supposed to know this town—where's the nearest blacksmith?"

"The nearest? Well, there's a mender in the bazaar, but the best ones are . . ."

The Old Man was off, striding purposefully down the street leaving Hort to hurry after him.

It wasn't a market-day; the bazaar was still sleepy with many stalls unopened. It was not necessary for Hort to lead the way as the sharp, ringing notes of hammer striking anvil were easily heard over the slow-moving shoppers. The dark giant plying the hammer glanced at them as they approached, but continued his work.

"Are you the smith?" Panit asked.

This earned them another, longer, look but no words. Hort realized the question had been ridiculous. A few more strikes and the giant set his hammer aside, turning his full attention to his new customers.

"I need a Nya trap. One of these." The Old Man thrust the trap at the smith.

The smith glanced at the trap, then shook his head. "Smith; not carpenter," he proclaimed, already reaching for his hammer.

"I know that!" the Old Man barked. "I want this trap made out of metal."

The giant stopped and stared at his customers again, then he picked up the trap and examined it.

"And I'll need it today—by sundown."

The smith set the trap down carefully. "Two silvers," he said firmly.

"Two!" the Old Man snorted. "Do you think you're dealing with the Kittycat himself? One."

"Two," the smith insisted.

"Dubro!"

They all turned to face the small woman who had emerged from the enclosure behind the forge.

"Do it for one," she said quietly. "He needs it."

She and the smith locked eyes in a battle of wills, then the giant nodded and turned away from his wife.

"S'danzo?" the Old Man asked before the woman disappeared into the darkness from which she'd come.

"Half."

"You've got the sight?"

"A bit," she admitted. "I see your plan is unselfish but dangerous. I do not see the outcome—except that you must have Dubro's help to succeed."

"You'll bless the trap?"

The S'danzo shook her head. "I'm a seer, not a priest. I'll make you a symbol—the Lance of Ships from our cards—to put on the trap. It marks good fortune in sea-battles; it might help you."

"Could I see the card?" the Old Man asked.

The woman disappeared and returned a few moments later bearing the card which she held for Panit. Looking over his father's shoulder, Hort saw a crudely drawn picture of a whale with a metal-sheathed horn proceeding from its head.

"A good card," the Old Man nodded. "For what you offer—I'll pay the two silvers." She smiled and returned to the darkness, Dubro stepped forward with his palm extended. "When I pick up the trap," Panit insisted. "You needn't fear. I won't leave it to gather dust."

The giant frowned, nodded and turned back to his work.

"What are you planning?" Hort demanded as his father started off again. "What's this about a sea-battle?"

"All fishing is sea-battle," the Old Man shrugged.

"But, two silvers? Where are you going to get that kind of money after what you said in the boat this morning?"

"We'll see to that now."

Hort realized they weren't returning to town but heading westward to the Downwinder's hovels. The Downwinders or . . . "Jubal?" he exclaimed. "How're you going to get money from him? Are you going to sell him information about the monster?"

"I'm a fisherman, not a spy," the Old Man retorted, "and the problems of the fishermen are no concern of the land."

"But . . ." Hort began then lapsed into silence. If his father was going to be closed-mouthed about his plans, no amount of browbeating was likely to budge him.

Upon reaching Jubal's estate, Hort was amazed at the ease with which the Old Man handled the slaver's underlings who routinely challenged his entry. Though it was well known that Jubal employed notorious cut-throats and murderers who hid their features behind blue-hawk masks, Panit was unawed by their arrogance or their arms.

"What do you two want here?" the grizzled gate-keeper barked.

"We came to talk to Jubal," the Old Man retorted.

"Is he expecting you?"

"I need an appointment to speak with the slaver?"

"What business could an old fisherman have with a slaver?"

"If you were to know, I'd tell you. I want to see Jubal."

"I can't just . . ."

"You ask too many questions. Does *he* know you ask so many questions?"

That final question of the Old Man's cowed the retainer, confirming Hort's town-refined suspicions that most of the slaver's business was covert rather than overt.

They were finally ushered into a large room dominated by a huge, almost throne-like, chair at one end. They had been waiting only a few moments when Jubal entered, belting a dressing-gown over his muscular, ebony limbs.

"I should have known it was you, Old Man," the slaver said with a half-smile. "No other fisherman could bluff his way past my guards so easily."

"I know you prefer money to sleep," the Old Man shrugged. "Your men know it too."

"True enough," Jubal laughed. "So, what brings you this far from the docks so early in the day?"

"For some the day's over," Panit commented dryly. "I need money: six silver pieces. I'm offering my stall on the wharf."

Hort couldn't believe what he was hearing. He opened his mouth to speak, then caught himself. He had been raised to know better than to interrupt his father's business. His movement was not lost on Jubal, however.

"You intrigue me, Old Man," the slaver mused. "Why should I want to buy a fish-stall at any price?"

"Because the wharf's the only place your ears don't hear," Panit smiled tightly. "You send your spies in—but we don't talk to outsiders. To hear the wharf you must be on the wharf—I offer you a place on the wharf."

"True enough," Jubal agreed. "I hardly expected the opportunity to fall my way like ripe fruit . . ."

"Two conditions," the Old Man interrupted. "First: four weeks before you own my stall. If I repay the money—you don't own my stall . . ."

"All right," the slaver nodded, "but . . ."

"Second: anything happens to me these next four weeks you take care of my wife. It's not charity; she knows the wharf and the Nya— she's worth a fair wage."

Jubal studied the Old Man a moment through hooded eyes. "Very well," he said finally, "but I sense there is much you are not telling me." He left the room and returned with the silver coins which rattled lightly in his immense palm. "Tell me this, Old Man," he asked suspiciously, "all these terms—why don't you just ask for a loan?"

"I've never borrowed in my life," Panit scowled, "and won't start now. I pay as I go—if I don't have enough I do without or I sell what I must."

"Suit yourself," the slaver shrugged, handing over the coins. "I'll be expecting to see you in thirty days."

"Or before."

The silence between father and son was almost habitual and lasted nearly until they had reached the town again. Strangely, it was the Old Man who broke the silence first.

"You're being quiet, boy," he said.

"Of course," Hort exploded. "There's nothing to say. You order things we can't pay for, sell your life-work to the biggest crook in Sanctuary and then wonder why I'm quiet. I know you don't confide in me— but Jubal! Of all the people in town . . . And that talk about conditions! What makes you think he'll stand by any of them? You don't trust soldiers but you trust Jubal!"

"*He* can be trusted," the Old Man answered softly. "He's a hard one when he's got the upper hand—but he stands by his word."

"You've dealt with him before? Nothing can surprise me now," Hort grumbled.

"Good," his father nodded. "Then you'll take me to the Vulgar Unicorn?"

"The Vulgar Unicorn!" He was surprised.

"That's right. Don't you know where it is?"

"I know it's in the Maze somewhere, but I've never been there."

"Let's go."

"Are you sure you want the Vulgar Unicorn, Old Man?" Hort pressed. "I don't think a fisherman's ever set foot in there. The people who drink at the Unicorn are mercenaries, cut-throats and a few thieves thrown in for good measure."

"So they say," the Old Man nodded. "Wouldn't be going there if they weren't. Now, you leading or not?"

All conversation stopped as they entered that infamous tavern. As he struggled to see in the darkness, Hort could feel the eyes of the room on him, sizing them up, deciding if he was a challenge or a victim.

"Are you gentlemen looking for someone?" The bartender's tone implied he didn't think they should stay for a drink.

"I want some fighting men," the Old Man announced. "I've heard this is the place."

"You heard right," the bartender nodded, suddenly a bit more attentive. "If you don't know who you want, I'll be glad to serve as your agent—for a modest fee, of course."

Panit regarded him as he'd regarded his fellow fisherfolk. "I judge my own people—go back to your dishes."

The bartender clenched his fists in anger and retreated to the other end of the bar as the Old Man faced the room.

"I need two, maybe three men for a half-day's work," he called loudly. "A copper now and a silver when it's over. No swords or bowmen—just axes or pole-arms. I'll be outside."

"Why are we going to talk to them outside?" Hort asked as he followed his father into the street.

"I want to know what I'm getting," the Old Man explained. "Couldn't see a thing in that place."

It took most of the afternoon but they finally sorted out three stalwarts from the small pack that had followed them. The sun was dipping toward the horizon as Panit gave his last man the advance coin and turned to his son.

"That's about all we can do today," he said. "You run along and see your friends. I'll take care of the trap."

"Aren't you going to tell me your plan?" Hort pleaded.

"Haven't got it all worked out yet," the Old Man admitted, "but if you want to see what happens, be on the dock at first light tomorrow. We'll see how smart this monster is."

Unlike the day before, Hort was at the dock well before the dawn. As the first tendrils of pre-dawn light began to dispel the night he was pacing impatiently, hugging himself against the damp chill of the morning.

Mist hung deep over the water, giving it an eerie, supernatural appearance which did nothing to ease Hort's fears as he alternately cursed and worried about his absent father. Crazy Old Man! Why couldn't he be like the other fishermen? Why take it on himself to solve the mystery of the sea-monster? Knowing the best way to combat the chill was activity he decided to launch the family's boat. For once, he would be ready when the Old Man got here.

He marched down the dock, then slowed, and finally retraced his steps. The boat was gone. Had Sanctuary's thieves finally decided to ply their trade on the wharf? Unlikely. Who would they sell a stolen boat to? The fishermen knew each other's equipment as well as they knew their own.

Could the Old Man have gone out already? Impossible—to be out of the harbor before Hort got there, the Old Man would have had to take the boat out at night—and in these waters with the monster . . . .

"You there!"

Hort turned to find the three hired mercenaries coming down the pier. They were a sullen crew by this light and the pole-arms two of them carried gave them the appearance of Death's own oarsmen.

"We're here," the leader of the trio announced, shifting his battle-axe to his shoulder, "though no civilized man fights at this hour. Where's the Old Man who hired us?"

"I don't know," Hort admitted, backing down from this fierce assemblage. "He told me to meet him here same as you."

"Good," the axe-man snarled. "We've appeared, as promised. The coppers are ours—small price for a practical joke. Tell that Old Man when you see him that we've gone back to bed."

"Not so fast," Hort surprised himself with his sudden outspoken courage as the men turned away. "I've known the Old Man all my life and he's no joker. If he paid you to be here, you'll be needed. Or don't you want the silver that goes with those coppers?"

The men hesitated, mumbling together darkly.

"Hort!" Terci was hurrying toward them. "What's going on? Why are there cut-throats on the dock?"

"The Old Man hired them," Hort explained. "Have you seen him?"

"Not since last night," the lanky fisherman replied. "He came by late and gave me this to pass to you." He dropped three silver coins into the youth's palm. "He said if he wasn't here by midday that you were to use this to pay the men."

"You see!" Hort called to the mercenaries as he held up the coins. "You'll be paid at midday and not before. You'll just have to wait with the rest of us." Turning back to Terci he lowered his voice to a conspiratorial whisper. "What else did the Old Man say—anything?"

"Only that I should load my heaviest net this morning," Terci shrugged. "What's going on?"

"He's going to try to fish for the monster," Hort explained as the Old Man's plan came clear to him. "When I got here his boat was gone."

"The monster," Terci blinked. "The Old Man's gone out alone after the monster?"

"I don't think so. I've been here since before first light. No, even the Old Man wouldn't take a boat out in the dark—not after the monster. He must be . . ."

"Look there! There he is!"

The sun had finally appeared over the horizon and with its first rays the mist began to fade. A hundred yards offshore a small boat bobbed and dipped and in it they could see the Old Man pulling frantically at the oars.

As they watched he suddenly shipped the oars, waiting expectantly. Then the boat was jerked around, as if by an unseen hand and the Old Man bent to the oars again.

"He's got it! He's got the monster!" Terci shrieked, dancing with delight or horror.

"No!" Hort disagreed firmly, staring at the distant boat. "He doesn't have it. He's leading it, baiting it into shallow water."

It was all clear to him now. The metal trap! The monster was used to raiding the Old Man's traps, so he fed it one that couldn't be crushed. Now he was teasing the unknown creature toward shore, dragging the trap like a child drags a string before a playful kitten. But this kitten was an unknown, deadly quantity that could easily attack the hand that held the string.

"Quick, Terci," Hort ordered, "get the net! It won't follow him onto the shore."

The lanky fisherman was gaping at the scene, his mind lost in his own thoughts. "Net the monster?" he mumbled. "I'll need help, yes, help . . . HELP!" He fled down the dock screaming at the still-dark, quiet huts.

This was not the Maze where cries for help went unheeded. Doors opened and bleary-eyed fishermen stumbled out to the wharf.

"What is it?"

"What's the noise?"

*"Man your boats! The Old Man's got the monster!"*

"The monster?"

"Hurry, Ilak!"

"The Old Man's got the monster!" The cry was passed from hut to hut.

And they came, swarming over their boats like a nest of angry ants: Haron, her sagging breasts flopping beneath the nightdress she still wore; Omat, his deformed arm no hindrance as he wrestled his boat onto the water with one hand, and in the lead, Terci, first rowing, then standing, in the small boat to shout orders at the others.

Hort made no move to join them. They were fishermen and knew their trade far better than he. Instead he stood rooted on the dock, lost in awe of the Old Man's courage.

In his mind's eye Hort could see what his father saw: sitting in a small boat on an inky sea, waiting for the first tug on the rope—then the back-breaking haul on the oars to drag the metal trap landward. Always careful not to get too far ahead of the invisible creature below, yet keeping its interest. The dark was the Old Man's enemy as much as the monster was; it threatened him with disorientation—and the mist! A blinding cloud of white closing in from all sides. Yet the Old Man had done it and now the monster was within reach of its victims' nets.

The heavy net was spread now, forming a wall between the mystery beast as it followed the Old Man and the open sea behind them. As the boats at either end of the net began to pull for shore, the Old Man evened his stroke and began to move steadily through the water . . . but he was tired now; Hort could see that even if no one else could.

"There!" Hort called to the mercenaries, he pointed toward the shore-line. "That's where they'll beach it! Come on!"

He led their rush down the dock. He heard rather than saw the net scoop up its prey; a cheer went up from the small boats. He was waiting waist-deep in the water when the Old Man's boat finally reached the shallows. Grabbing onto the cleats, Hort dragged the boat to the beach as if it were a toy while his father sagged wearily between the oars.

"The trap," the Old Man wheezed through ragged gasps, "pull it in before those fools get it tangled in their nets!"

The rope was cold and hard as cable, but Hort dragged the trap hand-over-hand away from the sea's grip. Not surprisingly, it was full of Nya that shimmered and flopped in the morning sun. Without thinking, Hort reached behind his father and dumped the fish into the boat's live-well.

All the boats were ashore now, and there was splashing and thrashing around the net in the shallows.

"What is it like?" the Old Man gasped; he could scarcely raise his head. "What's the monster like?"

"It looks to be a large crab," Hort announced, craning his neck. "The mercenaries have got to it."

And they had; waving the crowd back they waded into the water to strike at the spidery giant even before the net was on the shore.

"I thought so," the Old Man nodded. "There weren't any teeth marks on the traps. Some damn sorcerer's pet run loose," he added.

Hort nodded. Now that he could see the monster it fit the rumors he had heard from time to time in the town. The Purple Mage had kept large crabs to guard his home on the White Foal River. Rumor said he was dead now, killed by his own magic. The rumor was confirmed by the crab; it must have wandered downstream to the sea when its food no longer appeared.

"Whose catch is that?"

Hort turned to find two Hell-Hounds standing close beside him. Simultaneously he noticed the crowd of townsfolk which had gathered on the streets.

"Everybody's," the Old Man declared, getting his strength back. "They caught it. Or anybody's. Maybe it's Terci's—it's mangled his net."

"No, Old Man," Terci declared, approaching them. "It's your catch. There's none on the wharf who'd deny that—least of all me. You caught it. We netted and gaffed it for you after the fight."

"It's yours then," the Hell-Hound decided, facing the Old Man. "What do you plan to do with it?"

It flashed across Hort's mind that these soldiers might be going to fine his father for dragging the crab to the beach; they might call it a public nuisance or something. He tightened his grip on the Old Man's arm, but he'd never been able to hold his father.

"I don't know," Panit shrugged. "If the circus was still in town I'd try to sell it to them. Can't sell it for food—might be poisonous—wouldn't eat it myself."

"I'll buy it," the Hell-Hound announced to their surprise. "The Prince has tasters and a taste for the unknown. If it's poisonous it will still make table-talk fit for an Emperor. I'll give you five silvers for it."

"Five? Ten—times're hard; I've got debts to Jubal for my fish-stall," the Old Man bargained, no more awed by the Hell-Hounds than he had been by Jubal himself.

At the mention of the slaver's name, the tall Hell-Hound scowled and his swarthy companion sucked air noisily through his teeth.

"Jubal?" the tall man mumbled as he reached for his pouch. "You'll have your ten silvers, fisherman—and a gold piece besides. A man should have more than a slaver's receipt for this day's work."

"Thankye," Panit nodded, accepting the coins. "Take your watch to the marshes and swamps; there's never one crab but there's ten. Corner'em on dry land an' Kittycat'll eat crab for a month."

"Thanks for your information," the Hell-Hound grimaced. "We'll have the garrison look into it."

"Not a bad day's catch," the Old Man chortled after the retreating soldiers, "and Nya besides. I'll send two in luck-money to the blacksmith and the S'danzo and get new traps besides." He cocked his head at his son. "Well," he tossed the gold coin in the air and caught it again, "I've got this too, to add to your other gift."

"Other gift?" Hort frowned.

The smile fell from the Old Man's face like a mask. "Of course," he snarled. "Why do you think I went after that thing anyway?"

"For the other fishermen?" Hort offered. "To save the fishing ground?"

"Aye," Panit shook his head. "But in the main it was my gift to you; I wanted to teach you about pride."

"Pride?" Hort echoed blankly. "You risked your life to make me proud of you? I've always been proud of you! You're the best fisherman in Sanctuary!"

"Fool!" the Old Man exploded, rising to his feet. "Not what you think of me; what you think of yourself!"

"I don't understand," his son blurted. "You want me to be a fisherman like you?"

"No, no, no!" the Old Man leaped to the sand and started to march away, then returned to loom angrily over the youth. "Said it before—not everyone can be a fisherman. You're not—but be something, anything, and have pride in it. Don't be a scavenger, drifting from here to yon. Take a path and follow it. You've always had a smooth tongue—be a minstrel, or even a storyteller like Hakiem."

"Hakiem?" Hort bristled. "He's a beggar."

"He lives here. He's a good storyteller; his wealth's his pride. Whatever you do, wherever you go—take your pride. Be good with yourself and you'll be at home with the best of 'em. Take my gift, son; it's only advice, but you'll be the poorer without it." He tossed the gold coin to the sand at Hort's feet and stalked off.

Hort retrieved the coin and stared at the Old Man's back as he marched away.

"Excuse me, young sir?" Old Hakiem was scuttling along the beach, waving his arms frantically. "Was that the Old Man—the one who caught the monster?"

"That's him," Hort agreed, "but I don't think this is a good time to be talking to him."

"Do you know him?" the storyteller asked, holding fast to Hort's arm. "Do you know what happened here? I'll pay you five coppers for the story." He was a beggar, but he didn't seem to starve.

"Keep your money, Hakiem," the youth murmured, watching the now-empty beach. "I'll give you the story."

"Eh?"

"Yes," Hort smiled, tossing his gold coin in the air, catching it and putting it in his pocket. "What's more, I'll buy you a cup of wine to go with it—but only if you'll teach me how to tell it."

# The Vivisectionist

## Andrew Offutt

### 1

A minaret topped the Governor's Palace, naturally. The narrow, eventually pointed dome resembled an elongated onion. Its needle-like spire thrust up to pierce the sky. That spire, naturally, flaunted a pennon. It bore the device of Imperial Ranke (*Ranket Imperatris*). Below, the dome was clamped by a circular wall like upended herbivorous teeth. If ever the palace were attacked, that crenelated wall promised, beware archers in the embrasures between the merlons! Beware dumpers of boiling oil.

Every bit of it was haughty and imperious, insultingly imperial. And high.

Even from the top of the (lower) wall of the granary across the avenue from the wall surrounding the Governor's Palace complex, no grapnel could be hurled, for no human was so strong.

An arrow, however, could be shot.

On a night when the moon over Sanctuary was not a maiden's pale round breast but a niggling little crescent hardly worthy of the business end of a scythe, a bow twanged like a dying lute. An arrow rushed at the pennon spire of the Governor's Palace. After it, like the web-trail of an industrious spider or a wind-blown tent caterpillar, sped a silken cord so slim as to be invisible.

And then it was laboriously and time-consumingly drawn and dragged back, for the archer had missed his shot.

He aimed anew, face set for curses rather than prayers. Elevating his bow a bit, he drew to the cheek and, daringly endangering the springy wood, drew even farther. Uttering not a prayer but a curse, he released.

Away sped the arrow. It trailed its spidery line like a strand of spittle in the pallid moonlight.

It proved a night for the heeding of curses, if not the answering of prayers. That was appropriate and perhaps significant in Sanctuary, called Thieves' World.

The shaft streaked past the spire and reached the end of its tether if not its velocity. It snapped back. The line forced it into a curving attempt to return. It snapped around the spire. Twice, thrice, four times. The archer was dragging hard. Keeping taut the silken line bought at the expense of a pair of lovely ear pendants of gold and amethyst and chrysoprase stolen from—never mind. The archer pulled his line, hard. That maintained and increased tension, tightened the arrow's whipping about the spire which was, naturally, gilded.

Then all motion ceased. A mourning dove spoke to the night, but no one believed that dolorous call presaged rain. Not in Sanctuary! Not at this time of year. The archer leaned into his line, and braced his heels to lean his full weight on it. The cord was a taut straight-edge of immobility and invisibility under the unimposing one-ninth moon.

Teeth flashed in the dimness. The archer's, standing atop the granary behind the Governor's Palace of Sanctuary. His mop of hair was blacker than shadowed night and his eyes nearly so, under brows that just missed meeting above a bridged nose that just missed being falcate.

He collected his other gear, collected himself, swallowed hard, choked up all he could on his line until he was straining, stretched, on tiptoe.

Then he thought something rather prayer-like, and out he swung.

Out above the street made broad enough to accommodate several big grain wagons abreast he swung, and across it. The looming wall rushed at him.

Even with the bending of his knees until they were nearly at his chest, the jar of his impact with the unyielding wall was enough to rattle teeth and turn prayers to curses. Nothing broke, neither legs nor silken line. Certainly not the wall, which was of stone, quarried and cut to form a barrier four feet thick.

He went up the rope in a reverse rappel, step after step and hand over hand. Dragging himself up the wall, walking up the fine perfectly set stones, climbing above death, for that was the penalty for slipping. The street was far below and farther with each pulling step.

He never considered that, or death, for he never considered the possibility of slipping.

A mighty warrior he was not. As an archer he had many peers and many betters. As a youth he was perfect, lean and wiry and strong. He was a highly competent thief in a citylet named for thieves. Not a cutpurse or a street-snatcher or an accoster; a thief. A burglar. As such, he was a superb climber of walls, without better and possibly without peer. He was good at slipping in by high-set windows, too.

His coloring and clothing were for the night, and shadows. They were old friends, he and shadows.

He did not slip. He ascended. He muscled himself atop the broad wall of the Governor's Palace, of Sanctuary. Unerringly, he stepped through the crenel, the embrasure between two merlons like blunt lower teeth. And he was at home, in shadow.

Now he gazed upon the palace itself; the palace of the golden Prince sent out from Ranke to (pretend to) govern Sanctuary. The thief smiled, but with his mouth closed. Here there were tigers in the form of guards, and young teeth would flash even in this most wan of moonlight. That precaution was merely part of his competence.

At that, he had lived only about a score of years. He was not sure whether he was nineteen or twenty or a bit older. No one was sure, in this anile town the conquering Rankans called Thieves' World. Perhaps his mother knew—certainly not the father he had never known and whom she had known casually, for this thief was a bastard by birth and often, even usually, by nature—but who knew who or where his mother was?

Below, within the wall lay ancillary buildings and a courtyard the size of a thoroughfare or a small community common, and guards. Across, just over there, rose the palace. Like him it was a shadow, but it loomed far more imposing.

He had broken into it once before. Or rather he had previously gained nocturnal entry in manner clandestine, for that other time he had help. A gate had been left unlocked for him, and a door ajar.

Entering that way was far easier and much preferable to this. But that time the opener of the gate had been bent on the public embarrassment and downfall of the Governor, and the thief was not.

Prince-Governor Kadakithis was no enemy, as a matter of fact, to this youth spawned in the shadows of the wrong end of town. The thief had rendered the Rankan prince two considerable services. He had been rewarded, too, although not in such a manner that he could live happily ever after.

Now, on this night of the most niggling of crescent moons, he stood atop the wall and took in his line from behind and below. It stretched upward still, to the pennon-spire. It remained taut. He had to believe that it would continue to do. Elsewise he was about to splatter onto the pave below like a dropped pomegranate, a fruit whose pulp is plentiful and whose juice is red.

When the line was again taut he yanked, dragged, braced, yanked, swallowed hard, and kicked himself off the wall into space. His stomach fell two storys to the pave; he did not. His soft-booted but padded feet struck another wall of cut fulvistone. Impact was no fun and he had to stifle his grunt.

Then he went up.

"D'jou hear something, Frax?" A voice like a horse-drawn sledge gliding over hard earth. Not stone, or sand, but packed dry earth.

"Mmm? Hm? Huh? Wha'?" A deeper voice.

"I said: Frax, did you hear something?"

Silence. (At sound of the voices the thief had frozen. Hands-forearms-torso atop the very palace; tail in space and legs adangle.)

"Uh-huh. I heard something, Purter. I heered her say 'Oh Frax you han'some dawg, you're the best. Now suck on thisun awhile, darling.' and then you woke me up, you bastard."

"We're supposed to be on guard duty, not sleeping, Frax, damn it. —Who was she?"

"Not gonto tell you. No I din't hear nothing. What's to hear? An army of Downwinders comin' over the friggin' walls? Somebody riding in on a hootey-owl?"

"Oh," Purter's higher voice said, with a shiver in it. "Don't say that. It's dark and creepy enough tonight."

"Stuporstishus rectum," Frax accused, with more austerity than skill, and lowered his head again onto his uplifted knees.

During their exchange the thief had got his rangy self onto the wall. He made hardly any sound, but those idiots would have drowned out something even as loud as snapping fingers. He wiggled through another embrasure and onto the defense gallery that ran around the top of the palace, below the dome and spire that rose on up, higher than the outer wall. Men trusted with guard duty, he was thinking contemptuously, heard something and blabbered. He shook his head. Idiots! He could teach these stupid soft-butted "soldiers" a thing or three about security! It took a civilian to know about the best security measures, in such a town as this. For one thing, when you thought you heard something, you shut the hell up and listened. Then you made just a little noise to pretend unconcern, and froze to catch the noisemaker in another movement.

The shadow of a shadow, he moved along the gallery, between the smooth curve of the dome and the crenelations of a wall. After thirty-one paces he heard the scuffing footsteps and tap-tapping pikestaff butt of a careless sentry. That persuaded him to squat, get as close to the wall as he could, and lie down. Flat, facing the wall, whose merlons rose above the gallery. He lay perfectly still, a shadow in shadow.

A spider wandered over his shoulder and up his cheek and began struggling in his black mop of hair, and was unmolested. The spider felt warmth, but no movement, not so much as a twitch. (If mental curses could have effect, the spider was a goner.)

The sentry ambled by, scuffing and tapping. The thief heard him yawn. Dumb, he thought, dumb. How nice it was of sentries to pace and make noise, rather than be still and listen!

The sentry having moved on leftward along the perimeter of the wall, the thief moved on rightward; northwestward. He'd an armlet of leather and copper well up his right upper arm, and a long bracer of black leather on that wrist. Each contained a nasty leaf-bladed throwing knife of dull blue-black. There was another in his left buskin, where sheath and hilt were mere decoration. He wore no other weapons, none that showed. Certainly he bore neither sword nor ax, and the bow lay at the base of the granary wall.

He stopped. Stepped into a crenel just above two feet deep. Stared, off into the darkness. Yes. There was the spire of the Temple of Holy Allestina Ever Virgin, poor thing. It was the first of the markers he had so carefully spotted and chosen, this afternoon.

The thief did not intend to enter the palace by just any window. He knew precisely where he was going.

The task of regaining line and arrow was more difficult than he had anticipated. He silenced snarls and curses. Knot a rope ten times and try swinging on it and the accursed thing might well work itself loose. Shoot an arrow to wrap a cord slimmer than a little finger around a damned gilded brass flagpole, and he had to fight to get the damned thing to let go!

Within four or six minutes (with silenced snarls and curses) he had sent enough loops and twitches ripple-writhing up the line to loosen the arrow. It swung once around the spire, twice, encountered the line, and caught. More curses, a sort of prayer, and more twitches and ripples riding up the line. Reluctantly the arrow ended its loving embrace of the pennon-spire. The line fluttered loose. Down came the arrow. It fell with a clatter that, to a shadowy thief in shadows, sounded like thunder on a cloudless day.

Sleepy sentries heard no thunder. Only he noticed. He reeled in line and arrow. In a crouch, he reached behind him into his snugly fitted backpack. From it he drew two cylinders of hardwood wrapped with black cloth. Around them he looped his line, arrow detached. He held silent for a time, listening. A fly hummed, restless and loud. The thief heard nothing to indicate that any of his actions had been noticed with anything approaching alarm.

Rising, he went on his way. Along the perimeter of the palace, along the flagged walkway betwixt dome and toothy wall.

Moving with a cat suppleness that would have been scary to any observer, he reached his second marker. Nicely framed between two merlons, he could see it, away off in the distance. The purple-black shape of Julavain's Hill. Again he smiled, tight of lip.

A merlon became a winch, aided by the two wooden cylinders brought for the purpose. They would pay out the silken cord and prevent the stone from slicing it. Its other end he secured to his ankles. And froze, waiting while the sentry clumped by. He was not importantly thumping his pike's butt, now. He no longer cared to keep himself awake. The thief gritted his teeth against the ghastly noise of the hardest of wood grating over harder flagstones. The porker was dragging his pike!

Then silence was thick enough to cut with a knife, of which the thief owned an abundance. He waited. And waited.

At last he stepped, still crouching, into the crenel. Turning, he carefully winched himself, backward, down the wall. Down and down, until he came to a particular window. It was cut in the shape of a diamond. That decision had involved more than esthetics; the damned thing was harder to enter.

Most carefully indeed, he turned. He paid out the cord with his hands until he was quite upside down outside that window. Blood flowed into his head while he strained muscles and vision until he was assured that the chamber was uninhabited.

Then, grinning, Hanse the thief flipped down and dropped lightly into the bedchamber of H.R.H. Kadakithis, Prince-Governor of Sanctuary.

He had done it again! And this time all on his own and without aid. He had breached the wall, eluded the guards, broken into the palace, and was in the very privatemost chamber of the Prince-Governor himself!

*Well, lord Prince, you wanted to see Shadowspawn—here he is, awaiting you!* Thus he thought while he freed his ankles of expensive silken line and removed his gloves. At least this time no bedmate waited here for her youthful lord.

It was all Hanse could do to keep from laughing aloud in sheerest prideful delight.

"A nice-looking girl left this here for you, Hanse," Moonflower the Seer had told him. "She got it from another—along with a coin for her trouble—who got it from still another."

Hanse raised his dark, dark brows and hooked a thumb in the shagreen belt he wore over a screamingly red sash. From one side of the belt was slung a dagger. An Ilbarsi knife, long as his whole arm, hung down his other leg.

"This you . . . *Saw,* Passionflower?"

She smiled, a hugely fat and grossly misnamed woman who overflowed two cushions atop a low stool. She saw him as a boyish boy and had ever let him turn her head with his charm, which she was almost alone in seeing.

"Oh no," Moonflower said almost archly, "I needed to go to no such trouble. I know things, you know."

"Oh, I know you know things, you clever darling," he told that gross dumpling in her several skirts, each of more than one unrepeated color. "And this time you're going to let me know how you know, I know."

She nodded at the wax-sealed walnut shell he was idly tossing in his left hand. "You know me too well, don't you, you naughty scamp! Smell it."

Up went his close-snuggling brows again, and he brought the shell to his nose. He rolled his eyes. "Aha! Perfume. A good one. Times are good for the only true mage of Sanctuary, then."

"You know that is not my perfume," she said, not without a sideward turn of her blue-tressed head to give him an arch look.

"*Now* I know that," Shadowspawn said, jocular and easygoing and almost cute in the sunlight, "because you tell me so. The walnut was given you by a well-off girl wearing good perfume, then. Betwixt her breasts, I'll bet, where she bore this charming charm."

She lifted a dimpled finger. "Ah! But that is the point. The scent on that charm is not mine, and the girl who gave it me wore none at all."

"Oh Moonflower, pride of the S'danzo and of Sanctuary! By Ils if the P-G knew of your genius, he'd not have that ugly old charlatan at court, but you, only you! So. By the perfume you know that there was a third woman, who gave this and a coin to another to give to you to give to me." He wagged his head. "What a game of roundabout! But what makes you think this thing was given her by still another, to begin with?"

"I saw the coin," Moonflower said, all kittenish inside a body to block a door or bring groans to a good steed.

"It bore still another scent?"

Moonflower laughed. "Ah Hanse, Hanse. I *know* that. Soon you will know too, surely, once you open the walnut shell. Surely it contains a message from someone who wanted no one to know he sent it to you."

"He?"

"Do you care to make a wager?"

He who was called Shadowspawn clutched the walnut to him in mock terror. With his other hand he clutched his purse theatrically. "Wager with you about your wisdon? Never! No one has accused me of being stupid." *Well, almost no one,* he mentally added, thinking of that burly stranger, Tempus the Hell-Hound . . . Tempus the . . . what?

"Be off with you and open it privily then. You're standing between me and paying clients!"

There were none present, Hanse assured himself before he said, "In a moment," and thumb-nailed the brownish wax along the lip-like closure of the walnut shell. He knew Moonflower was frowning, believing that he should be more secretive, but he also knew what he wanted to do. A gesture, merely a gesture. The scrap of extra fine leaf-paper he took out and poked, still folded, into his sash. Pressing the shell closed and thumbing the wax into a semblance of seal, he proffered it to the S'danzo seer who consistently proved that she was no charlatan.

"For Mignureal," he said, pretending shyness. "To scent her . . . her clothing, or something?"

For a moment the flicker of a frown appeared on Moonflower's doughy face, for her big-eyed daughter was quite taken with this dangerous youth from Downwind, whose means of income was no secret. Then she smiled and accepted the scented shell. It swiftly vanished into the vast cleavage of what she called her treasure chest, under her shawl.

"You're such a nice boy, Hanse. I'll give it to her. Now you git, and inspect your message. Maybe some highborn lady wants a bit of dalliance with your handsome self!"

The rangy young man called Shadowspawn had left her then. Smile and even pleasant expression left his face and he swaggered like a Mrsevadan gamecock. Face and walk were part of his image, which none would dare say might stem from insecurity. Still, Moonflower's words would not have made him smile anyhow. He was not handsome and knew it, as he knew that his height was no more than average. The biggest thing about him was his ego—although his lips, which some thought were sensuous, were to him too full. His nickname others had given him. He did not dislike it; his mentor Cudget Swearoath had told him a nickname was good to have—even such a one as "Swearoath." Hanse was just a name; *Shadowspawn* was dramatic, with a romantic and rather sinister sound that appealed to the youth.

He left Moonflower remembering how he had indeed dallied with a beauty of means. Highborn she was not, though she had been from the palace, and richly garbed. Hanse had been touched both in his ego and in his greed, by her attentions. Only later had he discovered that it was not truly he she was interested in. She and a fellow plotter were in the employ of someone back in Ranke—the emperor himself, perhaps envious or wary of Kadakithis's good looks?—who wanted to discredit and destroy the new Prince-Governor, him they called Kittycat. They had elected to use Hanse in their plot; Hanse had been their dupe!—for a while.

But that was done with, and on this later day he left Moonflower and swaggered along the streets. His eyes were hooded and the weapons all too obvious on him. Some stepped off the narrow planking of the sidewalk for him, and (quietly) cursed themselves for it. Still, they would do it again. In appearance, all tucked in behind his eyes and abristle with sharp blades, he was "about as pleasant as gout or dropsy," as a certain merchant had once described him.

Well, he was alive. Both the lovely plotter and her traitorous Hell-Hound co-conspirator were not. Further, Kadakithis was grateful. And now, as Hanse discovered to his astonishment back in his quarters, the Prince-Governor had actually sent him a note!

Hanse recognized the seal and the scrawl at the bottom from other documents. Since Prince Kadakithis knew that Hanse could not read, the bit of fine paper contained not writing, but clever drawings. The Governor's seal, with a hand extending from it, beckoning to a dark splotch. It was man-shaped—a shadow. Under that was an untidy jumble of (turnip slices?) with straight lines raying up from them. Shadowspawn's frown was a momentary thing. Then he was nodding in comprehension—he hoped.

"The P-G wants me to come calling on him, and here's a promise of reward: shiny coins. He sealed up the message in the walnut shell and gave it to one of his harem, with instructions. No one should see Hanse the thief receive a message from the Prince-Governor, else Hanse's name become Plague and he be avoided the same. So that girl found another, and passed on the walnut and a coin, with her lord's instructions: 'Take this to Moonflower for Hanse.' "

And she had actually done it, without prying open the shell in an attempt to gain greater treasure than one coin! Well, miracles had happened before, Hanse mused, gazing pensively at the strange message. Had she opened the shell, she'd likely have discarded the note.

Or nervously pressed it back into the shell to scuttle to Moonflower with it. *Maybe someone does know that Hanse received a message that shows a beckoning hand from the Rankan seal, and a pile of coin. I hope she's the quiet sort! If I knew who she is, I'd scare her into silence. But then maybe she didn't open it at all . . .*

*The point is, I hate to walk into the palace, day or night. How would that look? Me!*

*Besides, someone inside probably spies for someone out here, and the word would be passed. Hanse just walked right up and in, and he was passed, too! Better watch him; maybe he's a spy for that golden-haired Rankan* boy *in the palace!*

And so Hanse had thought on that, and begun to grin, and then to plan, and out he went to reconnoiter and plan, and now he had *broken* in, all unseen and unknown, to await his summoner in the latter's own privy apartment!

And now, sitting there waiting, Hanse reflected and contemplated the more, and his face clouded. The prickling in his arms started slowly, and grew.

Unwittingly the tool of that pretty Lirain who had so cleverly seduced or "seduced" him (with no trouble at all!), he had gained this apartment before, also by night and secretly. That time he had stolen the very symbol of Rankan power, that wand called the Savankh. Eventually all that had turned out, and governor and thief reached an understanding. By way of reward, Hanse was granted pardon for all he might have done—once he had assured the royal youth that he had never slain. (He had, since. It afforded him little enjoyment or pride.) Hanse also came out of that painful adventure with a nice little fortune.

Unfortunately it was in two saddlebags currently reposing at the bottom of a well. He hoped those saddlebags were of good leather.

Now he had broken in here twice. This time he had proven that he could enter this apartment without help from inside or out. What then, when Kadakithis gave thought to that?

Hanse had respect for the youthful Rankan's mind. It even possessed a devious quality. Hanse had seen and felt proof of that, when as Kadakithis's unwilling agent he had participated in the ruin of the two plotters, Bourne and Lirain.

Suppose, the frowning Hanse mused, that Kadakithis pondered, and kept thinking.

There existed in Sanctuary one who could gain his chambers and thus his royal and gubernatorial self, at will. At any time, and never mind guards and sentries! Suppose that one chose to come again, as thief?—or was hired to do, as assassin? Would such a possibility not tend to prey on Kadakithis's good mind? Might he not decide that he was less than wise to trust him called Shadowspawn, a thief and ruthless besides? Might he not go even further in his thinking, and decide—wisely, as he would see it—that all things considered, Hanse was more dangerous than valuable?

In that case, the Prince-Governor might very well conclude, he and thus Sanctuary and thus Ranke were better off without such worries, such a possibility. In that event, it might occur to him that the world were better off without Hanse's continued presence in it. Nor would the world take heed of the timely demise of a cocky young thief.

Hanse swallowed, blinked. Sitting stiffly on a divan in the luxurious apartment, he put it all through his mind again and chased its tail. He came to his own conclusion.

I have been a fool. I did all this for my pride, to be such a clever fellow. I am a clever thief, but a stupid fellow! Being here thus when he comes in could gain me another signature on another document from him—this time my death-order! Oh damn, plague and pox, what have I done!?

Nothing, he thought as he rose with a great sigh, that could not be undone . . . he hoped. All he had to do was betake himself from here so that neither Kadakithis nor anyone else would ever know he had broken in. He glanced around and swallowed hard. It certainly was hard and against the grain not to steal something!

And so Shadowspawn went to the window, and wearily began the process of breaking out of the Governor's Palace and its grounds.

2

"It develops that I need help," Prince-Governor Kadakithis said, "and I cannot see a way to threaten it out of anyone."

"Including me?"

"Including you, Hanse. Furthermore, if you won't help, I can't see how I can punish you either."

"I'm glad to hear it. But I didn't know there were things a governor couldn't do, much less a prince."

"Well, Shadowspawn, now you know. Even Kittycat isn't all powerful."

"You need help and the Hell-Hounds can't provide it?"

"That is close, Hanse. The *Imperial Elite Guardsmen* cannot help me with this. Or so I perceive it."

"I sure do wish you would sit down, Highness, so I can."

Kadakithis walked across the rich carpet of his privatemost chamber and sat on the edge of the peacock spread of his bed. He gestured. "Do take that divan, Hanse, or those cushions as it pleases you."

Hanse nodded his thanks. He sank among the cushions, curbing a grin at their luxury. Last night he had sat on the divan, and only he knew it. This day he chose the luxury of the jumble of stuffed Aurveshan silk. (Quag the Hell-Hound had been on duty at the gate. He had recognized the hooded blind beggar, who winked at him. Having been secretly apprised that Hanse was invited, Quag conducted the blind beggar to His Highness. The hooded robe lay on the bed beside the Prince now, who had congratulated Hanse on the cleverness of his entry. Hanse forbore to tell him how much more clever he had been last night.)

Now he decided that he could afford a modicum of daring: "Either I'm hearing sideways or you just told me you need me for something the Hell-Hounds—I mean Imperial Elites—can't do. Or that your Highness can't trust them with? Or that you don't want them to know about."

Revelation: "Or . . . something illegal?"

"I will not affirm or deny anything that you have said." That said, the Prince merely gazed at him. The boy did a good job of looking enigmatic, Hanse mused, overlooking the fact that they were about the same age.

"If the Prince will forgive my saying it . . . his Chief of Security is surely not one to balk at such a . . . mission."

The Prince continued to stare. One pale eyebrow rose slightly under that disgustingly handsome shock of yellow hair. And then Hanse was staring.

"Tempus! It's *about* Tempus, isn't it! I haven't seen him for weeks."

Kadakithis turned his gaze on an ornate Yenizedish tapestry. "Hanse: neither have I."

"He is not on a mission for your Highness?"

"Just use the pronoun for me, Hanse, and we can save whole days of our lives. No. He is not. He is missing. Who might wish him to be missing?"

Hanse was wary of being used as informant, but saw no reason not to answer that one. "Oh, half the people in town. Maybe more. About the same number that would wish the governor to be missing. Your pardon of course, Governor. Or the Emperor. Or Ranke."

"Hmm. Well, empire is built on conquest, not love, however often they are the same. But I have striven to be decent here. Fair."

Hanse considered. "It is possible that you have been fairer than we might have expected."

"Nicely put. Carefully chosen words. You may well become a diplomat yet, Shadowspawn. And the *Hell-Hounds?* What of them?"

Hanse smiled briefly at the slim noble's calling his elite guards by the people's name for them; indeed, even the Hell-Hounds called themselves Hell-Hounds these days. It was a dramatic name with a romantic and rather sinister sound that appealed to their sort.

"Shall I answer that, to one from Ranke, with all the power there is? What power have I?"

"You have influence with the Prince-Governor, Hanse, and with his Chief of Security. You uncovered the plot against me and helped break it up. You regained that awful fear-rod, and it cost you. Recently you helped Tempus in a matter, too. Now we are even in one area at least, aren't we?"

"Even? I? Me? Hanse of Sanctuary and the Emperor's brother?"

"Stepbrother," the Prince corrected, and fixed Hanse with a wide-eyed gaze, all blue. It reminded Hanse of his own ingenuous pose. "Yes. Now we have both killed. I, Bourne. You . . . the night Tempus lost his horse."

"The Prince-Governor is not without knowledge," Hanse observed.

"Another careful, diplomat's phrasing! Now: Tempus set himself to destroying the minions of that Jubal fellow. Do you know why?"

"Maybe Tempus is a racist," Hanse said, trying to look wide-eyed and ingenuous.

It didn't appear to be working. Damn. This golden-locked boy was smarter than Moonflower, despite her extra-human ability. Hanse sighed. "You know. Jubal is a slaver and those weird-masked employees of his are feared. He has respect, and power. Tempus works for you, for Ranke's power."

"Let's don't go making wagers on that. Would you say his killing of those in the blue bird-masks might be called murder, Hanse?"

"It might if it was one of us," Hanse said, to the gleaming top of a low table. "Surely not for him that calls us Wrigglies, though."

The Prince failed to disguise his little start. "Strong words, Hanse of Sanctuary. And to one who does *not* call the Children of Ils 'Wrigglies'!"

"Yes, and I really wish I hadn't said it. As a matter of fact I wish I wasn't here at all. How can I share confidences here? How can I say my mind to you, when you aren't a you, but both prince and governor?"

"Hanse: we have been through some things together."

*In a manner of speaking,* Hanse thought. *You weren't poked with that damned terror-stick, and you didn't spend half the night down a well and the other on a torturer's table!*

"I might even consider myself in your debt," Kadakithis went on.

"I am getting awfully uncomfortable, my lord of Ranke," Hanse said elaborately. "Will my lord Prince tell me why I am here?"

"Damn!" Kadakithis regarded the carpet and heaved a great sigh. "I've an idea it would be a waste of time to offer you wine, my friend. So I—"

"*Friend!*"

"Why yes, Hanse," Kadakithis said, all large of eye and open-looking. "I call you friend. We are even of an age."

Hanse erupted to his feet in a jerk that was still admirably sinuous. He paced. "Oh," he said, and paced. "Oh gods, Prince—don't call me friend! Don't let anyone else hear that!"

The Prince looked very much as if he wanted to touch him, and was sure that Hanse would shrink away. "How lonely we both are, Hanse. You *won't* have any friends, and I can't! I dare trust no one, and you who could trust—you reject even an extended hand."

Hanse was almost stricken. Friends? He thought of Cudget, dead Cudget. Of Moonflower. Of Tempus. Was Tempus a friend? Who could trust Tempus? Who could trust anyone wearing the title "governor?"

"Ranke and Sanctuary are not friends," he said slowly, quietly. "You are Ranke. I am of Sanctuary, and . . . more. Not, uh, noble."

"Trusted friend of the governor? The thief Shadowspawn?"

Hanse caught himself about to say "Thief? Who, me, Governor?" and stopped the words. Kadakithis knew. Nor was he Moonflower or that melon-peddler Irohunda, to be taken in by Hanse's cultivated (and seldom used) boyish act. But . . . *friend?* It was a frightening word, to Shadowspawn from Downwind and the Maze.

"Let's try to be bigger than Ranke and Sanctuary. Let's *try,* Hanse. I am reaching out. Speaking plainly: Tempus declared war on Jubal—*not on my orders*—and Jubal retaliated or tried to. You were there and you didn't run. Tempus lost a horse and gained a friend. You defended Tempus, helped him. More hawk-masks died. Are you in danger for that, from Jubal?"

"Probably. I've been trying not to think about that."

"And me?"

"The Empire's governor in Sanctuary knows to go forth armed and with guards, because he is governor," Hanse said, not so enigmatically.

"Diplomatic, careful words again! —And Tempus?"

It was then that Hanse knew why he was here. "You . . . you think Jubal has Tempus!"

The Prince regarded him. "Hanse, some people don't try to be particularly likable. Tempus seems to try *not* to be. I cannot imagine calling him friend." Kadakithis paused to be certain Hanse grasped his implication. "Still, I represent the Empire. I govern for Ranke, subject to the Emperor, Tempus serves and represents me, and Ranke. I do not have to love him, or like him. *But!* How can I tolerate anyone's taking action against any of my people?" Kadakithis made a two-handed gesture while Hanse thought: *How strange that I think more of Tempus— Thales—than the Prince-Governor he serves!* "I cannot, Hanse! Nor can I use the Hell-Hounds to investigate, not in a really sensitive matter such as this. Nor can I launch an attack on Jubal, or even arrest him— not and govern the way I wish to do."

*He really does want to do well, to be friends with Sanctuary! What a strange Rankan!* "You could call him in for questioning." Hanse was hopeful.

"I had rather not." The young Rankan called Kittycat shot to his feet with admirable use of legs alone, if not with a thief's sinuous grace. "I had rather not acknowledge his existence, can you see that?" He waved a hand in a rustle of aquamarine silk sleeve, took a pace, turned his earnest face on Hanse. "I am governor here. I am Empire. He is—"

"Gods, Prince, I'm only a damned thief!"

Kadakithis frowned and glanced around, ignoring Hanse's look of horror at his blurted words. "Did you hear someone say something, just then?"

"No."

"Neither did I. As I was saying. Tempus doesn't mean that much to me and I don't mean that much to Tempus. Tempus, I fear, serves Tempus and whatever he fancies is his destiny. I might not even miss him. Still, there are some things I dare not allow, dare not tolerate. Oh how I wish you could understand a bit of how difficult it is, being born royal, and holding this job!"

Hanse, who had never held any job, tried. And without trying, he looked earnest and sympathetic. With a prince!

"Now I think that you are Tempus's friend, Hanse. Would Jubal torture him?"

Hanse felt himself about to develop a taste for strong drink. Looking at the other very young man's sash—an Ilsigi sash—he nodded. Abruptly he wanted to curse. Instead he felt an unwonted and unwanted prayer come cat-sidling into his mind: *O Ils, god of my people and father of Shalpa my patron! It is true that Tempus-Thales serves Vashanka Tenslayer. But help us, help us both, Lord Ils, and I swear to do all I can to destroy Vashanka Sister-wifer or drive him hence, if only You will show me the way!*

And Hanse blinked, and hurled that ridiculous and unwelcome thought bodily from his mind. Prayers indeed!

"Hanse . . . consider the limits to my power. I am not a man named Kadakithis; I am governor. I *cannot* do anything about it. *I* cannot."

Hanse looked up to meet those cerulean eyes. "Prince, if someone broke in here to kill you right now, I'd probably defend you. But I would not try to sneak into Jubal's keep for half your fortune and all your women."

"Alone against Jubal? Lord, neither would I!" Kadakithis came to him then, and laid hands on a thief's shoulders. His eyes were intense and large. "My only request of you, Hanse, is . . . I just wish you'd agree to try to learn where Tempus is. That's all. Your way, Hanse, and for a lot less reward than half my fortune and the women I brought here."

Hanse backed from under those hands, from those staring eyes so full of sincerity. He paced to the bed, and the hooded robe of a blind beggar.

"I wish to leave by the fourth window down, Prince. That way I can let myself onto the roof of your smokehouse. If you were to call in your sentinels for review, I'd be out of here by the time they reached your presence."

Kadakithis nodded. "And?"

"And I—I don't want any reward but don't dare ever tell anyone I said that, or remind me! You'll hear from me—" he whirled and skewered the other very young man with a gaze like an accusation—"*friend.*"

Kadakithis was wise enough to nod without smile or comment. Besides, he looked more as if he wanted to cry, or reach out.

"I understand your reason, Hanse. But, are you sure you can manage to break out of here . . . the *palace?*"

Hanse turned away to roll his eyes. "With your help, Prince, I *may* be able to do it. I'd hate to have to try to break *in,* though!"

3

It might have taken a trained investigator from Ranke a week, or a lifetime. It might have taken a Hell-Hound a month or two lifetimes (a Tempus lifetime?), or a couple of days with the aid of shining ugly instruments of suasion. It took a thief of Sanctuary less than a full day to collect the information. Had he had letters, he'd have made a list.

Since he was unlettered, he must reckon and account in his head, once he had talked with this one and that one and some others. Only one realized that he was actively seeking information, and that was because Hanse let her know. Now he made his list, in his head, while he sprawled on his own bed and stared at nothing in particular.

Tempus did not get on with the other Hell-Hounds.

Tempus waged private war on Jubal. It was his own decision. (Not a good one; Jubal's business profited Thieves' World and Empire as well.)

Jubal was a merchant who dealt in human merchandise. He provided some few to that scrawny Kurd fellow of whom even hardened Sanctuarites spoke susurrantly and with glances cast uncomfortably this way and that.

In the barracks, Tempus had had serious trouble with Razkuli and that snarly-growly Zalbar. (Quag had mentioned that to a certain woman under the most intimate of circumstances. A bad but common time for the imparting of confidences.)

Stulwig Northborn had spent a shining coin bearing the Emperor's likeness. Such coinage was not all that common here, although it was welcome. People of the governor's staff occasionally spent such coins. Likely then someone had bought something of Stulwig; someone from the palace. Stulwig dealt in potions and drugs and worse.

Harmocohl Dripnose had most recently seen two men conveying a sizable burden to the lovely gardened home of Kurd. Harmocohl's impression was that the two were hood-cloaked Hell-Hounds.

Hell-Hounds were elite Imperial guardsmen and did not deal with such as Stulwig or Kurd. Indeed, at least one of them hated Kurd. Hardly likely that Hell-Hounds would deliver a human package to him. Unless there was someone they hated more than the dark experimenter.

Tempus was missing.

The word was out that Jubal heroically sold no more human merchandise to Kurd the vivisectionist . . . a man with a Rankan accent.

Why would such as Jubal cut off such a source of revenue? For moral reasons, because Kurd did evil things to people? Hardly. Because Jubal had made a deal with other enemies of Tempus? Zalbar and Razkuli, perhaps? Because Tempus was now in the mysterious experimenter's foul and reeking hands, perhaps?

In an ugly dark stenchy room Hanse learned more of Kurd and his business. Kurd claimed to be dedicated to the god Science. Medicine. That required experimentation. But Kurd was not content to experiment with the wounded and victims of accidents. The pallid fellow created his own. And, Hanse thought with rather more than distaste, Kurd could occupy himself for a lifetime with one whose wounds—Hanse suspected and thought he knew—healed with inhuman speed and completeness. Make that superhuman, or preternatural. Tempus-call-me-Thales was a man of war who had participated in many battles. Yet there were no scars on the man. Not one.

Tempus/Thales.

"You, I own, can call me anytime," he had told Hanse, and "my friend," he had called Hanse, and "Just tell me not to call you friend," he had dared Hanse. And Hanse had not been able to tell him that, thus revealing and silently replying that he was close onto desperate for friends, a friend; for someone to care about him. For someone to care about.

Hanse sprawled supine on his bed in an upstairs room in the heart of the Maze, and he pondered what he had learned. He rose to pace and chew his full lower lip and ponder, with his soul and heart and longing all naked in his eyes so that it was good no one was there to see, for Hanse wanted others to see only what he deliberately projected.

*All I need do is report all this to Kitt—to Kadakithis,* he thought. The Prince-Governor who had begun his term here by announcing that there would be law and order and safety for citizens and had hanged, among others, one Cudget Swearoath, mentor (and father image?) to Hanse. The P-G did not like Tempus (and father image?) to Hanse.

It was all Hanse need do. Just report what he had learned and now suspected. Then it was up to Kadakithis. He had the power and the resources. The men and the swords. The Savankh.

Surely that was as far as Hanse's responsibility extended, to Kadakithis and to Tempus. If he had any responsibility to that krrf-snorting bully.

And . . . suppose H.R.H. Kadakithis, P-G, did nothing? Or if his Hell-Hounds, the charming Razkuli and Zalbar, received their orders but only pretended to act. Did not Rankans protect their own? Did not soldiers obey authority? Was there not honor among those thieving over-Lords?

If not, then Hanse's world would be a-teeter. Despite his pretenses there had to be trust and some sort of order, didn't there, and trustworthiness? Hanse frowned and looked about almost wildly. An animal in a cage it feared but could not escape, yet also feared what lay beyond the bars. Even the spawn of shadows did not want to live in a world that askew and a-teeter. If it existed, if the world was truly a thing of Chance and Chaos, he preferred not to know. Fighting it, he had learned to trust Tempus. He had been *forced* to trust Kadakithis, because he was down a well up at Eaglenest. Later, disbelieving and resisting, he had learned that he *could* trust the Rankan. That disturbed his haven of cynicism and was hard to admit. But was not cynicism merely a mask on an idealist seeking more, seeking perfection, seeking disproof of his cynical assumptions?

*Far better just to report what I know and leave it at that and go on about my business.* That would be enough. Tempus already owed him a debt, anyhow, and had promised him a service.

Shadowspawn began collecting his materials for a night of stealth, of breaking and entering. It was a thief's business and these were the tools. Yet he knew that he was not preparing for theft.

*You are a fool, Hanse,* he told himself with a curse in Shalpa's name, and he agreed. And he continued with what he was doing.

At the door he stopped, blinking. He looked back with a frown. Only now did he remember the look Mignureal had given him just two hours ago, and her strange words. They meant nothing and connected to nothing. "Oh, Hanse," she had said with a strange intensity on her girlish face. "Hanse—take the crossed brown pot with you."

"With me where?"

But she had to flee, for her glowering mother was calling.

Now Hanse stared at the brown crock with the etched pair of X's. Mignureal did not know about it. She could not. Mignureal had mentioned it specifically! She was Moonflower's daughter . . . Name of the Shadowed One, she must have some of the power too!

Hanse turned back to pick up that well-stoppered container, a fired pot a bit larger than a soldier's canteen. *Why, Mignureal? Why, Lord Ils?*

He had acquired it months ago, easily and quickly, without knowing what it contained. Mignureal had never seen it and could not know about this container of quicklime. She could not know where he was going this night for he had only just decided (and that without quite admitting it to himself); she was Moonflower's daughter . . .

Stupid, cumbersome, senseless, he thought while he slipped the crock into a good oilskin bag he had lifted in the bazaar. He secured it to his belt so that it rested high on one buttock. And he touched the sandal of Thufir tacked above the door, and went forth.

The white blaze of the sun had hours since become yellow in its daily waning, and then orange. Now it quatted low and seemed to spray streamers of crimson across the darkening sky. It did not look at all like blood, Hanse told himself. Besides, soon it would be dark and his friends would be everywhere, in black and indigo and charcoal. The shadows.

*I could use a good sword,* the shadow thought, blending into another shadow. An eerie feeling still lay on him, from that business with Mignureal. Surely not even Kurd deserved quicklime! *This long "knife" from the Ilbarsi Hills is a good tool,* he thought, to keep his mind on sensible, practical matters. *But it's time I had a good sword.*

*I'll have to try and steal one.*

*"Thou shalt have a sword,"* a voice said sonorously inside his head, a lion within the shadowed corridors of his mind, *"if thou free'st my valued and loyal ally. Aye, and a fine sheath for it, as well. In silver!"*

Hanse stopped. He was still and dark as the shadow of a tree or a wall of stone. He was good at it; six minutes ago four cautious people had passed close enough to touch him, and never knew he was there.

*I want nothing of you, incestuous god of Ranke,* he thought, almost speaking while a thousand ants seemed at play along his spine. *Tempus serves you. I do not and will not.*

*Yet you do this night, seeking him,* that silent voice that was surely the god Vashanka's said. And a cloud ate the moon.

*No! I serve—I mean . . . I do not . . . No! . . . Tempus is my . . . my . . . I go to aid a fr—man who might help me! Leave me and go to him, jealous god of Ranke! Leave Sanctuary to my patron Shalpa the Swift, and Our Lord Ils. Ils, Ils O Lord of a Thousand Eyes, why is it not You who speaks to me?*

There was no reply. Clouds rolled and they seemed dark men astride dark horses that loped with manes and long tails aflow. Hanse felt a sudden chill absence of that presence in his mind. In a few seconds he was praying not to gods but cursing himself for giving heed to the delusions of a dark night, a night badly ruled by a moon pale as a Rankan concubine and now covered like the whore she was. The Swift-footed One ruled this night.

And Hanse went on, not in shadows now for there were no shadows; all the land was one vast shadow. Out of Sanctuary. Past lovers who neither saw nor heard this son of Shalpa the Shadowed One. On, to the beautifully tended gardens surrounding the house of a pasty-faced walking skeleton called Kurd and worse. The little crescent of moon pretended to return. It was only a ghost struggling weakly against clouds like restless shadows blotting the sky.

The well-tended, scented gardens provided a pleasant if unneeded cover. A gliding anthropomorphic shadow amid herbaceous shapes like looming shadows. Hanse went right up to the house. It too was dark.

*No one wants to visit Kurd. No one considers trying to steal from Kurd. Why should it not be easy, then? Kurd must think he needs no precautions or defenders!*

Still, he kept his lips over his teeth when he smiled. He glided into the fragrant shrubs, odd deciduous shrubs with long thin branchlets, set up close against Kurd's house exulting in how simple it was, and then the bush's trailing tendrils moved, rustling, and turned, and twined, and clutched. And clamped. And Shadowspawn understood then that Kurd was not without exterior defenses.

Even as he struggled—fruitlessly, against frutescence—he knew that the knowledge was gained too late. Whether this thing was bent on strangling him or twisting his limbs until they broke or merely holding him until someone came, it was more horribly effective than human guards or three watchdogs. Amid silent rustling horror Hanse tugged at the tendril more slender than a brooch-pin, and only cut his fingers. His knife he only dulled, sawing at a purposeful tendril that gave but refused to be cut. And they moved, twining, rustling, insinuating themselves between his arms and body and around his legs and arms and torso and—throat!

That one he fought until his fingers bled. It was relentless. *O ye gods, no, no, not like this*—he was going to die, silently strangled by a damned skinny plant's tendril!

He was, too. His "N—" disposed of his last breadth. He could not draw another. As his eyes started to bulge and a dull hum commenced to invade his ears on the way to becoming a roar and then eternal silence, it occurred to him that Kurd's garden could do more than strangle him. If it continued to tighten, it would slice in and in until it beheaded a strangled corpse.

Hanse fought with all his strength and the added power of desperation. As well have resisted the tide, or the sand of the desert. His movements became more restricted as his limbs were more and more constricted. Dizziness began to build like storm clouds and the hum rose to the roar of a gale.

So did the clouds above, and great big drops of water commenced to fall from the laden sky. That was just as eerie and impossible, for rain in Sanctuary fell in accord with the season, and this was not that season. The land was weeks away from the time called Lizard Summer, when lizards fried or were said to fry in their own juices, out on the desert.

What matter? Plants loved rain. And this one loved to kill. And it was killing Hanse, who was losing consciousness and feeling while his hearing became restricted to the roar inside his head. More rain fell and Hanse, dying, tried to swallow and could not and did what he thought he could never do: he began to give up.

Memory came like a white flash of late summer lightning. He heard her words as clearly as he had hours ago. *"Hanse—take the crossed brown pot with you."*

Even that blazing flare of hope seemed too late, for how could his bound arms detach the bag from his belt, open it, open the crock inside, and give this predatory plant a message it might understand?

Answer: he could not.

He could, however, dying, jerk his forearm four or five inches. He did, again and again, breathless, dying, losing consciousness but still moving, puncturing the leather bag again and again and banging the point of his knife off the pot which was smooth, glazed, well made, and O damn it all too damned *hard!*

It broke. Shards punched through knife holes and widened them to let quicklime spill down in a candent stream. Hanse was sure it hissed in the moist grass about the moist base of the strangler plant—but Hanse could not hear that hissing or anything else save the roar of a surf more powerful than life could withstand.

He slumped, dead now with streamers of caustic steam rising above his legs—and a suddenly frenetic shrub began waving and snapping its tendrils about as if caught by the very Compass Bag itself, whence issues the wind of every direction at once. In those whipping throes it not only released its prey, it hurled him several feet backward. He lay sprawled, away from the plant and clear of the smoking corrosive death about its base, and the soles of his buskins smoked. Rain pelted his face and he lay still, still, while the killer plant died.

*It was not raining in Sanctuary but out of a clear night sky came a sizzling bolt that hardly rocked the structure that grounded it. The graven name* VASHANKA, *however, abruptly disappeared from the facade of that structure, which was the Governor's Palace.*

4

*Oh damn, but my damned head aches!*
*Pox and plague, that's rain on my face and I'm getting soaked!*
*Holy cess—I'm* alive!

None of those thoughts prompted Hanse to move, not for a longish while. Then he tried opening his mouth to let rain assuage a sore throat, and choked on the fifth or sixth drop. He sat up hurriedly. His grunt was not from his head, which felt fat and swollen and stuffed to bursting. He rolled swiftly leftward off a source of sharper pain. He had been lying on his back. Under him, thonged to his belt, had been the ruins of a nice leathern bag of broken pottery.

*If I don't bleed to death I'll be picking pieces of pottery out of my tail for a week!*

That thought made him angry and with a low groan he rose to glare triumphantly on the faintly smoking remnant of a destroyed shrub. Its neighbor looked almost as bad. Shadowspawn took no chances with it. Avoiding shrubs and indeed anything herbaceous that was larger than a blade of grass, he went to the nearest window. Just as he completed his slow slicing of the sheet of pig's bladder stretched over the opening, he heard the awful sound from within. A groan, long and wavery and hideous. Hanse went all over gooseflesh and considered heading for home.

He did not. He peeled aside the ruined window and peered into a dark room containing neither bed nor person. Mindful of his punctured and lacerated buttock, he went in. There was nothing to do about his head. He had, after all, been strangled to death. Or come so close that the difference wasn't worth considering—save that he was alive, which was absolutely all the difference that mattered.

After a long measured while of standing frozen, listening, staring in effort to make his eyes see, he moved. He heard nothing. No groan, no movement, no rain. The moon was back. It was not in line with the window, but it was up there and a little light sneaked in to aid a thief.

He found a wall, a jamb. Squatted, then went lower, wincing at rearward pain, to ensure that no light showed under the door. The latch was a simple press-down hook. He took his time depressing it. He took more time in slowly, slowly pulling open the door. It revealed a corridor or short hall.

While he wondered whether to go right or leftward, that ghastly sound of agony came again. This time a pulpy mumble underlay the moaning groan, and once again Hanse felt the icy, antsy touch of gooseflesh.

The sound came from his right. He slipped his knife back into its sheath, patted other sheathed knives, and undid the thong at his belt to get the bag off. That hurt, as a shard of pottery emerged from his clothing, and him. That hand he moved very slowly, mindful of the clink of broken pottery. He squinted before he glanced back, because he did not want his enlarged pupils to shrink.

The window showed a pretty night, small-mooned but dark of sky, without clouds or rain. Without even knowing that the rain had been confined to Kurd's grounds, Shadowspawn shivered. Did gods exist? Did gods help?

Hanse took a long step into the corridor and turned right. The bag swung at the end of its thong from his right hand. Just in case someone popped up, that might make him look less deadly: anyone sensible would assume him to be normally right-handed.

As he reached the end of the hall with a big door ahead and another on his left, someone popped up. The side door opened and light rushed forth. It flared from the oil lamp in the hand of a gnome-like man who wore only a long ungirt tunic; a nightshirt.

"Here—" he began and Hanse said "Here yourself" and hit him with the wet, rent bag of broken pottery. Since it struck the fellow in the face, he moaned and let go the lamp to rush both hands to his bloodied face. "Damn," Hanse said, watching hot oil slosh onto the man's tunic and bare legs and feet. It also splashed wall and door and ran along the floor, burning. At the same time, a third groan of unendurable agony rose behind the other door, the big one still closed.

"Master!" Hanse screeched, high-voiced. "FIRE!" And he shoved the squatty fellow backward, kicked the burning lamp in after him, and yanked the door shut. Instantly he attacked the other one, and soon entered Hell.

Part of a man lay on a table, a short skinny fellow. He was even shorter and skinnier now, bereft of both legs and both arms, all his hair, and his left nipple with part of the pectoral. Even as Hanse shuddered, he knew there was only one form of rescue for this wretch. Ignoring the shining sharp instruments Kurd used, Hanse drew the arm-long blade those crazies up in the Ilbars Hills called a knife, got his best two-handed grip, and struck with all his might. Blood gushed and Hanse clamped his teeth against vomit. He had to strike again to complete the job. Now only a torso lay on the table, and a shuddering Shadow-spawn clung to the weapon as he squinted around a chamber full of tables and thoughtfully provided with graded runnels in the floor, for the carrying off of blood.

"Thales?"

Two groans replied. One of them ended with "help," weak as a kitten. It was not Tempus's voice, but Hanse went to that table.

"He—he—he's cut off my right arm and . . . and three fingers of my my l-l-le-eft hannnd . . . just to . . . just to . . ." An enormous body-shaking shudder refused to let the man finish.

"You do not bleed. Your legs? Feet?" Hanse was squinting without really wanting to see.

"I—I—they . . . there . . ."

"Think," Shadowspawn said, swallowing hard. "I can cut these straps or your throat. Think, and choose." He started to turn away.

"I am . . . ali-i-ive . . . I can wa-a-alk . . ."

Hanse sliced off the man's restraining straps. "I seek Tempus."

"You seek death here, thief!" a voice said, and light flooded the chamber.

Hanse didn't pause to reply or look to see who bore the light. He turned, plucking forth a guardless knife like a leaf of steel, and threw. Only then did he really look at the man in the doorway; throw once to disconcert, the second time with aim. Lean and more than lean the man was, pallid skin taut. A man in a voluminous nightshirt, a man to get a chill from a south wind in June. A man who held a cocked crossbow in one hand, awkwardly, and a closed lamp or lanthorn in the other, sleeve sliding back to show an arm of bone plated with parchment. Kurd.

He was ducking the whizzing knife that missed by several inches. The lanthorn swung wildly, splashing lunatic flashes of yellow light off walls and floor and tables with ghastly stains. The dope should have put the light down first, Hanse thought, plucking out another sliver of sharp steel. With both hands on that little crossbow Kurd might be danger-ous. Instead his arm was nailed to the door by a knife that caught cloth but only raked skin—there was no flesh—so that the monster cried out more in fear than in pain. The crossbow hit the floor, thunked, and sent its bolt thunk-twanging into a wall or a table leg or—Hanse didn't care.

"I'm here for Tempus, butcher. Just stand there and provide light. Move and I'll throw again." He showed Kurd a third bright blade, sheathed it. "You'd look good with another navel, anyhow." Then he went to the source of the third groan. "Oh, oh gods, oh, oh gods why is this *allowed?*"

No god answered the anguished query torn from Shadowspawn by the sight of Tempus.

Big blond Tempus answered, scarless and armless, and the answer came from a mouth without a tongue. He managed to make Hanse un-derstand that three pins were stuck into each stump. Hanse steeled himself to pull them out before turning to gush vomit onto the grooved floor of Kurd's laboratory of torment, and whirled back to send such a glare at the vivisectionist that Kurd shivered and stood still as a statue, lanthorn held high.

Hanse cut Tempus loose and helped him sit up. The big man did not bleed. He bore various cuts, all of which looked old. They were not. He made stomach- and heart-wrenching sounds, ghastly noises that Hanse interpreted as *"I'll heal,"* which was just as ghastly. What *was* this man?

"Can you walk?"

More noises. Repeated. Again. Hanse thought he understood, and bent to look. Yes. Minus some toes, Tempus had said. He was. Three. No, four. The middle one was gone from the left foot.

"Thales, there's only me and I can't carry you. I freed another and he can't help. What shall I do?"

It took Tempus a long while to make him understand, trying to form words without a tongue, and once Kurd moved. Hanse turned to see the other freed wretch fleeing past the vivisectionist. Hanse threatened and Kurd froze. He held the lantern in a quivering hand at the end of a wavering arm.

*Strap Kurd to a table,* Tempus had said. *Where's servant?*

Kurd answered that one, once he had a knife at his flat gut. His gardener and sole retainer was unconscious.

"Oh," Hanse said, "he'll want to be bound, then," and worked the blade out of sleeve and door. With a knife in either hand, he gestured. "Hang the lanthorn."

"You can't—"

Hanse poked him with sharp steel. "I can. Run complain to the Prince-Governor as soon as you can. You can also die now, which would be a shame. But I'll try to stick you in the belly, low, just deep enough so you'll be a day or three about dying. Of gangrene, maybe. *Hang that lanthorn, monster!"*

Kurd did, on the hook that was, naturally enough, beside the door. He turned to meet Hanse's foot driving straight up between his skinny shanks. It impacted with a jar.

"Something for your balls, if you have one," Hanse said, and didn't even glance at the man who sank all bulge-eyed and gasping to his knees, with both hands in the predictable position. Hanse hurried to where the gardener lay, not even covered by the blanket his master had used to smother the fire. By the time Hanse finished trussing him with strips of his nightshirt, the gnomish fellow would starve before he freed himself.

Minutes later his master was strapped to one of his own tables. Hanse gagged him, because Kurd had left off threatening to plead and make the most ridiculous promises. Hanse returned to Tempus.

"They couldn't get loose for a roomful of gold, Thales. Now how in the name of every god am I to get you out of here and back to town, friend?"

Tempus required five minutes and more to make himself understood. *Don't. Lay me back. I'll heal. The toes first. Tomorrow I'll be able to walk. Wine?*

Hanse laid him back. Hanse fetched wine and blankets and some sort of gruelly pudding. Knowing that Tempus hated his helplessness, Hanse fed him, helped him guzzle about a gallon of wine, arranged him, covered him, checked Kurd and his servant, made sure the house was locked, and roamed it.

Surgeon's tools, a bag of coins, and a pile of bedding he piled outside the door to the chamber of scientific experimentation. He would not lie in a monster's bed, or on one of those tables! He slept, at last, on the floor. On bedding from the gardener's chamber, not Kurd's. He wanted nothing of Kurd's.

Valuable knives and the bag of money were different.

He awoke at dawn, looked in on three sleeping men, marveled, and left that place that was nine times more horrible by day. He found a sausage, considered, and chose flatbread instead. Only the gods and Kurd knew what sort of meat comprised that sausage. In a shed Hanse found a cart and a mule. He had to do some chopping and some sweating. At last he got Tempus out of the ruined house and into the cart padded with hay. Hanse covered him amid shudders. Tempus's cuts looked days older, nearly healed.

"Would you like a few fingers or a nose or something of Kurd to accompany you out of here, Thales?"

Almost, Tempus frowned. " 'O," he said, and Hanse knew it was a no. "You want to, uh, leave them for . . . later?" Tempus's reply was almost a *yes, for me.*

Hanse got him out of there. He used much of Kurd's money to buy the place and services of a tongueless, nearly blind old woman, along with some soft food, wine, blankets and cloak, and he went away from them with a few coins and hideous memories. The coins bought him expensive treatment from a leech who dared not chuckle or comment as he cleaned and bandaged a buttock with multiple lacerations, which he said would heal beautifully.

After that Hanse was sick in his room for the better part of a week. The remaining three coins bought him anesthetic in the form of strong drink.

For another week he feared that he would encounter Tempus on the street or someplace, but he did not. After that, amid rumors of some sort of insurrection somewhere near, he began to fear that he would never see Tempus, and then of course he did see him. Healed and scarless. Hanse went home and threw up.

He traded a few things for more strong drink, and he got drunk and stayed that way for a while. He just didn't feel like stealing, or facing Tempus, or Kadakithis either. He did dream, of two gods and a girl of sixteen or so. Ils and Shalpa and Mignureal. And quicklime.

# The Rhinoceros and the Unicorn

## Diana L. Paxson

"So why did you come back?" Gilla's shrill retort interrupted Lalo's attempts to explain why he had not been home the night before. "Has every tavern in Sanctuary shown you the door?" She planted her fists on her spreading hips, the meaty flesh on her upper arms quivering below the short sleeves of her shift, and glared at him.

Lalo stepped backwards, caught his heel on the leg of his easel, and clattered to the floor in a tangle of splintering wood and skinny limbs. The baby began to cry. While Lalo gasped for breath, Gilla took a long stride to the cradle and clutched the child to her breasts, patting him soothingly. Echoes of their older children's quarrels with their playmates drifted from the street below, mingling with the clatter of a cart and the calls of vendors hawking their wares in the Bazaar.

"Now see what you've done!" said Gilla when the baby had quieted. "Isn't it enough that you bring home no bread? If you can't earn an honest living painting, why don't you turn to thievery like everyone else in this dungheap of a town?" Her face, reddened by anger and the heat of the day, swam above him like a mask of the demon-goddess Dyareela at Festival time.

*At least I have that much honor left!* Lalo bit back the words, remembering times, when one of his merchant patrons had refused to pay, that the limner had let fall the location of rich pickings while drinking in the Vulgar Unicorn. And if, thereafter, one of his less reputable acquaintances chose to share with him a few anonymous coins, surely honor did not require him to ask whence they came.

No, it had not been honor that kept him honest, thought Lalo bitterly, but fear of bringing shame to Gilla and the children, and a rapidly deteriorating belief in his own artistic destiny.

He struggled up on one elbow, for the moment too dispirited to stand. Gilla sniffed in exasperation, laid down the child and stalked to the other end of the single room in the tenement which served as kitchen and chamber for the family, and, too rarely, as the painter's studio.

The three-legged stool groaned as Gilla sat down, set a small sack on the table, and began with ostentatious precision to shell peas into a bowl. Late afternoon sunlight shafted through the shutters, lending an illusory splendor to the tarnished brocade against which his models used to pose, and leaving in obscurity the baskets of soiled clothing which the wives of the rich and respectable (terms which were, in Sanctuary, roughly synonymous) had graciously given to Gilla to wash.

Once, Lalo would have rejoiced in the play of light and shadow, or at least reflected ironically on the relationship between illusion and reality. But he was too familiar with the poverty the shadows hid—the sordid truth behind all his fantasies. The only place he now saw visions was at the bottom of a jug of wine.

He got up stiffly, brushing ineffectually at the blue paint smeared across the old stains on his tunic. He knew that he should clean up the pigments spilling across the floor, but why try to save paint when no one wanted his pictures?

By now the regulars would be drifting into the Vulgar Unicorn. No one would care about his clothing there.

Gilla looked up as he started towards the door, and the light restored her greying hair to its former gold, but she did not speak. Once, she would have run to kiss her husband goodby, or railed at him to keep him home. Only, as Lalo stumbled down the stairs, he heard behind him the vicious splatter of peas hitting the cracked glaze of the bowl.

Lalo shook his head and took another sip of wine, carefully, because the tankard was almost empty now. "She used to be beautiful . . ." he said sadly. "Would you believe that she was like Eshi, bringing spring back into the world?" He peered muzzily through the shadows of the Vulgar Unicorn at Cappen Varra, trying to superimpose on the minstrel's saturnine features the dimly-remembered image of the golden-haired maiden he had courted almost twenty years ago.

But he could only remember the scorn in Gilla's grey eyes as she had glared down at him that afternoon. She was right. He was despicable—

wine had bloated his belly as his ginger hair had thinned, and the promises he had once made her were as empty as his purse.

Cappen Varra tipped back his dark head and laughed. Lalo caught
the gleam of his white teeth in the guttering lamplight, a flicker of silver
from the amulet at his throat, the elegant shape of his head against the
chiaroscuro of the Inn. Dim figures beyond him turned at the sound,
then returned to the even murkier business that had brought them there.

"Far be it from me to argue with a fellow-artist—" said Cappen
Varra, "but your wife reminds *me* of a rhinoceros! Remember when
you got paid for decorating Master Regli's foyer, and we went to the
Green Grape to celebrate? I saw her when she came after you . . . Now
I know why you do your serious drinking here!"

The minstrel was still laughing. Suddenly angry, Lalo glared at him.

"Can you afford to mock me? You are still young. You think it
doesn't matter if you tailor your songs to the taste of these fleas in the
armpit of the Empire, because you still carry the *real* poetry in your
heart, along with the faces of the beautiful women you wrote it for!
Once already you have pawned your harp for bread. When you are my
age, will you sell it for the price of a drink, and sit weeping because the
dreams still live in your heart but you have no words to describe them
anymore?"

Lalo reached blindly for his tankard, drained it, set it down on the
scarred table. Cappen Varra was drinking too, the laughter for a moment gone from his blue eyes.

"Lalo—you are no fit companion for a drinking man!" said the minstrel at last. "I will end up as sodden as you are if I stay here!" He rose,
slinging his harp case over his shoulder, adjusting the drape of his cloak
to a jauntier flare. "The *Esmeralda's* back in port from Ilsig and points
north—I'm off to hear what news she brings. Good evening, Master Limner—I wish you joy of your philosophy . . ."

Lalo remained where he was. He supposed he should go too, but
where? If he went home he would only have to face Gilla again. Idly he
began to draw on the table, his paint-stained forefinger daubing from a
little pool of spilt wine. But his memory had sought the past, when he
and Gilla were painfully saving the gold pieces that would deliver them
from Sanctuary. He remembered how they had planned what they
would do with the wealth sure to come once the lords of Ranke recognized his talent, the images of transcendent beauty he had dreamed of
creating when he no longer had to worry about tomorrow's bread. But
instead, they had had their first child.

He looked down, and realized that his finger had been clumsily out-lining the pure profile of the girl Gilla had been so long ago. His fist smashed down on the table, obscuring the lines in a splatter of wine, and he groaned and hid his face in his hands.

"Your cup is empty . . ." The deep voice made a silence around them.

Lalo sighed and looked up. "So is my purse."

Broad shoulders blocked the light of the hanging lamp, but as the newcomer turned to shrug off his cloak his eyes glowed red, like those of a wolf surprised by a peasant's torch at night. Beyond him, Lalo saw the tapster's boy slithering among the crowded tables towards the new customer.

"You're the fellow who did the sign outside, aren't you?" said the man. "I'm getting transferred, and a picture for my girl to remember me by would be worth the price of a drink to me . . ."

"Yes. Of course," answered Lalo. The tapster's boy stopped by their table, and his companion ordered a jug of cheap red wine. The limner reached into his pouch for his roll of drawing paper, weighted it with the tankard to keep it from curling up again. The stopper of his ink bot-tle had dried stuck, and Lalo swore as he struggled to open it. He picked up his pen.

Swiftly he sketched his first impression of the man's hulking shoul-ders and tightly curled hair. Then he looked up again. The features blurred and Lalo blinked, wondering if he had already had too much wine. But the hollow in his belly cried out for more, and the tapster's boy was already returning, ducking beneath a thrown knife and detour-ing around the resulting struggle without spilling a drop.

"Turn towards the lamp—if I'm to draw you I must have some light!" muttered Lalo. The man's eyes burned at him from beneath arched brows. The limner shivered, forced himself to focus on the shape of the head and noted how the lank hair receded across the prominent bones of the skull.

Lalo looked down at his drawing. What trick of the light had made him think the fellow's hair curled? He cross-hatched over the first out-line to merge it into a shadowy background and began to sketch the profile again. He felt those glowing eyes burning him. His hand jerked and he looked up quickly.

The nose was misshapen now, as if some drunken potter had pressed too hard into the clay. Lalo stared at his model and threw down his pen. The face before him bore no resemblance to the one he had drawn!

"Go away!" he said hoarsely. "I can't do what you ask of me—I can't do anything anymore . . ." He began to shake his head and could not stop.

"You need a drink." Pewter clinked against the tabletop.

Lalo reached for the refilled tankard and drank deeply, not caring anymore whether he would be able to earn it. He felt it burn all the way down to his belly, run tingling along his veins to barrier him from the world.

"Now, try again," commanded the stranger. "Turn your paper over, look well at me, then draw what you see as quickly as you can."

For a long moment Lalo stared at the oddly attenuated features of the man before him, then bent over his work. For several minutes only the scratching of swift penstrokes competed with the clamor of the room. He must capture the glow of those strange eyes, for he suspected that when he looked at his companion again, nothing but the eyes would be the same.

But what matter? He had his payment now. With his free hand he reached for the mug and drank again, shaded a final line, then pushed the drawing across the table and sat back.

"Well—you wanted it . . ."

"Yes." The stranger's lips twitched. "Everything considered, it's quite good. I understand that you do portraits," he went on. "Are you free to take a commission now? Here's an earnest of your fee—" He reached into the folds of his garment, laid a gold piece shining on the table, quickly hid his misshapen fingers once more.

Lalo stared, reached out gingerly as if expecting the coin to vanish at his touch. Fortified by the wine, he could admit to himself how very odd this episode had been. But the gold was hard and cool and weighed heavily in his palm. His fingers closed.

The stranger's smile stiffened. He drew back suddenly, away from the light. "Now I must go."

"But the commission!" cried Lalo. "Who is it for, and when?"

"The commission . . ." the man seemed to be having trouble enunciating the words. "If you have the courage, come now . . . Do you think that you can find the house of Enas Yorl?"

Lalo cringed from his snarl of laughter, but the sorcerer did not wait for him to reply. He had cast his cloak around him and was lurching towards the door, and this time the shape the cloak covered was hardly human at all.

Lalo the limner stood in Prytanis Street before the house of Enas Yorl, shivering. With the setting of the sun, the wind off the desert had turned cold, although there was still a greenish light in the western sky. Once he had spent two months trying to capture on canvas the translucent quality of that glow.

The rooftops of the city made a deceptively elegant silhouette against the sky, topped by the lacy scaffolding of the tower of the Temple of Savankala and Sabellia nearby. Insulting to local prejudices though the new temple might be, at least it promised to be magnificent. Lalo sighed, wondering who would paint the murals within—probably some eminent artist from the capital. He sighed again. If he had gone to Ranke it might have been himself, returning in triumph to his birthplace.

But that consideration forced his attention back to the edifice that loomed before him, its shadows somehow darker than those of the other buildings, and the job that he had come here to do.

Terrors coiled like basilisks in the corners of his mind. His legs trembled. A dozen times during his journey across the town they had threatened to buckle or turn in the opposite direction, and the wine had been sweated out of him long ago.

Enas Yorl was one of the darker legends of Sanctuary, although, for reasons which the episode in the Vulgar Unicorn had amply illustrated, he was rarely seen. Rumor had it that the curse of some rival had condemned him to the existence of a chameleon. But that was said to be the only limit on his power.

Had the sorcerer's offer been some perverted joke, or part of some magical intrigue? *I should take the gold to Gilla,* he thought, *it might be enough to buy us places in an outward-bound caravan . . .*

But the coin was only a retainer for a service he had not yet performed, and there was no place he could flee that would be beyond the reach of the sorcerer. He could not return the money without facing Enas Yorl, and he could not run away. Shaking so that he could hardly grasp the intricately-wrought knocker, he let it fall upon the brazen surface of the door.

The interior of the building seemed larger than its outside, though the colorless mists that swirled around him made it hard to be certain of anything except the glowing red eyes of Enas Yorl. As the mists curdled and cleared, Lalo saw that the sorcerer was enthroned in a carven chair which the artist would have itched to examine had anyone else been sitting there. He was considering a slim figure in an embroidered Ilsig cloak who stood twirling a mounted globe.

Seas and continents spun as the stranger turned, stared at Lalo, then back at Enas Yorl.

"Do you mean to tell me that sot is necessary to your spell?"

It was a woman's voice, but Lalo had already noted the fine bones structuring the face beneath the scarred tanned skin and cropped hair, the wiry grace of the body in its male attire. So might a kitten from the Prince's harem have looked if it had been left to fight its way to adulthood in the alleys of the town.

Abruptly perceiving himself through the woman's eyes, Lalo straightened, acutely aware of his stained tunic and frayed breeches, and the stubble on his chin.

"Why do you need a painting?" she asked scornfully. "Isn't this enough to purchase the use of your own powers?" From a bag suspended around her neck she poured out a river of moonlight which resolved itself into a string of pearls which she cast rattling upon the stone-flagged floor.

"I could . . ." said the sorcerer wearily. He was smaller than he had been, an oddly shaped mound in the great chair. "If you had been anyone else, I would have given you a spell worth as much as that necklace, and laughed when your ship outran the land winds that carry the energies I use, and your beauty became ugliness again. The natural tendency of things is towards disorder, my dear. Destruction is easy, as you know. Restoration takes more energy."

"And your power is not great enough?" Her voice was anxious now.

Lalo averted his eyes as the sorcerer's appearance altered again. He was feeling alternately hot with embarrassment and chill with fear. Risky as involvement in the public affairs of wizards might be, to be privy to their personal affairs could only bring disaster. And whatever the relationship between the figureless sorcerer and the disfigured girl might be, it was obviously both extremely personal, and an affair.

"There is a price for everything," replied Enas Yorl once he had stabilized. "I can transform you without aids, but not while continuing to protect myself. Jarveena, would you ask that of me?" His voice was a whisper now.

The girl shook her head. Suddenly subdued, she let her cloak slip to the floor and seated herself. Lalo saw an easel beside him—had it been there before? He took an involuntary step towards it, seeing there a set of brushes of perfectly matched camel's hair, pots of pigment finely ground, a smoothly stretched canvas—tools of a quality of which he had only been able to dream.

"I want you to paint her," said Enas Yorl to Lalo. "Not as you see her now, but as I see her always. I want you to paint Jarveena's soul."

Lalo stared at him as though he had been struck to the heart but had not yet begun to feel the pain. He shook his head a little.

"You read my heart as you see the lady's soul . . ." he said with a curious dignity. "The gods alone know what I would give to be able to do what you ask of me!"

The sorcerer smiled. His form seemed to shift, to expand, and in the blazing of his eyes Lalo's awareness was consumed. *I will provide the vision and you will provide the skill* . . . the words echoed in Lalo's mind, and then he knew no more.

The stillness of the hour just before dawn hushed the air when Lalo again became conscious of his own identity. The girl Jarveena lay back in her chair, apparently asleep. His back and shoulder ached furiously. He stretched out his arm and flexed his fingers to relieve their cramping, and only then did his eyes focus on the canvas before him.

*Did I do that?* His first reaction was one he had known before, when hand and eye had cooperated unusually well and he had emerged from an intensive bout of work amazed at how close he had come to capturing the beauty he saw. But this—the image of a face whose finely arched nose and perfect brows were framed by waves of lustrous hair, of a slenderly curved body whose honey-colored skin had the sheen of the pearls on the floor and whose delicately up-tilted breasts were tipped with buds of dusky rose—this *was* that Beauty, fully realized.

Lalo looked from the picture to the girl in the chair and wept, because he could see only blurred hints of that beauty in her now, and he knew that the vision had passed through him like light through a windowpane, leaving him in the darkness once more.

Jarveena stirred and yawned, then opened one eye. "Is he done? I've got to go—the *Esmeralda* sails on the early tide."

"Yes," answered Enas Yorl, his eyes glowing more brightly than ever as he turned the easel for her to see. "The painting holds my magic now. Take it with you and look at it as you would look into a mirror, and after a time it will become a mirror, and all will see your beauty as I see it now . . ."

Shaking with fatigue and loss, Lalo sat down on the floor. He heard
the rustle of the sorcerer's robes as he moved to embrace his lady, and
after a little while the sound of the painting being removed and her
footsteps going to the door. Then Lalo and Enas Yorl were alone.

"Well . . . it is done . . ." The sorcerer's voice was fleshless, like
wind whispering through dry leaves. "Will you take your payment
now?"

Lalo nodded without looking at him, afraid to see the body to which
that voice belonged.

"What shall it be? Gold? Those baubles on the floor?" The pearls
rattled as if they had been nudged by the sorcerer's current equivalent
of a toe.

*Yes, I will take the gold, and Gilla and I will go and never set eyes
on this place again* . . . The words were on his lips, but every dream he
had ever known was clamoring in his soul.

"Give me the power you forced on me last night!" Lalo's voice
strengthened. "Give me the power to paint the soul!"

The laughter of Enas Yorl began as the whisper in the sand that
precedes the simoom, but it grew until Lalo was physically buffeted by
the waves of pressure in the room. And then, after a little, there was silence again, and the sorcerer asked, "Are you quite sure?"

Lalo nodded once more.

"Well, that is a little thing, particularly when you are already . . .
when there is such a strong desire. I will throw in a few extras—" he
said kindly, "some souls for you to paint, perhaps a commission or
two . . ."

Lalo jerked as the sorcerer's hands closed on his head, and for a moment all the colors in the rainbow exploded in his brain. Then he found
himself on his feet by the door with a leather satchel in his hand.

"And the painter's gear . . ." continued Enas Yorl. "I have to thank
you not only for a great service, but for giving me something to look
forward to in life. Master Limner, may your gift reward you as you deserve!"

And then the great brazen door had shut behind him, and Lalo found
himself in the empty street, blinking at the dawn.

The desert shimmered glassily with heat, appearing as insubstantial
as the mists in the house of Enas Yorl, but the moist breath of a fountain cooled Lalo's cheeks. Dazed by the contrasts, the limner found
himself wondering whether this moment, or indeed any of the past three

days, were real or only the continuation of some sorcerous dream. But if that were so, he thought as he turned back to the echoing expanse of Molin Torchholder's veranda, he did not want to wake.

Before the first day after his adventure had passed, Lalo had received requests for portraits from the Portmaster's wife and from Jordis the stonemason, newly enriched by his work on the temple for the Rankan gods. In fact the first sitting was to have been this morning. But yesterday's summons had taken precedence; and so it was that Lalo, uncomfortable in worn velveteen breeches that were loose in the shanks and pinched his waist, his embroidered wedding vest, and a shirt which Gilla had starched so that it scraped his neck every time he turned his head, waited to be interviewed for the honor of decorating Molin Torchholder's feasting hall.

A door opened. Lalo heard light footsteps above the plash and gurgle of the fountain, and a young woman with precisely coiled fair hair beckoned to him.

"My Lady?" he hesitated.

"I am the lady Danlis, ancilla to the mistress of this house," she answered briskly. "Come with me . . ."

*I should have known,* thought Lalo, *after hearing Cappen Varra sing her praises for so long.* But that had been some time ago. As he followed her straight-backed progress along the corridor Lalo wondered what vision had made Cappen fall in love with her, and why it had failed.

A startled slave looked up and hastily began gathering together his rags and jars of wax paste as Danlis ushered Lalo through a door of gilded cedarwood into the Hall. Lalo stopped short, taken aback by the abundance of color and texture in the room. Figured silken rugs littered the parquet floor; gilded grape vines laden with amethyst fruit twisted about the marble columns that strained against the beamed ceiling; and the walls were draped with patterned damask from the looms of Ranke. Lalo stared around him, wondering what could possibly be left to decorate.

"Danlis, darling, is this the new painter?"

Lalo turned at a rustle of silks and saw hastening across the carpets a woman who was to Danlis as an overblown rose is to the bud of the flower. She was followed by a maid, and a fluffy dog spurted ahead of her, yapping fiercely and knocking over the pots of wax which the slave had set aside.

"I'm *so* glad that my lord has given me permission to get rid of these *dreary* hangings—so bourgeois, and as you see, they are quite faded now!" The lady went on breathlessly, her trailing skirts upsetting the pots which the slave had just finished righting again. The maid paused behind her and began to berate the cowering servant in low fierce tones.

"My Lady, may I present Lalo the Limner—" Danlis turned to the artist, "Lalo, this is the Lady Rosanda. You may make your bow."

"Will you take long to finish the work?" asked the Lady. "I will be happy to advise you—everyone has always complimented me on my excellent taste—I often think that I might have made an excellent artist—if I had been born into another walk of life, that is . . ."

"Lord Molin's position requires a worthy setting—" stated Danlis as her mistress paused for breath. "After the initial . . . difficulties . . . construction of the new temple has proceeded smoothly. Naturally there will be celebrations in honor of its completion. Since it would be impious to hold them in the temple, they must take place in surroundings which will demonstrate whose genius is responsible for the achievement which will establish Sanctuary's position in the Empire."

Lady Rosanda stared at her companion, impressed, but Lalo scarcely heard her, already abstracted by consideration of the possibilities of the place. "Has Lord Molin decided on the subjects that I am to depict?"

"*If* you are chosen—" answered Danlis. "The murals will portray the goddess Sabellia as Queen of the Harvest, surrounded by her nymphs. First, of course, he will want to see your sketches and designs."

"I might model for the Goddess . . ." suggested Lady Rosanda, twitching an improbably auburn curl over one plump shoulder and looking arch.

Lalo swallowed. "My Lady is too kind, but modeling is exacting work—I wouldn't consider asking someone of your refinement to spend hours posing in such uncomfortable positions and scanty attire . . ." His panic eased into relief as the lady simpered and smiled. His own vision of the Goddess was characterized by a compassionate majesty which he doubted Lady Rosanda could even visualize, much less portray. Finding a model for Sabellia would be his hardest task.

"Now that you understand the work, how much time will you require?"

"What?" Lalo forced himself to the present again.

"When can you bring us the designs?" Danlis repeated tartly.

"I must consider . . . and choose my models . . ." he faltered. "It will take two or three days."

\* \* \*

"Oh, Lalo . . ."

The limner jerked, turned, and realized that he had come all the way from Molin Torchholder's well-guarded gatehouse to the Street of the Goldsmiths without conscious direction, as if his feet were under a charm to carry him home.

"My dear friend!" Puffing a little, Sandol the rug dealer drew up beside Lalo, who looked at him in bewilderment. It had not been 'my friend' the last time they met, when Sandol had refused to pay the full price for his wife's portrait because she said it made her look fat.

"I have wanted to tell you how much enjoyment your painting brings us. As they say, a work of art is a lasting pleasure—Perhaps we ought to have a portrait of myself to balance my wife's. What do you say?" He wiped his brow with a large handkerchief of purple silk.

"Well of course I would be happy—but I don't know just when—my time may be occupied for a while . . ." answered Lalo, confused.

"Yes indeed—" Sandol smiled unctuously. "I understand that your work will shortly grace a much more august residence than my own. My wife was saying just this morning what an honor it was to have been painted by the man who is decorating Molin Torchholder's feasting hall!"

Suddenly Lalo understood. The news of his prospective commission must be all over town by now. He suppressed a grin of triumph, remembering how he had humbled himself to this man to get even a part of his fee. Perhaps he should do the picture—the rug merchant was as porcine as his lady, and they would make a good pair.

"Well, I must not discuss it yet . . ." replied Lalo modestly. "But it is true that I have been approached . . . I fear that an opportunity to serve the representative of the gods of Ranke must take precedence over lesser commitments." Interested commentary followed them like an echo down the busy street, apprentices telling their masters, silk-veiled matrons whispering to each other as they tried on rings.

"Oh indeed I *do* understand," Sandol assured him fervently. "All I ask is that you keep me in mind . . ."

"I'll let you know," said Lalo graciously, "when I have time." He increased his pace, leaving the rug merchant standing like a melting icicle in the sea of people behind him. When he had crossed the Path of Money into the Corridor of Steel, Lalo permitted himself a discreet skip or two.

"Not only my feet but my entire life is charmed now!" he told himself. "May all the gods of Ranke and Ilsig bless Enas Yorl!"

Sunshine glared from the whitewashed walls around him, flashed from polished swords and daggers displayed in the armorer's stalls, glittered in myriad points of light from linked mail. But the brilliance around him was less dazzling than the vistas opening to Lalo's imagination now. He would have not merely a comfortable living, but riches; not only respect, but fame! Everything he had ever desired was within his grasp . . .

Cutpurses flowed around him like shadows as he passed through an alleyway, but despite the rumors, his purse still swung slackly, and they drew back again without his having noticed them. Someone called out to him as he passed the more modest establishments near the warehouses, but Lalo's eyes were blinded by his visions.

It was not until his feet had carried him onto the Wideway that edged the harbor that he realized that he had been hailed by Farsi the Coppersmith, who had loaned him money when Gilla was sick after the birth of their second child. He thought of turning back, but surely he could visit Farsi another time. He was too busy now.

Plans for the new project were boiling in his brain. He had to come up with something that could transcend the rest of Molin's decor without trying to compete with its vulgarity. Colors, details, the interplay of line and mass, rippled before his mind's eye like a painted veil between him and the sordid streets of the town.

So much would depend on the models he chose for the figures in the design! Sabellia and her nymphs must display a beauty that would uplift the imagination even as it pleased the eye, an air at once both regal and innocent.

Lalo slipped on a fishhead. He flailed wildly for a moment, then regained his balance and stood panting and blinking in the bright sun. "And where will I find such maidens in Sanctuary?" he asked himself aloud. "Where mothers sell their daughters into whoredom as soon as their breasts begin to show?" Even the girls who retained some outward beauty were swiftly corrupted within. In the past, he had found his models among the street singers and the girls who eked out a weaver's paltry daylight wages on their backs, at night. He would have to look elsewhere now.

He sighed and turned his face to the sea. It was cooler here, and the changing wind brought a fresh sea breeze to compete with the rotting fish odor of the shore. The blue water sparkled like a virgin's eye.

A woman with a child in her arms waved to him, and after a moment Lalo recognized Valira, come to the shore for an hour or two of sunshine with her baby before it was time for her to ply her trade with the sailors there. She lifted the child for him to see, and he noted with a pang that although her eyes were painted, and glass beads glittered in her hennaed hair, her arms were still childishly thin. He remembered when she had been one of his oldest daughter's playmates, and had often come to Lalo's house for supper when there was no food at her own.

He knew about the rape that had started Valira in this profession, the poverty that kept her there, but her cheerful greeting made him uncomfortable. She had not chosen her fate, but she could not escape it now. Her existence clouded the bright future he had been envisioning.

Lalo waved briefly at Valira and then hurried on, at once relieved and ashamed when she did not call out to him.

He continued along the Wideway, past the wharves where the foreign ships were berthed, pulling at their moorings like a nobleman's horses tethered outside a peasant's sty. Some of the merchants had spread out their wares on the docks, and Lalo threaded his way among knots of people bickering over prices, exchanging insults and news with equal good humor. A few City Guards lounged against a piling, weariness and wariness mingling in their faces as they surveyed the motley crowd. They were accompanied by one of the Prince's Hell-Hounds, his expression differing from theirs only in that it became, if possible, even more supercilious when he looked at his men.

Lalo passed without stopping the abandoned wharf near Fisherman's Row which had become his favorite place for meditation over the years. He had no need of it now—he had too much to do! Where could he find models? Perhaps he should visit the Bazaar this afternoon. Surely he could find some honest maidens there . . .

He hurried up the Street of Smells towards his home, but stopped short when he saw his wife hanging out laundry in the building's courtyard, talking over her shoulder to someone hidden behind her. He approached cautiously.

"Did the interview go well, dear?" asked Gilla brightly. "I've heard that the Lady Rosanda is most gracious. You're quite favored by the ladies today—see, here's Mistress Zorra come to call on you . . ."

Lalo winced at the edge in her voice, then forgot her as she moved and the caller came towards him. He received in quick succession an impression of a trim figure, a complexion that glowed like the roses of Eshi, copper-bright hair and a pair of dazzling eyes.

He swallowed. The last time he had seen Mistress Zorra was when she had accompanied her father to collect their rent, which was three months overdue. He tried to remember whether they had paid last month's rent on time.

"Oh, Master Lalo—you've no need to look so apprehensive!" Zorra blushed prettily. "You should know that your credit is good with us after so many years . . ."

*After so much gossip about my new prosperity, you mean!* He thought, but her smile was infectious, and after all she was not responsible for the stinginess of her sire. He grinned back at her, thinking that she was like a breath of spring in this summer-parched street. Like a nymph . . .

"Perhaps you can help me to maintain my credit, mistress!" he replied. "Would you like to be one of my models for the paintings in Molin Torchholder's Hall?"

How delightful it was to be the dispenser of largesse, thought Lalo as he watched Zorra dance away down the street. She had been painfully eager to break all previous engagements so that she could come to him the next day.

*Was that how Enas Yorl felt when he gave me my desire?* he wondered, and wondered also (but only for a moment) why, in doing so, the sorcerer had laughed.

"But why can't I pose for you in Molin Torchholder's house?" Zorra pouted, glanced at Lalo to see if he was watching her take off her petticoat, and let the garment slip to the floor.

"If my patrons could detach their walls and send them here for decoration, I doubt they would let even me in the door . . ." replied Lalo abstractedly, transferring paint from paintpots to palette in the precise order he always used. "Besides, I'll need to make several studies from each model before I decide on the final design . . ."

Morning sunlight shone cheerfully on the clean-swept floor, cleared now of strangers' laundry, gleamed on Lalo's palette knife and glowed through the petals of the flowers he had given to Zorra to hold.

"That's right—" he said, draping a wisp of gauze around her hips and adjusting the angle of her arms. "Hold the flowers as if you were offering them to the Goddess." She twitched as he touched her, but his awareness of her flesh was already giving way to his perception of her body as a form in space. "Generally I would do only a quick sketch or two," he explained, "but this must be complete enough to give Lord

Molin an idea of what the finished work will be like, so I'm using color . . ."

He stepped back, seeing the picture as he had visualized it—the fresh beauty of the girl in the sunlight with her bright hair flowing down her back and her arms filled with bright flowers. He picked up his brush and took a deep breath, focusing on what he saw.

His awareness of the murmur of conversation at the other end of the room, where Gilla and their middle daughter were preparing the noon-meal, faded. He did not turn when one of his sons came in, was shushed by his mother and sent outdoors. The sounds slid past him as his mind stilled, as the tensions of the past days slipped away.

Now he was himself at last, serenely confident that his hand would obey his eye, that both would reflect the perceptions of his soul. And he knew that not the commissions, but this confidence in himself, was the true gift of Enas Yorl. Lalo dipped his brush in the paint and began to work.

The bar of light had moved halfway across the floor when Zorra abruptly straightened and let her flowers fall to the floor.

"This had better be worth it!" she complained. "My back hurts, and my arms are falling off." She flexed her shoulders and bent back and forth to ease the strain.

Lalo blinked, trying to orient himself. "No, not yet—it's not finished—" he began, but Zorra was already moving towards him.

"What do you mean, I can't look? It's my picture, isn't it?" She stopped short, staring. Lalo's eyes followed her gaze back to the picture, and appalled, he let the brush slip from his hand.

The face that looked at him from the easel had eyes narrowed with cupidity, lips drawn back in a predatory grin. The red hair flamed like a fox's brush, and somehow the rounded limbs had been distorted so that she looked as if she were about to spring. Lalo shuddered, looking from the girl to the picture and back again.

"You whoreson maggoty bastard, what have you done to me?" She rounded on him furiously, then turned back to the picture, snatched up his palette knife, and began to stab at the canvas. "That's not me! That's hateful! You hate women, don't you? You hate my father, too, but just you wait! You'll be living with the Downwinders by the time he gets through with you!"

The floor shook as Gilla charged towards them. Lalo staggered back as she thrust between him and the half-naked girl, squeezed Zorra's wrist until the little knife clattered to the floor.

"Get dressed, you hussy! I'll have no such language where my children can hear!" snapped Gilla, ignoring the fact that they heard far worse every time they went into the Bazaar.

"And you too, you bloated sow!" Zorra pulled away, began to struggle into her clothes. "You're too gross for even Amoli to hire—I hope you end on the streets where you belong!" The door slammed behind her and they heard her clatter down the rickety stairs.

"I hope she breaks her neck. Her father still hasn't fixed those stairs," said Gilla calmly.

Lalo bent stiffly to pick up his palette knife. "She's right . . ." He took a step towards the mutilated picture. "Damn him . . ." he whispered. "He tricked me—he knew that this would happen. May all the gods damn Enas Yorl!"

Gilla looked at the picture and began to laugh. "No . . . really," she gasped, "it's an excellent likeness. You only saw her pretty face. I know what she's been up to. Her fiancé killed himself when she threw him over for that gorilla from the Prince's guard. The vixen is out for all she can get, which the picture makes abundantly clear. No wonder she hated it!"

Lalo slumped. "But I've been betrayed . . ."

"No. You got what you asked for, poor love. You have painted that wretched girl's soul!"

Lalo leaned on the splintery railing of the abandoned wharf, staring with unfocused eyes into the golden dazzle cast upon the waters by the setting sun as if by wishing hard enough he could become one with that beauty and forget his despair. *I have only to climb over this flimsy barrier and let myself fall . . .* He imagined the feel of the bitter waters closing over him, and the blessed release from pain.

Then he looked down, and shuddered, not entirely because of the cooling wind. The murky waters were littered with obscene gobbets that had once been part of living things—offal flushed down the gutters from the shambles of Sanctuary to the sea. Lalo's gorge rose at the thought of that water touching him. He turned away, sank down with his back against the wall of a shanty the fishermen sometimes used.

*Like everything else I see,* he thought, *whatever seems fairest is sure to be most foul within!*

A ship moved majestically across the harbor, passed the lighthouse and disappeared around the point. Lalo had thought of shipping out on such a vessel, but he was too unskilled for a sailor, too frail for a common hand. Even the solace of the taverns was denied to him. In the Green Grape they would congratulate him on the success that was impossible now, while the clients at the Vulgar Unicorn would try to rob him, and beat him senseless when they discovered his poverty. How could he ever explain, even to Cappen Varra, what had happened to him?

The planks on which he was sitting shook beneath a heavy tread. Gilla . . . Lalo tensed, waiting for her accusations, but she only sighed, as if releasing pent hope, or fear.

"I hoped I'd find you here . . ." Grunting, she eased down beside him, unslung and handed him an earthenware pot with a narrow spout. "Better drink this before it gets cold."

He nodded, took a long swallow of fragrant herb tea laced with wine, then another, and set the pot down.

Gilla pulled her shawl around her, stretched out her legs and settled back against the wall. Two gulls swooped overhead, squabbling over a piece of flesh. A heavy swell set wavelets lapping against the pilings below them, then there was silence again.

In the shared stillness, warmed by the tea and by Gilla's body, something that had been wound tight within Lalo began to ease.

"Gilla . . ." he said at last, "what am I going to do?"

"The other two models failed?"

"They were worse than Zorra. Then I started the portrait of the Portmaster's wife . . . Fortunately I got the sketch away before she could see it. She looked like her lapdog!" He drank again.

"Poor Lalo," Gilla shook her head. "It's not your fault that all your unicorns turned out to be rhinoceroses!"

He remembered the old fable about the rhinoceros who looked into a magic mirror and saw there a unicorn, but it did not comfort him. "Is everything beautiful only a mask for rottenness, or is it only that way in Sanctuary?" He burst out then, "Oh Gilla, I've failed you and the children. We're ruined, don't you understand? I cannot even hope any more!"

She turned a little, but did not touch him, as if she understood that any attempt at comfort would be more than he could bear.

"Lalo . . ." she cleared her throat and started again. "It's all right—we'll get by some way. And you haven't failed . . . you haven't failed our dream! You made the right choice—don't I know that it was me and the children in the first place that kept you from what you were meant to do?

"Anyhow—" she tried to turn her emotion to laughter, "if worst comes to worst *I* can model for you—just for you to get the basic lines of the figures, of course," she added apologetically. "After all these years I doubt I have any flaws that you don't already know . . ."

Lalo set down the teapot, turned and looked at her. In the light of the setting sun Gilla's face, into which the years had carved so many lines, was like a weathered image which some worshipper had gilded in an attempt to disguise its age. This bitter line for poverty endured, that, for the death of a child . . . Could all the sorrows of a world have marked a goddess more?

He laid his hand on her arm, seeing the size of her body, but feeling the strength in it, and the flow of energy between them which had bound him to her, even more than her beauty, so many years ago. She sat still, accepting his touch, although he thought she would have been well-justified in turning away.

*Do I know you?*

Gilla's eyes were closed, her head tipped back to rest against the wall in a rare moment of peace. The deepening light upon her face seemed now to come from within. Lalo's eyes blurred. *I have been blind,* he thought, *blind, and a fool . . .*

"Yes . . ." he fought to steady his voice, knowing how he would paint her, where he would look for others to be his models now. His breath caught, and he reached out to her. She looked at him then, smiling questioningly, and received him into her embrace.

A hundred candles blazed in Molin Torchholder's Hall, set in silver candelabra wrought in the shape of torches upraised in clenched fists. Light shimmered in the gauzy silks of the ladies of Sanctuary, gleamed from the heavy brocades worn by their lords, flashed from each golden link of chain or faceted jewel as they moved across the floor, nearly eclipsing the splendor of the room.

Lalo observed the scene from a vantage point of relative quiet beside a pillar, tolerated for his role in creating the murals whose completion the party was intended to celebrate. Everyone of wealth or status who craved the favor of the empire was there, which these days amounted to most of the upper crust of Sanctuary, everyone wearing the same mask of complacent gaiety. But Lalo could not help wondering how, if he had painted this scene, those faces would have appeared.

Several merchants for whom Lalo had worked in the past had wangled invitations, although most of his former clients would have felt as out of place in this gathering as he did. He recognized a few friends, among them Cappen Varra, who having just finished a song, was now warily watching Lady Danlis, who was far too busy being charming to a banker from Ranke to notice him.

Several other acquaintances from the Vulgar Unicorn had somehow managed to get hired as extra waiters and footmen. Lalo suspected that not all of the jewels that winked so brightly tonight would leave the house in the hands of those who had brought them, but he did not feel compelled to point this out to anyone. He braced himself as he recognized Jordis the stonemason shouldering his way towards him through the glittering crowd.

"Well, Master Limner, now that you've finished serving the gods, you'll have a bit more time for men, eh?" Jordis smiled broadly. "The space on my wall that's waiting for my picture is still bare . . ."

Lalo coughed deprecatingly. "I'm afraid that in my concentration on heavenly things I've lost my touch for earthly excellence . . ." The stonemason's expression told him how pompous that sounded, but it would be far better for everyone to think his head had been turned by his new prosperity than for them to guess the truth. The solution to his dilemma that had enabled him to complete the job for Lord Molin had forever barred him from Society portraiture.

"Heavenly things . . . ah, yes . . ." Jordis' eyes had moved to one of the nymphs painted on the wall, whose limbs were supple and rounded, whose eyes shone with youth and merriment. "If I could make a living gazing at such lovelies, I suppose I'd refuse to paint old men too!" He laughed suggestively. "Where do you find them in this town, eh?"

*Selling their bodies on the docks . . . or their souls in the Bazaar . . . slaving in your kitchen or scrubbing your floors . . .* thought Lalo bitterly. This was not the first time this evening that he had been asked who his models were. The nymph at whom Jordis was now leering so eagerly was a crippled beggar girl whom he had probably passed in the street a dozen times. On another wall the whore Valira proudly presented a sheaf of grain to the Goddess, while her child tumbled like a cherub about her feet. And the Goddess they worshipped, who dominated all of the facile splendor in this room, was his Gilla, the rhinoceros who had been revealed as something greater than any unicorn.

*You have hearts but you do not feel . . .* Lalo's eyes moved over the dazzle of apparel and ornament in which Lord Molin's guests had disguised themselves. *You have eyes but you do not see.* He murmured something about an artist's perspective.

"If you want a room decorated, I'll be happy to serve you, but I do not think that I will be doing portraits any more." Ever since he had learned to see Gilla, his sight had been changing. Now, when he was not painting, he could often see the truth behind the faces men showed the world. He added politely, "I trust that your work is going well?"

"Eh? My work—oh yes, but there's not much left for a stonemason now! What remains will require a different sort of craft . . ." His chuckle held a hint of complicity.

Lalo felt himself flushing, realizing that Jordis assumed he had been fishing for information about the new temple—the greatest decoration job that Sanctuary had ever known. *Wasn't I?* he wondered. *Is it unworthy to want my goddess to adorn something more worthy than this jumped-up engineer's feasting hall?*

His mouth dried as he saw Molin Torchholder himself approaching him. Jordis bowed, smirked, and melted back into the crowd. Lalo forced himself to stand up and meet his patron's eye, for Lord Molin's excess flesh covered a powerful frame, and there was something uncomfortably piercing about his gaze.

"I have to thank you," said Lord Molin. "Your work appears to be a success." His eyes roved ceaselessly from the crowd to Lalo's face and back again. "Perhaps *too* successful," he went on. "Next to your goddess, my guests appear to be the decorations here!"

Lalo found himself trying to apologize and froze, terrified that he would blurt out the truth.

Molin Torchholder laughed. "I am trying to compliment you, my good man—I would like to commission you to do the paintings on my new temple's walls . . ."


"Master Limner, you appear to be in good spirits today!"

Lalo, who had just turned from the Path of Money into the Avenue of Temples, on his way to make an initial survey of the spaces he was to decorate in the new temple to the Rankan gods, missed a step as the soft voice spoke in his ear. He heard a dry chuckle, felt the hairs rise on his neck and bent to peer more closely at the other man. All he could see beneath the hooded caravaneer's cloak was the gleam of crimson eyes.

"Enas Yorl!"

"More or less . . ." his companion agreed. "And you? Are you the same? You have been in my thoughts a great deal. Would you like me to change the gift I gave to you?"

Lalo shivered, remembering those moments when he would have given his soul to lose the power the sorcerer had bestowed upon him. But instead, his soul had been given back to him.

"No. I don't think so," he answered quietly, and sensed the sorcerer's surprise. "The debt is mine. Shall I paint you another picture to repay it?" He added, "Shall I paint a portrait of *you,* Enas Yorl?"

The sorcerer halted then, and for a moment the painter met fully the red gaze of those unearthly eyes, and he trembled at the immortal weariness he saw there.

Yet it was not Lalo, but Enas Yorl, who was the first to close his eyes and look away.

# Then Azyuna Danced

## Lynn Abbey

### 1

He was a handsome man, somewhat less than middle-aged, with a physique that bespoke a soldier, not a priest. He entered the bazaar-stall of Kul the Silkseller with an authority that sent the other patrons back into the dusty afternoon and brought bright-eyed Kul out from behind his bolts of cloth.

"Your grace?" he fawned.

"I shall require a double length of your finest silk. The color is not important—the texture is. The silk must flow like water and a candleflame must be bright through four thicknesses."

Kul thought for a moment, then rummaged up an armload of samples. He would have displayed each, slowly, in its turn, but his customer's eyes fell on a sea-green bolt and Kul realized it would be folly to test the priest's patience.

"Your grace has a fine eye," he said instead, unrolling a half-length and letting the priest examine the hand and transparency of the cloth.

"How much?"

"Two gold coronations for both lengths."

"One."

"But, your grace has only recently arrived from the capital. Surely you recall the fetching-price of such workmanship. See here, the right border is shot with silver threads. It's certainly worth one-and-seven."

"And this is certainly not the capital. Nine Rankan soldats," the priest growled, reducing his offer further.

Kul whisked the cloth out of the priest's hand, spinning it expertly around the bolt. "Nine soldats . . . the silver in the cloth is worth more than that! Very well. I've no choice, really. How is a bazaar-merchant to argue with Molin Torchholder, High Priest of Vashanka? Very well, very well—nine soldats it is."

The priest snapped his fingers and an adolescent temple-mute scurried forward with the priest's purse. The youth selected nine coins, showed them to his master, then handed them to Kul who checked both sides to be certain they weren't shaved—as so much of Sanctuary's currency was. (It was not fitting that a priest handle his own money.) When Kul slipped the small handful of coins into his waist-pouch, Torchholder snapped his fingers a second time and a massively built plainsman ducked under the stall's lintel, holding the door-cloth until the priest departed, then taking the bolt from the silent youth.

Molin Torchholder strode purposefully through the crowded bazaar, confident the slaves would keep pace with him somehow. The silk was almost as good as the merchant claimed, and in the capital, where better money flowed more freely, would have brought twice what the merchant had asked. The priest had not risen so high in the Rankan bureaucracy that he failed to savor a well-finessed haggling.

His sedan-chair awaited him at the bazaar-gate. A second plainsman was there to hold his heavy robes while he stepped over the carved-wood sides. The first had already placed the silk on the seat and stood beside the rearmost poles. The mute pulled a leather-wrapped forked stick from his belt, slapped it once against his thigh and the entourage headed back to the palace.

The plainsmen went to wherever it was that they abided when Molin didn't need their services; the youth carried the cloth to the family's quarters with the strictest instructions that the esteemable Lady Rosanda, Molin's wife, was not to see it. Molin himself wandered through the palace until he came to those rooms now allotted to Vashanka's servants and slaves.

It was the latter who interested him, specifically the lithe Northern slave they called Seylalha who practiced the arduous Dance of the Consort at this time each day. The dance was a mortal recreation of the divine dance Azyuna had performed before her brother, Vashanka, persuading him to make her his concubine rather than relegate her to the traitorous ranks of their ten brothers. Seylalha would perform that dance in less than a week at the annual commemoration of the Ten-Slaying.

She had reached the climax of the music when he arrived, beginning the dervish swirls that brought her calf-length honey-colored hair out into a complete, dazzling circle. The tattered practice rags had long-since been discarded, but she was not yet twirling so fast that the priest could not appreciate the firmness of her thighs, the small, upturned breasts. (Azyuna's dance must be danced by a Northern slave or the movements became grotesque.) The slave's face, Molin knew, was as beautiful as her body though it was now hidden by the swinging hair.

He watched until the music exploded in a final crescendo, then slid the spy-hole shut with an audible click. Seylalha would see no virile man until the feast-night when she danced for the god himself.

2

The slave had been escorted to her quarters—more properly: returned to her cell. The beefy eunuch turned the key that slid a heavy bolt into place; he needn't have bothered. After ten years of captivity and especially now that she was in Sanctuary, Seylalha was not likely to risk her life in escape-attempts.

He had been there watching again; she knew that and more. They thought her mind was as blank as the surface of a pond on a windless day—but they were wrong. They thought she could remember nothing of her life before they had found her in a squalid slave-pen; she'd merely been too smart to reveal her memories. Neither had she ever revealed that she could understand their Rankan language—had always understood it. True, the women who taught her the dance were all mutes and could reveal nothing, but there were others who had tongues. That was how she came to learn of Sanctuary, of Azyuna and of the Feast of the Ten-Slaying.

Here in Sanctuary she was the only one who knew the whole dance but had not yet performed it for the god. Seylalha guessed that this year would be her year—the one fateful night in her constricted life. They thought she didn't know what the dance was. They thought she performed it out of fear for the bitter-faced women with their leather-bound clatter-sticks. But in her tribe nine-year-olds were considered of marriageable age, and a seduction was a seduction regardless of the language.

Seylalha had reasoned, as well, that if she did not want to become one of those mutilated women who had trained and taught her she'd best get a child from her bedding with the god. Legend said Vashanka's unfulfilled desire was to have a child by his sister; Seylalha would oblige the god in exchange for her freedom. The Ten-Slaying was a new-moon feast; she bled at the full-moon. If the god were man-like after the fashion of her clan-brothers, she would conceive.

She knelt on the soft bed-cushions they provided her, rocking back and forth until tears flowed down her face; silent tears lest her guardians hear and force a drugged potion down her throat. Calling on the sungod, the moongod, the god who tended the herds in the night and every other shadowy demon she could remember from the days before the slave-pens, Seylalha repeated her prayers: "Let me conceive. Let me bear the god's child. Let me live! Keep me from becoming one of *them!*"

In the distance, beyond walls and locked door, she could hear her less-fortunate sisters speaking to each other on their tambours, lyres, pipes and clatter-sticks. They'd danced their dance and lost their tongues; their wombs were filled with bile. Their music was a mournful, bitter dirge—it told her fate if she did not bear a child.

As the tears dried she arched her back until her forehead rested on the soft mass of her hair beneath her. Then, in rhythm to the distant conversation, she began her dance again.

3

Molin paced around the marble-topped table he had brought with him from the capital. The mute who always attended him hid in the far corners of the room. Molin's wrath had touched him three times and it was not yet high-noon.

The injustice, the indignity of being the supreme priest of Vashanka in a sink-hole like Sanctuary. Construction lagged on the temple: inept crews, unforeseen accident, horrendous omens. The old Ilsig hierarchy gloated and collected the citizenry's irregular tithes. The Imperial entourage was cramped into inadequate quarters that shoved his household together. He was actually sharing rooms with his wife—a situation neither of them had ever desired and could no longer tolerate. The Prince was an idealist, an unmarried idealist, whose belief in the bliss of that inconvenient state was exceeded only by his naivete with regard to statecraft. It was difficult not to enjoy the Prince's company, however, despite his manifold shortcomings. He had the proper breeding for a useless younger son, and only the worst of fates had brought him so perilously close to the throne that he must be sent so depressingly far from it.

In Ranke, Molin had a fine house—as well as rooms within the temple. Rare flowers bloomed in his heated gardens; a waterfall coursed down one interior wall of the temple drowning out the street-noises and casting rainbows across this very table when it had resided in his audience chambers. Where had he gone wrong? Now he had a tiny room with one window looking out to an air shaft that must have sunk in the cesspools of hell itself and another one, the larger of the two, overlooking the gallows. Moreover, the Hounds were elsewhere this morning and yesterday's corpses still creaked in the breeze.

Injustice! Indignity! And so, of course, he must clothe himself in the majesty of his position as Vashanka's loyal and duly-initiated priest. Kadakithis must find his way to these forsaken quarters and endure them as the priests did if Molin was to acquire better lodgings. The Prince was late—no doubt he'd gotten lost.

"My Lord Molin?" a cheerful voice called from the ante-chamber. "My Lord Molin? Are you here?"

"I am, my Prince."

Molin gestured to the mute who poured two goblets of fruit tea as the Prince entered the room.

"My Lord Molin, your messenger said you wished to see me urgently on matters concerning Vashanka? This must be true, isn't it, or you wouldn't have called me all the way out here. Where are we? No matter. Are there problems with the temple again? I've told Zalbar to see to it that the conscripts perform their duties . . ."

"No, my Prince, there are no new problems with the temple, and I have turned all those matters over to the Hounds, as you suggested. We are, by the way, in the outer wall of your palace—just upwind of the gallows. You can see them through the window—if you'd like."

The Prince preferred to sip his tea.

"My purpose in summoning you, my Prince, has to do with the upcoming commemoration of the Ten-Slaying to take place at the new-moon. I wished certain privacy and discretion which, frankly, is not available in your own quarters."

If the Prince was offended by Molin's insinuations he did not reveal it. "Do I have special duties then?" he asked eagerly.

Molin, sensing the lad's excitement, pressed his case all the harder. "Extremely special ones, my Prince; ones not even your distinguished late Father, the Emperor, was honored to perform. As you are no doubt aware, Vashanka—mayHisnamebepraised—has concerned Himself rather personally in the affairs of this city of late. My augurists report that on no less than three separate occasions since your arrival in this accursed place His power had been successfully invoked by one not of the temple hierarchy."

The Prince set down his goblet. "You know of these things?" he asked with open-faced incredulity. "You can tell when the god's used His power?"

"Yes, my Prince," Molin answered calmly. "That is the general purpose of our hierarchy. Working through the mandated rituals and in partnership with our God we incline Vashanka's blessings toward the loyal, righteous upholders of tradition, and direct His wrath toward those who would deny or harm the Empire."

"I know of no traitors . . ."

". . . And neither do I, my Prince," Molin said, though he had his suspicions, "but I do know that our God, Vashanka—mayHis-namebepraised—is showing His face with increasing frequency and devastating effect in this town."

"Isn't that what he's supposed to do?"

It was difficult to believe that the vigorous Imperial household had produced so dense an heir; at such times as this Molin almost believed the rumors that circulated around the Prince. Some said that he was at least as clever and ambitious as his brother's advisers feared; Kadakithis was deliberately botching this gubernatorial appointment so he would have to be returned to the capital before the Empire faced rebellion. Unfortunately, Sanctuary was more than equal to the most artfully contrived incompetence.

"My Prince," Molin began again, snapping his fingers to the mute who immediately pushed a great-chair forward for the Prince to sit in. This was going to take longer than anticipated. "My Prince—a god, shall we say any god but most especially our own god Vashanka—mayHisnamebepraised—is an awesomely powerful being who, even though He may beget mortal children on willing or unwilling women, is quite unlike a mortal man.

"A mere man who runs rampant in the streets with his sword drawn

and shouting sedition would be an easy matter for the Hounds to control—assuming, of course, they even noticed him in this town . . ."

"Are you saying, my Lord Molin, that such a vagrant *is* plowing
through my city? Is that why you've called me here, really? Does my
suite harbor a viperous traitor?"

It must be an act, Molin decided. No one could attain physical maturity with only Kadakithis' apparent intelligence to guide him. He *had* attained maturity, hadn't he? Molin's plans demanded it. He was known
to have concubines, but perhaps he merely talked them to sleep? It was
time for a change of tactics.

"My Dear Prince, as hierarchical superior here in Sanctuary I can
flatly state that the repeated incidents of divine intervention, unguided
as they are by the rituals performed according to tradition by myself
and my acolytes, constitute a severe threat to the well-being of your
people and your mission to Sanctuary. They must be stopped by whatever means are necessary!"

"Oh . . . oh!" the Prince's face brightened. "I believe I understand.
I'm to do something at next week's festival that will help you get control again. Do I get to bed Azyuna?"

The light in the young man's eyes reassured Molin that the Prince did
understand the purpose of a concubine. "Indeed, my Prince! But that is
only a small part of what we shall do next week. The Dance of Azyuna
and the Divine Seduction are performed at the festival each year. Many
children are born of such unions, many serve their ersatz-father with
great dignity—I myself am a son of the Consort. But, under *extreme* circumstances the Dance of Azyuna will be preceded by the most sacred
recreation of the Ten-Slaying itself. Vashanka—mayHisnamebepraised—
rediscovers His traitorous brothers plotting to overthrow the divine authority of Savankala, their father. He slays them on the spot and takes
Azyuna, at her insistence, to bed at once as his consort. The child of
such a union—if there were any—would be well-omened indeed.

"My Prince, the auguries indicate that such a child will be born here
in Sanctuary—of all places—and our God's activity here would lend belief to this. It is imperative that such a child be born within the strictures
of the temple; it would be fitting if the child's natural father were
you . . ."

The Prince turned the color of the fruit tea, though his complexion
quickly leveled off at a unique shade of green. "But Molin, that's general's work—killing surrendered officers of the enemy. Molin, you don't
expect me to kill *ten* men, do you? Why, there aren't more than ten

Vashankan priests in this whole city. I'd have to kill you. I couldn't do it, Molin—you mean too much to me."

"My Dear Prince," Molin poured another goblet of fruit tea and signaled the mute to bring a stronger libation for the next round. "My Dear Prince, while I would never hesitate to lay down my life for you or the Empire should, gods forfend, the need ever arise—nonetheless, I assure you, I am not about to make the supreme sacrifice at this time. There is nothing in the most sacred tomes of ritual dictating the nature or rank of the ten who must be slain—save that they must be undeformed and alive at the start."

At that moment there were shouts outside Molin's larger window and the all-too-familiar sound of the gallow's rope snapping another neck.

"Very simply, my Prince, cancel these daily executions and by the Ten-Slaying I'm sure we'll have our quota."

The Prince blanched at the thought of Sanctuary denizens whose activities so exceeded the norms of this none-too-civilized place that his judges would condemn them to death.

"They would be bound and drugged, of course," Molin consoled his Prince, "as is part of custom, if not tradition. Our hierarchy has suffered the discomfort of having the wrong man survive," Molin added quickly, without mentioning that they had also suffered the inconvenience of losing all eleven to their wounds before the ritual could be completed. The hierarchy had acquired an immense practicality over the generations when its own interests were concerned.

Kadakithis stared blankly into the corners of the room; he had stared briefly out the window but the busy gallows had not brought the peace of mind he sought. Molin entertained hopes of getting new quarters in the near future. The mute offered them a fresh goblet of the local wine— a surprisingly potable beverage, given its origins. But then the priorities of the populace were such that the wine should be far better than their cheese or bread. Molin himself offered the strong drink to the Prince.

"Molin—I cannot. If it were just the Dance . . . well, no, not even then." The Prince squared his shoulders and simulated a stance of firm resolve. "Molin, you are wrong—it would not be fitting for a Prince of the blood. I mean no slurs, but I cannot be seen consorting with a temple slave at a public festival."

Molin considered the refusal; considered taking Vashanka's role himself—he'd seen the temple slave in question. But he had been honest with the Prince; it was of the utmost importance that the child be properly conceived.

"My Prince, I do not ask this lightly, any more lightly than I informed my brethren in Ranke of my decision in this matter. The slave is of the best Northern stock; the rite is held in strictest mystery.

"The Hand of Vashanka rests heavily on your prefecture, my Prince. You cannot have failed to notice His presence. The daily auguries show it plainly. Your own Hell-Hounds, the very guardians of Imperial Order, are not immune to the dangers of Vashanka's unbridled presence!"

The High Priest paused, staring hard into Kadakithis' eyes, forcing the young governor to acknowledge the rumors that flew freely and were never disputed. Molin could trace his ancestry to the god in the time-honored way, but what about Tempus? The Hell-Hound bore Vashanka's mark, but had been whelped far beyond the ken of the priesthood.

"Who are we to channel the powers of the gods?" the Prince responded, his gaze unfocused, his manner uncomfortably evasive.

Molin drew himself up to his full height, some finger-widths taller than the Prince. His back straightened as if the beaten gold headdress of his office balanced on his brow. "My Prince, we *are* the channels, the only true channels. Without the mediation of a duly consecrated hierarchy the bonds of tradition which make Vashanka—mayHisnamebepraised—our God and us His worshippers would be irreparably sundered. The rituals of the temple, whose origins are one with the God Himself, are the balance between mortal and immortal. Anyone who circumvents the rituals, for any reason however well-intentioned . . . , anyone who does not harken to the call of the hierarchy in its needs subverts the proper relationship of god and worshipper to the damning harm of both!"

Again the experienced Imperial Hierarch stared down on the young, awestruck Prince. Molin was only half-conscious of overstating the case for stringent observation of the rituals. Vashanka's displeasure when He was not properly appeased was extensively documented. The rituals were all intended to bind a capricious and hungry deity.

The crowd outside Molin's window raised its voice and shut down their conversation; the day's verdicts were being proclaimed. There would be two more hangings on the morrow. Kadakithis started when his name was used to justify the awful punishments the Empire meted out to its criminals. He shrank back from the window as a huge black crow landed on the sill, swiveling its head in a lopsided stare of dark curiosity. The Prince shooed it back to the gallows.

"I will do what I can, Molin. I will speak with my advisers."

"My Dear Prince, in matters regarding the spiritual well-being of the Imperial Presence in Sanctuary, I am your *only* trusted adviser."

Molin regretted his burst of temper at once; though the Prince gave him smooth verbal assurances, the Vashankan priest was now certain that the Hound, Tempus, would know by sundown.

Tempus: a plague, a thorn, a malignancy to the proper order of things. A son of Vashanka, a true-son no doubt, and utterly unfettered by the constraints of ritual and hierarchy. If even a fraction of the rumors about him were to be believed; if he had survived dissection on Kurd's tables . . . It could not be believed. Tempus could not be so far beyond the hierarchy's reach.

Well, Molin thought after a moment, I'm a true-son too. Let the Prince run to him in sweating anxiety. Let him consult with Tempus; let them conspire against me—I'll still succeed.

Generations of priests had bred generations of true-sons to Vashanka. The god was not quite the blood-drinker he once was. Vashanka could be constrained and, after all, Molin's side of the family was far bigger than Tempus'.

He watched the Prince leave without feeling panic. The crow returned to the window-ledge as was its daily custom. The bird cawed impatiently while Molin and the mute prepared its feast: live mouse dipped in wine. The priest watched the bird disappear back to the Maze rooftops, staring after its flight long after his wife had begun to shout his name.

4

Seylalha stood perfectly still while the dour-faced women draped the sea-green froth around her. The women would not hesitate to prick her sharply with their bodkins and needles, though they took the greatest of care with the silk. They stepped back and signaled that she should spin on her toes for them.

Deep folds of material billowed out into delicate clouds at her slightest movement. The texture of the cloth against her skin was so unlike the heavy tatters of her usual attire that for once she forgot to watch the intricate dance-language of her instructors as they discussed their creation.

The time must be drawing near; they would not dress her like this unless it was almost time for her marriage to the god. The moon above her cell was a thin crescent fading to blackness.

They got their instruments and began to play. Without waiting for the sharp report of the clatter-sticks, Seylalha began to dance, letting the unhemmed ends of the silk swirl out to accompany her as she moved through the hundreds of poses—each painfully inured in her muscles. She flowed with the atonal music, throwing her soul into each leap and turn, keenly aware that this meaningless collection of movements would become her only, exquisite plea for freedom.

When she settled into the final frantic moments of the dance the sea-green silk was caught in her flying hair and lifted away from her body until it was restrained only by the brooches at her neck and waist. As she fell into the prostrate bow, the silk floated down, hiding the rhythmic heaving of her exhausted lungs. The clatter-sticks were silent, without nagging corrections.

Seylalha separated her hair and stood up in one graceful movement. Her teachers were motionless as well as speechless. Never again would she be the bullied student. Clapping her own hands at the quiet women, Seylalha waited until the nearest one crept forward to unpin the twisted silk and accompany her to her bath.

5

It was inky night and even the light of two dozen torches was insufficient to guide the procession along the treacherous, rutted streets of Sanctuary in safety. Molin Torchholder and five other ranking members of the hierarchy had excused themselves from the procession and waited in the relative comfort of the stone-porch of the still incomplete Temple of Vashanka. Behind the priests a great circular tent had been erected. The mute women could be heard tuning and conversing with their instruments. As the bobbing torches rounded into the plaza the women were silenced and Molin, ever-careful with his elaborate headdress, mounted a small dais on the porch.

The girl, Seylalha, shrouded in a cloak of feathers and spun gold, clutched the side-rail of the open platform as six bearers recruited from the garrison struggled with the rough-hewn steps. She lurched violently to one side, spilling the luxuriant cloth almost to the ground, but her dancer's reflexes saved her from an ill-omened tumble. Ten felons from the city dungeons, drugged into a stupor, clambered past—oblivious to the past and present as well as the limited future. Their white robes were already soiled by numerous falls in the muddy streets but none had seriously injured himself.

At the rear of the procession, wearing another mask of hammered gold and obsidian, Prince Kadakithis groped his way to the tent. He glanced at Molin as he passed though their masks made subtle communication impossible. It was enough, for Molin's purposes, that the Prince himself was entering the tent. He tied the cloth-door of the tent closed and braced three crossed spears against the lintel.

The Hell-Hounds formed an outer perimeter—the Hell-Hounds save for Tempus, whom Molin, with self-congratulations, had had assigned to other duties in the palace; the man might not do as he was told, but he wouldn't be near this ritual. The Hounds held their drawn swords before them; they would administer the coup-de-grace should anyone leave or enter the tent before sunrise. Molin reminded them of their obligations in a voice that carried well beyond the unfinished walls.

"Those Ten whom Vashanka destroyed have been disgraced and remain unworshipped to this day; their very names have been unlearned. But the wraith of a god is far stronger than the spirit of a mortal man. They will feel their deaths again and converge upon this site seeking an unwitting or feeble mortal whom they can usurp and use against their brother. It is your duty to see that this does not occur!"

Zalbar, captain of the Hell-Hounds bellowed his comprehension of Molin's order.

6

The women, and they were all dressed as women though Seylalha knew some of them were the eunuchs who routinely guarded her, crept forward to remove the heavy cloak from her shoulders. She shook the cramped silk and knotted her fingers in anticipation. A partition of fine netting separated the musicians from the other participants in this drama, but their sounds were familiar and oddly soothing. The carpet on which she had always danced lay slightly to one side of the center of the tent and behind the carpet was a mound of pillows to which the burly "women" directed her.

The white-robed men were invited to partake of a banquet laid out on a low table and fell over each other rushing to the sumptuous food. The masked figure who stood apart from the rest and seemed distinctly uncomfortable under his splendid robe was led to a separate table where only stale bread and water had been laid and an ugly, heavy short-sword awaited him.

So, that was the god, Seylalha thought, as the mask was lifted from his face. He was weak-chinned—but what civilized man did not show the stains of his rich foods and soft bed? He was, at least, a whole man.

The man-god would not look at her, preferring to watch the darkest, least penetrable recesses of the tent. Seylalha knew fear for his curiously absent passions. Sliding off the cushions she struck the first position of her dance, expecting the musicians to lift their instruments.

But the musicians reached for their clatter-sticks and the eunuchs guided her rudely back to the cushions. She shook their hands away, aware that they dared not hurt her, but then her attention, and the attention of everyone in the tent, was riveted to a newcomer, a more appropriate man-god who had eased out of the darkness and held an unsheathed dagger in his left hand.

He was tall, massive, etched with the harsh lines of a rough and feral man. The one whom she had mistaken for the man-god embraced the newcomer with hearty familiarity.

"I was afraid you wouldn't show up, Tempus."

"Both you and He had my word. Torchholder is a canny man; he distrusts me already—I could not walk in right behind you, my Prince."

"She is beautiful . . ." the Prince mused, glancing to Seylalha for the first time.

"You've reconsidered? It would be for the best if you did . . . even now. Her beauty means nothing to me. None of this means anything to me except that it must be done and I must do it."

"Yes, you're the one to do it . . . though she is more tempting than I would have thought possible."

The chiefmost of the gowned eunuchs moved to separate the men, giving the interloper a stiff punch on the shoulder. Seylalha, who could read the language of movement, froze in terror as the feral stranger turned, hesitated and plunged the dagger deep into the eunuch's chest all within the space of a few heartbeats. The other "women" who saw little more than a blur of movement, wailed and groaned in terror as the dead eunuch collapsed to the rough ground. Even the white-robed feasters ceased their eating and became a frightened knot of sheep-like men.

"It will be as I warned you, my Prince—not merely the Ten but all the others. If you've no taste for bloodshed it would be best if you depart now. My men await you. I will do my father's work."

"What of Zalbar? I knew nothing about that until Molin addressed them."

"They did not see me; it is unlikely they will see you."

The one who had been called the Prince slunk into the darkness. The other retrieved his dagger from the corpse.

"Our Imperial Prince is not one for rituals of bloodshed and violence," he said to everyone in the tent. "He has asked me to take the role of my father in his stead. Would any here gainsay my right to act for Vashanka and my Prince?"

The question was purest rhetoric. The bloody corpse was testimony to the price of gainsaying this intruder. Seylalha wrenched a heavy tassel from one of the pillows and shredded it behind her. She clung to the belief that her life had been an arrow directed to this night, her dance would be her salvation; but that belief was shaken as the eunuchs who had ruled her for so many years cowered in fear and the feasting men made a doomed attempt to find hiding places.

With an unpleasant smile the man-god strode to the table where he ripped a mouthful of bread from the loaf, drained the beaker of salted water and lifted the crude sword. He shifted it once or twice in his hand, his fingers adjusting to its awkward balance. With the same smile still on his lips he advanced toward the terrified men in white.

Screaming, despite the drugs, they raced through the tent as he winnowed through their numbers. The wisest, least drugged, plunged through the netting into the company of musicians. The man-god stalked his ersatz-brethren as if the darkness did not exist and with a vicious determination that bespoke his acceptance of the role. He shoved the shrieking women aside with his free hand and delivered the final strokes with the bloody sword. The killing completed, he set about gathering the heads of his enemies and placing them in a gory heap on the banquet table—a task made no easier to do or watch by the edgeless sword he wielded.

Still kneeling among the pillows, Seylalha drew the sheer silk tightly

around herself, twisting the loose ends about her arms until she had become a sea-green statue, for the cloth did nothing to conceal her beauty
and little to conceal her pale, quivering fear. When the blood-smeared
stranger who was more god than man had placed the last trophy upon
the table he vented his divine violence on the woman-garbed eunuchs.
Seylalha pulled the pins from her hair; the honey-brown cascade covered her eyes and hid her from the sight of the guardians lying butchered on the ground. She took fistfuls of hair and pressed them against
her ears, but that was not enough to block the knowledge of how the
half-men had died. As she had done so many times as a child and as a
woman, she began to rock back and forth, keening softly to gods whose
names she had long since forgotten.

"It is time, Azyuna."

His voice broke into her prayers. His hand clamped over her wrist
and drew her inexorably to her feet. Her legs shook and she could not
remain upright except through his hold on her. When he shook her
slightly she only closed her eyes tighter and swayed limply in his grasp.

"Open your eyes, girl. It is time!"

Obedient to the outside will Seylalha opened her eyes and shook
back her hair. The hand that gripped her was clean. The voice that
commanded her had something of that forgotten wild land of her birth
in it. His hair was the same color as her own, but he was not a man
come to claim his bride. She hung from his grip as mute and fearful as
the quiet women behind the torn netting.

"You are obviously the one to make Azyuna's pleas—however little
you resemble her. Do not force me to hurt you more than I must already!" he whispered urgently, leaning close to her ear, his breath as
warm and thick as blood. "Or have they not told you the whole legend?
I am myself, I am Vashanka—we both grow impatient, girl. Dance because your life depends on it."

He flicked her wrist and sent her sprawling to the blood-dampened
carpet. She brushed her hair away with a forearm made red from his
grip. The man-god had shed the somber clothing he had worn for the
killing and stood near the pillows in a clean gold-worked tunic, but the
crude sword still hung by his thigh—a rusty blush on the white tunic to
mark where its cleaning had not been complete. She read the tension in
his legs, the minute extension of his left hand toward the sword-hilt, the
slight lowering of one eyebrow and remembered that the dance was her
freedom.

Seylalha brought one hand through the tangled mane of her hair, pointed two fingers to her musicians. They struck a ragged, jarring chord to mark their own apprehensions but the tambourist found her throbbing drone and the dance began.

At first she felt the uneven ground beneath the rug and the damp spots upon it, just as she saw those icy eyes and the outstretched fingers. Then there were only the years of practice, the music and the desperation of the dance itself. Three times she felt herself collapse on a misplaced foot; three times the music saved her and, writhing, twisting, she caught herself with will-driven muscles that dared not feel their torture.

Her lungs were on fire, her heartbeat louder than the droning tambour and she danced. She heard only the pounding rhythms of the music and her heart; she saw Azyuna, dark and voluptuous, as she had first performed it before her long-toothed, blood-stained brother.

The god Vashanka smiled and Seylalha, honey-hair and sea-green silk twined together, began the dervish finale of the dance. There was a salt-metal taste in her mouth when she doubled into a barely controlled collapse on the carpet, limbs trembling and glimmering with sweat in the torchlight.

Darkness hovered at the end of her thoughts, the total darkness of exhaustion and death; a freedom she had not anticipated, but in the still-bright center of her thoughts she saw first the bloody god, then the white-and-honey stranger, both smiling, both walking slowly toward her. The sword was gone.

Strong arms parted the hair from her shoulders, lifted her effortlessly from the carpet and held her close against cool, dry skin. A leaden arm shook off its tiredness and found his shoulder to rest on. Had Azyuna loved her brother so deeply?

"Release her! I'm the proper sister for your lusts." A voice which was not Seylalha's filled the tent with images of fire and ice.

"Cime!" the white-and-honey man said while Seylalha slid helplessly back to the carpet.

"She is a slave, a temple's pawn—their tool to capture you and Vashanka both!"

"What brought you here?" the man's voice was filled with wonder as well as anger and, perhaps, a trace of fear. "You did not know . . ."

"The smells of sorcery, priests and the timely knowledge of intrigue. I owe you this much. They mean to bind the God."

"They meant to fill the lily-Prince with Vashanka and gain a Prince if not a child. Their plans are sufficiently thwarted."

Seylalha twisted slowly, raising an arm slightly to see past her hair to the tall, slender woman with the steel-streaked hair. Her breath came easier now; the dance had not killed her—only the god could give her freedom now.

"Mortal flesh is no bond—as you well know. Vashanka's children bear a special curse . . ." the man-god said, taking a step toward the woman.

"Then we'll complete their sorry ritual and damn the curse. They'll kill the slut when she bleeds again and for us—who knows? A god's freedom?"

The woman, Cime, jerked the knot loose from her vest, revealing a body that belied the steel in her hair. Seylalha felt the man step further away from her. Cime's words echoed mockingly in her ears. She had envisioned Vashanka falling upon his dark sister, this man-god would do no less. And she, Seylalha, would lie unbroken until the full moon. While brother and sister advanced slowly toward each other Seylalha's toes closed over the hilt of the discarded sword and dragged it into her reach. With serpentine swiftness and silence she shot between the pair, facing the woman, breaking the spell that drew them together.

"He is mine!" she screamed in a voice so seldom used that it might have belonged to Azyuna herself. "He is mine to bring my child, my freedom!" She held the sword to the other woman's breast.

The sister stepped back, anger, thwarted desire and more burned in her eyes, but Seylalha saw the fear in her movements and knew she had won. The man's fingers wove through her honey hair, closing on the neck brooch that held the cloth at her shoulder, ripping it from the soft silk.

"She's right, Cime. You can't lure me with His freedom; I've felt it for too long already. We'll play Torchholder's little game to the end and let the Face of Chaos laugh at us all. The girl's won her child, so leave— or I'll let her use the tent-peg on you."

Cime's face was fury unbounded, but Seylalha no longer cared. The sword dropped from her fingers as soon as his arms lifted her a second time and carried her, without interruption, to the pillows. She grasped his tunic and tore it back from his shoulders with a determination equal to his own. The mute women gathered their instruments and found a compelling harmony with which to fill the tent.

Seylalha lost herself with him until there was nothing beyond the pillows and the memory of the music. The torches were long since exhausted and in the darkness her god-lover was neither awesome nor cruel. He might have intended rape and pain, but her passion for a child and freedom consumed him and he lay asleep across her breast. Her body curved against his and though she had not meant it to happen, she fell asleep as well.

He grunted and jerked upright, leaving her puzzled and cold on the pillows. Wariness tightened the muscles of his leg. She raised herself up on one elbow without learning the source of his sudden concern.

"Cover yourself," he instructed, thrusting his torn tunic at her.

"Why?"

"There'll be a fire here," he spoke as if repeating words that swam in his head already. "By Wrigglies, Cime or what . . . we're betrayed."

He gripped her arm and hauled her to her feet as the tent burst into flames around them. Clutching the tunic to her breast, Seylalha molded herself against him. He was motionless for less than a second; the fire swept through the roof-cloth and raced toward the carpet and pillows where they stood. Sparks jumped toward her long hair; she screamed and flailed at the flames until he put them out with his hands and hoisted her rudely in his arms.

The firelight leeched all gentleness from his face, replacing it with pain and a glint of vengeance. One of the beams that supported the tent cracked down before them, sending a blaze of fire up past his knees. He cursed names that meant nothing to her as he walked through the inferno.

They broke through the ring of flames into the predawn moistness of the port-city air. She coughed, realizing she had scarcely breathed since he had lifted her. With the gasps of cool air she caught the bitter scents of singed hair and charred flesh.

"Your legs?" she whispered.

"They'll mend; they always do."

"But you're hurt now," she protested. "I can walk—there's no need to carry me."

She twisted to be free of him but his grip grew tighter and unfriendly. She began to fear him again as if their moments together in the tent had been a dream. The pinching fingers holding her arms and thighs could never have been gentle.

"I have not hurt you," he snarled. "Of more women than I care to remember you alone had demands that would sate me. You've gotten your freedom and I've gotten rest in a woman's arms. When it is safe I'll put you down, but not before."

He carried her past the scattered stones of the unfinished temple and out into the open land beyond the limits of Rankan Sanctuary toward

the houses left to ruins since Ilsig abandoned the town. She shivered
and shed quiet tears, but clung tightly as he assaulted the uneven,
overgrown fields in the gray predawn light. He stopped by a crumbling
wall and set her down upon it.

"The Hounds patrol here at dawn; they'll find you and bring you
safely to the Prince and Torchholder."

She didn't ask to go with him, holding the request firmly within herself. The one for whom she had danced was gone, probably forever, and
the one who remained was not the sort a dancer-slave would be wise to
follow. And there was the child to consider . . . Still, she could not
turn away from him as he glared at her. His face softened slightly, as if
her lover might live somewhere behind that grim visage.

"Tell me your name," he demanded in a voice half-gentle, half-
mocking.

"Seylalha."

"A Northern name, isn't it? A pretty name to remember."

And he was gone, striding back across the fallow gardens to the
town. She wrapped the torn, scorched tunic around her bare shoulders
and waited.


7


Molin Torchholder hurried down the polished stone corridors of the
palace; his new sandals slapped the soles of his feet and echoed in the
empty hallways. The sound reminded him of his slaves' leather-wrapped
sticks and that reminded him of how few slaves were left in the temple
since the mysterious fire had taken so many lives the night of the Ten-
Slaying two weeks before.

He had sent a messenger to the capital the next day with a full report
of the events as he understood them. He'd written and sealed it himself.
The Prince could not have sent word faster; no post could have returned in that time. There was no reason to think that Kadakithis or the
Emperor himself would be thinking about Vashanka today. But the
Prince's summons had been preemptive, so Molin hiked the long, empty
corridors with a worried look on his face.

The Ten-Slaying had convinced him to take his prince more
seriously. When the charred tatters of cloth and wood had cooled

enough to let the Hounds investigate the blaze, they had found a heap of blackened skulls in one place and the bodies of the ten felons scattered throughout the burned wreckage. For one who had expressed a distaste for bloodshed, Kadakithis had recreated Vashanka's vengeance to the final letter of the legends—a precision not required and which Molin could not even remember describing to the Prince.

Tempus stood beside the Prince's throne, back in town after another unexplained absence. The massive, cruel Hell-Hound did not look happy—perhaps the strains of the Sacred Brotherhood's loyalty were beginning to show. Molin wished, for the last time, that he knew why he had been summoned, then nodded to the herald and heard himself announced.

"Ah, Molin, there you are. We'd been wondering what was keeping you," the Prince said with his usual charm.

"My new quarters, while much appreciated, seem to be several leagues from here. I'd never thought there could be so much corridor in a small palace."

"The rooms are adequate? The Lady Rosanda . . ."

"The girl who danced Azyuna's Dance—what has become of her?" Tempus interrupted and Molin turned his attention at once from the Prince to the Hell-Hound.

"A few burns," he responded cautiously, seeing displeasure in Tempus' eyes. The Hound had called this interview; Molin no longer doubted it. "Minor ones," he added. "What little discomfort she may have experienced seems to have passed completely."

"You've freed her, haven't you, Molin?" the Prince chimed in nervously.

"As a matter of course, though it's too soon to tell if she'll bear a child. I thought it best to take her survival as a sign of the god's favor—in the absence of any other information. You haven't remembered anything yourself, my Prince?" Molin faced the Prince but glanced at Tempus. There was something in the Hound's face whenever the Ten-Slaying was discussed, but Molin doubted he'd ever get to the bottom of it. Kadakithis claimed the god had so completely possessed him that he remembered nothing from the moment the tent was sealed until sunrise when he found himself in his own bed.

"If she is with child?" Tempus continued.

"Then she will live out her days at the temple with the full honors of a freedwoman and the living consort of our god—as you know. Her power could become considerable—though only time will tell. It depends on her, and the child—if there is a child."

"And if there is no child?"

Molin shrugged. "In many respects it will be no different. It is not in the temple's power to remove the honors we have bestowed. Vashanka saw fit to remove her from the inferno." It was easier to imagine Vashanka possessing Tempus than the Prince, but Molin had not become High Priest by speaking his mind. "We acknowledge her as First Consort of Sanctuary. It would be best if she had conceived."

Tempus nodded and looked away. It was the signal the Prince had been waiting for. He had been even more uncomfortable at this interview than Molin; Molin was used to hiding secrets. The Prince left the chamber without ritual, leaving the High Priest and the Hell-Hound together for a moment.

"I've talked with her often these past few days. Remarkable, isn't it, to discover that a slave has a mind?" Molin said aloud to himself but for Tempus' benefit. If the Hound had an interest in Seylalha the Priesthood wished to use it. "She is convinced she slept with the god—in all other respects she is intelligent and not given to false beliefs, but her faith in her lover will not be shaken. She dances for him still, in silence. I've replaced the silks, but women and eunuchs must come from the capital and that will take time.

"I watch her each evening at sunset; she doesn't seem to mind. She is very beautiful, but sad and lonely as well—the dance has changed since the Ten-Slaying. You must come and watch for yourself sometime."

# A Man and His God

## Janet Morris

### 1

Solstice storms and heat lightning beat upon Sanctuary, washing the
dust from the gutters and from the faces of the mercenaries drifting
through town on their way north where (seers proclaimed and rumor
corroborated) the Rankan Empire would soon be hiring multitudes,
readying for war.

The storms doused cookfires west of town, where the camp followers
and artificers that Sanctuary's ramshackle facilities could not hold had
overflowed. There squatted, under stinking ill-tanned hide pavilions,
custom weaponers catering to mercenaries whose eyes were keener than
the most carefully wax-forged iron and whose panoplies must bespeak
their whereabouts in battle to their comrades; their deadly efficacy to
strangers and combatants; the dear cost of their hire to prospective employers. Fine corselets, cuirasses ancient and modern, custom's best
axes and swords, and helmetry with crests dyed to order could be had
in Sanctuary that summer; but the downwind breeze had never smelled
fouler than after wending through their press.

Here and there among the steaming firepots siegecrafters and commanders of fortifications drilled their engineers, lest from idleness
picked men be suborned by rival leaders seeking to upgrade their corps.
To keep order here, the Emperor's halfbrother Kadakithis had only a
handful of Rankan Hell-Hounds in his personal guard, and a local garrison staffed by indigenous Ilsigs, conquered but not assimilated. The
Rankans called the Ilsigs "Wrigglies," and the Wrigglies called the
Rankans naked barbarians and their women worse, and not even the
rain could cool the fires of that age-old rivalry.

On the landspit north of the lighthouse, rain had stopped work on Prince Kadakithis's new palace. Only a man and horse, both bronze, both of heroic proportions, rode the beach. Doom criers of Sanctuary, who once had proclaimed their town "just left of heaven," had changed their tune: they had dubbed Sanctuary Death's Gate and the one man, called Tempus, Death Himself.

He was not. He was a mercenary, envoy of a Rankan faction desirous of making a change in emperors; he was a Hell-Hound, by Kadakithis's good offices; and marshal of palace security, because the Prince, not meant to triumph in his governorship/exile, was understaffed. Of late Tempus had become a royal architect, for which he was as qualified as any man about, having fortified more towns than Kadakithis had years. The Prince had proposed the site; the soldier examined it and found it good. Not satisfied, he had made it better, dredging deep with oxen along the shore while his imported fortifications crews raised double walls of baked brick filled with rubble and faced with stone. When complete, these would be deeply crenelated for archers, studded with gatehouses, double-gated and sheer. Even incomplete, the walls which barred the folk from spit and lighthouse grinned with a death's head smirk toward the town, enclosing granaries and stables and newly whited barracks and a spring for fresh water: if War came hither, Tempus proposed to make Him welcome for a long and arduous siege.

The fey, god's breath weather might have stopped work on the construction, but Tempus worked without respite, always: it eased the soul of the man who could not sleep and who had turned his back upon his god. This day, he awaited the arrival of Kadakithis and that of his own anonymous Rankan contact, to introduce emissary to possible figurehead, to put the two together and see what might be seen.

When he had arranged the meeting, he had yet walked in the shelter of the god Vashanka's arm. Now, things had changed for him and he no longer cared to serve Vashanka, the Storm God, who regulated kingship. If he could, he was going to contrive to be relieved of his various commissions and of his honor bond to Kadakithis, freed to go among the mercenaries to whom his soul belonged (since he had it back) and put together a cohort to take north and lease to the highest bidder. He wanted to wade thigh-deep in gore and guts and see if, just by chance, he might manage to find his way back through the shimmering dimensional gate beyond which the god had long ago thrust him, back into the world and into the age to which he was born.

Since he knew the chances of that were less than Kadakithis becoming Emperor of Upper and Lower Ranke, and since the god's gloss of rationality was gone from him, leaving him in the embrace of the curse, yet lingering, which he had originally become the god's suppliant to thwart, he would settle for a small mercenary corps of his own choosing, from which to begin building an army that would not be a puerile jest, as Kadakithis's forces were at present. For this he had been contacted, to this he had agreed. It remained only to see to it that Kadakithis agreed.

The mercenary who was a Hell-Hound scolded the horse, who did not like its new weighted shoes or the water surging around its knees, white as its stockings. Like the horse, Kadakithis was only potential in quest of actualization; like the horse, Kadakithis feared the wrong things, and placed his trust in himself only, an untenable arrogance in horse or man, when the horse must go to battle and the man also. Tempus collected the horse up under him, shifting his weight, pulling the red-bronze beast's head in against its chest, until the combination of his guidance and the toe-weights on its hooves and the waves' kiss showed the horse what he wanted. Tempus could feel it in the stallion's gaits; he did not need to see the result: like a dancer, the sorrel lifted each leg high. Then it gave a quizzical snort as it sensed the power to be gained from such a stride: school was in session. Perhaps, despite the four white socks, the horse would suit. He lifted it with a touch and a squeeze of his knees into a canter no faster than another horse might walk. "Good, good," he told it, and from the beach came the *pat-pat* of applause.

Clouds split; sunrays danced over the wrack-strewn shore and over the bronze stallion and its rider, stripped down to plated loinguard, making a rainbow about them. Tempus looked up, landward to where a lone eunuch clapped pink palms together from one of Prince Kadakithis's chariots. The rainbow disappeared, the clouds suppressed the sun, and in a wrap of shadow the enigmatic Hell-Hound (whom the eunch knew from his own experience to be capable of regenerating a severed limb and thus veritably eternal; and who was indubitably deadlier than all the mercenaries descended on Sanctuary like flies upon a day-old carcass) trotted the horse up the beach to where the eunuch in the chariot was waiting on solid ground.

"What are you doing here, Sissy? Where is your lord, Kadakithis?" Tempus stopped his horse well back from the irascible pair of blacks in their traces. This eunuch was near their color: a Wriggly. Cut young and deftly, his answer came in a sweet alto:

"Lord Marshal, most daunting of Hell-Hounds, I bring you His Majesty's apologies, and true word, if you will heed it."

The eunuch, no more than seventeen, gazed at him longingly. Kadakithis had accepted this fancy toy from Jubal, the slaver, despite the slavemaster's own brand on its high rump, and the deeper dangers implied by the identity of its fashioner. Tempus had marked it, when first he heard its lilting voice in the palace, for he had heard that voice before. Foolish, haughty, or merely pressed beyond a bedwarmer's ability to cope: no matter; this creature of Jubal's, he had long wanted. Jubal and Tempus had been making private war, the more fierce for being undeclared, since Tempus had first come to Sanctuary and seen the swaggering, masked killers Jubal kept on staff terrorizing whom they chose on the town's west side. Tempus had made those masked murderers his private game stock, the west end of Sanctuary his personal preserve, and the campaign was on. Time and again, he had dispatched them. But tactics change, and Jubal's had become too treacherous for Tempus to endure, especially now with the northern insurrection half out of its egg of rumor. He said to the parted lips awaiting his permission to speak and to the deer-soft eyes doting on his every move that the eunuch might dismount the car, prostrate itself before him, and from there deliver its message.

It did all of those, quivering with delight like a dog enraptured by the smallest attention, and said with its forehead to the sand: "My lord, the Prince bids me say he has been detained by Certain Persons, and will be late, but means to attend you. If you were to ask me why that was, then I would have no choice but to admit to you that the three most mighty magicians, those whose names cannot be spoken, came down upon the summer palace in billows of blackest smoke and foul odors, and that the fountains ran red and the sculptures wept and cried, and frogs jumped upon my lord in his bath, all because the Hazards are afraid that you might move to free the slayer-of-sorcerers called Cime before she comes to trial. Although my master assured them that you would not, that you had said nothing to him about this woman, when I left they still were not satisfied, but were shaking walls and raising shades and doing all manner of wizardly things to demonstrate their concern."

The eunuch fell quiet, awaiting leave to rise. For an instant there was total silence, then the sound of Tempus's slithering dismount. Then he said: "Let us see your brand, pretty one," and with a wiggling of its upthrust rump the eunuch hastened to obey.

It took Tempus longer than he had estimated to wrest a confession from the Wriggly, from the Ilsig who was the last of his line and at the end of his line. It did not make cries of pleasure or betrayal or agony, but accepted its destiny as good Wrigglies always did, writhing soundlessly.

When he let it go, though the blood was running down its legs and it saw the intestine like wet parchment caught in his fingernails, it wept with relief, promising to deliver his exhortation posthaste to Kadakithis. It kissed his hand, pressing his palm against its beardless cheek, never realizing that it was, itself, his message, or that it would be dead before the sun set.

2

Kneeling to wash his arm in the surf, he found himself singing a best-forgotten funerary dirge in the ancient argot all mercenaries learn. But his voice was gravelly and his memories were treacherous thickets full of barbs, and he stopped as soon as he realized that he sang. The eunuch would die because he remembered its voice from the workshop of despicable Kurd, the frail and filthy vivisectionist, while he had been an experimental animal therein. He remembered other things, too: he remembered the sear of the branding iron and the smell of flesh burning and the voices of two fellow guardsmen, the Hell-Hounds Zalbar and Razkuli, piercing the drug-mist through holes the pain poked in his stupor. And he recalled a protracted and hurtful healing, shut away from any who might be overawed to see a man regrow a limb. Mending, he had brooded, seeking certainty, some redress fit to his grievance. But he had not been sure enough to act. Now, after hearing the eunuch's tale, he was certain. When Tempus was certain, Destiny got out its ledger.

But what to write therein? His instinct told him it was Black Jubal he wanted, not the two Hell-Hounds; that Razkuli was a nonentity and Zalbar, like a raw horse, was merely in need of schooling. *Those* two had single-handedly arranged for Tempus's snuff to be drugged, for him to be branded, his tongue cut out, then sold off to wicked little Kurd, there to languish interminably under the knife? He could not credit it. Yet the eunuch had said—and in such straits no one lies—that though Jubal had gone to Zalbar for help in dealing with Tempus, the slave

trader had known nothing of what fate the Hell-Hounds had in mind for
their colleague. Never mind it; Jubal's crimes were voluminous. Tempus
would take him for espionage—that punishment could only be administered once. Then personal grudges must be put aside: it is unseemly to
hold feuds with the dead.

But if not Jubal, then who had written Tempus's itinerary for Hell? It
sounded, suspiciously, like the god's work. Since he had turned his back
upon the god, things had gone from bad to worse. And if Vashanka had
not turned His face away from Tempus even while he lay helpless, the
god had not stirred to rescue him (though any limb lopped off him still
grew back, any wound he took healed relatively quickly, as men judge
such things). No, Vashanka, his tutelary, had not hastened to aid him.
The speed of Tempus's healing was always in direct proportion to the
pleasure the god was taking in His servant. Vashanka's terrible rebuke
had made the man wax terrible, also. Curses and unholy insults rang
down from the mind of the god and up from the mind of the man who
then had no tongue left with which to scream. It had taken Hanse the
thief, young Shadowspawn, chance-met and hardly known, to extricate
him from interminable torture. Now he owed more debt than he liked to
Shadowspawn, and Shadowspawn knew more about Tempus than even
that backstreeter could want to know, so that the thief's eyes slid away,
sick and mistrustful, when Tempus would chance upon him in the
Maze.

But even then, Tempus's break with divinity was not complete.
Hopefully, he stood as Vashanka in the recreation of the Ten-Slaying
and Seduction of Azyuna, thinking to propitiate the god while saving
face—to no avail. Soon after, hearing that his sister, Cime, had been
apprehended slaying sorcerers wantonly in their beds, he had thrown
the amulet of Vashanka, which he had worn since former times, out to
sea from this very shore—he had had no choice. Only so much can be
borne from men, so much from gods. Zalbar, had he the wit, would
have revelled in Tempus's barely-hidden reaction to his news that the
fearsome mage-killer was now in custody, her diamond rods locked
away in the Hall of Judgment awaiting her disposition.

He growled to himself, thinking about her, her black hair winged
with gray, in Sanctuary's unsegregated dungeons where any syphilitic
rapist could have her at will, while he must not touch her at all, or raise
hand to help her lest he start forces in motion he could not control. His
break with the god stemmed from her presence in Sanctuary, as his endless wandering as Vashanka's minion had stemmed from an altercation

he had over her with a mage. If he went down into the pits and took her, the god would be placated; he had no desire to reopen relations with Vashanka, who had turned His face away from His servant. If Tempus brought her out under his own aegis, he would have the entire Mageguild at his throat; he wanted no quarrel with the Adepts. He had told her not to slay them here, where he must maintain order and the letter of the law.

By the time Kadakithis arrived in that very same chariot, its braces sticky with Wriggly blood, Tempus was in a humor darker than the drying clots, fully as dark as the odd, round cloud coming fast from the northeast.

Kadakithis's noble Rankan visage was suffused with rage, so that his skin was darker than his pale hair: "But *why?* In the name of all the gods, what did the poor little creature ever do to you? You owe me a eunuch, and an explanation." He tapped his lacquered nails on the chariot's bronze rim.

"I have a perfect replacement in mind," smiled Tempus smoothly, "my lord. As for why . . . all eunuchs are duplicitous. This one was an information conduit to Jubal. Unless you would like to invite the slaver to policy sessions and let him stand behind those ivory screens where your favorites eavesdrop as they choose, I have acted well within my prerogatives as marshal. If my name is attached to your palace security, then your palace *will be* secure."

"Bastard! How dare you even imply that *I* should apologize to *you?* When will you treat me with the proper amount of respect? You tell me all eunuchs are treacherous, the very breath after offering me another one!"

"I am giving you respect. Reverence I reserve for better men than I. When you have attained that dignity, we shall both know it: you will not have to ask. Until then, either trust or discharge me." He waited, to see if the Prince would speak. Then he continued: "As to the eunuch I offer as replacement, I want you to arrange for his training. You like Jubal's work; send to him saying yours has met with an accident and you wish to tender another into his care to be similarly instructed. Tell him you paid a lot of money for it, and you have high hopes."

"You have such a eunuch?"

"I will have it."

"And you expect me to conscion your sending of an agent in there— aye, to aid you—without knowing your plan, or even the specifics of the Wriggly's confession?"

"Should you know, my lord, you would have to approve, or disapprove. As it lies, you are free of onus."

The two men regarded each other, checked hostility jumping between them like Vashanka's own lightning in the long, dangerous pause.

Kadakithis flicked his purple mantle over his shoulder. He squinted past Tempus, into the waning day. "What kind of cloud is that?"

Tempus swung around in his saddle, then back. "That should be our friend from Ranke."

The Prince nodded. "Before he arrives, then, let us discuss the matter of the female prisoner Cime."

Tempus's horse snorted and threw its head, dancing in place. "There is nothing to discuss."

"But . . . ? Why did you not come to me about it? I could have done something, previously. Now, I cannot . . ."

"I did not ask you. I am not asking you." His voice was a blade on whetstone, so that Kadakithis pulled himself up straight. "It is not for me to take a hand."

"Your own sister? You will not intervene?"

"Believe what you will, *Prince*. I will not sift through gossip with any man, be he prince or king."

The Prince lost hold, then, having been "princed" too often back in Ranke, and berated the Hell-Hound.

The man sat quite still upon the horse the Prince had given him, garbed only in his loinguard though the day was fading, letting his gaze full of festering shadows rest in the Prince's until Kadakithis trailed off, saying, ". . . the trouble with you is that anything they say about you could be true, so a man knows not what to believe."

"Believe in accordance with your heart," the voice like grinding stone suggested, while the dark cloud came to hover over the beach.

It settled, seemingly, into the sand, and the horses shied back, necks outstretched, nostrils huge. Tempus had his sorrel up alongside the chariot team and was leaning down to take the lead-horse's bridle when an earsplitting clarion came from the cloud's translucent center.

The Hell-Hound raised his head then, and Kadakithis saw him shiver, saw his brow arch, saw a flicker of deepset eyes within their caves of bone and lid. Then again Tempus spoke to the chariot horses, who swiveled their ears toward him and took his counsel, and he let loose the lead-horse's bridle and spurred his own between Kadakithis's chariot and what came out of the cinereous cloud which had been so long descending upon them in opposition to the prevailing wind:

The man on the horse who could be seen within the cloud waved: a flash of scarlet glove, a swirl of burgundy cloak. Behind his tasseled steed he led another, and it was this second gray horse who again challenged the other stallions on the beach, its eyes full of fire. Farther back within the cloud, stonework could be seen, masonry like none in Sanctuary, a sky more blue and hills more virile than any Kadakithis knew.

The first horse, reins flapping, was emerging, nose and neck casting shadows upon solid Sanctuary sand; then its hooves scattered grains, and the whole of the beast, and its rider, and the second horse he led on a long tether, stood corporeal and motionless before the Hell-Hound, while behind, the cloud whirled in upon itself and was gone with an audible "pop."

"Greetings, Riddler," said the rider in burgundy and scarlet, as he doffed his helmet with its blood-dark crest to Tempus.

"I did not expect *you*, Abarsis. What could be so urgent?"

"I heard about the Trôs horse's death, so I thought to bring you another, better auspiced, I hope. Since I was coming anyway, our friends suggested I bring what you require. I have long wanted to meet you." Spurring his mount forward, he held out his hand.

Red stallion and iron gray snaked arched necks, thrusting forth clacking teeth, wide-gaped jaws emitting squeals to go with flattened ears and rolling eyes. Above horse hostilities could be heard snatches of low wordplay, parry and riposte: ". . . disappointed that you could not build the temple." ". . . welcome to take my place here and try. The foundations of the temple grounds are defiled, the priest in charge more corrupt than even politics warrants. I wash my hands . . ." ". . . with the warring imminent, how can you . . . ?" "Theomachy is no longer my burden." "That cannot be so." ". . . hear about the insurrection, or take my leave!" ". . . His name is unpronounceable, and that of his empire, but I think we all shall learn it so well we will mumble it in our sleep . . ." "I don't sleep. It is a matter of the right field officers, and men young enough not to have fought upcountry the last time." "I am meeting some Sacred Band members here, my old team. Can you provision us?" "Here? Well enough to get to the capital and do it better. Let me be the first to . . ."

Kadakithis, forgotten, cleared his throat.

Both men stared at the Prince severely, as if a child had interrupted adults. Tempus bowed low in his saddle, arm outswept. The rider in reds with the burnished cuirass tucked his helmet under his arm and approached the chariot, handing the second horse's tether to Tempus as he passed by.

"Abarsis, presently of Ranke," said the dark, cultured voice of the armored man, whose hair swung black and glossy on a young bull's neck. His line was old, one of court graces and bas-relief faces and up-swept, regal eyes that were disconcertingly wise and as gray-blue as the huge horse Tempus held with some difficulty. Ignoring the squeals of just-met stallions, the man continued: "Lord Prince, may all be well with you, with your endeavors and your holdings, eternally. I bear reaffirmation of our bond to you." He held out a purse, fat with coin.

Tempus winced, imperceptibly, and took wraps of the gray horse's tether, drawing its head close with great care, until he could bring his fist down hard between its ears to quiet it.

"What is this? There is enough money here to raise an army!" scowled Kadakithis, tossing the pouch lightly in his palm.

A polite and perfect smile lit the northern face, so warmly hand-some, of the Rankan emissary. "Have you not told him, then, O Riddler?"

"No, I thought to, but got no opportunity. Also, I am not sure whether we *will* raise it, or whether that is my severance pay." He threw a leg over the sorrel's neck and slid down it, butt to horse, dropped its reins and walked away down the beach with his new Trôs horse in hand.

The Rankan hooked his helmet carefully on one of the saddle's silver rosettes. "You two are not getting on, I take it. Prince Kadakithis, you must be easy with him. Treat him as he does his horses; he needs a gen-tle hand."

"He needs his comeuppance. He has become insufferable! What is this money? Has he told you I am for sale? I am not!"

"He has turned his back on his god and the god is letting him run. When he is exhausted, the god will take him back. You found him pleasant enough, previously, I would wager. He has been set upon by your own staff, men to whom he was sworn and who gave oaths to him. What do you expect? He will not rest easy until he has made that mat-ter right."

"What is this? My men? You mean that long unexplained absence of his? I admit he is changed. But how do you know what he would not tell me?"

A smile like sunrise lit the elegant face of the armored man. "The god tells me what I need to know. How would it be, for him to come running to you with tales of feuding among your ranks like a child to his father? His honor precludes it. As for the . . . funds . . . you hold, when we sent him here, it was with the understanding that should he feel you would make a king, he would so inform us. This, I was told you knew."

"In principle. But I cannot take a gift so large."

"Take a loan, as others before you have had to do. There is no time now for courtship. To be capable of *becoming* a king insures no seat of kingship, these days. A king must be more than a man, he must be a hero. It takes many men to make a hero, and special times. Opportunities approach, with the upcountry insurrection and a new empire rising beyond the northern range. Were you to distinguish yourself in combat, or field an army that did, we who seek a change could rally around you publicly. You cannot do it with what you have, the emperor has seen to that."

"At what rate am I expected to pay back this loan?"

"Equal value, nothing more. If the Prince, my lord, will have patience, I will explain all to Your Majesty's satisfaction. That, truly, is why I am come."

"Explain away, then."

"First, one small digression, which touches a deeper truth. You must have some idea who and what the man you call Tempus is, I am sure you have heard it from your wizards and from his enemies among the officials of the Mageguild. Let me add to that this: Where he goes, the god scatters His blessings. By the cosmological rules of state cult and kingship, He has invested this endeavor with divine sanction by his presence. Though he and the god have their differences, without him, no chance remains that you might triumph. My father found that out. Even sick with his curse, he is too valuable to waste, unappreciated. If you would rather remain a princeling forever, and let the empire slide into ruin apace, just tell me and I will take word home. We will forget this matter of the kingship and this corollary matter of a small standing army, and I will release Tempus. He would as soon it, I assure you."

"Your *father*? Who in the God's Eye *are* you?"

"Ah, my arrogance is unforgivable; I thought you would know me. We are all so full of ourselves, these days, it is no wonder events have come to such a pass. I am Man of the God in Upper Ranke, Sole Friend to the Mercenaries, the hero, Son of the Defender, and so forth."

"High Priest of Vashanka."

"In the Upper Land."

"My family and yours thinned each other's line," stated Kadakithis baldly, no apology, no regret in his words. Yet he looked differently upon the other, thinking they were of an age, both wielding wooden swords in shady courts while the slaughter raged, far off at the fronts.

"Unto eradication," remarked the dark young man. "But we did not contest, and now there is a different enemy, a common threat. It is enough."

"And you and Tempus have never met?"

"He knew my father. And when I was ten, and my father died and our armies were disbanded, he found a home for me. Later, when I came to the god and the mercenaries' guild, I tried to see him. He would not meet with me." He shrugged, looking over his shoulder at the man walking the blue-gray horse into blue-gray shadows falling over the blue-black sea. "Everyone has his hero, you know. A god is not enough for a whole man; he craves a fleshly model. When he sent to me for a horse, and the god approved it, I was elated. Now, perhaps, I can do more. The horse may not have died in vain, after all."

"I do not understand you, Priest."

"My Lord, do not make me too holy. I am Vashanka's priest: I know many requiems and oaths, and thirty-three ways to fire a warrior's bier. They call me Stepson, in the mercenaries' guild. I would be pleased if you would call me that, and let me talk to you at greater length about a future in which your destiny and the wishes of the Storm God, our Lord, could come to be the same."

"I am not sure I can find room in my heart for such a god; it is difficult enough to pretend to piety," grated Kadakithis, squinting after Tempus in the dusk.

"You will, you will," promised the priest, and dismounted his horse to approach Tempus's ground-tied sorrel. Abarsis reached down, running his hand along the beast's white-stocking'd leg. "Look, Prince," he said, craning his neck up to see Kadakithis's face as his fingers tugged at the gold chain wedged in the weight-cleat on the horse's shoe. At the end of the chain, sandy but shining gold, was an amulet. "The god wants him back."

## 3

The mercenaries drifted into Sanctuary dusty from their westward trek or blue-lipped from their rough sea passage and wherever they went they made hellish what before had been merely dissolute. The Maze was no longer safe for pickpocket or pander; usurer and sorcerer scuttled in haste from street to doorway, where before they had swaggered virtually unchallenged, crime lords in fear of nothing.

Now the whores walked bowlegged, dreamy-eyed, parading their new finery in the early hours of the morning while most mercenaries slept; the taverns changed shifts but feared to close their doors, lest a mercenary find that an excuse to take offense. Even so early in the day, the inns were full of brawls and the gutters full of casualties. The garrison soldiers and the Hell-Hounds could not be omnipresent: wherever they were not, mercenaries took sport, and they were not in the Maze this morning.

Though Sanctuary had never been so prosperous, every guild and union and citizen's group had sent representatives to the palace at sunrise to complain.

Lastel, a/k/a One-Thumb, could not understand why the Sanctuarites were so unhappy. Lastel was very happy: he was alive and back at the Vulgar Unicorn tending bar, and the Unicorn was making money, and money made Lastel happy, always. Being alive was something Lastel had not fully appreciated until recently, when he had spent aeons dying a subjective death in thrall to a spell he had paid to have laid upon his own person, a spell turned against him by the sons of its deceased creator, Mizraith of the Hazard class, and dispelled by he-knew-not-whom. Though every night he expected his mysterious benefactor to sidle up to the bar and demand payment, no one ever came and said: "Lastel, I saved you. I am the one. Now show your gratitude." But he knew very well that someday soon, someone would. He did not let this irritation besmirch his happiness. He had gotten a new shipment of Caronne krrf (black, pure drug, foil stamped, a full weight of it, enough to set every mercenary in Sanctuary at the kill) and it was so good that he considered refraining from offering it on the market. Having considered, he decided to keep it all for himself, and so was very happy indeed, no matter how many fistfights broke out in the bar, or how high the sun was, these days, before he got to bed . . .

Tempus, too, was happy that morning, with the magnificent Trôs horse under him and signs of war all around him. Despite the hour, he saw enough rough hoplites and dour artillery fighters with their crank-bows (whose springs were plaited from women's hair) and their quarrels (barbed and poisoned) to let him know he was not dreaming: these did not bestir themselves from daydreams! The war was real to them. And any one of them could be his. He felt his troop-levy money cuddled tight against his groin, and he whistled tunelessly as the Trôs horse threaded his way toward the Vulgar Unicorn.

One-Thumb was not going to be happy much longer.

Tempus left the Trôs horse on its own recognizance, dropping the reins and telling it, "Stay." Anyone who thought it merely ripe for stealing would learn a lesson about the strain which is bred only in Syr from the original line of Trôs's.

There were a few locals in the Unicorn, most snoring over tables along with other, bagged trash ready to be dragged out into the street.

One-Thumb was behind his bar, big shoulders slumped, washing mugs while watching everything through the bronze mirror he had had installed over his stock.

Tempus let his heels crack against the board and his armor clatter: he had dressed for this, from a box he had thought he might never again open. The wrestler's body which Lastel had built came alert, pirouetted smoothly to face him, staring unabashedly at the nearly god-sized apparition in leopard-skin mantle and helmet set with boar's tusks, wearing an antique enameled breastplate and bearing a bow of ibex-horn morticed with a golden grip.

"*What* in Azyuna's twat are *you?*" bellowed One-Thumb, as every waking customer he had hastened to depart.

"I," said Tempus, reaching the bar and removing his helmet so that his yarrow-honey hair spilled forth, "am Tempus. We have not chanced to meet." He held out a hand whose wrist bore a golden bracer.

"Marshal," acknowledged One-Thumb, carefully, his pate creasing with his frown. "It is good to know you are on our side. But you cannot come in here . . . My—"

"I am here, *Lastel*. While you were so inexplicably absent, I was often here, and received the courtesy of service without charge. But now I am not here to eat or drink with those who recognize me for one who is fully as corrupt as are they themselves. There are those who know where you were, *Lastel,* and why—and *one* who broke the curse that bound you. Truly, if you had cared, you could have found out." Twice, Tempus called One-Thumb by his true name, which no palace personage or Mazedweller should have known enough to do.

"Marshal, let us go to my office." Lastel fairly ramped behind his bar.

"No time, krrf-dealer. Mizraith's sons, Stefab and Marype; Markmor: those three and more were slain by the woman Cime who is in the pits awaiting sentence. I thought that you should know."

"What are you saying? You want me to break her out? Do it yourself."

"No one," said the Hell-Hound, "can break anyone out of the palace. *I* am in charge of security there. If she were to escape, I would be very busy explaining to Kadakithis what went wrong. And tonight I am having a reunion here with fifty of my old friends from the mercenaries' guild. I would not want anything to spoil it. And, too, I ask no man to take me on faith, or go where I have not been." He grinned like the Destroyer, gesturing around. "You had better order in extra. And half a piece of krrf, your courtesy to me, of course. Once you have seen my men when well in hand, you will be better able to conjecture what might happen should they get *out* of hand, and weigh your alternatives. Most men I solicit find it to their benefit to work in accord with me. Should you deem it so for you, we will fix a time, and discuss it."

Not the cipher's meaning, nor the plan it shrouded, nor the threat that gave it teeth were lost on the man who did not like to be called "Lastel" in the Maze. He bellowed: "You are addled. You cannot do this. I cannot do that! As for krrf, I know nothing about . . . any . . . krrf."

But the man was gone, and Lastel was trembling with rage, thinking he had been in purgatory too long; it had eroded his nerves!

4

When the dusk cooled the Maze, Shadowspawn ducked into the Unicorn. One-Thumb was not in evidence; Two-Thumbs was behind the bar.

He sat with the wall supporting him, where the storyteller liked to sit, and watched the door, waiting for the crowd to thicken, tongues to loosen, some caravan driver to boast of his wares. The mercenaries were no boon to a thief, but dangerous playmates, like Kadakithis's palace women. He did not want to be intrigued; he was being distracted moment by moment. As a consequence, he was very careful to keep his mind on business, so that he would not come up hungry next Ilsday, when his funds, if not increased, would run out.

Shadowspawn was dark as iron and sharp like a hawk; a cranked crossbow, loaded with cold bronze and quarrels to spare. He wore knives where a professional wears them, and sapphire and gold and crimson to draw the eye from his treasured blades.

Sanctuary had spawned him: he was hers, and he had thought nothing she did could surprise him. But when the mercenaries arrived as do clients to a strumpet's house, he had been hurt like a whore's bastard when first he learns how his mother feeds him.

It was better, now; he understood the new rules.

One rule was: get up and give them your seat. Hanse *gave* no one his seat. He might recall pressing business elsewhere, or see someone he just had to hasten over to greet. Tonight, he remembered nothing earlier forgotten; he saw no one he cared to bestir himself to meet. He prepared to defend his place as seven mercenaries filled the doorway with plumes and pelts and hilts and mail, and looked his way. But they went in a group to the bar, though one, in a black mantle, with iron at chest and head and wrists, pointed directly to him like a man sighting his arrow along an outstretched arm.

The man talked to Two-Thumbs awhile, took off his helmet with its horsehair crests that seemed blood-red, and approached Hanse's table alone. A shiver coursed the thief's flesh, from the top of his black thatch to his toetips.

The mercenary reached him in a dozen swinging strides, drawing a stabbing sword as he came on. If not for the fact that the other hand held a mug, Shadowspawn would have aired iron by the time the man (or youth from his smooth, heartshaped face) spoke: "Shadowspawn, called Hanse? I am Stepson, called Abarsis. I have been hoping to find you." With a grin full of dazzling teeth, the mercenary put the ivory-hilted sword flat in the wet-rings on the table, and sat, both hands well in evidence, clasped under his chin.

Hanse gripped his beltknife tightly. Then the panic-flash receded, and time passed, instead of piling all its instants terrifyingly on top of one another. Hanse knew that he was no coward, that he was plagued by flashbacks from the two times he had been tapped with the fearstick of Vashanka, but his chest was heaving, and the mercenary might see. He slumped back, for camouflage. The mercenary with the expensive taste in accouterments could be no older than he. And yet, only a king's son could afford such a blade as that before him. He reached out hesitantly to touch its silvered guard, its garnet pommel, his gaze locked in the sellsword's soulless pale one, his hand slipping closer and closer to the elegant sword of its own accord.

"Ah, you do like it then," said Stepson. "I was not sure. You will take it, I hope. It is customary in my country, when meeting a man who has performed heroically to the benefit of one's house, to give a small token." He withdrew a silver scabbard from his belt, laid it with the sword, which Hanse put down as if burned.

"What did I ever do for you?"

"Did you not rescue the Riddler from great peril?"

"Who?"

The tanned face grinned ingenuously. "A truly brave man does not boast. I understand. Or is it a deeper thing? That—" He leaned forward; he smelled sweet like new-mown hay "—is truly what I need to know. Do you comprehend me?"

Hanse gave him an eagle's look, and shook his head slowly, his fingers flat on the table, near the magnificent sword that the mercenary Stepson had offered to give him. *The Riddler?* He knew no one of that name.

"Are you protecting him? There is no need, not from me. Tell me, Shadowspawn, are you and Tempus lovers?"

"Mother—!" His favorite knife leapt into his palm, unbidden. He looked at it in his own grasp in consternation, and dropped his other hand over it, and began paring his nails. *Tempus! The Riddler?* Hanse's eyes caressed the covetable blade. "I helped him out, once or twice, that's all."

"That is good," the youth across from him approved. "Then we will not have to fight over him. And, too, we could work a certain bargain, service for service, that would make me happy and you, I modestly estimate, a gentleman of ease for at least six months."

"I'm listening," said Shadowspawn, taking a chance, commending his knife to its sheath. The short sword too, he handled, fitting it in the scabbard and drawing it out, fascinated by the alert scrutiny of Abarsis the Stepson's six companions.

When he began hearing the words "diamond rods" and "Hall of

Judgment" he waxed uneasy. But by then, he could not see any way that he could allow himself to appear less than heroic in the pale, blue-gray eyes of the Stepson. Not when the amount of money Stepson had offered hung in the balance, not when the nobly fashioned sword he had been given as if it were merely serviceable proclaimed the flashy merce-nary's ability to *pay* that amount. But too, if he would pay that, he would pay more. Hanse was not so enthralled by the mercenaries' mys-tique to hasten into one's pay without some good Sanctuary barter. Watching Stepson's six formidable companions, waiting like purebred hunting dogs curried for show, he spied a certain litheness about them, an uncanny cleanliness of limb and nearness of girded hips. Close friends, these. Very close.

Abarsis's sonorous voice had ceased, waiting for Hanse's response. The disconcertingly pale eyes followed Hanse's stare, frank now, to his companions.

"Will you say yea, then, friend of the Riddler? And become my friend, also? These other friends of mine await only your willingness to embrace you as a brother."

"I own," Hanse muttered.

Abarsis raised one winged brow. "So? They are members of a Sacred Band, my old one; most prized officers; heroes, every pair." He judged Hanse's face. "Can it be you do not have the custom, in the south? From your mien I must believe it." His voice was liquid, like deep run-ning water. "These men, to me and to their chosen partners, have sworn to forsake life before honor, to stand and never retreat, to fall where they fight if need be, shoulder to shoulder. There is no more hallowed tryst than theirs. Had I a thousand such, I would rule the earth."

"Which one is yours?" Hanse tried not to sneer, to be conversational, unshaken, but his eyes could find no comfortable place to rest, so that at last he took up the gift-sword and examined the hieratic writing on its blade.

"None. I left them, long ago, when my partner went up to heaven. Now I have hired them back, to serve a need. It is strictly a love of spirit, Hanse, that is required. And only in Sacred Bands is a mercenary asked so much."

"Still, it's not my style."

"You sound disappointed."

"I am. In your offer. Pay me twice that, and I will get the items you desire. As for your friends, I don't care if you bugger them each twice daily. Just as long as it's not part of my job and no one thinks I am joining any organizations."

A swift, appreciative smile touched Abarsis. "Twice, then. I am at your mercy."

"I stole those diamond rods once before, for Tem—, for the Riddler. He'll just give them back to her, after she does whatever it is she does for him. I had her once, and she did nothing for me that any other whore would not do."

"You *what?* Ah, you do not know about them, then? Their legend, their curse?"

"Legend? Curse? I *knew* she was a sorceress. Tell me about it! Am I in any danger? You can forget the whole idea, about the rods. I keep shut of sorcery."

"Hardly sorcery, no need to worry. They cannot transmit any of it. When he was young and she was a virgin, he was a prince and a fool of ideals. I heard it that the god is his true father, and thus she is *not* his sibling, but you know how legends are. As a princess, her sire looked for an advantageous marriage. An archmage of a power not seen anymore made an offer, at about the time the Riddler renounced his claim to the throne and retired to a philosopher's cave. She went to him begging aid, some way out of an unacceptable situation, and convinced him that should she be deflowered, the mage would not want her, and of all men the Riddler was the only one she trusted with the task; anyone else would despoil her. She seduced him easily, for he had loved her all his young life and that unacceptable attraction to flesh of his flesh was part of what drove him from his primogeniture. She loved nothing but herself; some things never change. He was wise enough to know he brought destruction upon himself, but men are prone to ruin from women. In passion, he could not think clearly; when it left him he went to Vashanka's altar and threw himself upon it, consigning his fate to the god. The god took him up, and when the archmage appeared with four eyes spitting fire and four mouths breathing fearful curses, the god's aegis partly shielded him. Yet, the curse holds. He wanders eternally bringing death to whomever loves him and being spurned by whomsoever he shall love. She must offer herself for pay to any comer, take no gift of kindness on pain of showing all her awful years, incapable of giving love as she has always been. So thus, the gods, too, are barred to her, and she is truly damned."

Hanse just stared at Stepson, whose voice had grown husky in the telling, when the mercenary left off.

"Now, will you help me? Please. He would want it to be you."

Hanse made a sign.

"*Would* want it to be me?" the thief frowned. "He does not *know* about this?" There came the sound of Shadowspawn's bench scraping back.

Abarsis reached out to touch the thief's shoulder, a move quick as lightning and soft as a butterfly's landing. "One must do for a friend what the friend cannot do for himself. With such a man, opportunities of this sort come seldom. If not for him, or for your price, or for whatever you hold sacred, do this thing for me, and I will be eternally in your debt."

A sibilant sound, part impatience, part exasperation, part irritation, came sliding down Shadowspawn's hawkish nose.

"Hanse?"

"You are going to *surprise* him with this deed, done? What if he has no taste for surprises? What if you are wrong, and he refrains from aiding her because he prefers her right where she is? And besides, I am staying away from him and his affairs."

"No surprise: I will tell him once I have arranged it. I will make you one more offer: Half again the doubled fee you suggested, to ease your doubts. But that is my final bid."

Shadowspawn squinted at the heartshaped face of Stepson. Then, without a word, he scooped up the short stabbing sword in its silver sheath, and found it a home in his belt. "Done," said Hanse.

"Good. Then, will you meet my companions?" The long-fingered, graceful hand of Stepson, called Abarsis, made a gesture that brought them, all smiles and manly welcomes, from their exile by the bar.

5

Kurd, the vivisectionist who had tried his skills on Tempus, was found a fair way from his adobe workshop, his gut stretched out for thirty feet before him: he had been dragged by the entrails; the hole cut in his belly to pull the intestines out was made by an expert: a mercenary had to be at fault. But there were so many mercenaries in Sanctuary, and so few friends of the vivisectionist, that the matter was not pursued.

The matter of the Hell-Hound Razkuli's head, however, was much more serious. Zalbar (who knew why both had died and at whose hands, and who feared for his own life) went to Kadakithis with his friend's staring eyes under one arm, sick and still tasting vomit, and told the Prince how Tempus had come riding through the gates at dawn and called up to him where he was checking pass-bys in the gatehouse: "Zalbar, I've a message for you."

"Yo!" Zalbar had waved.

"Catch," Tempus laughed, and threw something up to him while the gray horse reared, uttered a shrill, demonic scream, and clattered off by the time Zalbar's hand had said *head: human;* and his eyes had said, *head: Razkuli's* and then begun to fill with tears.

Kadakithis listened to his story, looking beyond him out the window the entire time. When Zalbar had finished, the Prince said, "Well, I don't know what you expected, trying to take him down so clumsily."

"But he said it was a message for me," Zalbar entreated, caught his own pleading tone, scowled and straightened up.

"Then take it to heart, man. I can't allow you two to continue feuding. If it is anything other than simple feuding, I do not want to know about it. Stepson, called Abarsis, told me to expect something like this! I demand a stop to it!"

*"Stepson!"* Tall, lank Zalbar snarled like a man invoking a vengeful god in close fighting. "An ex-Sacred Bander looking for glory and death with honor, in no particular order! *Stepson* told you? The Slaughter Priest? My lord Prince, you are keeping deadly company these days! Are all the gods of the armies in Sanctuary, then, along with their familiars, the mercenary hordes? I had wanted to discuss with you what could be done to curb them—"

"Zalbar," interrupted Kadakithis firmly. "In the matter of gods, I hold firm: I do not believe in them. In the matter of mercenaries, let them be. You broach subjects too sensitive for your station. In the matter of Tempus, I will talk to him. You change your attitude. Now, if that is *all* . . . ?"

It *was* all. It was nearly the end of Zalbar the Hell-Hound's entire career; he almost struck his commander-in-chief. But he refrained, though he could not utter even a civil goodbye. He went to his billet and he went into the town, and he worked wrath out of himself, as best he could. The dregs he washed away with drink, and after that he went to visit Myrtis, the whoremistress of Aphrodisia House who knew how to soothe him. And she, seeing his heart breaking and his fists shaking, asked him nothing about why he had come, after staying away so long, but took him to her breast and healed what she might of his hurts, remembering that all the protection he provided her and good he did for her, he did because of a love spell she had bought and cast on him long since, and thus she owed him at least one night to match his dreams.

6

Tempus had gone among his own kind, after he left the barracks. He had checked in at the guild hostel north of the palace, once again in leopard and bronze and iron, and he was welcome there.

Why he had kept himself from it for so long, he could not have reasoned, unless it was that without these friends of former times the camaraderie would not have been as sweet.

He went to the sideboard and got hot mulled wine from a krater, sprinkling in goat's cheese and grain, and took the posset to a corner, so the men could come to him as they would.

The problem of the eunuch was still unsolved; finding a suitable replacement was not going to be easy: there were not many eunuchs in the mercenaries' guild. The clubroom was red as dying day and dark as backlit mountains, and he felt better for having come. So, when Abarsis, high priest of Upper Ranke, left his companions and approached, but did not sit among, the mercenaries Tempus had collected, he said to the nine that he would see them at the appointed time, and to the iron-clad one:

"Life to you, Stepson. Please join me."

"Life to you, Riddler, and everlasting glory." Cup in hand, he sipped pure water, eyes hardly darker never leaving Tempus's face. "Is it Sanctuary that has driven you to drink?" He indicated the posset.

"The dry soul is wisest? Not at the empire's anus, where the water is chancy. Anyway, those things I said long ago and far away: do not hold me to any of that."

The smooth cheek of Stepson ticced. "I must," he murmured. "You are the man I have emulated. All my life I have listened after word of you and collected intelligence of you and studied what you left us in legend and stone in the north. Listen: 'War is sire of all and king of all, and some He has made gods and some men, some bond and some free'.

Or: 'War is ours in common; strife is justice; all things come into being and pass away through strife'. You see, I know your work, even those other names you have used. Do not make me speak them. I would work with you, O Sleepless One. It will be the pinnacle of my career." He flashed Tempus a bolt of naked entreaty, then his gaze flickered away and he rushed on: "You need me. Who else will suit? Who else here has a brand and gelding's scars? *And* time in the arena as a gladiator, like Jubal himself? Who could intrigue him, much less seduce him among these? And though I—"

"No."

Abarsis dug in his belt and tossed a golden amulet onto the table. "The god will not give you up; this was caught in the sorrel's new shoe. That teacher of mine whom you remember . . . ?"

"I know the man," Tempus said grimly.

"He thinks that Sanctuary is the endpoint of existence; that those who come here are damned beyond redemption; that Sanctuary is Hell."

"Then how is it, Stepson," said Tempus almost kindly, "that folk experience fleshly death here? So far as I know, I am the only soul in Sanctuary who suffers eternally, with the possible exception of my sister, who may not have a soul. Learn not to listen to what people say, priest. A man's own mistakes are load enough, without adding others'."

"Then *let* me be your choice! There is no time to find some other eunuch." He said it flatly, without bitterness, a man fielding logic. "I can also bring you a few fighters whom you might not know and who would not dare, on their own, to approach you. My Sacred Band yearns to serve you. You dispense your favor to provincials and foreigners who barely recognize their honor! Give it to me, who craves little else . . . ! The Prince who would be king will not expose me, but pass me on to Jubal as an untrained boy. I am a little old for it, but in Sanctuary, those niceties seem not to matter. I have increased your lot here. You owe me this opportunity."

Tempus stirred his cooling posset with a finger. "That prince . . ." Changing the subject, he sighed glumly, a sound like rattling bones. "He will never be a Great King, such as your father. Can you tell me why the god is taking such an interest?"

"The god will tell you, when you make of the Trôs horse a sacrifice. Or some person. Then He will be mollified. You know the ritual. If it be a man you choose, I will gladly volunteer . . . Ah, you understand me, now? I do not want to frighten you . . ."

"Take no thought of it."

"Then . . . though I risk your displeasure, yet I say it: I love you. One night with you would be a surfeit, to work under you is my long-held dream. Let me do this, which none can do better, which no *whole* man can do for you at all!"

"I cede you the privilege, since you value it so; but there is no telling what Jubal's hired hawk-masks might do to the enunch we send in there."

"With your blessing and the god's, I am fearless. And you will be close by, busy attacking Black Jubal's fortress. While you are arresting the slavemaster for his treasonous spying, whosoever will make good the woman's escape. I understand your thought; I have arranged for the retrieval of her weapons."

Tempus chuckled. "I hardly know what to say."

"Say you look kindly upon me, that I am more than a bad memory to you."

Shaking his head, Tempus took the amulet Abarsis held out to him. "Come then, Stepson, we will see what part of your glorious expectations we can fulfill."

7

It was said, ever after, that the Storm God took part in the sack of the slaver's estate. Lightning crawled along the gatehouses of its defensive wall and rolled in balls through the inner court and turned the oaken gates to ash. The ground rumbled and buckled and bucked and great crumbling cracks appeared in its inner sanctum, where the slaver dallied with the glossy-haired eunuch Kadakithis had just sent up for training. It was profligate waste to make a fancy boy out of such a slave: the arena had muscled him up and time had grown him up, and to squeeze the two or three remaining years of that sort of pleasure out of him seemed to the slaver a pity. If truth be known, blood like his came so rarely to the slavepens that gelding him was a sin against future generations: had Jubal gotten him early on—when the cuts had been made, at nine, or ten—he would have raised him with great pains and put him to stud. But his brand and tawny skin smacked of northern mountains and high wizards' keeps where the wars had raged so savagely that no man was proud to remember what had been done there, on either side.

Eventually, he left the eunuch chained by the neck to the foot of his bed and went to see what the yelling and the shouting and the blue flashes and the quivering floorboards could possibly mean.

What he saw from his threshold he did not understand, but he came striding back, stripping off his robe as he passed by the bed, rushing to arm himself and do battle against the infernal forces of this enemy, and, it seemed, the whole of the night.

Naphtha fireballs came shooting over his walls into the courtyard; flaming arrows torqued from spring-wound bows; javelins and sword-play glittered nastily, singing as they slew in soft susurrusings Jubal had hoped never to hear there.

It was eerily quiet: no shouting, not from his hawk-masks, or the adversaries; the fire crackled and the horses snorted and groaned like the men where they fell.

Jubal recollected the sinking feeling he had had in his stomach when Zalbar had confided to him that the bellows of anguish emanating from the vivisectionist's workshop were the Hell-Hound Tempus's agonies, the forebodings he had endured when a group of his beleaguered sell-swords went after the man who killed those who wore the mask of Jubal's service for sport, and failed to down him.

That night, it was too late for thinking. There was time enough only for wading into the thick of battle (if he could just find it: the attack was from every side, out of darkness); hollering orders; mustering point leaders (two); and appointing replacements for the dead (three). Then he heard whoops and abysmal screams and realized that someone had let the slaves out of their pens; those who had nothing to lose bore haphazard arms, but sought only death with vengeance. Jubal, seeing wide, white rimmed eyes and murderous mouths and the new eunuch from Kadakithis's palace dancing ahead of the pack of them, started to run. The key to its collar had been in his robe; he remembered discarding it, within the eunuch's reach.

He ran in a private wash of terror, in a bubble through which other sounds hardly penetrated, but where his breathing reverberated stentorian, rasping, and his heart gonged loud in his ears. He ran looking back over his shoulder, and he saw some leopard-pelted apparition with a horn bow in hand come sliding down the gatehouse wall. He ran until he reached the stable, until he stumbled over a dead hawk-mask, and then he heard everything, cacophonously, that had been so muted before: swords rasping; panoplies rattling; bodies thudding and greaved men running; quarrels whispering bright death as they passed through the dark press; javelins ringing as they struck helm or shield suddenly limned in lurid fiery light.

*Fire?* Behind Jubal flame licked out the stable windows and horses whistled their death screams.

The heat was singeing. He drew his sword and turned in a fluid motion, judging himself as he was wont to do when the crowds had been about him in applauding tiers and he must kill to live to kill another day, and do so pleasingly.

He felt the thrill of it, the immediacy of it, the joy of the arena, and as the pack of freed slaves came shouting, he picked out the Prince's eunuch and reached to wrest a spear from the dead hawk-mask's grip. He hefted it, left-handed, to cast, just as the man in leopard pelt and cuirass and a dozen mercenaries came between him and the slaves, cutting him off from his final refuge, the stairs to the westward wall.

Behind him, the flames seemed hotter, so that he was glad he had not stopped for armor. He threw the spear, and it rammed home in the eunuch's gut.

The leopard leader came forward, alone, sword tip gesturing three times, leftward.

*Was* it Tempus, beneath that frightful armor? Jubal raised his own blade to his brow in acceptance, and moved to where his antagonist indicated, but the leopard leader was talking over his shoulder to his front-line mercenaries, three of whom were clustered around the downed eunuch. Then one archer came abreast of the leader, touched his leopard pelt. And that bowman kept a nocked arrow on Jubal, while the leader sheathed his sword and walked away, to join the little knot around the eunuch.

Someone had broken off the haft; Jubal heard the grunt and the snap of wood and saw the shaft discarded. Then arrows whizzed in quick succession into both his knees and beyond the shattering pain, he knew nothing more.

8

Tempus knelt over Abarsis, bleeding out his life naked in the dirt. "Get me light," he rasped. Tossing his helmet aside, he bent down until his cheek touched Stepson's knotted, hairless belly. The whole bronze head of the spear, barbs and all, was deep in him. Under his lowest rib, the shattered haft stuck out, quivering as he breathed. The torch was brought; the better light told Tempus there was no use in cutting the spearhead loose; one flange was up under the low rib; vital fluids oozed out with the youth's blood. Out of age-old custom, Tempus laid his mouth upon the wound and sucked the blood and swallowed it, then raised his head and shook it to those who waited with a hot blade and hopeful, silent faces. "Get him some water, no wine. And give him some air."

They moved back and as the Sacred Bander who had been holding Abarsis's head put it down, the wounded one murmured; he coughed, and his frame shuddered, one hand clutching spasmodically at the spear. "Rest now, Stepson. You have got your wish. You will be my sacrifice to the god." He covered the youth's nakedness with his mantle, taking the gory hand from the broken haft, letting it fasten on his own.

Then the blue-gray eyes of Abarsis opened in a face pale with pain, and something else: "I am not frightened, with you and the god beside me."

Tempus put an arm under his head and gathered him up, pulling him across his lap. "Hush, now."

"Soon, soon," said the paling lips. "I did well for you. Tell me so . . . that you are content. O Riddler, so well do I love you, I go to my god singing your praises. When I meet my father, I will tell him . . . I . . . fought beside you."

"Go with more than that, Stepson," whispered Tempus, and leaned forward, and kissed him gently on the mouth, and Abarsis breathed out his soul while their lips yet touched.

9

Now, Hanse had gotten the rods with no difficulty, as Stepson had promised he would be able to do, citing Tempus's control of palace personnel as surety. And afterward, the young mercenary's invitation to come and watch them fight up at Jubal's rang in his head until, to banish it, he went out to take a look.

He knew it was foolish to go, for it was foolish even to *know,* but he knew that he wanted to be able to say, "Yes, I saw. It was wonderful," the next time he saw the young mercenary, so he went very carefully and cautiously. If he were stopped, he would have all of Stepson's Sacred Band as witnesses that he had been at Jubal's, and nowhere near the palace and its Hall of Judgment.

He knew those excuses were flimsy, but he wanted to go, and he did not want to delve into why: the lure of mercenary life was heady in his nostrils; if he admitted how sweet it seemed, he might be lost. If he went, perchance he would see something not so sweet, or so intoxicating, something which would wash away all this talk of friendship and honor. So he went, and hid on the roof of a gatehouse abandoned in the confusion. Thus he saw all that transpired.

When he could in safety leave his roost, he followed the pair of gray horses bearing Tempus and the corpse ridgeward, stealing the first mount he came to that looked likely.

The sun was risen when Tempus reached the ridgetop and called out behind: "Whoever you are, ride up," and set about gathering branches to make a bier.

Hanse rode to the edge of the outcropping of rock on which Tempus piled wood and said: "Well, accursed one, are you and your god replete? Stepson told me all about it."

The man straightened up, eyes like flames, and put his hand to the small of his back: "What do you want, Shadowspawn? A man who is respectful does not sling insults over the ears of the dead. If you are here for him, then welcome. If you are here for me, I assure you, your timing is ill."

"I *am* here for him, *friend.* What think you, that I would come here to console you in your grief when it was his love for you that he died of? He asked me," Hanse continued, not dismounting, "to get these. He was going to give them to you." He reached for the diamond rods, wrapped in hide, he had stolen.

"Stay your hand, and your feelings. Both are misplaced. Do not judge what you do not understand. As for the rods, Abarsis was mistaken as to what I wanted done with them. If you are finishing your first mercenary's commission, then give them to One-Thumb. Tell him they are for his benefactor. Then it is done. Someone of the Sacred Band will seek you out and pay you. Do not worry about that. Now, if you would honor Abarsis, dismount." The struggle obvious in Tempus's face for control was chilling, where nothing unintentioned was ever seen. "Otherwise, please leave now, friend, *while* we are yet friends. I am in no mood for living boys today."

So Hanse slid from the horse and stalked over to the corpse stage-whispering, "Mouth me no swill, Doomface. If this is how your friends fare, I'd as soon be relieved of the honor," and flipped back the shroud. "His eyes are open." Shadowspawn reached out to close them.

"Don't. Let him see where he goes."

They glared a time at each other above the staring corpse while a red-tailed hawk circled overhead, its shadow caressing the pale, dead face.

Then Hanse knelt stiffly, took a coin from his belt, slid it between Stepson's slightly parted lips, and murmured something low. Rising, he turned and strode to his stolen horse and scrambled clumsily astride, reining it round and away without a single backward glance.

When Tempus had the bier all made, and Abarsis arranged on it to the last glossy hair, and a spark nursed to consuming flame, he stood with clenched fists and watering eyes in the billows of smoke. And through his tears, he saw the boy's father, fighting oblivious from his car, his charioteer fallen between his legs, that time Tempus had hacked off an enemy's arm to save him from the ax it swung; he saw the witch-bitch of a sorceress the king had wed in the black hills to make alliance with what could not be had by force; he saw the aftermath of that, when the wild woman's spawn was out of her and every loyal general took a hand in her murder before she laid their commander out in state. He saw the boy, wizard-haired and wise, running to Tempus's chariot for a ride, grasping his neck, laughing, kissing like the northern boys had no shame to do; all this before the Great King discharged his armies and retired home to peace, and Tempus rode south to Ranke, an empire hardly whelped and shaky on its prodigious feet. And Tempus saw the

field he had taken against a monarch, once his liege: Masters change.
He had not been there when they had got the Great King, dragged him
down from his car and begun the Unending Deaths that proved the
Rankans barbarians second to none. It was said by those who *were*
there that he stood it well enough until his son was castrated before his
eyes, given off to a slaver with ready collar . . . When he had heard,
Tempus had gone searching among the sacked towns of the north,
where Ranke wrought infamy into example, legends better than sharp
javelins at discouraging resistance. And he saw Abarsis in the slaver's
kennel, the boy's look of horror that a man of the armies would see
what had been done to him. No glimmer of joy invaded the gaunt
child's face turned up to him. No eager hands outflung to their re-
deemer; a small, spent hero shuffled across soiled straw to meet him,
slave's eyes gauging without fear just what he might expect from this
man, who had once been among his father's most valued, but was now
only one more Rankan enemy. Tempus remembered picking the child
up in his arms, hating how little he weighed, how sharp his bones were;
and that moment when Abarsis at last believed he was safe. About a
boy's tears, Abarsis had sworn Tempus to secrecy. About the rest, the
less said, the better. He had found him foster parents, in the rocky west
by the sea temples where Tempus himself was born, and where the gods
still made miracles upon occasion. He had hoped somehow the gods
would heal what love could not. Now, they had done it.

He nodded, having passed recollection like poison, watching the fire
burn down. Then, for the sake of the soul of Stepson, called Abarsis,
and under the aegis of his flesh, Tempus humbled himself before Vashanka and came again into the service of his god.

10

Hanse, hidden below on a shelf, listening and partaking of the funeral of his own fashion, upon realizing what he was overhearing,
spurred the horse out of there as if the very god whose thunderous voice
he had heard were after him.

He did not stop until he reached the Vulgar Unicorn. There he shot
off the horse in a dismount which was a fall disguised as a vault,
slapped the beast smartly away, telling it hissingly to go home, and

slipped inside with such relief as his favorite knife must feel when he sheathed it.

"One-Thumb," Hanse called out, making for the bar, "What is going on out there?" There had been soldierly commotion at the Common Gate.

"You haven't heard?" scoffed the night-turned-day barman. "Some prisoners escaped from the palace dungeon, certain articles were thieved from the Hall of Judgment, and none of the regular security officers were around to get their scoldings."

Looking at the mirror behind the bar, Hanse saw the ugly man grin without humor. Gaze locked to mirror-gaze, Hanse drew the hide-wrapped bundle from his tunic. "These are for you. You are supposed to give them to your benefactor." He shrugged to the mirror.

One-Thumb turned and wiped the dishrag along the shining bar and when the rag was gone, the small bundle was gone, also. "Now, what do you want to get involved in something like this for? You think you're moving up? You're not. Next time, when it's this sort of thing, come round the back. Or, better, don't come at all. I thought you had more sense."

Hanse's hand smacked flat and loud upon the bar. "I have taken enough offal for one day, cupbearer. Now I tell you what you do, Wide-Belly: You take what I brought you and your sage counsel, and you wrap it all together, and then you squat on it!" And stiff-kneed as a roused cat, Shadowspawn stalked away, toward the door, saying over his shoulder: "As for sense, I thought *you* had more."

"I have my business to think of," called out One-Thumb, too boldly for a whine.

"Ah, yes! So have I, so have I."


11


Lavender and lemon dawn light bedizened the white-washed barracks' walls and colored the palace parade grounds.

Tempus had been working all night, out at Jubal's estate where he was quartering his mercenaries away from town and Hell-Hounds and Ilsig garrison personnel. He had fifty there, but twenty of them were paired members of three different Sacred Bands: Stepson's legacy to him. The twenty had convinced the thirty nonallied operatives that "Stepsons" would be a good name for their squadron, and for the cohort it would eventually command should things go as everyone hoped.

He would keep the Sacred Band teams and spread the rest throughout the regular army, and throughout the Prince's domain. They would find what clay they chose, and mold a division from it which the spirit of Abarsis, if it were not too busy fighting theomachy's battles in heaven, could look upon with pride.

The men had done Tempus proud, already, that night at Jubal's, and thereafter; and this evening when he had turned the corner round the slave barracks the men were refitting for livestock, there it had been, a love-note written in lamb's blood two cubits high on the encircling protective wall: *"War is all and king of all, and all things come into being out of strife."*

Albeit they had not gotten it exactly right, he had smiled, for though the world and the boyhood from out of which he had said such audacious things was gone to time, Stepson, called Abarsis, and his legacy of example and followers made Tempus think that perhaps (oh just perhaps) he, Tempus, had not been so young, or so foolish, as he had lately come to think that he had been. And if thus the man, then his epoch, too, was freed of memory's hindsightful taint.

And the god and he were reconciled: This pushed away his curse and the shadow of distress it cast ever before him. His troubles with the Prince has subsided. Zalbar had come through his test of fire and returned to stand his duty, thinking deeply, walking quietly. His courage would mend. Tempus knew his sort.

Jubal's disposition he had left to Kadakithis. He had wanted to take the famous ex-gladiator's measure in single combat, but there was no fitness in it now, since the man would never be quick on his feet, should he live to regain the use of them.

Not that the world was as ridiculously beautiful as was the arrogant summer morning which did not understand that it was a Sanctuary morning and therefore should at least be gory, garish, or full of flies buzzing about his head. No, one could find a few thorns in one's path, still. There was Shadowspawn, called Hanse, exhibiting unseemly and proprietary grief over Abarsis whenever it served him, yet not taking a billet among the Stepsons that Tempus had offered. Privately, Tempus thought he might yet come to it, that he was trying to step twice into the same river. When his feet chilled enough, he would step out onto the banks of manhood. If he could sit a horse better, perhaps his pride would let him join in where now, because of that, he could only sneer.

Hanse, too, must find his own path. He was not Tempus's problem, though Tempus would gladly take on that burden should Shadowspawn ever indicate a desire to have help toting it.

His sister, Cime, however, *was* his problem, his alone, and the enormity of that conundrum had him casting about for any possible solution, taking pat answers up and putting them down like gods move seeds from field to field. He could kill her, rape her, deport her; he could not ignore her, forget her, or suffer along without confronting her.

That she and One-Thumb had become enamored of one another was something he had not counted on. Such a thing had never occurred to him.

Tempus felt the god rustling around in him, the deep cavernous sensing in his most private skull that told him the deity was going to speak. *Silently!* he warned the god. They were uneasy with each other, yet, like two lovers after a trial separation.

*We can take her, mildly, and then she will leave. You cannot tolerate her presence. Drive her off. I will help thee,* spake Vashanka.

"Must you be so predictable, Pillager?" Tempus mumbled under his breath, so that Abarsis's Trôs horse swiveled its ears back to eavesdrop. He slapped its neck, and told it to continue on straight and smartly. They were headed toward Lastel's modest eastside estate.

*Constancy is one of My attributes,* jibed the god in Tempus's head meaningfully.

"You are not getting her, O Ravening One. You who are never satisfied, in this one thing, will not triumph. What would we have between us to keep it clear who is whom? I cannot allow it."

*You will,* said Vashanka so loud in his head that he winced in his saddle and the Trôs horse broke stride, looking reproachfully about at him to see what that shift of weight could possibly be construed to mean.

Tempus stopped the horse in the middle of the cool shadowed way on that beautful morning and sat stiffly a long while, conducting an internal battle which had no resolution.

After a time, he swung the horse back in its tracks, kicked it into a lope toward the barracks from which he had just come. Let her stay with One-Thumb, if she would. She had come between him and his god before. He was not ready to give her to the god, and he was not ready to give himself back into the hands of his curse, rip asunder what had been so laboriously patched together and at such great cost. He thought of Abarsis, and Kadakithis, and the refractory upcountry peoples, and he promised Vashanka any other woman the god should care to choose before sundown. Cime would keep, no doubt, right where she was. He would see to it that Lastel saw to her.

Abarsis's Trôs horse snorted softly, as if in agreement, single-footing through Sanctuary's better streets toward the barracks. But the Trôs horse could not have known that by this simple decision its rider had attained to a greater victory than in all the wars of all the empires he had ever labored to increase. No, the Trôs horse whose belly quivered between Tempus's knees as it issued a blaring trumpet to the dusty air did so not because of its rider's triumph over self and god, but out of pure high spirits, as horses always will praise a fine day dawned.

# Things the Editor
# Never Told Me

## Lynn Abbey

I had just administered the coup de grace to my latest THIEVES'
WORLD offering—my third—when Bob asked if I'd like to have the last
word in SHADOWS OF SANCTUARY. It was an offer I couldn't refuse, though I'd no idea how I would put into words the experiences of
working on all three THIEVES' WORLD volumes. After many unsuccessful attempts at getting this essay down on paper, I began to suspect that maybe Bob hadn't known the right words either. He was smiling when he made the offer, and he doesn't usually give up a by-line
that easily. Sigh. Another example of Things the Editor Never Told Me.

Actually, a lot of things the editor didn't tell us were things he didn't
know himself. We were all naive about the mechanics of a franchised
universe back at Boskone of 1978 when the THIEVES' WORLD project was created. It sounded wondrously uncomplicated: we would exchange character sketches and refer to a common street map; Bob
would write us a history; Andy Offutt would create our gods. We only
had to go to ground and write our five—to—ten thousand words. Fat
Chance. Unexpected discovery number one: Sanctuary isn't an imaginary anything; it's a state of mind recognized by the American Psychi-
atric Association.

We thought we'd gone to ground—it turned out that we'd gone over-
board. Bob hadn't told us the things we'd really need to know, and none
of us wanted to dictate to the guy who'd created this fun-house, so each
of us made great use of the little vicissitudes of life that would add
"grit" and "realism" to our stories. My not-gypsy read not-Tarot cards,

dealt with necromancers, stole a corpse and witnessed the usual street violence.

It didn't seem too bad until I found the entire book oozing out of my mailbox and read the volume in its entirety. We had Crom-many drugs, magicians, vices, brothels, dives, haunts, curses and feuds. Sanctuary wasn't a provincial backwater; it wasn't even the Imperial armpit; it was the Black-Hole of not-Calcutta. Things could only get worse . . . .

And they did. Bob told us the second volume would be called TALES FROM THE VULGAR UNICORN—the very name incites depravity. And we rose to the occasion—or perhaps we fell. I explored the unpleasant pieces of my S'danzo's past, gave her a berserker for a half-brother and created Buboe, the night bartender down at the Vulgar Unicorn. Well, Bob said we were supposed to have a scene down at the ol' V.U.—but One-Thumb was hors de combat in the bowels of Sanctuary and no one knew who was running the joint. (I recall one of my confreres created someone called Two-Thumbs—I think that was from spite.) Buboe—a buboe isn't a *person,* a buboe is the rather large glandular eruption that accompanies the terminal stages of the Black Plague; opening it insures death for the opener and the openee.

TALES didn't ooze out of the mailbox; it ate right through the metal. I haven't seen all the stories for volume three yet, but I'm confident the downward spiral has continued. Each set of stories brings new oddments of human behavior, new quirks of character that the authors wouldn't dare put in a universe for which he or she was solely responsible. In Sanctuary, though, where guilt is shared along with the glory, one volume's innuendo becomes the next volume's complete story.

And frankly, nastiness is interesting. If I tell you that the smell of rotting blood can linger for years you might not notice what I don't tell you. Consider for a moment some of the things none of the authors know for sure: the weather in Sanctuary—daily and seasonal. It must be strange. If the Downwinders are downwind of the town then the prevailing wind is off the land—try convincing any coast-dweller of *that.*

As far as the city itself is concerned, I've always imagined it as a sort of late medieval town, out-growing its walls. The Maze is built like the Shambles in York, England, where each storey gets built out over the lower one so everybody can drop their slops directly into the street instead of on their neighbor. There are those who seem to think Sanctuary's like Rome. (Nonsense, Ranke is Rome—or is it that Rome is rank?) They imagine that the town has the rudiments of sewer systems, that the villas are attractive, open buildings and that at least some of the streets are paved. There also seems to be a Baghdad-by-the-sea approach, with turban'd tribesmen and silk-clad ladies, as well as a few indications that we might be dealing with a Babylonian building-style. Since so many of our stories are set in the dark, I suppose it doesn't matter that we don't really agree on what the city looks like.

Of course, nobody, including the Empire, knows how big Sanctuary really is. Anytime one of us needs a secret meeting place we just create one—Sanctuary is either very large or very cramped. You can live your whole life in the Maze or the Bazaar, and yet it only takes fifteen minutes to walk from one end of town to the other—or does it? I'm not sure.

Take the Bazaar, for example. I've spent a fair amount of time in that Bazaar and I don't know exactly how it's put together. Part of it is a farmer's market (though I haven't the faintest idea where the farmers are when they aren't at the Bazaar). Other parts are like the cloth-fairs of medieval France, where merchants sell their wares wholesale. Still other parts resemble the permanent bazaars of the Middle-East. Rather than trouble myself with philosophical questions, like how many angels can dance on the head of a pin, someday I've got to figure out how many S'danzo can live full-time in the Bazaar.

Moving from angels to gods for a moment—it seems probable that anyone living in Sanctuary would have a personal relationship to the gods—nothing like worship or faith, mind you. The people seem homeric in their religion: the last thing an ordinary citizen wants is dealing with the gods; worship is designed to keep the deities at bay. We have at least two major pantheons represented in the temples and the gods know how many priesthoods trying to control them. They tell me there's a fellow out in California who has made a coherent mythology for the religions of Sanctuary. He's putting his theology into Chaosium's *THIEVES' WORLD* game, but nobody's saying where they're putting the intrepid mythmaster.

Then there's currency—or why we call it THIEVES' WORLD. Since no one knows how the currency works, the townsfolk have no choice but to steal from each other. We sort of agree that there are copper coins, silver coins and gold coins—but we don't know their names or their conversion rates. We say: a few copper coins; or we get very specific and say: nine Rankan soldats—just in case someone else is writing about soldats that weren't minted in Ranke. But how many soldats make a shaboozh—or does it work the other way around? It probably does.

Someday I'll create a money-lender for the town; making change in Sanctuary has got to be an art form. It won't do any good, though. Citizens and authors alike will find reasons not to visit my money-lender. They'll set up their own rates of exchange. The Prince will debase the currency. Vashanka will start spitting Indian-head nickels in his temple. I won't let that stop me. If the editor won't tell me how these things are to be done, I'll just have to start telling *him*.